Winter,Spring/Summer 2000

TriQuarterly 107/108

TRIQUARTERLY IS AN INTERNATIONAL JOURNAL OF WRITING, ART AND CULTURAL INQUIRY PUBLISHED AT **NORTHWESTERN UNIVERSITY.**

Subscription rates (three issues a year)—Individuals: one year $24; two years $44; life $600. Institutions: one year $36; two years $68. Foreign subscriptions $5 per year additional. Price of back issues varies. Sample copies $5. Correspondence and subscriptions should be addressed to ***TriQuarterly***, **Northwestern University**, 2020 Ridge Avenue, Evanston, IL 60208-4302. Phone: (847) 491-7614.

The editors invite submissions of fiction, poetry and literary essays, which must be postmarked between October 1 and March 31; manuscripts postmarked between April 1 and September 30 will not be read. No manuscripts will be returned unless accompanied by a stamped, self-addressed envelope. All manuscripts accepted for publication become the property of ***TriQuarterly***, unless otherwise indicated.

 Printed in the United States of America by Edwards Brothers Printing.; typeset by ***TriQuarterly***. ISSN: 0041-3097.

National distributors to retail trade: Ingram Periodicals (La Vergne, TN); B. DeBoer (Nutley, NJ); Ubiquity (Brooklyn, NY); Armadillo (Los Angeles, CA).

Reprints of issues #1–15 of ***TriQuarterly*** are available in full format from Kraus Reprint Company, Route 100, Millwood, NY 10546, and all issues in microfilm from University Microfilms International, 300 North Zeeb Road, Ann Arbor, MI 48106. ***TriQuarterly*** is indexed in the *Humanities Index* (H.W. Wilson Co.), the *American Humanities Index* (Whitson Publishing Co.), Historical Abstracts, MLA, EBSCO Publishing (Peabody, MA) and Information Access Co. (Foster City, CA).

TriQuarterly is pleased to announce that the following awards and honors have been given to the following authors for work that has appeared in the magazine in the past year:

Beth Ann Fennelly was awarded a Pushcart Prize for her poem "The Impossibility of Language" (TQ 105).

A.A. Srinivasan was awarded a Pushcart Prize for her short story "Tusk" (TQ 105).

The following poems will appear in *Best American Poetry 2000*:
Erin Belieu's "Choose Your Garden" (TQ 103)
Richard Blanco's "Mango, Number 61" (TQ 103)
Yusef Komunyakaa's "The Goddess of Quotas Laments" (TQ 105)

Paul Breslin was awarded an Illinois Arts Council Literary Award for his poem "To a Friend Who Concedes Nothing" (TQ 105).

Joshua Weiner was awarded an Illinois Arts Council Literary Award for his poem "Kindertotenlieder" (TQ 106).

Please note: Due to a backlog of material* TriQuarterly *will not resume reading unsolicited submissions until October 1, 2001. In the meantime all manuscripts will be returned unread.

We wish all writers well and look forward to reading their work next year.

Contents

Theater

Portfolio

Poetry

Cover: "Untitled, 1999," lithograph by Mark Strand

Reading Isaac Babel's Diary on the Lower East Side

Edward Hirsch

Morning in the subway, morning in the train,
filthy sunlight on the window, the stale smell
of summer air, sweating bodies, rootlessness.

Farewell, dead men, I'm sinking my teeth into life
and crossing the square, holding my notebook
aloft like a prize, a freshly won trophy.

Describe the usual face of an old market,
a sour apple, two peddlers munching cherries,
a young woman in a white hat lifting her skirt

and wading through a nasty puddle, her style,
the century, Spinoza grinding an eyeglass
in his unimaginable shop, Ukrainian Dickens.

He spans the Pale of Settlement with his hands:
everything repeats itself, governments profess
Justice, and everyone—he winks at me—steals.

Outside, a backyard stocked with chickens.
His daughter married a stork, his son emigrated.
Ill-fated Galicia, ill-fated Jews, stubborn, paling.

I'm sinking my teeth into life—farewell, dead men—
and talking to a Russian woman who needs to borrow
some sugar. Sweet anemic tea and two apple tarts.

Accidentally brushing an elbow against her breast.
Conversation in the corner about rising prices,
unbearable costs. The pogrom in Zhitomir:

begun by Poles, then continued by Cossacks.
45 Jews assembled in the open marketplace,
marched into the slaughteryard, butchered.

Their tongues cut out, their cries. Picture
a mother dropping her child from a burning window,
and the yardman who caught him, bayonetted.

I leave shaken, but the story repeats itself
further to the East, Jews plundered at Belyov,
their bewilderment, gravestones toppled at Malin,

Pelcha, Boratyn, the remains of a synagogue
in Dubno, a temple in ruin, lamentations
clustered together in the ashes, Brody looted,

all of it as when the Temple was destroyed,
how the prophet cried out—*and we eat dung,*
our maidens are ravished, our menfolk killed . . .

Life flows on—wretched, powerful, immortal—
and voices blur across the century, bodies
crowded into steerage to Liverpool or Glasgow

or New York, Little Galicia of the tenements
from Grand to Houston. Refugees, peddlers,
prayers for the dead in the next building,

a girl who died from terror after the rape,
the pillage, her mother threshed by grief,
her father swaying, familiar doleful chants

from the benches, an eternal lamp burning
on the windowsill, its reflection in glass,
all the mirrors turned to face the wall.

The promise of a township, village, borough
where many Jews go walking arm in arm
late afternoons in mid-July, the Old World

guiding the New to a corner synagogue.
The Sabbath wanes. I've lost my place
in the prayerbook, the songs my grandfather

taught me, the bliss of a *tsaddik's* face,
a candle stricken with flame. I've found
an ancient people, still singing at dusk.

Then it's night on the avenues, streetlamps,
this unquenchable carnal lust. The train.
The walk back on quiet, deserted streets.

Remember everything. Describe the streets,
the Hebrew grammar unopened on the desk,
the bearded faces of old Jews, young Jews,

the all-night rattle of a typewriter
penetrating the air. Everything changes,
everything repeats itself in time.

The Rest of Your Life

John Barth

"Sounds like the beginning of a story," in my busy wife's opinion, and I quite agreed, although just what story remained to be seen.

What had happened, I'd told her over breakfast, was that the calendar function on our home computer appeared to have died. When I called up the word-processor's stationery format, for example, the date automatically supplied under my "business" letterhead read *August 27, 1956.* Likewise on our other letterhead formats, our e-mail transmissions and receptions—anything on which the machine routinely noted month, day, and year. I had first noticed the error while catching up on personal and business correspondence the evening before this breakfast-time report (the date of which, by weak coincidence, happened to be *July 27, 1996*, just one month short of the fortieth anniversary of that letterhead date). Wondering mildly how many items I might have dispatched under that odd, out-of-date heading—for as my wife would now and then remind me, I had become less detail-attentive and generally more forgetful than I once was—I made the correction both on the correspondence in hand and on the computer's clock/calendar control . . . and then forgot to mention the matter when Julia came home from her Friday-night aerobics group. Up at first light next morning as usual in recent years, I let the "working girl" sleep on (her weekend pleasure) while I fetched in the morning newspaper, scanned its headlines over coffee—Olympic Bomb Investigation Continues, TWA 800 Crash Cause Still Unknown—set out our daily vitamins and other pills and the fixings of the breakfast that we would presently make together, then holed up in my home office to check for e-mail and do a bit of deskwork until she was up and about. Again, I noticed, the date read August 27, 1956. I corrected it and experimentally restarted the machine.

August 27, 1956. Must be a dead battery, I opined over our Saturday-morning omelet.

Looking up from the paper's Business section: "Desktop computers have batteries?"

Some sort of little battery, I believed I remembered, to keep the clock going when the thing's shut down. Maybe to keep certain memory-functions intact between start-ups, although I hadn't noticed any other problems thus far. Not my line; I would check the user's manual.

"How come it doesn't default—Is that the right word?"

Default, yes. (Words *were* my line.)

"How come it doesn't default to the last date you set it to, or come up with a different wrong date each time? Why always August Whatever, Nineteen Whenever?"

Twenty-Seven, '56. Good question, but not one that I could answer.

Encouragingly: "Sounds like the beginning of a story."

Yes, well. We finished breakfast, did our daily stretchies together (hers more vigorous than mine, as she's the family jock), refilled our coffee mugs, and addressed our separate Saturday chores and amusements: for Julia, first her round-robin tennis group, then fresh-veggie shopping at the village farmers' market, then housework and gardening, interspersed with laps in our backyard pool; for yours truly, a bit of bookkeeping at the desk and then odd jobs about the house and grounds, maybe a bit of afternoon crabbing in the tidal cove that fronts our property. Then dinner *à deux* and our usual evening routine: a bit of reading, a bit of television, maybe an e-mail to one of our off-sprung offspring, maybe even a few recorder-piano duets, although we make music together less frequently than we used to. Then to bed, seldom later than half past ten.

Then the Sunday. Then a new week.

We had done all right, Julia and I; even rather well. Classmates and college sweethearts at the state university, we had married on our joint commencement day—shortly after World War II, when Americans wed younger than nowadays—and promptly thereafter did our bit for the postwar baby boom, turning out three healthy youngsters in four years. I had majored in journalism, Julia in education, and although she'd graduated summa cum laude while I had simply graduated, after the manner of the time she had set her professional credentials mostly aside to do the Mommy track while Daddy earned us all a living. I had duly done that, too: first at a little New England weekly, where I learned what college hadn't taught me about newspapering; then at an upstate New York daily; then at a major midwestern daily, where on the strength of a Nieman Fellowship year at Harvard (the young American journalist's next-best thing to a Pulitzer prize) I had switched from the Metro desk to Features; then at the Sunday magazine of Our Nation's Capital's leading rag—from which, as of my sixty-fifth birthday this time last year, I retired as associate editor to try my hand at free-lancing. Over those busy decades, as our nestlings fledged and one by one took wing, Julia had moved from subbing in their sundry schools to part-time academic counseling—whatever could be shifted with my "career moves" and expanded with the kids' independence—thence to supervisoring in the county school system and most recently, since our move from city to country, to fulltiming as Assistant Director of Development for a small local college. No journalist or educator expects to get rich, especially with three college tuitions to pay; but we had husbanded (and wifed) our resources, invested our savings prudently along with modest inheritances from our late parents, and watched those investments grow through the prosperous American decades that raised the Dow Jones from about 600 to nearly 6000. Anon we had sold our suburban-D.C. house at a jim-dandy profit and more or less retired—half of us, anyhow—to five handsomely wooded acres on the high banks of a cove off the Potomac's Virginia shore, complete with swimming pool, goose-hunting blind, guest wing for the kids and grandkids, His and Hers in the two-car garage, and a brace of motorboats at the pier: one little, for crabbing and such, the other not so little, for serious fishing with old buddies from the *Post*. Enough pension, dividend, and Social Security income to keep the show going even without what I scored for the occasional column or magazine-piece, not to mention Julia's quite-good salary. Her own woman at last, as she liked to tease, *she* meant to keep on fulltiming until they threw her out: the Grandma Moses of development directors.

What's more, this prevailing good fortune, not entirely a matter of luck, applied to our physical and marital health as well. Both had survived their share of setbacks and even the odd knockdown, but in our mid-sixties we were still mentally, physically, and maritally intact, our midlife crises safely behind us and late-life ones yet to come, parents in the grave and grown-up children scattered about the republic with kids and mid-life crises of their own. On balance, a much-blessed life indeed.

And by no means over! Quite apart from the famously increasing longevity of us First-Worlders, J and I had our parents' genes going for us, which had carried that foursome in not-bad health right up to bye-bye time in their late eighties and early nineties. Barring accident, we had an odds-on chance of twenty-plus years ahead: longer than our teen-age grandkids had walked the earth.

"Time enough to make a few more career moves of my own," Julia teased whenever I spoke of this.

August 27, 1956. I recorrected the date, went on with my work, with the weekend, with our life; took the Macintosh in on Monday for rebattery-ing or whatever and made shift meanwhile with Julia's new laptop and my trusty old Hermes manual typewriter—stored in our attic ever since personal computers came online—until the patient was cured and discharged. The problem was, in fact, a dead logic-board battery, the service person presently informed me, and then tech-talked over my head for a bit about CMOS and BIOS circuitry. He couldn't explain, however, why the date-function defaulted consistently to August 27, 1956, rather than to the date of the machine's assembly, say (no earlier than 1993), or of the manufacture of its logic board. Did electronic data-processors in any form, not to mention PCs and Macintoshes, even exist on August 27, 1956?

Truth to tell, I don't have all that much to do at the desk these days, and so "making shift" was no big deal. Indeed, while both Julia and Mac were out of the house I turned my fascination with that presumably arbitrary but spookily insistent date into a bit of a project. We veteran journalists do not incline to superstition; a healthy skepticism, to put it mildly, goes with the territory. But why August? Why the 27th? Why 1956? Was something trying to tell me something?

Out of professional habit I checked the nearest references to hand, especially the historical-events chronology in my much-thumbed *World Almanac*. In 1956, it reminded me, we were halfway through what the almanac called "The American Decade." Dwight Eisenhower was about to be landslided into his second presidential term; Nikita Krushchev was de-Stalinizing the USSR; Israel, Britain, and France were about to snatch back the Suez Canal from Egypt, which had nationalized it when we-all declined to finance President Nasser's Aswan dam; the Soviet-U.S. space race was up and running, but *Sputnik* hadn't yet galvanized the competition; our Korean war was finished, our Vietnamese involvement scarcely begun . . . et cetera.

What couldn't I have done back in my old office, with the Post's mighty databases and info-sniffing software! But to what end? Since the computer-repair facility was associated with "Julia's college," I contented myself with a side-trip to the campus library when I drove in to retrieve the machine. A modest facility ("But we're working on it," my wife liked to declare), its microfilm stacks didn't include back numbers of my former employer; they did file the *New York Times*, however, and from the reel *Jul. 21, 1956–Dec. 5, 1956* I photocopied the front page for Monday, August 27. Soviet Nuclear Test in Asia Reported by White House was the lead story, subheaded U.S. Contrasts Moscow's Secrecy With Advance Washington Warnings. Among the other front-page news: British Charge Makarios Directed Rebels in Cyprus and Eisenhower Stay in West Extended (the President was golfing in Pebble Beach, California, from where the nuclear-test story had also been filed). The lead photo was of the newly nominated Democratic Presidential and Vice-Presidential candidates, Adlai E. Stevenson and Estes Kefauver, leaving church together with members of their families on the previous day; the story below, however, was headlined TV Survey of Conventions Finds Viewing Off Sharply, and reported that neither the Republican nor the Democratic national conventions, recently concluded, had attracted as many viewers on any one evening as had Elvis Presley and Ed Sullivan.

So: It had been a Monday, that day forty Augusts past (its upcoming anniversary, I had already determined, would be a Tuesday). I showed the page to Julia over lunch, which we sometimes met for when I had errands near her campus.

"Still Eight Twenty-Seven Fifty-Sixing, are you?" She pretended concern at my "fixation" but scanned the photocopy with mild interest, sighing at the shot of Stevenson (whose lost cause we had ardently supported in the second presidential election of our voting life) and predicting that *this* year's upcoming political conventions, so carefully orchestrated for television, would lose far more viewers to the comedian Jerry Seinfeld than that year's had to Elvis Presley. And she pointed out to me—How hadn't I noticed it myself?—that the Soviet nuclear-test story had been filed "Special to the *New York Times*" by a sometime professional acquaintance of ours, currently a public-television celebrity and syndicated columnist, but back then already making his name as a young White House reporter for the Baltimore *Sun*.

While I, I reminded Julia, was still clawing my way up from the Boondock *Weekly Banner* to the Rochester *Democrat and Chronicle*. Don't rub it in.

"Who's rubbing?" She ordered the shrimp salad and checked her watch. "It was an okay paper already, and you made it a better one. Which reminds me . . . "And she changed the subject to the college's plan to install fiber-optic computer cables in every dormitory room during the upcoming academic year, in order to give the students faster access to the Internet. Her scheduled one o'clock meeting with a potential corporate sponsor of that improvement cut our lunch-date short; I wished her luck and watched her exit in her spiffy tailored suit while I (in my casual khakis, sportshirt, and Old Fart walking shoes), finished my sandwich and took care of the check.

Yes indeedy, I mused to myself, homeward bound then: the dear old *Democrap and Chronic Ill*—as we used to call it when things screwed up at the city desk. Heroic snow-belt winters; summers clouded by the "Great Lakes effect," though much pleasanter in August than our subtropical summertime Chesapeake, and blessedly hurricane-free. The inexhaustible energy of an ambitious twenty-six-year-old, chasing down story-leads at all hours, learning the ins and outs of our newly adopted city as perhaps only a Metro reporter can, yet at the same time helping Julia with our three preschoolers, maintaining and even remodeling our low-budget first house, and still finding time over and above for entertaining friends, for going to parties and concerts (a welcome change from Boondockville)—time for everything, back when there was never enough time for anything! Whereas nowadays it sometimes seemed to me that with ample leisure for everything, less and less got done; July's routine chores barely finished before August's were upon me.

Once Mac was back in place (and correctly reading, when I booted him up, *August 6, 1996*) I did a bit more homework with the aid of some time-line software that I used occasionally when researching magazine pieces. By 1956, it reminded me, the world newly had or was on the cusp of having nuclear power plants, portable electric saws, Scrabble, electric typewriters and toothbrushes and clothes dryers, oral polio vaccine, aerosol spray cans, home air conditioners, aluminum foil, lightweight bicycles with shiftable gears and caliper brakes, wash-and-wear fabrics, credit cards, garbage disposers, epoxy glue, frisbees, milk cartons, pantyhose, ballpoint pens, FM radio, and stereophonic sound systems. Still waiting in the wings were antiperspirants, automobile air conditioning and cruise control, aluminum cans, birth control pills, bumper stickers, pocket calculators, decaf coffee, microwave ovens, felt-tip pens, photocopiers, home-delivery pizza, transistor radios, home computers (as I'd suspected), contact lenses, disposable diapers, running shoes, Teflon, scuba gear, skateboards, wraparound sunglasses, audiocassettes (not to mention VCRs), touchtone telephones (not to mention cordlesses, cellulars, and answering machines), color and cable television, Valium, Velcro, battery-powered wristwatches, digital anythings, and waterbeds.

"Disposable diapers," Julia sighed that evening when I spieled through this inventory: "Where were they when we needed them?"

Fifty-Six was the year Grace Kelly married Prince Rainier the Third, I told her, and Ringling Brothers folded their last canvas circus tent, and the *Andrea Doria* went down, and Chevrolet introduced fuel-injected engines. Harry Belafonte. The aforementioned Elvis. *I Love Lucy*. . . .

"I *did* love Lucy," my wife remembered. The early evening was airless, sultry; indeed, the whole week had been unnaturally calm, scarcely a ripple out on our cove, and this at the peak of the Atlantic hurricane season, with Arturo, Bertha, Carlos, and Danielle already safely behind us, and who knew whom to come. Back in '56, if I remembered correctly, the tropical storms all bore Anglo female names; I'd have to check.

We were sipping fresh-peach frozen daiquiris out on our pier while comparing His and Her day, our summer custom before prepping dinner. As Julia was now the nine-to-fiver, I routinely made the cocktails and hors d'oeuvres and barbecued the entree as often as possible, although it was still she who planned the menus and directed most of the preparation. She'd had a frustrating afternoon; hadn't hit it off with that potential co-sponsor of the college's fiber-optic upgrade, an Old Boy type whose patronizing manner had strained her professional diplomacy to the limit. Excuse her, she warned me, if the male-chauvinist bastard had left her short of patience.

Enough about 1956, then, I suggested.

"No, go on. Obsessional or not, it soothes me."

Steak eighty-eight cents a pound, milk twenty-four cents a quart, bread eighteen cents a loaf. Average cost of a new car seventeen hundred bucks—remember our jim-dandy Chevy wagon?

"A Fifty-Five bought new in Fifty-Six, when the dealer was stuck with it." Our first new car, it had been: two-tone green and ivory. "Or was it a Fifty-Six bought late in the model year?"

A bargain, whichever. Median price of a new house—get this—eleven thousand seven hundred. I think we paid ten five for Maison Faute de Mieux.

"Dear Maison Faute de Mieux." Pet name for our first-ever house, afore-referred to. "But what was the median U.S. income back then?"

Just under two thousand per capita per annum. My fifty-six hundred from the *D and* C was princely for a new hand.

Julia winced her eyes shut in mid-sip. Headache? I wondered.

"Unfortunate choice of abbreviations." It had been in '56 or '57, she reminded me (as I had unwittingly just reminded her) that she'd found herself pregnant for the fourth time, accidentally in this instance, and we had decided not only to terminate the pregnancy by dilation and curettage —D & C, in ob/gyn lingo, and a code-term too for abortion in those pre-*Roe v. Wade* days—but to forestall further such accidents by vasectomy. "Shall we change the subject?"

Agreed—for a cluster of long- and well-buried memories was thereby evoked, of a less nostalgic character than our first house and new car. Duly shifting subjects, What's that floating white thing? I asked her, and pointed toward a something-or-other drifting usward on the ebbing tide.

"Don't see it." With her drink-free hand Julia shaded her eyes from the lowering sun. "Okay, I see it. Paper plate?"

It was an object indeed the diameter of a paper or plastic dinner plate, though several times thicker, floating edge-up and nine-tenths submerged in the flat calm creek. On its present leisurely course it would pass either just before or just under the cross-T where we sat, a not unwelcome diversion. Our sport-fishing boat, *Byline*, was tied up alongside; I stepped aboard, fetched back a crabber's dip-net, and retrieved the visitor when it drifted within reach.

"Well, now."

It was, of all unlikely flotsam, a *clock*: a plain white plastic wall clock, battery powered (didn't have those back in '56). Perhaps blown off some up-creek neighbor's boathouse? But there'd been no wind. Maybe negligently Frisbee'd into the cove after rain got to it? Anyhow quite drowned now, the space between its face and its plastic "crystal" half filled with tidewater (hence its slight remaining buoyancy), and stopped, mirabile dictu, at almost exactly 3:45, so that when I held it twelve o'-clock high, the outstretched hands marked its internal waterline like a miniature horizon.

Time and tide, right? Then, before I'd even thought of the other obvious connection, Julia said, "Now we're in for it: not only August twenty-seventh, but *three forty-five* on August twenty-seventh. A.M. or P.M., I wonder?"

We tisked and chuckled; during our coveside residency a number of souvenirs had washed up on our reedy shoreline along with the usual litter of plastic bags and discarded drink-containers from the creek beyond— wildfowl decoys, life vests, fishermen's hats, crabtrap floats—but none so curious or portentous. In a novel or a movie, I supposed to Julia, the couple would begin to wonder whether some plot was thickening; whether something was trying to tell them something, and whether 3:45 A.M. or P.M. meant Eastern Daylight Time in 1956 or 1996.

"At three forty-five A.M. Eight Twenty-Seven '96," Julia declared, "your loving wife intends to be sound asleep. You can tell her the news over breakfast." And she wondered aloud, as we moved in from the pier to start dinner, what we had each been up to at 3:45 in the afternoon of August 27 forty years ago in Rochester, New York.

Another memory-buzz, and it was well that we were single-filing, for I felt my face burn. Would it not have been that very summer, if not necessarily that month . . . but yes, right around the time of "our" abortion. . . .

Without mentioning it to Julia, I resolved to check out discreetly, if I could, a certain little matter that I hadn't had occasion to remember for years, perhaps even for decades. My intention had been to drop the dripping clock *trouvée* into our trash bin, but as I passed through the garage en route to setting up the patio barbecue oven (didn't have those in '56, at least not with charcoal-lighting fluid and liquid propane igniters) I decided to hang it instead on a nearby tool-hook, to remind me to notice whether anything Significant would happen to happen at the indicated hour three weeks hence.

Not that I would likely need reminding. Unsuperstitious as I am and idle as was my interest in that approaching "anniversary," I was more curious than ever now about what—in Julia's and my joint time-line if not in America's and the world's—it might be the fortieth anniversary of. I was half tempted to ask the *Democrat and Chronicle*'s morgue-keepers to fax me a copy of the paper's Metro-section front page for August 27, 1956, to see what had been going on in town that day (but the reported news would be of the day before; perhaps I ought to check headlines for the 28th) and whether I myself had bylined any Rochester stories while my more successful friend was filing White House specials to the *Times*. But I resisted the temptation. Frame-by-framing through Julia's college's microfilm files had reminded me how each day's newspaper is indeed like a frame in time's ongoing movie. We retrospective viewers know, as the "actors" themselves did not, how at least some of those stories will end: that Stevenson and Kefauver will be overwhelmed in November by Eisenhower and Nixon; that the U.S.-Soviet arms race will effectively end with the collapse of the U.S.S.R. in 1989. Of others we may remember the "beginning" but not the "end," or vice versa; of others yet (e.g., in my case, Britain's troubles with Archbishop Makarios in Cyprus) neither the prologue nor the sequel. But who was to say that what would turn out to be the *really* significant event of any given day—even internationally, not to mention locally—would be front-page news? Next week's or month's lead story often begins as today's page-six squib or goes unreported altogether at the time: Einstein's formulation of relativity theory, the top-secret first successful test of a thermonuclear bomb. And unlike the President's golf games, what ordinary person's most life-affecting events—birth, marriage, career successes and failures, child-conceptions, infidelities and other betrayals, divorce, major accident, illness, death—make the headlines, or in most instances even the inside pages? I reminded myself, moreover, that such "frames" as hours, day-dates, year-numbers—all such convenient divisions of time—are more or less our human inventions, more or less relative to our personal or cultural-historical point of view: What would "August 27, 1956" mean to an Aztec or a classical Greek? Oblivious to time zones and calendars, though not to astronomical rhythms, the world rolls on; our life-processes likewise, oblivious to chronological age though not to aging.

8/27/56. No need to consult the *D&C*: prompted by some old résumés and certain other items in my home-office files, my ever-slipperier memory began to clarify the personal picture. In the late spring of that year, Julia and I and our three preschoolers had moved to our first real city—in our new Chevy wagon, it now came back to me, bought earlier in Boondockville on the strength of my Rochester job offer, and so it had been a leftover '55 after all. After checking neighborhoods and public-school districts against our freshly elevated budgetary ceiling, we had bought "Maison Faute de Mieux," its to-the-hilt mortgage to be amortized by the laughably distant year 1986. And on July 1 I had begun my first more or less big-time newspaper job, for which I'd been hired on the strength of a really rather impressive portfolio from what I'm calling the Boondock *Weekly Banner*. No *annus mirabilis*, maybe, 1956, but a major corner-turn in my/our life: formal education and professional apprenticeship finished; family established and now appropriately housed; children safely through babyhood and about to commence their own schooling; our six-year marriage well past the honeymoon stage but not yet seriously strained; and my first major success scored in what would turn out to be a quite creditable career (for if I could point to some, like that *Times*/PBS fellow, who had done better, I could point to ever so many more who'd done less well) in a field that by and large served the public interest, not just our personal welfare. Reviewed thus, in the story of both our married life and my professional life the summer of '56 could be said to have marked the end of the Beginning and the beginning of the Middle.

Over that evening's cocktail-on-the-pier, "You left something out,"

Julia said, and my face reflushed, for I had indeed skirted a thing or two that my day's digging had exhumed. But what she meant, to my relief, was that it had been that same summer—when George Jr. was five, Anne-Marie four, and Jeannette about to turn three—that their mother had felt free at last to begin her own "career," however tentatively and part-time, by working for "pay" (i.e., reduced kiddie-tuition) in our daughters' nursery school.

Right she was; sorry about that.

"It may seem nothing to you, George, but to me it mattered."

Properly so.

She looked out across the cove, where the sun was lowering on another steamy August day. "I've often envied Anne-Marie and Jeannette their *assumption* that their careers are as important as their husbands'."

I'm sure you have. By ear I couldn't tell whether "their husbands" ended with an apostrophe. The fact was, though, that if our elder daughter and her spouse, both academics, had managed some measure of professional parity in their university, our younger daughter's legal career had proved more important to her than marriage and motherhood; she'd left her CPA husband in Boston with custody of their ten-year-old to take a promotion in her firm's Seattle office. Even Julia's feelings were mixed about that, although the marriage had been shaky from the start.

More brightly, "Oh, I forgot to tell you," she said then: "I asked this computer-friend of mine at work about that date-default business? And he said that normally the default would be to the date when some gizmo called the BIOS chip was manufactured, which couldn't be before 1980. BIOS means Basic Input-Output System? But this guy's a PC aficionado who sniffs at Macintoshes. Anyhow, he's putting out a query on the Net, so stay tuned."

I was still getting used to some of Julia's recent speech habits: those California-style rising inflections and flip idioms like "stay tuned" that she picked up from her younger office-mates and that to me sounded out of character for people our age. But I suppressed my little irritation, told her sincerely that I appreciated her thoughtfulness, and withdrew to set up the charcoal grill before the subject could return to Things Left Out.

On 8/27/56, yet another bit of software informed me next day, the Dow Jones Industrial Average had been 579, and *Billboard* magazine's #1 pop recording in the USA had been Dean Martin singing "Memories Are Made of This." Whatever other desk-projects I had in the works—and my "retirement," mind, had been only from daily go-to-the-office journalism, not from the profession altogether—were stalled by distraction as the Big

Date's anniversary drew nearer. In "the breakaway republic of Chechnya," as the media called it, a smoldering stalemate continued between rebel forces and the Russian military, whose leaders themselves were at odds over strategy. In Bosnia a sour truce still held as election-time approached. Julia found another possibly interested corporate co-sponsor for her college's fiber-optic upgrade. The queerly calm weather hung over tidewater Virginia as if Nature were holding her breath. There would be a full moon, my desk calendar declared, on the night after 8/27/96; perhaps we would celebrate the passage of my recent lunacy. On Sunday 8/18, trolling for bluefish aboard *Byline* with pals from the *Post*, I snagged my left thumb on a fish hook; no big deal, although the bandage hampered my computer keyboarding. My "little obsession" had become a standing levity since Julia (without first consulting me) shared it as a tease with our friends and children. George Jr., who worked for the National Security Agency at Fort Meade, pretended to have inside info ("We call it the X-File, Dad") that extraterrestrials were scheduled to take over the earth on 8/27/96. Picking up on her brother's tease, his academic sister e-mailed me from Michigan that the first UFOs had secretly landed on 8/27/56; their ongoing experiments on our family—in particular on its alpha male—would be completed on the fortieth anniversary (as measured in Earth-years) of that first landing. We'll miss you, Dad.

"So guess what," Julia announced on Friday, August 23. "I had lunch again today with Sam Bryer—my computer friend? And he found out from some hacker on the Net that all Macintoshes default to 8/27/56 when their logic-boards die because that's Steve Whatsisname's birthday—the founder of Apple Computers? Steve Jobs. A zillionaire in his thirties! Sam says everything about Macintoshes has to be cutesy-wootsie."

Aha, and my thanks to . . . Sam, is it? Sam. To myself I thought, Lunch again today with the guy? and tried to remember when I had last lunched with a woman colleague. The bittersweet memories then suddenly flooded in: a certain oak-paneled restaurant in downtown Rochester, far enough from the office for privacy but close enough for the two of us to get back to our desks more or less on time; a certain motel, inexpensive but not sleazy, on the Lake Ontario side of town; the erotic imagination and enviable recovery-speed of a healthy twenty-six-year-old on late-summer afternoons when he was supposed to be out checking the latest from Eastman Kodak or the University. It occurred to me to wonder whether it might have happened to be exactly at 3:45 P.M. EDST on August 27, 1956, that a certain premature and unprotected ejaculation had introduced a certain rogue spermatozoon to a certain extramural ovum: "Our imperious desires," dear brave Marianne had once ruefully quoted Robert Louis Stevenson, "and their staggering consequences."

For the sake of the children, as they say—but for good other reasons, too—Mr. and Mrs. had chosen not to divorce when the matter surfaced; and except for one half-hysterical (but consequential) instance, Julia had not retaliated in kind. The Nieman Fellowship year in Cambridge, not long after, had welcomely removed us from the Scene of the Crime as well as testifying to my professional rededication; its prestige enabled our move to St. Louis (the *Post-Dispatch*), thence to D.C., excuse the initials—and here, forty years later, we were: still comrades, those old wounds long since scarred over and, yes, healed.

Tell your pal Sam, I told my wife, that Eight Twenty-Seven is Lyndon Johnson's and Mother Teresa's birthday, too, though not their upcoming fortieth, needless to say. Virgos all. Birthstone Peridot. What's Peridot?

Julia, however, was communing with herself. "My pal Sam," she said deprecatingly, but smiled and sipped.

Who knows what "really" happened when the Big Day came? The explanation of my computer's default date, while mildly amusing, was irrelevant to the momentous though still vague significance that it had assumed for me, and in no way diminished my interest in its anniversary. By then my fishhook wound, too, was largely healed. Julia and I made wake-up love that morning—she had been more ardent of late than usual, and than her distracted husband. I cleared breakfast while she dolled up for work and then, still in my pajamas and slippers, lingered over second coffee and the Tuesday paper before going to my desk. Another sultry forecast, 30 percent chance of late-afternoon thundershowers. Second day of Democratic National Convention in Chicago; Hillary Rodham Clinton to address delegates tonight. Cause of TWA 800 crash still undetermined; Hurricane Edouard approaching Caribbean. I decided to try doing an article for the Post's Sunday magazine—maybe even for the *New York Times* Sunday magazine—about my curious preoccupation, which by then had generated a small mountain of notes despite my professional sense that I still lacked a proper handle on it, and that those of my associated musings that weren't indelicately personal were too . . . philosophical, let's say, for a newspaper-magazine piece. I've mentioned already that the Really Important happenings, on whatever level, aren't necessarily those that get reported in the press: the undetected first metal-fatigue crack in some crucial component of a jetliner's airframe; the casual mutation of one of your liver cells from normal to cancerous; the Go signal to a terrorist conspiracy, coded innocuously in loveseekers' lingo among the Personals. But my maunderings extended even from *What's the significance of this date?* through *What's the significance of the whole concept of date, even of time?* to *What's the significance of Significance, the meaning of Meaning?*

Never mind those. I quite expected 8/27/96 to be just another day, in the course of which we Americans (so said some new software sent by our Seattle-lawyer daughter) would per usual eat forty-seven million hot dogs, swallow fifty-two million aspirin tablets, use six point eight billion gallons of water to flush our collective toilets, and give birth to ten thousand new Americans. But I was not blind to such traditional aspects of Forty Years as, say, the period of the Israelites' wandering in the desert, or the typical span of a professional career—so that if, as aforesuggested, 8/27/56 had been for mine the end of the Beginning and beginning of the Middle, then 8/27/96 might feasibly mark the end of the Middle and thus the beginning of the End. I was even aware that just as my "little obsession" therewith had assumed a life of its own, independent of the trifle that had prompted it, so my half-serious but inordinate search for Portent might conceivably generate its own fulfillment—might prompt Julia, for example, this late in our story, to settle a long-dormant score by making, as she herself had more or less joked, "a few career moves" of her own; or might merely nudge your reporter gently around some bend, distancing me from her, our family and friends and former colleagues, so that in retrospect (trying and failing, say, to make a marketable essay out of it or anything else thenceforward) I would see that August 27 had indeed been the beginning of the end because I myself had made it so.

Just another day: the first for many, for many the last, for many more a crucial or at least consequential turning-point, but for most of us none of the above, at least apparently. I ate an apple for lunch; phoned Julia's office to check out *her* Day Thus Far and got her voice-mail message instead: a poised, assured, very-much-her-own-woman's voice. As is my summertime post-lunch habit, I then ran a flag up our waterfront pole from the assortment in our "flag locker," choosing for the occasion a long and somewhat tattered red-and-yellow streamer that in the Navy's flag code signifies Zero; it had been a birthday gift to me some years past from George Jr., who jokingly complained that I read too much significance into things and therefore gave me something that literally meant Nothing. After an exercise-swim I set out our crab traps along the lip of the cove-channel and patrolled them idly for a couple of hours from *Sound Bite*, our noisy little outboard runabout—inevitably wondering, at

3:45, whether my wife and Sam Whatsisname, Sam Bryer, might actually be et cetera. At that idea I found myself simultaneously sniffling and chuckling aloud with . . . oh, Transcendent Acceptance, I suppose.

Not enough crabs to bother with; they seemed to be scarcer every year.

At about 4:30—as I was considering whether canteloupe daiquiris or champagne would make the better toast to Beginning-of-the-End Day when Julia got home—the forecast thunderstorm rolled down the tidal Potomac, dumping an inch of rain in half an hour, knocking out our power for twenty minutes, and buffeting the cove with fifty-knot gusts, as measured on the wind gauge in our family room. Busy closing windows, I absent-mindedly neglected to fetch in the Zero flag before the storm hit; as I watched nature's sound-and-light show from our leeward porch, I saw the weathered red and yellow panels one by one let go at their seams in the bigger gusts and disappear behind curtains of rain. By five the tempest had rolled on out over the Chesapeake, the wind had moderated to ten and fifteen, and the westward sky was rebrightening. Our dock bench and pool-deck chairs would be too soaked for Happy-Hour sitting; we would use the screened porch. I reset all the house clocks and hauled down the last shredded panel of George Jr.'s flag, thinking I might mount it on a garage or basement wall behind that waterlogged clock as a wry memorial to the occasion: my next-to-last rite of passage, whatever.

Normally my wife got home from work by half past five; that day I was well into the six o-clock news on television—Russians resume pullout from Grozny; Syria ready to resume talks with Israel; big hometown welcome expected for First Lady's convention appearance—when the garage door rumbled up and Julia's Volvo rolled in. Often "high" from her day at the office, she arrived this time positively radiant, forgetting even (I noted as I went to greet her) to reclose the garage door as usual from inside her car. Tugging her briefcase off the passenger seat with one hand while removing her sunglasses with the other, "Any champagne in the fridge?" she called. She kneed the car door shut—I pressed the garage-door wall button—gave me an exaggerated kiss hello, and exhilarated past me into the kitchen. Plopped down her briefcase; peeled out of her suit-jacket; yanked the fridge open; then stopped to grin meward, spreading her arms victoriously.

"Congratulate me! I *nailed* the guy! Fiber optics, here we come!"

Well, I did congratulate her—wholeheartedly, or very nearly so. I popped the bubbly; toasted her corporate co-sponsoral coup; let her crow happily through half a glass before I even mentioned what I'd thought she would be celebrating, perhaps prematurely: the unremarkable close of what had proved after all to be just another day. When I did finally bring that matter up, it was via the heavyhanded portent of the thunderstorm and George Jr.'s flag.

"So here's to Nothing," Julia cheered, and although she topped off our glasses and bade us reclink them, her mind was obviously still on her successful courtship of that potential college-benefactor. Presently she excused herself to change out of office clothes and take a swim, she announced, before hors d'oeuvres and the rest of the champagne. I wasn't even to *think* of starting the charcoals for the veal grillades and marinated eggplant wedges; she was flying too high to fuss with dinner yet.

So *I'll* fuss, I volunteered, but contented myself with merely readying the grill for cooking. Our pool is well screened from the neighbors, and we skinny-dip on occasion, though not as a rule—since who knows when a delivery- or service-person might drive up, or the lawn-mowing crew. But presently out she frisked jaybird-naked, did my triumphant mate, and like a playful pink porpoise dived with a whoop into the pool's deep end.

"Come on in!" she all but ordered me after a bit. "Drop your drawers and take the plunge!" Not to spoil her fun, I did, but couldn't follow through when, to my surprise, she made to crown her triumph with a spot of submarine sex.

On 8/27/96 the Dow Jones closed up seventeen, at 5711. We ate late; watched the First Lady's convention speech on television (Julia raising her fist from time to time in a gesture of solidarity); decided not to wait up for the ensuing keynote address. Instead, nightcap in hand, we stepped outside to admire the moon over our cove—still officially one night shy of full, but looking already as ripe as a moon can look.

So, said I: That's that.

"What's what?" She truly had no idea what I was referring to.

Old Eight Twenty-Seven Et Cetera.

"Oh, right." She inhaled, exhaled, and with mock gravity said "You know what they say, George: *Today is the first day of the rest of your life.*"

How right she was.

The Death of Nu-Nu

Mitch Berman

1

No one at the Café Lucca knew the man's name, so you will not learn it from me. No, none of us, neither the regulars nor the waiters, knew his name, though all of us knew him; or at least we knew who he was.

He would enter the café, glancing not so much at as over the regulars, who looked, or glanced, or did not look back at him according to our own habits. He appeared to have little desire to see us, and none to be seen by us.

He was about sixty, more tall than not, more bald than not, more handsome than not. He was thin and his face was thin, with tanned skin stretched to an unglossy tightness around prominent high cheekbones and slightly sunken cheeks and temples. I believe that his eyes, through goldrimmed bifocals, were blue. He had superb and unvarying posture. All his movements were executed with a firm premeditation that suggested good health, but nothing left of youth.

He dressed in a way that would pass him through New York City anonymously, recognized instantly and only as being of that social class which must subscribe to, but not necessarily enjoy, the ballet and the opera. There was never any scuffing, nor too much shine, on his black penny-loafers; there was never any lint or loose thread on his navy blazer or creased charcoal trousers. I disliked him slightly because it was impossible to have strong feelings about him.

He would establish himself at Table 8—and if it were not available, he would shift uneasily and soon depart, leaving a tip that was even smaller than usual—fix his eyes to the headlines of his clean unfolded copy of *The New York Times*, accept his cappuccino and baba au rhum with such modest word or gesture as the waiter required, then turn to the crossword puzzle and rapidly complete it, in ink. Only then would he read anything else in the paper, and he seemed to read everything else, from the first page of the news to the last of the classified. He never stayed less than an hour or more than two. When, after years of faithful attendance, he took an extended absence from the Café Lucca, I did not notice he was gone. And now I will withdraw from the story, though I am still telling it. I remain at the Lucca, if you wish to picture me there, at Table 1, in the corner by the radiator. My drink is double espresso, hot in winter, iced in summer. I am usually writing.

2

The man was in Florida for the eighteen months when he did not come to the Café Lucca. The day after he arrived for what was to be only a week with his sister's family in Boca Raton, he fell ill at her dinner table and was taken to Roosevelt Memorial Hospital. He had an aneurysm—a kind of overfilled water balloon—directly over the motor strip in his brain, and the doctors warned that the necessary surgery would risk paralysis. He was knocked out, drilled and sawed like a wood-shop project, chopped up, screwed down, sewn up, pronounced as good as new. His motor strip was intact, and after a week of observation at Roosevelt Memorial, he was farmed out to a private room in the Coconut Grove Nursing Home.

The Coconut Grove was on one of the busier streets in Boca, and although there were no coconuts, he could see, if he opened his fourth-floor window and bulged his face hard left into the screen, a wedge of Ocean Avenue on which there was a traffic light that was rarely triggered by crossing cars, a bus-stop bench and a Benetton store. Wake-up was at 7, lights-out at 10. Meals were served at 8, 12 and 6; at least once a day a Jell-O Surprise would be placed before him, with a maraschino cherry staring up out of it.

He missed the coffee first, or rather the smell of the coffee, or rather all the smells of the Café Lucca back in New York. As he got stronger, gave up the wheelchair, took solid food, these smells carried back to him, the way desert dust drifts on a high wind to a distant city: the smell of the freshly ground coffee beans, or not quite, but that smell mixed with the general and pervasive smells of cooking, basil or garlic or wine and always onions, with the specific, nearby, intimate smells of his rum-soaked pastry, the steam from his cappuccino, the vinegary scent that arose when he unfolded the *Times*, or not quite, but all these smells mixed with fresh air, for the Lucca's front door and the transom window above it would remain open at this time of year. He had never thought of the air in Manhattan as fresh, but it was, at least in early autumn, when the winds dried out and crackled the leaves, when the leaves crackled dry and fell loose on the ground, when his feet crackled the leaves on the sidewalks. He could still see his penny-loafers among those leaves, firm, sweeping, capable; now his feet were tentative, shuffling, pale, paled by fluorescent light in brown corduroy slippers against green marble-patterned linoleum. When he had first entered the Coconut Grove he had been overpowered by the cherry antiseptic used to swab the floors, but as he got accustomed to it, he came to smell it only as the absence of clean air: he would open his window, lean the side of his face against the screen, and inhale the Boca air, watching people go in and out of Benetton, watching the summer sale come and go, watching the stock trucks unload the fall line and the window dressers push it up front in the picture windows, watching the winter wools and flannels arrive; watching people who walked by and particularly those who settled on the bus bench, including a stout elderly woman who came Thursdays at 3:40 with a straw handbag full of soap opera magazines and two large Winn-Dixie shopping bags, one containing jars of Cremora and the other containing six-packs of Old Milwaukee beer, and as he compounded these ingredients, imagining her life, the bus would pause there and consume the woman in one bite, leaving behind a belch of sticky-sweetish diesel fumes, the same fumes that had enveloped the Café Lucca when the red double-decker tourist buses had pulled away from the curb of Bleecker Street, and he wondered whether people at the Lucca had conjectured about him as he had about the Cremora Lady: he inhaled the air from his window, and even the outside air, with its close and fresh-rotten hint of the Atlantic, even the outside air, half-smelled, mixed in with the odor of the Coconut Grove, smelled of something, smelled slightly, if he were quiet and were listening, of the café, of escape, of home. He could not stay there indefinitely, half of him in the nursing home, half in the town, all of him back in the café; the seaside humidity had rust-roughened the screen, after a while the screen roughened his cheek, and once a mosquito bit him through it.

When he closed the window and turned out the light, he closed the window on the Coconut Grove, on Boca Raton, on Florida, and went back to fall, back to winter, back to a place where there were falls and winters, back to Manhattan, back, finally, always, to the café. He explored the café as he never had—never had to do—before, in the way a stroke victim does not so much relearn the functions of his body as consciously learn them for the first time.

He knew, had always known, had never known he knew, everything about the Café Lucca: the name not only of the owner, a squat young Tunisian man with curly black hair and black-lashed black eyes like apostrophes, but of his wife and two small daughters; the names of all the waiters, though he rarely used them; and the names, occupations, tables and usual orders of the other regulars, though he never spoke to them. He discovered he knew these things because each of his fantasies encapsulated a complete and sequential visit to the café, and in them the cappuccino and baba au rhum did not materialize on his table of their own accord, but were, as in life, placed there by a waiter whom, as in life, he had to thank, to pay, to tip. Just as what he'd always taken to be the smell of the Lucca was constituted of many smells, so too the sound of the Lucca was composed of many sounds that he could now separate as one can unravel the colored threads from the edge of a woven scarf: the thin clatter of radio disco from behind the counter, the thick clinking of Buffalo China on Buffalo China, the burble of conversation, the frequent ring of the house phone—electronic—and the occasional ring of the pay phone—acoustic—and the constant arguments between the coffee lady, who yelled at everyone in a Maltese accent, and the waiters, who defended themselves in Russian, Spanish and Arabic accents, or when they were really angry, in Russian, Spanish or Arabic.

He knew, most of all, about the cat. Nu-Nu was a young male, not quite fully grown, a cross between an orange tabby and a Siamese. From the tabby he had the orange and white markings; from the Siamese a long, pointed face and an aloof demeanor. When the radiator was on, he slept either stretched out atop it on a carpet-covered pallet or curled up like a frozen shrimp on a chair beside it; when it was off, he stayed out of sight, baking himself into a woozy trance among the compressor coils beneath the ice-cream freezer. Being a young cat he was, when not sleeping, uncontrollable, sharpening his claws on the vinyl booth upholstery, tackling the ankles of the coffee lady, who fed him by hand and called him *sabieh tighei*—"sweetheart" in Maltese—heaving onto his back to bite and kick the black rubber runner that tongued through the café on rainy days, pausing to flash his crazed challenging white-rolling eyes at onlookers before kicking and biting some more, walking a tightrope along the sill of the wainscoting beneath the tall-paned display windows in urgent, violent, propulsive pursuit of lazy summer flies, sashaying a zigzag through the forest of chair-legs to sniff and rub his cheeks against the handbags and jackets that hung down to his level, and slinking low and weasel-like out the door to stalk pigeons from the shadows under the cars standing on busy Bleecker Street. Though the man had never touched the cat, he knew by sight all the textures of his fur, from the vein-shot translucent velvet of the ears to the fine striations of orange and white on his head to the coarse hairlike locks that stood straight out from his crooked shank when he curled up. He resolved to pet the cat in all of those places, and find out if they felt as they looked. The cat was an undemanding, undiluted pleasure of the café, and the pier to which the man moored his ambitions to return.

He always approached the Café Lucca from the northern tip of Father Demo Square, the brick-paved triangular plaza, edged with park benches, which lay across Bleecker Street: in spring or in fall, the door flung open, the cat prowling freely indoors and outdoors, a sidewalk passerby propping a foot on the low iron railing to chat with a customer sitting outside; in summer, the door closed, the air-conditioning on, the cat salted away, the drinks iced; in winter, sealed up again, a glass bubble of light and activity across the becalmed streets, the windows dull-bright, clouded with condensation, while behind them, in that damp and reassuringly too-hot heat, in that Lucca smell, in that sound, the customers were loud and collegial, their heavy clothes lumped up on the backs of chairs, one of the tourists hailing the waitress and one of the regulars weaving between the tables, dropping a word to those he knew, and the occasional lightning of a camera's flash shocked all of it into black-and-white, a freeze-frame from which it was slow to defrost, to regain color and resume motion, while Nu-Nu slept on his pallet in the Sphinx position, compact as a loaf of bread, only a whisker twitching: it was an oasis at all hours and in all seasons, and the cat was the heart of it. Unlike this slow humid death-by-the-clock cherry-flavored prison, the Lucca was vibrating with life.

The cherry smell had insinuated itself, once again, into his consciousness because he had been returning frequently to the nursing home from new tests at the hospital. Whenever the sliding glass double-doors of the Coconut Grove opened to him—the lobby had once been a bank, and the more cynical residents said the antiseptic covered up the smell of money—a blast of cherry air-conditioned freon slowed him down, made him groggy. The very air in the Coconut Grove was doped.

Finally, as if it had taken all this time to nerve themselves up, the doctors broke the news to him. He had a tiny astrocytoma—a malignant brain tumor—that had been obscured by the aneurysm. It was in a better spot than the aneurysm, and they anticipated an uneventful surgery.

As they had the first time, the doctors guessed wrong. Surgery left the man quivering and spasming on the operating table, and then in intensive care, where, after eight days, he stopped moving entirely, stopped breathing on his own, and entered a coma from which the doctors gave him, in the manner of TV weathermen predicting rain, a 10 percent chance of survival.

He heard them from the depths of his coma, as a man buried beneath a heavy snowdrift might hear—or think he hears—the voices of his would-be rescuers far above him: slowed, distant, distorted, unreal. *Down here, still here. . . .* His brain struggled to form the idea behind the words, could not put together the actual words, had no chance of making his lips form the words or of pushing any breath through them. Like a man rusted into a suit of armor, his body was his entire world. Home and the café were incalculably distant. He could hear only the doctors' consultations, in tones sapped of any urgency, and he imagined the rest, in flashes, in pieces, weaving them together into a long poisoned dream:

They keep finding the cancer has spread. So they're amputating pieces of me: first they hack off my toes, then my feet, then one leg up to mid-shin, more and more and more, cutting off and cutting up my body. For some reason that I do not question, they're not using a surgical saw, but a highly polished aluminum nut scoop.

They haven't given me an anesthetic, just an Andes Mint. Though I'm supposed to be numb, I can feel it, can feel impact, not pain: I can feel collision. They're chunking into me, chipping away at me as if I am rock and the cancer is ore. My body shakes and the bedsprings squeak with the impact. Dismantling me for the parts. Jarring me.

Jarring me. Brain here, in the wide-mouth; heart in the Mason; eyes in the baby-food jars. Not pickles, mayo, creamed corn: brain, heart, eyes. I keep telling you. Ignore the labels; shop well; here was once a man; here was once an organ donor. Organ donor. I checked the box on the card. There in my wallet. Organ donor.

I'm the meal at a buffet. The diners, each of whom needs an organ transplant, roll up to me in wheelchairs, looking me over, nostrils flared. Hungry. They are hungry. Each has a highly polished aluminum nut scoop.

The last thought he had before awakening was that his phone bill must be seriously overdue.

"Mih . . . mih," he told the nurse, or at first only his lips told her, without any voice behind them. He had been dreaming a long time, had worked up a great hunger, and now he couldn't say what he wanted. He wanted an Andes Mint.

It was two weeks before he got his voice back, five before he could eat solid food, seven before he was sent back to the Coconut Grove, much longer than that before he finally got it through his head that his dreams of dismemberment and mutilation had not been real, that no one had taken any of him away, removed anything, cut any of him off.

It seemed they had. It seemed they must have. He would stand before his bathroom mirror—the medicine cabinets, with three small palm trees etched into the back of the glass, had been salvaged from a Miami hotel—wondering at how different he was, how much less of him there was.

People ordinarily have the chance—are forced—to get used to their deterioration over time, even when it is accelerated by illness. But these changes had taken place in him overnight: over one long night. Though he was discernibly the same individual, all his substance was gone. Most of the little hair he had still had left had disappeared, and what was left had turned pure white. Reddish-brown spots cropped out on his head and neck. His arms and upper legs were gray and stringy. The cheeks that had once been chiseled were now chiseled away, fallen, sunken, and the skin dangled, flaccid, from his cheekbones. His whole lower face had atrophied, while his forehead, eyes and glasses remained as always, looking as though they'd grown. His face, on which he had liked to model incisive, debonair expressions in the Café's Lucca bathroom mirror, was shaped like a light bulb.

His fantasies of returning to the Lucca had come back to him, cat first. They had seemed to have left him, cat last, out of a sense of courtesy, as if not to dangle before his helpless body things it could not have, pleasures that were out of the question for a man in a coma but that were again becoming possible for a man who was improving every day, increasingly possible, likely, inevitable, until the day when the doctors pronounced that his cancer was in remission, that it might or might not come back, and that he might as well go home.

3

The man wore a navy peacoat, though it was a warm Saturday afternoon in late spring; he got cold easily now. The Café Lucca was busy, and the owner, short-handed, was waiting all the tables himself. Immediately after the man's arrival a tour bus pulled up outside, blocking out the sun, and disgorged forty Italians who rushed in, filled every available pore of space in the café like water saturating a sponge, upended espressi under which they had placed their faces, and rushed out. The man decided to believe he'd been lost in the flurry, and now that he'd been served no one had reason to stop and notice him. The owner, who had put on some weight, went back and forth, busing the tables, joined by the coffee lady. Five of the regulars were scattered around at their old customary tables, waxworks in their constancy, like some tableau rehydrated from the dried stuff of memory: the recently retired telephone repairman, fat and bearded like a Santa Claus not yet gone gray, with his collection of daily crosswords, his carafe of white wine and the glass he always kept half full; the writer with his ratty manuscript ripped from spiral-bound notebooks, knee jumping to his blaring Walkman; the elderly founder of the café with his enormous belly and suspenders hoisting his pants over it, speaking nasal, staccato, birdlike Italian to his wife, who answered him in English; the muscular ex-cop with his tight black T-shirt, dyed black hair and gradient sunglasses, who read nothing but sat preposterously erect, arms folded across his chest, visually patrolling Father Demo Square. He wondered if any of them had seen him come in. He looked down, plucking a thread off his pants and pulling his coatsleeves out over his fraying shirt cuffs. The sky over Father Demo was bright blue, and the air so clear that the leaves of the young trees stood out cleanly individuated. Puffed-up male pigeons chased females between the legs of the park benches. A couple he knew walked slowly by on the sidewalk—floated by, their legs cut off beneath the wainscoting—arm in arm, almost close enough to touch. His impulse, which surprised him, was to wave to them, but he did not do it. The possibility that they would not return his greeting left him paralyzed.

Had he changed so much? And yet he felt the same inside. The same as the regular who'd returned to the café four times a week from an apartment on East Eighty-first Street, the same as the dreamer who'd returned to the café every day from a hospital bed thirteen hundred miles away, returning as a pigeon returns, mangy and addled, to the place where its keeper lived and died: he felt not only the same urge to return to the café but felt *the same*, the same as the one who had, the night before he'd been taken to the hospital, sat beside his sister on her overstuffed floral love seat under the fluted green glass shade of their Aunt Lil's bridge lamp, leafing through family albums that glowed faint chalky green, through the crumbling, flaking, peeling, paling, dissolving turn-of-the-century albumen prints of the posed and seated ancestors, through the decades and through the generations to the 20s, the 30s, when there had appeared in the small square Brownie prints an infant which had looked nothing like he looked today—nothing like him except for the concave temples, the blue of the eyes, the inward turn at the corners of the mouth—a baby, a child, a boy only three feet tall, four feet, five: he felt himself today, as he sat in the Lucca, to be the same person who had, eighteen months before, sat beside his sister, paging through the 40s and 50s, paging through the greenglass black-and-whites on into faded into fading color, on into the 60s into the 70s, telling his sister stories that, no matter how small the child in the pictures, always began with "I," calling that boy, that child, that baby "me," as if there were nothing—no years, no changes, no lost teeth or lost time—between himself and that unrecognizable infant; he felt himself today, now, in the café, to be the same person who had cried for milk, taken naps, resisted naps, listened to the talking box, watched the blue light, watched the colored light, walked on leaves, crossed words, taken naps again, sat under green glass, smelled cherries, smelled ocean, had an aneurysm, had an astrocytoma, had an amputation, had an Andes Mint. He reflected, finally, on all the old people he had seen come into the Lucca, who shuffled instead of walked, wheezed instead of laughed, who had lost their color, who had lost their moisture, who had withered as a leaf withers from spring to fall and then had withered more, from green to brown to brown-gray, from flexible and stained-glass luminescent to rigid-dry and brittle and opaque, who had withered as a spring leaf turns to a fall leaf turns to a winter leaf turns to flakes, to dust, crushed by the heel of a man who walks on unnoticing, who walks on unknowing into seasons beyond knowing, whose shoe rots off his foot, whose skin rots off his bones, who walks on, stalks on, staggers on, past vigor and volition, who falls on, bowed and curled by gravity, who falls on, falls down, falls; he thought of the old people, and how he had become one of them. And how the younger observer, looking at the washed-out colors, the reined-in steps, the stopped-up gestures, the tics and tremors, listening to the parch and phlegm, to the phrases that must be repeated to them and the phrases that they must repeat, assumes from what he sees and hears that the disappointments of the old must also, internally, take on this thinned, diminished quality, and how the younger observer cannot know that he is very wrong.

The man turned his attention back to the *Times*, but not for long. He had tried his hand at the crossword puzzle, but it had struck him as pointless, so he hadn't finished. The place was quaint, bustling, youthful, and though he knew everything and everyone in it, as unrecognizable to him as he seemed to everyone in the café. Though in his mind he had never left the Lucca, it had changed: and as he had apparently lost his vividness, his identity, his reality to the people in the café, so had the café lost its reality to him. It was faded and removed from him; it was part of his past. Or not yet part of his past: waves of anticipation continued to swell up and carry him, as if his return to the café hadn't happened yet and could still be looked forward to; and each wave broke into the acknowledgment, the realization, the resignation that his return was now taking place, had already taken place, was all but over; until finally the two joined together, the anticipated return and the knowledge that it had already happened and that there was nothing left to anticipate, into a blunt-faced, hollow, bottom-dropped-out sensation of having wanted something so much and enjoyed it so little that it was as if it had never happened at all. He was like a child who prays all year for a certain Christmas present, who counts down the days, who counts off the minutes, who hangs all the decorations, who sings all the carols, and then, at the appointed hour, does not get his present.

Nu-Nu was nowhere to be seen. The man had been here for an hour, had looked around several times, at first surreptitiously, because he did not wish to seem as if he were soliciting attention, and then openly, because it did not make any difference. The cat had not appeared. Undoubtedly he'd long since been run over during one of his pigeon-hunting forays out on Bleecker Street, and no one else even remembered him.

He thought of asking the owner what had happened to the cat, but he doubted the owner would hear him even if he called him by his name; whether any of them could hear him, or see him, or whether he had become completely transparent, invisible and imperceptible in word or action, to everyone in the café.

It was time to leave. He did not bother getting the check, but put a ten-dollar bill on the table, weighted it down with the sugar dispenser, and departed without saying a word; if anyone had been watching him, the watcher would have seen that the firmness and decision which had always undergirded the man's movements were gone, that he had hitched and hesitated as he had stood, looking around, and pushed the chair back, and that, despite the slowness with which he moved, he had got the scuffed toe of his shoe caught on the door jamb and stumbled slightly on his way out.

The owner emerged from the kitchen, saw that the customer at Table 8 had vanished, lurched as if to chase after him, then looked down and saw the money, newspaper and half-eaten baba au rhum. As he stood there, gazing out on Bleecker Street, Nu-Nu appeared from underneath the ice-cream freezer where he had been sleeping. Full grown now, neutered, sedate and already beginning to get a little fat, he rubbed his face on the owner's ankles, did not seem to notice that the owner did not seem to notice, found his favorite chair with its circular black vinyl cushion hot from the sun, lay down on it curled up tightly like a frozen shrimp, and went back to sleep.

Fold Here and Detach

John Blades

I knew there'd be trouble when I found the sheet of stamps on the dining room table, strategically placed next to the stack of envelopes. Abbie had left them there, in plain sight, so I couldn't ignore or pretend to overlook them. She had written the notes for me, thanking relatives and friends for their cards and expressions of sympathy. She had put them in envelopes and sealed them. She had addressed the envelopes in her deceptively casual script. Why hadn't she gone ahead and put the stamps on them? Why had she left the stamps on the sheet for me to separate—to deperforate?

I knew why. I could hear her in the kitchen, preparing lunch. I could hear her chopping and slicing vegetables. I needed fiber, she insisted, roughage to drive the oxidants and free radicals out of my system, as if her own system were in any less immediate need of dedoxidization and deradicalization. Humming along with the radio, she was turning the flower duet from "Lakme" into a discordant trio—a quartet if you added the fibrous, pulpy sound of carrots and zucchini being mutilated, lettuce being decapitated, peppers and squash being eviscerated. In other circumstances, the accompanying music might have been sedating, but now its single purpose was to harass and agitate.

I wanted another cup of coffee, but I knew better than to enter the kitchen—not until after I'd stamped the letters. Even then, I knew from long and grievous experience that it was best to avoid the kitchen, at all costs, at least while Abbie was in there. That was where most of the major confrontations seemed to start, usually over some insignificant matter, like coffee grounds or soup spoons or napkin rings.

The song ended, along with her humming. Her cutting knife was momentarily still. In the queasy silence, I could sense that she was listening for my reaction. I waited until she turned on the food processor, contrarily transforming the pulp and the fiber into a disagreeable but digestible puree, before I made a move toward the stamps. I wanted to do this as quietly and quickly as I could, to have it done—*a fait accompli*—before she could detect any signs of anger and frustration and use them as an excuse to intervene.

No matter how squeezed and pressed, I couldn't allow myself to act precipitously, without the necessary reconnaissance and preparation. I slowly circled the table before deciding that the best strategy was to approach the stamps frontally, without any flanking maneuvers or peripheral diversions.

First I extended my arm, sighting down my fingertips. There was only the slightest tremor—nothing abnormal. I checked my nails. They didn't need trimming, though I took a second to remove a potentially disfiguring speck of grease. I dried my hands on my pants. I couldn't risk disturbing the glue with clammy fingers.

From the tabletop, multiple images of Albert Einstein looked up at me, like faces in a miniature funhouse mirror. Another of her malign little jokes, I was convinced, calculated to rattle and shake. She could easily have purchased nature or evironmental stamps, with benign, idealized, pacifying illustrations of birds and animals. Instead, she came home from the Post Office with a bewilderingly polymorphus gallery of celebrities, athletes, statesmen, buccaneers, artists, capitalists, and politicians, from Hitchcock to Lindbergh, Poe to Rockwell. I had to admit that Einstein brought a little more gravity to this perverse rank and file, but his face was such a caricature of scientific muddle that I was both revolted and disturbed.

When I'd expressed a preference for the more generic issue, ideally those imprinted with only the price of the stamp and the American flag, she'd questioned my patriotism. "It's just a way of commemorating the achievements of great Americans. Surely you don't have a problem with that?"

"I have no problem with Einstein," I said, "or any dead scientist or president. I'll go along with Babe Ruth and, in a pinch, John Wayne. But Marilyn Monroe and Elvis—that's carrying things too far. Who's next—Homer Simpson?"

"Your problem is negativism," she said. "Keep nattering on and on with those unhealthy, seditious thoughts and you'll become a Post Office poster boy yourself—but not on any commemorative stamps."

My problem was not so much whose face was on the stamps as how they were packaged—cheek to cheek, on sheets of one hundred, ten deep and ten wide, connected by perforations so infintesimal they were invisible to my naked eye. The only way I could verify their existence was with a magnifying glass.

Examining the Einstein commemorative under its lens, I counted (and recounted) the number of perforations on a vertical edge: thirteen of them, ominously enough. On closer examination, it became apparent that the perforations were at once too small and too numerous for the stamps to be neatly detached. Larger and fewer perforations, it followed, would facilitate separation, resulting in fewer mutilations, defacements, eyestrain, and warped nerve endings, to say nothing of uniformly more attractive envelopes and postcards.

If this was obvious to me, it must have been just as obvious to the postal officials in charge of perforations. Given the bureau's grave and steadily deteriorating financial condition over the years, which was all too evident from the escalating cost of stamps and corresponding decline in services, there was only one conclusion to be drawn: that the Post Office was systematically reducing the size of perforations in order to save money.

Worse, it was further apparent that this downsizing was being done covertly, without Congressional knowledge or authorization. Under extreme pressure to cut costs, the Post Office had resorted to desperate and illegal means. This, in turn, necessitated the utmost secrecy to avoid public detection, and almost certain insurrection.

It was an unnerving discovery, as well as a sticky one. Sweat had collected on my fingertips while I was counting the perforations. In the process, I'd smeared the glue on four stamps, leaving them too damp to be pasted to envelopes.

I quickly tore off the impaired stamps, two each at diagonal corners of the sheet, and put them in the pocket of my warm-up jacket. I could only hope that Abbie wouldn't check to be sure that the number of stamped envelopes equaled the number of missing stamps. There was also a real danger that she'd check my jacket pocket, so I'd need to dispose of the rejects at the earliest opportunity.

For now, I had more pressing worries. The more I thought about the Post Office duplicity, the more scandalous and politically explosive it seemed. My evidence for this was circumstantial, at best, admittedly based on unreliable eyesight and an optically problematic magnifying glass. For absolute confirmation, I'd need a micrometer, which would enable me to measure the distance between perforations, their diameter, and with some elementary calculations, their circumference.

But I didn't need to go to such lengths, not when further (if inexact) corroboration for my suspicions was likely to be found near at hand.

Rummaging through the desk in the living room, I was able to retrieve packet after packet of letters, notes, and cards, all secured with rubber bands and filed away, year by year, decade by decade, by the brutally meticulous and obsessive Abbie.

I found it curious, to say the least, that she had methodically tossed out all the envelopes, and along with them the stamps, after so scrupulously filing away the correspondence itself, a practice, I began to suspect, that was not simply meant to save space. Luckily enough, I came upon a single surviving stamped envelope, one that must have slipped between the sheets of a letter, eluding certain destruction.

The stamp was twenty years old, with a face value of thirteen cents. But by another stroke of exceptional fortune, I found that the vertical size of the recovered stamp was one inch, exactly matching the Einstein, so that I was able to compare the number of perforations. I could barely keep my hands from trembling as I held the magnifier to the edge and counted them: eleven and a half—one and a half fewer than the Einstein.

By any rational measure, I had all the proof I needed that the Post Office had been secretly fudging on perforations. This may not have been a cosmic revelation but it filled me with a profound sense of elation, one that surely equalled Einstein's at the moment he arrived at $E = MC^2$.

That didn't make the task ahead of me any easier, but it helped restore my confidence and faith in my powers of recuperation. Now I knew that my condition was neither physical nor psychogenic—what Abbie so blithely dismissed as a "perforation complex." It was environmental, a handicap imposed on me by the U.S. Post Office.

Whatever satisfaction I could take from this discovery was brief, interrupted by Abbie's query from the kitchen. "What's taking you so long in there? Lunch is almost ready."

She had insisted that the letters be stamped by lunch: not half of them, not even three-quarters or two-thirds. She refused to negotiate or compromise. Not a bite to eat, she said, until I'd finished every last one.

I had to proceed quickly, but not counterproductively so. Another of Abbie's stipulations was that the job had to be cosmetically correct—no rips or tears, with each stamp separated precisely on the line of perforation, so that each of the tiny semicircles was intact. "Appearances count," she said. "No detail is too fine to escape the judgment of others. How would you like to receive a letter with a torn stamp? You'd lose all respect for the sender."

"The world is full of ragged edges," I told her. "People with ragged edges. People who walk sideways and think crooked thoughts. People with erratically perforated minds and bodies."

I tried to persuade her that there'd be a minimum of stress and strain if only she'd buy stamps by the roll, pointing out the obvious: That I'd have one edge per stamp to deperforate, rather than three or four. I could deal with rolls of stamps, even the little booklets. But I choked at the mere sight of the sheets—seized by emotional gridlock.

No matter how sweetly and logically I put this to her, Abbie wouldn't listen to reason. "Sheet stamps are much more therapeutic," she said. "You need something that will strengthen your manual and digital skills and repair your mental faculties." I dared not even mention self-adhesive stamps to her—they were synonymous with sloth, corruption, debauchery.

"You find fault with everything," she said: "your food, your clothes, your haircuts, your manicures. There's nothing I do that pleases you. Now you're complaining about the stamps I buy. Well, you can just buy your own stamps. And groceries. And . . ."

She knew I couldn't do any of that. I've been given stringent instructions not to leave the house. And I couldn't rely on anyone else. All my loved ones have gone, leaving me in the care of Abbie, who used to love me, I think.

I had to get down to the business at hand. I held the sheet of stamps to the light, so the perforation line would be clearly defined. But I'd put myself into an impossibly awkward position, trying to detach the stamps with my hands above my head, squinting. On my very first attempt, I managed to tear the stamp well beneath the perforation, giving Einstein a buzz cut.

It was an unsightly disfigurement and, in all probability, a disqualifying one, for mailing purposes. Even in the unlikely event it passed Abbie's inspection, it was almost certain to be rejected by the Post Office sorting machine.

I placed the sheet of stamps on the table, but my efforts to separate them were further impeded by the residue of wax and dust on its surface. I fared no better with the next half-dozen stamps, inflicting progressively graver damage on Einstein—severing his ears, the dewlap below his chin, the chin itself—until I'd finally torn a stamp almost in half, well below Einstein's hairline, lobotimizing the father of atomic science.

With each such mishap, I deposited the maimed stamp into the pocket of my warm-up jacket. As their number grew, I regretted all the more that I'd been forced to give up my robe. While I'd grudgingly agreed with

Abby that it had grown foul and shabby, it was still more comfortable than the jacket, if not nearly so fashionable, and over the years the robe had acquired an expansive and pacifying shape that fit the contours of my body.

More important, for my immediate purposes, the robe had larger pockets, so that it could have accommodated far more stamps than the pockets of the warm-up jacket. They were already close to capacity, not just with stamps but with Kleenex, rubber bands, paperclips, and rolls of antacid. The robe had yet another advantage in that it was made of terry cloth, which meant it it would have absorbed the muck from the accumulating stamp collection.

For what my pockets held now were wet and gummy clots, unpleasant to touch and multiplying as exponentially, as rapaciously, as horror-movie blobs. While I'd gone about my business, I'd been too preoccupied to notice the sweat running down my forehead, dripping off my nose and chin and onto the sheet of stamps. I had to discard a half-dozen on account of sogginess.

Once I became aware of the meltdown, I stopped to cool off, struggling to get my head and hands together. With a few moments to reflect, I was able to see the whole picture, with all the clarity and logic of a geometric axiom. Given: As the quantity of perforations increases, their size and quality decrease proportionately.

This qualitative decline, I had no doubt, was due to another clandestine cost-cutting expedient by the Post Office, a switchover to cheaper and inferior equipment. Further investigation, I was confident, would disclose that its perforating machines had been manufactured in South Korea.

The more I thought about it, the more apparent it became that this devolution was occurring across the board, coast to coast, around the globe. Putting it crudely but irrefutably, perforations had gone to hell everywhere, not just at the Post Office but in every corporate nook, cranny, and fissure of American commerce and industry.

This had cost me plenty in recent years, I now realized, in terms of personal anguish as well as dollars. At its most costly, I had forfeited $11 million, which was the amount I would have won in a magazine discount SWEEPSTAKES, if my GRAND PRIZE ENTRY TICKET hadn't been disqualified as a direct result of aberrant perforations.

The letter notified me that all I had to do to claim my GUARANTEED GRAND PRIZE was to affix four stamps to the enclosed TRANSMITTAL FORM. Each of the stamps entitled me to a discount magazine subscription. But the stamps were defectively perforated and fiendishly difficult to detach. Exhausted and demoralized by the effort, I'd done a sloppy job of pasting them to the entry form, so the stamps, already in tatters, were askew, way off-center, overlapping the edges of the box.

I read over the rules one last time before returning the form and saw that it had been clearly spelled out: "Stamps that are imprecisely detached and improperly aligned will be disqualified." I deposited the envelope in the mailbox, knowing in my heart that it was a futile gesture, that I'd just blown $11 million. If the grand prize did elude me, however, I could be certain the magazines would arrive in my mailbox without delay.

On a less monumental scale, I'd had tortuous difficulty with other forms of correspondence—not just contest entries but dividend checks, public television pledges, phone, gas, and electric bills—that bore the sly command, "Fold here and detach," "Return this portion with your remittance," "Tear along dotted line," or any of its infinite and perplexing permutations.

Following the instructions on the monthly income check from my brokerage was an increasingly harrowing experience. "Detach on the perforated blue line," it instructed. What blue line? If there really was a line at the top of the check, I failed to locate it, even after I'd increased the magnification on my glasses from 250 to 300—a figure that seemed especially portentuous, since it corresponded to my cholesterol level and my weight.

The perforations on the check were no more visible than the alleged blue line. At best, they were faux perforations, designed to thwart detachment and redemption. If that was the brokerage strategy, it was highly effective in my case. The checks had been accumulating in my desk for many months, their raw and unsightly edges making them impossible to cash.

The drawer also held a cache of other uncashed checks and unpaid bills, all of them in hideous states of deterioration and deperforation, along with numerous threatening letters, FINAL NOTICEs warning me about the imminent cancellation of my vital services—heat, water, sewage, insurance. All essential life support systems were about to be shut off.

I would attend to these after lunch, after I finished stamping the letters Abbie had left me. But practice was only making me more and more imperfect. I'd failed to make a single mucilaginous conjunction between stamp and envelope.

I noticed that I'd missed my pocket with two or three stamps, which were now sticking to my warm-up jacket. I could also feel stamps attached to my forehead, cheeks, and chin, as crusty and ragged as scabs. Turning my neck, I detected a scab-like rustle in my hair.

I heard Abbie putting the plates on the table, and I knew the food was going to be cold and congealed before I could sit down to eat. I knew I was finished before I'd even started.

Sweat was irritating the perforations on my chest, making them bristle and itch. They criss-crossed my torso, from stem to stern, still raw and vulnerable. I felt as if the slightest strain or pressure would cause them to split, like a defective zipper, exposing my endangered heart, exposing every bleeding, pulsing, quivering organ within my chest and abdominal cavity.

I had to take emergency measures. Though I'd abused, defaced and slimed individual stamps, I noticed that I'd been unconsciously detaching them from the sheet itself in a precise and symmetrical manner, so that the remaining stamps formed a lower-case "t"—or, the more I examined it, a cross. If this is my cross, I told myself, then I will bear it as efficaciously as I'm able.

I unzipped my warm-up jacket. I could see that the cruciform sheet of stamps nearly matched the shape of my sutures, the bodily perforations and blue lines. I affixed the philatelic bandage to my bare chest. There was no need to lick the stamps. Despite the slippery hair and scar tissue, the stamps made a tight seal, relieving the pressure from within. It was only a temporary rescue operation, I realized, but it would be my salvation.

I couldn't expect any approbation—or sympathy—from Abbie, who had grown impatient and was about to enter the room to see what was delaying me. As if she didn't already know. I could hear her footsteps, mushy and ominous, as if she were squashing grapes or avocados beneath her slippers. I dreaded the impending scene—the recriminations, the denunciations, the humiliations. But I found some consolation in knowing just how Abbie would react, that there were far worse punishments than being sent off to my room without lunch.

Seven Types of Ambiguity

Dan Chaon

Age 49:
This is a braid of human hair. The braid is about two feet long, and almost two inches wide at the base. It seems heavy, like old rope, but is not brittle or rough. Someone has secured each end with a rubber band, so the braid itself is still tight—the simplest braid, which any child can do, three individual strands twined together, A over B, C over B and A, etc. It smells of powder. There is a certain violety scent which over the years has begun to reek more and more of dust. The color of the hair is like dry corn husks. At first, Colleen thought it was gray.

But it must have been blonde, she now thinks. There was a newspaper clipping among the effects in her father's strongbox, concerning the death of a girl who would have been Colleen's aunt: her father's older sister, though he'd never mentioned her, that she could remember. The clipping, which is dated October 9, 1918, is a little less than an eighth of a column. "Death came to the home of Julius Carroll and wife Sunday evening and claimed their daughter, Sadie, aged eleven years, who had been ill with typhoid fever for two weeks. All that loving and willing hands could do did not save the child." The article goes on to describe the funeral, and to offer condolences. Perhaps erroneously, Colleen has come to believe that the braid belonged to that long-ago girl. There is no one to ask, no one alive who can confirm anything. She found it recently, curled in the bottom of a trunk along with some of Colleen's grandfather's papers. The braid wasn't labeled. It seems to have been removed rather abruptly, or at least uncarefully. The edges at the thickest end of the braid are ragged and uneven, as if it has been sawed off by a dull blade.

It reminds her of a conversation she'd had with her father years ago. She'd been very interested in genealogy at the time, and had sent him a number of charts, which he'd dutifully filled out to the best of his ability, but he'd really wanted no part of it. When she'd asked to interview him about his memories of their family, he'd balked. "I don't remember anything," he'd said. "Why do you want to know about this garbage, anyway? Let the dead rot in peace," he said. "They can't help you." She'd made some comment then, quoting something she'd read: Genetics is destiny, she told him. Don't you ever wonder where the cells of your body came from? she asked.

"Genetics!" her father said. "What's the point of it? All that DNA stuff is just chemicals! It doesn't have anything to do with what's real about a person." Anyway, he said, a cell is nothing. Cells trickle off our body all the time, and every seven years we've grown a new skin altogether. The whole thing, he said, was overrated.

Nevertheless, for years now she has carried the braid with her. She keeps it in an airtight plastic bag, in a zippered compartment of her suitcase. No one else knows that she carries it with her, and most of the time she herself forgets that it is there. She cannot recall when, exactly, the braid began to travel with her, but it has become a kind of talisman, not necessarily good luck, but comforting. Occasionally, she will take it out of its bag and run it through her hands, like a rosary. The braid has traveled all over the world, from Washington D.C. to the great capitals of Europe, from Mali to Peru. She supposes that this is ironic.

For the last ten years, she has worked for an international charitable organization which gives grants to individuals who, in the words of the foundation's mission statement, "have devoted themselves selflessly to the betterment of the human race." For years, she has anonymously observed candidates for the grants, and written reports on them. Her reports are passed on to a committee which divides its endowed moneys among the deserving. It is a great job, but it leaves her lonely. She is divorced, and she rarely speaks to her grown son. Most of the relatives that she remembers from her youth died a long time ago. There are a number of regrets.

Age 42:
She is in a motel room in Mexico City when her son, Luke, calls. "Mommy?" he says, in a voice that is drunk or drugged. He is twenty years old, telephoning from San Diego, where he had been a student before he dropped out. The last that Colleen had heard, he was working as a gardener for a lady gynecologist from Israel and living in a converted greenhouse out behind the woman's house.

"She's really weird," her son says now, trying to carry on a normal conversation through his haze. "Like, when I'm clipping the hedges or something, sometimes she lies out on a lawn chair, totally naked. I mean, I'm no prude, but you'd think she could wait until I was done. It's not a pretty sight, either. I mean, my God, Mom, she's older than you. I'm starting to wonder if she's trying to come on to me."

He is drunk, Colleen thinks. What sober person would talk about this kind of thing with his mother? But the comment about her age sinks in, and she hears her voice grow stiff: "It must be really grotesque, if she's older than me," Colleen says.

"Oh, Mom!" Luke says. Yes: there is the petulant slur in his voice, a wetness, as if his mouth is pressed too close to the phone. "You know what I mean." And then, as is Luke's habit when he is intoxicated, his voice strains with sentiment. "Momma, when I was little, I thought you were the most beautiful woman in the world. I just idolized you. You remember that blue dress you had? With the gold threads woven in? And those blue high heels? I thought that you looked like a movie star." Any minute now, Colleen thinks, he will start bawling, and it disturbs her that she can't muster much compassion. He has used it up, expended it on the histrionics of his teenage years, on the many, many ways he has found to need "help" since going off to college. He has already been treated once for chemical dependency.

"Oh Mommy," Luke says. "I'm so screwed up. I'm so lost." He takes in a wet breath. "I really am."

"No you're not, Honey," Colleen says. She clears her throat. He is still a kid, she thinks, a child yearning for his mother, who has been cold. But what else can she say? They have had these conversations before, and Colleen has learned that it is best to simply pacify him. "You'll find your way," Colleen says, soothingly. "You've got to just keep plugging away at it. Don't give in." Of course, Colleen thinks, the truth is that Luke is clearly wasting his life. But he'd never listened to any advice when he was sober, and to say anything when he was drunk would only lead to an argument. She considers asking Luke if he is on anything. But she knows that he will deny it—deny it until he is desperate. What could Colleen do for him at such a distance, anyway? "Are you all right, baby?" Colleen whispers. "Is everything okay?"

Luke is silent for a long time, trying to regain his composure. "Oh," he says. And his voice quavers. "Yes—I'm fine, I'm fine. I'm not doing drugs, if that's what you're thinking."

"I'm not thinking anything. You just sound—"

"What?"

"Sad."

"Oh." He thinks about this. Then, as if to contradict Colleen, his voice brightens. "Well," he says, "How are things going for you? Anything exciting happening?"

"No," Colleen says. "The usual." He is her son, and she has failed him.

"How's grandpa?" Luke says. "Is he still holding up?"

"He's okay," Colleen says. She pulls the shade, shutting out the lights of Mexico City. There is nothing special about this place, nothing particularly outstanding about the candidate she is observing, a man who runs a free AIDS clinic for street people, but who is not nearly selfless enough to be awarded money by her firm. Does Luke realize how endless the world's supply of sorrow and hard luck stories is? Does he ever think that even if he were a saint, he might not be worthy of notice among a planet of billions? She is so tired. She can't believe how far away she is, how distant from the people that she should love.

Age 35:

"Why does everyone have to be so smart-alecky," her father says, and throws his tennis shoe at her TV screen. "That was a steaming pile of crap."

He has been drinking a lot since he came to her house, sitting alone in her guest room—the only place he is allowed to smoke—sipping at a never-empty tumbler of Jack Daniels. She has seen him drunk before, but he has never been this belligerent, this temper-prone.

"That didn't even make any sense," he says. He is referring to the video they just watched together, which she'd loved, and which she'd thought he would like too. "Why can't they just tell a good story anymore," he says sullenly. She can't believe that he actually threw his shoe at her television.

"Dad," she says. "You can't just throw things! This is my home!"

"Jesus H. Christ," he says, and stalks out of the room.

He has been staying with her for almost a month. She hadn't known he was coming: he just pulled into the driveway one morning. He'd been trying to get ahold of her for over a week, he said, and Colleen had frowned. "How did you try to get ahold of me," she wondered. "Smoke signals? Telepathy?"

"Well," her father said. "You're damn phone's always busy. How many boyfriends do you have, babygirl?" He tried to smile, tried to ease things a bit by evoking this old pet name from her childhood. But he knew that things were not as simple as that. The last time he'd stayed with her, they'd fought constantly; he'd left one night after an argument and hadn't called her for almost two months.

The argument had been about her son, Luke. Her father thought she was spoiling him; she said that she didn't dare to leave Luke alone with him because he drank so much. Each had hurt the other's feelings, which was how it often was. Neither one could bear the other's disapproval.

After a time, she goes to his room. He is sitting on the bed, smoking, and he looks at her balefully as he lifts his tumbler to his mouth. He has taken off his toupee and it lies beside him on the bed, like a fur cap. She could have never imagined him wearing a hairpiece; he has always been embarrassed and scornful of male vanity, but she sees that he is right to wear it. He is completely bald, except for a few fine tufts wisping here and there over his pinkish scalp, like the head of a four-month-old baby. Without the toupee, he looks awful—frightening, even.

He is going to live a while longer. The cancer, much to the doctors' surprise, is gone. It is not merely in remission; as far as they can tell, it has completely left his body. Sometimes, he seems aware that something miraculous, or at least vaguely supernatural, has happened to him. But not often—more frequently, he seems frazzled, even haunted by his good fortune, and he turns even more fiercely toward his old habits.

"I brought your shoe," she says. He looks at her, then down.

"I'm sorry I didn't like your program," he says. "I guess I didn't understand it."

"Well," she says. "You've never been one for ambiguity."

He frowns. He knows these "two-dollar words," as he calls them—he has done crossword puzzles all his life—but he disapproves of people actually using them. He thinks it's showing off.

"*Ambiguity*," he says. "Is that what you call it?"

"Dad," she says, quietly. "What's wrong with you? You never used to . . . go off on little things like that. It's not good."

He shrugs. "I guess I'm just getting old. Old and cranky." His hands shake as puts the nub of a Raleigh cigarette to his lips, and she thinks of how badly she needs him to be normal and happy, to be an ordinary father. *Don't be this*, she thinks urgently. She is a divorced woman with a thirteen-year-old son, and she works forty hours a week as an administrator at a charity organization, where all she thinks about is helping people, helping, helping, helping. She does not want him to need her, not right now. But she can see that he does. His eyes rest on her, gauging, hopeful.

"I don't have anywhere to go, Colleen." he says. "I don't know what to do with myself. I'm sixty-two years old, and I'm damn tired of working construction."

"Well," she said. "You know that you can stay here . . ." But she hesitates, because she knows it's not true. He can't stay here if he's going to drink and smoke like this. He knows this, and his eyes deepen as he looks at her. She doesn't love him as much as he'd hoped—she sees this in his eyes, sees him think it, struggling for a moment. Then he lifts his tumbler and tastes his drink again.

"That's all right," he says.

Age 28:

From time to time, she loses her temper. Like this one time, he pushes her, for no reason, teeth gritted: "Leave me alone!" he says, and that gets to her. Oh, I'll leave you alone, she thinks. See what it's like, see how you like to be alone.

She knows it is wrong, even as she presses her back to the bark of the tree that conceals her. It is a bad thing, but her anger buoys her, makes her breathing tight and slow. She isn't hurting him, she thinks. She is teaching him a lesson.

It takes him a while to realize that she is gone. It is a warm day in early summer, a little breezy. From her hiding place, she can see the wobbly reflection of the sun and clouds floating in Luke's inflatable swimming pool. Luke plays without noticing for some time. Then, as if he's heard a sound, he stands straight and alert. "Mom," he says. He scopes the yard and the roads and the pasture beyond. They live a few miles outside of the small college town where she is studying for her Master's degree; the nearest neighbor is a mile away. "Mom?" He says again, but she doesn't move. An army man drops from his hand into the grass, near where the hose makes a sinewy, snake-like curve through the lawn. "Mommy?" he says, more anxiously. Her heart beats, quick and light, as she presses herself into the shadows. She has the distinct, constricting pleasure of having disappeared—a pleasure that, since her divorce, has occupied her fantasies with odd frequency: to leave this life! To vanish and be free!

And, more than that, as he begins to panic—there is a kind of tingly relief. For what if he hadn't noticed that she was gone? What then?

She lets it go on too long, she knows. He is almost hysterical, and it takes a long time to get him calmed down—rocking him, his face hot against her shoulder, whispering: "What's wrong? It's okay. Don't cry!" A kind of warm glow spreads through her. "I thought you wanted Mommy to go away," she whispers—Horrible! Horrible!—she can sense that it is wrong but she keeps on, running her hand through his hair, long-nailed, thin fingers: vampire fingers. "I thought you wanted Mommy to go away," she murmurs. "Isn't that what you said?" And then she begins to weep herself, with shame and fear.

Age 21:
She is just out of college, staying at her father's house for a week or so, when the tornado hits. It is the most extraordinary thing that has ever happened to her. Parts of the roof are whisked away. The windows implode, scattering shards of glass across the carpets, the beds, into the bathtub. Apparently, there had been a beehive in the upper rafters, because dark lines of honey have run down the kitchen walls.

Colleen and her father have been hidden in the cellar, among rows and rows of dusty jars: beets and green beans and apple sauce that Colleen's mother had canned, or that her grandmother had canned, when her father was a boy. Some of the jars go as far back as 1940, their labels written in a faded, arthritic cursive. Her father has been planning to get rid of this stuff for as long as Colleen has been alive. She had been warned, as a child, never to open anything from the cellar. Her mother had heard of poisonous gas coming out of ancient, sealed containers.

She recalls this, sitting on the cool earthen floor that reminds her of childhood. As the storm roars overhead, she and her father huddle close together.

When they come up to see the world, after the howling has stopped, it is raining. There are no trees standing as far as they can see, only the flat prairie and branches and stumps everywhere, as if each tree had burst apart—as if, Colleen thinks poetically, there were some terrible force inside them that they finally could not contain.

"Jesus H. Christ," her father keeps saying. He goes to the door of the house, and Colleen follows after him. The rain is falling into the kitchen, dripping off scraps of insulation that hang down like kudzu. Her father touches the kitchen wall and puts his finger to his mouth. "Honey!" he says, and laughs. The room is full of the smell of honey, and the sound of water. She doesn't know what to say. It is the house that both she and her father grew up in, and it is destroyed.

Her father finds his bottle of Jack Daniels under the kitchen sink; he finds ice, still hard, in the refrigerator's freezer; and he pours them each a drink.

"At least the liquor's okay," Colleen's father says. "There's one blessing we can count."

Colleen smiles nervously, but accepts the drink that's offered to her. She had thought that this would be a rest period in her life—that it would be the last time she really lived at home, and that there would be a number of conversations with her father that would bring closure to this stage of her life. She had been a psychology major, and is very fond of closure. She likes to think of her life in segments, each one organized, analyzed, labeled, stowed away for later reflection: Another stage along her personal journey. Nevertheless, a tornado seems a melodramatic way to end things. She would have preferred some small, epiphanic moment.

Her father settles into the kitchen chair beside her, leaning back. The sky is beginning to clear; cicadas buzz from the dark boughs strewn about the lawn. Through the hole in the roof, they can see a piece of the evening sky. The constellations are beginning to fade into view.

"Well," her father says. He puts his palm on top of her hand, then removes it. He sighs.

"Now what?"

Age 14:

"Here's babygirl, with her nose in a book!" Colleen's father crows. "As usual!"

She is stretched out on her bed and looks up sternly, closing the book quickly over her index finger, hoping maybe that he will let her alone. But it is not likely. He is standing in the doorway, in a clownish, eager mood. He does a weird little dance, hoping to amuse her, and she is terribly embarrassed of him. Still, kindly, she smiles.

"What good is sitting alone in your room," he sings, and capers around. She leans her cheek against her hand, watching him.

"Dad," she says. "Settle down." She takes a tone with him as if he is a little boy, which has become their mode, the roles they act out for one another. Her mother has been dead for a little over a year, and this is how things go. They have accepted that she is smarter than he, more capable. They have accepted that things must somehow continue on, and that she will leave him soon. He says that she is destined for great things. She will go on to college, and become educated; she will travel all over the world, as he himself wanted to; she will follow her dreams. They don't talk about it, but she can see it—in the morning, as he sits hunched over his crossword puzzle, sipping coffee; after dinner, as he sits, watching the news, rubbing salve onto his feet, which are pale and delicate, the toes beginning to curve into the shape of his work boot. She can feel the weight of it as he stands in her doorway, looking in, trying to get her attention. He dances for a moment, and then he stands there, arms loose at his sides, waiting.

"Do you want to go out to Dairy Queen and get a sundae," he says, and she looks regretfully down at her book, where the hobbit Frodo is perhaps dead, in the tower of Cirith Ungol.

"Okay," she says.

She is a pretty girl. Older boys have asked her out on dates, Juniors and Seniors, though she is just a Freshman, and she is flattered, she takes note, though she always turns them down. Her hair is long, the color of wheat, and her father likes to touch it, to run the tips of his fingers over it, very lightly. These days, he only touches her hair very rarely, such as when she's sitting beside him in the pick-up and he stretches his arm across the length of the seat. His hand brushes the back of her head, as if casually. He believes that she is too old to have her father touch her hair. He will only kiss her on her cheek.

Their little house is just beyond the outskirts of town, and as they drive through the dark toward Dairy Queen, she wonders if she will ever not be lonely. Perhaps, she thinks, being lonely is a part of her, like the color of her eyes and skin, something in her genes.

Her father begins humming as he drives. The dashboard light makes his face eerie and craggy with shadows, and his humming seems to come from nowhere: some old, terribly sad song—Hank Williams, Jim Reeves, something that almost scares her.

Age 7:

On Saturday after supper, Colleen's father asks her if she'd like to go on over and see his place of employment. He tilts his head back, draining his beer. He smiles as he does this, and it makes him look sly and proud. "It's a nice night," he says. "What do you say, babygirl?" He seems not to notice as Colleen's mother reached between his forearms to take his plate. He is not inviting *her*.

Colleen is not sure what is going on between them. It is an old story, though, extending back in time to things that happened before Colleen was born—things Colleen's mother should have gotten, things she is still owed. Every once in a while, it begins to build up. Colleen can feel the heat in her mother's silences.

But her father doesn't appear to notice. He gives Colleen's hair a playful tug, and makes a face at her. "I'm only taking you, babygirl, because you're my favorite daughter."

Colleen, who is sensitive about being teased, says: "I'm your only daughter."

"You're right," her father says. "But you know what? Even if I had a hundred daughters, you'd still be my favorite."

Colleen's mother looks at him grimly. "Don't keep her up too late," she says.

Colleen' s father works for the Department of Roads, and he drives her out to a place where a new highway is being built. The road is lined with stacks of materials, some of them almost as tall as houses; and with heavy machinery, which looks sinister and hulking in the dusk. Her father stops his pickup near one of these machines, a steamroller, which she has seen before only in cartoons. He wants to show her something, he says.

Just at the edge of the place where the road stops, they are building a bridge. The bridge will span a creek, a tiny trickle of water where she and her father occasionally come to fish. Every few years or so, the creek has been known to flood, and so it has been decided that the bridge will be built high above it. The bridge, her father says, will be sixty feet off the ground.

The skeleton of the bridge is already in place. She can see it as they walk toward the slope that leads down to the creek. Girders and support beams of steel and cement stretch over the valley that her father tells her was made by the creek—over hundreds of years, the flowing water had worn this big groove into the earth. They have cleared earth where buffalo and Indians used to roam, he says, and then he sings: "Home, Home on the Range."

She is only vaguely interested in this until they come to the edge of the bridge. It *is* high in the air, and she balks when her father begins to walk across one of the girders. He stretches his arms out for balance, putting his one foot carefully in front of the other, heel to toe, like a tightrope walker. He turns to look over his shoulder at her, grinning. He points down. "There's a net!" he calls. "Just like at the circus!"

And then, without warning, he spreads his arms wide and falls. She does not scream, but something like air, only harder, rises in her throat for a moment. Her father's body tilts through the air, pitching heavily, though his arms are spread out like wings. When he hits the net, he bounces, like someone on a trampoline. "Boing!" he cries, and then he sits up.

"Damn!" he calls up to her. "I've always wanted to do that! That was fun!" She watches as he crawls, spider-like, across the thick ropes of net, up toward where she is standing, waiting for him. The moon is bright enough that she can see.

"Do you want to try it?" her father says, and she hangs back, until he puts his hand to her cheek. He strokes her hair, and their eyes meet. "Don't be afraid, babygirl," he says. "I won't let anything bad happen to you. You know that. Nothing bad will ever happen to babygirl."

"I know," she says. And after a moment, she follows him out onto the beam above the net, cautiously at first, then more firmly. For she does want to try it. She wants to fly like that, her long hair floating in the air like a mermaid's. She wants to hit the net and bounce up, her stomach full of butterflies.

"You're not afraid, are you?" her father says. "Because if you're afraid, you don't have to do it."

"No," she says. "I want to."

Her father smiles at her. She does not understand the look in his eyes, when he clasps her hand. She doesn't think she will ever understand it, though for years and years she will dream of it, though it might be the last thing she sees before she dies.

"This is something you're never going to forget, babygirl," he says. And then they plunge backward into the air. They fall, screaming together.

Author

Stephen Dixon

Headline on the *Times'* obituary page says "Joshua Fels, 76, modernist author of abstruse, labyrinthine novels, is dead." The obit covers three-quarters of the page and includes a critique of his work by the paper's cultural affairs editor, a list of his novels and years they were published, and excerpts from some of them. A large photo of him—slim build and chiseled craggy face—sitting at his writing desk in a polka-dot tie and what looks like a tailored suit, holding a lit cigarette and facing the camera but looking away. The caption gives the year of the photo, "when his literary reputation took a sharp rise." That was the year his third novel came out and won both major fiction prizes, but can't be the year the photo was taken. His hair's dark and full and he looks no more than forty, while when I. met him that same year his hair was gray, not as full, and he looked his age: 52. Critics, literary scholars and well-known serious fiction writers are quoted. He's called immensely inventive and virtuosic, a novelist of vast range, complexity, erudition and wit, with a masterful use of language and an audacious, original style.

Arguably, the greatest American writer since Faulkner, one critic says. Maybe since Melville, another says, "and it's conceivable, partly because of the difficulty of his work though mostly because of his brilliance, that he'll become one of the most influential novelists we've ever had." Fels lived in London and Martha's Vineyard the last ten years, the obit says, and is survived by his fourth wife, three children from his three previous marriages, several grandchildren, and a sister in Buffalo, NY. His first novel, "which weighed in at a dense 893 pages of only seventeen paragraphs and no chapters," was universally panned, except in England, but quickly developed a cult following. Despite this underground success and the many printings of his book that resulted from it, he didn't publish another novel for twelve years. All his books are now in print and have become contemporary classics. He recently completed an interconnected story collection, his editor says, which is longer than anything he's written and is the most innovative and demanding work he's done, and it'll be published at the end of the year.

I. met Fels more than twenty years ago. He was going with a high school teacher in a small town on the Hudson about twenty miles from New York, and she invited him to a party there on one of the weekends he was staying with her. He was introduced to the host, who asked what he did. "Well that's a piece of luck for the partygiver," the host said. "Josh Fels is coming. Lives down the hill, and as far as I know you'll be the one other person here who tinkers on a typewriter that way and knows something about literary publishing. I should remember to introduce you, or maybe you know him." I.'s girlfriend asked how come she didn't know Fels lived in town, and the host said "Probably because he's sworn all his friends and the local real estate agents to secrecy, so, shh, don't breathe it to anyone beyond these walls or we might lose him. I assume he doesn't want fledgling writers pecking on his door with manuscripts, and other unwanted encounters that hotshots like him must face. Even in the one interview he's given, when the question of his residence came up he said 'Just say a village along one of New York's main fluvial arteries where none of the streets are named, everyone has an unlisted phone number, no one comes to his front door if he's not expecting anyone, and a couple of residents have illegal guns.' I was surprised myself when he accepted my invitation. I think he only did because his wife's been out of town for two weeks, he's deep into the ending of his new novel, and he wanted a short break from his solitude." "Getting back to what you asked me," I. said. "I'm of course familiar with his work, though I don't even know what he looks like, since he's never had an author's photo on one of his books." (He checks the obit photo credit; "Judith Fels," maybe one of his wives, or even a daughter or his mother, but not his sister, since the obit gave her name as Phoebe. But how'd the newspaper get it? Anyway:) "I'm sure he does that so he won't be recognized by complete strangers," the host said. "It hasn't reached the point where fans are tearing off his clothes for souvenirs when they find out who he is, but just by his having alluded to that to me, I bet it's come close to it." "Yeah, maybe that's the reason," I. said. "Why, what else could it be, other than a strong aversion to being photographed?" "Who can say if this no-photo and -show and rare-interview business isn't just another way of drawing attention to your books. Not a unique one today but one that's come to be respected for serious writers and much written about. But what do I know? Although I'm no fledgling—I've been flapping my writing wings hummingbirdlike for more than fifteen years—even if my first book's only now coming out, but from a publishing house so small that the owner of this one-man operation answers the phone in different voices to give the impression he has a staff. Since my book will have an author's photo on its softcover, I can never again hide entirely from the public. At least not for the next ten years or so, unless I lose all my hair because the reviews are so bad or my face is disfigured beyond repair for some reason—let me think of one: distracted by a part of a new story I'm going over in my head, or at the point in my work where I've just finished a story and am coming up with the idea for a new one, I walk into an electric fan." "Funny. Now, if you don't mind, tell me what you think of Fels' work. You know, we all know he's celebrated and revered for his novels—I don't know if I pronounced that right: *ear, ev* —but I'm interested in what another experienced writer has to say about it. And be frank now; I won't be telling him one way or the other what you say. Not because I won't value it but because I know that what people think of his fiction—critics, book reviewers and scholars particularly—is the last thing he wants to read or hear." "His work? It's good, of course; it's really good." "That's it? One word sums up thirty years of work? Which books particularly do you or don't you like, and then what parts of those books particularly? Form, structure, style—isn't that what writers talk about when they're not talking about publishers, agents, advances? Not Fels, with that last unnecessary crack, and probably not you either, but do you like his style, for instance? Does he as a writer move you, bore or excite you, do other things to you?" "I've read all his books. There aren't many in number but there are a lot of pages. Though I admit that some parts of his stuff I quickly flipped through, but I do that with lots of writing and especially long books. But his work, summing it all up, is very intelligent and his style is interesting at times, and his dialog's tops. As for the form and structure, I don't know; they seem to work. 'Architecture.' I'm sure his is good also, but I really don't know what the work means when it's used about a work of literature. Look, I'm not good with the language of criticism. Critical language. Whatever they call it. I'm a meat and potatoes reader, you can say, when it comes to fiction. I just know that if a work hits me, I keep reading it, and if it excites me, of course I feel it, and if it overwhelms me—meaning, it's so powerful and original and readable that there's almost nothing I want to do but read it, which doesn't happen often—well, the reaction is obvious: I'm overwhelmed and I read it every chance I get and never flip through or skip, no matter how long the work is. That's not how I feel about any of Fels' work, though. His is good, maybe very good; he's probably an important writer." "But not a great or an excellent writer, you're saying, the way some distinguished critics and all those honors and awards have built him up and portrayed him?" "Excellent, great, very good, good; he's close to all of those at different times, maybe. Excellent in some ways and just very good to good in others, but never less than good, which is saying a lot, I feel. Or maybe a few passages and a page here and there are a little less than good, but you could say that about any writer, I suppose: Ovid, Shakespeare, Joyce, Proust, Dickens for sure—all those contrivances and coincidences in his work and the occasional inflated language, even if they were the accepted conventions then. As for Proust, I actually haven't read enough of him, or let's just say not all that much of him, or maybe even I'm saying I've read all want to of him, at least for the time being, for I find him fluffy and fussy and a bit boring. 'Spun sugar' I call some of it, which comes from a line in one of the first three *Remembrance* novels, I think—no, it'd have to, since that's all I've read of his, and only half of the third. But that lack of appreciation, or you could call it understanding—the lack of—could come from my own limitations, and he really is great, as Fels might be, though right now, from what I've read, not to me." "You mean both of them?" the host said. "Well, honestly, what writer can really be called great except Shakespeare and Keats and Virgil and Tolstoy and I guess you gotta throw Joyce in there, and a couple of others?" "Plenty more, I'd think, but I get what you mean. Have a good time, and speak to you later. Hey, where'd your pretty gal go?" I.'s girlfriend had long ago left them to speak to some other people and get a drink, and also, he was sure, to get away from his blathering about literary matters. "Just because you write fiction doesn't mean you know literature," she once said. "You often rely on gut feeling and come out sounding uninformed if not lowbrow and bitterly envious." He'd forgotten also that she'd done her master's thesis on Dickens in New York and loved that writer's work, every contrivance and line. He said what he did about Fels because he wasn't going to say nothing or what he really thought of the work. Forget even the possibility of greatness regarding Fels or some lack of his own understanding, was what he thought then and still believes. No writer's great if you have to have postgraduate degrees in seven different disciplines to understand most of his work. Besides, saying what he really thought would have been impolite and made for a somewhat uncomfortable evening after that and no intro to the author, probably, and he wanted to meet him if it came about without him pushing himself on Fels or urging the host to introduce them. Just to see what he was like and particularly how a writer handles such fame, but not to get in good with him for any self-serving purpose. Fels wouldn't like his work even if he did, for some reason, get to read it. In fact, even if Fels, if they had gotten to speak, had asked to see some of his work, he would have begged off, saying something like "Really, I want to spare you, and I also know how busy you must be with your own writing and all the things that go along with it, but thanks." If Fels had insisted, saying something like "Come on, I like reading unpublished manuscripts of younger writers," and he wouldn't have said this, but also "As an established writer who's had his share of good breaks, I almost feel duty-bound to from time to time," and then "and it's possible I can do something for you with my book editor and agent, providing I like it, of course," he would have said all right, and taken down his address, but he doesn't think he would have sent him anything; their work was just too unalike. (Kafka, he thought right after the host left him, he should have mentioned him and probably even Chekhov and Gogol and, though this would have sounded silly and naive, Homer, whoever he was, as other great writers.) Fels' fiction—and I.'s opinion on this deepened over the years—was extremely erudite, witty, well-crafted and tricky, et cetera—fiction of the fifties, I. called it, even when it was written in the nineties—and he did his research, that's for sure—probably spent a year or two per book just on that—while I.'s research consisted mostly of making sure the streets and dates and such were right, if he was writing about a real city and time, and to call a thing by the right word or term, such as "athletic bag" for the bag you carry your gym equipment in (he'd called a sports store to make sure, or are they called sporting or sports good stores or athletic shops? For that one, if he wanted to use it in his fiction, he'd go to the category section of the yellow pages). And despite all the modernist moves or fixtures or whatever they're called, in Fels' fiction, such as self-reflexiveness and periodic lists and longueurs, a word that'd be in Fels' work but not I.'s, he was a bit old-fashioned as a writer, with long introductions to scenes and plenty of atmosphere and description and explaining and the plot going from A to B to C and so on, though I. still had a tough time staying with it because of the density of the prose and lengthy sentences and enormous paragraphs and unconventional punctuation and devices like quotation marks within quotation marks within quotation marks and sometimes seven- or eight-person dialogs with no attribution for each line of dialog most times and everyone sounding alike. He was also a humorous writer but not in a way I. liked. That smart-alecky almost uppercrust English tongue-in-cheek cheeky humor, and he also seemed like a misanthrope in his fiction, with just about no character likable or sympathetic in any way. (Come to think of it, not Dante, Cervantes and Rabelais on his "great" list either, since he found them to be imaginative cold fish with flashes of compassion and, for the last two, humor that he thought mostly cartoonish and slight.) Oh, he's not explaining himself well (and what about Montaigne and Sophocles and most of Yeats and Camus and lots of Conrad, Coleridge, Dostoevsky, Swift, Blake and DeFoe?). Or to put it more plainly (and enough with this idiotic list, particularly when he quickly wants to sack Swift and say "lots" instead of "most" of Yeats and "almost all" of Blake, and he forgot-somewhere in there to put in Bernhard, Beckett, Eliot and Wordsworth), or just in a different way: Fels' first novel was two to three times longer than it should have been, or that's how it felt even if he couldn't finish it, though he did go back to it several times to try. Didn't even get through half of it, though that was still more than four hundred packed pages, but he could tell, by flipping through and periodically dipping in to the rest, that it wasn't going to pick up. So what's he saying? That the language in it was arch, artificial, pretentious, smug—most of, he's saying—and the story was plodding and the book as a whole seemed intent on being labeled a masterpiece when it was actually a big bloated tiring boor. (He knows he said he was through with the list, but how could he leave out Horace, Catullus, Whitman, whoever wrote "Ecclesiastes" and "Job" and "The Song of Songs" and certain early passages of the Bible?) Now he remembers a photo of Fels in the *Village Voice* more than thirty years ago. He even remembers where he was when he read the article the photo was in. On his fold-out bed in his crummy one-room apartment on New York's Upper West Side. He even remembers the rent: eighty-six dollars and two cents, and ten dollars a month for gas and electricity. He had to stick the rent check through the slot in the landlady's mailbox and slip the ten dollars in cash in an envelope under her apartment door. She said she'd rather keep it a secret why she wanted a check for one and cash for the other and in the ways she wanted them given to her—he remembers saying it'd be easier for him to pay both at once and in the same monetary form, preferably the teller's check—but it probably had something to do with taxes or separating the business expenses from the rent or just part of her eccentricity. He also wasn't going to make a big deal of it, since that was a very low rent and charge for utilities even then. Anyway, Fels had been part of a literary symposium at Judson Church downtown. (More than likely, I. had a glass of wine on the night table when he read the article, and a small plate of celery and carrot sticks, which he almost always prepared for himself when he drank and read in bed during the afternoon, and a sour pickle he'd slice up if he had one around. And it had to be the afternoon, or early evening. He never read a newspaper in bed late at night because he didn't want to go to sleep with newsprint ink on his hands or have to get out of bed to wash them if he felt himself falling asleep. And if he did have a glass of wine by his side, then it had to be late afternoon at the earliest, since he never started drinking alcohol of any sort—and still doesn't today except if he's taken out to lunch by his editor or agent, let's say and then, just to be polite or to unwind, he'll have a single glass of wine—before five or six P.M.) The photo seemed to have been taken from the rear of the audience or maybe even from the front row of the balcony, for there were many rows of people between the camera and the front of the church and he could barely make out the faces of the people on stage. The article singled out Fels as one of the discussants—a rare appearance in public, it called it, and a rare photo of him, the caption said. Maybe Fels had made that one of his stipulations for participating in the symposium: that the photographs of the panel be taken from so far back that he wouldn't be recognizable in them. Even at that time—it was several years after the first novel had come out, the one with few reviews and continuous small reprinting and finally major appreciations in important intellectual journals—he was already something of a literary celebrity in New York or at least had a cult following there and probably on many American college campuses, as well as being a best-selling author in England and Europe. He remembers now when he first heard of Fels. A writer friend a few years older than I.—they'd met in '61 at the only writers conference I. had ever attended, one they both got full fellowships to or they never would have gone—had told him about Fels' first novel and was flabbergasted he'd never heard of it, since it was one of the three or four best novels written since *Ulysses*, and that includes one or the other of Kafka's two best posthumously published novels and the big one by Musil and the last half of Proust's. I. wanted to read it and the friend said he'd have to buy his own copy, if he could find one in a store, or borrow it from a library, and for that, if the 42nd Street branch didn't have it, he might have to go to the Widener or Library of Congress, because the friend would never loan his own rare first edition hardcover in a million years.

But what's he going on about? I. isn't his initial ("I am not I.," he's tempted to say, but that's not the person he's writing this in) and Joshua Fels, it should go without noting, isn't the name of the writer whose obituary he read today. He had met this writer who died yesterday (checks the obit and sees it was yesterday and not some day before, so it was probably written a while back and just the latest details had to be added) about twenty-five years ago (reconstructs in his head—not "reconstructs" but pinpoints or something a whole bunch of factors—now that had to be the first time he's used that word, as was "reconstructs," which he ended up not using—to determine the year they met, and it was exactly twenty-five years ago) and in the way he said (girlfriend, summer, party at a town on the west side of the Hudson about a half-hour's drive from the city, host he spoke to at the door and what they said, or did he first speak to her beside the swimming pool in back, or was that just a small man-made fishpond with goldfish inside?) But the question's still: what's he getting at with all this? Something about memory, he thinks, and how events just seem to pop back from some buried spot when the mind's been triggered by something like an obituary of someone you knew or were acquainted with in some way, and also about being a young writer (actually, not so young; 38, but still, with five or six book-length manuscripts by then, no book published after trying to place one for around fifteen years) snubbed by an older well-known writer and how he felt about it and what it meant to him, if those two aren't the same thing. Oh, stop with the crypt of memories swinging open and all that. Fine, then what? Simply this: He finished something yesterday—okay, a short story—wanted to start something new today—story, novel, two-page short-short: what did he care? A fiction of any length—even a play if it was possible—because he gets agitated with himself and grumpy with his family if at the end of the day after the one he finished a fiction he still doesn't have something to work on the next day. In other words—but he thinks he explained that okay. So he woke up knowing he was going to try to start a new work today (he's still on winter break from school so has more time than usual to write), made his kids breakfast and drove them to their schools, prepared his wife's breakfast (all he'd have to do later is heat it up) and a salad for the family for tonight's dinner, made his daily mug of miso soup (broth, really, since it's just boiled water, heaping teaspoon of miso and a little grated ginger. Supposed to be good for the prostate, he read in a *New York Times* science article a few years ago, but just get on with this), sipped the soup or broth while reading today's *Times* in his easy chair in the living room (perhaps he should have said that the paper's delivered and he went out to the end of the driveway to get it right after he made the kids breakfast, since he doesn't want to chance driving over the paper when he takes them to school—and *papers*, for they also get the *Baltimore Sun*—nor chance that his neighbors, who live in the only house up the hill and share the driveway, drive over them), turned to the obituary page (that last parenthetical sentence could be clearer, and he knows it's going to take work), the first section he looks at after reading the headlines and a few paragraphs of what seem like the most important articles on the front page (and settle for "soup," as "broth" seems too weak a word for it and soup is what he calls it), and saw the obit of Fels, he'll probably continue to call him (the name has no conscious double meaning and seems like an apt one for the type of guy he was and his patrician background), dropped the paper on the floor (soup was finished and the tea kettle was just about to whistle), and going into the kitchen to put the miso mug in the sink and pour the water for his coffee (he'd set up the two-cup drip pot with coffee grounds last night because he likes getting a jump on his early-morning chores: kids' and wife's breakfasts, water and food for the cat, tonight's salad, getting the newspapers, several other things like shaving and calisthenics, and sometimes he even prepares his wife's breakfast and his miso soup, minus the water, the night before and refrigerates them, and sometimes the entire salad, washed and dried and in a bowl with a damp dish towel on top to keep it fresh, or just washed and in the dish towel and next morning he'd cut it up into the bowl and then put the towel he used to wrap the salad in on top) he thought he'd try to write the first draft of a story about his encounters with Fels at the party and also what it was like (for one reads plenty, or let's say a lot's been written about starting-out writers but not much about one this age) to be a not-so-young-anymore unpublished writer, except for around ten stories in little to very small magazines, and while he was pouring the water a first line came to him which he wanted to jot down soon as he finished pouring because it seemed a good one to start off with, one that would lead to another one and so on, and which he might forget, but forgot to: "Headline in the paper today said 'Famous Innovative Writer Dead,'" got his manual typewriter and a stack of paper off his desk in the bedroom (wife was sleeping stentorously—a word a student of his wrote in a story last week and he said in class "What the heck you using a word like that for? It sounds like a sleeping dinosaur. 'The husband was snoring in bed,' or 'The husband was in bed, snoring,' or 'was asleep, snoring, in bed,' or something like that, but don't get so godamn—I was going to say 'goshdarn,' but that would have seemed so fake coming from a person like me—fancy, and I'm saying that for all of you"—and the room was dark because the curtains were still closed, so did this quietly and carefully as he could because he didn't want her to wake and ask him to help get her up now), set the typewriter and paper on the dining room table, went back to close the bedroom door and then the louver doors separating the living room from the hallway outside the bedroom, brought in his mug of coffee, got his pen out of his pocket and put it on the table, forgot to get his Ko-Rec-Type tabs off the desk but that's all right, he thought, this will only be a first draft or however far he gets in it before his wife wakes up and calls for him, sipped some coffee and started to type.

He could have done that so much more simply: He finished writing something yesterday, wanted to start writing something today, saw the obituary and started to write.

Even simpler: ". . . wanted to start on something today," and the rest of it.

So what did it feel like being snubbed by that writer?

He really didn't care, if he remembers correctly, thought nothing of it then, it now comes back to him, even laughed about it a little later to his girlfriend—"You won't believe the way Mr. Bigtime Famous Author just high-hatted me," and when she said "What'd he do, not that I'd know who he is unless someone pointed him out to me. That him, the handsome natty one in the blue blazer and Topsiders?" and he said "Yeah, he moored his sailboat in the driveway. We were introduced, all very nice and chummy, and he treated me like an enormous lump of elephant dung, something he wanted to get away from fast for all the obvious reasons," and she said "And to name a few?" and he said "My size, origin, the ugly sight of me, of course my smell, and that if he lost his balance or was feeling a bit tipsy he might fall in to me." But high-hatting elephant dung? Doesn't work. And better to just write what happened than say, before he says how he felt, what happened. That doesn't make much sense and he forgets what he intended to say with it, though if he analyzed the line he's sure he could figure it out and say what he'd intended, but just move on.

Fels arrived at the party (I., he'll continue to call him, since he has to call him something or he'll get him mixed up with Fels or someone else, actually heard people around him say "Fels is here." "Someone says she just saw Fels at the food table." "You know who's at this party? Fels. I'd heard there was a possibility of his showing up, but I never thought he would. A fantastic writer, even though I only understand every other line he writes and am not even so sure about that") and tried not to smile—no, that's not fair; he just didn't smile—or show any expression but an uninterested one when the host grabbed I.'s arm (I. was walking past, didn't know the guy talking to the host was Fels but had been on the lookout for him, figuring a writer might look different than the other people at the party) and said—this was by the swimming pool or fishpond—"Joshua, I'd like you to meet another writer, someone relatively new to our little community,' and gave I.'s name. They shook hands. I. said "It's a pleasure, sir." No, he wouldn't have said that. He probably said, since it's something he almost always says—a fair guess: nineteen out of twenty times, and for the past thirty years, when he's introduced to someone the first time—"Nice to meet you," and smiled. Fels said "Thank you," or something, the no-smile blank look, and turned around, seemed to be searching for someone, seemed to locate that someone in a crowd of people at the bar nearby, which was where I. had been heading, excused himself to the host, didn't look again at I., and headed for the bar, and I. said to the host "Vel, dat vuzz a fine how-do-you-do if I ever hurd one," and the host said "Why, what's wrong?" and I. said "Nossing, vat could be wrong? I got my gatkers on backvards? I don't sink so, it don't feel like it, but maybe I'll get to tayk vit him later, if I could only lose dis accent furst," and the host said "Yeah, what is it with the accent, though it's a very good one, whatever kind it is." Then: "See you later, gotta do my host-mosting," and left, and I. watched Fels. Fels asked the bartender for a drink, then was spoken to by one of the guests and looked at this man as if he couldn't place him. Still, he smiled, then laughed, got his drink and clinked glasses with the man and then with the woman next to the man, and talked to them for a few minutes, or let's say he was still busy talking to them, smiling and laughing and patting the man's upper arm, when I. looked away. Point is: that encounter was all by accident. Fels—I. could tell by his reaction to them from the start didn't know who the hell these people were, though they for sure knew who he was, or at least the man did, and they had probably even sought him out once they'd heard he was here. I. imagined the conversation while he was looking at them. "Mr. Fels"—"Please, we're at the same party and were invited by the same people, so call me Joshua"—"Joshua, then, all right, though it isn't easy to, but Joshua, we—I mean I—I mean both of us, my wife and I, since we've both read you (so the wife did know who Fels was), simply want to say how much we admire your work and that we'd like to drink to you and your next book, which we hear is close to being finished," and Fels: "Thank you, but tonight the less said about my work, past, present and future—" and the man: "Of course, anything you say, sir," and Fels: "And please, no 'sir' either, if you also don't mind, and I hope I'm not being too demanding. Even though I'm invariably older than almost everyone I converse with, that 'sir' address always makes me feel bloody ancient," and the man: "Really, we understand, and I'm terribly sorry," and Fels: "Now look at me; I've put you on the defensive. Please, let's get past these weary time-consuming civilities and social empathies and talk about something more important, which would be anything but my work," and the man or woman: "Whatever you wish, sir—excuse me," and they all laughed and started talking about other things: the town, weather, what they're planning to do this summer (it was a Fourth of July party, I. now remembers, and the host even set off an elaborate fireworks display near the end of it, one that could probably have been seen from across the river), what work the man and woman do, a book either the man or woman had read and which wasn't Fels', they want to assure him, so don't think they're going to violate his request not to talk about his work. . . . Later, I. was heading for the bar and saw Fels there ordering a drink. I. thought it's obvious the guy doesn't want to talk to me, but that shouldn't stop me from getting a drink when I want one. When Fels got his drinks—a glass in each hand—and turned around and saw I. a couple of feet from him, he quickly looked away and excused himself past some people. That clinches it, I. thought. All I was going to do was nod hello but the guy wouldn't even give me time for that. Maybe he thinks that because I'm a writer I'll want to talk about writing and from that get around to asking if it'd be too much of an imposition for him to read one of my manuscripts or we'll start talking shop and I'll ask if he knows of a good literary agent or book editor I can send my work to, and what about his, "Do you think he or she would be interested in looking at something from a writer who considers himself a serious one and who's never had a book published but has been trying to for close to fifteen years? Or maybe it has nothing to do with me, I. thought. Give the guy the benefit of the doubt. Maybe he told someone a minute ago that he's getting a refill at the bar—"May I get you one too?"—and he'll be right back, and considers himself a man of his word. *Is* a man of his word. He hates people-hopping at these parties, he could have told this person, and much prefers sitting to the side with someone and having a long deep conversation on a subject they both know something about or one he up till then knew little about but learned from this person and found very interesting. (Just thought of some more for his list: Dickinson, Murasaki, probably Baudelaire, Melville and Rimbaud, and if Euripides instead of Sophocles then Sophocles just a rung below, and of course Chaucer if he didn't already have him on it, and at the bottom of the greats, Céline, Celan, Mandelstahm, Hamsun and Undset, and okay, Dostoevsky.) That was the last time I. saw Fels. When he and his girlfriend were leaving, the host said to him "Did you and Joshua ever get to talk?" and I. said "I don't think he took to that idea very much, or maybe I'm mistaken, but no, we never got around to it, though not because I went out of my way to avoid him. I did get to see what he drinks. Margaritas if you have tequila, gin and tonics if you don't. I don't know what he would have drank if you didn't have tonic," and the host said we always have tonic, even in winter, and limes. Well, that's unfortunate you found him that way, and I'm surprised too. I know he can show a steely exterior to semi-illiterates who practically boast they don't know a book from a brick. But to most people, once you get to talking to him, he can be a puppy inside, and someone whose fame hasn't affected him one whit. He left before my great fireworks display because he has to rise early tomorrow if he's to meet the deadline he's set for himself on his new book. His publisher has spring-listed it the third year in a row and Joshua doesn't want to disappoint them this time." "That's a concern I should only have," I. said, "plus about a tenth of the handsome advance I'm sure he got and also a publisher who'd be so forgiving and indulgent. I guess they must want the book a lot so don't want to say anything to lose him," and the host said to I.'s girlfriend "He kidding me?" and she said "I think not."

There was a second time, he now remembers. At a book party in a huge rare and used bookstore in downtown New York. The writer of the book also managed the store and got the owner to host the party with his publisher. A couple of hundred people must have been there, mostly writers, editors and agents. Eventually the place got so crowded that someone stood at the door, only letting people out. Fire regulations, he kept shouting, "we're way over capacity," though when a prominent writer appeared at the door, and this might have happened a number of times, he said "For her I gotta break the rules and let in, which I'm sure the rest of you waiting will understand." I. had done a lot of browsing in the store and got to know the manager that way, so was invited but told to get there early or he might not get in. He was living with the same girlfriend in an apartment a few blocks away, but she had gone to St. Louis with her daughter to visit her maiden great-aunt who was quite old and sick and planning to leave most of her inheritance to them, and whom she hadn't seen for many years. New paragraph? He met a woman at the food bar. "They were both reaching for the stuffed grape-leaf tray, their hands collided, he said "Sorry," and withdrew his hand, she said "No, you first; your hand was there before mine," and he said "Wouldn't think of it; please." Anyway, she got a leaf, then he got one which turned out to have no rice or anything in it. "Look at this; oily and empty. I'd complain to management except he's the one the party's for, so shouldn't be disturbed at such an event with something this trivial, and besides, I should feel lucky to be here at all with such an illustrious crowd. It's like a magazine pullout or two-page spread of who's who in writing today. You must know the kind, where all the writers are lined up in rows and at the bottom of this spread are their names, best-known book titles, most prestigious honors and awards, and what size advance their last book got." "Were you in one of these photos and I'm showing my ignorance in not knowing who you are?" and he said "Not by a long shot, and that isn't because I don't write or have never been published. To me it's such an asinine ignominious thing to be part of, a group literary photo. I wouldn't have posed in one even if by some rare chance I'd been asked." "So you're a fiction writer who's probably had a book out recently from a small publisher, with a small printing, small to no advance and barely a review." "You nailed the nose, lady, except for the reviews. There were none, but then it's only been around for six months. The best thing I can say about the way my first and only book came out is that I didn't have to pay to get it published. And you, a writer?" and she said "Married to one." He asked "Who?" and she said "I could easily tell you, or you could play match-the-writer-with-his-wife, but you'd have to scout the room first." "Henri Michaux," he said without looking around, and she said "Wrong continent, I know he's not dead, and he is one of my all-time favorites, like my husband. But why'd you say him?" "I wanted to try out my pronunciation of his name, but that's ridiculous. I apologize for acting dopey." "Joshua Fels," and he said "Oh, I don't know him though we did once meet, but really no more than a handshake. And if I hadn't met him, your match-the-spouse game would have been virtually impossible, since I hear he doesn't sit or stand for photos or anything for a book jacket like that. That must be why, because I'm sure they asked him, he wasn't in the recent *Esquire* spread on American writers. Though maybe he also wasn't in it for the same reasons of asininity and whatever the second one was that I gave. It was at a July 4th party two years ago. You might have been there too and we were never in the same room or the same area outside together." (All that could have been done—much quicker. Just should have said: "Two years later he was at . . ." Or better: "They met again, he now remembers. Two years later he was at a big crowded book party in New York, though he first got to talking to Fels' wife. She was about twenty years younger than he, very pretty, lively and smart." Or no description of her. And she was actually beautiful, and tall and slim and well-built; he at first thought she was a fashion model. But just: ". . . to talking to Fels' wife.") "I didn't know Josh then; we only got married this year. But I know the party you mean. The Abramowitzes. We like that town so much that we bought the house from his ex-wife after she'd acquired it as part of their divorce settlement the year before. They hold it every July 4th; we were at the last one. Fabulous fireworks. I'm curious, though, and it's not something I can very well talk about yet with Josh's friends and our neighbors, what your impression of his ex-wife was, if you met her. I never have but I understand she was quite witty and attractive, and Josh said that unlike me, she loves parties." "Really, far as I could make out, he seemed to have come alone. In fact I'm sure of it, because I remember something about being told his wife was out of town for the night with their child and that was why he'd be able to get up early the next morning to write. No, what am I talking about, that's actually me and the woman I live with, but tonight. She flew to St. Louis with her daughter and tomorrow I get to have an uninterrupted day of work." (Best to skip all that and go back to ". . . talking to Fels' wife.") He told her where he'd met Fels and she asked what his connection to the hosts was. "The woman I'm with now in New York used to teach high school in that area and had a small rowhouse in town, which she still owns and we go to almost every other weekend. In fact if you're living in the house Mr. Fels had then, you've probably driven past hers a number of times." He gave the street. "Sure," she said, "I pass it a couple of times a day at least." Just around then Fels said to her "Enjoying yourself, darling?" But before he came over to them, I., out of nowhere, said "I know this has nothing to do with anything we were talking about—and if you think I'm hogging your time or you just want to move on to see who else you may want to speak to, please say so—but I've been curious lately as to what certain people involved with or interested in literature think are the greatest writer since Creation, and that should include not only poets and novelists and such but, if their styles warrant it, essayists, historians, philosophers" . . . all of which, of course, he never said. Though for about thirty seconds he thought it a different way of getting in a few of the names he might have missed, but got the timing screwed up. She could have said "For starters, Milton, Goethe and Flaubert," and he could have said "Milton should be an obvious choice, but I could never read him for more than a few pages without wondering where I was in the work or feeling a bit stomach-sick or sleepy. As for the other two, and maybe Musil, I might agree with you. But please," he would have said if he had actually asked her this—and there's always a slight chance he did and then for more than twenty years forgot he had even thought of it—"because I can imagine what your husband would think of such a ridiculous question, if it's at all possible, forget I ever asked it." (But to go back: "Just around then Fels said to her 'Enjoying yourself, darling?'" or used her first name, which I. forgets and will probably never remember, since the names of the first three wives aren't given in the obituary and "Toba," the surviving wife, can't be it, since it's such an unusual name that when he saw it in the paper he would have remembered it.) She said yes and that she's been having a very nice conversation with this man. She apologized to I. for having to ask his name again, or maybe they hadn't exchanged names till then, and said "My husband, which you must have guessed, Joshua Fels," and I. said "Nice to meet you," and they shook hands. "We've already briefly met," and Fels said "We have?" and gave that look of "This certainly comes as news to me," and I. said "Not tonight but a while back," and she said "That's right, at the Abramowitzes', I forgot to mention it. Not only that, dear, but his close woman friend has a house a short distance from ours, one we pass regularly in the car," and gave the street name, which I. also forgets. "We should have them for drinks one of the next few weekends when they're staying there," and Fels said "Good idea. You make all the arrangements, though check with me beforehand to make sure I'm not previously engaged," and smiled at her or something and walked away without looking at him again. I. wanted to say to her "Listen, we'll forget about the drinks, but nice try, for it might've turned out okay." Or "Christs, I don't care if he is your husband, but that's the second damn time—we're talking two for two, lady—he's given me the big brush-off while I was standing next to him. What is it with the guy? Can't he just say, if he wants to beat it away fast, 'Nice to meet you, goodbye'?" Or "God, what a freaking—excuse me, and I'm actually holding myself back—snob. Talk about being dismissed? And almost you too for suggesting we visit. He wants to see my girlfriend and me about as much as he wants a crippling case of stomach cramps this very minute." Or—But forget it. "So," she said, "let me have your woman friend's name and her phone number up there," and she wrote it down in a little address book. "This is terrific and a wonderful stroke of luck meeting you here. If I pass by your house and see the light's on—it's dark otherwise, am I right?—then I'll know you're around and I'll call you. Yours is which of those rowhouses?" and he said "Facing them, one on the extreme right with the abandoned refrigerator on the porch." "I'd love to get to know a congenial young couple in the area who are also literary and artistic," because he'd told her his girlfriend's also a printmaker. "In town, Josh seems to know mostly lawyers, doctors and people who move around other people's money, several of whom are quite as literate as doctors and lawyers used to be but reluctant to talk with us about what they read. It could be they're too intimidated by Josh's book reputation to discuss literature in front of him and that he seems to have read every serious piece of writing ever written, but I don't think you'd act toward him that way. And one weekend evening soon would be ideal, since Josh is busy all week writing or doing other literary business and only starts to unwind on Saturdays after five. Now you should circulate, covertly provoke 'And what do you do?' questions about yourself, spread your name around and get your last book and future projects known. I'm not an expert on it—all the reapings Josh gets seem to drop out of an envelope into his lap—but I bet you'll never have a better opportunity than here to get the publishing and book-reviewing and grants-giving world interested in you. I'd spread the word about you myself, but I'm not familiar with your work. I will be, though. Who was it who said 'Any writer'—I'm standing in for Josh with this saying, and I know he'll back me—'who doesn't buy another writer's book is either pathetically penurious or a cad'?" "Kipling, it sounds like," he said, "or maybe Galsworthy or Wilde," and thinks "Kipling; good, especially three or four of the *Jungle Book* stories, but not great." Fels' wife never called. Did he expect her to? Sure, why not? She seemed sincere about it and too smart and meticulous to forget. Repeating their phone number twice to make sure she got it down right. Fels must have said when I.'s name came up for drinks at their house, "I'm really chock-full of writer acquaintances and friends, darling. Maybe when one of them drops dead we can replace him with this young man as they do with members of the Arts and Letters Academy, and you did buy his book." But what's he being so rough on him for? Fels might have said he's not in the mood to meet anyone new now (hasn't I. felt that way a number of times?), pleasant as this young man seemed and he's sure his woman friend is. And he has a book to finish and another one to research and write, so he wants—for the next twenty years, he'll say, and he's only being facetious about this by half—to keep his social obligations down to something he can control. "But you want to see them so much? Just say I'm overextended right now and offer my apologies and then meet them at a local cafe or pub. Because you know what can happen if we have them here. It'll be interesting for all of us up to a point. And then, after some trepidation, they'll invite us in return, and I wouldn't want to possibly hurt or offend them by saying no, just as I don't want this invitation thing to snowball. Best, I'd say, to appear insincere from the beginning by not phoning them as you had planned. You run into him again and he brings up the matter about the lights on in their house and that was the signal you'd established that they were there, you say that for some reason you thought they were in the city and the lights were on to ward off burglars. Though what am I putting these narrow-minded thoughts into his head, as if either of them would ever think you insincere? Simply don't invite them and let them supply the reasons why, which I'm certain will be nothing short of magnanimous: 'Fels might not be well.' Or 'He's known for being somewhat unsociable and a bit of a loner, so let's not take it personally.' And the one I'd think the young man would empathize with and respect the most: 'He's busy with his work, just like I'd be if I had the time and could afford it.'" A few months later, I., while reading a book on the porch of his girlfriend's house (James' short stories: brilliant mind but the writing quite turgid and stodgy), saw Fels and his wife drive past in an open convertible, Fels in the passenger seat and looking as if he was holding down his hair with his hand. After that, he saw Fels' wife drive past alone a couple of times, staring straight ahead. If she had looked his way, he would have waved.

Now I. remembers another time he met Fels, this one a quickie. The following spring or summer—anyway, it was warm, shorts and T-shirt weather, and it couldn't have been the following fall, for by then he and this woman had broken up. Fels coming out of the small market in town, carrying a bag of groceries, and I. heading for the store. I. said hello and Fels looked up, didn't smile or nod, gave no sign he recognized him, kept walking, stopped at a bicycle leaning against a wall, divided up the groceries into the two baskets on either side of the rear wheel and threw the empty grocery bag into a trash container, unlocked the bike and peddled off. "Damn, you got me again," I. said, Fels too far away by now to hear him, and I. hadn't intended him to. And then wanted to yell in a funny Russian accent like the guy on a comedian's radio show more than forty years ago—the Mad Russian the guy was called, on the show for less than a minute each week—"How do you do? *How do you do? How do you do!*" but thought "Don't. He'll come back indignantly and say something like, and maybe even give some indication he knows whom he's speaking to, 'Was that gibe supposed to be meant for me?'"

And another time, this one a real meeting, and he thinks the last time he saw Fels. Thinks hard and thinks yes, the last. I. was married by then and his wife had known Fels' third wife. Or maybe she was his fourth and the one he was married to when he died was his fifth and the obit had the count wrong. That can happen when you don't list all the names. But the wife after the one I. had met at that book party in New York, that he's almost sure. I.'s wife and she had been in a women's college together. The woman was about three years ahead of her and had tutored her in some subject or another. No, that's not how it went. Then why'd he think it? It just came to him and he thought it was right and was even going to say "some subject like calculus or astronomy or Chinese." So where'd they know each other from? A dinner party that Fels and this woman had given in their apartment in New York. (Wait a second. —No no, forget that, the chronology's right. The book-party wife and the one before her lived with Fels in the Hudson River house. Then Fels lived with the dinner-party wife in New York City and no doubt another place, and Fels and his fifth wife lived in England and Martha's Vineyard and probably some other place, or maybe at the end he was living alone in these places but he and the fifth wife hadn't got divorced. But how could I. have forgotten that his wife, a year or so before he knew her, had gone to this dinner party and met Fels? He just forgot, that's all. It completely slipped his mind and was replaced by something he didn't know he was making up.) His wife had been taken to the party by a well-known English poet, more well known today for his essays and critical books and translations of Greek tragedies and Scandinavian plays. But at the time—I. remembers reading about it around then and for a few years after in newspapers and cultural journals—it was said he stood a fair chance of getting a Nobel and that he was reportedly shortlisted for it once or twice. Some of his poetry—is this necessary? Maybe none of the stuff about the poet is, except to show how I.'s wife got to the party, but just finish the thought because maybe something will come out of it. I. thought some of his poetry was vigorous and exciting for its sensuality and ferocity and honesty and even the brutal or just vehement way he spoke about art and poverty and women, especially his two previous wives, and so I. would say he had five or six exceptional poems and he loved the guy's clarity but overall as a poet (and he never cared much for literary criticism, and a good translation of a play shouldn't be too hard if you know the language or have first-rate literals) he wouldn't call him great. There, that's something what he hoped he'd land on by continuing with it. The poet used to see I.'s wife (of course, before she knew I.) for about two years every time he came to the States on a reading tour or university lecture or week's poet-in-residenceship at one or just to see her and his American publisher, which meant they saw each other about four times a year. She also spent several months in London with him once. She even thought they might end up getting married then. But the guy was a philanderer, even when she was living with him, and drank too much and often got angry and insulting when he did and sometimes violent—not hitting her; just throwing around chairs and books and breaking a finger when he slammed his hand through a headboard—so she decided better to just see him occasionally till she was seriously involved with someone else, and only in New York. The party, though. But one more thing about him, now that it's in his head. The last time the poet called her—this was a few months after she and I. had met—I. answered the phone and said she wasn't home and who should he say had called? and the poet gave his name, but his full name rather than the two initials and surname he used for his published work, and asked whom he was speaking to and I. said "A friend of hers," and the poet said "Just looking after her plants and cats?" and I. said "No, I live here now, so those are only two of my household duties when she doesn't see to them," and the poet said "By living there, and please don't think me presumptuous or snoopy, does that mean you're not simply renting a spare room to help her out with the rent or borrowing a couch and some linen for a week or sleeping on the floor for a few nights?" and I. said "That's right; our clothes hang side by side in the bedroom closet and with her approval I've commandeered her bottom dresser drawer," and the poet said "Well, that's a damn pity for me. But I think it's wonderful for her and I wish you two the most brilliant future together. Tell her I'll try calling again next time I'm passing through, and perhaps I can take both of you out to lunch." (New paragraph? No, just that will do.) The two women (Fels' wife and I.'s future) sat next to each other at the dinner table. That's it: they discovered they'd gone to the same college, though Fels' wife had graduated a few years before I.'s had entered the school, and they talked for hours about their teachers and courses and interests and poetry and translations and theater, and met once after that for lunch and had a lively time together then too. Then something happened—I. forgets what. But he does remember she said she never saw Fels except at this party and he barely said a word to her other than "May I get you a drink?" and later "May I refresh your glass?" so involved was he with other people, particularly the poet, and she was also seated at the opposite end of the long table from him, though he seemed like an engaging fellow and extremely funny, had everyone around him laughing and even breaking up at things he said. "I almost wished, though I was enjoying myself plenty at my end of the table, that I'd been seated closer to him because of all I was missing. I also found him to be very attractive, looking at least fifteen years younger than someone there said he was. How old is he now?"

"Did he drink a lot?" I. remembers saying then, and she said "I didn't notice, and in what we were just talking about, why's it matter?"

So where was he? He really went off then. *The last time he saw Fels.* Right. The last time was in front of FAO Schwarz when it was still on 58th Street, he thinks, and Fifth. I. and his wife and their first child (not even ten months then but standing, though at the time seated on I.'s shoulders) were outside the store around Christmastime when they saw Fels and his dinner-party wife heading toward it. I.'s wife saw them first, and of course I. wouldn't have known who the woman was, and said "Look, Joshua Fels and his wife, what's her name? . . . darn, it'll be embarrassing if I can't remember it," and he said "I don't know, which one? I only met one of them, the second or third or whichever one she was—I know she wasn't the first—and I forget her name too. You of course mean the one you had dinner with at their apartment before you met me," and she said "Got it," and called out the woman's name just as they were about to enter the revolving door. They turned to her—several people on line behind them said something, so they stepped out of the way. The woman waved to his wife and said something to Fels. He made some kind of hand motion—I. didn't, and still doesn't, know what it meant; sort of throwing up one hand, but the same motion one would make if he were throwing up both hands, if that's clear—and she came over and Fels looked at the door spinning fast with nobody inside and then opened the regular door to the side and went in. The two women kissed. I.'s wife introduced him and their child. Fels wasn't in the lobby. Or else I. couldn't see him among all the people there—anyway, he wasn't standing by the doors and windows there, so might have gone inside. The woman said "My goodness, look at this gorgeous thing and those blond locks. You lucky stiff. I wanted one so much. But Josh already had so many that he said one more would break his back. Literally, he meant too. That he was too old for carrying them on his shoulders; that grandchildren were much lighter for that." I. said "I'm getting too old for it too, I think," and set his daughter down. "Upey, upey," she said, raising her arms, and he hoisted her back up. The women talked about things they'd done the last few years. A photography book on doll furniture the woman did; a book-length translation of poetry his wife did. Oh yes, the woman saw it. Teaching; people they both knew; the poet: he's doing fine, Josh sees him more than she does, but he seems to be writing less poetry and more about it these days. "If we're going to talk some more," I. said to his wife, "don't you think we should go back inside the store? It's probably getting too cold for her," pointing up to his daughter, "and I don't think she's old enough yet to know how to complain about it." "It's not so bad out," his wife said, "and she's bundled up like a bear against the cold." "If he really thinks—" and his wife said "No, she'll be fine." Did he say that—well, of course also for his daughter's sake—but to get inside and maybe see Fels and be introduced to him again and they'd talk? Was that what his wife was trying to prevent because she sensed that Fels didn't want to talk to anyone (not coming over with his wife) and she knew I. wanted to talk to him? No, that couldn't have been what she thought but probably was what he did. "Oh, look, hubby shows his illuminated face," and she waved to the store, and there was Fels, ceiling light beamed directly on his head, behind a lobby window, looking at them and pointing to his watch. Come join us, her wave now said. He threw up that same hand again, the left. He a lefty? I. still didn't know what the motion meant though. Maybe something like "I don't want to. Why do you insist on doing things I don't? We're wasting time. We will be wasting time. (Reverse those. First time: "will"; second: "we're.") It's always the same. You want to, I don't. You want to (hand shoots up again), I don't." But get to the point with all this. Really isn't one. He's recounting the last time he saw Fels. Putting in almost everything he remembers about it. Not to prolong it but to describe. Why? To get a real picture. And while remembering, finds himself remembering more. Things he didn't know he remembered, had never thought of or hadn't for years. The illuminated face: new. She actually said that, or words close. New too: ceiling light beaming on Fels' face but mostly onto the top of his head, turning his gray hair bright blond which, I. thinks, it must have been when he was a young man. Wasn't wearing a hat that night? (And it was night, did he say that? Or dark, around five or six.) Probably not. Or he was, he now remembers—a fedora of sorts—but took it off, no doubt, when he went into the store. But "to the point," because this *is* getting slow. So speed it up. They were introduced. (Obviously—but then again, not so "obviously," since they ((the two women and I. and his kid)) could have gone into the store—Fels came over. Actually: same "they" were approaching the store when Fels left it through the regular door and headed for them.) Introduced. Fels' face? Just get on with it. Shaking hands. "There's absolutely no reason why you should remember this, but we've met before (I.)." "Oh, have we (Fels)? I've an atrocious memory for such things, growing worse with age for it and everything else. It's also been the kind of strange, hectic day that would contribute even further to my memory loss." All right, Fels' face: dyspeptic (a word used fairly commonly in Fels' fiction, along with pudibund and conundrum and fatidic, spelling literary fake) when he walked over, and aloof or put off or bemused, except for quick on-and-off smiles appearing solely around his mouth, while he was there. So, was the descript worth it? Again, hardly, and slowed this down even more. "Harrying's what the day's truly been like (Fels' wife). And then, after all that happened earlier, which Josh would kill me if I revealed so much as a part of"—"No, I wouldn't, dear; though perhaps a small amputation" ("mutilation"?)—"to want to come here to buy presents for his grandchildren and buck the mobs outside and in?" "I love my grandkids (Fels to her). Sometimes more than I loved my own children when they were kids, something I'd like you to forget I confessed. But are children just getting sweeter and smarter with each generation, and if so, where does that put mine when we were kids? In the precociously know-nothing ogre class like our parents said? So I'm saying that almost anything's worth bucking to prevent their disappointment come Christmas day if they arrived to find us giftless (still only to his wife)." "In fact (I.), about what I was saying before, we've met twice, not counting today or seeing you in the local grocery store in that town you lived in upstate." "Twice, now (Fels)? My poor memory's really going to get a workout from you and look shot. When was all this?" I.'s wife's glance said she thought I. was about to say something sarcastic about the previous brush-offs, and not to. But I'll fool her (I. Oh, go to regular tags. Getting "thought" in this way looks too clumsy). I'm going to act respectful and maybe even a bit obsequious, he thought, and in no way allude to those two times when he practically spit on me. All right: no more than ignored. "The last time was at that Strand bookstore book party for the manager of it," I. said. "I think it took place just a little before that terrific relatively short novel of yours came out." "That party," Fels said, "is almost a total blank. If we stand here for thirty seconds more with no further mnemonic elbowings, it'll be completely erased. I'm sorry it's not you I forget, or want to, but the entire affair. It was loud, overcrowded and a horrendous ordeal to get to the bar. But I do remember thinking throughout it, and it's conceivable this thought nudged out the rest, of all those beautiful old books and bound galleys and reviewer copies being ruined by spilled drinks and dripping dips. What a dumb idea that was, having a party there." "You're probably right; I didn't think of it that way. The first time I met you, though, was a couple of years before that. Around the time you were finishing *Recapitulations*. A July 4th party at—well, I forget their first names, but the Abramowitzes, near where you used to live, or for all I know, still keep your house." "I've been to their parties a number of times on that holiday," Fels said, "so by now I can't distinguish one from the next. They all have a minimum of a hundred-fifty people at them and end the same way: lots of rockets ejaculating in the sky and a final big bam!" "It's true; this one had that too, and was pretty crowded. But there's a third time, I just remember," I. just now remembers saying. "At the Academy and Institute of Arts and Letters' May ceremony and banquet, where you were being inducted into whichever one of those two is the more august body and I was getting an award in literature." "Could that be right?" Fels said. "I've only been to one of their events, when I got that same literature award a hundred years ago. But I never showed up for either of my inductions, so you must have me mixed up with another older writer." "Truth is, I wasn't being serious about it. Just a case of—my professed literature award, I mean, if I'm even using 'professed' right there, and I've no idea why I brought up that induction business—of 'don't I wish.'" "I see," Fels said, "I see, or think I do." "I was wondering also," I.'s wife said, "since I don't think I ever heard you mention that award and certainly not in that context. But what I still can't quite grasp is what made you bring it up now." "As I said," I. said, "a don't-I-wish, which is no doubt as close as I'll ever get to it. But that's not enough?" He looked at her and the others. She was shaking her head, Fels was looking off at the traffic, and Fels' wife was staring at him and then did some movement with her face that seemed to say "Don' t look at me; I don't know." "Okay, what can I say," I. said to his wife. "It was stupid, clearly stupid. So excuse me, but I have my bad-joke and low-intelligence moments too. Hey," squeezing his daughter' s hands, "even through the mittens I can feel her little fingers getting frozen, so we should go." "Yes," Fels said, "don't let the child catch a cold. Goodbye, my sweet darling," he said to her, and kissed one of her hands and said to his wife "Did you ever see such a doll?" and nodded to I. and his wife and headed for the store. Fels' wife said "I don't want Josh to go in alone. He'll get peeved at me if I can't find him and he has to hunt for me through the place," and asked I.'s wife for her phone number, said "I don't have to write it down, I'll remember," and waved goodbye to them and their daughter and hurried after him.

Painted Cities

Alexai Galaviz-Budziszewski

Hanging Gardens

Rom has his colors down like no one else in the hood. Turned the west face of Speedy's Corner Store into a three-dimensional dreamscape, complete with galaxies, shooting stars and black holes which appear to bore right through the brick wall they're sprayed on. How he gets his colors to catch light like that, especially at night, when the orange of the street lamps reflect off his murals in iridescent gleams, is mystery to everyone. Awestruck, they watch him perform, red bandana maroon with sweat, clothes and skin speckled with over-spray: baby blue, crimson red, hi-glo yellow.

Speedy had seen the job Rom did on the alley wall of St. Stephen's rectory. The Christ on the Cross mural: overpowering not because of the crown of thorns, the blood dripping wounds, or the long, pouting stare Catholics are accustomed to; but overwhelming because of the way Christ looms above, as if frescoed on the concave surface of a spoon. Around Christ galaxies spin, shooting stars streak, and his white gown flows in a cosmic wind. To this day the mural is a routine stop on the North Side's bus tours into the heart of the city. Speedy's mural though, is as yet undiscovered, still pristine.

Whereas most of Rom's pieces are commissioned by area businesses or churches, maybe even the public, if Rom takes to heart the suggestions he hears while working: "Hey, bro, how about dedicating to my girlfriend, Flaca," "How about to my mother," "My grandmother who died yesterday," his dedication to Aurelia Marcos, a ten-year-old girl who disappeared the summer before last, simply appeared one morning without warning on the octagonal, brick kiosk that sits before the old Bohemian church on Eighteenth and Peoria.

The neighbors called the mural "poignant," though many were unsure of what the word meant. It wasn't negative though, most were sure of that, so the word was used over and over in description of the dedication until months later when the word dropped from favor through sheer boredom of use.

In the mural, a caricature of Aurelia sits alone on the wood bench her grandfather made for her many years before and placed in front of the ground floor apartment he lived in. How Rom knew this intimate detail of the Marcos family, no one knows, but they chalk it up to artist intuition. Anyone passing the scene views the bench, the brick-molded asphalt siding of her grandfather's building, and knows immediately the scene takes place in summer, that there is an open fire-hydrant somewhere near and that the scents of the neighborhood: frying tacos, boiling pots of garlic-spiced *frijoles*, cool Lake Michigan breezes transported by miles of sewer pipe, layer the atmosphere.

She sits playing with her hair and everyone remarks how Aurelia *could* just sit for hours, contented, smiling to herself occasionally when something funny came to mind. "But she never cried," her mother says, "No, never." Yet, in the dedication, as contented as Aurelia seems, chrome tears run down her high cheeks. This is where poignancy takes place.

Within the basket of each tear a city appears, like a hanging garden. Upon close inspection the image is revealed as a portrait of the neighborhood itself, shot from above, minute down to steeples and the path of the el as it snakes down Twenty-First Street. How he got his spray down to such fine points no one will ever know, and this is an issue of contention among the local graffiti artists: whether or not Rom actually broke the rules and employed brush. But the haze is there, the over-spray, the tell tale sign of aerosol art, which, in this case, lends to the already translucent tears, the cities held within glass bulbs, like holiday paper weights filled with liquid, begging to be flipped and allowed to snow.

The tears don't stop at the cheeks. They continue to fall: two, mid-air. Eventually, one glances off Aurelia's white knee and multiplies in a flash, producing more tears, finer tears, smaller cities. The silver droplets reach the painted cement sidewalk and absorb into what now appears to be a vast city in and of itself, splayed out beneath the reflective sheen of Aurelia's black patent leather shoes. Corridors of street lights, side-streets, meet at infinite points around the kiosk. At times, the neighbors say, the painted cities come alive, movement can be seen, the els slithering like hobby railroads, the neighborhood's lowriders stop and go on the boulevards.

Rom takes no credit for his murals. Never signs them, unless somewhere in the jumble of letters at the bottom of his pieces the name ROM is encoded. The neighbors call this humility, though many are unsure of what the word even means. They use it anyway, while they wait for miracles.

Residue

Could've been Death himself, the grim reaper, descending into the basketball court that night. Could've been ready to pull out any number of weapons, automatics, pumps, side-by-sides—everyone knows the grim reaper don't use sickles no more.

Grim reaper *looked* like he grew up south side, way he pimped down the alley ramp into Barret Park. Even though ole' boy was walking slow, that slight bump in his step was all south side, Twenty-second and Damen to be exact, could name the street corner by that walk alone.

First thought was he'd been living in somebody's basement. Jose Morales, valedictorian at Juarez High School thought it, and Sleepy too, twelve-year-old, droopy eyed, Party-Boy in training. Everyone in the park that night thought it. That, and how the world got awful small sometimes. Like just last week, when Beany from the Two-Ones found out his old lady was doing some dude where she worked downtown. Xerox repairman wound up being Juice from the Party-Players over on Allport, Beany's best friend when they came-up together on Eighteenth. Two days later Juice was found tied to an alley lamp post, alive but beaten. Beany's out hunting for his old lady now; he's got something more serious in mind for her.

But it figured the grim reaper was living in the neighborhood. Probably renting out a musty, concrete, basement for a buck-fifty a month, utilities included, stolen from a next door neighbor. Might have assumed the name Julio Ramirez, or Juan Calderon, one of those generic Mexican names nobody'd suspect it was Death himself, coming in at strange hours. Whoever owned the building, the landlord living in the front highest apartment, like they always do, probably thought Death was just a good worker. Probably thought he was some *mojado* busting his ass making calculators in Elgin for fourteen hours a day, wiring cash back home to Mexico, supporting seven growing children and a wife named

Iris, or Esmeralda, some name that brought to mind young beauty, though she herself was tired and worn. Landlord probably thought to hire Death too, being he was such a good worker. Give him twenty bucks to patch the front sidewalk, holes so big kids be falling down there, assumed kidnapped until someone heard the screaming.

And all along it was the grim reaper, filling in holes, living in the neighborhood, existing incognito.

Jr. Chine said it first, to no one in particular: "Hey, bro, that's Coco." Exactly how he knew the grim reaper was really Coco was impossible to tell. Why his mind had shifted from the Face-of-Death to that skinny Party-Boy lived round the block was impossible to tell, but they were good friends, and good friends can generally sense one another, like when you know a hit's pulling down the street five minutes before you actually see the car, cab darker than the street itself, orange street light thick as humidity.

It had been Jr. Chine's shot. He'd had the ball on the low-post, about to release his patented base-line jumper, dramatic for its disregard of the backboard, its confidence as it cycled through the air then swooped the chain-mesh net. The ball dropped from his hands like a whistle'd been blown, and it trotted, each bounce accompanied by the twang of an over inflated ball, toward the stinky field-house, down the slope of the compressed basketball court into the slot between the Cyclone retaining fence and the back of the brick building, where ball players, drunks and wicky-stick fiends pissed, the piss collecting over generations, reeking, giving the field-house its neighborhood moniker, "Stinky."

The figure's hands were hidden in his sweater's pockets. The deep hood hung low over his brow and his arms were locked at the elbows. Material was being stretched down as if the figure were cupping his balls, making the body seem even more ominous, an open mouth screaming, melting. If the crowd on the court could've seen the hands, a positive identification could've been made. They would've known for sure it was Death: long, white fingers, black fingernails, or they would've known it was really Coco: bleeding crucifix tattoo on the web of his right hand, Party-Boys etched in old English script like a banner over the crucifix. Jr. Chine approached the descending figure cautiously, his own right hand gripping the .25 automatic stuffed in the pocket of his cut-off shorts. He flipped the safety off, though, like always, he questioned immediately whether he'd actually flipped it on, and was now about to die feeling stupid. If he lived, he vowed, he'd memorize which action was the correct one, get the "safety" situation down pat, like he had the clip-loading maneuvers down pat, practicing for hours as he lay in bed, popping the clip in and out, in the dark, sightless, the clicks of the release mechanism working like second nature. He side-stepped towards the figure. His steps shortened as he neared. And suddenly Jr. Chine's vision went third person. Everything, the game, those standing behind, the cigarette Jr. Chine had left smoldering until he was back down court, disappeared from view, and he could see it all, himself, the situation, as if he was living his own movie.

"Coco, what the fuck are you doing?" Jr. Chine said. And a tiny voice came from the hooded figure. "Hey, bro, we need to find Angel."

"Who the fuck are you?" Jr. Chine said, now loud and boisterous, his adrenaline sky high. He bobbed and weaved as he moved around the figure. "Take off that hood so I can hear you." Jr. Chine's hands were wet. Around the grip of the gun his hand had become cold though the rubber grip itself remained hot. He pulled the gun from his pocket and held it stiff-arm at his leg.

"It's me, bro," the voice said a little louder, the hooded head following Jr. Chine as he juked and stuck.

"Coco?" Jr. Chine asked.

"Yeah."

Jr. Chine cocked his body ready to spring into action then reached out and peeked under the hood. It *was* Coco, though with all the welts, the fluvial bruises around his eyes, the fresh slices to his cheeks it was hard to tell. Jr. Chine's trigger arm went limp, his elbow finally unlocked after what felt like hours. Vision reeled itself back in. The burning in his arm remained but he relaxed and put the small gun back in his pocket.

"Hey, bro," Coco said. "Angel's on his way to kill Susan."

"Susan who," Jr. Chine said.

"His lady, bro."

Underground

There are cities down there, Little Egypt said so. He said they're smaller cities, not nearly as many people, but they have traffic and els, just like we do up here.

The subway used to connect. Little Egypt said that too. That the blue line used to take a steep dive right after LaSalle Street and descend into the cities, neighborhoods stacked on top of one another, deep into the earth, like department store floors. "But then," he said, "they built downtown, John Hancock and all that. Now the subway just flies right over, Jackson Boulevard, Monroe. People up here don't even care anymore."

I saw Little Egypt's suitcase once. He kept it stored beneath his bed, packed and ready to go if he ever got the call to leave. "My grandfather took this baby all around the world," Little Egypt said; he hoisted the suitcase onto his bed. "Should handle a trip below I'd think." He patted the swollen hide then curled out his bottom lip and nodded.

Inside were a lot of shorts. On the underside of the top-flap a Zip-Loc bag had been taped. A thick, purple cross had been drawn on it and beneath the cross, FIRST AID was written in large block letters. He untaped the bag and split the seal. Band-Aids, gauze, a spray-can of Bactine, a pamphlet on snake bites, poured out over his blue comforter. A few sets of chopsticks from *Jade of the East* Chinese poured out as well. I lifted a set. Along the paper wrapper *Jade of the East* was written in familiar oriental script. A local address followed, then a picture of a Chinese temple, layered, like a playing-card house. "That's my grandmother's favorite restaurant," Little Egypt said. He took the set of chopsticks from me and tore off the temple end. He split the sticks. "They make great splints." He placed one along his thin forearm. "And communication tools." He tapped out Morse code: "S.O.S," he whispered. "And great weapons too." He did a pirouette then waved the chopsticks in my face, "Hi-ya," he snarled. "But they don't really fight down there." He straightened and put the chopsticks back in their paper sleeve. "Really, it's a more peaceful society."

Double-D batteries were taped like shot-gun shells along the inside wall of the suitcase. From between his piles of T-shirts and shorts he pulled a red, plastic flashlight. He offered it to me and I flicked it on, casting a sharp yellow beam against his white wall. "I've had that puppy for years," Egypt said. "Never failed me. Not once." He curled out his lower lip again and shook his head. "Never." I flicked off the lamp and handed it back to him, grip first, the way one does a pistol or switchblade. "—I mean, they have lights down there and everything," Little Egypt said. He tucked his flashlight back in between his clothes. "But it's better to be safe than sorry." He pulled a roll of clear-packing tape from a bureau drawer and retaped the first-aid kit to its position on the underside of the top-flap.

Sometime later, one morning before school, Little Egypt was at my door, suitcase at his side. He was dressed in his church clothes: a red knit sweater, tan slacks and brown loafers so polished they seemed wet. It was early spring, the sun was unaccustomly high and bright.

"Just wanted to say bye," Egypt said. He smiled, his row of tiny teeth nearly fluorescent. I offered to walk him and I quickly dressed and washed my face. Over the running water of our kitchen sink, I heard Egypt on our front stoop whistling.

We walked down May Street.

"I left a note for my grandmother," Little Egypt said. "She should see it when she gets back from church. I'll write her, of course. I just didn't want to be too specific, tell her exactly where I'm going. Sometimes," Little Egypt said, "a man just has to break free." I nodded.

We passed the graffiti covered field-house of Dvorak Park—the pool—shards of broken glass catching sunlight along the concrete deck.

"That's one thing I won't miss," Little Egypt said, looking to the pool. "The pollution. They got a system down there, you know. Cleans all the streets. They never even heard of graffiti." He gave a nod as if there were a valuable lesson in this. The shower-room walls held messages: *Ambro Love. Flaca, You know I Still Love You, Junebug.*

At Twenty-first Place we turned the corner and walked towards the abandoned junk yard. "Well," Egypt sighed. He put his suitcase down. "I guess this is it." He stuck out his hand. "I'll be sure to write, and I hope to see you again some time." He clicked his tongue twice and winked. He lifted his suitcase then turned and walked down the quiet street. As he walked the heavy suitcase bounded off his short leg; he held out his opposite arm like a cantilever. I realized then how small he was.

He stopped half-way down the block in front of the junkyard office. He stepped off the curb to a familiar sewer grate, one I myself had looked into often as I combed our neighborhood for loose change. The smell of wet-metal spilled over the junkyard's corrugated walls—rust, oil. In the distance an el rumbled across Eighteenth Street, traffic whined on the Dan Ryan, a truck ground through its gears on Twenty-second. I heard everything in echo, my ear to the city, one giant seashell.

"Hello!" Egypt called down into the grate. He was in a squat, his suitcase alongside him. He looked to me and smiled, then waved. The brown of his church shoes stood out red in the morning sun.

"Hello," he called again. "Anyone down there!"

At that moment I realized I was about to lose my only friend.

The City That Works

Puppet plays guitar. He strums his strings on Eighteenth Street and Wolcott, in the narrow gangway between Zefran's funeral home and the El Milagro tortilla factory. There at night, the notes bounce up the brick walls around him and create an echo that Puppet believes he'll one day record and sell for millions of dollars.

He plays old tunes: Ritchie Valens ballads; Johnnie and Santo "Sleepwalks." He thinks he's romantic. When the els rumble by, he continues playing, convinced, somehow, his music is affecting the travelers: making a pickpocket reconsider as he slips his trigger hand towards a sleeping passenger's pocket.

Puppet can play the first few bars of Ritchie Valens' ballad "Donna" like an expert, the rest he fumbles through, and he returns to the chorus like it's his lifeboat, and the hair on the back of his neck stands on end. He wonders if those on the outside, those at either end of the dark gangway, where the orange of the street lights glows in long, vertical slits, are feeling it too. Often, when he steps out of the gangway, he expects entranced crowds to be gathered there: beautiful women with tears in their eyes and a love for him undying. Of course, there never is, just the hum of the city at night, things on auto-pilot, neon signs, street lights, the clicking of stop lights. Overhead another el rumbles by like a strip of film, only one or two of the yellow frames actually holding a silhouette.

Across the alley, in a bedroom on the top floor of a three flat, a young girl is finally able to sleep. She turns from her open window and faces the darkness. She hugs her pillow. "I love you Ritchie Valens," she says. "I love you."

After Cowboy Chicken Came to Town

Ha Jin

"I want my money back!" the customer said, dropped his plate on the counter, and handed me his receipt. He was a fiftyish man, of stout girth. A large crumb hung on the corner of his oily mouth. He had bought four pieces of chicken just now, but only a drumstick and a wing were left in the plate.

"Where are the breast and the thigh?" I asked.

"You can't take in people like this." The man's bulbous eyes flashed with rage. This time I recognized him; he was a worker in the nearby motor factory.

"How did we take you in?" the tall Baisha asked sharply, brandishing a pair of long tongs. She glared at the man, whose crown barely reached the level of her nose.

He said, "This Cowboy Chicken only sounds good and looks tasty. In fact it's just a name, has more batter than meat. After two pieces I still don't feel a thing in here." He slapped his flabby side. "I don't want to eat this fluffy stuff anymore. Give me my money back."

"No way," Baisha said and swung her permed hair, which looked like a magpie's nest. "If you haven't touched the chicken we'd refund you the money. But—"

"Excuse me," Peter Jiao said, coming out of the kitchen together with Mr. Shapiro.

We explained to him the customer's demand, which Peter interpreted to our American boss. Then we all remained silent to see how Peter, our manager, would handle this.

After a brief exchange with Mr. Shapiro in English, Peter said to the man in Chinese, "You've eaten two pieces already, so we can only refund half your money. But don't take this as a precedent. Once you've touched the food, it's yours."

The man looked unhappy but accepted the offer, still muttering, "American dogs." He referred to us, the Chinese employed by Cowboy Chicken.

That angered us. We began arguing with Peter and Mr. Shapiro that we shouldn't have let him take advantage of us this way. Otherwise all kinds of people would come in to sample our food for free. We didn't need a cheap customer like this one and should throw him out. Mr. Shapiro said we ought to follow the American way of doing business—you must try to satisfy your customers. "The customer is always right," he had instructed us when we were hired. But he had no idea who he was dealing with. You let a devil into your house, he'll get into your bed. If Mr. Shapiro continued to play the merciful Buddha, this place would be a mess soon. We had already heard a lot of complaints about our restaurant. People in town would say, "Cowboy Chicken is just for spendthrifts." True, our product was more expensive and far greasier than the local braised chicken, which was cooked so well that you could eat even the bones.

Sponge in hand, I went over to clean the table littered by that man. The scarlet Formica tabletop smelled like castor oil when greased with chicken bones. The odor always nauseated me. As I was about to move to another table, I saw a hole on the seat burned by a cigarette, the size of a soybean. It must have been the work of that son of a dog. Instead of refunding his money, we should've detained him until he paid for the damage.

I hated Mr. Shapiro's hypocrisy. He always appeared good-hearted and considerate to customers, but was cruel to us, his employees. The previous month he had deducted forty yuan from my pay. It hurt like having a rib taken out of my chest. What had happened was that I had given eight chicken breasts to a girl from my brother's electricity station. She came in to buy some chicken. By the regulations I was supposed to give her two drumsticks, two thighs, two wings, and two breasts. She said to me, "Be a good man, Hongwen. Give me more meat." Somehow I couldn't resist her charming smile, so I yielded to her request. My boss caught me stuffing the paper box with the meatiest pieces, but he remained silent until the girl went out of earshot. Then he dumped on me all his pee and crap. He said, "If you do that again, I'll fire you." How I was frightened! Later, he fined me, as an example to the other seven Chinese employees.

Mr. Shapiro was an old fox, good at sweet-talking. When we asked him why he had chosen to do business in our Muji City, he had said he wanted to help the Chinese people, because in the late thirties his parents had fled Red Russia and lived here for three years before moving on to Australia; they had been treated decently, though they were Jews. With an earnest look on his round, whiskery face, Mr. Shapiro explained, "The Jews and the Chinese had a similar fate, so I feel close to you. We all have dark hair." He chuckled as if he had said something funny. In fact that was capitalist baloney. We don't have to eat Cowboy Chicken here, or appreciate his stout red nose and his balding crown, or wince at the thick black hair on his arms. His company exploited not just us but also thousands of country people. A few villages in Hebei Province grew potatoes for Cowboy Chicken, because the soil and climate there produced potatoes similar to Idaho's. In addition, the company had set up a few chicken farms in Anhui Province to provide meat for its chain in China. It used Chinese produce and labor and made money out of Chinese customers, then shipped its profit back to the U.S. How could Mr. Shapiro have the barefaced gall to claim he had come to help us. We have no need for a savior like him. As for his parents' stay in our city half a century ago, it was true that the citizens here had treated Jews without discrimination. That was because to us a Jew was just another foreigner, not different from other white devils. We still cannot tell the difference.

We nicknamed Mr. Shapiro Party Secretary, because just like a Party boss anywhere he did little work. The only difference was that he didn't organize political studies or demand we report to him our inner thoughts. Peter Jiao, his manager, ran the business for him. I had known Peter since middle school. At that time he had been named Peihai Jiao, an anemic, studious boy with few friends to play with. Boys often made fun of him because he had four tourbillions on his head. His father had served as a platoon commander in the Korean War and had been captured by the American army. Unlike some of the POWs who chose to go to Canada or Taiwan, Peihai's father, out of his love for our motherland, decided to come back. But when he had returned, he was discharged from the army and sent down to a farm in a northern suburb of our city. In reality all those captives who had come back were classified as suspected traitors. A lot of them were jailed again. Peihai's father worked under surveillance on the farm, but people rarely maltreated him, and he had his own home in a nearby village. He was reticent most of the time; so was his wife, a woman who didn't know her dad's name because she had been fathered by some Japanese officer. Their only son, Peihai, had to walk three miles to town for school every weekday. That was why we called him Country Boy.

Unlike us, he always got good grades. In 1977 when colleges reopened, he passed the entrance exams and enrolled at Tianjin Foreign Language Institute to study English. We had all sat for the exams, but only two out of the three hundred seniors from our high school had passed the admission standard. After college, Peihai went to America, studying history at the University of Iowa. Later he changed his field and got a degree in business from that school. Then he came back, a completely different man, robust and wealthy, with curly hair and a new name. He looked energetic, cheerful, and younger than his age. At work he was always dressed formally, in a Western suit and a bright-colored tie. He once joked with us, saying he had over fifty pounds of American flesh. To tell the truth, I liked Peter better than Peihai. I often wondered what in America had changed him so much—in just six years from an awkward boy to a capable, confident man? Was it American water? American milk and beef? The American climate? The American way of life? I don't know for sure. More impressive, Peter spoke English beautifully, much better than those professors and lecturers in the City College who had never gone abroad and learned English mainly from textbooks written by the Russians. He had hired me probably because I had never bugged him in our school days and because I had a slightly lame foot. Out of gratitude I never talked about his past to my fellow workers.

On the day Cowboy Chicken opened, about forty officials from the Municipal Administration came to celebrate. A vicemayor cut the red silk ribbon at the opening ceremony with a pair of scissors two feet long. He then presented Mr. Shapiro with a brass key the size of a small poker. What's that for? we wondered. Our city didn't have a gate with a colossal lock for it to open. The attendees at the ceremony sampled our chicken, fries, coleslaw, salad, biscuits. Coca-Cola, Pepsi, and orange soda were poured free like water. People touched the vinyl seats, the Formica tables, the dishwasher, the microwave, the cash register, the linoleum tile on the kitchen floor, and poked their heads into the freezer and the brand-new rest rooms. They were impressed by the whole package shipped directly from the U.S.A. A white-bearded official said, "We must learn from the Americans. See, how they have managed to meet every need of their customers. Everything was thought out beforehand." Some of them watched us frying chicken in the stainless steel troughs, which were safe and clean, nothing like a soot-bottomed cauldron or a noisy, unsteady wok. The vicemayor shook hands with every employee and told us to be cooperative with our American boss. The next day the city's newspaper, the *Muji Herald*, published a lengthy article about Cowboy Chicken, describing its appearance here as a significant breakthrough in the city's campaign to attract foreign investors.

During the first few weeks we had a lot of customers, especially young people, who, eager to taste something American, would come in droves. We got so much business that the cooked-meat stands on the streets had to move farther and farther away from our restaurant. Sometimes when we passed those stands, their owners would spit to the ground and curse without looking at us, "Foreign lackeys!"

We'd cry back, "We eat Cowboy Chicken every day and we've gained lots of weight."

At first Mr. Shapiro worked hard, often staying around late until we closed at ten-thirty. But as the business was flourishing, he lay back more and stayed in his office for hours on end, reading newspapers and sometimes chewing a skinny sausage wrapped in cellophane. He rested so well in the daytime and had so much energy to spare that he began to date the girls working for him. There were four of them, two full-timers and two part-timers, all around twenty, healthy and lively, though not dazzlingly pretty. Imagine, once a week, on Thursday night, a man of over fifty went out with a young girl who was willing to go anywhere he took her. This made us, the three men hired by him, feel useless, like a bunch of eunuchs, particularly myself because I had never had a girlfriend, though I was almost thirty. Most girls were good to me, but for them I was just a nice fellow deserving more pity than affection, as if I weren't able to handle my crippled foot all right. For me, Mr. Shapiro was just a dirty old man, but the girls here were no good either, always ready to sell something—a smile, a few sweet words, and perhaps their flesh.

The day after Mr. Shapiro had taken Baisha out, I asked her about the date, curious to see besides money what else made this paunchy man so expert at handling girls. What's more, I was eager to find out whether he had bedded them in his apartment after dinner. That was illegal. If he had done it, we'd have something on him and could turn him in when it was necessary. I asked Baisha casually, "How many rooms does he have?" My hands were busy taking plates out of the dishwasher and piling them up on a table.

"How could I know?" she said and gave me a suspicious stare. I must admit, she was smart and had a mind quick like a lizard.

"Didn't you spend some time with him yesterday evening?"

"Yes, we had dinner. That was all."

"Was it good?" I had heard he had taken the girls to Lucky House, a third-rate restaurant near the marketplace.

"So-so."

"What did you eat?"

"Fried noodles and sautéed beef tripe."

"Well, I wish somebody could give me a treat like that."

"What made you think it was his treat?"

"Was it not?" I put the last plate on the pile.

"I paid for what I ate. I won't go out with him again. He's such a cheapskate."

"If he didn't mean to spend money, why did he ask you out?"

"He said this was the American way. He gave the waitress a big tip though, a ten, but the girl wouldn't take it."

"So afterwards you just went home?"

"Yes. I thought he'd take me to the movies or a karaoke bar. He just dusted off his big butt and said he had a good time. Before we parted on the street, he yawned and said he missed his wife and kids."

"That was strange."

Manyou, Jinglin, and I—the three male employees—talked among ourselves about Mr. Shapiro's way of taking the girls out. We couldn't see what he was up to. How could he have a good time by just eating a meal with a girl? This puzzled us. We asked Peter whether all American men were so stingy, but he said that like us they would pay the bill in such a case. He explained, "Probably Mr. Shapiro wants to make it clear to the girls that this isn't a date, but a working dinner."

Who would buy that? Why didn't he have a working dinner with one of us, the male employees? We guessed he might have used the girls, because if he had gone to a fancy place, like Four Seas Garden or the North Star Palace which had special menus for foreigners, he'd have had to pay at least five times more than a Chinese customer. We checked with the girls, who admitted Mr. Shapiro had asked them to order everything. So he had indeed paid the Chinese prices. No wonder he had a good time. What an old fox. Still, why wouldn't he take the girls to his apartment? Though not every one of them was a beauty, just the smell of the youthful flesh should have turned his old head, shouldn't it? Especially the two part-timers, the college students, who had fine figures and educated voices; they worked only twenty hours a week and wouldn't condescend to talk with us very often. Probably Mr. Shapiro was no good in bed, a true eunuch.

Our business didn't boom for long. Several handcarts had appeared on Peace Avenue, selling spiced chicken on the roadside, near our restaurant. They each carried a sign that declared: "Patriotic Chicken—Crispy, Tender, Delicious, 30% Cheaper Than C.C.!" Those words were not false. Yet whenever we saw their signs, we couldn't help calling the vendors names. Most citizens here, especially old people, were accustomed to the price and taste of the Patriotic Chicken, so they preferred it to ours. Some of them had tried our product, but they'd complain afterward, "What a sham! So expensive, this Cowboy thing isn't for a Chinese stomach." And they wouldn't come again. As a result, we mainly had fashionable young people as our clientele.

One day Mr. Shapiro came up with the idea of starting a buffet. We had never heard of that word. "What does it mean?" we asked.

Peter said, "You pay a small amount of money and eat all you can."

Good, a buffet would be great! We were all ears. Our boss suggested nineteen yuan and ninety-five fen as the price for the buffet, which should include every kind of Cowboy Chicken, mashed potato, fries, salad, and canned fruit. Why didn't he price it twenty yuan even? we wondered. That would sound more honest and also make it easier for us to handle the change. Peter explained this was the American way of pricing a product. "You don't add the last straw to collapse a camel," he said. We couldn't understand the logic of a camel or a horse or an ox. Anyway, Mr. Shapiro fell in love with his idea, saying even if we didn't fetch enough customers, the buffet would help spread our name.

Peter wasn't enthusiastic about it, but we all said it was a brilliant idea and would definitely make us famous. Of course we knew it wouldn't work. We supported it because we wanted to eat Cowboy Chicken. Mr. Shapiro was such a skinflint that he would never give us a discount when we bought chicken for ourselves. He said the company's policy didn't allow any discount for its employees. On the other hand, our friends, when buying chicken here, often asked us to do them a favor—giving them either some choice pieces or a discount, but we dared not do anything for them. Now came an opportunity, so without delay we put out notices and passed the word about the buffet, which was to start the following week. For a whole weekend, we biked around town in our free time to make sure the news could reach our relatives, friends, and whomever might benefit from it.

It dropped two feet of snow on Sunday night, and traffic was paralyzed the next morning, but we all arrived at work on time. Mr. Shapiro was worried, assuming the severe weather would keep people indoors. We assured him that they were not hibernating bears and would definitely show up. Still anxious, he stood outside the front door with the fur earflaps of his hat tied around his jaw, smoking and looking south and north at the people shoveling snow along the sides of the street. Strips of smoke and breath hung around his head. We all had on dogskin or cotton-padded trousers in such weather, but he wore only woolen pajamas underneath jeans. It was glitteringly cold outside; the wind tossed the phone lines which whistled like crazy.

With his protruding mouth pointed at Mr. Shapiro, Manyou said to us, "See how hard it's to be a boss in America. You have to worry about your business all the time."

"Boy, he's scared," I said.

"For once he's working," added Feilan, who was a plump girl, but had a pleasant apple face with two dimples on it. Unlike us, she hadn't gone to high school because she had flunked two of the entrance exams.

We set the buffet stand in a corner and fried piles of chicken. Gradually people arrived. When about a dozen customers had sat down to their meals, Mr. Shapiro looked relieved, though he couldn't stop rubbing his cheeks and ears which must have frozen numb. He retreated into his office for coffee, but he had no idea that this was just the first skirmish of a mighty battle. As the morning went by, more and more people came in, and we could hardly cook enough chicken and fries for them. The room grew noisy and crowded, undoubtedly reaching its maximum capacity. Still our boss was happy. Encouraged by the bustling scene, he even whistled in his office, where he, in presbyopic glasses, was reading the *China Daily*.

My father and uncle were among the first dozen customers. Both could hardly walk when done with eating. After they left, my brother brought over six young men from his electricity station; they all had a soda or a beer in their pockets so that they wouldn't have to buy a drink. Without delay they began to attack the buffet; they ate as though this were their last supper on earth. I kept count of their accomplishment—on average they each finished at least a dozen pieces of chicken. Even when they were done and leaving, every one of them held a leg or a wing in his hand. Baisha's family had come too, including her father, uncles, and aunts. So had the folks of Manyou, Jinglin, Feilan. The two part-timers had no family in town, but more than ten of their schoolmates turned up. In the back corner a table was occupied by five people, whose catlike faces showed they belonged to Peter's clan. Among them was a young woman of at least seven months' pregnancy; she was Peter's sister, surely her unborn baby needed nutrition.

We all knew the buffet was heading for disaster, but we couldn't care too much and just continued deep-frying chicken and refilling the salad and mashed potato bowls. Once in a while we also went over to the buffet stand and picked a piece of chicken for ourselves, because today nobody could keep a record. At last we too could eat our fill. I liked the chicken better with soy sauce and slapped plenty on. The employees shared a bottle of soy sauce, hidden under the counter.

By midday some people in the marketplace had heard of this rare bargain, and they came in, all eating like starved wolves. Most of them were from the countryside, selling and buying stuff in town; surely they had never dreamed that any restaurant would offer such an abundant meal.

Peter wasn't around most of the time. He had to be at the Tax Bureau in the morning, and in the afternoon he went to the bank to fetch our wages. When he returned at four o'clock, his face darkened at the amount of food consumed by the buffet— twenty boxes of chicken and eighteen sacks of fries were gone, which should have lasted three days. He went to inform Mr. Shapiro, who came out of his office and looked disconcerted. Peter suggested we stop the buffet immediately. Our boss's face reddened, his Adam's apple going up and down as though he were guzzling something. He said, "Let's offer it just for a while. We're not sure if we lost money or not."

We closed twenty minutes early that night in order to count the money. The result didn't surprise us: we lost seven hundred yuan, exclusive of our wages.

In spite of his misshapen face, Mr. Shapiro insisted on trying the buffet for another day. Perhaps he meant to show who was in command, reluctant to admit the buffet was a flop. That suited us fine, since not all of our people had come yet.

The next day Mr. Shapiro sat on a chair outside his office and watched the customers stuffing themselves. He looked like a giant bull dog, vigilant and sulky, now shaking his head, now smiling exaggeratedly. At times his face turned grim, his eyelids trembling a little. A few men from my father's office showed up, and two of them even attempted to chat with me in front of my boss. This scared me. I responded to their greetings and questions cursorily for fear that Mr. Shapiro might detect my connection with them. Fortunately he didn't know our language, so he noticed nothing.

After my father's colleagues left, a tall, thirtyish man in a buff corduroy jacket turned up. Having paid for buffet, he left his fur hat on a table, then walked across to the stand, and filled a plate with drumsticks and breasts. As he was about to return to his seat, Mr. Shapiro stopped him and asked, "Why did you come again?"

The man happened to know some English and said with an friendly grin, "First time customer."

"You ate a ton of chicken and mashed potatoes just now. How come you're hungry so soon?"

"What's this about?" The man's face changed.

Peter came over, but he wasn't sure if the man had been here. He turned to us and asked, "Is this his second time?"

Before we could answer, the man flared up, "This is my hundredth time, so what? I paid."

Manyou laughed and told Peter, "There was a fella here just now in the same kind of jacket, but that was a different man."

"That's true," I picked up. I knew the other man, who was an accountant in my father's bureau. This fellow fuming in front of us was a genuine stranger, with a beeper on his belt. He must have been a cabdriver or an entrepreneur.

Peter apologized to the man, told him to go ahead and eat, then he explained the truth to Mr. Shapiro, who had been so edgy that some customers began to look identical to him. "How the hell could I tell the difference?" our boss said. "To me they all look alike—all are real Chinese with an alligator's appetite." He laughed heartily, like a young boy.

Peter interpreted his words to us, and we all cracked up.

We lost about six hundred yuan on the second day, so this was the end of the buffet. Lucky for us, Mr. Shapiro didn't withhold our wages, which we all received the next day. This was the beauty of working for Cowboy Chicken—it had never delayed to pay us, unlike many Chinese companies, especially those owned by the state, which simply didn't have enough cash to pay their employees full wages. My mother often got only 60 percent of her salary from her weather station, which could not increase its clientele, or run a night school, or have any power over other companies. She'd sigh and say, "The longer I work, the more I lose."

At the sight of my monthly wages—468 yuan, my father became heartbroken. He'd had a drop too much that night, full of self-pity. Waving a half-smoked cigarette, he said to me, "Hongwen, I've joined the revolution for almost forty years, and I now earn only three hundred yuan a month. But you just started and draw a larger salary. This makes me feel duped, duped by the Communist Party I've served."

My youngest brother butted in, "It's never too late to quit, Dad."

"Shut up!" I snapped. He was such an idiot he couldn't see the old man was really suffering. I said to my father, "You shouldn't think that way. True, you're not paid a lot, but your job is secure, like a rubber rice bowl that nobody can take away from you or smash it—even a tank cannot crush it. Every day you just sit at your desk drinking tea and chatting away, and at the end of each month you take home a full salary. But I have to work my ass off for a capitalist who pays me by the hour."

"You make so much and always eat high-protein food. What else do you want?"

I didn't answer. In my heart I said, I want a job that pays a salary, and want to be like some people who go to their offices every morning for an eight-hour rest. My father kept on, "Cowboy Chicken's so delicious. If I could eat it and drink Coke every day, I'd have no need for socialism."

I wouldn't argue with him. He was beside himself that night. Indeed I often had some tidbits at the restaurant, mainly fries and biscuits, and as a result I seldom ate dinner when I came home, because I wanted to save some food for my family. That was why my father assumed I was stuffed with chicken every day.

After the disastrous buffet, Mr. Shapiro depended more on Peter, who in fact ran the place single-handedly. To be fair, Peter was a able man and had put his heart into the restaurant. He began to form a lot of connections in town and persuaded people to have business lunches at our place. This made a huge difference. Because their companies would foot the bills, those business people would order table loads of food to treat their guests to hearty American meals, and then they'd take the leftovers home for their families. By and by our restaurant gained a reputation in the business world, and we had a stable clientele. So again Mr. Shapiro could stay in his office in the morning drinking coffee, reading magazines, and even listening to a tape to learn the ABC's of Chinese.

One afternoon the second son of the president of Muji Teachers College phoned Peter, saying he'd like to hold his wedding feast at our restaurant. I knew of this dandy, who had divorced his hardworking wife the year before, otherwise his current bride, a young widow who had given up her managerial position in a theater four years ago in order to go to Russia, wouldn't continue their relationship. Now they had decided to marry, and he wanted something exotic for their wedding dinner, so he picked Cowboy Chicken.

Suspicious about the request, Mr. Shapiro said to Peter, "We're just a fast-food place, not equipped to cater a wedding banquet."

"We must not miss this opportunity. A Chinese man would spend all his savings on his wedding." Peter's owlish eyes glittered.

"Well, we'll have to serve alcoholic beverages, won't we? We have no license."

"Forget that. Nobody has ever heard of such a thing in China. Even a baby can drink alcohol here." Peter looked impatient.

Manyou, who could speak a little English, broke in, "Mr. Shapiro, Peter is right. Men of China use all moneys for wedding, big money." He seemed embarrassed by his accent and went on biting his hangnails.

So our boss yielded. From the next day on, we began to prepare the place for the wedding feast. Mr. Shapiro called Cowboy Chicken's headquarters in Beijing to have some cheesecakes, ice cream, and Californian wines shipped to us by the express mail. Peter hired two temps and had the room decked out with colorful ribbons and strings of tiny light bulbs. Since it was already mid-December, he had a dwarf juniper and candlesticks set up in a corner. We even hung up a pair of large bunny lanterns at the front door, because the Year of Rabbit was almost here. Peter ordered us to wear clean uniforms for this occasion—red sweaters, black pants, and maroon aprons.

The wedding banquet took place on Thursday evening. It went smoothly, since most of the guests were from the college, urbane and sober-minded. The bride, a small woman in her mid-thirties, wore an air-blue silk dress, her hair permed and her lips rouged almost violet. She smiled without stopping. It was too bad that her parents hadn't given her beautiful eyes; her eyes must have gone through cosmetic surgery which had produced their tight, thick double lids. Baisha said the woman owned two gift shops in Moscow. No wonder she wore six fancy rings and a tiny wristwatch in the shape of a heart. With so many diamonds and so much gold on her fingers, she must have been lazy, not doing any housework. From her manners we could tell she had seen the world. By comparison, her tall groom looked like a bumpkin despite his fancy outfit—a dark-blue Western suit, a scarlet tie studded with tiny magpies, and patent-leather boots with brass buckles. He had a hoarse voice, often laughing with a bubbling sound in his throat. When he laughed, you could hardly see anything on his face except his mouth, which reminded me of a crocodile. His gray-haired parents sat opposite him, quiet and reserved, both being senior officials.

The man officiating at this banquet talked briefly about the auspicious union of the couple. Next, he praised the simple wedding ceremony, which had taken place two hours ago. After a round of applause, he turned to our boss and said, "We thank our American friend, Mr. Ken Shapiro, for providing us with such a clean, beautiful place and the delicious food. This is a perfect example of adapting foreign things to Chinese needs."

People clapped again. All our boss could say was "Thank you" in Chinese. He looked a little shy, his cheeks pink and his hazel eyes gleaming happily.

As people were making the first toast, we began to serve chicken, every kind we had—crispy, spicy, barbecued, Cajun, and Cowboy original. An old woman opened a large paper napkin with a flowered pattern on it, and observed it for a long time as though it were a piece of needlework on lavender silk which she was reluctant to spoil. A bottle of champagne popped and scared the bridesmaid into screaming. Laughter followed.

"Boy, this is hot?" the groom said, chewing a Cajun wing and exhaling noisily.

They all enjoyed the chicken, but except for the champagne they didn't like American wines, which were too mild for them. Most women wouldn't drink wine; they wanted beer, Coca-Cola, and other soft drinks. Fortunately Peter had stocked some Chinese liquor and beer, which we brought out without delay. We had also heated a basin of water, in which we warmed the sorghum liquor for them. Mr. Shapiro raved to his manager, "Great job, Peter!" He went on flashing a broad smile at everyone, revealing his white teeth. He even patted some of us on the back.

I liked the red wine, and whenever I could, I'd sip some from a glass I had poured myself. But I dared not drink too much in case my face might change color. When the guests were done with chicken, fries, and salad, we began to serve cheesecake and ice cream, which turned out to be a big success. Everybody loved the dessert. An old scholarly-looking man said loudly, "Ah, here's the best American stuff!" His tone of voice suggested he had been to the U.S. He forked a chunk of cheesecake into his mouth and smacked his thin lips. He was among the few who could use a fork skillfully; most of them ate with chopsticks and spoons.

That was the first time we offered cheesecake and ice cream, so all of us, the employees, would take a bite whenever we could. Before that day, I had never heard of cheesecake, which I loved so much I ate two slices. I hid my glass and plate in a cabinet so that our boss couldn't see them. As long as we did the work well, Peter would shut his eyes to our eating and drinking.

For me the best part of this wedding feast was that it was subdued, peaceful, and short, having lasted only two hours, perhaps because both the bride and the groom had married before. It differed from a standard wedding banquet, which is always raucous and messy, drags on for seven or eight hours, and often gets out of hand since quarrels and fights are commonplace among the drunk. None of these educated men and women indulged in alcohol. The only loudmouth was the bridegroom, who looked sort of retarded. I couldn't help wondering how come that wealthy woman would marry such a heartless ass, who had abandoned his two small daughters. Probably because his parents had power, or he was good at tricking women. He must have wanted to live in Moscow for a while and have another baby, hopefully a boy. Feilan shook her head, saying about him, "Disgusting!"

When the feast was over, both Mr. Shapiro and Peter were excited with flushed faces. They knew we had just opened a new page in Cowboy Chicken's history; our boss said he was going to report our success to the headquarters in Dallas. We were happy too, though sleepy and tired. If the business was better, we might get a bigger raise the next summer, Mr. Shapiro had told us.

That night I didn't sleep well and had to go to the bathroom continually. I guessed my stomach hadn't got used to American food yet. I had eaten fries and biscuits every day, but had never taken in ice cream, cheesecake, red wine, and champagne. Without doubt my stomach couldn't digest so much rich stuff all at once. I was so weakened that I wondered if I should stay home the next morning.

Not wanting to dampen our spirits of success, I hauled myself to the restaurant at nine o'clock, half an hour late. As we were cutting vegetables and coating chicken with spiced flour, I asked my fellow workers whether they had slept well the night before.

"What do you mean?" Baisha's small eyes stared at me like a pair of tiny daggers.

"I had diarrhea."

"You stole too much food, and it serves you right," she said with a straight face, which was slightly swollen with pimples.

"So you didn't have any problem?"

"What makes you think I have the same kind of bowels as yours?"

Manyou said he had slept like a corpse, perhaps having drunk too much champagne. To my satisfaction, both Jinglin and Feilan admitted they had suffered from diarrhea too. Feilan said, "I thought I was going to die last night. My mother made me drink two kettles of hot water, or I'd be sure dehydrated today." She held her sides with both hands as if about to run for the ladies' room.

Jinglin added, "I thought I was going to poop my guts out." Indeed, his chubby face looked smaller than yesterday.

As we were talking, the phone rang. Peter answered it. He sounded nervous, and his face turned bloodless while tiny beads of sweat were oozing out on his stubby nose. The woman caller complained about the previous evening's food and claimed she had been poisoned. Peter apologized and assured her that we had been very careful about food hygiene, but he would investigate this matter thoroughly.

The instant he put down the phone, another call came in. Then another. From ten o'clock on, every few minutes the phone would ring. People were lodging the same kind of complaints against our restaurant. Mr. Shapiro was shaken, saying, "Jesus, they're going to sue us!"

What did that mean? we asked him, unsure how suing us could do the complainers any good. He said the company might have to pay a lot of money. "In America that's a way to make a living, for some people," he told us. So we worried too.

At noon the college called officially to inform Peter that about a third of the wedding feasters had suffered from food poisoning, and that more than a dozen faculty members couldn't teach that day. The bridegroom's mother was still in the Central Hospital, taking an intravenous drip. The caller believed the food must have been unclean or passed the expiration dates, or probably the ice cream had been too cold. Mr. Shapiro paced back and forth like an ant in a heated pan, while Peter remained quiet, his thick eyebrows knitted together.

"I told you we couldn't handle a wedding banquet," our boss said with his nostrils expanding.

Peter muttered, "It must've been the cheesecake and the ice cream. I'm positive our food was clean and fresh."

"Maybe I shouldn't have gone the extra mile to get the stuff from Beijing. Now, what should we do?"

"Don't worry. I'll explain it to them."

From then on, whenever a complainer called, Peter would answer personally. He said that our food had been absolutely fresh and clean and that some Chinese stomachs couldn't stand dairy products. That was why more than two thirds of the previous night's diners had not felt anything unusual.

His theory of Chinese stomachs was sheer nonsense. We had all drunk milk before and had never been poisoned like this. Three days later, a 1200-word article appeared in the *Muji Herald*. Peter was its author. He wrote that there was this substance called lactose, to which many

Chinese stomachs were allergic because our traditional diet had very little dairy food. He even quoted from a scientific journal to prove that the Chinese had different stomachs from the Westerners'. He urged people to make sure they could endure lactose before they ate our dairy items. From now on, he declared, our restaurant would continue to offer ice cream, but also a variety of non-milk desserts, like Jell-O, apple pies, pecan pies, canned fruit.

I was unhappy about the article, because I had thought the company might compensate us for the suffering we had gone through. Even a couple of yuan would help. Now Peter had blown the opportunity. When I expressed my dissatisfaction to my fellow workers, Feilan said to me, "Don't be so small-minded like a housewife, Hongwen. As long as this place's in good shape, we'll make more money."

Bitch! I cursed to myself. But I gave a thought to her words. She did have a point, though. The restaurant had almost become our work unit now; we might all take a hit if it lost money. Besides, if I filed for compensation, I'd first have to admit I had pilfered ice cream and cheesecake. That would amount to asking for a fine and ridicule.

Soon Peter had Cowboy Chicken completely in his clutches. This was fine with us. We all agreed he could take care of the restaurant better than Mr. Shapiro. We nicknamed him Number-Two Boss. Since the publication of his article that had quieted all complaints, more and more people ate here, and some came mainly for our desserts. Young women were partial to Jell-O and canned fruit while children loved our ice cream. Again we began to cater wedding banquets, which gradually became a source of our profit. From time to time people called and asked whether we'd serve a "white feast," the dinner after a funeral. We wouldn't, because it was much plainer than a wedding banquet and there wasn't much money to be made. Besides, it might bring bad luck.

When snow and ice had thawed away from the streets and branches began to sprout yellowish buds, Mr. Shapiro wouldn't go out with the girls as often as before. By now most restaurants in town treated him as a regular customer, charging him the Chinese prices. One day, Juju, the younger part-timer, said our boss had got fresh with her the previous evening when he was tipsy at Eight Deities Garden. He had grasped her wrist and called her, "Honey." She declared she wouldn't go out with him anymore. We told the girls that if he did anything like that again, they should report him to the police or sue him.

In late April Mr. Shapiro went back to Texas for a week to attend his stepdaughter's wedding. After he returned, he stopped dating the girls altogether. Perhaps he was scared. He was wise to stop, because he couldn't possibly contain himself at all times. If he did something indecent to one of the girls again and she reported him to the authorities, he would get into trouble, at least be fined. Another reason for the change might be that by now he had befriended an American woman named Susanna, from Raleigh, North Carolina, who was teaching English at Muji Teachers College. This black woman was truly amazing, in her early thirties, five foot ten, with long muscular limbs, and a behind like a small cauldron. She had bobbed hair, and most of the time wore jeans and a pair of earrings the size of a bracelet. We often talked about those gorgeous rings. Were they made of 14-carat gold? Or 18-carat? Or 20-carat? At any rate they must be worth a fortune. Later, in the midsummer, she took part in our city's marathon, almost beat the professional runners, and won the Friendship Cup, which resembled a small brass bucket. She was also a wonderful singer with a manly voice. Every week she brought four or five students over to teach them how to eat American food with forks and knives. When they were here, they often sang American songs she had taught them, such as "Pretty Paper," "Winter Wonderland," and "Silent Night, Holy Night." Their singing would fetch some pedestrians in. This was good for our business, so we were pleased to have her here. Mr. Shapiro gave them a 20 percent discount, which outraged us. We wondered why he kept a double standard. If there was the company's policy against discount, it must have applied only to Chinese employees. But we all agreed Susanna was a good woman. Unlike other customers, she gave us tips; also, she paid for her students' meals.

One afternoon in late May, Susanna and four students were eating here. In came a monkey-like man, who had half-gray hair and flat cheeks. With a twitching face he went up to Peter, his fist holding a paper ball. He announced in a squeaky voice, "I want to sue your company for ten thousand yuan."

This was the first time I had heard that a Chinese would sue somebody for money. We gathered around him as he unfolded the paper ball to display a fat greenhead. "I found this fly in the chicken I bought here," he said firmly, his right hand massaging his side.

"When did you buy the chicken?" Peter asked.

"Last week."

"Show me the receipt."

The man took a slip of paper out of his trouser pocket and handed it to Peter.

About twenty people formed a half circle to watch. As the man and Peter were arguing, Mr. Shapiro and Susanna stepped out of his office. Seeing the two Americans, the man wailed at Peter, "Don't dodge your responsibility. I've hated flies all my life. At the sight of this one I puked, then dropped to the floor and fainted. I thought I'd recover soon. No, the next evening I threw up again and again. That gave me a terrible headache and a stomach disorder. My ears are still ringing inside, and I've lost my appetite completely. Since last Wednesday I haven't gone to work and have suffered from insomnia every night." He turned to the spectators. "Comrades, I'm a true victim of this capitalist Cowboy Chicken. See how skinny I am."

"Like a starved cock," I said. People laughed.

"Stop blustering," Peter said to him. "Show us your medical records."

"I have them in the hospital. If you don't pay me the damages I'll come again and again and again until I'm fully compensated."

We were all angry. Feilan pointed at the man's sunken mouth and said, "Shameless, you're not a Chinese."

Baisha said, "Ten thousand yuan for a fly? How could you dream of that? Even your life isn't worth that much."

When a student had interpreted the man's accusation to Mr. Shapiro and Susanna, our boss turned pale. He moved closer and managed a smile, saying, "Sir, if you have concrete evidence, we'll be willing to consider your demand."

The student interpreted those words to the man, on whose face a vile smile appeared. We were angry at Mr. Shapiro, who again acted like a number-one Buddha. If you run into an evil man, you have to adopt uncivil measures. Our boss's hypocrisy would only indulge this crook.

"Excuse me," Manyou cried and arrived with a bowl of warm water. He put it on the counter and said to the man, "I'm going give your fly a hot bath, to see if it's from our place." He picked up the insect with a pair of chopsticks and dropped it into the bowl. We were all puzzled.

A few seconds later, Manyou announced, "This fly is not from Cowboy Chicken because, see, there isn't any oil on the water. You all know we sell only fried chicken."

Some spectators booed the man, but he wouldn't give way. He fished out the fly with his hand and wrapped it up, saying, "I'm going take you to court no matter what. If you don't offer a settlement, there'll be no end of this."

With a false smile Jinglin said to him, "Uncle, we're one family and shouldn't be so mean to each other. Let's find a quiet place to talk this out, all right? We can't negotiate in front of such a crowd."

The man looked puzzled, flapping his round eyes. Jinglin hooked his thick arm around the man's neck while his eyes signaled at me. Reluctantly the crook moved away with him.

I followed them out the front door. It was slightly chilly outside, and the street was noisy with bicycle bells, vendors' cries, and automobile horns. A few neon lights flickered in the north. After about fifty paces, we turned into a small alley and then stopped. Jinglin smiled again, revealing his rotten teeth, and he took out a small pocketknife and a ten-yuan note. He opened the knife and said to the man, "I can pay you the damages now. You have a choice between these two."

"Don't make fun of me! I ask for ten thousand."

"Then I'll let you taste this knife."

The man wasn't frightened by the two-inch blade. He grinned and asked, "Brothers, why help the foreign devils?"

"Because Cowboy Chicken is our company, and our livelihood depends on it," I answered.

Jinglin said to him, "You're the scum of the Chinese! Come on, choose one."

The man didn't lift his hand. Jinglin said again, "I know what you're thinking. I can't stab you with such a small thing, eh? Tell you what, I know your grandson who goes to the Second Elementary School, and I can catch him and cut off his little pecker with this knife. Then your family line will be gone. I mean it. Now, pick one."

The crook was flabbergasted, looking at me and then at Jinglin, whose fat face became as hard as though made of copper sheet. With a trembling hand he picked the money and mumbled, "Foreign dogs." He turned, hurrying away. In no time he disappeared in a swarm of pedestrians.

We both laughed and walked back to the restaurant. Across the street, three disheveled Russian beggars were playing the violin and the bandora. Different from most Chinese beggars who would cry woefully and accost people, those foreign musicians were reticent, just with a cartwheel hat on the ground to collect money, as though they hadn't cared if you gave or not.

We didn't tell our boss what we had done; we just said the man was satisfied with a ten-yuan note and wouldn't come again. Susanna and her students applauded when they heard the news. Peter reimbursed Jinglin the money on the spot. Still, Mr. Shapiro looked suspicious and was afraid the man would return.

"He won't trouble us anymore," Peter said, smiling.

"Why are you so sure?" asked our boss.

"I have this." With two fingers Peter pulled the crook's receipt out of his breast pocket.

We all laughed. Actually even with the receipt in hand, that old bastard wouldn't have dared come again. He wasn't afraid of Jinglin exactly, but feared his four brothers, who were all stevedores on the riverbank, good at fighting and never hesitant to use a club or a dagger or a crowbar. That was why Jinglin, unlike the rest of us, could get rid of him without fearing any retaliation.

Later we revealed to Peter what we had done in the alley. He smiled and promised he wouldn't breathe a word to Mr. Shapiro.

As our business became stable, Peter had grown into a local power of sorts. For months he had been building a house in the countryside. We wondered why he wanted his home to be four miles away from town. It would be costly to ride a motorcycle back and forth every day. One Sunday morning, Baisha, Feilan, Manyou, Jinglin, and I set out to see Peter's new home. We pedaled abreast on the wide embankment along the Songhua River, humming movie songs and cracking jokes. Birds were crying furiously in the willow copses below the embankment, while at a distant jetty a team of men sang a work song, unloading timber from a barge. Their voices were faltering but explosive. It hadn't rained for weeks, so the river was rather narrow, displaying a broad whitish beach. A few boys fishing there lay on their backs; around them stood some short bamboo poles planted deep into the sand. When a fish bit, a brass bell on one of those poles would jingle. On the other shore, toward the horizon, four or five windmills were turning like sails; above them the gray clouds floated lazily like a school of turtles.

We knew Peter had a few American dollars in the bank, but we were unsure how rich he was. His house, though unfinished, staggered us. It was a three-story building with a garage in its back; it sat in the middle of two acres of sloping land, facing a gentle bend in the river and commanding a panorama that included two islands and the vast landscape on the other shore.

Peter wasn't around. Six or seven workers were hammering something rhythmically inside the house. We asked an older man, who looked like a supervisor, how much the house would cost.

"At least a quarter of a million yuan," he said.

"So expensive?" Manyou gasped. His large lashless eyes blazed.

"You know what, it can be more than that. We've never seen a home like this before."

"What kind of house is this?" asked Feilan.

"It's called Victorian. Mr. and Mrs. Jiao designed it themselves. It has two marble fireplaces, both imported from Hong Kong."

"Damn, where did he get so much money?" Baisha said and kicked a beer bottle with her white leather sandal.

We were all pondering the same question, which weighed down our hearts like a millstone. We didn't stay long, fearing Peter might turn up. On the way back we spoke little to one another, unable to take our minds off Peter's house. Obviously he made much more than we did, or he wouldn't have had the money for such a mansion, which was even larger than the mayor's. Before setting out, we had planned to have brunch together at a beer house, but now none of us had appetite anymore. We parted company the moment we turned away from the quay.

After that trip, I noticed that my fellow workers often looked sidelong at Peter, as though he were a hybrid creature. Their eyes showed envy and anger. They began learning English more diligently. Manyou attended the TV college at night, working on a textbook called *English for Today*, while Baisha and Feilan got up early in the morning, listening to the learners' program on the radio and memorizing English words and expressions. Jinglin wanted to learn genuine American English, which he said was more natural, so he was studying *English 900*. I was also learning English, but I was older than the others and didn't have a strong memory, so I could make little progress.

At work, they appeared friendlier to Mr. Shapiro and often poured coffee for him. Once Baisha even let him try some scallion pancake that was her lunch.

One morning, when we were not busy, I overheard Baisha talking with Mr. Shapiro in English. "Have you a house in U.S.A.?" she asked.

"Yes, I have a brick ranch, not very big." He had a cold, his voice nasal and thick.

"How many childs in house?"

"You mean children?"

"Yes."

"I have two and my wife has three."

"Ah you have five jildren?"

"You can say that."

Mr. Shapiro turned away to fill out a form with a ballpoint pen, while Baisha's narrow eyes squinted at his heavy cheek and then at the black hair on his wrist. She was such a flirt, but I was impressed. She was brave enough to converse with our boss in English! whereas I could never open my mouth in front of him.

Because we had seen Peter's mansion, our eyes were all focused on him. We were eager to find fault with him and ready to start a quarrel. But he was a careful man, knowing how to cope with us and how to maintain our boss's trust. He avoided arguing with us. If we didn't listen to him, he'd go into Mr. Shapiro's office and stay in there for a good while. That unnerved us, because we couldn't tell whether he reported us to the boss. So we dared not be too disobedient. Every night Peter was the last to leave. He'd close the shutters, lock the cash register, wrap up the unsold chicken, tie the package to the backseat of his Honda motorcycle, and ride away.

Ever since the beginning, the daily leftovers had been a bone of contention between Mr. Shapiro and us. We had asked him many times to let us have the unsold chicken at the end of the day, but he refused, saying the company's policy forbade its employees to have leftovers. We even offered to buy them at a half price, but he still wouldn't let us. He assigned Peter to take care of the leftovers alone.

It occurred to us that Peter must have taken the leftovers home for the construction workers. He had to feed them well, or else they might jerry-build his mansion. Damn him, he not only earned more but also got a perk. The more we thought about this, the more resentful we became. So one night, after he closed up and rode away, we came out of the nearby alley and pedaled behind him. Manyou was at the TV college that night and Jinglin had to look after his younger brother in the hospital who had just been operated on for a hernia, so they couldn't join us. Only Feilan, Baisha, and I followed Peter. He was going much faster than we were, but we knew where he was heading, so we cycled without hurry, chatting and laughing now and then.

In the distance Peter's motorcycle was flitting along the embankment like a will-o'-the-wisp. The night was cool, and a few men were chanting folk songs from their boat anchored in the river. We were eager to prove Peter had shipped the leftovers home, so that we could report him to Mr. Shapiro the next morning.

For a long while the light of Peter's motorcycle had disappeared. We stopped, at a loss. Apparently he had turned off the embankment, but where had he gone? Should we continue to head for his home, or should we mark time?

As we were talking about what to do, a burst of flames emerged in the north, almost two hundred yards away, at the waterside. We went down the embankment, locked our bicycles in a willow copse, and walked stealthily toward the fire.

When we approached it, we saw Peter stirring something in the fire with a trimmed branch. It was a pile of chicken, about twenty pieces. The air smelled of gasoline and burned meat. Beyond him, the waves were lapping the sand softly. The water was sprinkled with stars, rippling with the fishy breeze. On the other shore everything was buried in darkness except for three or four clusters of lights, almost indistinguishable from the stars in the cloudless sky. Speechlessly we watched. If there were another man with us, we might have sprung out and beaten Peter up. But I was no fighter, so we couldn't do anything, merely crouching in the tall grass and cursing him under our breath.

"If only we had a gun!" Baisha whispered through her teeth.

Peter was in a happy mood. With a ruddy face he began singing a song, which must have been made by some overseas Chinese:

> I'm not so carefree as you think
> My feelings never unclear
> If you can't see through me
> That's because again you waste
> Your love on a worthless man
>
> O my heart won't wander alone
> Let me take you along
> Together we'll reach a quiet place
> Where you can realize
> Your sweetest dream. . . .

For some reason I was touched by the song. Never had I known he had such a gorgeous baritone voice, which seemed to come a long way from the other shore. A flock of ducks quacked in the darkness, their wings splashing the water lustily. A loon let out a cry like a wild laugh. Then all the waterfowl turned quiet, and Peter's voice alone was vibrating the tangy air chilled by the night.

Feilan whispered, "What a good time he's having here, that asshole."

"He must miss his American sweetheart," Baisha said.

Feilan shook her chin. "Makes no sense. He's not the romantic type."

"Shh—" I stopped them.

When the fire almost went out, Peter unzipped his fly and pulled out his dick, peeing on the embers, which were hissing and sending up a puff of steam. The curve of his urine gleamed for a few seconds, then disappeared. He yawned, and with his feet pushed some sand over the ashes.

"Gross!" said Feilan.

Peter leaped on his motorcycle and dashed away, the exhaust pipe hiccuping explosively. I realized he didn't mind riding four miles to work because he could use some of the gasoline provided by our boss for burning the leftovers with.

"If only I could scratch and bite that bastard!" Feilan said breathlessly.

"Depends on what part of him," I said.

Baisha laughed. Feilan scowled at me, saying, "You have a dirty mind."

The next day we told all the other workers about our discovery. Everyone was infuriated, and even the two part-timers wouldn't stop cursing capitalism. There were children begging on the streets, there were homeless people at the train station and the boat house, there were hungry cats and dogs everywhere, why did Mr. Shapiro want Peter to burn meat like trash? Manyou said he had read in a restricted journal several years ago that some American capitalists would dump milk into a river instead of giving it to the poor. But that was in the U.S.A.; here in China, this kind of wasteful practice had to be condemned. I told my fellow workers that I was going to write an article to expose Ken Shapiro and Peter Jiao.

In the afternoon we confronted Peter. "Why do you burn the leftovers every day?" Manyou asked, looking him right in the eye.

Peter was taken aback, then replied, "It's my job."

"That's despicable," I snapped. "You not only burned them but also peed on them." My stomach suddenly rumbled.

Feilan giggled. Baisha pointed at Peter's nose and said sharply, "Peter Jiao, remember you're a Chinese. There're people here who don't have enough corn flour to eat while you burn chicken every night. You've forgotten your ancestors and who you are."

Peter looked flustered, protesting, "I don't feel comfortable about it either. But somebody has to do it. I'm paid to burn them, just like you're paid to fry them."

"Don't give me that crap!" Jinglin cut in. "You're a capitalist's henchman."

Peter retorted, "So are you. You work for this capitalist company too."

"Hold on," Manyou said. "We just want to reason you out of this shameful thing. Why do you waste chicken that way? Why not give the leftovers to the poor?"

"You think I enjoy burning them? If I gave them away, I'd be fired. This is the American way of doing business."

"But you're a Chinese running a restaurant in a socialist country," said Jinglin.

As we were wrangling, Mr. Shapiro came out of his office with coffee stains around his lips. Peter explained to him what we quarreled about. Our boss waved his hand to dismiss us, as though this were such a trifle that it didn't deserve his attention. He just said, "It's company's policy, we can't do anything about it. If you're really concerned about the waste, don't fry too many pieces and sell everything you've fried." He walked to the front door to have a smoke outside.

Peter said, "That's true. He can't change a thing. From now on we'd better not fry more than we can sell."

I was still angry and said, "I'm going to write to the *Herald* to expose this policy."

"There's no need to be so emotional, Hongwen," Peter said with a complacent smile, raising his squarish chin a little. "There have been several articles on this subject. For example, the *Beijing Evening News* carried a long piece last week about our company. The author praised our policy on leftovers and believed it would reduce waste eventually. He said we Chinese should adopt the American way of running business. In any case, this policy cannot be exposed anymore. People already know it."

That silenced us all. Originally we had planned that if Mr. Shapiro continued to have the leftovers burned, we'd go on strike for a few days. Peter's words deflated us all at once.

Still Jinglin wouldn't let Peter loose easily. When it turned dark, he pressed a thumbtack into the rear tire of the Honda motorcycle parked in the backyard. Peter called home, and his wife came driving a white Toyota truck to ship back the motorcycle and him. This dealt us another blow, since we hadn't expected he owned a brand-new pickup as well. Even some factories in our city couldn't afford such a vehicle. We asked ourselves, "Heavens, how much money does Peter actually have?"

We were all anxious to find that out. On payday, somehow Mr. Shapiro mixed Peter's wages with ours. We each received an envelope stuffed with a bundle of cash, but Peter's was always empty. Juju said Peter got only a slip of paper in his envelope, which was called a check. He could exchange that thing for money at the bank, where he had an account as if he were a company himself. In Juju's words, "Every month our boss just writes Peter lots of money." That fascinated us. How much did he get from Mr. Shapiro? This question had remained an enigma ever since we worked here. Now his pay was in our hands, and at last we could find it out.

Manyou steamed the envelope over a cup of hot tea and opened it without difficulty. The figure on the check astounded us: $1,683.75. For a good moment nobody said a word, never having imagined that Peter reaped an American salary, being paid dollars instead of yuan. That's to say, he made twenty times more than each of us! No wonder he worked so hard, taking care of Cowboy Chicken like his home, and tried every trick to please Mr. Shapiro.

That night after work, we gathered at Baisha's home for an emergency meeting. Her mother was a doctor, so their apartment was spacious and Baisha had her own room. She took out a packet of spiced pumpkin seeds, and we began chatting while drinking tea.

"God, just think of the money Peter rakes in," Jinglin said, and pulled his brushy hair, sighing continually. He looked wretched, as if ten years older than the day before. His chubby face had lost its luster.

I said, "Peter can afford to eat at the best restaurants every day. There's no way he can spend that amount of money."

Feilan spat the shells of a pumpkin seed into her fist, her eyes turning triangular. She said, "We must protest. This isn't fair."

Baisha agreed with a sigh, "Now I know what exploitation feels like."

"Peter has done a lot for Cowboy Chicken," Manyou said, "but there's no justification for him to make that much." He seemed still in a daze and kept stroking his receding chin.

"We must figure out a countermeasure," said Jinglin.

I suggested, "Perhaps we should talk with our boss."

"You think he'll pay each of us a thousand dollars?" Baisha asked scornfully.

"Of course not," I said.

"Then, what's the point in talking with him?"

Manyou put in, "I don't know. What do you think we should do, Baisha?"

I was surprised that he could be at a loss too, because he was known as a man of strategies. Baisha answered, "I think we must unite as one and demand our boss fire Peter."

Silence fell in the room, in which stood a double bed covered with a pink sheet. A folded floral blanket sat atop a pair of eiderdown pillows stacked together. I wondered why Baisha needed such a large bed for herself. She must have slept with her boyfriends on it quite often. She was such a slut.

"That's a good idea, I mean to get rid of Peter," Manyou said, nodding at her admiringly.

Still perplexed, I asked, "Suppose Mr. Shapiro does fire him, then what?"

"One of us may take Peter's job," said Manyou.

Feilan put in, "Are you sure he'll fire Peter?"

To our surprise, Baisha said, "Of course he will. That will save him fifteen hundred dollars a month."

"I don't get it," said Jinglin. "What's the purpose of doing this? Even if he fires Peter, he won't pay us more, will he?"

"Then, he'll have to depend on us and may give us each a raise," answered Baisha.

Unconvinced, I said, "What if the new manager gets paid more and just ignores the rest of us?"

Manyou frowned, because he knew that only Baisha and he could be a candidate for that position, which required the ability to use English. Feilan, Jinglin, and I couldn't speak a complete sentence yet.

"Let's draw up a contract," Feilan said. "Whoever becomes the new manager must share his wages with the rest of us."

We all supported the idea and signed on a brief statement, which said that if the new manager didn't share his earnings with the rest of us, he'd be childless and we could get our revenge in any way we chose. After that, Baisha went about composing a letter addressed to Mr. Shapiro. She didn't know enough English words for the letter, so she fetched a bulky dictionary from her parents' study. She began to write with a felt-tip pen, now and again consulting the dictionary. She was sleepy and yawned incessantly, covering her mouth with her left palm and disclosing her hairy armpit. Meanwhile, we cracked pumpkin seeds and chatted away.

The letter was short, but seemed to the point. Even Manyou said it was good after he looked through it. It stated:

Our Respected Mr. Kenneth Shapiro: We are writing to demand you to fire Peter Jiao immediately. This is our united will. You must respect our will. We do not want a leader like him. That is all.

Sincerely,
Your Employees

We all signed our names and felt that at last we could stand up to that capitalist. Since I'd pass our restaurant on my way home, I took charge of delivering the letter. Before we left, Baisha brought out a bottle of apricot wine, and together we drank to our solidarity.

I dropped the letter into the slot on the front door of Cowboy Chicken. After I got home, for a while I was light-headed and kept imagining the shock on Mr. Shapiro's pudgy face. I also thought of

Peter, who, without his current job, might never be able to complete his outrageous mansion. But soon I began to worry, fearing Baisha might become the new manager. Compared with Peter, she had a volatile temper and was more selfish. Besides, she couldn't possibly maintain the connections and clientele Peter had carefully built up, not to mention develop the business. Manyou wasn't as capable as Peter either. Sometimes he could be very clever in trivial matters, but he had no depth. He didn't look steady and couldn't inspire trust in customers. To be fair, Peter seemed indispensable to Cowboy Chicken. I wouldn't have minded if Mr. Shapiro had paid him five times more than me.

We all showed up at work at eight-thirty the next morning. To our surprise, neither Mr. Shapiro nor Peter betrayed any anxiety. They acted as if nothing had happened, and treated us the same as the day before. We were baffled, wondering what they had planned for us. Peter seemed to avoid us, but he was polite and calm. Apparently he had read the letter.

We expected that our boss would talk with us one by one. Even if he wouldn't fire Peter, he might make some concessions. But for a whole morning he stayed in his office as if he had forgotten us altogether. He was reading a book about the Jews who had lived in China hundreds of years ago. His calm appearance agitated us. If only we could have had an inkling of what he kept up his sleeve.

When the day was at last over, we met briefly at a street corner. We were confused, but all agreed to wait and see. Feilan sighed and said, "I feel like we're in a tug-of-war."

"Yes, we're in a mental war, so we must be tough-minded and patient," Manyou told us.

I went home with a stomachache. Again my father was drunk that night, singing revolutionary songs and saying I was lucky to have my fill of American chicken every day. I couldn't go to sleep until the wee hours.

The next day turned out the same. Peter assigned each of us some work, and Mr. Shapiro still wouldn't say an unnecessary word to us. I couldn't help picturing his office as a giant snail shell into which he had shut himself. What should we do? They must have devised a trap or something for us. What was it? We had to do something, not just waiting like this, or we'd be liquidated soon.

That night we gathered at Baisha's home again. After a lengthy discussion, we agreed to go on strike. Baisha wrote a note, which read:

Mr. Shapiro: Because you do not consider our demand, we decide to strike at Cowboy Chicken. Begin tomorrow.

We didn't sign our names this time, since he knew who we were and what we referred to. I was unsure of the phrase "strike at Cowboy Chicken," but I didn't say anything, guessing that probably she just meant we'd leave the place unmanned. Again I delivered the letter. None of us went to work the next morning. We wanted the restaurant to lose some business and our boss to worry a little so that he'd be willing to cooperate with his workers. But we had agreed to meet at one o'clock in front of Everyday Hardware, near Cowboy Chicken, then together we'd go to our workplace and start to negotiate with Mr. Shapiro. In other words, we planned to strike only for half a day.

After lunch we all arrived at the hardware store. To our surprise, a squad of police was standing in front of Cowboy Chicken as if a fire or a riot had broken out. They wouldn't allow people to enter the restaurant unless they searched them. What was going on? Why had Mr. Shapiro called in the police? We were puzzled. Together we walked over as if we had just returned from a lunch break. The front of the restaurant was cordoned off, and three police were stationed at the door. A tall policeman stretched out his arm to stop us. Baisha asked loudly, "Hey, Big Wan, you don't remember me?" She was all smiles.

"Yes, I saw you," Wan said with a grin.

"We all work here. Let us go in, all right? We have tons of work to do."

"We have to search you before letting you in."

"I've nothing on me. How do you search?" She spread her arms, then lifted her long skirt a little with one hand, to show she didn't even have a pocket.

"Stand still, all of you," said Wan. A policewoman moved over Baisha a black gadget like a miniature badminton racket without its strings.

"Is this a mine detector or something?" Jinglin asked the policewoman.

"A metal detector," she said.

"What's going on here?" Baisha asked Wan.

"Someone threatened to blow this place up."

We were all horrified by that, hoping it had nothing to do with us.

The police let us in. The moment we crossed the doorsill, we saw that an old couple stood behind the counter, taking care of orders. Damn it, Peter had brought his parents here to work! How come he wasn't afraid a bomb might blow them to pieces? In a corner, Susanna and two student-like girls were wiping tables and placing silver. They were humming "We Shall Overcome," but stopped at the sight of us. In the kitchen the two part-timers were frying chicken. Dumbfounded, we didn't know how to respond to this scene.

Mr. Shapiro came over. He looked furious, his face almost purple. He said with his spit flying about, "You think you can frighten me into obeying you? Let me tell you, you are all terminated!"

I didn't know what his last word meant, though I was sure it had a negative meaning. Manyou seemed to understand, his lips twitching as if he were about to cry. He gulped and couldn't say a word.

Peter said to us, "We can't use you anymore. You're fired."

"You can't do this to us," Baisha said to Mr. Shapiro and stepped forward. "We are founders of this place."

Mr. Shapiro laughed. "What are you thinking of? How much stock do you have in this company?"

What did he mean? We looked at one another, unable to fathom his meaning. He said, "Go home, don't come anymore. You'll receive this month's pay by the mail." He turned and walked away to the men's room, shaking his head and muttering, "I don't want any terrorists here."

Peter smiled at us with contempt. "Well, the earth won't stop spinning without the five of you."

I felt the room swaying like a lumbering bus. I had never thought I could be fired so easily: Mr. Shapiro just said a word, then gone was my job. The previous fall I had quit my position in a coal yard in order to work here. Now I had become a total loser, and people would laugh at me.

The five of us were terribly distressed. Before we parted company on the street, I asked Manyou to spell for me the word Mr. Shapiro had used. With his fountain pen he wrote on my forearm, "Terminated!" There was no need for an exclamation mark.

At home I looked up the word in my pocket dictionary, which says "finished." My anger flamed up. That damned capitalist believed he had finished with us, but he was mistaken. We were far from terminated—the struggle was still going on. I would ask my elder brother to cut the restaurant's electricity first thing the next morning. Baisha had said she'd have one of her boyfriends create some problems in Cowboy Chicken's mail delivery. Manyou would visit his friends at the garbage center and ask them not to pick up trash at the restaurant. Jinglin had declared, "I'll blow up Peter's Victorian!" Feilan hadn't decided what to do yet.

This was just a beginning.

That Winter

Fred G. Leebron

It was the winter that once again he did not reach into the upper rack of year-end bonuses, the winter that his dad suffered through prostate cancer and his sister discovered that she was going to die, the winter that returning from seeing her in New York he endured three flat tires within ninety minutes. Three flat tires, his friends said. How could that be? And he would patiently explain the crummy patching job from the guy in Liberty Corners, the underinflated donut that blew after only a mile, the rain pouring down through the fog as he sat on the shoulder of 78 in the eight-year-old Civic wagon with his wife and their five-year-old and one-year-old and waited for help, for rescue. It was the winter of inch after inch of rainwater in the basement of their new home, it was the first winter of his new job in a new town, it was the winter when he woke every morning feeling oppressed and paranoid only to discover that by the end of each day his presentiments were justified. It was the winter when questions of death and life became so paramount for him that he actually tried to address them himself, that he spent evenings with his wife pondering aloud whether anyone should ever judge anyone else and yet wasn't a person's judgment what made him that particular person, the winter that he wondered if people denied the fact of their death even as they irreversibly slid toward it, the winter that he and his wife bandied about words like grace and mercy and debated just what the fuck they meant. It was a winter when he fought his rage and tried to titrate it as if it were an analgesic, the winter that his sister's doctor told him that for pain management he liked to go to narcotics early on in the process, and they both understood to what process he referred. It was the winter of death, a lot of imminent death, a lot of rain that had nothing to do with growth and everything to do with being buried, the winter that his kids astonished him with their resilience and obliviousness. It was the winter that he understood that everyone sat at a window, the window between what they were and what they could be, what they had and what they wanted, their own nature and the nature of an ongoing world.

It began with a phone call after a business trip, or perhaps it began years before, at the first opalescence inside his sister, that grew along her spine in prickly metastases, or even before then, within the unknown gland the name of which even an autopsy might fail to reveal, when the cells split, when her life divided. But that Saturday he sat managing his kids while his wife worked at the office. And the phone rang. Sylvie was building Tinker Toys. Henry wrestled the cat into the fridge. Wearily he rose from the step where he sat surveying them and retrieved the receiver.

"Hello," he said flatly, not hiding the fatigue, the annoyance, the it's-a-Saturday-leave-me-alone tone.

"Hey, Sweetie."

His mind backed up, not quite recognizing. "Hey."

"It's Elizabeth."

His middle sister. Of course. "Oh, hi. How are you?"

"Good, good. How was your trip? You sell a lot?"

"Never enough," he admitted.

"Isn't that how it is?"

"Oh yes." The small talk irritated him, but he stuck with it. She didn't call that often, she lived in London. For years they'd been close. But the distance had brought distance, though she'd come for the last family Thanksgiving.

"Is your lovely wife around?"

He marveled at the Anglo inflection. "No. She's at the office since I've been gone all week."

"And you're stuck with the kids."

"I wouldn't say stuck." He glanced at their perfect little heads. How beautifully they were playing. In that week of hotels he'd missed them, missed the way they smelled, how they crawled over him and drooled on him, how they laughed. "How'd your tests go?"

She'd been troubled by muscle stiffness and back pain for seven months. She'd visited an osteopath and a chiropractor, and at Thanksgiving an American doctor had recommended a battery of evaluations. They suspected something chronic, was what he recalled.

"Well, actually," she said, "that's why I'm calling. They didn't go so well."

"Oh," he said. He'd sat again on the step, the kids partially in view in the living room. He felt something odd going up inside his mind.

"I have advanced cancer," she said. "It's not curable."

"What," he said. "What does that mean?"

"He said it's two or three years on, moving slowly."

"Well," he said. He was struggling. He saw what was rising inside him and it was some kind of brick wall trying to shut her out, saying she lived far away, she lived in London, she was sick, he wasn't, his kids weren't, his wife wasn't, that his side of the brick wall was okay, that he could keep it okay. "Can they manage it?" he managed. "I mean, what are you saying?"

"It was the bone scan," she said clearly. "They said I've got something like forty tumors on my spine. Beyond that, I don't know."

"How's Richard?" he struggled to ask, feeling his forehead, how real and foreign it seemed at the same time.

"Richard is shattered," she said.

"Oh," he said again. In his mind, right inside his head, to his horror he saw the solidity of the brick wall. "What happens next?"

"A biopsy." God she was in control. "More tests. We'll get some results maybe Wednesday. They want to find the primary. Although," she paused, "and this is kind of odd, they said the fact that it was already in the bone meant that the original source may already be healed."

"Weird," he said.

"I'm sorry I had to tell you last. I called everyone else Thursday, when I knew, but I heard you were out of town and I didn't want to lay this all on your wife."

"That was kind of you." What else could he say? That Thursday night he was out drinking beer with a new road buddy and doing a bit of Percodan.

"So," she said. "I guess I should be going."

"I'll call you after the doctor's appointment," he said. "I love you."

"I love you, too."

She hung up. He dialed his wife at the office.

"When are you coming home," he tried, his voice eroding.

"Well, I thought I'd—"

"—Come home," he said.

"What is it?"

"Just come home," he cried.

It was Chanukah. It was Christmas. It was a lot of gifts under the tree in a lot of different homes up and down the east coast. It was New Year's and sharing a half bottle of champagne and pouring the rest down the sink before turning in at eleven. It was long mornings that started at four or three and lasted five hours before he could pry himself from bed while his wife handled the children. It was gently cajoling, cajoling gently his sister back to the East, to New York, for a second opinion at the famously aggressive Tomkins Morrow Cancer Center while the rest of the family battered her about British passivity and incompetence. It was turgid phone calls with his mother, his other sisters, his brother, each of them preaching to the already converted on the need for Elizabeth to return to live in the States, where the care was better, where they could be with her. Tiredly he listened as they took her reluctance as personal rejection. He felt he knew what it was. That she didn't want to give into the cancer, that she didn't want it to change her life. And he thought, somewhere in his mind where the brick wall could have been, that she'd have to come to them, that she'd have to cross whatever barrier there was so they could face whatever there was to face together. How he dreaded and wanted that to happen.

It was New York, in the first sopping week of January, he and his wife and the kids staying at a buddy's apartment in Chelsea while the buddy stayed with his girlfriend in the Village and Elizabeth and Richard stayed uptown near Columbia where their brother worked, and the other sisters trained in from D.C. and Philadelphia, the family gathering as if for a funeral.

The day of the appointment he took his sister for a morning swim at the 92nd Street Y. Within a chlorinated vault he sat in a short balcony and watched her swim. There were a dozen other sickly looking swimmers, most in their sixties or seventies, and he wondered if they had cancer, too. She side-stroked facing him, and he tried to study her, the ringed eyes, the pale face. Was she really, truly dying? Could you die at forty having exercised every day, eaten right, done nothing to excess? Their mother was searching for blame, for fault. She complained there was something environmental wrong with London or the computers at his sister's office. The cancer books said you had to surrender your wrath. The cancer books said you had to live one day at a time, drink eight glasses of water, research the clinical trials, stay positive, acquire and strengthen your faith. They were written by survivors, people who had been handed death sentences yet had kept on living five, ten, fifteen, endless years. You wanted to believe them. You had to believe them. There were doctors who could do all the research for you, doctors who would charge $20,000 for their specially tailored cures, doctors who weren't even doctors. She swam with water cloaking her face.

In the lobby afterwards she walked slightly stooped.

"Do you have my wallet?" she said.

"I thought you had it."

"No, I gave it to you."

He ran back to the pool. The lifeguard waved to him as soon as he saw him. She'd entrusted him with her wallet and he'd nearly blown it. As he thanked the lifeguard he was trembling with gratitude and self-loathing.

Driving toward Columbia, each pothole jarred her pain loose and she moaned. I'm sorry, he kept saying. I'm sorry. He wondered how many people in New York had cancer. He'd done enough browsing in bookstores and clicking through the internet to rattle off that men had a one in *x* chance of getting it in a lifetime, women a one in *y*, the average life expectancy with cancer of an unknown primary was *z* and occurred in anywhere between *a* and *b* of all diagnosed cancers. Blah, blah, blah. She didn't want to hear the statistics. She hadn't wanted to come for this fancy second opinion. Ignorance could give her strength. Their family history was prostate cancer, he'd told one Tomkins Morrow screener. Well, the guy remarked drily, we can rule that out. It took him a short while to learn why that was. He was dumb and he was smart. He just wanted to be smart.

Upstairs in his brother's apartment, the children ran up and down the long hallway. His father sagged in a chair, his jowled face looking sad and exhausted. What they said about his own cancer was newly formulaic—that he would die of other shortcomings (his weight, his heart, his kidneys) before it could kill him. Twenty years before he had sat with his father in a car in late spring, while his sister and his mother shopped at a chaotic county flea market, and his father had sighed deeply and with tired eyes looked at him in the rearview mirror. "You know," he said, "I'm at the winter of my life." "You're fifty-one," his son had said, "what do you mean?" "I mean," he'd said, "I'm on my way out." For twenty years now, he'd been in this state of surrender and yet kept on living. The cancer authors wouldn't know what to make of the success of his defeatism.

In the hall his wife hid a look of mild harassment. His sister lay silent on a white couch.

"Can I get you anything?" he asked. She shook her head. "A glass of water?" She assented. They had to leave in twenty minutes for the appointment that had taken him two weeks of phone calls to schedule. He fed his sister sips of water, as if nursing her for the next performance. The children skittered and shrieked in the hallway. His wife kept coming in, quietly reminding them of the time. In a back room, his sister's husband fed e-mail to his London office. His sister drank a little more water. He *really* didn't want to hurry her.

"Okay." She winced as she rose from the couch. "I'm ready."

The line into the parking garage under Tomkins Morrow lasted twenty minutes, and along the corridors to their designated office suite were waiting room after waiting room packed like bus stations at Thanksgiving. Apparently, there were two kinds of people: those who had cancer, and those who were going to get it. At Tomkins Morrow the "cure" rate was well into double digits, and one thing was certain: even if you were essentially alone, sometimes it could be pretty hard to feel that way.

After an hour's wait beyond the scheduled appointment, the four of them—his mother, his sister, her husband, and he—were shown to an examining room. A nurse came in, thoughtful, smiling, and issued a warm and heartfelt greeting. She was like some kind of stewardess on a plane into the stratosphere of world-renowned oncological care. A quarter hour later came the Fellow, Eastern European. He interrogated Elizabeth in a friendly fashion, drew the curtain around her, examined her, and then informed them that shortly the Boss would come. Evidently the Boss was a cross between a rock star and the service manager at an auto repair center, a guy who didn't get his hands dirty but told you what the problem was and how much it was going to cost. Within ten minutes he arrived, tall, clipped brown hair fringed with gray. He looked at the ground as he walked. He strode right up to Elizabeth, snapped the curtain around her, felt in unknown places, whipped the curtain open, and pronounced himself ready to talk. At that point his pager beeped. He plucked up the desk phone, spoke briefly, rang off.

"That was what I was afraid of," he said. "I have a conference call. We'll move you all to another room and I'll be in as soon as I can."

In a corner office five stories up, overlooking a fruit stand and a hot dog cart, they talked giddily about how hungry they should be and how they could all hold off eating. The busy hum of people and machines sounded hopeful and American. At a certain point Elizabeth dialed another hospital and proceeded to try to schedule a third opinion. In the hallway they heard the Boss preparing to enter. Behind him trailed the Fellow.

The six of them sat at a small round table.

"I've reviewed all the results," the Boss said, crisply, matter-of-factly. "I think the physician in London did an excellent job working you up, and I confirm the diagnosis."

There followed a thirty minute Q and A where the Boss looked at his watch only once and everyone tiptoed around prognosis, choosing to land on issues of chemotherapy, hormone therapy, and the fact that searching for the primary rarely identifies it. Finally, Elizabeth's mother could wait no longer. She wanted to know: Where would the care be best?

"Wherever home is," the Boss said. "London is as good as New York in all aspects of treatment. In some ways, they're even ahead of us."

The brother was stunned. Tomkins Morrow was saying it was no better, Tomkins Morrow was declining to pursue. He looked long at the Boss. He was writing her off. Her case had no hope. The brother was devastated.

As he drove Elizabeth and Richard uptown, they forced shreds of conversation.

"I'm glad he said the care in London was excellent," Elizabeth said.

"That justifies the whole trip," said Richard.

By this time the brother understood that chemotherapy could kill you or make you stronger, that it was a complicated choice, that it was the only chance—and the most minute chance at that—for cure.

"Is there any roast turkey back at the apartment?" Elizabeth asked.

He nodded his head. She needed to keep her weight up. She needed to drink eight glasses of water a day. And sometime within the next three weeks, she needed to make a decision. There'd be radiation for pain. Beyond that, he could see nothing good. The books said you had to project yourself into that small surviving percentile. You had to lead the fight against your own disease. Elizabeth called it dis-ease. Once, when he was trying to arrange return tickets for them and they wanted the cheapest rate, he told her that the conditions weren't appropriate for sick people. "I am not sick," she said. "I'm sorry," he said, "I just don't think you can fly standby." "Oh," she said quietly, "that *is* right."

Back in their brother's apartment, he looked secretly at his wife and shook his head. His sister lay again on the white couch. The care in London was good. The big deal doctor had confirmed the diagnosis. Everything was fine.

Weeks and weeks. Months that could not quite make a season. Checks written for $275, $1800, to various alternative programs. The brother recalled the story of a movie star stricken with cancer, who traveled wherever he'd heard of a cure. Coffee enemas in Mexico, shark cartilage in Cuba, protein injections in the Bahamas. He died within the allotted time. Everybody dies, the brother consoled himself. I believe that the mind is merciful, his wife said. That she'll accept it with peace. At night, sometimes, he heard his wife talking on the phone to her sister about his sister, about her state of mind or her ovaries, and he wanted to rip the phone from her hand and scream, *that's my sister you're talking about.* Privacy, dignity—these were only abstractions. Did he get on the phone to his brother about her sister's wily boyfriend or her last dysplastic pap smear? He couldn't say anything to her. She flew with him on grueling trips to London, she sat with him in his sister's feng shui'd bedroom and talked about all the trivial things his sister yearned to discuss—celebrity weddings, interior design. On the flights home she reached across the armrest and held his hand and wouldn't let go. He needed her. He loved her. He just didn't want anyone judging his sister. What she tried. What she thought. What she wanted.

He wrote letters to various companies about the three blown tires and waited for checks in the mail. He tried to quit drinking. He tried to reach eight glasses of water a day. In the evening he mopped the basement and marveled how anyone had missed the fact that the sump pump did not occupy the lowest point in the floor. He e-mailed Elizabeth. She believed in God. She believed that God was everywhere. He told her about making Cajun meatloaf or shrimp with portabello mushrooms. He gossiped with her about his more successful colleagues. He signed every e-mail, I love you. She e-mailed, I love you, too.

He was offended by people who would ask if she had any children, as if that would make her illness that more unearned. He understood it was almost utilitarian—how many would be left behind, how many would be inconsolable? It was just weeks ago that he'd felt enraged by the year-end magazine features, Fifty Who Made a Difference, Twenty-five Who Have Left Us Bereft, as if only so few mattered in the annual summed obituaries. Again, it was utilitarian—how many lives had the lost lives diminished? In New York he had been harmed most by his buddy's girlfriend's clear-eyed pronouncement, as she crossed her legs, lit a cigarette, and looked him squarely in the heart: that perhaps this struggle was the reason his sister was brought to her life in the first place. The facts were these: she had no children, her job was in middle-tier investment banking. Why else should she be alive, but to face some form of the unspeakable?

He hated most the sense of the future, that for the world beyond his window there was always next week, next month, next year. Sometimes he found himself wishing for the mobs at Tomkins Morrow. How silent and polite they were, the only waiting room he'd ever been in where people actually moved so that families could sit together. Like Auschwitz, a friend told him.

Each morning he woke groping for an exit from this dream. They used to shoplift Lifesavers together from the Acme on Woodbine, when he was six and she was ten. In the dark room over the garage she practiced kissing on him before she pursued it with the sixth-grade boys—how he curled into her arms in the loud Naugahyde chair and she kept kissing him and kissing him, her pursed lips sloppily finding his face in the darkness. Ten years later they planned an elaborate tour of Europe together. They took a train all the way from Germany to Greece, boarded a ferry to an island, climbed steps to a white villa, purchased rooftop accommodations for fifty cents each. The next morning she awoke covered in hives or bites, scratching furiously. They tried to ignore and outlast the bumps, but within a day they multiplied like chicken pox and spread she said even to her genitals, and just a week after their trip had begun they had to bail out all the way back home to the States. When he was in college in New Jersey, he visited her once every few weeks in New York, where they ate and drank in tapas bars and he pretended that he liked her friends from work. One New Year's Eve they dressed up and went to all the parties, told everyone they were each other's dates. That kind of crap.

Before he was born, an uncle whom he would be named after lay dying of cancer, his brain growing mishmashed. Close the Venetian blinds, he'd ask, when he meant, Turn off the television. His wife, sweet-faced, utterly gentle, attended him. They were childless. "A man as sick as I am," he managed to say once, quite clearly, "does not tell his wife his thoughts." What did that mean, Elizabeth's brother now wondered. Regret? Bitterness? Hatred? If life were the continuous pressure to understand—why do I love her, why does she love me, why do I hate my job, why do I love my children, why, why, why—then what did it mean to know it was going to end? He did not believe that you could take that understanding with you. What would be left between them when he stood beside her that last time in London? Was the purpose of accrued memory something like mercy, as his wife suggested? Or was mercy the release from exhaustion and pain? Couldn't denial—the instinct that even as you slipped under you still might emerge again—be merciful? Was grace acceptance or wishful thinking? He wanted to *know*. He couldn't know.

"We're all going to die," his New York buddy had said. "Isn't that wild? I mean, all of us are going to die."

It was the only solace he could find, that kind of universality. One's love could endure, one's work—a day, a week, a month, a year, a decade. One Hundred Who Made the Millennium—would be the next headline.

He did not think that anyone he knew would be among them. Wasn't there comfort in that, in the essentially cozy, futile, hermetic quality of everyone's life? In eighth grade, a cranky Ukranian classmate, the skin of his stomach doubled into two belly-buttons by some past barbaric surgery, turned to him and sneered. "How many people do you think *really* care about you, really know you? What do you say, 100, 150?" He snickered. "I don't think so. You know what I think?" And the brother shrugged, wide-eyed. "I think twenty, max, if that. That's what I think."

"Sweetie," his sister called across the ocean past Valentine's Day, nearer the Millennium. "It all matters. Everything matters."

"I can't believe you haven't turned to God yet," a colleague said, studying him, the pointy chin of her face pointed at him. "Everybody turns to God in some form at times like these. Everybody."

He couldn't find God. He didn't have the impulse to look.

"Up until now," his brother said, "we've all been pretty lucky." Five siblings around their forties, two parents nearing their seventies. It was easy to see what he meant. The first wretchedness.

"You have to keep on living." Now who was saying that? Some idiot. He looked at his children and knew it to be true. He wanted to live. He looked at his wife and knew that there was so much more between them, unexplored, unknown, that he needed to reach, that he wanted to reach. He wanted her, he wanted the children.

"I hope you're finding a way to release your anxiety," Elizabeth wrote in an e-mail. "I don't want you to stress out about this."

She was dying, oh God she was dying. It was the winter that death was everywhere, that he woke every morning and could not escape it, that he kept feeling he was missing everybody, that he had to keep living, that death descended, that it was descending, that it hadn't yet arrived. It was the winter that death was everywhere. He never wanted it to end.

Chrysalis

David H. Lynn

James Blessingame, District Court Judge Blessingame, slipped out his back door, tiptoed through the strip of garden along the drive, and peered stealthily around the front corner of his house, spying on the old man who'd been casing the vicinity for at least ten minutes.

Only by chance had the judge stopped home during the afternoon. An unexpected recess—the lead attorney in a case before him had gone into labor the night before—provided a rare weekday chance for Blessingame to desert his chambers, drop by the house to gather up athletic gear, and head to his club. Now, his toes prodding a small rhododendron in crimson bloom, he realized his fist still clutched a drooping jockstrap. Glancing about in fear that someone, one of his neighbors, might notice, he stuffed it into a pocket.

Ten minutes earlier he'd spotted the old man strolling casually up and down the sidewalk. The vision was so preposterous that it nearly failed to snag the judge's attention, his mind distracted by an annoying dispute over office space with a senior colleague; by an attractive new member of the bar (black eyes, navy suit so modestly slit it promised rare secrets); by whether to dispense with the workout after all and plummet directly to a rubdown and sauna as a way of dissipating the tension that pricked tiny scalpels into the muscle of his neck. From the kitchen he was gazing absently through the length of his house, through hallway and living room, when he happened to make out the stranger's vague shape through a front bow window.

No, the man wasn't a derelict. Nor did he strike Blessingame as delusional as the judge strode angrily along the hallway. Then he sighed and halted. Someone, he decided, must have played a trick on the old man, twisting him round off Woodward Avenue with false directions. Or he'd failed in deciphering a map and spun himself silly on these residential streets. Or boarded the wrong bus, climbing down at this unlikely stop.

But that wasn't it either. This man knew where he was. Blessingame, peering forward toward the window but not allowing himself to be seen, could make that out too. For some reason—perhaps the old man's bizarre behavior provoked a reciprocal secretiveness—the judge didn't simply charge through the door and confront him. He was curious and wanted to observe just how far the fellow would go.

It wasn't merely being white that cast the stranger so clearly out of place. Some white families—mostly older couples to be sure—still lived scattered among these few blocks of Harper Woods on the northern crease between city and hostile suburbs. Back and forth this one had been wandering, sizing up the neighborhood, studying the house. He tried to appear casual, at ease. Instead, he managed to seem both furtive and painfully awkward.

Once upon a time he must have been a big man with strong shoulders. Yet the hint of a stoop made him seem frail in a gray suit that had grown too full. His hair (he still had that, a full head of it the judge noted with some chagrin) was iron gray and dramatically swept back. Between two fingers he was fastidiously pincing the brim of an old-fashioned fedora, another failed attempt to make himself less conspicuous.

The afternoon was hazy, humid. School hadn't let out. No one lingered or played in the street, no one strolled along the sidewalk or even peered, so it seemed, from behind windows of the other homes to note the sly old man. Now from the corner of his garden James Blessingame watched as the stranger nodded, apparently reorienting himself, reacquainting himself. Slowly, slowly, ever so casually, he was edging his way up the front walk.

At the fieldstone steps the visitor climbed stiffly but quickly now, no longer glancing back. Nor, once on the porch, did he knock to announce himself. He perched the fedora like a sentinel on the wicker settee and turned to hunch intently at the door.

Judge Blessingame leaned farther out. He couldn't quite spy what the old man was working at. He slipped still closer. The bizarre fellow was scratching—prying with a nail file or small screwdriver at something on the door post.

"Pardon me—would you kindly explain just what the hell you're doing to my house?" Blessingame's voice boomed deep.

Startled, the visitor stiffened but didn't quake or collapse. Bracing one hand against the door, he turned to confront his accuser. His left eye seemed damaged—it wouldn't open quite fully. Yet he appeared neither meek nor apologetic. "I'm surprised it's still here," he said as if it were an accusation. "You live in this house?"

"I own this house." Blessingame approached, mounting the steps. "What's that you've found? Why shouldn't it be there?"

"I doubt you'd have any use for such a thing—a *mezuza*. But you haven't removed it. No one has."

"Pardon?"

The old man pointed. He scratched again at a small cylinder set in the door frame at an angle, perhaps two inches long, painted over many times, hardly more than a defect in the wood by now. A fleck of white paint fell away revealing only a slightly paler shade.

"Huh." The judge studied it without drawing closer. "Now I figured that was some kind of buzzer. You know, broken or rusted. Been planning to fix it too, but not till time comes to repaint the rest. Thanks to you, it'll be sooner than I'd imagined. You do know you're trespassing, Mister—?"

Defiance as well as impatience crept into the old man's eyes. His jaw stiffened. "Naturally I will reimburse you for any damage. Hazzan. My name is Theodore Hazzan. How do you do?"

"I'm sure you will. Blessingame's mine. James Blessingame. Welcome to my house." He didn't manage to keep the irony from his tone, but Hazzan seemed neither to notice nor care. His eagerness to return to the task was paramount.

"What did you say this box is?"

"A mezuza. They're fastened to door posts and entryways. By Jews, of course. Not your people. By Jews."

"Yes. Yes." The judge nodded. "I remember—the Lord commands the Israelites to mark their doors in Egypt. But with blood, wasn't it? So the Angel of Death will spare their first-born. I'd no idea they were still doing it. Not this way either."

Hazzan merely gestured with his nail file at the self-evident ornament.

"That's fine, whatever they may do," Judge Blessingame continued. "But no Jews live here anymore, not in this house."

In truth, the unexpected turn of the conversation made him uneasy. He'd known, of course, that this had been a Jewish neighborhood, supposed even that Jews built this very house in which he took such pride. None of that bothered him. It made no difference. He was grateful for the care and solid good taste they—whoever they were—had exercised.

And he had nothing against Jews either. At least not in the sense that people usually supposed or that some of his own friends did. No, it was true he could be impatient with particular Jews he'd encountered in college and law school; later too, professionally and in service organizations trying to salvage something of this decaying city. But such impatience, (which he vigilantly, politically secreted away), festered in his chest and jaw only because these particular Jews could be so damn *earnest*. How desperately they'd be keening to do the right thing. No desire even for public acknowledgment of their good deeds. No, they yearned to keep living off the glories of the 60s, marching and riding buses and even dying for the rights of their Black brothers. Well that was fine as far as the judge was concerned. But Jews, at least the Jews he dealt with day to day, knew nothing, knew shit about being Black today. And he was sick—this was the truth he admitted to himself only now on the front porch of his own house, peevish and weary and fed-up—he was sick of them trying so damn hard.

"Inside lives a little piece of paper," the old man was stubbornly continuing as if Blessingame hadn't spoken. "Parchment actually. A prayer, a blessing."

"Parchment actually." Blessingame again didn't manage to hide his exasperation. "I'm glad for the lesson, but you must understand that this is of no use to me. I assume it's not even proper for the likes of me, for my people as you say, to have one of these things on my door."

He was surprised by his own peevishness. The old man bothered him, got under his skin. Tiny blades were worrying themselves again into the muscle of his neck. And a bone-deep weariness seemed to have welled up, as if lying in wait for such a moment (and loneliness too, but any acknowledgment of that hovered on the horizon of awareness) and opened him raw.

"If this—*mezuza*—was yours or your family's, feel free to take it. Here, I'll get a decent screwdriver and we'll pry it off for you. I can touch up the paint myself this weekend."

"No, that's not the point," the old man snapped. "And there is nothing to take anymore. Just the case. Without the scroll it's hollow, worthless."

"Empty or not, worthless or not." He wondered how the old man knew it was empty, but he was tiring of this. A sauna and rubdown—the opportunity was fast disappearing. "Mr. Hazzan. What if I remove it myself? I'm not offended it doesn't belong on a Black man's house, if that's the problem. Either take it yourself or let me remove and dispose of it, but I have no more time for this today."

The accusation and dismissal seemed almost to strike the old man. He winced and raised a hand, shaking his head. "I must sit," he waved. And lowered himself heavily onto the porch, leaning on one arm, his knees spread awry. His bad eye squeezed shut into a squint that set his whole face akilter.

Good Christ, thought Blessingame stepping closer, worried the old man might pass out or collapse entirely. That would have worse consequences than mere inconvenience. "Look here, do you need an ambulance?"

"No, no. I'm okay. It's warm today," he said with a broken smile. "A glass of water, maybe?"

"You just sit there until you're okay," the judge ordered. He reached into his pocket but realized that the front door key was on a ring still hanging in the back door lock. Hurrying down the steps and through the garden once more, he filled a glass in the kitchen, and strode quickly through the house his family and friends had thought him mad to buy—unless there was a girlfriend or plans for a girlfriend, perhaps a family, that none of them knew about. A house this size for a single man, even a man of his accomplishments. . . .

Blessingame came to a halt and pursed his lips. Knowing the old man was waiting for him on the front porch cast a shadow across the sun. Suddenly he felt the weight of years he hadn't noticed settling about him, and the chill of loneliness—of aloneness—he'd been too busy to acknowledge. Yes, in fact there had been a woman, one in mind when he bought this house. Not that his family and friends knew she existed. She, Marjorie, was an attorney he'd met in San Diego—the law school brought him as a speaker and she'd been in the audience. She asked a tough question after the talk and then another, and they'd thrashed the matter out over coffee, ignoring students and professors standing around impatiently. He'd extended his stay, taken holiday leave. For four days they breathed only each other. And after six months of secrecy and cross-country flights and delicious planning, she'd arranged to join a local firm. No reason to admit to the senior partners why she was making the move. No reason for Blessingame to tell her about this house—it was an impetuous surprise even to himself. He'd signed the contract on it hours before her plane landed, as if the fact of it would allow him to grasp Marjorie close too before they could discover all the reasons that would drive them apart. (A black judge depending on reappointment; a white attorney held to a different standard than her senior partners.) Instead, the fact of the house festered into an insupportable burden. She never moved in but visited from her tiny apartment. After a few furtive and disappointing meetings, the poison of those practical reasons leeched them even of the language for parting.

The stabbing sadness of the memory startled Blessingame. For an instant he puzzled at the glass in his hand. Then he remembered the old man. Sad and freshly irritated, he tugged the front door open and failed to take his usual pleasure at the heft of its heavy wooden swing.

Hazzan hadn't moved. He was panting lightly. Accepting the glass without looking up, he gulped several gulps of water. Some dribbled onto his tie. He flicked at the beads absently.

"Take your time," the judge said sternly, an impatient nurse with a cantankerous patient. "Rest until you're feeling better."

His lips rubbery and blue, the old man was still panting. He gestured at the door frame. "I came to do something."

"I've told you already—take it. Feel free. No charge. We'll have it off in no time."

But Hazzan was shaking his head. He dug at his jacket pocket. "I don't want it. Just to put this back." Gently he drew forth an envelope and from the envelope, gently, a small ragged scrap.

"Ah," said Blessingame. "Ah." His voice changed. "That, I take it, belongs inside. And you come to have it, how?"

"I stole it."

The judge glanced smartly at the small cylinder buried beneath successive coats of hardened enamel. Why was it that only now did he consider the possibility that Theodore Hazzan was disturbed in some way after all, perhaps a certifiable nut case? "You stole it," he repeated. "Not anytime recent, you didn't."

The old man didn't respond. He was staring out toward the street, his thoughts on something other than this conversation, this distraction.

"Years and years ago. A lifetime since then," he said at last. "We didn't live in Harper Woods, our family. My father worked tool-and-die down-river. For him the day was not a good day unless he could cross the door with his hands black with honest dirt and grease, my mother waiting with a bowl and soap for him to wash first thing. *He* didn't make money enough to live in such a place as Harper Woods."

Blessingame grunted, defensive about his own position here. The Jews he knew weren't tool-and-die, not unless they owned the plant, and he found it hard to conjure the image of this man's father and his righteously dirty hands. Yet he couldn't suppress a confession of his own. "Down-river you say? Matter of fact, most of my family still live down-river. You believe my Dad worked the Rouge River plant thirty-five years?"

His visitor nodded or shrugged, the judge couldn't tell, but the old man seemed hardly to hear.

"Anyway, what's your father got to do with you stalking my house?" said Blessingame more curtly.

Hazzan lifted his hands and dropped them on his knees once more. "I came first to this house when I was seventeen. I needed a job and jobs were hard to come by, unless I followed my father to the union and the shop—and I did not want to leave school. So I did a terrible thing."

"Stealing that piece of paper was so awful?"

The old man wagged his head at the ludicrous notion and then nodded at the door. "I asked the man who owned this house for a job."

"But you said they were Jews. You were both Jews, right?—what was so wrong?"

Hazzan wagged a hand this time. "I could think to ask this rich man because he had once been my father's friend. As a boy I knew him as Uncle. I would hear stories of them going to *shul*—synagogue, you understand?—as boys together, of waiting on sidewalks and fighting for jobs. For my father this was good, this was life—this battle, this struggle, the hard work and his family. But Uncle Arthur didn't like the dirty hands or the freezing so much. He was a smaller man, with fair skin and delicate hands, a musician. Who can blame him?" Hazzan seemed to be asking the question of some judge other than the one before him.

"With dimes and pennies, help too from his wife's family I suppose, he bought his own tool-and-die shop. It grew—how it grew. What was necessary to attract business he did, and he did too what was necessary to keep his workers from taking too much. No union organized his floor, not ever.

"Perhaps they had fought and argued before—how could I know? I was still too young. But I remember the night my father came home in a dark rage because Uncle Arthur had forced the union out. Who do you think one of the organizers was? Papa said nothing, threw nothing. But his lips were white and he forgot to remove his overcoat. I had never seen him such a way. My mother was actually frightened. Not of him but for him. Never did I see my father's friend again—never was his name spoken in our house—not until I found my way to his shop and asked for help.

"Uncle Arthur was surprised, delighted to find his long-lost nephew in his doorway, as if I was the black sheep who disappeared so long ago. He took me in his arms. And before I knew I should never take his work he hired me. As a favor to my father, his all-but-brother—that's how he would have it.

"My father! Finally I got up the nerve to tell him—and he stared at me. He stared at me and turned away and—this I had never seen him do, never—he leaned into the street and he spit and he turned away from me."

Hazzan paused. He ran a hand across his face and sipped at the water his host had fetched him. He did not notice that Blessingame, sighing, had settled next to him on the steps.

"This porch—I painted this porch," he continued. "Not sloppy like this, but with love, every stroke. Because I loved this man Arthur Lewis. Can you imagine that? He read—*everything*—and Mozart and Brahms, he knew them like friends. From outside these windows I listened to him listen. More—he'd stood up to my father and paid the price for his betrayal—cut off like dead. And he built this new world for himself. Well, I was standing up too.

"Those bricks in the walk?" he demanded with off-hand defiance. "One by one, a perfect dance from one to the next, I drew the walk and laid those bricks. I can still feel them raw at my fingertips. I knew this house even better than he did. Better than you do. Better!" He was furious, staring now at Blessingame.

With hardly a pause Hazzan shifted ground, but suddenly he seemed stealthy again or embarrassed. He was gazing out across the street. "Arthur Lewis also had a daughter, Elsa, two years younger than me."

"Ah," Blessingame said again, his impatience and boredom kindled once more. For such tired testimony as this, Hazzan's first love, he was to sacrifice his precious afternoon?

"No," Hazzan snapped. "Nothing like that—it wasn't that way. You don't understand. It was for her father's sake. So he would think well of me. So I could watch and study him, even talk with him when there was chance—I tutored Elsa in mathematics, and then, later, I escorted her to concerts and movies. *As a favor to my uncle*, don't you see? He was arranging nothing between us, and forbidding nothing either. Me he didn't take seriously as a threat to his precious daughter. My father's son, a poor boy from down-river, I was too grateful to be any threat. They knew they could count on me. And because he asked me, I was such a good boy, so respectful. Such a fool.

"You expect me to say Elsa was beautiful like a dream. But no, not beautiful. Not even pretty perhaps—I knew it then, but it did not matter. For a long time I hardly noticed her as anything but a child, she was so shy and gray and quiet, a little girl, nothing more than her father's daughter. At first. But later her eyes, they showed me secret fire, dark fire, with a temper too that seemed crazy.

"Naturally—it was part of my job—I would be correcting her little mistakes, with arithmetic maybe, here and there. When with no warning it was this howling storm sweeping Elsa up in a rage and she shrieking at me, swearing at me, calling me names I'd never heard, never imagined, so that I became the young one, naive and innocent. She scared me with those wild moods. And she laughed at my face then, and kissed me, and I was the young one.

"Sometimes, when she was cruel, she ignored me or made me walk behind her. But if I dared walk away, oh she wouldn't stand for that—she flung herself about my neck. She would cling to me and rub herself against me. Here on these steps, she snatched my hair and kissed me in the moonlight, daring her parents to see.

"So yes, this much you were right." He waved a hand, conceding. "This house itself became our only confidant. We knew its secret places and it knew our secrets too. I'd spot its roof down the street as I approached, before these trees had grown so tall, either in the daytime to work openly or in the evening, late and secret, and a sweat of fear and yearning spread across my chest."

The judge glanced about uneasily. He wasn't sure in any event that he wanted his neighbors spying him talking this way to a crazy old man, a Jew come back to the promised land no less. But there seemed no way to stop him, and—this the truth that made him most uncomfortable—the story had caught him up as a reluctant witness after all. He needed to hear it through.

But why? he wondered, exasperated with himself now. None of this had anything to do with him and yet he needed to hear it through. Was it the coincidental stories of working-class fathers and sons with aspirations for flight? Or was it the still vibrating echoes of Marjorie deep in his ear? Once conjured, she seemed to be refusing easy dismissal to safe and distant memory.

"For nearly two years this was our way," Hazzan was saying. "Today, well, such a thing wouldn't be possible. But that was a different world.

"Our secret seemed powerful and strange. We treasured it not because we were afraid but because this way it stayed so strong. We didn't say the words even to each other—we didn't need to.

"Her father, her parents finally they began to suspect. When? They could tell. Perhaps they were not surprised after all. But they said nothing to me. They changed nothing openly. I was still welcome to do my little jobs here and to tutor Elsa. I wasn't going to challenge them then. As long as they would let us be, I would risk nothing.

"We *knew* each other, Elsa and me—you understand? We didn't have to speak even, we knew each other so well."

Blessingame was nodding silently, lips pursed.

"Slowly, so subtly, Uncle Arthur went to work against me with gentle poisons. He never forbid. No, he knew it wouldn't work. Forbidding would only drive Elsa to me. He knew his daughter too. But slowly, over months, he let her see that it was only a choice, simple and clear. That she was to choose between the family and me, between his world and the one I offered.

"But why did he do this? I loved the man.

"Look, you see the sky through that tree, and the road with these houses, and my car down the block, the green one, yes. None of this is as clear to me as my memory of Elsa hurrying along the pavement toward our rendezvous in the sandwich shop over on Woodward Avenue. Her scarf, blue, bright bright blue, the breeze tugs at it and she fights hand-on-head to hold it in place. I'm sitting in the window of the sandwich shop, waiting and watching, and I see her hurrying along the street to meet me. But she isn't my Elsa. She isn't the same girl. Something in her walk. Something in her mouth. Still, she sits down opposite me, smiling, but her eyes, they won't look up at me. They aren't dark with fury and fire and love—they're hidden and flat. I bob and shift and try to catch her eye, to make her see me, but she won't see. If she will look, if she will see *me*. . . . But she won't allow it."

Hazzan pulled a handkerchief from his pocket and wiped at his nose, his hand trembling. "And what I could not understand then was very simple—that Else had made her choice and chosen, well, not me. This made no sense. It has never made sense. With all we shared, all we knew of each other, how could she abandon me so easily?"

Blessingame sighed and rubbed his eyes. An inspiration, an insight deep as his own pulse had come to him in the last few moments as they sometimes did on the bench, but this one gave him no satisfaction. "Sounds to me like maybe that's what your Uncle Arthur had in mind, or something like from the beginning," he mused. "Maybe once he realized you and his daughter were—*close*—this could be one final way of rubbing your old man's nose in it, paying him back—through you, by doing this to you." The judge shrugged.

Hazzan tilted his head to the side, considering. He glanced up at Blessingame intently, head cocked so his good eye, sharp blue, could get a clear look, as if making the man out for the first time. He nodded his head. He shook his head. Then he took up the thread of his story again, as if afraid to let it go just yet. He needed to follow it through as well.

"What could I do? I was in a rage, but against who? I couldn't be so angry with Elsa. But she didn't have the courage to step across with me into another world. I couldn't even be angry yet with him, Arthur Lewis. Not yet. I felt humiliated and ashamed.

"That night, very late, I rode my bicycle out to this house. I didn't know what I was going to do or what I wanted to do. Maybe she would be waiting for me. . . . But, ah, I knew better. I was crazy with pain. But, but. I didn't know what to do and I had to do something.

"The moon was very full and cold. All she had to do was look out the window. Any of them could look out—I didn't hide. Clear as day, better than I see today I could see these bricks and steps. Yet I was blind too. I stumbled over there on the walk and the bike clattered to the ground. I froze. But nothing happened. Silence. They were mocking me—they couldn't hear, wouldn't take notice of me even if I was sneaking up like a thief in the night, like a murderer. So, like a thief, I stole up these steps and my knife pried the mezuza away from its place and I stole the parchment out from it and I pushed the empty case back. I don't think I even knew what I was doing. A thief, I stole away with the blessing on this house and it has haunted me, more in recent years even than then. We are funny creatures, we men, haunting ourselves this way."

Hazzan fell silent, caught up in his own thoughts, weighing his own words as well as the disturbing notion that the judge had unexpectedly planted in his mind. "Was I only his toy after all? His puppet? Was he pulling strings and dancing me so I didn't even know I danced as he wished, all to hurt my father, his old friend? My father who would scarcely sit in a room with his son after this.

"Maybe this is right.

"Maybe you are right.

"A puppet—Arthur Lewis made me dance in fire and I had no clue." He smiled grimly in amazement and shook his head.

Blessingame sat silently by him on the front steps of the house. He was thinking about crossing between worlds and how easy it was and how impossible it could be. He imagined a delicate membrane between Marjorie and himself, gossamer in San Diego but all too leaden once they returned here. Tough with expectation and custom, it lay heavy, suffocating. Never were they able to pierce through to each other, or they hadn't known how.

For several minutes neither man spoke. At last Blessingame rose and fetched a screwdriver and a hammer. Without looking at Hazzan he chipped at the mezuza on the door post. He was gentle but deliberate, like a sculptor seeking to discover a form secreted in the stone. Flakes of paint dropped away. Slipping, his blade gouged the wood of the door frame. A second time it veered off the surface, gouging a pocket in his fist. "Damn," he muttered.

Another stab and a bright gash of brass lay exposed. Sweating now, frustrated and resentful, thinking of the girl Elsa and the woman Marjorie, Blessingame worked with a savage care to draw the screws without stripping them. He didn't want Marjorie resurrected for him. It had taken years enough—out of all proportion to their days together—to bury the absence of her. Now the fresh memory—so quick, so vivid he could smell her as if she'd just stolen away from his side—only brought home to him that he was older and lonely and alone. Nor did he appreciate this old man, this Jew, catching him up this way in stories and memories that had nothing to do with him. The small cylinder remained fixed to the door frame as if loath to be torn free.

Once more he pried at it with the blade. Abruptly, casually, it dropped into his palm.

All this while Hazzan sat on the steps of the porch without watching what his host was doing. Perhaps he took it for granted. Perhaps he was thinking of something else entirely.

Blessingame studied the cocoon in his palm. Its back was loose, a hinge at one end. Pushing with his nail, he peered inside to inspect the long-abandoned shell, its butterfly already fled. Instead, his eyebrows shrugging high, he discovered a tiny scroll of paper, parchment actually.

Thrown off balance, he turned awkwardly towards his guest, thrusting the cylinder out. Only at the last instant did he snatch it back—still the old man was staring off toward the trees—dig the scroll free with his nail, and tuck it into his shirt pocket.

"Here," he said, pushing the hollow mezuza at Hazzan.

The old man seemed startled, even terrified to be confronted with the physical reality of the ornament. "No," he said, shaking his head. "You must think me crazy. I must be out of my head after all these years."

He rose from the steps, refusing to touch the mezuza still extended in the other's hand, and picked up his hat from the wicker settee. "I'm sorry," he said. "I don't know why."

He paused again and took a deep breath, a full breath. "Yes, maybe yes, I do. I buried my wife not long ago, you see." He raised a hand defensively. "It was all right. A blessing really. She had been in great pain. But, well, when it was finished I had time and I was thinking of many things, and I realized that this, here, was something else I needed to finish at last."

He walked to the bottom of the steps and turned back to his host. "You have been kind to listen. What I needed was to tell someone. That's what I see. It wasn't really a story until now. And only in the telling do I see too what a silly, stupid little story it has been, clutched to my heart like something precious, a secret little prick of pain, all these years. After all these years I realize better how Arthur Lewis made me dance. And the anger doesn't rise again, it disappears like smoke. Phff, what does anger matter any more? It is too late." He patted his breast pocket. "I think I will keep this blessing after all, for however long. You keep the mezuza." He fumbled for his wallet. "I am sorry about your paint. Here, I must, allow me."

Blessingame, silent, lips pursed, stood at the top of his steps and allowed the other to reach up to him with a ten-dollar bill. "That cover it?" Hazzan asked.

"You're in the clear," said the judge.

The Long Way Home

Kathryn Ma

No one in my family knows it was me who set the fire. I did it deliberately, meaning this: I made a loose pile of my sister's eight most precious things—one for each year I bore her existence—struck a match and coaxed forth a blaze. I was eight years old; my sister Joanna was ten. I didn't know the house would go. The beds, the sofa, the green glass plates my mother used to serve cake. But I knew the match would lead to fire, and fire to destruction of possessions held dear. I was not so sorry watching it all happen. I was sorry later, the next 21 years.

My parents think it started at a faulty closet light. I will tell them today how it really happened. I have chosen today as carefully as I cupped my hand and blew, delivering my message with one long, giving breath. The paper caught, the fabric, too. They will learn all about it at five o'clock.

It's warm and sunny, a good day for confession.

"I'm here," I call as I head up the walkway to my parents' second house. My father won't remember that I told them I would visit, but my mother looks out the window, waves a happy hand. They live in the flats, in a two-bedroom box built to match its neighbors. Not as nice as their first house, but still, says my father, when anyone complains—a house. A house.

"He's wonderful today," my mother tells me. "His old self." She forgave him years ago, six weeks after his own tearful confession; since then, she looks for signs of the man she forced herself to absolve.

"Look, Dad." I hold up from my shopping bag a fat triangle of brie. His doctors have forbidden it, making it all the more worthy of his lust.

"Plenty ripe I hope," he says. He's sniffing at the package like a dog.

"Oozing," I assure him; he smacks his drooping lips. For my mother I've brought coffee beans and chocolates and embroidery needles I've already threaded in fifteen different shades of orange and red. She's working on a sunset, "Southwestern," she informed me, "for the little pillow on Dad's old chair." I imagine the outline of one noble cactus and layers of color indicating sky.

These are not bribes or offerings of peace. It is part of my job to supply delectables; I've been doing so now for more than ten years. Joanna brings her troubles, and I bring the bounty. A husband, five years older, and a promise of grandchildren in one or two years. Words of assurance on health and money; even money itself, when my parents need it. I work as a bookkeeper. I've learned accountability and caution.

"Joanna's coming." My mother has settled into her chair, under the only decent lamp in the room. I'm fetching her needlework; with my back to her, I make an extravagant face.

"I thought she was away. In Oregon or something." I'm not all that surprised. My sister has a taste for drama, a sixth sense for spectacle and final acts. She's discovered two suicides and seen a boy drown.

My mother pulls the lamp closer. She spreads her needlework over her bulbous knees. She's got skinny legs and feet that slip into girls' buckle sandals, but her knees look huge, the caps like eggshells waiting to be cracked.

"Oh you girls," she says. I'm dismayed to hear her mantra spoken with more humor than grief. Once our battles were my mother's greatest sorrow. Joanna would hate as much as I to have become a source of gentle exasperation, or worse yet, bemusement.

"Well I'm glad she's coming," I tell my mother, but already she's bent over the array of needles I've brought her, the gleam of gluttony brightening her eyes. She chooses one threaded in pale orange and slides it into her needlework with an addict's ecstasy. In the kitchen I hear my father snuffling cheese; here in the living room, my mother's swooning. Be content with the little things in life. It's practical advice, glossed by modesty and a hint of devotion. My father quotes it like Scripture to anyone dull enough to listen. I've taken up the cause, embraced it as my own. Where would I be without the little things? Eight little things brought me here. I could name you each if I had to.

It's four-thirty; I could call my father in and tell them outright, but that isn't the way I've got it planned. I perch on the loveseat wedged between my parents' chairs. I want to wait until five, which is the time it happened, while my mother was getting supper, and Joanna walking home from Trisha Blume's house. Ritual should be part of confession, memory part of penance.

"Do you remember Trish Blume?" I ask my mother. She nods right away; she lives better in the beforetime, unencumbered by The Tragedy and Dad's Big Mistake.

"Joanna's friend," says my mother. "She played the piano, something you girls wouldn't do."

"I looked her up once. She wasn't in the phone book, and the school couldn't find her."

"She was two years ahead of you."

"I liked her," I say.

"No you didn't." She jerks the needle; is she peeved at me, my fatuous declaration, or the thread, snarled like fishing line on a treacherous branch? I'm relieved to hear her annoyance; this is the mother I've known and loved.

"She was friendly when Joanna wasn't around."

"Harry," calls my mother. She has to call twice before my father hears. "Come away from that cheese, you've had enough." He shuffles into the room, his gums still working. He once was tall and carried his stoutness forward, now his spine bends him over like a firm hand on the back of his neck. I am short, like my mother, but I have sturdy legs and strong, square shoulders. I share a face with Joanna—wide cheekbones, blunt brow. In family pictures, only Joanna and I look related.

"Susie is asking about Trisha Blume." My father nods and creaks into his chair.

"A nice girl," says my father. He motions for me to bring him his paper. "You were all sweethearts. Joanna, Susie and Trish."

"Remember that Joanna was at Trisha's the night of the fire?" My father frowns at his paper; my mother covers her mouth.

"Why bring that up?" She drops her hand, starts smoothing her knees again, ironing out the past. "Why bring that up at a time like this?"

"No one was hurt, because Joanna was at Trisha's. That was lucky, don't you think?"

"You were hurt," says my mother. I have six-inch patches of grafted skin on the inside of my forearms. They are shiny but flesh-colored. When I put lotion on, they polish up and glisten. My sweater caught as I was jumping for the door.

"I forget they're even there." I tuck my wrists behind, though my arms are clothed in cotton.

"Three skin grafts," says my mother, disbelieving. She raises her voice. "Insurance paid for that, thank God. Otherwise we never could have managed."

My father opens his paper, sticks his head inside. I'm sorry she brought it up, but I knew it might happen. I'll make it better in a minute; it's almost five o'clock. Mother forgave him, but can't resist exposing him from time to time. They had no insurance on the house. My mother called, screamed at the agent. Policy cancelled, he kept on repeating, until finally she put down the phone. A year of premiums had gone unpaid. It took them six years to pay back the bank, another five to make a down payment. They borrowed money from her parents, and my mother took work as a bookkeeper's assistant.

The back door bangs; it's Joanna. I realize I've been hoping she'll get here in time. She kisses Mother, gives Dad a rough pat.

"You never use the front door," says my mother mildly.

"Sand," she replies, holding up her shoes. She's been at the beach, her dark hair is tangled. She carries their house key loose in her pocket. Has she lost her bag again or was her van broken into? No doubt another roommate has ripped her off. She shoves the key back into her pocket and appraises me.

"You look fancy," she says. I took extra effort before I left my house. My same dark hair is smoothed back with a band; my shoes are polished, and I'm wearing a soft skirt.

"I'm glad you're here. I have something to say."

"Before I have a beer?"

"Let me just say it, then you can drink," but Joanna ignores me, heads for the kitchen.

"It's cocktail hour," she calls back. The refrigerator opens and slams. I count to twenty, then twenty-five. She reappears with the beer, crackers and the rest of Dad's brie. She eats standing up, balancing her beer on a chipped plate.

I try again. "I have something I've been wanting to say." The room feels warmer than it did ten minutes ago. I have to go to the kitchen and get a glass of water. I'm determined to keep going, to get through what I've planned. We are ready for the relief of truth. Ready to speak it, ready to receive. I'm glad Joanna is here. For all my practicing, I'll only be able to do this once. I'm sorry, I mean to tell them. They'll have to forgive me; I've been atoning all these years.

"Are you all right?" asks my mother when I come back into the room. "She's been talking about the strangest things."

"About me?" Joanna smirks, tilts the beer bottle over my head.

"No, your father," says my mother. "And his silly old mistake."

"God, Susan." Joanna straightens the beer bottle, takes a drink. "That's tacky."

"Mother brought it up, not me."

"You feed him cheese, you dig up the past. Dad," says my sister. "She's trying to kill you."

I take a breath. I see my mother's spotted hands busy with her needle.

"But don't worry," Joanna continues, "I'll light a candle for you tonight. One for Mother, two for Dad."

"You, at church?" Joanna is looking straight at me, licking her fingers like she's tugging off a glove.

"No." She's smiling. "In my tub." I kick myself; I've been in her bathroom, seen the claw-footed bathtub and dozens of candles scattered about.

"Say what?" says my father, emerging from his newspaper. He sniffs the air again, his whiskers twitching. I see my mother's lip curl; Joanna freezes. We're all watching him in faint disgust, expecting a tongue or a rough, greedy pant.

"Go on, go on." He's wagging his head, congenial and forgiving. "You're all my sweethearts, my three good girls."

They look at me, waiting, and then the penny drops. My head is halved: the brain floats; the mouth turns to lead. I want to scream, but I can't, I've gone silent, after years of plugging up. Were I my mother, I'd release my famous furies. A champion, my mother, at sudden attack. She would choose without pattern—Joanna, my father, or me—and begin her assessment in a clear, staccato voice. Too noisy, too quiet, too quarrelsome, and then there's your father, only good for sowing sand. Righteousness turned to shouting, shouting turned to spew. We held very still throughout the barrage; sudden movement, we figured, might bring a hard slap. She never hit Joanna or me, but once we saw her fling a dish. Dad ducked, unnecessarily. She threw like a girl of her generation. The dish hit the window and shattered them both.

"The night of the fire," I finally begin. Joanna perks up, steps closer.

"I've been thinking about how it happened."

"It's ancient history," my mother sighs. My father looks at me mournfully, I see his shoulders slump, but his sad little act doesn't reach me. I've paid his penance, more than he's paid mine.

"Joanna said she was coming home from Trisha's. Remember that? The long way home?"

"I was," says Joanna.

"But no one saw you or knew where you were."

"I came through the woods. To the back door."

"We were in front." I'm telling my parents. "Joanna came from the house when she joined us in the front yard."

"I went right through the house. In the back door, out the front." She's watching me, fascinated, so am I. My story is unravelling like a good intention, finding new form in the telling, and the telling itself is bringing me such pleasure, pleasure not known for 21 years.

"She said you were lucky," my mother comments. "Just a little bit earlier, she was saying how much luck."

"I think she did it," I say. "I think Joanna was in the house the whole time, that she lit a fire in our closet and couldn't put it out. I found matches in her snap wallet, hidden in her purse."

"That's priceless," says Joanna.

"We don't need to talk about this, do we?" Even in a chair, my father can't straighten. "Do we, Susie?" He rubs his head with a clumsy paw. He spent the insurance money at the track, the secret nest egg that never hatched. All of it? screamed Mother. All of the money, gone like that? Dad beat his head with softened fists. The horses, oh Jesus. Every one of them let me down.

"I'll tell you what," says Mother. I hear the bite and feel a flutter. I look to Joanna, but she looks away from me. Don't leave the room, I silently pray. She doesn't. Neither of us ever turned our back on our mother, even when we were old enough to walk away.

"Here's my heart." Mother pats the arm of her chair. "Here's all of you." She jabs in a needle and gives it a twist. "Susie. Joanna. Dad. Susie. Joanna. Dad." Every name gets a needle, every needle gets a twist. Mother is screaming by the time she's finished, and Dad is curled, his head to his knees.

"Are you happy?" asks Joanna. She's looking again, straight at me. Oh I am. I am. I knew my mother would come to my rescue. She and anger are dear old friends.

"Calm down," Joanna says to Mother. "Take a breath." Mother does, gulping air. Joanna talks to her, bringing her back. She picks up Mother's sewing, which has fallen to the floor.

"You girls," says my mother, not angry anymore, but not bemused either. Joanna smoothes the sewing across our mother's lap. Only the little things demand their attention. Mother selects a needle from the studded arm of her chair.

"See to your father," she tells Joanna. She can't keep out the disdain, but Dad doesn't notice, he's still bent and curled.

"Come on, Dad." Joanna lifts him from his chair and points him toward the kitchen.

"I'm sorry," sobs my father. "I'm still so sorry I did it." Words I meant to utter and screams I meant to shout. Joanna walks, one arm at his shoulders, another at his waist. I hear her coax him with something to eat.

I stay where I am on the loveseat. The story I told has closed me down like a box. My mother glows beneath her lamp, the righteous woman at her needle. If I were to slide my hands up my arms, I could finger ancient scars, but to move, to touch, would admit to what I've done. Nothing will happen if I sit very still.

Joanna makes supper, and the three of them eat. I can hear Joanna's voice, instructional and low. After dark, she sends our parents up to bed. The water runs in the kitchen, drawers are opened, plates scraped. Joanna finishes the dishes and comes into the room. My mother switched off her lamp when Joanna called her to the kitchen, so I'm in the dark, sitting.

"You were right about the matches," says Joanna. She's brought a bottle of wine and two glasses. She pours and hands me a glass. Shoves it right into my face so I have to take it.

"'Blume's the Best,'" she says. "From Trisha's father's restaurant."

"Two books," I say.

"Trish and I used to smoke his cigarettes. In the woods, taking the long way home."

"I never tried a cigarette. Not the whole time I was a child."

"You were so good," says Joanna. She moves to Mother's chair, snaps on the light. She's sitting where Mother sat, but she doesn't look anything like her. I find I can move my feet and turn my head. I hold the glass stiffly and watch Joanna drink.

"You're not happy anymore, are you?" asks Joanna.

I shake my head, no.

"It only lasts a moment," she says. "Then it goes."

I feel a giving way, at the jawline, in the knees. My shoulders drop, and my belly loosens. Not the relief I came for tonight, but my mouth is mine again, my hands set free. I lower the glass to the coffee table. Joanna leans forward and stares into my face.

"You have a lot to tell me," she says. "I think you'll do it."

I touch my sister's shoulder, but it isn't enough, so I leave the loveseat, crouch in front of her chair. I lean till my forehead is pressed to Joanna's chin. It rests there for a second. We both pull back.

"Drink up," says Joanna. "It's cocktail hour somewhere in the world."

Had I been asked at my conception whether I wanted a sister at all, I would have answered truthfully, no thank you Lord, let me be. Look what the Lord brought me, against my fervent wishes: a mother, for anger, a father, for tears. And a sister, Lord, for the weals of love. Delivereth my balm, a burning branch.

Neighbors

Josip Novakovich

Marko Sikic drove to his grocery store on the street of Proletarian Brigades in Nizograd, Croatia. Ordinarily he walked the five blocks to his work, but now he didn't want to face the people in the streets. Croatia had declared independence from Yugoslavia, and he as a Serb didn't know what that amounted to for him. He wanted to be inconspicuous in the street, but even in his Volkswagen Golf, that proved difficult. He nearly backed into his neighbor, a retired math teacher, who had limped from the blind spot, obviously fully expecting the advantages accorded to pedestrians by law and order, as though any law and order had remained. When Marko suddenly spotted the torso in gray, he braked, and stopped a couple of feet before the tilted geometrician, who circumscribed his threats in the air with a knotty walking stick. The teacher had ordinarily been friendly.

When Marko walked into his shop, he immediately became cheerful; he enjoyed talking with customers. He flirted with women, and did it not just to sell to them, but because he loved the mutual ego boost and cheer that often resulted from it. (After a good flirtation, he felt handsome, and if there was no customer around, he combed his hair upward; it was still strong, and black, with only a few grays above his ears; his blue eyes contrasted well with the black hair and eyebrows.) He loved seeing each customer enter and scrutinize his shelves, and he attempted to guess by how the eyes moved, where the hands were, and how calm they were, whether and what the customer would buy.

Croats and Czechs and Hungarians kept buying in his shop even after the war began (in August 1991), but the Serbs who had remained in the town didn't. They avoided the appearance of banding together, and if they shopped, they went to the large ill-lit state-owned store in the center of the town.

An old friend of his, Bruno—a former soccer player for Dinamo Zagreb—came to his shop, and joked, "Could I have some patriotic beer, Nizograd Pivo?"

Marko laughed, "Maybe you'd like some plum brandy? That's even more patriotic."

"So," said Bruno, still smiling, "I hear that you're happy about the Serb invasion?" The smile only emphasized sharp creases cutting through his cheek muscles, and spidery crow-feet around his dark heavily-lidded eyes.

"Oh, no, where do you get that idea, my friend?"

"People overheard you gloating when Yugoslav jets flew over the town. And if the jets bombed, do you think the pilots would have worried whether you were here? They assume that most real Serbs have left anyway."

Marko frowned and his breathing became quick and shallow. True, when a dozen MiG jets flew over the town, he relished the mighty vibrations that came from the sound; the explosions of the sound barrier awed him, reassured him, but he didn't remember saying anything about it. Was Bruno provoking him, trying to read his mind? And Bruno did have a point; Marko could have left. Serb militia had come to him urging him to join their ranks or at least to move out of town. He'd heard stories in a nearby village about Serb soldiers cutting off two fingers from those who refused to leave so they'd keep showing the Serb three-finger victory salute. Villages that had no Serbs left in them could be set on fire and bombed by the Serb army without fear of killing their own. Still, there were so many Serbs in town, that the idea of bombing struck him as far-fetched. "I don't think there will be any bombing. That's just a show."

"Nice to hear you say that. So you have any Nizograd Pivo? I need lots, just in case they do bomb," Bruno said as if repeating the question, and maybe he was repeating it. Marko piled five half-liter amber bottles over the counter.

"How about another round?"

Marko piled five more bottles, and he noticed that Bruno's hands shook slightly, as he placed the bottles in a large plastic sack, where they clanked vulnerably. Strangely, Marko liked the signs of nerves; he wasn't the only one on the defensive; there was a camaraderie of the nervous and the compromised between them that promised limits to insincerity. Or was Bruno suffering from DTs?

"Why don't you come over to drink a couple of these?" said Bruno. "Like in the good old days. We could compare our new stamps."

"I'll try," said Marko. Although they had often drunk together, Marko knew that this time he would not visit. Maybe there would be a trap in

Bruno's place—maybe a couple of Croat thugs would knock him down. Sure, they were friends, but this was a new world disorder; what was more important, friendship or patriotism? That varied from person to person, and you never knew, actually. Well, he should be able to trust Bruno, at least, he rebuked himself. Bruno laughed in good cheer, or simulating good cheer, and said, "There are many new stamps now—Slovenian, Croatian—and soon there'll be Macedonian, Bosnian; wonderful times for us philatelists, wouldn't you say? Maybe even good days for joke collecting. Any new jokes?"

"Can't think of any."

"Jesus, things must then be really bad!" Bruno shook his head.

On the way back home, Marko was circumspect, driving slowly, attempting not to see the Croatian police on the street corners and the red chess board, Croatian emblem, on the walls, beneath the slogans, Croatia for Croats! and below the pictures of Tudjman, who, instead of resembling a father of a nation, looked like a vengeful law professor who's just come out of jail.

Marko had feared it would come to this grim state of affairs, and out of that fear he had voted for secession from Croatia, secretly, as most Serbs had done in the Krajina (the swath of Croatia with mixed Croatian and Serbian population, which used to form the buffer zone between the Ottoman and the Austro-Hungarian Empires). Milosevic in Belgrade claimed that if Croatia became an independent country, Krajina should be annexed to Serbia to protect the minority Serbs, and now the Yugoslav and Serb armies were moving into Krajina without Croatia's being able to stop them. If Krajina became Serbia, that would be nice, Marko thought. He'd be right at home. He was anyway—more so than he'd be in Serbia, where he'd visited only a couple of times, and where he'd been insulted in a bakery for using the Croatian word "kruh" for bread (Serbs say "hleb"); to live there, he'd have to change his speech.

The following night, Marko remembered what Bruno had said about bombs not being able to tell nationality. When the sirens came on, he went into the basement with his wife and two kids, partly because that was the martial law, and partly because he felt uneasy.

"Dad, will nuclear bombs blast the town?" asked the five year old, Danko.

"No."

"So why are we going into the basement?"

"To pretend that we are bombed."

"Cool!" Danko said. "But I wish they'd drop at least one."

"Shut up, both of you!" said Dara.

"Why do we all have to play stupid boy games now?" asked Mila, the six-year old daughter.

"Good question," said Dara. "That's because some boys grow to look like men but remain destructive boys."

The kids wanted to keep the light on to play checkers. The phone rang upstairs.

"Who could be calling now?" said Dara.

"I'll go and see," said Marko.

"No, don't. It might not be safe."

In the meanwhile, the phone rang the fourth time, and the message machine came on.

"We know you are there. That's all right. But please turn off the light. Or do you want us to turn it off for you?"

Marko turned off the light.

"Sons of whores, those damned cops. They probably think I keep the lights on to signal to the pilots!"

Just then, there was an amazing explosion that shook the foundations of the house with the ground, as though a major earthquake had struck, as thought different layers of the earth struggled, quarrelled, and ground over each other. Shards of bricks shattered their basement windows. Half of a brick flew in, and smashed a ten liter bottle of homemade wine from Marko's little vineyard in the hills. The red wine splashed them all, but none were hurt by the flying glass. The smell of wine was too weak to wash out the smell of fire and explosives and smoke. Before they could orient themselves, there was another blast that sent waves of hot air through the cracks in the basement windows.

"Damned bandits!" shouted Marko. "Damned Serb bandits!"

Dara's teeth chattered.

"I'm not going to forgive Milosevic this," he said. "I take this personally."

"Why, there's nothing personal in this. Bombs dropped. . . ."

"There would have been if I personally died. Or if you did."

Half an hour later, there was another round of bombing. Half ton bombs were being dropped on the machine-parts factory.

In the morning, Marko, exhausted and jittery, surveyed the air-raid damage. His house had lost one side of the roof, which was plainly blown off, all the windows were shattered. Half of the stucco on his brick walls had peeled off, and many bricks were damaged.

The house next door no longer existed, and instead of it, there was a hole in the ground lined up with red and charcoal bricks and shattered pipes. Smoke arose out of the ashes, and in that smoke, Marko thought he discerned burnt out plastic, rubber, and flesh, yes, no doubt flesh, perhaps human, perhaps animal, probably both. His neighbor, the retired math teacher, had lived with his ten cats. Thirty-five years before, he'd taught Marko fifth grade math, in a reign of terror, which Marko resented then, but appreciated now; in his business it helped to be able to calculate quickly in his head. And as the old man had aged, Marko had liked him, more and more, and occasionally, they had stood in front of their homes, and chatted, looking across the street at the town market, or into the park with steam rising in the distance from a hot spring. Now, the neighbor's cats, that was a different matter; they raised hell in their mating in February, and they were so needy that they came over to Sikic's doors and windows, and meowed, usually at three in the morning. Mila and Danko, even as toddlers grabbed the cats, and carried them, sometimes by the tail, sometimes by hind legs, and rarely right. Once, an orange tabby scratched Mila's eyelid. As the eyelid swelled, the parents rushed to the hospital, and fortunately the eye was intact. So Marko was not about to feel sorry for these cats, but for the neighbor he did.

Fragments of the neighbor's bones were found under the stones and bricks, mixed with fragments of cat bones, and one would have needed a forensic expert to sort out man and cat. So the math teacher's relatives and Marko gathered the bones, and placed them in a little coffin for an infant, and since the cemetery on the hill was too close to Serb positions, it took considerable courage to bury the box in the ground. Serbs in the hills could mistake them for Croat soldiers setting up a canon. Not having much time, they dug a shallow hole, and left the box there, with yellow soil and rocks over it, to await peace, when it could be placed deeper in the ground, and when the mathematician's picture could be found, to be set into a gilded oval frame—like a chick back into its egg—and placed on the glazed tombstone over the bones of man and cat. But for now, nobody had his picture, and there was no time for glazing the stones. To everything there's a season, a time to love, and a time to hate, a time to work, and a time to rest, and now was the time to blast stones, not to glaze them. And now was no time to linger and walk slowly, but to run.

The following night, there were more air-raid sirens. "Let's all huddle together," suggested Dara in the dark, "to keep fear away from us." Her voice came to Marko together with the fluorescent hiss and firefly luminosity of the electronic clock.

"We don't need to be that desparate," Marko said. "Hey, it's almost midnight. Let's listen to the news ."

But before the news came on, they went back to bed, for there had been no explosions, and they both fell asleep, and then woke up when Danko screamed. He crawled in bed with them, and although he'd been weaned a long time before, he probed with his hands to find breasts, and by mistake, he attempted to suck on Marko's nipple, but neither of the males found that comforting, and so Danko groped for Dara's breasts. "What did you dream, Sweetie?" she asked, but he wouldn't answer. He leaned his cheek on her breast, his ear over the nipple, and fell asleep, smiling, perhaps comforted by the murmur of the rivulets of milk from his babyhood.

In the morning, they found out on TV that there was a truce worked out by the United Nations and Cyrus Vance and by the British Lords talking in fine lispy baritones about how unbecoming it was for small nations to wage wars, how tribal, and primitive and savage, while at the same time the British Lords supported various air raids of their own in far flung regions, and while their own enforcements of unity at home resulted in quite a bit of discord and bombing.

And, after the truce, for several days, people walked in the streets, unafraid of mortar fire. Marko took advantage, despite the cold November weather, to replace the tiles on his roof, and he got the glass for his windows, and even patched up the stucco.

Passersby teased him, seeing him work like that, "Boy, are you an optimist? What's wrong with you?"

"What did you say, optometrist? A kind of visionary, you mean? Yes, you're right."

One dusty morning, Marko drove to Hungary, where groceries were much cheaper. He couldn't go straight north to Hungary, but had to deviate west, to Bjelovar, from where the roads north were clear. He envied the Hungarians—all over the place there were loud and bright ads for American and German companies, the roads were freshly asphalted; women bravely wore extremely short mini-skirts, despite the cold weather and feverish men's eyes. That could have been us, he thought, if we knew how to get along.

He drove into Pecs, and after buying sausages, cheese, canned goulash and hot peppers, and many other popular items for his store, he took a walk down a fashionable street, and ran into a bar, Playboy Club. He walked in, and five women in bikinis swarmed around him, offering him flutes of champagne. He retreated suspecting they would take his money, basically mug him. Still, where were the men? Well, why would they need the clubs when their women were undergoing a sexual revolution? He strolled in the streets, and was tempted to talk to a woman who seemed to smile at him, but that struck him as inane. But then, why did it? he wondered.

On the way back, when he crossed into Croatia, it was dark, and although he thought he knew the roads well, at one point he wondered whether he had crossed into Serb territory. Now, he shouldn't fear, he thought, he could tell them he was a Serb, but he had no papers to prove that. His ID would state that he lived in Croatia. He ran into a ramp barring train tracks, and wondered whether to wait. Perhaps it was an ambush. And then the train passed, brightly lit, with no passengers visible. Were they lying on the floor, so snipers from the woods wouldn't shoot them? Where were the engineers? Perhaps it was a ghost-train barreling across the Balkans like a smart bomb. After the train, the bell clanged and the red-and-white-striped ramp lifted. Was there anybody observing the crossing and seeing him? He turned around, and it was dark on all sides, and his breathing grew shallow. When he was a child, his grandmother had told him about monsters that lurked in the dark, and he grew so terrified, that at night he didn't dare set his foot on the floor, for fear that out of the dark, the Horned Witch, who had only one tooth, would snatch him and drag him into the underworld, to boil him in a clay pot with snakes, spiders, and death-cap mushrooms, so the devils could slurp his melted and spiced eyes, tongue, and heart. Because of that fear of the dark beneath his bed, he hadn't dared to go to the bathroom at night, and sometimes, after drinking too much tea with honey, he wetted in his bed, or woke up, struggling till dawn not to. And just so now, he felt a terrible urge to urinate, but didn't dare to stop; everywhere in the dark he imagined snipers, mines, and toothless men with long knives.

He kept driving west on small roads without edge-markings, and several times, with his heart pounding arrhythmically, he almost slid off the road. Only when he hit the major roads going to Zagreb, which, despite the war, emanated a pink aura into the foggy sky as though advertising its Eros, did he find his bearing to go toward the Orient.

When he got home, he slammed the car door, and turned on the flashlight to go in through the front, and he saw red graffiti written on the pavement in front of his house, Serbs Go Home. Next to the graffiti were new grenade markings, resembling a large flower, with one bulbous hole and scars, emanating straight out, like petals—away from the hills from which the grenade was lobbed. He wondered whether his family was all right, and he rushed inside. They were all playing dominoes in the candlelight.

The pavement sign haunted him even more than the grenade scars. The following day he didn't go to work, but stayed in bed, drank tea, and often went to the bathroom, to shave (as though that would clean all the trouble out of the way) which he did three times that day (his beard was strong, but one shave per day would do), and he brushed his teeth a dozen times. During each cup of tea he urinated several times, as though all the icy anxiety in him could be melted and dissolved and pressed out and drained, down into the subterranean traffic of filth and offal, to flow far away. There was no bombing that day, and he got several calls from his customers, mostly Croats, who were wondering whether he'd keep his store open. Most stores were closed, and it was hard to buy food, so they begged him to stay open. And yet, he was not sure whether they really begged him or gleefully and luridly tempted him into a trap, or whether they waited for him to lose his nerve and to flee, so there would be one less Serb in town, which eventually, he was sure, they all hoped would be purely Croatian.

Still, many people needed groceries, and while starving, they would not worry about his Serbdom. And so, in the morning, the next day, he went to work, and opened his shop. He had record sales. Although most people frowned, and without saying a word, bought their goods, some expressed their appreciation for his staying open. And some even told him jokes. Bruno, his old friend—so old that Marko now remembered how in fifth grade they measured their penises together with a ruler—told him this one: "A Serb, a Croat, and a Bosnian are the only survivors of a shipwreck. They are holding onto a wood-plank and freezing. A goldfish swims up to them, and the Bosnian catches it, but it slips out of his hands, and then the Croat and the Serb catch it together, if you can believe it, one holding the tail, and the other the neck, if a fish has a neck. Goldfish says, Fine and gentle people, please let me go. Ordinarily I do the three wish routine but there are three of you, so each one gets one wish. The Serb says, Oh, please put me in the middle of a tavern, dancing kolo, with accordion music and a gravel-voiced pevaljka. Done, said the fish, and the Serb vanishes in the wind, straight to a Serb tavern with a wild female singer. The Croat says, Oh, put me on an Adriatic beach, with a jug of bevanda, and make the winds blow from the South. And the fish says, I can't guarantee about the winds, because it's the second wish, but I'll put you on your beach. He disappears in a warm wind and lands on a nude beach in Croatia, where he's disappointed that there are no naked German women as there used to be. And the Bosnian says, I'm so lonely. Could you please get both of them back here? Sure, said the fish. Done."

And the whole day passed in good cheer, as though there was not a worsening war taking place. The next morning, Marko walked to his shop, whistling cheerfully. He passed by an old stuccoed house, which in the rains had lost some of the sandy layers, and now, a sign from 1945, in insistent red, appeared, *Comrade Stalin Great Friend and Protector of Small and Oppressed Nations*. And on a new bank emerged the sign, beneath bullet riddles, *Life We'll Give, But Trieste, Never!* Again in red. Of course, Tito gave Trieste back to Italy in exchange for Western protection against Stalin. *Comrade Tito Loves Children*. He had never noticed these signs before; perhaps the buildings were painted frequently enough to hide the slogans, but now, the unwashable history lurked and jeered. Marko smiled, finding the old printed signs next to graffiti-like crooked and jittery ones—Long Live President Dr. Tudjman and Croatia for Croats—humorous.

But he did not smile for long. In front of his shop lay heaps of shards. Perhaps a bomb hit the pavement and the windows were shattered? But when he came closer, he realized that was not the case. Inside the shop, all the shelves where shattered, the merchandise gone. Plum jam jars lay shattered on the floor with jam splashed, dark red, and gluey, like spilled brains. The cash register was gone. He'd taken the money along with him the night before, but the register was worth a lot. The door leading to the storage room was smashed, and splinters lay scattered on the floor.

He kneeled, with his knee bleeding on a small shard, but he didn't mind the pain. He wept. Damnation! This is the end. What's the point? It would be better if they'd killed me, at least I wouldn't have to suffer.

What should I do, what should I think that I should do? How could I think? What's there to think? You can think only if you believe in some truths. I neither believe anything nor doubt anything. This wreck is the truth, and it's finished, done.

But still, he wondered, Who did it? Who didn't do it? Serbs destroyed the town from the outside, Croats demolished it from the inside.

He walked home slowly. On the way, he noticed another shop, also Serb owned, totally demolished. Krystallnacht plagiarized.

At home, he told his wife what had happened.

"Jesus, even the Croats are insane," she said.

"What do you mean, even?"

"This is it, we got to leave!"

"No way. Where would you go? Travel requires money. Who could I sell my shop to now?" Still, all he could see was the limy clock-light, and he spoke to it, as if to a single ray of reason placed in the dark history.

"But let's go to safety." Dara pleaded. "This is horrible."

"Where? We couldn't afford to go to America."

"How about Hungary?"

"Hungarian is not even an Indo-European language. You want to live in a place where you don't understand anybody?"

"Yes, that would be wonderful! What did all this soulful understanding here get us? Here all of you have been bragging about big Slavic souls for decades, drinking yourself into blackouts to prove how chummy you were, and where are your chums now? Knifing each other. So yes, Hungary sounds great to me."

"You can't look at it objectively now. We've had a lot of fun, no matter what, in this damned federation of ours. Turn on the radio, let's see what the world says."

"Surely not that we are having fun now."

"Where would you go? In a world like this, what difference does it make where you go?"

"It's not like this in Germany and Austria."

"With our luck, as soon as we got there, it would be like this. They're sick of foreigners, exiles, Southerners; if I had a shop there, they'd firebomb it, I'm sure. Or they'd find some kind of exile camp, more or less a concentration camp, in the outskirts of Vienna, to keep us in for years on cheap sausages and water."

"You are a pessimist."

"Realist. A realist resembles a pessimist because life always leads to death. Life unavoidably ends in the worst case scenario—disease and death. So how's one to be optimistic?"

"At least we have each other, and we have our kids, and we are all healthy!"

"You call this healthy? I'm sure I have an ulcer, cancer, and if I don't this very minute, it'll grow in me. All this explosive cancer all around us can't stay only outside, it will creep in, has crept in, and it's eating me. Don't talk about health."

They didn't tell the kids anything.

At night, there were more sirens and they went back into the basement, and sat on crates of sugar and salt.

Danko said, "I hope they drop a bomb on my kindergarten."
Marko slapped him over his mouth with a backhand.
"What did you do that for?" asked Dara.
The boy cried and wailed.
"I'm sorry," Marko said. "That was an awful thing to say, I couldn't control it."
"He's just a kid."
"I know. I am sorry."
"You should be ashamed of yourself."
"O.K., enough of that." He picked up Danko, and wanted to cuddle him, but Danko bit him, and wouldn't let go. Marko pinched him, until he did. Marko's forearm was covered in warm son-spilled blood.
"See, evil has crept into all of us," he said.
"Oh, now the universe is responsible for your bad temper."
"Precisely."
"I'm hungry," said Danko.
"You have no excuse to hit our lovely child."
"Don't talk, feed him if you want to prove a point."
At least that wasn't a problem. Marko had stored quite a few supplies in the basement, but he didn't have the can opener handy so he climbed up the stairs, to get one, and as he climbed he vaguely remembered that he shouldn't take risks. What if there was an explosion now? Well, now he'd welcome it. God, please, let there be one!
He brought along spoons as well, and so the whole family feasted on refried beans and pickled peppers. They stayed in the basement until dawn, which brought light even into the dusty basement—not enough light for Marko to see the particles of dust drifting, but enough to realize that the night was over. And indeed, there were no more explosions from the aircraft or from the hills. By now everybody was asleep, the attackers, and the attacked, perhaps even God, but that did not prevent the light growing from its indigo blue into a gray haze.
Marko and Dara carried their sleeping children upstairs; Marko the older one.
"Time to sleep," Dara said.
"Yeah, right. I have a day off. Maybe a life off. Plenty of time. I don't even need to sleep." As he walked he noticed that he had a morning erection; perhaps fear had somehow translated into sexual arousal. This could be addressed somehow, and why not most simply? He said, "How about sex?"
"Are you serious?"

"Hell, yeah, the survival of the species is in question. Besides, the kids are asleep."

"Let me think about that."

"About what?"

"Sex." She yawned.

"It's not an intellectual quandary. You'll fall asleep."

"Let me at least take a bath, I haven't had one in days."

"I haven't either. How could it bother us now? We haven't sweated."

"Well, it bothers me. You better take a bath, too."

Later, in sex, he quickly ran out of breath, gasped, and rolled over, thinking he was having a heart attack. Damn, can't even do that any more! Soon however he regained breath, and, after she merely touched his abdominal muscles with her nails, his abdomen twitched and his erection came back. He renewed his efforts, and tried to recall a Hungarian in a windblown mini-skirt, any Hungarian, but he remembered no images, only concepts about images. His wife could appear overweight, but she didn't seem so to him; he found her proportionate, fleshly, voluptuous, and he liked her wild frizzy hair tickling his neck and ears and back while he clasped her. His amorous efforts didn't last more than several heart beats, and he rolled over and panted again. He was tempted to be embarrassed, but what would be the point of shame? In his heightened sense of threat, his body didn't wait for anything, in digestion, sex, breathing—everything was heightened. He didn't measure his blood pressure, but was sure it would be at least 200/120. Ten minutes later, he measured his pulse, and it was over a hundred, as though he were an astronaut just landed on the moon, and he might just as well have been one, on a moon of blossoming craters, the dark side of the moon, which the earth did not see, and did not bother to see, for where was that earth with its global villages to stop the current accelerated disasters?

Dara moaned, and he wasn't sure whether she was having a nightmare or whether she had stealthily continued to stimulate herself, to make up for his lapse.

Still, after all the sexual twitchings, and gasps, and contemplation about various pressures, he grew calm, and breathed slowly, feeling safer and safer, or more and more indifferent to whether he was safe, and so he fell asleep, with images from wakefulness dancing in various colorful forms, with falling leaves becoming schools of yellow fish, swimming deeper and deeper, and this sinking sensation was for a time comforting and pleasant. Sleep, wonderful sleep! Marko was aware of welcoming and praising his fuzzed-up consciousness. But not for long—for he was not safe, not even in sleep, where his dreams ambushed him in a kaleidoscope of blood and jam through which he tried to swim, to extricate himself, toward light, but the light turned into shards which cut into his eyes, spilling them. He woke up, sweating and shivering, relieved that it was all just a bad dream—nothing was cutting into his eyes, except the light from the window. He wasn't glued by his blood to the shards of his shop. The pleasure of waking up used to consist in some subliminal awareness that after a nightmare there would be the bright sunny denial—the rays of daylight would melt away the ghosts. He'd frequently had bad dreams, but even amidst them, he was somehow aware that all he needed to do was to wake up, and he'd be safe. And now, waking up didn't help, for the more alert he was, the more he realized that the actual threats were perhaps bigger than he had imagined. What if he stepped out in the street and a Croat soldier shot him? Maybe they'd start shooting civilian Serbs. Who's to say that stealthily they couldn't take them into the woods and shoot, massacre, burn, bury? What if, after he took several steps, a grenade fell, lobbed from the mountain from his own compatriots. What if . . . and it was not much if, to his mind now, but more likely, when. What will happen when a grenade falls . . .

The phone rang. His wife walked toward it, but he grabbed her, and said, "Don't answer. "

"Why not?"

"You don't know who is calling."

"That's the point."

"I don't want to know."

The phone rang again, and Marko guarded it, lest a family member should answer. He was glad that the answering machine didn't work; the blast that had obliterated the neighbor's house had sent a surcharge of electricity and ruined the machine. So at least he didn't have that apparatus of treachery that allowed anybody to speak right in the middle of his home, whether he welcomed it or not. Still, they are attacking me whichever way they can, Marko thought. With light, with darkness, with sound, with silence, from without and within.

"Go get yourself a bottle of beer," said his wife. "You are getting too weird, relax."

"That's not a bad idea, except, I think that if I drank one bottle of beer, I'd vomit it; just the thought of it turns my stomach." And he burped as though he'd had a case of beer.

"So, you plan to sit here, and grow crazier and crazier? We better go. At this point, even going to Serbia would be better. At least nobody is bombing it."

"True, but you're a Croat."

"They needn't know."

"They would."

"How? And so what?"

"Everybody knows everything."

"There you go again. Let's just pack."

She looked at him with contempt, her eyes almost closed, as though she needed to refract him through her eyelashes to analyze what insubstantial rays he was made of. He wondered whether she was contemptuous because of his poor sexual prowess. She looked pretty with the light creating a refracting aura through her hair, with tinges of greens and blues. And so the contempt was all the more irritating. She thinks I can't do anything, that I'm to scared to go anywhere. Am I? No, it takes more courage to stay than to run. But, look, she's sure that I can't go, and she's just taunting me, out of habit, sadism, hatred; maybe even she hates me for being a Serb. Maybe she doesn't want to go, she just wants to create some blame for me.

"All right, by God, let's do it!" he shouted, shrieked.

She recoiled back from him, in surprise. Perhaps she had counted on him saying no. He enjoyed the surprise. Plus, indeed, a change of any kind might be better than waiting, cooped up, until something irreparable could happen as it already had.

Silently, with their hands trembling minutely, they loaded up family documents, pictures, a few inherited things, such as her cuckoo clock, his grandfather's saber with fancy silverwork, several children's toys (worthless, but precious to the children at the moment), shoes, silverware, children's first drawings.

"Where are we going?" asked Mila.

"We are going skiing in the Slovenian Alps, just like the last year," said Marko.

"That's great!" she said. "Did you pack my boots? Woolens?" She looked at the packed car mistrustfully.

"Don't lie to the child," Dara said.

"Now how do you know that we won't end up there, ha?" Marko said.

Danko agreed to go anywhere cold only if he got a bar of chocolate. Marko gave it to him, and the boy chewed it and sucked on it, and as it melted, drew brown lines on his cheeks and pants, trying to clean his fingers.

"Impossible child," said Marko.

"Let him be," said Dara. "You got problems much less sweet than chocolate stripes. Wonderful, sweet boy!" She smoothed his hair, and the boy smacked his lips and glowed from motherly love and chocolate, clearly an agreeable amalgam.

As they drove out of town westward at sunset, they would pass by Marko's shop. He wondered whether to take side streets to bypass the shop, but as he looked down a few of them, they looked so desolate that they gave him a creepy sensation.

On street corners strolled many soldiers. In the beginning, there had been only Croatian police, now there was some kind of Croatian army, assembled from who knows where. By physiognomies, Marko could tell there were foreign mercenaries here—Dutch and British soccer hooligans, with tattoos on their forearms and cheeks—and there were Croats from the Hercegovina mountains, bonier and taller than the Croatian Slavonian peasants. They were total strangers, invaders in the name of defense. Maybe some of them plundered, maybe all of them did.

He certainly wouldn't miss these men, nor his shop, for that matter. He thought he wouldn't bother to look at the shop. What would be the point? He wouldn't look at it as though he were leaving Sodom before the fire and brimstone. But as they neared his shop, he slowed down for several people jaywalking and carrying something toward the location of his shop.

Red light from the sun flickered and flashed from where his shop should be. When he passed the glare, he noticed that his shop had new glass windows and a clean wooden door. He stopped and walked out of the car.

"Oh, there you are!" said Bruno through his pursed lips, which, instead of a cigarette, held large nails.

"What's going on? Who's taking over my shop?" asked Marko.

"I've been trying to call you like crazy, but you don't pick up the damned phone!"

"So, who has stolen my shop?"

"Nobody, man. We all agreed that it was a terrible thing that happened to you, and so we are rebuilding your shop."

"How's that? First you tear it down and then you build it?"

"Listen, we are all old townsfolk here. It's the outsiders who got into the war to pillage and plunder. They hope to plunder in the Serb villages, but for now, before they succeed to get there, they'll plunder here. You think it matters to them who is who? No, they want booty, war booty. It's business. Your goods are already sold, probably on the way to Serbia, and the money is in some soldiers' pockets."

"You think?"

"Yes, that's right," said another old schoolfriend of his, Ivan, who flunked out of Zagreb School of Engineering and now ran a junkyard west of town.

"They couldn't plunder your yard, though," Marko said.

"No!" laughed Ivan. "I chose my profession wisely. Got a proper training too."

"Well, why are you doing this? Who's paying for this?" Marko asked, turing his palms upward to point at the glaring glass.

"Come on. Nobody! We got spare parts here and there," said Marko. "If we were reasonable, we'd be rich. When the war's over, you can sell us beer at a discount—that'll be fair exchange."

Marko shook his head, amazed.

Bruno said, "Wait, I have a good one. Jovan, a Serb from our parts, flies to Chicago to visits his best friend, Bobo. As they meet, Jovan kisses Bobo on one cheek. . . ."

"Oh, please, spare me. I'm too shocked for jokes."

Ivan said, "It's only the tenth time he's telling this one."

"That's the only way to remember jokes," said Bruno. "Repeat them ten times."

Marko examined the new pine door, which was smoothly cut out of fresh wood that smelled of resin, and looked naked-white, virginal.

"Thanks guys, I don't know what to say and how to thank you. You've blown my mind!"

Marko walked back to the Volkswagen and told his wife that his old friends were rebuilding his shop.

"Don't get your hopes up," she said. "I am not going to wait for more explosions. Let's keep going."

He slowly and grindingly turned on the ignition, and they continued driving. They passed by several shops, a bakery, a bar, most of which were Croat owned. They were all demolished. Some were being repaired, others stayed gaping, wounded, obscene, and kept smoldering, with wet rancid smoke barely rising above the ground, drifting dustily.

What to say? Was the sight reassuring? Yes, Marko found it reassuring. He was not singled out. And now, he believed what he'd seen, was even touched.

"What are you waiting for?" Dara said. "You are changing your mind?"

"Yeah, maybe it's all going to be all right here. I have friends."

"You find all this comforting? Well, they'll burn down your shop again. They are just waiting for you to fill it up with sausages and cheese first. Let's keep going!"

Marko drove on, slowly, hoping to come up with a good argument to turn back, not to drive in a loop through Hungary into Vojvodina and Serbia.

Suddenly, after a curve, he saw flames. He stopped. There were two oil barrels, with the flames providing the light and heat. Check point. But whose? Either way, he didn't want to be checked and interrogated. But they must have seen the car, despite his turning the lights off. In the dark, the stars were sharp, wonderfully luminous, like floating celestial eyes, with fluttering rays for eyelashes. Too bad he couldn't enjoy the moment of beauty in the darkness, or perhaps because of the darkness, he in fact did enjoy it? What if it turned out to be his last moment? In the cosmic sense, it made no difference.

"What are you paralyzed for?" asked Dara. "Don't you see who it is? Don't you listen to the radio?"

He stared ahead at the checkpoint, and discerned that the four soldiers, two seated, and two strolling, wore helmets. Blue Helmets! The U.N. had set up checkpoints, to separate the warring parties. He laughed with relief. No need to be cosmic yet. A sign appropriate for a wall flashed in his mind: U.N. Friend and Protector of Small and Oppressed Nations. He drove, the Nepali soldiers stopped him, and asked him in English something he didn't understand. One soldier read in the dictionary. "Oruzje? Bombe?"

"Of course not," Marko said.

They searched the trunk. "Slivovitz?"

"No," he said. He looked on the side, and faced a machine-gun barrel poking above white sandbags. The looming eye of the gun gave him a start, and his heart skipped a beat.

Several minutes after the passed the checkpoint, Marko suddenly felt terribly sleepy, depressed, defeated. Would there be a whole series of checkpoints? Guns, borders, an infinity of obstacles.

"Watch how you drive!" said Dara. "You almost drove off the road!"

"I know it. I'm tired. It's getting late. Are you sure you want to keep going; you want to look for a hotel in Hungary?"

"Not that I want to, but that's the thing to do."

"I think it's much simpler to go back and sleep in our house."

"Well, maybe you are right. Better than in a ditch where we could end up if you keep driving like this. All right, but then we could start early in the morning. "

And so they drove through the U.N. checkpoint, where they were asked the same questions, as though in the ten minutes of absence they might have loaded up the trunk with grenades.

On the way back, they saw flames leaping out of the windows of many houses. They realized that the houses on fire belonged to the Serbs who had left and joined the Serb army. Anxiously they drove home, wondering whether the same thing had happened to their house. What were the U.N. soldiers doing. Observing?

Their house was intact. It was cold, and they had run out of heating oil. They all cuddled in one bed, covered with a thick down cover, and in the morning emerged like chicks of different birds from various eggs in the same nest, shivering in the cold. Marko called up Bruno, and soon Bruno brought him thirty liters of heating oil, and told him a dozen new jokes, all of which seemed to lack punch lines. "Stop it," said Marko. "Whoever gave you confidence in your sense of humor?"

"Clearly not you, party pooper."

Eventually, the Serb army fled from the Western Slavonian hills, during the Croatian army's first blitz offensive. Now, there were no more sirens, and people no longer spent nights in their basements but left them to their rightful inhabitants, sprouting onions, rats and cats. The townspeople could relax, but they seemed to have forgotten the art of relaxation. Many had grown thin in the war, from anxiety and bad nutrition, but some, including Marko, had put on a lot of weight. He used to live differently; everybody used to live differently; people used to walk in the town park and in the town square, but the war knocked out the habit. The siege had changed the lifestyle. People now lived like Americans; they watched more television than before (and there were more channels now), and they ate bigger meals, as if the war had created an incurable appetite in the newly independent nation. Bruno, too, had put on weight. And so, no wonder, the two old friends got together to eat in a basement cafe. As Bruno entered, his hair shining from being combed with water, he kissed Marko on his left cheek, then on the right, then again on the left, and so on, until Marko said, "Wait a minute, I know we were close, but what's going on?"

"Hush!" Bruno put his finger on his lips. "It's better that they think we are gays than Serbs!" And he laughed.

"Jesus, now you've taken up practical jokes."

"That's the joke you didn't let me finish, so I thought I'd act it out."

"Oh, thanks a lot," said Marko, drying his cheeks against his shoulders.

"See, it works for you. You are as squeamish as when you were a kid. I remember, nobody was allowed to touch you."

The two men sat down, drank beer (Marko's treat, of course) and they didn't feel satisfied with a meal of grilled chevapi and onion. They reminisced about the old days when they had eaten better and wilder; it was King Bolete season. Considering that they had remained friends even during the war, now that it was over, they trusted each other completely, even if Bruno's jokes had deteriorated. As they were finishing the spicy minced meat, they had little to say, and Marko was bored and tired. So, when Bruno suggested that they gather mushrooms in the park, Marko livened up. If nothing else, the walk could give him some fresh air and energy and free him from a clogged-up and groggy sensation.

They walked past the railroad tracks and steaming hot springs, past the hospital wing that had been blown by a ton bomb the same night that Marko's neighbor perished. Marko was a little uneasy. "Let's not go too far, there could be mines here."

"Not here, further up, outside of the town, yes, but not here. Chetniks never had control of the park."

They stared at the ground, at the colorful leaves, trying to make out round shapes of ceps. They came to a place where a cross was raised, with an inscription, which read, *To Virgin Mary, who appeared to me on this spot and spoke to me when I wanted to kill myself.* A flower wreath hung over the cross. Both men laughed at the sight; there was an inflation of Virgin Mary appearances. Could only one virgin do so much work? The cross was made with old planks of wood, perhaps from an old barn, hammered together with rusty nails, some of which bent because the wood was hard, probably oak, and the man nailing the wood perhaps had an unsteady, hurried, hand. A blue picture of the Virgin, with her head tilted, was nailed to the cross; even the white frame had grown blue in the rains. She pursed a narrow mouth with beautifully wavy and stung lips and raised her pointed fingers on the right arm timidly, not even up to her ear. And as the two friends laughed, and walked further up the hill, Marko stepped on a piece of metal, which squealed against his sole. He looked down, and he saw a round edge, a halfmoon, of a mine tilting under his shoe. He gasped in terror, expecting the mine to go off any second. "Run, my friend," he said to Bruno. "I'm standing on a mine!"

"Mother!" shouted Bruno, and ran several paces, hid behind a tree, and looked at Marko's feet.

"Don't move, " he shouted. "I'll run and get help! "

In fright, Marko was unable to move anyhow, and he perhaps wouldn't have moved, or would have jumped off, who knows, but he reached a state beyond decisions, instantly. Scorching pain as lightning shot up his neck, and another branch blazed down his left arm. Something hit him across the chest, slammed his ribs, knocked his air out and froze his lungs. The force of the bursting blood in his stopped heart jolted him forward, and he fell, with his nose plunging into the yellow leaves of beeches. His sideburns and ear scraped the cap of a cloudy-white mushroom, the destroying angel. The mine didn't go off. But his life did, and as it did, the destroying angel glowed whiter. And the wind blew silently, carrying the washed up piece of paper with the image of the fleshly narrow mouth, above the fibrillating yellow leaves.

from Blonde

Joyce Carol Oates

Pin-up 1945

The look on Glazer's face! His buddies on the *Liberty* would rag the kid mercilessly how he'd been leafing through the January '45 *Stars & Stripes* with this peeved, bored expression until turning a page he stared, bug-eyed, and his jaw truly *dropped.* Whatever was in those pulp pages had the effect on Glazer like an electric shock might've had. Then this croaking noise from him, "Jesus. My wife. *This is my w-wife!*" The magazine was snatched from him. Everybody gawking at GIRL DEFENSE WORKERS ON THE HOME FRONT and this full-page photo of the sweetest-faced girl you'd ever seen, darkish curls springing out around her head, beautiful wistful eyes and moist lips in a shy, hopeful smile, she's wearing a denim coverall snug on her young sizable breasts, and her amazing hips, with little-girl awkwardness she's holding a canister in both hands as if to spray the camera. *Norma Jeane works a 9-hour shift at Radio Plane Aircraft, Burbank, California. She is proud of her work in the war effort— "Hard work but I love it!" Here, Norma Jeane in the fuselage assembly room. Here, Norma Jeane in a pensive moment thinking of her husband Merchant Marine Seaman Recruit Buchanan Glaser currently stationed in the South Pacific.* Ragging the poor kid teasing him the name was printed Glaser not Glazer how's he so sure this little girl is his wife?—and there's a struggle over the magazine, almost it gets ripped Glazer rushes at us glaring-eyed and excited—"You fucks! Cut it out! Gimme that! *That's mine!*"

There, in Sid Haring's English class at Van Nuys High, a sniggering cadre of boys passing a magazine among them, and the furrow-browed youngish teacher confiscated it from them, tossed it into a desk drawer, until later that day he leafed through it to where the boys, dirty-minded he didn't doubt, had earmarked a page, and seeing the photo Haring pushed his glasses against the bridge of his nose and stared: Norma Jeane? Despite her heavy makeup and "sexy" pose he recognized her at once. His former student! Here was Norma Jeane Baker, so shy she hadn't been able to speak in class, tilting her head to one side with a dark-lipsticked mouth in a drunken dreamy smile and eyes half-shut in ludicrous ecstasy. This child, no more than sixteen? seventeen? in what appeared to be a translucent ruffled nightie to mid-thigh, and high-heeled shoes, and she's clutching beneath her pointed breasts a dumbly smiling panda. *Ready for a cold night's cuddle?* Sid Haring stared at the photo for a long moment sitting numbly on the edge of his desk. "I might have saved her. But how?" Like a guilty man he glanced at the window of his door in worry someone might be watching. "It isn't my fault. Is it?" He would rip the offensive photo into shreds, tear up the magazine and toss it into his wastebasket but instead he tore out the photo and tossed out the magazine; he took care not to wrinkle the full-page glossy photo of his former student but slipped it into a manila folder for safekeeping at the very bottom of the bottom drawer of his desk.

And in April, in Culver City, there was Detective Frank Widdoes of the Culver City Police Department searching the pigsty trailer of a rape-murder suspect, and Widdoes was in a furious mood holding his nose with one hand and with the other looking through a pile of girlie magazines, and there in *Pix* where the magazine was folded open to a two-page feature he saw— "That girl! Norma Jeane." The girl he'd interviewed. Pretending to believe she might have information in a murder case. She'd been so pretty, so sweet, so trusting; as his own daughter wasn't ever trusting with him any longer, or any other female of his acquaintance. "Norma Jeane Baker." Widdoes hadn't seen Norma Jeane in a year and already she looked much older. Makeup thick as a crust, and the sweet little-girl face beneath. She was posed in a bathing suit that showed practically everything she had and left just enough to the imagination, and ludicrous high heels; one of the shots was frontal, a stunner, and the other was the classic Grable pin-up stance, the girl peering coyly over her shoulder at the viewer, hands on hips, with a wink; there were red bows on the white bathing suit and in the girl's hair which was a darkish mass of tumbled, shellacked-looking curls. In the first photo she was holding a beach ball provocatively offered to the viewer and her mouth was pursed for a kiss. *What's the best cure for the blues? Our Miss*

April knows. Widdoes felt a dull pain in his chest. Not like a bullet but like he'd been hit by a blank, wadded-up cardboard out of a gun barrel. His partner asked him what found there and Widdoes said savagely, "What d'you think I'm finding? In a shithole you find shit." Unobtrusively he would roll up *Pix* to stick in a pocket for safekeeping.

In May, in his trailer office back of the smoldering junkyard on Reseda, in Van Nuys, Warren Pirig who'd been Norma Jeane's foster father stared at the cover of the new *Swank*. The cover! "Norma Jeane. Je-sus." His girl. The one he'd given up, and never once touched. The one he still dreamt of sometimes. Except she was older, more filled out, staring back at him boldly as if now she knew the score, and liked what she knew. Or anyway that's how she was posed. In a dampened and very tight T-shirt with USS SWANK in red across the front, and nothing else: the white T-shirt to her thighs, and high-heeled red shoes. Her darkish-blond hair was swept up onto her head and a few stray curls hung down. You could see every contour of her young body, her big round soft-looking breasts with defined nipples, the shadowy bush of pubic hair, the slight swell of the belly. A flush came over Warren's face. His Norma Jeane, his foster daughter he'd given up to get married at barely sixteen, at his wife's insistence, and now what? what's this mean? Her young husband was in the service and here's Norma Jeane showing tits and ass like a whore. "It isn't my fault for goddam sure. Whose?" Warren felt a powerful stab of desire and at the same time a profound disgust as if he'd gotten into something rotten. His beefy fingers itched with the impulse to do hurt. To who?

Still, he took care to preserve *Swank*, April '45. Hiding it in a drawer with old financial records.

Later that month there came Elsie Pirig into Mayer's Drugs, and the cashier called excitedly to her, to show her the new issue of *Parade*— "This is her, isn't it? That girl of yours? The one who got married a couple of years ago?" Elsie stared into the opened magazine. Norma Jeane! "Oh my God. Ohhh." Norma Jeane's hair had been plaited like Judy Garland's in *The Wizard of Oz* and she wore snug corduroy slacks and a powder-blue "handknit sweater set" and she was swinging on a country gate in an awkwardly posed but charming shot; in the background were browsing horses. *Spring in our beautiful San Fernando Valley! For instructions in how to knit this lovely sweater set in cotton wool see p. 89.* Norma Jeane was very young and very pretty but if you looked closely (as Elsie did, for sure!) you could see the tension in that bright, broad smile.

Norma Jeane was a shy backward sort of girl, what's she doing posing for pictures? In a magazine like *Parade*? Elsie was so upset she stalked out of Mayer's clutching the magazine, forgot to pay for it, drove straight to Mission Hills to see the girl's mother-in-law Bess Glazer, no time even to telephone beforehand. "Bess! Look! Did you know about this? Look who it is!"—breathlessly thrusting the copy of *Parade* into the older woman's startled face. Bess saw, and frowned, she was surprised, yes but not very surprised. "Oh, her. Norma Jeane." Elsie was shocked: Bess took it so calmly. Without a word leading Elsie through the house shaded against the powerful sun of southern California and into the brighter kitchen where out of a drawer she retrieved the January issue of *Stars & Stripes* with the feature GIRL DEFENSE WORKERS. And there was Norma Jeane, again! "Ohhh. Why didn't anybody tell me?" Elsie sank onto a chair like one kicked in the belly. Her own daughter, her foster-daughter she'd loved, in coveralls so tight you could see the curve of her buttocks, smiling at the camera in a way, Elsie would swear, Norma Jeane had never smiled at anyone in real life. *As if whoever held that camera was her closest friend.* Or maybe it was the camera that was her closest friend. A wave of emotion washed over Elsie. Twenty years taking in foster kids for the county, and never once had any of the kids turned out special, until now: Norma Jeane Baker, looking like a professional photographer's model in *Parade* and *Stars & Stripes* and God knows where else. Oh, why hadn't Norma Jeane shared this wonderful news with her? Bess was saying, with her sour-prune look, "Bucky sent this home. He's proud of it, I guess." Elsie said incredulously, "You mean you're *not*?" Bess said, sniffing, "Proud of such a thing! I should say not. The Glazers think it's shameful." Elsie was shaking her head indignantly. "*I* think it's wonderful. *I'm* proud. Norma Jeane's going to be a model—a movie star, maybe! You just wait." Bess said meanly, "She's supposed to be my son's *wife*. Her wedding vows come *first*."

You'd have to be pretty dumb, Elsie Pirig was thinking, with a smirk, to put anything else first, if you looked like Norma Jeane in these photos.

As the long dream of the war ended. Norma Jeane's year of wonders began.

Her photos in *Stars & Stripes*, *Pageant*, *Pix*, *Parade*, *Sir!*, *Salute*, *Yank*, *Swank*, *Click*, *Laff*. Beginning with the *Stars & Stripes* feature as a single lighted match might start a vast conflagration in which the match is consumed almost immediately. Phones ringing off the hook! Interested parties, all male, telephoned the editors of *Stars & Stripes* wanting to know about "Norma Jeane" from Radio Plane: was she a model? a starlet? did she have an agent? what was her last name? These calls were shunted off to the freelance Hollywood photographer Otto Öse who'd done the shoot for the magazine and who would take credit for discovering Mrs. Bucky Glazer a.k.a. Norma Jeane Baker—"Out of oblivion, in Burbank."

Otto Öse checked with Radio Plane which provided him with an address for the girl though not a telephone number and one evening in late January there was Otto slouched behind the wheel of his '38 black Buick roadster in front of the melancholy woodframe dwelling in which, evidently, she lived. A young married woman, still in her teens, living alone in such a place: almost, Otto felt sorry for her. On principle he disliked females, certainly he distrusted females, the more attractive the more seductive, the more seductive the more he distrusted them, whose souls were but flesh and whose very flesh was suffused with that pitiless blind will of which the great Schopenhauer spoke, tempting men to confuse sexual longing with a spiritual love, and tempting even intelligent men to confuse "love" with their own self-worth. Oh, Otto Öse had been forewarned! *A woman is a snare to be despised.* Yet seeing the girl trudging along the sidewalk from the trolley stop, a cold lightly falling rain, yet she seemed oblivious of the rain, too tired maybe, dispirited, in a bulky khaki jacket and a scarf tied tightly around her head, and carrying a lunch pail—a tin lunch pail, like a schoolgirl!—he stared at her with involuntary sympathy. *Yet she's of the enemy. Beware!* He rolled down his window and called to her, teasing, "Hey, baby! Smile pul-*ease*." Didn't have his camera but he made finger-motions as if taking pictures and the girl stared at him and flinched; in that instant recognizing him, though it had been many months since he'd visited Radio Plane and inveigled her into having her picture taken, and he'd never told her his name. He took so many pretty girls' pictures, and forgot them one by one, like L.A. County morgue shots he sometimes took, faces, bodies, faces, bodies, names but arbitrarily attached, one corpse is equivalent to another corpse as one pretty girl to another, and the less-than-pretty were never photographed, as if invisible or in fact non-existent, of no possible consumer worth, thus no worth to Otto's shrewd eye; except, it seemed, this Norma Jeane was turning to be something special, and a credit to Otto Öse. "Baby, c'mere. You know me, your old friend Otto Öse. Have I got a sweet surprise for you."

Hesitantly she came to his car. He presented her with three copies of *Stars & Stripes* which she hadn't yet seen, though the issue been out for weeks. As she stared at the GIRL DEFENSE WORKERS feature he told her about the calls. Magazine editors were asking about her. Modeling agencies. She'd heard of *Pageant*, right? *Yank*, *Salute*, *Pix*? "We're talking twenty bucks a bang, Norma Jeane." The girl didn't hear. She was staring at the photographs as if she had no idea who they were of, what they meant. Was she slow-witted? He remembered her extreme shyness. Just the kind of female to mold to your wishes. He hoped her husband would stay away for a long time but, too bad, the war was winding down, he'd be shipped soon. Unless he got killed. Norma Jeane licked her lips, which looked nothing like the sensuous lips in the photographs, "Oh gosh, Mr.—Oz? these pictures are . . ." Norma Jeane spoke so softly, Otto almost couldn't hear. She must have been tired from her nine-hour shift at Radio Plane, she showed so little enthusiasm. Otto said exuberantly, "Pretty good, eh? Without studio lighting. Without make-up." She said politely, "Sometimes snapshots of me look O.K. but they aren't really me. Like this isn't." Otto said, "What? Sure that's you. Who else?" Norma Jeane said, "Oh but I c-couldn't do it another time. It was just luck I guess." Otto said, irritated, "Like hell it was luck, baby. I take that as an insult. I'm a professional photographer and I make my own fuckin luck. When I take a girl's photo it's *taken*, and it's *taken* the right way. No dumbass luck involved, kid." Otto spoke in his vehement-jazzy voice which he maybe meant, maybe didn't mean; it was like playing saxophone, if you're going to play sax at all you might as well play it with all you've got. The effect on Norma Jeane was gratifying. She apologized quickly, saying, "I mean . . . I'm not really this pretty. I wish I was! She looks so sure of herself here. But you remember me, I wasn't. I'm not." Otto examined the girl in *Stars & Stripes* and the girl shivering beside the roadster, her nostrils reddened from a cold, her lipstick flaked, who smelled of talcum powder gummed with sweat, plastic dope, and said bluntly, "Kid, you're right. At the moment you look, frankly, like hell. But you're photogenic, see? That's what we've discovered." "'Photogenic'—means you kind of t-trick the camera," Norma Jeane said, "so you look better than you really are." The photographer laughed, and poked her beneath the chin as you'd poke a child who by chance has given a clever answer, though not necessarily the right answer. "Baby, that's the Hollywood secret in a nutshell. Maybe the secret of all religion, culture. 'A trick to make things look better than they really are.'" He laughed. He liked Norma Jeane, almost. She wasn't as dumb as she looked. He said, "Norma Jeane, if you're a photographer's model who looks like shit but your photos look good, then *you look good*. Because a model is her photos, nothing more. Like a movie star is her movie self, nothing more.

But don't look puzzled, kid. We're in it for the dough, trust me. *I'll* do the metaphysical-ontological brooding. *You* do what you're told." He should invite her to sit with him in the car, she'd been standing in the rain all this while shivering, but the truth was, Otto Öse so liked to hear himself talk, when he had a subject about which he felt strongly, he wasn't much aware even of his listeners. He lit another cigarette and said, reminiscing, as if the events he were recounting had happened years ago and not only a few weeks ago. "I should've called you, kid. About the photos. I handed everything over to the editor and got my check and cashed it and figured that's that. But when I looked at the contact sheets, they were so good of you, I couldn't believe what I had. The other girls were O.K. But they just faded away next to 'Norma Jeane.' Then, the prints. The guy who does my developing whistled saying? 'Je-sus, Otto! Where'd you find this sexpot?' and I said, 'What sexpot?' thinking he was kidding me, 'Y'mean the little dope girl at Radio Plane?' and I looked at the prints, and I thought, 'Am I crazy?' But at the magazine all the calls were about *you*." The girl was shivering and blowing her nose into a ragged tissue. She laughed a squeaky scared laugh that sounded wise for her years. "No, Mr. Oz. The calls were about *you*."

His name, he told Norma Jeane, was OTTO ÖSE. He spelled it for her.

The way he pronounced his name you knew he was somebody important. Or would one day be.

Norma Jeane asked shyly, "Is that a real name?"

"'Real'? I live in Hollywood, Baby. We're as 'real' as required."

What did such an answer mean? Norma Jeane was thinking he was like a gnome or a troll in a fairy tale. You asked them questions and they gave riddle answers. They told the truth, but not a truth you could decipher.

Still, she'd climbed into the roadster. After ten minutes he noticed her shivering, and invited her inside, and her first thought was *No I better not*, thinking of Bucky Glazer, how hurt and jealous Bucky would be, but the next she knew she was inside Otto Öse's car, and excited, not liking the way he looked at her, but it made her laugh the way he looked at her, with mock familiarity, intimacy, his left eyelid drooping in a wink. His mouth twitchy with smiles. *Like we're looking at each other close up, like on pillows. Pillow talk!* Otto Öse was saying, "You look like the kind of girl the sharks are gonna swarm over. You heard of feeding frenzy in the ocean? What you need, Norma Jeane, is a big-shark protector. Like me."

Otto Öse boasted he'd been photographing girls—"gurls"—for thirty-six years (but he couldn't be that old, this must be one or his jokes) and there was no shortage of good-looking "gurls" arriving in Hollywood every day by bus, train, car, hopeful of being discovered like Lana Turner at the drugstore, that American-success-story bullshit but once in a while a girl came along who struck the right people—that's to say men—as special, and maybe, just maybe, she really was special. What was special to a few men might be special to millions of men. Men were the test—"The average asshole, I mean. Why not take advantage of the situation? As I said, twenty bucks a shot." Norma Jeane shook her head in wonder. "Twenty *dollars*? After deductions I make not quite nine a day." And the work was exhausting and the smells of the dope room were giving her serious headaches. She'd wake in the night coughing and unable to catch her breath. And when the War ended—for sure, she'd be out of a job. No matter how good Norma Jeane was at her work, no matter how her foreman praised her, when the men returned they'd be given their old jobs back. With raises.

Well, that was only just. Wasn't it? Men serving their country.

Her old job was *Mrs. Bucky Glazer*.

(At first she'd written to Bucky every day practically, wetting her stationery with tears. Oh, she'd missed him! Her Daddy-honey. Her tireless Big Thing. She'd included little poems out of her journal—"In you/ The World is new./ Without you/ Where am I?"—but out of tact perhaps Bucky never referred to these, so she stopped sending them. Men didn't cared much for poetry, she knew. In turn Bucky wrote to Norma Jeane much less frequently, fact-filled but brief letters about the *Liberty* and his crew-mates and what he'd seen of the Pacific, which wasn't much, and how he was missing home after all, couldn't wait for a leave, Bucky's handwriting sloping down the page like a stumbling man with erasures and crossed-out words and misspellings, so Norma Jeane was distracted trying to make sense of what she read. Poor Bucky! They'd given him a diploma at Mission Hills High maybe because he'd been a star athlete but his writing skills were about seventh grade.)

Otto Öse was saying, "You deaf? I said twenty bucks, I mean twenty bucks." He exhaled smoke impatiently. With a little experience, a portfolio it's called, you'll be pulling twenty-five, thirty. Of course, you need connections. Say I interest one of the girlie-glossies like *Swank*, we'll make more. A *Swank* cover, we're talking fifty bucks for you up front."

Otto Öse wasn't telling Norma Jeane what he'd be making, if she was making fifty.

Norma Jeane looked at Öse fearfully. Almost, like a child she wanted to press her hands over her ears, climb out of his car and run away. The

Dark Prince! She stared out over the rooftops and ragged palm trees of the city at the lights of the RKO twenty miles away, in yearning. But now he'd actually come for her, she wasn't ready.

Öse was saying, "Tomorrow, then. I'll get *Pageant* to send a taxi prepaid to this address." Norma Jeane laughed, this was so preposterous. "*Tomorrow?* Oh, but—I'm w-working tomorrow." "Oh no, you're not, baby," Öse said, "you're calling in sick." "What! I'll get docked my pay." "Fuck your lousy pay. *Pageant's* paying you—and me. Didn't I tell you, twenty bucks up front?" "Yes, but—that isn't real, is it?" "What the fuck isn't 'real'? You got bricks for brains, sweetheart? I tell you a simple fact and not the most improbable fact, not a Ripley's Believe-It-Or-Not fact, and you look at me with those dopey goo-goo eyes and say, 'Oh is it r-real?'" Cruelly Öse mimicked Norma Jeane's breathy voice and stammer. Norm Jeane laughed, it was so rude. So mean. So intimate. Like truly this stranger knew *her*. Weakly she said, "But, Mr. Öse—what should I w-wear? I don't have anything really nice." Öse laughed, poking her another time beneath the chin. "Clothes ain't gonna be your problem, baby. Clothes is only gonna get in the way."

"Let's celebrate! *I'm* thirsty."

It was past 6:30 P.M., and dusk. Without waiting for Norma Jeane's reply, Öse started the roadster and drove through Burbank to a roadhouse a few miles away. Norma Jeane was faint with hunger but was thinking if only she could have a bath! wash her hair! change into some nice clothes that didn't smell of dope! she'd be more in a mood to celebrate. But Öse was boasting of the magazine work he'd done, contract "starlets" he'd photographed for RKO, Twentieth-Century Fox, The Studio, modeling agencies with which he was connected; Norma Jeane could only listen. In the roadhouse, Öse ordered rum-and-cokes for them both, though Norma Jeane protested she didn't drink. Öse grinned at her, leaning his hawkish face across the booth. "'Don't drink'—what's it, some loony religious principle? Like Old Yahweh gives a serious crap what you, or any of us, puts in your mouth? in your gut?" Norma Jeane was embarrassed, and didn't know how to reply; but when the rum-and-cokes came, she refused to drink. Öse lifted her glass to her mouth, as you might do with a small stubborn child, but Norma Jeane shook her head, annoyed, and pushed his hand away—"I said *no*, Mr. Öse! *I don't drink.*" "Don't tell me, let me guess—you're Christian Science?" Öse laughed. Norma Jeane bit her lip, and refused to answer; and Öse took the rum-and-coke for his own. "Call me 'Otto,' baby. 'Mr. Öse' is my old man buried in a cornfield back in Nebraska."

When their dinners came, Öse only picked at his, continuing to drink, and to light up his parchment cigarettes, which were in fact small slender cigars, while Norma Jeane ate hungrily. She hated Öse watching her with his sharp hawk-eyes! Observing, with approval, "You eat like a healthy little filly, baby. But go easy on the starches. You're the kind of basically boneless girl whose gonna get thick in the middle by age thirty-five—if you live that long." Norma Jeane swallowed a large mouthful of baked potato, and flared up, "Why do you say *that*, Mr. Öse? Everything you say is laced with meanness like rat poison. You said that before." "Said what before?" Öse asked. "About me not living long." "Hell I did. When? I didn't." "You *did*! At the factory. You said, 'Maybe you won't live long.' I didn't like that." "Well hell, I'm sorry," Öse said affably. "You can live—forever! Into the twenty-first century! When the rest of us are dust! *Viva*!" With a flourish he drained his third glass of rum-and-coke. Norma Jeane was trembling with anger, yet at the same time placated. Strange, how Öse seemed to know her more intimately than Bucky ever had, though she'd lived with Bucky for more than two years and she'd made love with Bucky more times than she could have counted! As if the photographer even without his camera could peer into her soul where Bucky Glazer had never once glanced. As if lovemaking between a man and a woman was no more than a certain duration in time and when it was over, it was over. *But a baby, having a baby out of your actual body—that would be real, wouldn't it?*

Norma Jeane heard herself saying suddenly, "W-What I wanted was a baby, and my husband didn't. I would still love him, if—" Her voice trailed off, Öse was staring at her with such a look of incredulity and dislike. "What? You're not pregnant, are you?" Norma Jeane said, "N-No. I meant—" "You're sure you're not pregnant?" "Of course I'm sure. What I'd wanted—" "If you're pregnant, sweetheart, level with me now. Just tell Otto the truth." "I said no I'm not! Don't you listen? I was only saying—" Öse interrupted, "If we get a deal going, you and me, and there's magazines lined up, don't you tell me one day, 'Ohhhh Mr. O-Öse, I'm knocked up!'—'cause I'm gonna be seriously pissed to hear that. There's been a time, with you Okie gur-rls"—he pronounced the word as if it were a mild amusing obscenity, "—I've got to feeling like an abortion-broker instead of a photographer: on the phone making arrangements with Jew doctors, giving teary little gur-rls one hundred bucks to get their innards scraped clean 'cause they were too dumb to tell the guy, what you gotta clearly tell the guy, *use a rubber on the dick*! *Or it's dick verboten*."

Norma Jeane's fork clattered onto her plate. "Mr. Öse—"

"'Otto,' I said. It ain't hard, c'mon— '*Ot-to*'—a spondee."

"—I hate you."

Öse laughed, expelling smoke out of his nostrils and mouth.

"Oh no, you don't. Not Norma Jeane."

Instead of driving Norma Jeane home to the boarding house, Öse pulled off the road into a desolate wooded area on the outskirts of Burbank. In the near distance, on a raised bed, a long rattling freight train was passing. It was past nine-thirty and Norma Jeane was dazed with exhaustion. Quickly she said, "Mr. Öse, Otto—I want to go right home. I don't want to be here. I'm a m-married woman—" Öse said affably, his hoarse voice slurred with drink, "Then nothing's gonna surprise you, baby, right? Two years married you said to this high school stud, you've been banged fourteen hundred sixty times minimum, what's the big deal?" Öse reached for Norma Jeane who was cringing against the car door and she raised both elbows to ward him off. He grunted, struck in his skinny chest; Norma Jeane was stronger than he'd expected. "Please, Mr. Öse! Please don't." Öse laughed, his face hot. In the roadhouse he'd pushed his dinner away half eaten, he'd been drinking steadily and he'd been in the men's room so long Norma Jeane began to worry he'd passed out there or was badly sick and how would she get home? He'd returned after ten minutes with damp-combed spiky hair and a look about his face like he'd dipped it in cold water with partially good results. But he'd driven the funky little Buick roadster with drunken aggressiveness. In the parked car he was arguing, "Y'know who Otto Öse is, baby? Your only friend. Nobody in a girl's life like for instance your overseas hubby or your folks—if you got folks: you Okies split up a lot, populating our jails and public institutions—wants you to *do well*. On your own, with a 'career.' They want you to *fail*; they want you to fall on your *ass*. But not Ot-to Öse! I want you to *succeed*. It's nickels and dimes today, big bucks tomorrow—maybe. But there is no way to Big Bucks except by me, Otto. 'The way is strait, the eye of the needle is narrow.' Ask Mary Baker. Y'hearing me? Or just playing dumb?"

Norma Jeane tried to open the door, but the handle wouldn't turn.

Öse said, touching her shoulder, "There's nothing to be afraid of with *me*. I *promise*. I never force girls to do what they don't truly want to do. Not once in forty years! Not like this madman-pervert who raped and murdered and 'dismembered' a girl in West Hollywood last Saturday, a 'starlet' at M-G-M. Heard about her? Same guy, they think, cut up a girl in Culver City a few months ago. Otto Öse ain't nothing like *that*."

Norma Jeane said, "Please let me out! Or—take me home. *I don't want to be here.*"

Öse said, with a pretense or hurt, "Hey, I thought we were gonna celebrate. Baby, C'mon! Have mercy." In his position behind the wheel he shifted, grunting as he unzipped his trousers; his long legs got in the way, he banged a knee and cursed. Norma Jeane sat paralyzed, staring. In all her life she'd only made love with one boy and that was Bucky Glazer and the look on her face of fear, disgust, revulsion must've been so genuine, Öse saw and relented, in the way of a screen comic in close-up, "Aw shucks, baby, what'd ya think? You been misjudging me? All Otto's got for you gurls is—" as out of the crotch of his trousers he extracted a small tubular object and held it out to Norma Jeane, on the palm of his hand.

A roll of film.

Next morning Norma Jeane was picked up at her boarding house by a pre-paid Checker Cab and driven to Otto Öse's studio in West Hollywood. Through 1945 she would do more than two dozen magazine and advertising features with the photographer. She would earn between ten and thirty dollars for most sittings, as much as fifty for a cover. (What did Otto Öse earn? Norma Jeane never thought to ask.) By the time of the German surrender in May she would be signed up with the Preene Modeling Agency of Hollywood. By the time of the Hiroshima and Nagasaki bombings in August, she would be signed up with a Hollywood film agent.

She'd have earned much more than she was earning if she'd been willing to pose nude, but this she absolutely refused. "Oh no. *I will never.*"

Finding Ruth

Chaim Potok

She did not often go to parties but, as luck would have it, decided to attend that one. She walked the five blocks from her apartment to the turn-of-the-century white clapboard house, climbed the creaky stairs to the first-floor landing, and opened the door onto a rhapsody of sensations: talk, heat, music, scents. The apartment was crowded. Two small table fans labored futilely against the heat. Eager for a familiar face, she noticed the unfamiliar man at the window, who, at about six foot three, was the tallest person in the room. He wore blue jeans and a black T-shirt and stood angled forward, staring out the open window at the hot night. Then she saw someone she knew and made her way through the crowd. She was filling a paper plate with food, when she heard behind her, "Hi, I'm Dylan Hart."

Close up he was strikingly tall, even for her.

She said, "I'm Keren Edwards."

"Nice to meet you, Karen."

"Keren. With two e's."

"Keren."

"There are three hundred years of Kerens in my family."

"Really? I'm the first Dylan. Where is your family from?"

"Vermont. Yours?"

"New York. Where are you in the university?"

"I'm finishing third year law. And you?"

"Physics," he said. "Quantum mechanics."

"I don't know anything about quantum mechanics."

"I don't know anything about law. Anything good to eat, Keren?"

"Try the hummus and eggplant."

He had narrow bony shoulders. Long light-brown hair lay uncombed over a smooth forehead. His face was long and thin; his wide-set eyes, separated by a deep v-shaped wedge above the straight nose, were a translucent green. The slightly turned-down corners of his mouth gave him a dour look. He reached for a paper plate. She stood watching him load up on hummus and eggplant. He nodded at her and walked away. She saw him move nimbly through the crowd, holding his plate at shoulder-height, and go over to where he had stood earlier at the window.

She wandered through the room, occasionally talking to a friend. She found herself drifting toward the window, where he stood rocking back and forth on his feet. He wore loafers and no socks.

She said, "Hi, I'm Keren Edwards."

He looked startled. It took him a moment to turn away from wherever he had been and focus upon her.

"Keren with two e's. The hummus and eggplant are good."

"I didn't prepare the food, I'm only eating it. Is Dylan after Bob or Thomas?"

"Thomas. My mother's passion in her college days."

"What do your folks do in New York?"

"My father makes money. What do your folks do in Vermont?"

"My father makes souls."

"Is that soles with an e?"

"My father is a Presbyterian minister."

"I don't know anything about Presbyterians."

"I don't know anything about making money."

He looked at her a moment: the straight blond hair worn in a bob to just below the ears; the long slender neck; the hazel eyes; the little-girl's face; and the tall full woman's body. "Lucky you," he said, and looked back out the window.

She spotted a member of her environmental law seminar at the other side of the room. It could not have taken her much more than a minute to cross the room through the crowd. She looked back. He was nowhere to be seen.

Two days later she ran into him again, at a cafe on Harvard Square. It was a sweltering evening, the air malign under drooping trees, the streets dusty and crowded. Gasoline fumes floated like yellow fog in the lamppost lights. They were repaving the square, almost every other day reconfiguring the streets with orange traffic cones. To run into him that way she had to have chosen certain streets over others, carefully navigated the traffic cones, determined which lights she would wait at—gone through countless stops, turns, and hesitations. The first time, the party, as luck would have it, chance. But now, twice—

She walked slowly toward him. He was sitting alone at a sidewalk table, bent over a cup of coffee and a yellow pad, writing with concentration.

She hesitated only briefly. "Will I disturb you if I say 'Hi' again?"

He straightened. It took him an effort to remove his eyes from what he had been writing and fix them on her. He said, "Karen."

"Keren."

"Right, Keren. With two e's."

"I was passing by."

"Well, hi. Again."

He wore blue jeans and a red T-shirt, and shoes without socks. She had not noticed before how thin his arms were, his fingers long and delicately boned. He held a ballpoint pen in his right hand. She saw that the page he had been working on was filled with equations.

He said quietly, "You're disturbing me. Of course, you're disturbing me. But sit down, sit down."

He put the pen into the pocket of his T-shirt and closed the pad.

A waiter came over.

"Jack, another one for me, and—" He looked at Keren.

"Cappuccino, please."

The waiter went away.

On the clogged torn-up tar-smelling street drivers honked their horns. Punks roamed the crowded sidewalk and a teenager flashed by on a skateboard.

She asked, "Are you here for the summer?"

"Working on a project. And you?"

"I have a job with the Environmental Protection Agency in Boston."

"Chasing bad corporations?"

"Right now it's mostly research. What are you writing your dissertation on?"

He hesitated briefly. "Elusive particles. Electrons deflected by photons and traveling backward and forward in time."

"I have no idea what you just said. Did I hear you say backward and forward in time?"

"An electron is a sub-atomic particle that can go in any direction, at any speed, forward or backward in time, once it encounters a photon, a quantum of radiant energy. Unusually capricious, the electron."

"What do you do with the capricious electron?"

"I chase them."

The waiter came over with their order. When he left, she said, "I made it through high-school physics mostly thanks to the grace of God."

A group of teenagers walked past the cafe, some smoking, their baseball caps on backwards. On the street the traffic was stalled.

He looked at her curiously. "Is that a figure of speech, or are you religious?"

"I'm a somewhat lapsed Christian."

"I'm Jewish."

"Are you an observant Jew?"

"Very definitely not."

"What do you believe in?"

"I believe in atoms."

"Atoms? How can you believe in atoms?"

"Minute particles that move around perpetually, repelling and attracting each other."

"But atoms you *know*. What do you *believe* in?"

He was holding his cup, jiggling it slightly, peering at the ripples that moved across the surface of the coffee.

"In my junior year at Princeton, I had a brief, intense battle with myself, and decided that I believed in my work and not much else."

She sipped from her cup.

He said, looking at her, "I don't remember meeting anyone from Vermont before. Is that the way you all talk up there?"

Her hand trembled as she put the cup down. "Up there, there are regional variations. Does everyone sound the same in New York?"

He leaned forward in his chair. "Is it fair to say that we don't seem to have anything in common?"

"Well, we're both tall."

"So are giraffes."

"I had great sympathy for giraffes when I was growing up. Did you know that giraffes give birth simply by standing and dropping their young? The infant giraffe has a way to fall before he hits the ground."

"At least he's moving in an uninterrupted straight line. But aside from being tall, we really don't have anything in common. So there's not much point to our seeing each other, is there?"

She finished her cappuccino.

"Will I see you again?" he asked.

"Only if you learn to pronounce my name with two e's,"

"Keren," he said. "Keren."

He called two days later and they arranged to meet for coffee at a cafe on Mount Auburn Street near Adams House. She took a sidewalk table.

It was early evening. She sat and waited. The construction crews had finished the day's labor on the square: a strip of street paved; another section torn up; a bewildering new array of traffic cones. A hot wind blew brown dust across the dry sidewalks. She smelled the dust in the stifling air and suddenly saw him darting and weaving among the crawling cars on the street. He carried a briefcase, clasping it tightly to himself shoulder high with both arms as if it were a child. He had on blue jeans and a green T-shirt, and shoes without socks. He was unshaven, flushed and sweaty.

"Sorry to be late."

"It's all right. I wasn't waiting long."

"How've you been?"

"I'm okay. How are you?"

"Tired, exasperated."

"Chasing electrons?"

"And other elusive things."

A waiter in a white shirt and dark trousers came over to them. "What can I get you guys?"

"Coffee black, three sugars."

She ordered a cappuccino.

The waiter left.

She said, "Three sugars, Dylan?"

"Jolts my electrons."

"Sends them backwards and forwards in time?"

"I hope not backwards."

"When do you expect to finish?"

"What?"

"The dissertation."

"Maybe December, maybe next summer."

"And then?"

He shrugged. They sat looking at the traffic.

The waiter came with their order. "Thanks," Dylan said. "Sure thing," said the waiter.

The lamppost lights came on. Throngs of people made their way silently along the sidewalks. You could walk with ease along the tops of the cars stalled on the street. The cafe was crowded.

She said, "My parents are coming in for the graduation."

"Proud of their lawyer daughter?"

"They struggled to give me this education. I'm the first woman in our family to have made it this far."

"The first in three hundred years of Kerens? Are they proud of you working for the E.P.A.?"

"Actually, my father wants me to work for the church."

"Aha, parental payback time. My father doesn't want me doing science, he wants me to learn the business. More than a hundred years of financiers, investment bankers, and power brokers in my family. I'm the first scientist. A major disappointment. I am no good with money. I was always trying to get to the point of things right off. I could never get to the point of things when it came to money."

"What things were you trying to get to the point of?"

"Everything. Our TV set, the car, the lawn mower, the safe, computers, lab equipment, the laws of physics, lasers, microscopes, missiles, space vehicles, electrons, neutrinos. Everything."

"Were you ever interested in getting to the point of God?"

"God? Hardly."

"I believe in an interfering God."

He was silent a moment. "I thought you said you were a somewhat lapsed Christian."

"An interfering God is not exclusively a Christian idea."

"I don't know really what the words 'interfering God' mean."

"I believe that grace is God's way of enhancing a human being's potential in the natural world."

"You do? And we haven't even gotten to talking about Jesus yet."

"That's the part that's lapsed."

He studied her a moment, then drank from his cup. "Keren with two e's," he said. "Short form of Kerenhappuch, one of the daughters of Job. I looked it up. Has the name really been in your family for three hundred years?"

"Yes, absolutely. Borne by pious, stalwart New England women, on my mother's side. The kind that made the cloth for their families, knit the stockings and leggings, spun and wove wool and flax, carried pails of water from the well, cooked, and had ten children. On *my* father's side, there was Jonathan Edwards, the Connecticut minister who—"

"I know about Jonathan Edwards. About the middle of the eighteenth century. He stirred up the church in the colonies. The Great Awakening, it's called. Big spiritual revival, an inner revolution. On my father's side, there was this near mythic character who helped put up barricades in Berlin in the failed 1848 revolution, ran off to America, worked selling cheap clothes from pushcarts for a while, went into the real estate business, began buying apartment houses, and then built tenements in Manhattan and became very rich."

She put her hands on her lap.

"Your cappuccino is getting cold."

She drank unsteadily from her cup.

"Now we have giraffes and revolutionaries in common," he said.

"How do you know about Jonathan Edwards?"

"The only good non-science teacher I ever cared about was the woman who taught American history in our high school. Mrs. Emily Wright. A wise and wonderful woman from an old New York WASP family."

She finished the cappuccino. Her face was flushed and there was a sheen of perspiration on her forehead and upper lip.

He sat looking at her. "Where do you live?"

"Near Radcliffe Yard. You don't have to walk me."

"I think I'll go back to the lab. There's a problem I can't seem to get to the point of."

"Electrons?"

"Retaliatory Unassisted Transmission Headings."

She laughed. "I'm sorry—"

"It has to do with lasers and guidance systems." He paid the bill and reached for the briefcase. "I enjoyed talking to you, Karen. Keren."

She watched him thread his way through the traffic in the street.

He called her the following evening.

"I can't be there tomorrow."

"I don't expect you to."

"Good luck and congratulations."

Her parents were staying in a hotel near the square. The evening before graduation they took her to dinner in a place just off Mount Auburn Street, around the corner from the cafe where she had been with Dylan; an expensive Italian restaurant they could ill afford. Her father, very tall in a dark suit and white shirt and tie, and with a haggard ivory-white face and a full head of neatly combed graying hair, carried himself with care-worn dignity. She had not seen her parents since Christmas. Her heart ached at how much her father had aged.

He cleared his throat. He had begun having trouble with his "golden box," as he called it, his voice. "You should come home, daughter. Come home and take the position with Larry Dugan. In four years, five years, when he retires, you'll begin to be a force in the church."

"I don't think so, Father."

"Dugan is searching. Dugan will find someone else."

"I hope he finds someone good. I truly do."

"Stubborn, stubborn. Always stubborn. High school, college. Stubborn."

Her mother, a tall handsome woman with a firm mouth and stern blue eyes, said, "Father, we mustn't quarrel on this joyous occasion."

"Come home, have a career, meet someone, raise a family. Isn't that what all young women want today?"

"Are you seeing anyone, Keren?" asked her mother.

"No, Mother."

Her mother said, "Let's thank the Lord for His blessings, and for the special grace He bestows upon our beloved youngest daughter."

Her father cleared his throat. "We'll pray together," he said, bowing his head.

Her parents went home soon after the graduation. She went to a party and said goodbye to friends. He did not call that day nor the next. She sat alone in her small apartment, thinking, There is no cause and effect at work here, nothing logical. The humid air pressed on her skin. The void inside her grew.

Four days went by. Then, a week. Why should he call? She had no claim on him. Nothing had been exchanged between them.

She found his name in the phone book. He lived not far from the square. She called but the phone went unanswered. The next day she called the graduate physics department.

"We have no Dylan Hart," a woman's voice answered. "You must mean Michael D. Hart."

"If that's the only Hart."

"I'll put you through to his lab."

"Who?" said a man's voice.

"Michael D. Hart. Dylan Hart."

"Are you a friend of Dylan's?"

"Yes."

"What did you say your name was?"

"Keren Edwards. I just graduated from the Law School."

"Well, Karen, Dylan's away."

"Away? As in out of town?"

"Away."

"Do you know for how long?"

"With Dylan we never know how long."

"Sorry to trouble you."

"No trouble at all."

Mornings she walked the brick-paved streets from her apartment to

Harvard Square. Men worked jackhammers tearing up the ground. There were cement mixers and hot-tar carriers and steamrollers. Earth-moving trucks choked the street. The Cambridge sky was iron, the air gritty with tar and soil. A pall of yellow dust hung over the square. She breathed the dust and entered the subway and rode to Boston. In the office she worked as an assistant to a lawyer who was determining if a chemical plant was violating federal regulations. Evenings she studied law books: she would need to pass her bar exams to sign court documents and to appear in court. Her floor fan stirred the smothering air. From time to time she raised her eyes from the books, feeling keen longing like a weight on her chest. But, really, nothing had been said. They had met twice by chance and once by intent. Could anything be read into that? Michael D. Hart. Did he do that often, go away like that? Through the haze of acute craving, she heard the phone ring.

"Hi," a man's voice said. "Karen?"

"Keren." She was half-asleep. "Yes."

"It's Dylan."

Suddenly fully awake. "Dylan. Hello."

"I was out of town and just got back." He sounded tired.

"Is your family all right?"

"It had nothing to do with my family. How are you?"

"I'm well."

"Are you free tomorrow evening? Can you meet me at the Pamplona at six?"

At ten past six he climbed the stairs to the cafe and found her waiting for him at a table on the terrace near the outside wall. She had to look twice to recognize him. He was wearing a charcoal gray suit and a white shirt and gray tie, and polished black shoes without socks. His hair was combed. There was an ugly welt along the right side of his forehead.

He said, "Hi. I'm Dylan Hart."

"Hello, Dylan. What did you do to your head?"

"Low ceiling on the commuter plane to Chicago."

"You took a commuter from here to Chicago?"

"On my way back yesterday from a gold mine near Spearfish in the Dakotas."

"You were in the Dakotas?"

"Beautiful country."

"What were you doing in a gold mine in the Dakotas?"

"Working in a neutrino laboratory. Parts of that gold mine and that puddle-jumping commuter are very definitely not for tall people. Are you hungry? I'm starved. Let's not stay here. There's a nice place nearby."

They walked along the street. He had a long brisk stride. She followed beside him easily. Currents of humid air drifted through the street, carrying the smell of the river. The street was crowded with summer-session people still walking around awed by Cambridge.

"You look good in a suit," she said. She wanted to ask why he didn't wear socks, but decided not to.

"Debriefing in Boston. Government bigwigs. You look good, as always."

She felt herself filled with a rush of warmth. He brought her to the same Italian restaurant where she had eaten dinner with her parents the evening before the graduation. Wine-red carpeting with pale orange floral patterns; subdued chandelier lighting; tasseled table lamps with softly burning electric lights inside Tiffany-style shades; plush chairs; a magical trompe-l'oeil Venice on delicately textured wall paper: the campanile in the Piazza San Marco, the Grand Canal and the Church of Santa Maria della Salute, a gondolier on a bridge, the Palace of the Doges, gondolini in a regatta, the lion of Saint Mark, the clock tower with its face of gold and enamel bearing signs of the Zodiac. It was before the dinner hour.

They were seated without a reservation. About half a dozen couples were at tables.

The waiter came over and they ordered drinks.

"It's good to see you, Keren."

"Good to see you, Dylan. You look exhausted. Do you go away like this often?"

"With very little notice sometimes."

"To the gold mine?"

"And other places."

"My father used to be an itinerant preacher. He traveled a lot when we were kids."

"How many kids were you?"

"I have two older sisters. One lives in Los Angeles and teaches in the church. The other is a missionary in Africa."

"Is that what you all do at some time, missionary work and teaching?"

"Many, not all."

"And that's what your father wants you to do?"

"He wants me to do legal work for the church and become a lobbyist."

"What did you tell him?"

"I said I didn't think so."

"You would rather police the polluters. Oil refineries, sewage plants, nitrogen oxide emissions. Karen, the E.P.A. watch person."

"My father never once asked me what I do at the E.P.A. He thinks it's government interference with our stewardship of the earth."

Their drinks came.

"Cheers," he said.

"Cheers."

"I have one younger sister."

"What does she do?"

"She makes money. Nearly everyone in my family makes money or is part of the support system for those who make money."

The waiter came over for their food order.

"Everything is good here," Dylan said. "I like the veal. Environmentally sound."

When the waiter had gone, she said, "I really shouldn't have talked that way about my father. He's an educated and decent man."

"Karen, my father is Columbia and Yale. But he's a single-minded peasant when it comes to the world of finance. Give a peasant a giraffe and he'll harness it to a plow. He wants to know why I don't use all the science to help him develop his new title insurance company and help my sister with her mortgage servicing firm, instead of, instead of—"

"Chasing neutrinos in a gold mine."

"He doesn't know anything about that."

"What does your mother say?"

"My mother? My mother doesn't get involved. She reads Dylan Thomas."

"My mother used to read us stories from the Bible on the nights when my father was away and we were all alone in the house. We'd lie on the big double bed in my parents' bedroom, with my mother in her nightgown and long braids, and she'd read to us."

"You were brought up with Jesus on the cross? Didn't it give you nightmares?"

"No, no, she turned my father's leaving into occasions when she would read to us about the Hebrew Matriarchs. My father would read to us about Jesus, and my mother would read about Sarah, Rebekah, Rachel, and Leah. And Ruth the Moabite. It's what we had for bedtime stories instead of *Hansel and Gretel* and *Snow White* and *Rumpelstilskin* and *Cinderella*."

"Ruth the Moabite. Pious, stalwart Ruth—"

"You know the story of Ruth?"

"I went to an expensive, private Jewish high school in Manhattan."

"You had a WASP teacher in your Jewish high school?"

He finished his drink. "We had a few of them. There was Mrs.

Wright, who taught American history. There was patient Mr. Lawrence, in whose chemistry class I blew up a test tube trying out sodium in water. Brainy Mr. Roberts took me along to a math conference in Atlanta. Dapper Mr. Donaldson steered me toward physics. Some of my best teachers were WASPs."

"A WASP teacher taught you about Ruth?"

"No, that was Rabbi Simon. He had us act it out in class. Different students read the dialogue."

"What part did you read?"

"Actually, I was a passive listener. Very uninterested in Ruth."

"I loved her. I'd lie very still in that big bed with my eyes closed, listening to my mother read to us about a woman who marries a man in her own country who is not of her people, journeys with her mother-in-law to her husband's land after her husband dies, marries a kinsman named Boaz, and becomes the ancestress of King David. I'd imagine the harvest time, I'd see Ruth gleaning in the fields, I'd feel the sunlight and the heat, I'd see her lying down in the granary, I'd hear her talking to Boaz. My sisters thought it was a boring story. But I loved it. Madame Curie and Eleanor Roosevelt and Ruth were the only women I knew about who had somehow made their own destiny."

He was listening with his mouth slightly open, his eyes intent upon her face. The restaurant was beginning to fill up. Two couples recognized Dylan as they entered, and waved to him. The waiter came with their food. He was Italian, very solicitous. Prego. Parmizan? Ground pepper? More water? Bread? Everything molto bene? Enjoy the meal.

They ate quietly for a while.

He asked, "Do you like your salmon?"

"Very much."

"The veal is excellent. I like to come here whenever I get back from a trip."

"How often is that?"

"The fourth time this year."

"Where have you been?"

"Once, on a Pacific atoll, where I caught bronchitis. And twice in the desert in New Mexico, where I came back the first time with a bad case of sun-poisoning."

"And the gold mine, where you bumped your head."

"Well, actually, I bumped my head on that commuter flight to Chicago."

"Can I ask what you do?"

"I'm with the National Defense Program."

"You're a doctoral student, and you're working with the National Defense Program?"

"Actually, I'm doing post-doctoral work. Lasers and guidance systems. They recruited me."

"Retaliatory something-or-other?"

"Retaliatory Unassisted Transmission Headings."

"Retaliatory against what?"

"Ballistic missiles."

"Is it dangerous work?"

"Yes, but I'm not in the dangerous part of it."

"Are you with the—what do they call it—Strategic-something-or-other? Strategic Defense Initiative?"

He looked down at his plate. On the wall above his head, gondoliers guided their boats toward the Piazza San Marco and a little girl in a blue hat fed pigeons in the square.

"I'm afraid we might be going a bit past the line," he said.

They finished eating in silence.

"Do you want any dessert? Coffee? I'll get the check and walk you to your apartment."

Outside the light was fading. She thought she could still smell the river in the sultry air. She felt him beside her, tall and thin and somewhat loose-jointed.

She said, "I enjoyed being with you, Dylan."

"So did I. Good company, good food."

"But you still think giraffes and revolutionaries aren't enough common ground."

"Maybe we can add Ruth to the list. I have an aunt named Ruth, my mother's younger sister."

"Does she make money too?"

"Actually, no. She teaches comparative literature at Princeton."

"So now we have giraffes, revolutionaries, and Ruth."

They came to the square. The lamppost lights had come on and the cones shone on the newly surfaced pitch-black streets. The square teemed with summer people. In front of the store near the cafe where she had met Dylan by chance, a scruffy old man stood playing "Summertime" on a clarinet. At the table where she had interrupted Dylan's writing, she saw two women about her age, drinking coffee and talking.

They followed the traffic cones, which brought them to a brick-paved sidewalk. Two blocks down, they walked past a turn-of-the-century white clapboard house. An electric fixture burned over the porch door and two ground-floor windows were lit. The first-floor apartment where the party had taken place was dark.

She said, pointing up to the windows of the apartment, "I went because my place was unbearably hot and I was tired of my law books and just wanted to get out."

"Actually, I was invited by someone in my lab, who forgot to show up."

"No!"

"If he had come, I probably would have spent the evening with him and the people he wanted me to meet."

"I know you'll laugh at this, but my mother would say that was the hand of God. She would stop at the passage in the story of Ruth where it says that 'her hap was to light on a part of the field belonging to Boaz,' and she'd remind us that it didn't just *happen* that Ruth gleaned in the field of Boaz, it was the hand of God guiding her destiny."

"The hand of your interfering God."

"Leading Ruth to Boaz and the birth of David."

"Keren, most of the important events in our lives happen to us by chance."

"I don't believe that."

"I wonder where your interfering God was when the hap of the Jews of Europe was to light on Auschwitz."

"There are mysteries for which we don't have answers, Dylan."

"This is definitely not going into the list of things we have in common."

"Does that mean that you won't come up for a cup of coffee?"

"I'd like a cup of coffee," he said.

They approached a long section of sidewalk, not unusual in that neighborhood, where the brick paving had been pulled up and removed, revealing open earth.

"Careful," he said, taking her hand.

She felt the raw pebbled earth under her shoes and his fingers on her arm. Dear Lord, she thought, if Your hand isn't here, it isn't anywhere. They walked along the quiet street in the embowering darkness of tall trees whose roots were thrusting through the sidewalk pavement, and came to an old single house set back on a grassy lawn. He followed her up the front porch and through a wooden door and up two flights of dimly lit creaky stairs to a narrow landing with two doors. She opened the door to the right and they went inside.

The air was hot. She turned on lights. It was a studio apartment. To the left of the door a section was set off by a wall to form a tiny kitchen. She hurried to open windows and switch on the floor fan. He stood near the door, looking at the small kitchen table and two chairs, the bookcases against the wall, the easy chair and the futon, the shelf with her tape deck, the table with the small TV. On her walls were posters and photographs of redwood forests, Yellowstone, the floor of Bryce Canyon National Park, the Colorado River, the Grand Canyon, Arizona buttes, the Muir Woods. An orange and yellow throw rug lay in front of the futon.

"Please take off your jacket, Dylan, and make yourself comfortable."

He put the jacket on the futon, and loosened his tie. It was always a fascination to come into the apartment of a woman he had known only in cafes or bars or at dinner. The floors and walls and furniture told you more than the talk.

"I have French coffee, if you want. Strong coffee."

"Sure."

"And lemon chiffon cake."

"Sounds good."

"Sit down, Dylan. Please."

He sat at the kitchen table, watching her. She wore an A-line, scoop-neck, sleeveless pale-green linen dress, with a cameo brooch below her left shoulder, cream-colored on a caramel-colored background. He watched her quick, efficient movements at the sink and stove. A young and soft and pretty face, a gentle face. The short blond hair. The bright hazel eyes. That accent. A small Vermont town. A Bible-reading mother, a pulpit-pounding father. Something about her. An aura. Not so much the sexuality, though there was certainly that, and powerfully, but a grace, and a strong and unyielding solidity.

He said, "What is that brooch you're wearing?"

"It was my grandmother's, my mother's mother. She left it to me."

"Another of the Kerens?"

"Keren Anne Bradley. She had nine children. Worked for the church most of her life, and died at eighty-seven."

"Is there longevity in your family?"

"On both sides."

"There's none in mine, as far as I know. The men all die of heart-failure from too much work."

"Are you telling me that's one more item we don't have in common?"

He pointed toward the walls. "All these books on religion in your library. Required reading for Presbyterians?"

"Required reading for religion majors at the University of Pennsylvania."

"Rosenzweig, Buber, Heschel, and Levinas?"

"I did honors in contemporary Jewish thought."

"What did you write on?"

"The title of my thesis was, *The Event and the Other: Against Totality*."

"I have no idea what that means."

"I have no idea what Retaliatory Unassisted Transmission Headings means."

"Isn't this where we started?"

"No. This time I'm preparing the food. Do you want sugar in your coffee."

"Absolutely. Do your parents mind your Jewish studies?"

"Why would they mind? It was some of the people in the town who were small-minded, not my parents. It wasn't easy growing up as a girl with brains. And as the daughter of the minister who was bringing people to Jesus. The uppity Edwards girl. Too smart for us church folk. All those books she's reading. Those strange ideas in her head about women. Ruth was my salvation. I kept telling myself if Ruth could get out of her world, I could get out of mine."

She brought the coffee to the table.

"Let me help you with something."

"There are spoons and forks in that drawer."

He had been sitting with his legs crossed, the bare skin above his shoes showing. He stood and crossed to the cabinets and in the tiny space of the kitchen brushed against her. She gave him a brief look, color rising to her face. He brought the utensils to the table.

She said, "Three sugars isn't good for you, Dylan."

"I'll take two."

"Can I cut you a piece of cake?"

"Sure."

"How much of your work can you talk about?"

"Ask, and I'll tell you what I can."

"What do you do out in New Mexico and in the Pacific?"

"We test anti-missile missiles. We send missiles up and we try to knock them down with other missiles."

"With your retaliatory thing?"

"That's what we're testing."

"What does unassisted transmission headings mean?"

He said after a moment, "That's a name I invented. It's a guidance system to keep track of tens of thousands of highspeed objects and analyze billions of pieces of information coming to us from sensors and weapons platforms. We want to be able to destroy at least eighty percent of the enemy's missiles while leaving most of our own retaliatory capacity intact."

"Is it working?"

"No program like that can be written without the help of computers."

"Why are you doing it?"

"Because it's close to impossible. And because I'd rather we had it than the other side."

"Have you been able to knock anything down?"

"Actually, I'm afraid that now we may really be going past the line."

"All right, Dylan. I understand about lines."

"Did you bake this cake?"

"Yes. It's my mother's cake. I bake it for myself when things get difficult."

"Are things difficult?"

"The bar exams this July. Studying. Hours alone."

"I like the way you arrange things, Keren. The posters and photographs on the walls. That one of the Grand Canyon. Impressive."

"What's the point to saving us from missiles, Dylan, if there's no earth left to save?"

"Everything so neat. My place is a mess."

"My mother taught us to keep an orderly home."

"My mother never had to worry about that. Others did it for her."

"What does your mother do, besides read Dylan Thomas?"

"She reads Allan Ginsberg, and spends my father's money on charitable enterprises."

"What's her name?"

"My mother? Grace."

She laughed. "No!"

"Actually, her name is Lydia. Lydia Helen Kaplan Hart."

She sipped from her cup. "You know, if I had a different name, you might not have trouble with it."

"What do you mean, a different name?"

"I could take the name Ruth."

"I don't understand."

"If I added it. Keren Ruth. Or Ruth Keren. Ruth K. Edwards."

"Why would you do that?"

"They tell you to pick a new name. Somebody daughter of Abraham and Sarah."

He put his cup down. "I'm not asking—"

"It has nothing to do with you, Dylan. It started before law school."

"This is not an issue with me, Keren."

"I've been studying for nearly a year with a teacher in Boston."

"Do your parents know?" he asked after a pause.
"When the time comes, I'll tell them."
"I really don't think I'm ready—"
"I'm not asking you for anything, Dylan."
He gazed at her a moment. "Actually, I was getting used to Keren."
"Do you think you'll have a problem getting used to Ruth?"

Rose

Stephen Schottenfeld

It is the winter of '47 and Rose is always there. In our apartment, in our lives—Rose with her dumpy body, her puffball hair, and gigantic nerves. She was my father's sister and she lived down the street with her husband Murray—a union man (the schluffer, in her words)—and her two boys. And each day, Rose would come to our apartment and roll out her grievances. My mother would stand in the living room and listen, then remind Rose of the time not too long ago when a husband with steady wages and a pension was a godsend.

"Yes, there was," Rose would say. "But now there's more. Don't tell me there isn't. And Murray doesn't see it. Everyone's out there grabbing, and he just keeps going slow. He is not a progressive thinker. He is not an adventurous man. I'll tell you what he is—what he knows. He knows all the names of the ballplayers. He knows the batting averages, the pitchers. All kinds of statistics. He knows everything—he knows nothing."

My mother would shake her head and Rose would stare at the handwoven drapes or glance through the doorway at the new bedroom set. We had just hired a decorator and there were signs of him everywhere.

"Why did you marry him then?" my mother would say.

"Who should I have married? You make it like there was a line. There was no one else knocking, in case you didn't know. Murray was not elbowing through a crowd. He wasn't. And he kept after me. He kept coming around. Every day, there he was. And still, I tell you—everyone knows I did him a favor when I married him."

"I wonder how they know, Rose. But let me tell you something."

"Fine."

"Let me tell you something, Rose. Are you listening to me?"

"Go."

"You keep giving him an earful, it's no wonder he's deaf to you. The more you say, the less he'll do."

"What you know. If I didn't give him an earful, he wouldn't move. If I'm gruff with him, that's why it is."

"You don't give him a moment's peace. Not one. I've told you time and again he's a good father."

"Why shouldn't he be? But let me tell *you* something, Esther. You think they're not ashamed of him? You think they don't see what the other men are doing? Everyone else out there reading the stocks and him with the scores. Sure, he takes them to the ballgames, to the fights. He gives them time. But they're not stupid. They see what he is. A weak and insignificant man."

My mother shaking her head and Rose just standing there, hard-mouthed. "To say that about him—your husband. To stand here and say that. So what—he won't set the world on fire. That's not what he's looking to do. Leave him be. There are others out there who aren't so good."

"That's my consolation? That there's worse. It's easy for you to say, when my brother is buying up Knickerbocker Avenue . . ."

"One building, Rose . . ."

"Mister moneybags. With new furniture, new couches and drapes. With a fancy new restaurant every Saturday night. I've got the same appetite as you, Esther. I like to taste new things. Good living, just like the rest of us. So don't tell me about Murray. Don't tell me because you just don't know."

And Rose glaring at Mom—the fashion plate—because every few months Dad would take her to Loehmanns and she'd pick out all this finery, and Rose would see the stuff and rush to Klein's and dig around for a knockoff—the exact same dress, except the cut wasn't right or the color was shaded wrong, or even if it was the exact same dress, she just couldn't wear it well because she had a misshapen figure and she simply lacked grace. But still, she'd come back boasting, "I got the same dress, but you wouldn't believe the nothing it cost. I paid crumbs for it and it's just as nice." And my mother would grimace because the dress was close enough and now the two of them were like twins.

Rose was right about my father, though. About the money. In the following week, he bought another piece of property and, with Rose's urging, offered it to Murray—to manage it. Collect the rents, respond to complaints, keep the place clean, and make a nice chunk of change. It was a gift, but Murray knew it was coattail stuff; more importantly, he simply wasn't interested.

"What do I want with your property?" he said, and when my father mentioned that Rose might want a different answer, he said, "Let *her* manage it, then. I've got my work."

When Rose learned that Murray had rejected the offer, she marched over and asked what happened.

"What happened?" my father said. "He said no, what happened."

"Then you make him say yes."

"He is what he is, Rose."

Rose didn't stick around to tell my father what that was. She stormed off.

"She's gonna look for him one day," my father said, "he'll be hanging from the ceiling."

But it was Rose, not Murray, who was tormented. She had a slew of ailments, real and imagined. Bunions, indigestion, gall stones, palpitations, migraines, depression, fear of heights and crowds. She had an internist, a shrink, and other handlers; she kept them all very busy. And shortly after Murray said no to the management deal, Rose had her second breakdown. In the days leading up to it, she had stopped coming by, and we learned from Murray that he had come home—he worked the lobster shift at the *Times*—and found her screaming, panic-stricken. He tried calming her, he said, but she just got worse. He called her shrink and when the man arrived, he took a look at her, turned to Murray, and said that Rose needed to go in.

She was in the hospital for ten days. She returned stunned. Slowed speech, blunted nerves, dulled memory. For a week, my mother would go over there and tend to her—dress her, comb her hair. She was like a child, my mother would say, and we'd hear about Rose's blank face, her washed-out eyes, her draggy steps.

Rose wanted nothing to do with Murray—didn't want to see him, hear him, know he was there. So Murray stayed away. When he came home from work, he slept. When he woke in the early afternoon, he padded through the apartment, saying, "How's my Rosey? Better, right? She'll pull through just fine, a little rest is all. She's exhausted from it. Dog-tired, and why shouldn't she be? I call her chop-chop, because she's always in her heels and she's always in a rush. Rest. Rest is what she needs. You're not in pain, are you, Rosey?" And Rose not even looking at him, so Murray turned to my mother and said, "The only pain I like is *champagne*." And Rose bristling now because she'd heard that joke more than the telephone—just another example of Murray going nowhere. And Murray saying, "You're a doll to do this, Esther," as he scooted out the door for his billiards, or off to the bar for some baseball-talk with the elbow-benders (the lazies, Rose would say), to rehash the series—Gionfriddo's catch, Lavagetto's double, Branca's acework busted up in the fifth, and the various gopher balls slugged—and back in the apartment, Rose slumped in her straight chair, shaking her head, and my mother nodding, and Rose saying, "I don't see what's so goddamn funny," and my mother nodding some more, and Rose, pale-voiced but strengthening now, "In ten years, if he's ever made good, he can be the funnyman. Tell me every one of his stupid jokes, and I might laugh." And within days, Rose was as vigilant as ever.

She finally gave up on him. She had poked and prodded, but Murray would never change. In her eyes, he was a failure not because of his union job, but because he was so content with it. When he talked about engraving, about the cylinders and the handwork, the etching and the dabbing, you could hear his pride. He was not only a tradesmen, but an artist. But Rose didn't want to know from art; she wanted to know where it got you at the end of the day—which was damn far, my mother would tell her—but there was no convincing Rose. Murray's life was penny-ante stuff. He would never stack up to my father or the other men in the family. And every day that he worked his union job and played his billiards and watched his baseball and dawdled with the crossword, while everyone else was busy making a killing, was another day that their lives had receded a bit further.

Rose didn't divorce him; she just cropped him out of the picture. She stopped wasting any energy on him and channeled it all onto the boys—who already had a healthy dose of her. If she had married an irrelevant man, her children would more than compensate. This she was damn sure of. In fact, the more she considered it, the more it made sense, because that was what all my father's hard work was for, anyway—our great leap forward.

And this is where the story becomes my brother's—although my brother never felt that his life was his, so perhaps this story shouldn't be either. Regardless, any Brooklyn memory must begin with Rose. My older brother Milton was the same age as Rose's older son, Alan. They were rivals because Rose made it this way—she was ever-eager for her boys to outdistance us—and because my parents, in not disputing this competition, confirmed it. Alan was truly gifted. He had spent the past summer upstate at Camp Rising Sun for promising youths, which sounded like a farce until you heard Rose sing about it, and you immediately felt that the adolescent world comprised those shining stars who had gone there and would inevitably prosper and those misfits who hadn't and would certainly be passed over. My brother, who had not gone to Camp Rising Sun, but instead had worked in Dad's carpet store, was not a misfit. He was a solid student with similar grades, but he was clearly a step behind. Once, he had asked Alan which subjects gave him trouble and Alan responded, "In *that* school?" In the winter of '47, both were applying to college. It was obviously an anxious time.

Not just because of Rose, either. It was made anxious by my father, too, whose schooling ended at thirteen, when he emigrated from Austria. He first worked as a hotel hatchecker; one of his tasks was to run upstairs and notify some politician that the press had found out about the floozy in the room, and he might want to clear out. He learned floor covering from his older brother, Abe, then got a bank loan, rented some space, bought some rolls of linoleum and carpets, and started up the business. He became a leader in our community—founding member of the Kiwanis Club, vice president of the synagogue—but he lamented his education. When he gave speeches, he feared that his deficiencies would show through. He listened to the radio, for the language. As a young man, he clipped Woodrow Wilson's speeches out of the newspaper—not for the politics, but the eloquence. He believed so strongly in education. He spoke about it constantly. "You will not have my limitations," was his refrain.

In the winter of '47, I was in the tenth grade and I was too busy studying to notice much of anything. But when I talked to my brother, I could see that he was stumbling. After school, I'd sit at my desk. My brother would enter our room, talk distractedly, then leave.

"You must be excited for college," I'd say.

"I must be."

"Where do you think you'll go?"

"Huh?"

"Where do you think you'll go?"

"I'll go."

"Which place needs the best grades?"

"All of them."

"What kind?"

"Tops. The kind you're getting now. So don't you worry."

When Rose was outside with her boys and she spotted Jamesy, the local dimwit, she'd say, "Look at Mister dum-dum." Jamesy lived with his mother on Cypress Avenue; he was the closest thing to a street person in our lives. And each day, he'd lumber up the block until he found a stoop to sit against and drum his wooden sticks. He'd stay there for a good hour, muttering, smiling, tapping out some mindless paradiddle, and Rose would point to him and scare her boys. "Take a good look," she'd say. "This is without an education. The only job you'll get is keeper of the key to the men's room. Mister Custodian they'll call you."

Rose had a specific education in mind. Medicine. Perhaps because medicine and doctors played such a role in her life—although it might have been the typical prestige thing. For all I know, Alan and Jerry really wanted to be doctors, but when they mentioned it, there was a strong sense of recitation. One suspected it had been drilled into them. I shouldn't be so quick to judge; I wanted to be a doctor, too. My brother didn't know what he wanted—just not to be Dad.

"You know, if Dad were in school, he'd get lousy grades," he'd say.

"What's that supposed to mean?"

"He'd be real lost. He'd work like a dog, but he'd have a real hard time."

"He stopped in the seventh grade, what do you expect?"

He waved me away. I went back to my book. "Just remember," he said, "you can never study too hard. If you think you're studying too hard, that moment you're thinking about it, you're not studying at all."

"You sound like Rose."

He smiled. "Oh yeah?"

"You sound like Rose when she's crazy."

"I'll bet." He stood up. "Rose in fairyland." He crossed the room and mumbled, "What am I doing here?"

"Where you going?"

"Out the door. Outside. Out."

"It's cold."

"Good."

Mom wanted to move to Manhattan. We had the money now, and she wanted to get the hell away from Rose. But Dad wouldn't have it. "The store's here," he said. Most of the family was, too, and every Sunday he'd sit in the living room, with his black book, and call them. "Why don't you let them call *you* for once?" my brother would say, and my father responded, "What's the difference?" The only one who used the phone more than Dad was Rose. She called the family, her doctors, the high school guidance counselor, college administrators, city officials. She used it like a hotline.

She left one person off her list, though—her father. Zaideh lived in an apartment above the carpet store. He lived rent-free, courtesy of my father. My brother liked to go and talk with him. Perhaps they commiserated about Rose.

"You know what Zaideh said about Rose? 'A high opinion of herself, backed by nothing.' "

"That's his daughter," I said.

He smiled. "That's what he said. Do you know what your Zaideh does?"

"He's your Zaideh, too."

"I'm talking to you. Do you know about the basement? In the store?"

"No."

"Well, they got one. A trapdoor leads down to it. There's some carpets there, and these barrels with pickles and kraut. And wine. It's all Zaideh's. He makes it, keeps it down there. And during the day, he goes for a little taste. Except he doesn't stop with the sample. He's a drinker, you know. Not like Dad, with his glass of hot water. Dad finds him sometimes, up against a barrel, passed out."

"Near the pickles?"

"Huh?"

"Because he's pickled."

"That's clever, Nathan. You're a sharp one."

"Must smell pretty bad down there," I said.

"Zaideh's used to smell. Worked in a tannery."

"When?"

"In Austria."

"I was gonna say—hasn't worked since he got here."

"Brought the whole family over, is what he did."

"Dad would have made it himself."

"Fat chance, at thirteen? Anyway, Zaideh doesn't owe a thing. Just sit in his basement, eat his pickles, and fart."

"Sounds nice."

"If he wants a little air, steps outside. Smokes his cigar, drinks his schnapps. Kibitzes with the customers. Acts like the mayor of Knickerbocker Avenue."

"Heck of a contribution."

"You ever hear him, about how he rode around, schlugging goyim?"

"I heard it all. Fed his kids butter by the spoonful. Great stories. Dirt poor."

But he wasn't listening. "Zaideh with his trap door. You know what I call that? His escape hatch. Goes downstairs to his little hideaway. Like crawling down a hole. Just keep out. He's got the life."

"What's he got? Dad pays for everything. Apartment, car."

"Dad likes it that way. Gets something out of it. Gets to walk proud."

"So."

"Calls his store, 'M. Berman and Son.' It's his store and he won't even put his name on it. So selfless. Just remember, when you get your college degree, it'll say the same thing. Except this time, S. Berman."

"You too, then."

"Yeah, me too."

"Why do you talk about Dad like that?"

He waved me away. "I'm just talking." He stared out the window, at the alleyway. He turned back. "Anyway, that basement would be a great hangout. Got the wine right there and everything."

"Why do you want to get drunk so bad?"

"Why do I want to get drunk so bad?"

"Yeah."

"Why am I talking to you?"

"Fine. Go talk to mom."

"Those are my options."

"Talk to Jamesy then. He's outside."

"I saw him."

"Yeah, he'll agree with you. Except he nods his head all day, so it's not like it matters."

He turned to leave, then said, "You should go there sometime."

"Where? The basement?"

"Got the Old World down there."

"What do I want with the Old World?"

"Could learn something from it."

"I got enough to learn. History every day for an hour."

"Oh, that's your history?"

"My history? What's with you?"

"What?"

"Giving me this fatherland stuff. Dad's the only one who davens here."

"So."

"So, you talk a lot."

"Oh, yeah?"

"A lot of nonsense."

"Well, maybe I'm turning fanatic, right now."

"I doubt it. But in case you do, synagogue's that way."

"I know where it is."

And the next morning, he davened with Dad. I walked into the living room and saw them in the bedroom, side by side, swaying. I thought he was doing it just to spite me, so that night I joked, "I'll tell Mom to blow the shofar when dinner's ready." He just smiled and said, "You do that."

Each day, he davened. And about a week into it, I spotted him in a storefront, reading with Rabbi Feder. The rabbi sat there with his broad hat, reading his siddur, and my brother followed intently.

He brought books home. Buber and Torah and Talmud. One day he's talking about Zaideh, the next it's Kabbalah. It happened that fast. He read passages out loud, to see if they sounded as good as they looked on the page. He stayed with it for two months, until Rose came in with the letter.

Arms extended, the letter shaking in her hand. She was exultant. "Columbia!" she screamed. My mother went white. "Alan's going to Columbia!" She read the entire thing. My mother congratulated her. "Yes, yes," Rose said. "And an easier ticket to their medical school, once you're there." My brother left the room. He walked past them and stepped outside.

That night, at dinner, my father said, "You applied to Columbia?" He was merely stating it. My brother nodded. "We'll hear soon, then."

"This happens with the mail," my mother said.

Over the next few days, the others heard as well. Carlucci's boy to Fordham, Fazio's to NYU, Feldman's to City College.

My brother stopped davening. When I asked him why, he said, "How about you getting in there for once?" A few nights later, we were in our room and I looked up from my desk and saw him on his bed, staring at the wall. When he spotted me, he returned to his book. "There's a lot of ways to get distracted reading this stuff," he said. I nodded. I stared down at my textbook, but I could see he wasn't reading. A few minutes passed. "I've got my whole life to read this," he said, and he stood up and stepped to the window.

I watched him stare out at the alleyway.

"Zaideh keeps a kosher home," he said. "Except he never eats there." He shook his head, then turned to me. "Dad davens in the morning. He does his duck walks and his stretches, too. A bunch of movements, if you ask me." He glanced at my textbook. "I'm amazed how you study. You're non-stop, you know that."

I shrugged.

"Really, you are. I hear Dad talking about you. You're making him proud."

"You, too."

"Yeah. But there's only one report card in that wallet."

I looked away.

"Not your fault, Nathan. I'm just saying. He shows it to customers. Last summer, when I worked there, I saw him. Probably didn't mean it, but there I was. Feather in his cap, you are." He set his book on the nightstand and sat down on the bed. "You know, we should hang out sometime."

"Where?"

"Christ, out. You sound scared."

"No, I'm not."

"What do you think I'm gonna do to you?"

"Nothing. I was just asking. It'd be fun to do something."

"Yeah? We could catch a feature, then. Or better yet, we could go to the Garden, watch the fights."

"That sounds good."

"Yeah?" He stared at the floor. "Dad's never liked the fights. He likes the runners. Glenn Cunningham. You know about him? The miler?"

"A little."

"A little. Well, Glenn Cunningham's not supposed to be running. Was burned as a kid. Real bad. Doctors said he'd never walk. But he showed them. Did he ever. That farmboy beats everybody. Dad loves that stuff. He could care less about the running. The story, he loves. Real bootstraps stuff. Now if you could find a boxer, a real gimp, with no punch, except he's got this jaw, so he won't go down—that'd be a fighter for Dad. Champ or not, you'd have a fan."

I nodded.

"The fights. We should go soon. I'm not gonna be here much longer. Farewell to this place."

"Me, too."

"That's right. Boarding school. When do you head up there?"

"I thought September, but now they want me in the summer, to catch up."

"When?"

"June."

"How do you like that. You're getting out before me. Figures. Well, you might be going first, but I'm going farther."

"You think you'll go to Cornell?"

He shrugged. "Yeah. Cornell. Far, faraway Cornell."

I think my brother would have stopped davening even if not for Rose. When it came to Judaism, the younger family members went through the motions. Granted, there were a few with a stronger devotion, but for the most part, we knew we weren't here to be better Jews. But if my brother was looking for something—and he clearly was—perhaps Rose did get in the way just a bit. It's hard to consider God and tradition with Rose in your living room. My brother wanted rituals not merely separate but stronger than his surroundings. The competition, the striving; he simply couldn't cancel out everything. At least, not through Judaism.

Each day, the mail brought nothing and the house grew quieter. At the dinner table, my father mentioned a customer, my mother nodded, and we fell silent again.

And then my brother said, "I didn't apply."

I looked at him. His lips quivered.

My father's face chalked. "What?" he said, and he straightened in his chair.

"I didn't . . . do the applications."

But my father didn't get it. Perhaps because my brother had hedged, as if he too were hoping there was something more—he was so scared. But even if my brother had said it directly, my father would have still misunderstood him. He hadn't applied because he hadn't had to—that's what my father was thinking. He had found some school, some second-rater, that had made the process easier, because my brother always looked for short-cuts. And so this school, whoever it was—certainly not Columbia (my mom must have been thinking that, it's not Columbia, and already fearing Rose)—had somehow learned of my brother's marks; or perhaps it had something to do with the student paper —he was the editor—perhaps that's what it was, a writing scholarship. And this lesser school had contacted him, or his guidance counselor, and expressed interest, and my brother had jumped at the offer. My father could imagine all of this because he knew nothing about the process; the most important thing in his life and he simply knew nothing. So when my brother said he didn't apply, my father must have expected stupidity and laziness, never defiance, and he was prepared for disappointment, never betrayal.

"You didn't apply?" my father said, shifting in his chair.

"No."

"Where are you going then?" He turned to my mother. "What school accepts without applying?"

And that's what must have killed my brother, that at the moment he expected to crush my father, he simply confused him. He looked at me wearily. He laughed. He gave this false-fronted, sheepish grin. "No one," he said. And then he wept.

My father stammered, "No, no, you applied. You said you did. To Columbia. To NYU, Cornell . . ." My brother lowered his head and my father sputtered, "You told me, when I asked, the guidance counselor . . . those were the schools." My brother didn't answer, and my father shook his head so quickly. "No, no, no. Of course you did. Of course you applied. Why . . . What did you do, if you didn't apply?" He turned to my mother again. "What else was there to do?"

"Who can we talk to?" my mother said, so restrained, but my brother said nothing.

"Yes," my father said. "We'll talk to someone. Whoever it is. We'll fill out the applications right now. Where are they? Let me see them."

"They're not here."

"Bring them to me."

"I'm sorry."

"Bring them to me now!" He grabbed my brother's arm and tugged it. My mother reached to stop him. He turned to her and loosened his grip, and my brother pulled away.

"We'll go to the schools," my father said, trembling. "I'll explain to them—something has happened. What do I have to do, who do I talk to? There's a way to fix this." My brother stared down. My father said "Why?" over and over again, louder. "I don't . . . what did you do, if you didn't apply? What *was* there?" and he started bawling, the tears streaming down his face.

My brother stayed silent. He must have been thinking, "If this was so important to you, why did you make it so easy for me to fail?" Because my brother didn't know that he wouldn't apply until the moment it was done. The applications were due in a month and then a week and you could simply do nothing and wake up and it was over, and something larger had started.

My father wept—so completely, that when he finished, it was as if his life had emptied. My brother lifted his head and stared at him. The entire family had failed and it could have never been otherwise, so how could he have done this?

My father wiped his eyes. He looked sickened. I listened to his breaths catch in his throat. His nostrils flared. He turned and faced down my brother. With a shaken voice, he said, "This is what you give back to me?"

He stood up and crossed the room. He paused at the bedroom door. His jaw tensed. My mother watched him. He turned to her and said softly, "The Seder, in a week."

Each day, Rose was over, asking about it. No doubt she sniffed something. I watched my mom sidestep—"No, the mail hadn't come yet"—and when that lie lost all credibility, because everyone else had heard by now, she upped the falsework—we'd heard something good from NYU.

"What good?" Rose asked. "You mean in?"

Mom nodded, then added she didn't think it was the right one for Milton.

"What's wrong with it?" Rose asked.

"Nothing. We just want to see about the others. We're waiting."

Rose nodded. She sensed confirmation; she had done a better job with the kids, without the money. Alan was better, she was better. Murray was still a fool, but it didn't matter. She had triumphed.

The week was even quieter than the preceding one—like a shiva, except that everyone stayed away, including us. My father worked late, my brother went to the movies, I played punchball in the street, and my mother, when she wasn't fending off Rose, prepared the Seder meal. The Seder was always at Zaideh's, so Mom did most of the cooking there. She made the haroset, the matzot balls, and the tzimmes. The wine, of course, came from Zaideh's basement stash. In the past, my brother and I would visit his apartment and watch the carp—soon to be gefilte—swim around in the bathtub, but not this year.

The morning of the Seder, my brother completed his deception. We were at the table again, and he announced that he had enlisted in the navy. My father just huffed. He had had enough exploding; he simply couldn't muster the energy. He asked when he had decided this, and my brother said months ago. The navy—it sounded about as absurd as a clown college. My father asked a few more particulars. My brother said he'd be stationed in Chicago, he was leaving in July, and he'd serve for two years. "When you finish, you'll go to school," my father said, and my brother knew but to nod. My father was silent for a while, but I could see something break across his face. "Let me tell you why we come here," he said, but he teared up so quickly. He shook his head and left the room.

Zaideh's apartment was a railroad flat; the Seder table stretched across three rooms. Mom ran food from the kitchen and stayed away from Rose. But eventually Rose cornered her. She fessed up. Even Rose was thrown by it—although I can't say it ruined her evening. A little later, Murray told one of his jokes—"I'm reading a book on levitation; I can't put it down"—and Rose laughed.

The service began. We said Kiddush. We dipped parsley. We came to the four questions, which the Haggadah calls for only the youngest child to read, but our family never stopped there. We preferred three or four renditions. It was more like a bench show. Lou's son, Alvin, was the youngest, so he went first. He struggled. Next was David, who needed a bit of coaxing at the end. Marvin garbled the melody, but was altogether fine. Howard sang it flawlessly. The family applauded.

Dad led the narrative. His voice faltered as he read about the four kinds of children, but he soon steadied. We remembered our suffering in Egypt, in Europe. We sang *Dayenu*. We ate and told jokes. We ate some more. Lou rubbed his belly and said, "Why do I eat like this?" The afikomen was fetched. We sang *Had Gadya* and went home.

In the years that followed, my brother would finish his stint in the navy, enroll at NYU, drop out, then go to work for my father. They fought constantly. I was at college, then medical school, and I'd hear the complaints—my brother was lazy, he came in late, he spent the day moving problems from one spot on his desk to the next; my father was uncompromising and short-sighted. I waited for my brother to quit, for my father to fire him, but neither happened. My brother, with all his talk about getting far far away, and instead standing right next to Dad. Like those mornings they davened together, except now for the whole day.

And then, my brother met his wife. Someone like Rose, I guess, in that she pushed him, tirelessly. He became an even better businessman than my father who, no matter how hard he worked, was always held back by the Depression—the bankruptcy papers ever-imminent. He had survived it, but the memories forever shadowed him. My brother was not burdened by memory and was thus willing to extend himself. He saw the money in the suburbs. He followed it. The business thrived. My father stayed in Brooklyn and, in later years, his store was nothing more than an albatross. When he died, my brother sold it.

Why does the past reopen? It is fifty years later and now Brooklyn is the Old World, and Austria is beyond consideration. My children have married gentiles and my brother's have married money. But this is Rose's story, not my brother's, never mine.

In the month following the Seder, Rose asked my father for a tuition loan for Alan. He was not surprised by the request; he had long before set the money aside.

"I don't have the figures yet," she said.

"That's okay, Rose. Whatever it is."
"School should not cost so much."
He shrugged.
"I'll pay every penny. Every month, you get something back."
"I know."
She shook her head. "You give me too much," she said.
He looked away.
"You do." She squeezed his arm.
"What have I done wrong?" he asked.
"You?"
"To not go." He looked back. "Why would he not go?"
"You did nothing wrong."
He shook his head. "This is my disgrace?" he asked.
"Never," she said. She spoke so fiercely, all he could do was nod.

Tattletale

Frances Sherwood

My brother had taken nine years to die, made a career of it. By the end, he had borrowed money from everybody he knew, was charged up to the max at K-Mart, owed the IRS thousands of dollars, and had promised all sorts of different people the inheritance of the same objects in exchange for some favor or other. He had antagonized everybody. My other two brothers were totally fed up. One of J.J.'s sons was not speaking to him. The other, when Jean-Jacques refused to go to a hospice, had said: why can't you die like normal person. In fact, I heard that on his last day, J.J. had walked out of the hospital, had to be hauled back. He had a joke about using public transportation, meaning, of course, the ambulance; he was a regular with the rescue squad.

Leaving for California late that summer night, the box of ashes on my sister lap, I felt pregnant as if when the plane hit San Francisco, I would give birth to him, my big, fifty-five year old baby brother. Actually, I had already opened the plastic bag which had been shipped to me in Indiana via Federal Express, let fistfuls of ash sift between my fingers, thinking of how we had once played ring around the rosy, ashes, ashes, you all fall down. His ashes were soft as feathers, threaded with bits of bone, and compared to my mothers' ashes two years before, a lot. But then J.J. had always been overweight except for one year of his sickness. Why am I saying this? He would hate to be remembered that way, as true as it was. My childhood taunt was fatty, fatty, two by four, couldn't get in the bathroom door, so he had to do it on the floor. In fact, as early as seven and eight, he was hanging back in photos, hiding himself, his pants belted below the belly, his shirts stretched over his midriff. I feel terrible, but . . . well . . . he *was* fat.

And slow. Three years younger than I, he walked behind me on the way to school, and once there, I would see him on the little kids side on the fringe of games and shouting. When he did get to play, he was always It and always the rotten egg. He wet his bed until he was six, (I would pinch my nose, pee-you), sucked his thumb like a baby until he was eight, picking the fuzz from his blanket, stuffing it up his nose. His perpetually skinned knees from the races around the block scabbed over so many times they left permanent scars. He played with his food, would chew his meat and put it back on his plate in disgusting wads. Scared of the winged monkeys in Oz, the bathtub drain, the sucking flush of the toilet, he thought something lived under the bed, in the bedroom closets, and up in the tree by his window. He was even frightened of his stuffed Mary-Had-a-Little-Lamb toy. On one end it was a Mary and when you flipped it over during its wind-up song, under her skirts was the lamb. To him, it looked like a wolf and I would chase him all through the house with it until he surrendered.

Even though on car trips in our turquoise Pontiac, I beat him to the front seat, and he had to ride in the back, often getting carsick, when my parents sold the car, he went to the used car lot, carved his name on the right back bumper as if it was his. He loved animals, too. Our stupid dachshunds were Jean-Jacques' best friends despite I having the most dibs on getting to sleep with them. He was closer to animals (who do not care what you look like) than people, so close he thought they could understand human language as they did in our baby books—Peter Rabbit, the Owl and the Pussy Cat, Barbar the Elephant, Mr. Toad. Later, he was not surprised to learn through TV nature programs of the sensitivity of elephants, the intelligence of pigs, that lemurs mourn their dead. And I, Candida Marie as a kid? I coveted a pony I could ride in a ring like I did at the Monterey County State Fair every year.

Nobody was sure how J.J. got hepatitis. He told people it was a transfusion, but I thought it could have been any number of things—weird sex, dirty needles, for he was excessive in all respects and though I know alcohol does not cause infectious hepatitis, the benders he and his wife had gone on every weekend, I venture to point out, did not help. Their two kids got hot dogs and potato chips as their treat. Shortly before his diagnosis at forty-six, divorced and without a job, he was back with my mother, crowded into her trailer with her artifacts of a better time. He called me collect in Indiana, said he was taking care of her, she wasn't getting any younger. A couple of weeks later when my mother wrote me that the real story was he was dying, I knew the worry would kill *her*, and it did.

Needless to say, J.J. was her favorite from childhood; the underdog, he needed an ally. For instance, quizzed on his spelling words every Thursday night by our enlightened father, J.J. could would miss one, two, three meant a spanking. As a grown man, actually up until the month before he died, J.J. would reminisce: Candy (that's what he called me, the only one who called me that), Candy, Daddy beat me, you know. What I knew from day one was the name of the game, could spell con-sti-tu-tion, score in spelling bees and hustled straight A's out of the hat. Our second brother's strategy was to lay low. Seven years younger than I, three years younger than J.J., Locke stayed in his room, played with coke bottles like toy soldiers, and the fourth, John Stuart, seventeen years younger, the baby, born a year before my father died, was out of the running. We don't even have any baby pictures of him. My mother would take him out on the deck in her arms after work, tell him his father was in the stars. Yeah, sure, beginning his million year comeback.

Never one to waste time, I planned to use my trip west not only to scatter J.J.'s ashes with Locke and John Stuart, but also do a little San Francisco sight-seeing—the Japanese tea garden, Coit tower, a shrimp cocktail at Fisherman's Wharf, Ghiradelli chocolate—and get a load of this, catch my fortieth high school reunion down in Monterey which I regretted the instant I walked into our pre-reunion cocktail party. The worst part was not that I didn't recognize a soul, but that nobody recognized me, and I had been Sophomore Class President, for God's sakes. Granted it had been forty years, the reason being I wanted to be rich and famous before I made my appearance; no, all kidding aside, you could say I had more important things to do and was not that I wasn't popular. Teachers liked me, I was in with various cliques. Then for a couple of years it was boys, boys, boys.

At the actual reunion the next night in a Carmel Valley Country Club, the men gave the speeches, although the women had organized it. One man tried to auction off a former cheerleader's underpants as if we were still back in 1958 with no history to our name. I heard from people who had never left town (practically everybody) about former teachers who had nervous breakdowns, walked away from their families, became preachers in Montana, rode their bicycles around town all day, got cancer. Most of us were retired, now occupied with investment clubs, tango lessons, Bridge this and that. Not I, said the Little Red Hen. The day I die is the day I retire. One of my classmates, a former dentist bragged he hadn't been out of his swimming trunks in two weeks. We should have auctioned off those skivvies. As you can imagine, golf was the biggest thing and several guys had golf in their e-mail address. The center of attraction was Miquel Mollusca, the former star football player, who with manly bravado bought round after round of drinks for the guys. What are you drinking? was the question of the night. These dipsos clustered in a corner while the women at the tables held down the fort. Prizes were given for the longest marriage, the most grandchildren. I lost out as the person who had come the furthest distance to somebody who had come from Florida. For their information I wouldn't have even been there except I had to be in California, double-duty. And why should Florida count because he was retired? But I do have to admit I looked the best of the women except for the young trophy dates in skimpy dresses, blue nail polish. One of the men was in a blue silk bombardier jacket with KOREA embroidered on it. He had always been borderline; people don't change.

Except for a couple of guys who did not show up, (the smart ones), I was the only person with an LL.D., not to mention Ph.D. In passing I had almost picked up an M.B.A. It's hard to believe I was one of three professors in a class of two hundred. In the bios they wrote up, the space following my name was filled in, just like in my yearbook—Honor Band, Honor Orchestra, and Honor Roll, Chorus, Thespians, Softball Team, International Club, Girls State. Some of us had already died. My brother had died. In my humble opinion, a good use of a life involves planning. Who's Who in America, LL.D., Ph.D., author of two books on economics published by reputable academic presses, numerous articles in juried journals, certified CPR instructor, Master Gardener, member of a chamber orchestra, dog trainer, world traveler. I own a 1950 Jaguar named Marlena.

In J.J.'s defense, I will allow that our mother and father were less than perfect, in all justice, poorly qualified for parental duties. On the one hand, we, kids, wondered if we would ever measure up, working hard to master the rules and regulations so necessary for admission into the adult world, sitting up straight at the dinner table, keeping elbows at sides, no spills, cleaning our plate, requesting permission—may I please be excused—carrying out our plate, rinsing our plate, going to our rooms. On the other hand, despite good manners and best behavior, disorder, even disaster lay in wait at the center of the most ordinary occasion. The meals at which we had to sit up straight often came late at night, 10:00, 11:00, a sophisticated European hour according to our parents, who, by then, bleary and beery, were, ready to pick a quarrel over the least suspected slight. Another case in point is that although our house was filled with expensive, tasteful stuff, (my father was a professor, my mother a lawyer), we had dogs who never got housebroken. My mother made all my clothes; they never fit. She would squeeze out my blackheads, but I went to first grade with a dirty neck, waxy ears. Our rock garden of exotic succulents was overgrown with a tangle of weeds. Love birds one minute, the next our parents would veer off into taunts and threats, begin to throw records like flying saucers. J.J. and I huddled together in my bed, Locke at our feet. We worked him with our toes up and down, rubbed each other's backs, turning skin into map, laying hands on Texas, Canada itches, do France. Anywhere to be away from home. In the morning shattered 78s, old Ellingtons, Billy Holidays—shiny black triangles, Matterhorn-jagged edges lay scattered all over the floor.

I made the lunches. Chocolate cupcakes with squiggles of white icing down the middle. Was sure to include fruit, carrot sticks, carefully wrapped the sandwiches in wax paper, edges folded so they would not come undone. Yet try as I might, all unraveled when J.J. and I came home from school and he would eat a whole loaf of bread squashing the soft slices into little dough balls, popping them in his mouth, or biting a hole in circles of sliced baloney, nibbling to the rim. He would put on a record and dance ballerina style with arabesques and grand leaps, mocking my ballet lessons, making me finally collapse in a heap of giggles. Pirates was a favorite game; J.J. swabbed the decks with dash, walked the plank with panache, flopping down on the ground without complaint while I hunted for buried treasure, scanned the charts for possible hurricanes. I played hard, played for keeps, always won. Jacks and hopscotch, dolls and cowboys and Indians. Our family did not own a television because it was not good for us. An hour before my parents got home with Locke from the childcare center, J.J. and I'd rush like mad to clean the house, J.J. pooping out before he did his share. I told on him, he got punished. I practiced my flute while he sobbed softly in the next room and then, out of the goodness of my heart, I would let him sit on my bed while I did my homework. I even let him touch my radio.

There were so many false alarms that when J.J. actually died I couldn't believe it. He had come for Christmas in Indiana just the month before and as usual for the last nine years, spoke about the music he wanted at his funeral—R.E.M., some wavery New Age stuff, but as usual I had brushed him off, said for my funeral he could play "Happy Days are Here Again." He wanted to give me his animal collection, small figurines. I informed him I was at the age for getting rid of stuff. If he was dying, I could do him one better, take it in stride. But, I did get a huge Christmas tree for him, decorated with antique bulbs, drove him around the neighborhood where they went all out with Christmas lights, wheeled him in the mall, had a dessert party to which I invited his Indiana girlfriend. Yes, he had a girlfriend. He always had girlfriends, was a real charmer, led a seamy sexual life. He said his caretaker had the hots for him, but that he did not dirty his own backyard. That alone should have been enough to keep him alive. I bought him a new shirt, a book about a cats. Surely I would not give him presents if he was going to die. How could J.J. die? He was too big. He was my little brother. He liked to eat too much, so enjoyed the smokes I made him take outside. Once he toppled over during a smoking adventure, but the snow was soft and I was able to right him without difficulty. What I was scared of was he was going to cut himself, expose me to his tainted blood. He fell asleep in front of the television with his mouth open, and at night while I listened upstairs he would wander, naked, his cane bumping the floor like Father Time.

My other brothers, Locke and John Stuart, were in California busily living their lives during all this. J.J., I suspected, had borrowed them dry, panicked them periodically with false alarms, cries of wolf, dramatic previews of coming attractions, the latest grisly development of his disease. I really wasn't in contact much with them; to be honest, I hardly knew them for I left home at eighteen, the year after my father joined the celestial legion and J.J. became the reluctant man of the house. Locke, the middle brother, I suppose muddled along, and John Stuart learned to walk, all that stuff while I was up in Berkeley reading great American novels, hearing folk singers, occasionally breezing home, gradually emptying my room, spiriting on each visit one more souvenir off the shelf, thief of myself, knowing that I would not be back.

Then in the east for law school, graduate school, I lost track of them for about a decade. Later J.J. shared choice tidbits, no doubt to make me feel guilty, like the three of them clustered behind venetian blinds waiting for my mother to come home from work and J.J. taking John Stuart to the hospital—an eye operation. He had bled from the eyes, J.J. told me, and he was the only visitor in the hospital since my mother hated hospitals. I didn't know there was anything wrong with John Stuart's eyes.

It is shabby now, maybe it was then, our Monterey house; upstairs where my room was has been made into a separate apartment. In nearby Pacific Grove, originally a religious revival tent city, they have plaques on the cutesy little houses. Miss Hannah Mae Gibson, 1885, Mr. Clarence Habert, 1892, a little like they do in London for famous authors—Coleridge, Thomas Quincy, all the drug addicts. I wondered if years down the road they would put up a plaque, Candida-Marie Laporte,

1940, the year of my birth, or place a statue of me as they had for John Steinbeck, the local hero, on Central Avenue. And I had forgotten about the fog which was unremitting. Then on Monterey Wharf, (throngs of tourists in pastels clothes), while I was having battered artichoke hearts and a good stiff drink, the waitress, not knowing it was where I grew up, told me Monterey was for the newly married or nearly dead. I instantly got an attack of homesickness for the flat of Indiana, the high heat of summer, where the cicadas saw loudly in the tall grass, mosquitoes swirling in dizzy clouds at dusk, and tomatoes and sunflowers grow unabashedly big. I missed the secretary in our department who kept all in order, I missed porch life with my pets, the summer sky—Big Dipper, Little Dipper, Hercules with his sword promising a month of clear days and an eternity of cold light.

And here is the truly ugly part.

After I told J.J.'s girlfriend he died, she invited me over for dinner. She served thick pork chops and tapioca pudding with big pearly lumps we call fish eyes. She lit candles, I opened a bottle of wine. Then she told me about Vietnam.

Get this: J.J. mushrooming down from a helicopter, its beating dragonfly fins echoing the butterfly wings in his chest. Crawling on his belly through muck and slaughter, ordered to shoot children and women, old men, he got sick of it, got out, although the images renewed themselves every night, rose like Draculas, populated the country of his sleep with their sinister shadows.

It was terrible, Deborah said, for him.

J.J. had never been in Vietnam, never in the army at all. He had flat feet among other things.

Blond and shy, stick arms and knobby wrists, Deborah had old-fashioned astigmatism, blinked in bright sunlight. She and her mother, an elderly Mennonite woman in braids around her head sat in back of their antique shop waiting for customers all day. She had never been out of Indiana, hardly out of La Grange County until J.J. came along who introduced her to espresso lattes, the ins and outs of parapsychology, hip California lingo.

J.J. had a period of utter despair, she continued in her breathless account, but heroically, mustering all his strength, he managed to pick himself up, make a career designing hospitals in Japan.

Deborah kept a scrapbook of their affair—letters and pictures, pressed flowers from their trip to Hawaii, swatches of fabric. He was the hunter, she the gatherer.

When he was in Hawaii, she said, he went up in the mountains and looking down over the valley of Honolulu had a revelation. He realized that everybody needed light bulbs, hence his flourishing light bulb business.

This she spoke of in reverential tones, as if he were Moses on mountain top glimpsing the promiseland or Edison inspired. Oh, J.J., I thought, liar, liar, pants of fire.

The quilt, she finally mentioned, the quilt, her story now more appeal than recitation.

The quilt was a beautiful piece of work, made on Deborah's specifications by a team of Amish women, by hand, by lantern light and worth thousands of dollars.

He had sold it, actually to three different people who all claimed it, I had to tell her along with everything else, veracity will out.

I still love him, she protested.

Sure you do, I said.

Even the pastor of the church J.J., who was not the least religious, joined in the last fevered weeks of his life, had to be set straight. J.J. had been in the service, Bronze Star, Purple Heart, B.S., Magna Cum, U.C., Berekeley, M.S., Cal.Tech., A.A.E., American Association of Engineers she was prepared to repeat in his memorial service. I had to explain that it was a whole mythology he had concocted, reality being that J.J. barely graduated from high school, had gone to a community college for about a year, dropped out, sold those tacky, colored-coded, self-playing organs in a mall, worked for Montgomery Ward. Fact is he could never really hold a job. The disability insurance when he got sick saved his life so to speak.

I did not go to the so-called Celebration of Life Service, although I could picture the motley crew, mostly people of his support group—the terminally ill, chronically helpless, abysmally depressed—everybody hanging on by their teeth to their tiny shred of life, his caretaker, no doubt also believing he had been in Vietnam—all packed into a little room, Suite 101, in a strip mall, Church of Religious Science inscribed on the glass door. I did send flowers, a hundred dollar bunch, and the pastor sent me back the program.

Musical Prelude, J.J.'s favorite recordings
Welcoming
Reading of the 23rd Psalm
Spiritual Message
Musical Interlude

Words of Tribute
Moment of Silence
Benediction.

Jean-Jacques, the back of the program read, has passed on richer than when he came through the gate of birth. He carries within him the treasures of life and love on this plane. We bless him on his journey of eternal life.

After the Neptune Society of California assured us they were not contaminated, my two remaining brothers and I threw his ashes at the same inhospitable, California beach as my mother's ashes had been scattered. Three gray seals watched from a bunch of brown kelp. I had the fleeting impression that they were the spirits of my brother, my mother, my father, looking on at us still stuck on the shore of the world. Because J.J. had Hepatitis, Public Health cordoned off his apartment, had to rip up rugs and strip down the walls, toss all his clothing. But already, people had broken in. The woman who had been his caretaker and supposedly fancied him, had informed me by long distance phone that she would help me get things settled in California on a per diem basis, and that she had been promised the computer, the stereo, the television, the CD collection. Other people stole the promised quilt and everything else untouched by a bodily fluid. Nobody took his figurine animal collection. I took his blue glass elephant. Blue was his favorite color. The USDA Forest Service sent me notice of a Living Memorial. A tree was planted in his honor. As a life ends, a new life begins the diploma-like document stated. It made me think of when we played cowboys as kids. I would aim at him, bang, bang, you're dead. He had perfected his fall, would roll over obediently, play dead until I tickled him alive.

The Artificial Cloud

Justin Tussing

Munjoy hung in a clever, leather harness. Below him lay the whole Valley. He could see the two castles and the long wall that stood between them. Clouds slipped past like giant wet cats.

All morning Munjoy had used his spyglass to watch the girl play chess. The girl had been playing chess and losing. He thought her face was so void of emotion as to be indicative of a type of boredom reserved for the very poor and the very wealthy. She wore a brocaded dress that started, like a collar, just beneath her chin and piled around her feet; it extended down past her wrists, covering the back of her hands, concluding in loops through which she'd threaded her middle fingers. A line of buttons no bigger than a bee's eyes ran down the front of the dress. At the conclusion of each game her opponent reached across and unfastened a button; these were so closely spaced that, although they'd been playing all morning, the dress was open only as far as her clavicles. Munjoy assumed her opponent to be the King; the man dipped pieces of bread in a crock full of a black jelly; he had a mane of red hair which fell over his shoulders and he had a long beard which glistened from the jelly he'd spilled upon it. The man had ten fat, pink fingers and as many rings. This couple sat in a flagstone courtyard. All around them, Munjoy observed falcons, parrots, and egrets perched on carved, wooden stands; jesses fastened to the birds' legs were tied to their perches. The birds were universally tiny. Juveniles, thought Munjoy. A small flamingo snapped its black beak at a man who brushed its feathers with a red dye. The courtyard was in the center of a large castle. Pairs of uniformed guards protected the building's entrances.

Munjoy recorded his observations in a notebook. He wore a jumpsuit of bleached cotton that buttoned in back and which he had to be helped into. Munjoy was a dwarf and he had fingers like toes; buttons were a challenge. To maximize its camouflage, the jumpsuit had just a narrow rectangular eye slit. The loosely-woven cloth allowed Munjoy to breathe, but in order to eat he had to tug the hole over his mouth.

In addition to the spyglass, notebook, and pens, Munjoy carried a long, curved, cavalry sword and some provisions: hard cheese, water, and the circular loaf of bread which was traditional, meant to symbolize that future time when his country would have dominion over the Valley. Munjoy used colored inks to differentiate between agricultural, military, and political observations.

On an autumn day in the Eastern Land, the King noticed a cloud that resembled the head of a hound his father had once owned. He had been playing chess with his consort when he looked upwards in contemplation. There were many other clouds in the sky. "I name that cloud Hound's Head," he said, and then he pointed it out to the girl. When the man had finished winning the game he looked up and there was the cloud, where he had last seen it, where it stayed all afternoon (he presumed that naming it had somehow made it permanent). The most unique aspect of the cloud, the girl said, was its immutability. Neither suspected that what made the cloud remarkable was Munjoy.

Each morning, before dawn, Munjoy was strapped aboard the cloud. Each morning he was handed a brand new notebook by an engineer named Hurst, the day's date embossed in gold on the cover. He tried to make small talk with the man who maintained the cloud, but Hurst considered the dwarf simply luggage. So Munjoy situated himself in his hanging seat and, after making sure that all of his equipment was within reach, he gave the high sign with a mittened hand. Hurst launched the cloud.

Munjoy hated the mornings. The cloud gained altitude slowly, only a few hundred feet when it passed over the Town. Here Munjoy would smell the wood smoke leaking up the chimneys. He'd watch the dark, smoke-stained windows. His own house looked so empty to him. And the fact that Munjoy knew his house was empty made it much worse to him than the empty-looking houses where he knew neighbors slept. Then he was over the fields: potatoes, rye, and wheat. Approaching the Frontier, he'd see the small orange dots of the watch fires. By the time he'd passed over the Wall he would be quite high; he could see past the lowest mountain passes to other mountains with their redundant spires. Everything outside of the Valley looked cold. Then there would be a slight bump when the cloud reached the end of its tether.

Munjoy's dwarfism had given him a certain prominence. At the Harvest Festival, maiden girls would run up behind Munjoy and throw their skirts over his head, then run off shrieking. When he turned sixteen, the age at which other boys were conscripted into the Royal Guard, he started work as an ox driver at the King's granary.

The granary smelled sour—crushed rye and ox piss. The ox was named Sissy and he trudged an orbit around the building, harnessed to a long spar that turned the millstone. Munjoy followed behind with a stripped sapling that he never employed, except to scatter flies. Like a compass with a stone point, Munjoy and Sissy etched a single circle.

Then one day, when Munjoy showed for work, there was only the muddy circle where the mill had stood. The building had been dismantled and its separate parts stacked onto a pair of hay wagons.

"What's this?" Munjoy asked Hurst—the engineer stood by the loaded wagons and smoked a thin cigarette.

"Are you Munjoy?"

The dwarf nodded.

"Proclamation of the King, you've been drafted."

"To do what?"

"You can hitch your ox to one of those wagons, for a start." Hurst told Munjoy where to take the wagons.

Having only known circles, the ox had to dissect the road into a series of arcs. Munjoy felt bad for the animal. And Munjoy felt bad for himself, too. Hurst stopped them at a great domed barn, painted silver-gray, just before the talus at the base of the mountains.

"Do you swear allegiance to the King, the Sovereign, and most Just?" Hurst asked.

"I do," said Munjoy.

"When will the Western Land reign over the entire Valley?"

"It is inevitable," said Munjoy, "as long as Righteousness and Justice exist."

Then Hurst walked him into the barn.

Sometimes, as he made his observations, Munjoy imagined that there was a man beneath every cloud, an entire cloud army, and that they were united in a silent brotherhood. On such days, each cloud that passed over the mountains seemed like a triumph.

* * *

A conscientious spy, Munjoy made detailed observations. On his first flight he wrote: Military (red)

As I slipped over the boundary, I felt some anxiety, but the people seem to have taken no notice. Wise and wonderful is the King. The Wall appears to be of a width equal to its height. Twenty feet? Solid. A trench runs along the foot of the Wall and there is an earthworks studded with sharpened poles. Guard posts are located at regular intervals. A larger post (mess or command?) is connected to the outposts by a series of roofed tunnels. The roofs are thatched. There seem to be about two hundred men guarding the wall at any one time, each is equipped with a weapon, swords and hammers. I've observed individuals digging with the swords, possibly for potatoes. I've seen no ladders or ramps that might indicate an intention to surmount the Wall in the immediate future. The earthworks might disguise an attempt to tunnel beneath the Wall, but I see no movement—no pick-axes, no shovels.

Agriculture (green)

The crops have been planted. I recognize a variety of bean, clover, and tomatoes. Men, women, and children can be seen weeding the fields. I've noticed some individuals harvesting small lumps which I'd guess to be potatoes. There are shallow, square ponds which contain orange fish—a boy proceeds from one pond to the next with a wheelbarrow. He uses a shovel to scatter corn over the water. Far to the north there is a group of white animals grazing which could be sheep, goats, or possibly large fowl. They harvested their hay very early and it is moldering. Their horses are swaybacked.

Political (black)

I have located their sovereign. He sits on a patio of the castle and plays chess with a young woman. She loses each game. Their King sits in a sturdy leather chair—loops of rope at each corner allow posts to be inserted so that an honor guard can move him about the premises. The girl wears a dress that fastens in front with a single line of closely spaced buttons—for each game she loses she undoes a button. She has been losing for hours and the dress is open to a point just even with tops of her breasts. Men in military uniforms engage the pair in conversation for a few minutes then excuse themselves. Servants rub their King's feet with lotions and a chef comes out with ornate dishes designed to look like bird's nests, flowers, and turtles. Their King appears to be bored by everything except the girl; she appears bored with everything. Their King says something to her and she walks over beside him. He sticks his face into the opening of her dress like he's searching for a lost coin. Fortunate are we.

After his first flight, Munjoy was presented with a commendation from his King for "Services Towards the Restoration of the Valley." Munjoy's name was written in a fancy script above the King's seal and signature. The next day, the dwarf tucked the paper inside his undershirt as he was helped into his flying suit. The little man was harnessed beneath his cloud. The doors of the barn swung open and the lanterns spilled light into the dark morning. Munjoy felt essential.

Hurst approached Munjoy as he hung in the undercarriage. "We'll need to hold that paper for you," he said.

"Why?"

"In case of an accident," said Hurst, "so there can be nothing to connect you to the King."

"The tether," said Munjoy.

Hurst stuck his hand out and waited.

Munjoy passed the paper out the suit's eye slit.

As the tether paid out, Munjoy could feel Sissy's steps vibrating along the line.

The King made it his habit to wait outside the barn in his carriage so he could personally debrief Munjoy when the little man returned in the evening.

"Describe her again," said the King.

Munjoy picked up his notebook and re-read the passage: "She wears a crown of orange flowers. Miniature yellow butterflies alight on the flowers and fan her with their wings. When she moves they erupt in a cloud which stays just above her until she is still and they re-settle. For lunch she was served a platter of fingerling trout and she only ate the cheeks."

"She's magnificent," said the King. "I command you, continue."

"She is joined by her King. He wears dark woolen pants and no shirt. There are many scars on his back and chest. He stands next to her and she traces the scars with her fingertips. She talks to him for some time. A pair of servants come out and erect a privacy screen around the couple—there is no roof to this structure. They entertain one another in the customary fashion."

"He's a toad," said the King. "And a poor warrior. Of course, my skin is as free of blemishes as a baby's."

"I have no doubt," said Munjoy.

"From now on you needn't concern yourself with mundane observations. Do you understand?"

"I do." Munjoy looked at the notebook in his hands.

"Do you understand when I say, 'mundane.'"

"I understand."

"The girl," said the King. "Only watch the girl." He took the notebook from Munjoy. Then he rapped his knuckles on the wall of the carriage and the door opened; a page helped Munjoy out. Hurst waited outside. The engineer regarded Munjoy before the King summoned him.

Munjoy's observations became the property of the King and a state secret. If he wrote, as he did one day, "Today is my birthday, I am thirty-four," then that too became a secret.

When Munjoy arrived at the barn the next day, he found bushel sacks of sand attached to corners of the cloud's undercarriage. "To test the structure's capacity," Hurst informed him. "Our King is concerned whether the cloud is able to carry more precious cargoes." When the cloud was launched, the dwarf could feel Sissy's every plodding step as the animal unwound the tether. With this new weight, the cloud flew lower than before. So low that Munjoy could feel the heat of chimneys. When he passed above the Wall, from the light of the watch fires, he could see that the men on sentinel duty busied themselves with small tasks: he observed a man creating a crocheted doily and there was a man with a small knife who carved a linked chain from a solid block of wood. Out of respect for the solitary men, Munjoy didn't write these things down; the King would only view such details as weaknesses to be exploited.

There was quality to the tautness when the slack came out of the cloud's tether, almost a groaning.

All morning Munjoy glassed the patio, but there was no sign of the woman. A child swept the courtyard with a corn husk broom. Then Munjoy found her, sitting on top of a turret. A rope was wrapped around her waist and tied to a stone. She had a telescope balanced on the parapet and it pointed right at him.

The sight of the girl watching him stole his breath. With care not to lose sight of her, he moved his hand in a slow wave—she copied this gesture as if his reflection.

Munjoy saw her King appear behind her. The man watched the girl for a minute. As Munjoy watched, he reached around her and cupped his hands over her breasts. The girl spun about, startled. Her telescope tumbled end over end, until it smashed in the courtyard below. Munjoy watched the cords in the girl's throat as she yelled at the man. The man pointed into the sky and she swatted him. A servant appeared to untie the woman and escort her inside.

When the cloud began its retreat with a lurch. Munjoy thought of

Sissy, of the animal's subservience to the tether's reel. He remembered the notebook and he started to fill it.

It was after sunset before the cloud could be winched into the barn. Hurst released Munjoy from the harness and told him the King waited outside in his carriage. The King had requested that Munjoy bring the notebook.

Munjoy climbed into the carriage and took a seat across from the king. He read what he had written. There was a pause once he'd finished.

"Read it again," the King said.

"She doesn't appear until noon." Munjoy followed his finger on the page. "She limps and uses a cane."

"My poor bird," said the King.

"After lunch, an attendant arrived and put up a privacy screen. The attendant cleaned a number of sores and boils which were on the girl's spine."

"What kind of a man would beat such a girl?"

"I not certain they are evidence of a beating," said Munjoy.

"Absolutely," said the King. "They are nothing else."

"There are certain diseases and infirmities which cause abscesses and boils."

"I've solicited your observations, not your opinions. It is my intention to bring this girl here."

"Your Majesty," said Munjoy. "First I would have to get past the Wall and then there is the Countryside. Because of the obvious problems with visibility, I have very little knowledge of night defenses. The Castle itself is well guarded and has an interior that I know nothing more of than what I've inferred, right or wrong."

"Munjoy," said the King, "You've already circumvented those obstacles. You'll pluck her straight into the sky."

Munjoy decided the King had given this idea very little thought.

"I have spoken with my engineer and I'm certain that he can solve any technical problems."

All of the freedom that Munjoy had come to associate with being above the valley evaporated. "What if she refuses my rescue?"

"She's not being rescued by a dwarf in a cloud. She's being rescued by a king. You are only the vehicle. Besides, such an exceptional woman can only have contempt for those people. I shall introduce myself to her and entreat her to come. That will be sufficient. These details are nothing for you to concern yourself with."

"I'm your servant," said Munjoy.

"Once she is my Queen, the things that you've seen will be forgotten."
Munjoy nodded his head.
"I will compose a letter for you to deliver." Then the King leaned forward and grasped Munjoy by the shoulders. "Understand, I would attach myself to that contraption, if it weren't for other duties."
Munjoy bowed.
"You're excused."

Munjoy had just finished brushing Sissy when Hurst walked into the stall. Bluebottle flies covered welts on Sissy's back; they shimmered like sequins. Munjoy hung a step-ladder on a wooden peg.
"Whoever is driving him has to lay off the whip."
"You and the animal are both in a fine mess," said Hurst.
"We are." Munjoy scratched the animal's dewlap. "He has a great disposition because he's only known kindness."
"And they took the berries off him, that kills the fight."
"He's just like us, he's only limited by who he is."
"The King is only limited by what he can imagine."
"That's the problem," said Munjoy. "It has me stuck in a cloud."
"Where no one else has ever been."
"It's quite impossible to describe."
"Can you see over the mountains?"
"I can," said Munjoy.
"What's there?"
"More mountains."
"Do you know why he chose you?" Hurst asked.
"Because I'm the smallest."
"Because you're an orphan and an outcast. If there was an accident, who would miss you?"
Munjoy made a few swipes with the brush across Sissy's deep chest.
"When I designed the cloud, I always expected I'd be the pilot," said Hurst. "Our King forbid it."

The next morning, Munjoy waited by the ox's stall to see who was handling him. A boy walked into the stall carrying a cane-handled quirt. In one hand the boy grabbed the cord that fastened to the ring in the animal's septum. He gave three quick lashes and Sissy flipped one foot after the other; the ox's hooves kneaded the soft earth.
"He's like you or me, it takes him a while to get moving in the morning," said Munjoy.

"He's going now," said the boy, laying another stripe across the animal's haunches.

"I mean you shouldn't beat him," Munjoy said, stepping in front of the boy.

The boy stood half a head higher than Munjoy; he gave a sharp tug on the rein and Sissy came to a halt.

"He's my friend," said Munjoy. "Don't mistreat him."

"You've got a job and I've got a job," said the boy. "If the King orders me to beat him, then that's what I'll do. I'd tell him nice if I could, but all he understands is the whip." With that he swatted the back of Sissy's leg and took him out of her stall.

When Munjoy approached the cloud he noticed a large reel attached to the front of his harness. Metal crank arms jutted from each side and culminated in bone T-handles. Hurst fitted the device with a cover complete with sleeves for the cranks. With the engineer's assistance, Munjoy got into his jumpsuit and, together, they got him situated in his harness. A sheepskin pad protected Munjoy's chest from the sharp edges of the brass reel.

Hurst made sure that Munjoy's arms were long enough to turn the cranks. The man flipped a lever on the reel then grabbed a wire that stuck out from beneath the cover and walked out through the barn doors. The cranks spun as the wire paid out. Munjoy was instructed to turn the handles. He turned the cranks and the device slowly retrieved the wire.

"That's just a simple tool, a mechanical advantage," said Hurst. "Let me show you what I've been putting my heart into." The engineer wheeled a lorry underneath the cloud. An object was hidden beneath a shroud. With a flourish, he yanked the sheet away.

There on the cart sprawled a giant, black eagle; it had powerful, thick shoulders that became wings which flowed into fragile feather fingers. The head was cocked to one side and its eyes were green jewels. A curved beak was clamped on a golden bit which, in turn, was connected to a bridle; reins looped over the horn of the King's finest tooled-leather saddle. A latticework of gold highlights showed the details of every overlapping feather that formed the body. Talons, sharp as knives, finished feet that were tucked beneath the body. It was the most beautiful thing Munjoy had ever seen.

Hurst attached the bird to the wire from the reel; he turned the cranks and lifted the bird off the truck. Now he stuck a key into a hole in the bird's back. The bird's wings began a slow rhythmic beating and its head tracked a lazy, side-to-side arc. "I'm going to notify the King that you can see him."

Munjoy watched the metal bird imitating flight.

"I told you he'd come up with something appropriate," said the King.

"I have no imagination," said Munjoy. He could not understand how the machine's simple movements could contain such dignity.

"There are certain people who possess Vision and for them the world holds no limits. Hurst is such a person."

"How can one world contain such wonders?" Munjoy asked as the mechanical bird surveyed the barn.

"Do you know what the most destructive emotion is?" asked the King.

"Loneliness," said Munjoy.

"Yes," said the King.

Munjoy watched the bird.

"That's why I've sent you to get her."

"She's very wonderful," said Munjoy.

"Only I could appreciate her," said the King.

"I understand."

The King removed a document from his jacket and held it before Munjoy. "Put this in the bird's mouth and, when she is by herself, lower it to her." He passed the paper to Munjoy.

"As you command," said Munjoy

"Bring her to me." The King kissed Munjoy on the top of head.

Hurst launched the cloud into the blackness.

The black bird kept sentinel as Munjoy drifted out over the town. He could smell apple wood in the chimney smoke and he knew that the trees which hadn't produced fruit had been felled. It was late autumn.

The days had become shorter. The night sky appeared on the horizon, framed by the high mountains, like a cold portal, like something one might pass through. Munjoy lowered the mechanical bird so it skimmed over the Countryside. The sight of the bird passing over the watch fires satisfied the dwarf. Munjoy reeled the bird in, and man and machine passed over the Wall together.

Munjoy knew when he was over the Castle.

The night before, Munjoy had looked about his house for something he might bring with him on this flight, some talisman. Inside, the house was dim. It surprised him that none of his things did he remember as being given to him. He'd crawled into his bed, little more than a low nest, where a cat might choose to drop a litter. He could think of nothing that wouldn't seem a burden if he were to carry it above the Valley.

Munjoy found the girl alone on the parapet. In one hand she held the broken telescope and with the other she made a noncommittal wave, a stirring of the air. In the half-light Munjoy read the letter the King had entrusted him with: *I am the King of the Clouds. I have been watching you. I need you. Climb aboard this bird and I'll take you away with me. Together we shall live in splendor on the other side of the World.* The letter was unsigned. Munjoy took a pen out and on the bottom of the King's letter he signed his own name. Then he rolled the letter up and stuffed it in the bird's beak. He started the bird on its long descent.

Almost half an hour passed before the artificial bird neared the patio. The girl went back into the Castle. As the bird continued to descend, the real birds on the patio panicked. The little flamingo fell from its perch and flapped about upside down. A red-tailed hawk stooped on one foot and tried to remove its hood with its other talons. A gyrfalcon flew a tight circle at the end of its jesses.

Munjoy was cautious, hoping not to drop the bird all the way to the flagstones. The sunlight helped—he knew he just had to prevent the bird from reaching its shadow. When he stopped it, the girl emerged at the edge of the courtyard; she looked at the bird for a few minutes before she approached it. It seemed to Munjoy, in those moments while she stood across the courtyard, that the bird seemed greatly diminished. Munjoy realized that he'd only watched the girl from this rather awkward perspective. The girl walked across the courtyard and with a quick stab of her hand she snatched the paper from the bird's beak. As she unrolled the King's letter, Munjoy saw that the way she held it close to her face suggested she might be squinting.

Fifteen-hundred feet above her, Munjoy watched through his spy-glass as the girl lifted a leg over the bird. The King's finest saddle seemed no bigger than a milking stool beneath her. She was a giant. She clamped her legs around the bird and looked upwards. Munjoy started to turn the organ grinder.

Someone must have spotted the giantess once she'd cleared the castle's walls. People gathered in the patio to point up at her. Her king was there; he shouted. A group of soldiers took to assuming different formations. Munjoy's arms burned and burned; he found himself kicking his legs in an attempt to assist in cranking the enormous reel. He wanted just to watch her, but sweat running into his eyes made him blind.

For the first time, as she was retrieved into the cloud, the giantess could see past the snow-capped spires that surrounded the Valley. In her excitement, she spurred the tail feathers; they snapped off and fell like arrows into the crowd gathered beneath her. When Munjoy heard the giantess's laugh—the first thing to reach him from the world below—it gave him new energy.

"Munjoy," she called into the belly of the cloud.

The dwarf's arms were nothing but ether and fire, still he reeled until her huge hands latched onto his ankles. The giantess's touch sent electricity through the dwarf's exhausted body.

"I'm rescued," she said.

Munjoy couldn't speak. In his labor, the suit's eye slit had slipped around and hooked over his ear. He fumbled with his clothing so he might see her. He heard the cloth tearing, and the giantess peeled the hood over his head. Munjoy huffed the air.

"You're the King of the Clouds." Her hair was wild in the wind; it pointed its curly fingers in every direction. She had hungry green eyes.

"No," said Munjoy. He thought it likely his chest would explode.

"You'll take us out of the Valley."

"I'm just Munjoy. A dwarf."

The giantess couldn't stop her hands. She tore the seams out of his jumpsuit. Her fingers were all over the little man's body.

"You shouldn't touch me."

"Why?" she asked.

"I'm bringing you across the Wall so my King can make you his wife." Munjoy closed his eyes, he could barely stand to tell her. "He has no idea you're a giant."

"We're flying over the mountains," she said.

"This is not flying. It's a machine. See the tether?" Munjoy pointed at the line leading off into the distance. "Soon we'll be reeled in just like I reeled you in."

"Look," she said, pointing at a nameless place over the mountains. "That's where we're heading."

Munjoy couldn't begin to understand what he was feeling.

"You've chosen me. We're taking a journey," she said.

The dwarf felt a chill from the sweat cooling.

"From up here you can see anything and you saw me."

"I wanted you," said Munjoy.

"You have me. I'm with you. We're together. We just have to get past these mountains."

"I wanted to share this," said Munjoy. "We can see the whole valley."

"You're wonderful. I'll be yours forever. We only need to get over those mountains." The giantess's hands had found the heat between his thighs.

"That's everything," said Munjoy.

"Exactly." The giantess had climbed from the bird, into the cloud with Munjoy. She'd wrapped herself around him. She smelled of musk and green onions.

The tether shuddered; the wind moaned over it. Munjoy thought he could feel Sissy stumble. "I don't know if we have any hope," he said.

"Save us."

Munjoy unsheathed the sword. He couldn't reach the tether.

"Let me," the giantess said, extending a spar of an arm.

With the tether severed, the cloud sailed towards the mountains. In this one moment there was enough time for Munjoy to imagine a world with limitless hope. They could make it out of the Valley. The girl was strong; she would protect him. It seemed that everything was possible. Sissy was free—the ox could spiral through fields of sweet clover. With the right breeze, it seemed the cloud might stay aloft forever. Then it listed. It turned on its side. Munjoy saw the girl's destiny was tangled with his own; it was obvious, irresistible, and straight down.

On Rediscovering Henry James

George McFadden

Introduction

I have been aware of feeling better for the last three days or so; the reason, I think, is that I have begun again to reread Henry James—this time, his Men of Letters volume on Hawthorne. My problems with his changing prose style in 1894 were eased and cleared up in the comparison with the beautifully appropriate and direct language of that Hawthorne book written in 1878–79. Especially by the frequent presence of that other style grown more prevalent fifteen years later: the rather pompous rhetoric, more humorous than ironic, which makes light of James's wrath and scorn while at the same time giving it over-emphatic expression. It's all so tied up in James with his almost full recognition that he was making himself ridiculous by being so upset at the shortcomings (as they bore so annoyingly on himself) of his London theater audience and their devoted tools, the theater-managers. And, though it was a very powerful if not very serious source for himself of what he insisted was pure fascination of a highly artful nature, he went so far as to confess that what it was, most essentially, was "*fun*"—and serious enough in its unique effect: namely to serve as an anodyne against the most ingrained trouble and distress of his life. Somehow his struggle to conquer his theater audience by giving them pleasure (their kind) provided him with more heartlightening entertainment, sheer fun, than anything else he had ever done. Evidently the art he used upon them was a more palpable and overtly satisfying skill to James its possessor than was his genius for the novel. (It was deep unease over his novel-skills that had started the whole adventure with the London theater.)

What I found in reading James's *Hawthorne* was that he reports much the same process going on during the latter's years in Concord, living in the "Old Manse," and writing his "Mosses." James carries on a war, all through his biography, against the French critic Émile Montégut, what had treated Hawthorne as above all a deep pessimist. James points out that, on the contrary, when his two-to-four-hour-a-day writing stint was done, the author of those most "dismal" tales would idle away his time most pleasantly and read Voltaire and Rabelais! James quotes a passage from the *Notebooks* about looking up from his Rabelais and observing a pert little bird trying to come in to him through the window. No Raven, that little creature! James's point is that the imagined distance that separated Hawthorne's happy time in Concord from the Puritanical horrors of old Salem as he was picturing them was somehow therapeutic and cheering. This homeopathy is exactly what James means when he writes in his "Note" about the writing of his unperformed plays being a "family party" where, for once, "*ses siens*" did not need to assume a seemly posture and could be seen as they really were.

This whole section toward the end of Part IV of James's *Hawthorne* is a sort of reasoned forestatement of Joyce's claim (and Flaubert's, first) for the godlike *apatheia* of the artist, and one that applies equally to James "ciphering out" his plays, except that it is not godlike but realistic, humble, and human: the anomaly is, I think, on the whole, only superficial: "Our writer's imagination . . . was a gloomy one; the old Puritan sense of sin, of penalties to be paid, of the darkness and wickedness of life, had . . . passed into it. It had not passed into the parts of Hawthorne's nature corresponding to those occupied by the same horrible vision of things in his ancestors; but it had still been determined to claim this later corner as its own, and since his heart and his happiness were to escape it insisted on setting its mark upon his genius—upon his most beautiful organ, his admirable fancy. . . . When he was lightest at heart, he was most creative, and when he was most creative, the moral picturesqueness of the old secret of mankind in general and of the Puritans in particular, most appealed to him—the secret that we are really not by any means so good as a well-regulated society requires us to appear."

James wrote these words not long after writing his novel of 1875–77, *The American.* At the novel's heart is an instance of socially-unregulated behavior so delicately pictured by James that it has passed without recognition ever since. James the artist accepted this outcome, perhaps because he was willing that secrets, especially family ones, should not be vulgarized, and most especially not by their author, who is a member of the family par excellence. It was in 1878, though, that he told brother William of his intent to make much more use of the skills he had picked up in the French theaters. As much as anything else, these were skills of divulging well-kept secrets with the greatest possible impact on hundreds of people out front. And who shall deny that James's subsequent fiction is not full of the same? In literature, the classic, indeed the primitive, tribal form for divulging the secret of human depravity is in carnival, saturnalia, farce—the "fun" of literature.

The anomaly in James (even when he's at his best) which is likely to strike a repeated rereader, is the persuasively recurrent nature of personal relationships, especially family ones; and, perhaps even more baldly, the frequent recurrence of certain devices taken, without much disguise, directly from plays James had seen in Paris. What the parallel between James and Hawthorne brings out is the similarity between Puritanism in Hawthorne's case and the James family in Henry Junior's case. Their "heart" and "happiness" escaped, but a "mark" had been set on the "genius" of each, "his most beautiful organ, his admirable fancy." I think of James as a stronger genius than Hawthorne, because his lifelong effort to show how very human people can be in an extremely well-regulated society did pass beyond picturing others for his readers' benefit. It was an anomalous, even a contradictory effort, to let his readers in on the rarest, most *récherché* secrets of denizens of the *meilleur monde*, without ever "telling" them. They'd need to find out for themselves.

This is the reason James found this entry of Hawthorne's on his "mild taciturnity," as he says, so "touching"—"A cloudy veil stretches across the abyss of my nature. I have, however, no love of secrecy and darkness. I am glad to think that God sees through my heart, and if any angel has power to penetrate into it, he is welcome to know everything that is there. Yes, and so may any mortal who is capable of full sympathy, and therefore worthy to come into my depths. But he must find his own way there; I can neither guide nor enlighten him."

Unlike Hawthorne, James loved conversation and was anything but taciturn, despite his stammer. Oddly, though, at this time in his voluminous writing career, James was using the suppression, as well as the divulging, of secrets as a frequent motif, especially in his inveterate subject of relations within the family. But it is even more remarkable that almost from the beginning of his career as a creative writer he had been curtailing his efforts at guiding or enlightening his readers. In the process he had been creating a whole new audience for his novels—and, of course, for some other writers' novels. The process hadn't been an easy one for readers or author, and the strain had told during the eighties on them both. It would seem that James found, during this time and ever after, that the comparative vulgarization he derived from using his shtick of theatrical devices lightened his heart and enabled him to maintain his own "taciturnity" of artistic creation. "Reciprocity" is one of his pet words during this stretch. He offered it to his readers, in leaving them to "find their own way."

"Backward Clearness" in Chapters 39 and 40 of *Bostonians*

I had mixed up James's phrase "backward clearness" with my own version, "backward awareness." Coming across the passage in *The Bostonians* where the phrase "backward clearness" is actually used for the first time, I can see there may be a real difference between the two terms. Where Olive spends a long afternoon walking up and down the western shore of Buzzard's Bay while Verena and Ransom are out in a hired sailboat, we find her with bitter sorrow and pain realizing that, basically, Verena means more to her than she means to Verena; that whereas Verena's commitment to the women's rights movement and, therefore, to her was "for a time," her "passion" (the word is used) for Ransom is bound to supersede it and to be a permanent sort of barrier preventing the two women from being all-in-all to each other. In the language used here, James says she saw the past two years "in backward clearness" with a whole line of finger-posts standing out in full view, none of which she had noticed as she passed by, but now "mapping out . . . the geography" plain as could be.

This is different from what Isabel realizes in James's earlier-written novel. First she has a sort of backward premonition, or overdue recognition, when she notices Merle standing and Osmond seated, that their relation is and was more intimate than any mere sociability would allow for. But not until her sister-in-law puts it into words does Isabel "know" that she has been "used" by this intimate pair; and in fact she has now no sense of a detailed map for her past with Osmond, except for the image Ralph had put into words that were skewed by his own hatred and resentment, if not outright jealousy, of her husband: "ground in the mill of the commonplace." (They had been James's own words in his notebook, but when he changed his later chapters he gave the phrase to Ralph.) It is something of a question whether Isabel ever fully accepts Ralph's image, and there is good reason why she should not, as the reader finds with a moment's reflection.

By contrast, Olive's self-awareness is a slow development that had already come to a head three months ago (as James counts the time—really it's from March 28 to the present, beginning of September). Olive's self-understanding reached half-point in New York when she reversed her view taken in Cambridge, and conceded it would be in her interest and the Cause's to have Verena married to a man for whom she had no passionate attachment. James now actually reminds us of Olive's previous crisis in New York's Washington Square, and tells us that this one is different: this time Olive realizes flight will not save the situation, for Verena is "not to be trusted." Olive had trusted her revulsion from Ransom in New York, when supposedly she and he had been seeing one another "for the last time." But once again Verena has had a secret from her: Ransom's August letter, announcing his firm intention to renew his suit, and with marriage definitely in view. That very morning, moved by Miss Birdseye's death a week ago, Verena had said she had but "five words" and ten minutes for Ransom, to say their union was "impossible"—and this was the result, a long day, from ten A.M. till dark, out on the Bay with him all by themselves. Ransom had Verena "in his boat" with a vengeance!

What Olive now sees on her map of those past two years is the unreality of all her teaching effort with Verena, in Boston and in Europe, as if it were a total waste on her part of devotion, love, and hard work. But the reader should know that her backward vision now is anything but accurate. In the first place, those were the best two years of Olive's life. Even more, James ends by giving Olive the recognition that Verena had meant more to her all that time than she had ever done to Verena. In other words, Olive had taken more from Verena than she had given. This balancing of giving and taking is always on James's mind in his loving pair-ups. Jean Strouse tells us it was a James family habit. Our successful Yankee merchant's daughter, Olive, sharply reminds herself in these same pages of her two large monetary payments to Verena's parents, and takes a mean satisfaction in denying hospitality to the now expensively dressed Mrs. Tarrant. Olive has got what she paid for out of their child, and in her detached, unfeeling, Boston-calculating mind, Olive can honestly see she has no further rightful personal claim on Verena. Olive is also made to realize, in this calculating and cold side of her mind, that Ransom's male claim on Verena is "natural" and therefore (according to the mentality of her time) irresistible. Olive's remaining feeling for Verena, thus mapped out, is simply pity—pity coupled with a strong sense of her own superiority. Olive takes satisfaction in not being a victim of any such "natural" feelings for men, but on the contrary holds to nothing but contempt and hatred.

Chapter thirty-nine maintains the essential new tone of the whole January, 1886 installment, consisting of the last half of chapter thirty-eight and chapters thirty-nine and forty as well. These pages all are much more tautly written than the previous ones, indicating that James finally knows where he is going and means to get there with but one installment of overrun. The main thrust is Olive's response to Ransom's obduracy in his pursuit of Verena: she becomes in truth a fighting woman, who wins her own personal struggle against her false modesty and "superior" delicacy, and at last casts off her humbugging pose of being a helpless victim of the brutal male. James shows her becoming a woman of sincere courage and commitment, but at the cost of submitting herself to all the vulgarity of her frankly democratic appeal to the Boston public. Chapter thirty-nine ends with Olive stealing a march on the stupidly overconfident Ransom.

Chapter thirty-nine, judging by the sweeping pretensions of its crude rhetoric, is an altogether unworthy scramble for recovery by James, but it has the virtue of getting him and us back on solid ground. Instead of being made up of solid, lengthy paragraphs of unnovelistic diegesis, chapter thirty-nine offers five "two" scenes, in one of which Olive finally achieves maturity and solidity as a person. In another, we have a highly stageworthy curtain scene, with a triumphant line for Olive, three times repeated, and a final *cri déchirante* of the type with which Desclée would freeze the souls of playgoers at the Gymnase Dramatique.

Besides the dramatic *scènes à deux*, James takes the easy way out by shifting Ransom offstage for a week, via an exchange of notes with Verena. These decampings are always associated with broken engagements in James. Here he also has Miss Birdseye's death and burial to tuck away, hugely affecting for Verena but fairly trivial to Ransom. He uses delivery of the notes to inform us of Dr. Prance's exit and her picture of Olive and Verena moping in silent gloom. Ransom is at his worst, asininely cocksure of his now successful self, his power over Verena, his ability to please women, and his "chivalry," to all except Olive.

Bad as James's writing, as such, is in the several pages during which he presents this worst day of Olive's life, it's fascinating to see him throw his best devices into such a forlorn effort at recovery. He's like the general he makes of Olive, staking his best troops on a last charge. He wins, too; fortunately literary devices are not so mortal as battalions of men. My conviction is that he put this chapter together in a single operation of his craftskills. In the process he seems more or less impelled to make important choices. First, his chosen heroine is Olive, and he reverts to her chief experience, the walk from her personal agon with Mrs. Burrage, ending in her hour of reflection in Washington Square and her decision to "give Verena up" to Henry Burrage. Later, however, James fits her into Isabel's place, returning with Pansy from the carriage ride in which she felt as her own all the centuries-old sorrows of Rome: that's how Olive feels, after her busy morning of housekeeping and letter-writing subsequent to the sad burial of Miss Birdseye—which she'd been deceived into feeling had forever tied Verena to herself and their cause. At the knowledge, now certain, that she couldn't trust Verena she was desolated of all her mere personal hope and joy. James would like us to believe she's become a tragic figure, blinded like Oedipus to worldly satisfaction of any kind. Nevertheless, Olive is selfish, narrow-minded, and mean-spirited as ever, still incapable of rising above her superior sense of pity for Verena. As for the other half of the tragic catharsis: Olive feels no terror, but she sees that Verena does.

James is almost too good at analyzing Olive's emotional progress, from the nameless dread she felt at her first sight of Ransom, to her present gamut from settled gloom to frantic anxiety. He lays on the rhetoric so thick, however, that we really can't take this Olive very seriously. At least, not until she finally makes her way to her dark, dead silent house at nightfall, in a quite sudden seizure of agonized fear that Verena has drowned in the bay, and that her dead body will be found, in her white dress, washed ashore in some hidden cove. (James had waxed lyrical on such "coves" a few pages earlier.) Then, suddenly (James loves "suddenlys") Olive sees Verena:

> Verena was in the room, motionless, in a corner—the first place in which she had seated herself on re-entering the house—looking at her with a silent face, which seemed strange, unnatural, in the dusk. Olive stopped short, and for a minute the two women remained as they were, gazing at each other in the dimness. After that, too, Olive still said nothing; she only went to Verena and sat down beside her. She didn't know what to make of her manner; she had never been like that before. She was unwilling to speak; she seemed crushed and humbled. This was almost the worst—if anything could be worse than what had gone before; and Olive took her hand with an irresistible impulse of compassion and reassurance. From the way it lay in her own she guessed her whole feeling—saw it was a kind of shame, shame for her weakness, her swift surrender, her insane gyration, in the morning. . . . Distinctly, it was a kind of shame. . . . She wished to keep the darkness. It was a kind of shame.
>
> The next morning Basil Ransom rapped loudly.

The suddenness of the sharp contrast between this "dark scene" and the one between Olive and Ransom that follows it without a break until it gives Olive a triumphant act-four curtain, makes perhaps the most dramatic moment in the whole novel. Olive finally had felt "terror"—not tragic but comic terror, because while she thinks of losing Verena in death the loved one is actually there looking at her. It's the kind of resurrection Dumas fils used to end *le Démi-Monde*. The result is that she loses her sense of superiority and with it her (never tragic) pity. What she feels instead, as James quite marvellously says, is "an irresistible impulse of compassion and reassurance." With his seemingly infallible gift of using the same words we have seen used only recently, he employs the two terms that transform Olive from a consumer, a user, and a taker, into a giving, supportive, "feeling-with" person. "Reassurance" is rather formal for "support," but "compassion" has the status nowadays of an absolute buzz-word. The truth is that too much of Olive is social case-study rather than live personal fiction, but for its date it is a social case study of remarkable insight.

One of the benefits of this kind of structural comparison is to lead us to look back at James's presentation of Isabel. We see then how all the Jamesian devices that creakily ("unnaturally," as Olive comments) give effective dramatic shape to this chapter thirty-nine are more fully, and so naturally and movingly present in *The Portrait of a Lady*. And, in addition, they have a most important organic function. Not only do they signify a decisive change in the heroine, but they bring the novel to an end which isn't a closure.

James, in reusing his devices in this chapter, gave a precise name and a clear explanation of the importance of such an "hour of backward clearness" in his method of characterization. Olive's thought-processes have been cleared, in both instances, by the imminent threat of losing Verena: first to a husband, then, here, in death. The result of her first "walk-off" and its subsequent "hour of backward clearness" in Washington Square had been a first stage of growth in Olive's mature personality. She had managed to accept the partial loss of Verena to the Burrages as a compromise that made sense by comparison to the total loss she would suffer if Verena were united to Ransom. Now James shows her to us, five months later (he persists in making it only three months), and after the four last weeks in which she had to inure herself to the loss of Verena to Ransom for (at least) an hour each day. After the depths of rhetorical gloom to which James commits Olive and us for this long late-August day, and regardless of explicit claims for Olive's tragic stature, the mere fact of the matter is that she at last realizes that her mission, her own lifelong destiny, is not Verena's. She knows she cannot blame Verena for disloyalty to herself when the young woman is only obeying her inherent nature (we see Olive as a victim of her era). Even Ransom, she acknowledges with loathing, is only being true to the brutal nature of men. So much James tells us about Olive's new "clearness"; he begs off telling us any more, claiming his ignorance three times, like St. Peter. It is as if as narrator he were giving way to his own often-invoked principle of privacy and denying himself the right to authorial omniscience. Perhaps these denials finally made him conscious of his own preference for much less than omniscience, to the point where he erected "into a law," what he had made his earliest method.

Aside from this act of candor, author to reader, just how mechanical the mere plotting of this thirty-ninth chapter is can be shown by comparing it with, not his masterpiece this time, but the "fourth act" section of *The Europeans*, equally grotesque and as awkwardly meant to "shame" a heroine. James set Eugenia's shaming up by moving Robert Acton offstage to Newport, for a cooked-up reason. Just so he now moves Ransom off to Provincetown, with the motive of a note from Verena begging a few days in which she can think over his demands. Ranson returns to a meeting with Verena, which he has demanded in another letter. It lasts all day and results in deeply shaming her, as Eugenia was shamed by Acton's crass response on finding her with a clumsily-hidden Clifford when he returned. There is no improvement in dramatic logic, because Ransom's withdrawal and return are a mere James device better suited to the manners of society. There is, however, an important improvement in novelness, because the actual source of Verena's shame is not made clumsily explicit. The drama is all in the emotional transformation Olive, unlike Acton, is made to undergo.

Then, with the lapse of a night and most of a morning, but only a period between two paragraphs in James's text, we are shown Ransom's confrontation with a whole new Olive "mobilizing" her forces for a great victory in the war for women's rights. There had been no such dramatic "turn" in *The Europeans*. (Which, in its four installments, is a better work of art than *The Bostonians*, even though in it James is a less mature novelist.)

A rereader is likely to think Ransom's compulsions thinly disguise James's own need to wrap up a novel that had got out of hand from the start. His custom was to intersperse quite arbitrary periods of time purposely left vacuous. He could then engage in what he called "harking back to catch up," pretty much at will, until he'd brought his readers where he needed them to be for his continuation. The whole catching-up procedure, being spontaneous, to him wasn't arbitrary. Perhaps most of those who love to reread James enjoy the way he plays catch-up, once they become aware of what there is to enjoy by comparing his fictive doings with what they've come up with by the use of their own imaginations—which they may preen themselves by preferring to "the master's."

Isabel Returns to Rome

Late the following morning, upon her arrival at the station in Rome, Isabel followed an impulse. Sending her maid on with their things to the Casa Rocanera, she ordered her own vehicle to Pansy's convent. She was greeted warmly at the gate, with a degree of consideration that rather surprised her, and immediately taken to the apartment of her stepdaughter. This somehow seemed to have been enlarged by the opening of a door to include an additional room, where Pansy was discovered in the act of instructing a half-dozen very little girls in the art of arranging flowers. At Isabel's entrance she blushed, but with perfect composure made her small pupils curtsy and greet the Signora. Soon she had finished what she wished to do with them and sent them away, each with her little offering for a favorite altar. Then Pansy embraced her stepmother with a degree of ardor that rather took Isabel's breath away.

"Oh my dearest Isabel!" she exclaimed, with an emphasis that struck our heroine as a new note in the girl's very tempered register. But then Pansy drew back and looked, a trifle anxiously, into her eyes as she asked, "May I call you Isabel? I have been thinking of you, oh so very much, since you went away, and for a long time I have been thinking of you always as 'Isabel.' Do, please, let me call you that."

Pansy's voice, in English, seemed different now, more expressive and less controlled, though still a bit foreign, somehow. It was odd, for Isabel was rather sure she had few opportunities of speaking English with anyone—except her small pupils perhaps.

"Oh, do Pansy, call me Isabel. Have you missed me?" Kissing her stepdaughter on a cheek in which the blood was still freshly rising, Isabel realized she was taken aback, after all, at her evident strength of feeling. She had expected some, indeed, but not so much.

"Yes, I missed you terribly. I so much wished to write to you, you know."

Isabel at this felt a small stab of guilt. To write to Osmond had been out of the question. A note every once in a while to poor Pansy, on the other hand, would only have been gracious in her, and she realized too late that she would have been rather glad to spend some of her heavy hours in that way. She was really very fond of Pansy, after all, she now could see. "Haven't you had many visitors?"

Pansy, with another sign of change in her manner, looked at her with a half-sad little smile. "Not the kind I really want."

Isabel, who felt that her question had been more than answered, could not restrain a certain curiosity of her own. "Has Madame Merle been to see you?"

"Oh, yes. She came to say good-bye." Then, noticing that this did not satisfy, Pansy added, "She went back to America soon after you left. I thought you knew. She was very nice to me, really. She gave me some awfully pretty things. That's one of the reasons I've been so wanting to have you come back, Isabel. They are so lovely and I haven't been able to show them to anybody at all, almost."

On Isabel this artless speech struck tellingly. Once again she was moved to the inward reflection, "Poor Madame Merle." It was evident enough that this inwardness of sympathy was not shared by her young friend, however, from whose mind the image of that brilliant and elegant person had already vanished. The girl's indifference left our young woman with a sense of mission and challenge almost too great for her usual self-regard. One part of the mysterious structure of the past which Gilbert Osmond and Serena Merle and Pansy Osmond shared was now crystal clear: the girl's mother wished her to marry, and to marry the man she truly loved. Her father wished no such thing. He had wished her to marry to satisfy his own ambition, in a manner that Isabel needed to grit her teeth to think of again, it was so stupid, so insanely self-defeating, and yet so typical of him.

"I don't suppose the Countess Gemini has been to see you, has she? It's hard for her to make the trip to Rome, of course." As she said this, Isabel recalled the Countess's words to her, that she was a woman who had been used.

"No. Father doesn't like me seeing her, you know. We've hardly ever had anything to say to each other anyway. Actually, I've been seeing a good deal of papa—though not to talk to. He comes here often now."

Pansy looked at her stepmother as one who had something of major interest to communicate and who is trying to decide the difficult question of how to break possibly upsetting news. "I am surprised." Isabel cared more for Pansy's unease than anything else. "Has he taken a fancy to the dear nuns?"

Pansy smiled. "No, it's been the other way about. They've taken a fancy to him. Especially Mère Justine. She started a novena for him. At first it was for me, really, that he would relent and let me leave. But then he met Monsignor Pacelli, and now they are all praying for him."

"Praying for him?" Isabel could only wish success to the efforts of the good ladies, and feared she failed to entirely avoid expressing a mild skepticism. "Is there a particular saint for daughters with difficult fathers?"

Pansy blushed. "Oh no, it isn't exactly for me any more. Papa is taking instructions from Monsignor Pacelli." Then, seeing some incomprehension, she added, "To become a Catholic, you know."

At this Isabel was more than surprised, for nothing in her life with Osmond had prepared her for even a slight turn on his part toward religion of any denomination. Once turned, however, it seemed to her almost inevitable—in Rome, after all—that being a member of the official church would only be the thing to suit him. She was able to make very little of the development; what it would mean to Pansy she could not tell. But she saw that Pansy had more to communicate, and asked about the mysterious *monsignore*.

"He gives us older girls lectures in religion." Pansy seemed anxious to reassure Isabel. "He's very nice, not terribly old at all. One or two of the girls are in love with him." If it had been anyone but Pansy, Isabel might have thought she giggled a little.

"Does he talk to you about getting married?" Isabel suddenly wondered whether Ned Rosier was a Catholic. Pansy nodded. "I only hope he says the same things to papa that he says to us."

Isabel was silent a while. Then, smiling, "And what does Mother Justine think? Which saint gets the credit for this miracle?"

Pansy gave a little laugh. "Oh, it's not any saint. The nuns pray right to our Blessed Mother for something like that. They like papa but I don't believe they think he's an easy case. Besides, the *Monsignore* is very popular, lots of foreigners have taken instructions from him. The nuns make jokes about it."

"But Pansy, why do you suppose your Father has become interested?"

The girl now began to lose her gaiety. Her unaccustomed gossipy, even girlish manner reverted to the serious, composed mien Isabel well knew in her. But she was very earnest as she replied, "Papa was very upset for a while, I'm pretty sure. At first he came to see me more often than he had done ever before, and I even think he may have been lonesome. You had gone away, you know, so had Madame Merle. While he was here he struck up an acquaintance with Monsignore Pacelli, and they seemed to get along very well with each other. Maybe he just likes to talk to someone like that. His family are princes."

It came back to Isabel that Ralph had once likened Osmond to an exiled prince. She was sure at any rate that there was nothing the least bit vulgar in Monsignore Pacelli. "I suppose they have a lot to say about history and heresies and papal infallibility." Truly, though, she could not imagine Osmond discussing any of these topics, and turned to a more pertinent inquiry. "What has become of Mr. Rosier? I suppose you're not allowed to write." Pansy reddened. Isabel was pleased, however, that instead of becoming either anxious or sorrowful her face took on an expression she had not seen there before: a look of determination, of alertness that seemed conscious of something secret, a hidden resource that gave the pretty features a quite adult air for the moment.

"No, Isabel, of course I'm not allowed to receive letters from young gentlemen, especially Mr. Rosier. I haven't tried to write to him, either. But I do hear about him."

Isabel wondered how. "Surely the nuns don't talk about him?"

"Oh, no, though I'm sure they know about him. They are very careful about that sort of thing. As a matter of fact, Madame Merle mentioned Mr. Rosier."

"Was she sympathetic to him?"

"Not exactly sympathetic—you know how she is. She was encouraging though, to me I mean. She said she was glad to see that I was a courageous girl. Those were her words. It was funny, Isabel. All that time she was with me I had the feeling she was trying very hard to make me like her. I never have, you know." Again Isabel found Pansy looking her right in the eye with a newfound directness which on her part she found the least bit intimidating. She asked a temporizing question. "Don't you think she liked you?"

"Now I think maybe she always did. I'm sure she was never used to children. She always treated me in a very grown-up way. She never kissed me or hugged me the way people do when they are fond of little children. She did give me things, but they were always for things I'd outgrown, never pretty things, not like presents. But then papa never seemed to notice when I needed them, so really I should have been grateful."

"So you think she would be happy if you married Mr. Rosier?" This was as far as Isabel dared to go. "She didn't mention marrying him. But the last things she gave me are things I can wear when I get married."

Isabel found the best reply to this was to fold Pansy in her arms and impress a kiss on her cheek. As she did she had a vision of her part in Pansy's little drama. She too was a gift from Madame Merle to that young person, meant to serve her as a very special wedding present indeed. All Isabel had ever read about weddings and good fairies or bad fairies, present or absent at them, seemed to hover over their two heads as they embraced. She was clearly designed to be the fairy present at the wedding of Pansy, if there ever was to be a wedding at all; and, in that case, her presence would be the cunning outcome of a long train of scheming by—some fairy or other!

Our young woman, whose comic sense we have hitherto called in question, was yet nowise deficient in a sturdy ironic penetration even when directed at pretensions of her own. It was what had prevented her resenting very deeply the use to which that inordinate woman had so cleverly put her. She had had occasion, many times over the last several years, to recall almost the exact terms by which she gained her first impression of Gilbert Osmond. Madame Merle had been her informant then and she had said little but the truth. What Isabel was now able to see much too well for her own satisfaction was that the man's defects, serious and perhaps fatal as they were, had been named frankly enough but in such an artful way as to gratify the superior feeling of a vain, inexperienced girl. It was a blow for Isabel to think this, though she had known it in an unthinking sort of way for a long time, even before the Countess Gemini put it into words she could not but understand. Now she found that she could bear the thought as well as the reality, and all the better because she held in her arms another young woman, strangely like herself as she had been then, and strangely too the plaything of those who would put her to their use.

She held Pansy before her at arms' length and studied her with care. "I am taking a very good look at you, dear. I shall be able to give a fresh account of you to everyone concerned." And she laughed. It was a challenge; she felt revived.

Isabel had wondered only slightly about her reception at Palazzo Rocanera. It was heartwarming, though since the master of the house was not at home it was limited to the servants. In her own room and feeling, suddenly, quite tired, she lay upon the bed and allowed her mind to drift idly for some little while, without however falling into anything like sleep. She almost consciously evaded the problem that might have kept her quite wakeful—of the manner in which she should greet her husband when they should encounter each other again. Instead she rather lost herself in drowsy recollections, as if binding together the ties of memory which had seemed so strangely severed once she parted from Gardencourt. Her room, though cool as it was possible for a chamber to be in the Roman June, was altogether different from an English bedchamber; the marble, the stone was all about her. View there was none at all, of course, with doors and shutters closed. Yet her sense of being more at home now was stronger than ever, and as for Albany really that old home scarcely crossed her mind any more.

The thought of Caspar Goodwood came to her, not as a home thought at all, for she associated him with New England and factories, but because of his protestations that he and she would make their home wherever in the world she might wish. What liars men are, she thought without much resentment, when they are trying to make love to a woman. It was altogether impossible to imagine Caspar making his home in Rome. In her present mood this impossibility insensibly turned into a memory of her last dealing with Caspar—his kiss. For the first time she allowed herself to linger over the surprise of it, its unprecedentedness. No one had ever kissed her like that. Most of all, her own husband had never done it. Herein was a mystery that to Isabel was filled with sadness, but with a queer elusive tremor of hope. There was perhaps something left in her life with Gilbert, something neither of them had yet drawn upon that might come to redeem them from the dry hostility in which they were held. It had been so different that other May in Rome, was it but four years ago? She had been here with Ralph, and Gilbert had wanted to be with her, she remembered, and she had asked him to come from Florence and spend time with her. They had been very happy days for her—for him too, she was certain of that. She hadn't known, then, how rare it was for Osmond to be happy, to be pleased as he was those two weeks in Rome, seeing her every day. They had all been happy: Ralph could still get about, Henrietta and Bantling went everywhere; even Madame Merle, back in Florence, was able to spend a little time with her daughter. It was melancholy to feel as she did that Ralph was gone now, and so was Madame Merle, and that she was left to work out the unsolved problem of those three lives as best she could. Was the answer to figure largely in making up the sum of her own life, then?

If there was a part in life Isabel refused to play more strenuously than any other, it was the role of victim. It seemed to her that the source of most of the Contessa Gemini's hapless follies was the way she threw herself into the part of the wronged wife of a vicious husband. "Taking revenge," "finding excuses," was not for our young woman, she was certain. Neither did it suit Osmond, as she very willingly conceded. His continual air of restraint, of holding himself and his finer feelings in check while he endured the more or less grievous trials to which they were subjected—by his headstrong wife most of all!—was almost the worst trial she had to endure from him. So she was spared from taking vain satisfaction in notions of her own virtue in having resisted the amorous advances of others. Indeed she now recalled with peculiar sharpness the moment of elation, during that other spring in Rome, when Lord Warburton had repeated his proposal. It had made her think how much more fortunate she had been in waiting for Gilbert Osmond! That moment in the ruins of the Sacred Way, when she had felt she was happier, perhaps, than she should ever be again—how prophetic it had been!

Poor Isabel was now conscious of how very small a share of virtue she was entitled to claim for resisting amorous advances from Lord Warburton. With Caspar, though, the case was different. She had carefully avoided thinking of his kiss, blocking it off as the brutal invasion of her pure kindness to him it had at first seemed to be. Now she allowed herself to dwell upon its effect, its mysteriously combined repugnance and appeal to responses she had hardly been aware of possessing. This ignorance (the more flattering term innocence never occurred to her) she now found deeply disturbing, even a kind of accusation. She had been kissed often enough—in better days!—by her husband; they had loved each other, she had borne him a child. How had she been at fault? But the child had died. Isabel had never been able to open this part of her memory afterward; she had taken a desperate kind of refuge in forgetfulness, a forgetfulness that every one around her conspired to preserve her in, her husband most of all.

Her freshest experience at this moment, however, was of Pansy. The girl was limited, perhaps repressed, deprived, confined, frustrated of her dearest desire, but through it all, alive. She too was Gilbert Osmond's child, Serena Merle's child. But it was Isabel whom she loved, loved as her mother. It came to Isabel that Madame Merle would never have left Pansy with her if the fondness of their relation had not been apparent to her, as indeed this truly inordinate woman had planned it should become. It occurred to her also that Madame Merle had never given her anything in particular, during their few months of close companionship; rather oddly, she had not a single keepsake to remind her of the person who had completely shaped and altered her life. What she had given her was Pansy.

Another rueful smile, or half-smile rather, appeared on Isabel's lips, had there been a spectator to note it, as she told herself it was her fate to be the receiver of gifts, gifts perhaps too generously given by admirers more willful than kind. Mr. Touchett's gift of seventy thousand pounds, for which she was now to hold Ralph responsible; Mrs. Touchett's original gift of transporting her from her orphan home to the European fairyland; Ralph Touchett's arbitrary anticipation of the family beneficence in order to make sure she, Isabel Archer, a mere American girl, should do as she saw fit in perfect freedom of her will. At the last, she had given back to Ralph all that she could; she had defied her husband to do it.

There it was, before her mind at last. Her husband—how was she to meet him? It was not hard for her to guess how he would meet her, if she were to leave it up to him to set the tone of their reunion; no doubt with something only exceeding silence by the minimum of speech required to mingle unconcern with utter disapproval. Other wives, she knew well enough, might have wondered whether their spouses would come home at all to a house thus empty for some weeks. Osmond, however, was if anything too much inclined to keep to his own house, to his own vast apartment in fact, particularly since, from being simply in the choicest of taste, it had acquired the beginnings of an even princely touch. In their Roman establishment, where he was close to the obscurest as well as the most showy hoards of curiosities and antiquities, Osmond had ceased to be the entire gentleman of leisure. Steadily, but with the most careful economy, he had been acquiring things that even Isabel, who had small taste for "things," was fain to see a value in. The sums of money her English bankers paid into their account in Rome were mostly spent by Gilbert on these treasures, to Isabel's complete satisfaction, for she herself had yet to find a way of spending money that gave her any special pleasure.

Isabel, therefore, was led to decide she must make a beginning with Osmond that very day. A beginning of what, she was unable to say as yet: of some kind of new life, at any rate, between the two of them and in relation to her own strong sense of a responsibility for Pansy. Hitherto she had only arranged a mere fraction of her own life, amounting to little more than her "evening" each week. She must do better than that, she resolved. If possible, she would arrange it all, with enough to spare to accomplish the mission that had been left to her. She had been conscious recently of more tribulation in her life than she had ever endured, or even feared she might have to submit to. She had felt her humiliations with a proportionate keenness. With it all she felt a determination rising in her to gain control of matters at least where her stepdaughter's happiness was in jeopardy, whatever might be her own future lot. Rising from the bed, she rang for her maid. She would start here and now.

Long since a young Italian maid had been found for Mrs. Osmond, who was able to acquaint her with the present state of household affairs and all the notable events that had occurred in her absence, which indeed had not been many. Once again, however, it was the Monsignore Pacelli who provided the principal novelty, for he had graced Casa Rocanera more than once as the dinner guest of Signore Osmond, and in the course of sundry words with cook and the others had shown himself *simpaticissimo*. Isabel was informed, what was more striking, that the staff had been instructed to be prepared to receive the Monsignore at odd hours of the afternoon and perhaps for the night, whether or not the Signore should be at home. Without too much comment upon her maid's expressions at the unusualness of this variation from the common run, Isabel completed her simple preparations for the remainder of the afternoon and left the rest of the unpacking to her servant. She then visited the kitchen herself, for she had not felt called upon as yet to retain a housekeeper. For one thing, they had a skilled cook enlisted for them on first setting up by Madame Merle, but as they hardly gave dinners at all, Isabel had thought it wise to set no one between herself and this person. There was a sort of major domo, but one could call him almost retiring. Her husband's fondness for servants about the place had not grown since their first acquaintance. Isabel herself rather enjoyed her sessions with these good people, and something in their Italian worldly simplicity somehow fitted better with her American approachableness than did the perhaps more efficient, and certainly more obsequious, care of an English staff.

After renewing acquaintance and learning of some vital family developments, she inquired into preparations for the evening's meal. It was to be very special, she was told. They had been alerted to the likelihood that *il monsignore* would call later in the afternoon, for *il signore padrone* had made a wonderful find for their rooms and was just now supervising its delivery. It was a thing *il monsignore* would take great pleasure in, that was certain! And something else, besides. For Salvatore the cook had had a long discussion with the monsignor about a certain dish that was properly done only among Romans born, and he had been waiting with much eagerness for the occasion to show he was a true Roman.

The mistress of the house was duly impressed, and signified her entire approval. "We shall not have to worry greatly about tea, then, shall we?" she smiled. "Shall we send out for something special, though, just in case. You know some very holy men are fond of sweet things." There was an appreciative laugh, and the kitchen maid who always presided over the arrival of the tea things accepted the responsibility of procurement. Isabel was thus free to make any elaborations she might wish in her plans for the afternoon. First she visited rooms of the *piano nobile* where she was accustomed to receive her guests of a Thursday evening, and was decidedly pleased to find there a few new things hardly eye-catching but of a goodness that she expected of anything Gilbert took the trouble of acquiring. "Like me," she said to herself with a sigh. And for her he had taken trouble as well, Isabel reminded herself. So much care and trouble, it later seemed to her, that she used to marvel as if at a kind of perversity in the man, for he had never cared to take it again. "Then I must have made him like it," Isabel thought. There must have been something about her in that first spring in Rome; she had put Lord Warburton through the hoops, such was his infatuation for her then. So different he had been from the master of Lockleigh she had left behind! Meanwhile what had surprised her in the rooms was a brighter yet richer look to the hangings, of which many were new. Osmond had replaced the excellent but faded stuffs that only cognoscenti set a proper value on with others that to her eye were as valuable but quite new-made. She guessed that his new friend must have guided him to some present-day master of the craft.

With this accession of spirit, Isabel turned away, making for her own apartment in order to array herself somewhat more festively for the sake of their possible guest as well as to mark her reunion with her husband. She was, however, prevented by a slight commotion coming up the staircase from the court, and soon thereafter by the arrival of a person not at all unlike Osmond in age and looks, but dressed in clerical black—as it happened, though, of a careful, distinguished cut and, one would have said, fashionable rather than otherwise. His face, dignified as well, was that of a man at his ease anywhere, with an air of open good humor not so often to be seen under the priestly headgear of the one-time papal city. Clearly he was the monsignor, the favorite already of her kitchen, and Isabel turned cheerfully to welcome him.

"Ah, my dear lady!" he exclaimed with a most pleasant smile, and in very good English. "I am your husband's friend and your humble servant, Ettore Pacelli. It is such a great pleasure to meet you." Isabel was, upon the instant, most favorably impressed by this newcomer, so much so that she wondered whether his "humble servant" had not been offered as a little English pleasantry by one who was accustomed, as royal by blood and sacerdotal by ordinance divine, to the receipt of something more in the way of obeisance than she was likely to offer. In any case she felt herself smiling radiantly and offering her hand to his warm clasp. She then retraced her steps, conducting him into the *salone*, and giving voice to her thought of a few minutes ago.

"I am so very pleased to find that Mr. Osmond has redecorated this room. It was most fine before, of course, but for my taste, I'm afraid, a little bit somber for receiving one's friends." And she invited him to seat himself in her own favorite corner, which was cool and where flowers had been placed, as usual, she had been happy to notice earlier.

"I should say, for what little I know myself, Mrs. Osmond, that you and your husband have a very fine taste. You do honor to this old and very good house. Though rather somber." As he added the phrase, he smiled back at our young woman in such a way as to make her more certain that they had already shared a joke or two and, if her guest had his way, would have a part in many more.

"Have I been mistaken, then?" she smiled in return. "I wondered when I first saw the change whether *'il monsignore'* might not have have guided my husband's choice. They are so new-looking, so much of the present day. That's not Mr. Osmond's usual style."

"'*Il monsignore*'? Is that meant to reveal a hidden gift in your humble servant for choosing draperies? Well, Mrs. Osmond, since it is a very soft impeachment, I will admit it. I have had occasion to pick and choose among vestments—the uniform of our service, the livery of our Master, you know, and I am acquainted with some excellent artisans. But perhaps you are also right in judging that the room looks more welcoming now. But then it has the altogether more great advantage of the presence of its mistress."

And he smiled at Isabel as if he did not mean it as a compliment but, simply, meant what he said. He looked, indeed, as if he wished to say more, feeling perhaps as our young woman began to suspect that he might not soon again have such an opportunity to be alone with Mr. Osmond's wife. And shortly he spoke.

"Your husband, Mrs. Osmond, isn't naturally a cheerful man, I should say? Do forgive me; you may very well find my poor observations very far from the truth. But I have seen so many Italian men like him, especially in the last years. Mr. Osmond like them has the serenity of the Stoic, but no inner lightness of the mind, or soul shall we say, that opens one's heart to joy or, even, real peace within the spirit. I have friends like him, old companions, members of my family even. Not all of them are Catholics, either; I know a few who are entirely modern in their ideas. Some of these men are religious, but I must tell you, very, very few. I was very happy when your husband asked me to instruct him in the Catholic faith, although he did not seem like one of the religious ones at all. He seemed sadder than most—at that time, I mean, in your absence, my dear Mrs. Osmond. I thought then it was your absence that had saddened him most."

Isabel might have taken these confidences amiss, but somehow she did not. She did not derive from a native stock famed for their tenacity of reserve, as the reader is well aware. Thus, though she did not embrace the notion of confession, she felt that Gilbert's friend was entitled to know that he had some reason for lacking gaiety of spirit.

"I'm afraid, in a way, I may have been more responsible than I wished in that, though against my will. Mr. Osmond was opposed to my going to England; I don't know whether he may have mentioned it to you or not. I felt I could not allow an old and true friend of mine to depart from this world without being present at his death. Truly it was a debt I owed to him."

"That does make it clearer. When I tell you that Mr. Osmond seemed particularly impressed by our Catholic rejection of divorce, I may give a wrong impression—yes, I think I would. He may simply have felt an unusual anxiety over your return, perhaps; I'm sure, no matter for that, he will be overjoyed to see you. Does he know of it?"

The fact that his question seemed to expect a return in the negative did much to relieve Isabel of a measure of embarrassment as she replied: "No, I'm afraid I haven't been able to write at all, it was a very sad time for me, too." Then, as she saw he was about to take prompt steps toward vacating the field, in the very natural apprehension that his presence would be superfluous at the reunion of these two spouses, equivocal as he might very well fear its tone would be, Mrs. Osmond went on with firm, reassuring hospitality. "Please don't think of leaving before Gilbert returns—with his precious new trophy. I'm sorry to say I'm hardly equal to the responsibility of appreciating such things. If you go he'll be deprived of the best part of his pleasure in it."

As Isabel uttered these words she had an odd sense of gratitude to her companion, for she felt herself being not only gracious and one might say, wifely, but perfectly sincere in the sentiments she had expressed to him. She was led to speak a few more words. "I'm going to see if I can't make it up to him." She said, offering it as another pleasantry between them.

Making very little of it, Monsignor Pacelli kept his seat and began to look about him.

"Is it something destined for this chamber, do you suppose? Have you had time to notice the new things?"

"Perhaps not. Mr. Osmond had begun to take his own room in hand, his working place. I'm sure he will make it into a studio that will reflect his different interests, his own drawings as well as his acquisitions."

"Ah, yes. You know I admire his drawings very much. Now that we have photographs of everything, almost no one bothers to make those careful, lovingly detailed floral pieces. Those draughts your husband does of scenes one recognizes so fondly, in the mountains, or in some little city nook, they give such pleasure! Not like photographs at all, truly."

Strangely, at this praise Isabel now did rather feel she was blushing. "Ah, you make me feel just how inadequate I am to value what Gilbert does. Not that my failure is of any importance. I know that his drawing does not always meet with approval, though, even from those whose judgment he respects. I suppose what you say about photography is quite true."

"Ah, there is much about Mr. Osmond that takes one back to an older time," he said, evidencing no disapproval. "Perhaps a better time, too, at least for those who were able to enjoy it properly—like monsignori fortunate enough to be well situated in Rome," he added with a dismissive smile. "But you know, his drawings somehow remind me of that little girl of his, Miss Osmond. Very proper, nothing 'showy' as I think you say, but discreet, correct in a most appealing way."

"Oh yes," Isabel responded enthusiastically. "I saw her at the convent this morning, on my way home from the station. She does enjoy your lectures."

"Oh, she is a good little person. I try to put some helpful advice in her way; I know she can make use of it. She is not at all like some of those little convent girls, Mrs. Osmond, I can say to you in the greatest of confidence." This aside was accompanied with an air of mock secrecy, amusing indeed in a personage who might easily have passed for one of the more astute denizens of a papal court. "I hardly feel equal to several of the 'little girls' I deliver my wise messages to. So I pray for them. They will need it."

"Do you pray for Pansy too?" Isabel asked, in the same pleasant vein.

"Ah, now I am surprised. In general, yes, I pray for all those to whom I am offering instruction, including your good husband. But you mean I should pray for Miss Osmond more particularly?"

Isabel hesitated. "Perhaps it's none of my affair. But I rather imagine that Mother Catherine and Mother Justine are praying for her quite hard."

"Oh, Mrs. Osmond, of course it's your affair. I will never admit to think of you as a stepmother to that dear little person, or as not loving her as your own. *Belle-mère*, that is what you are to her, I am quite certain. And tell me, if you think it prudent, why she is in need of even more prayer than those holy nuns are bringing to bear?"

Isabel, indeed, might almost have told this most kind inquirer, but in the circumstances (to which his priestly garb could not but add a touch of solemnity) she could not altogether deem it prudent to do so.

"Oh, I'm sure you will know in due course, Monsignor Pacelli, or perhaps I'll tell you some day. I do agree with you about Pansy, of course. But I'm not sure myself just how things stand." And she looked him in the eye with a self-mocking, rueful smile. "I've not been on the scene for a whole month, after all."

He laughed, and they talked of other, less personal matters until Isabel excused herself in order to see that all was in order. If Monsignor Pacelli had a breviary to read it was not visible, and she left him alone with the other fine things Osmond had collected, indicating as she went the periodicals neatly placed within his reach. She did not, however, hurry away, nor did she make any effort to hurry back. Her husband's guest, now hers as well, would certainly be able to entertain himself for an indefinite period. One of the reasons she had been feeling at home, it now occurred to her, was the so much easier pace of life on Roman time. Nothing could have brought this fact into more precious relief than her last experience of Caspar Goodwood.

As she mounted the stairs to her own room she was reminded of the descent Caspar had made upon her when she had written him from Rome, announcing her engagement. He had run her to earth, so to speak, in Florence, a hard journey from Boston of three thousand miles, lasting seventeen days, and only to berate her unforgivingly for changing her mind without explaining matters to him. Halfway up the great staircase she came suddenly to a complete stop, poised on a marble tread. What if he had kissed her then? It was hard for her to understand his restraint, now that she knew. He had been too angry, that was the reason. He had been passionate then, too, and he had infected her with his passion, but it had been anger, not love. It was the wrong passion.

As she resumed her climb, Isabel remembered her own outburst of tears five minutes after Caspar left her—why had she cared? Her feelings were hurt by his rudeness, his brutality. Not so: she, too, had been very angry. What had been hurt was her pride, or somewhat more specifically, her confidence that she could at all times please herself in her relations with other people and yet always be in the right, always be her reasonable, sensible self. It was Caspar who made her feel suddenly responsible for the extravagant waste of his time and energy. Over a month of hard travel, only to spend five minutes insulting her! She had to contrast his passion with the patience of her other lover. It was American time against Italian time. But the least she could say in simple fairness was that Gilbert had spent a great deal of time and care, too, in pleasing her, Caspar no time at all. During the month of Caspar's transit she had seen Osmond almost every day and had enjoyed his company almost every minute of the time. Surely she was better off as she was, in Rome, than she should have been married to Mr. Goodwood and, in all likelihood, back in Boston.

Whether we ought to commiserate with her, or perhaps admire her for at last determining to face up to her situation and take matters into her own hands to the extent she was able, Isabel became aware as she finished the passage to her room that she might have been worse off as Mrs. Goodwood than as Mrs. Osmond—surely would have been, passion or no passion. Reflecting thus, she never needed to overcome an unconscious abhorrence that prevented her from thinking of herself as Lady Warburton. As she opened her own door it came to her that the big difference, now, was Pansy. Hardly sure she loved any man, now that Ralph was dead, she knew she loved Pansy; aware now, as she had never been before, of her own passion, she sensed the beginning of a radical change in what had always been her own complete self-sufficiency. Those men she had handled so imperiously—so unfeelingly, as she now realized—they had known something in life of which she had been quite ignorant.

Could it be possible that Gilbert too was one of them? Somehow she found it hard to believe that could have been the case. Still, Osmond, who left so much to be desired as a husband, for herself at any rate, was by all seeming a complete enough specimen of the man of the world not to be suspected of so primary a lack of experience. Surely he was not unacquainted with the other way of kissing a woman!

As Isabel seated herself before the glass she brought back to mind those first days of their rather brief engagement and married life. She had been convinced, though without thinking of it at all, they were in love; she knew she had been, and she could not believe even now that he had not been. He had given her every sign of caring; but why had he not given her that sign? Was it possible that she could not at that time accept such a sign from him—or, as was possible, had she in some unconscious way led him to withhold it, delay it, in the notion that it would be premature, unwelcome? It was a chilling thought, and she could not rid herself of it as she stared at her reflection, so very much changed from the image of that spring in Rome and Florence, now over four years ago. Somehow its place was taken by the image of Pansy, so alive and fresh, and with a new intentness of purpose to make so striking a difference from the Pansy of those days; and then, suddenly, in a kind of collapse of long-maintained resistance, the image of her little son, that sad tiny waif so unfitted for life she almost felt no right to grieve as she had wanted to do over his death. No wonder, no wonder, the dreadful thought now came, considering what he had been deprived of in his bringing to birth. With this, Isabel laid her head in her arms and, again, burst into tears, but not of anger. She cried as she had been unable to do those years ago, as indeed she had not done only a few weeks ago, deeply moved as she had been at the death of Ralph. She was able to remember almost nothing of those dreadful months when her infant boy had come into the world so ill-equipped for it and left it so soon. All had seemed a blessed oblivion during the last year, and she assumed someone must have been very good to her—someone not her husband. Pansy, she was sure, perhaps Madame Merle. Madame Merle was, at any rate, she mused with a measure of returning calmness, being kind indeed to her at present. The idea of her abandoning such a complete human person as was Pansy, her own natural child, to the woman who had supplanted her in the arms of the man, the father she must at one time have loved, who must at one time have loved her! It was almost stupefying. Isabel felt deeply, profoundly humble, most of all in the realization that she was grateful; her deep resentment at the deception practiced upon herself dissolved into nothingness in her knowledge, now at last, of all that lay behind it.

Promised Lands: A *Different Drummer*

Eric J. Sundquist

By 1967 William Melvin Kelley counted himself among those African American intellectuals who had turned the corner into radicalism. The splintering of the civil rights movement, the assassination of Malcolm X, and the rise of the Black Panthers had sparked increased denunciation of the integrationist goals identified with Martin Luther King, Jr. Color consciousness surmounted the ideal of color blindness, and Kelley joined those who argued that the philosophy of integration required an untenable contradiction. The black integrationist, wrote Kelley in an essay entitled "On Racism, Exploitation, and the White Liberal," concedes that "to the extent he is black, the black man is not a human being . . . because of his black skin, he can never be more than almost human." Proof that the liberalism of integrationists was doomed lay in the logic of Nazi Germany: "The German liberal, frustrated in his attempts to Germanize the Jew, saw the salvation of his dream of uniformity in Hitler's call for the extermination of the Jews. Only when there were no more Jews would everybody be truly German." We cannot risk discovering what white liberals will do, said Kelley, when they find out that their "dream of American uniformity" cannot be realized as long "as black people exist in America."

Kelley's invocation of the specter of genocide was hardly original in 1967, no more so than his turn to separatism, as a writer, or his ensuing expatriation to France. His reference to the delusion of Jewish assimilation in Nazi Germany, accompanied by the stereotypical observation that the stance of American Jews toward American blacks was one of exploitation, put Kelley in the mainstream of Black Power. Had he chosen, Kelley might have written a novel like Bernard Malamud's *The Tenants*, whose lacerating portrait of the crisis between blacks and Jews, mediated by the rhetoric of the Holocaust, is rendered in the form of hyperbolic allegory. Few writers of the day surpassed Kelley's ability to layer realism with dense abstraction. But his later experimental novels—*dem* (1967) is a piercing satire on racial mixing, *Dumsfords Travels Everywheres* (1970) postmodern work inspired by *Finnegan's Wake*—failed to win a significant audience, while his first and finest novel, *A Different Drummer* (1962), faded from view after brief acclaim. Although the angry separatism and appeal to Nazi Germany to which Kelley felt driven by 1967 are only latent in *A Different Drummer*, this distinctly African American narrative epitomized the uncertainties of black freedom in the early 1960s and forecast the increasing fragility of pluralism in postwar America.

If we style freedom first of all a revolution in consciousness, there is no more exhilarating variation on the Exodus than that incorporated into *A Different Drummer*, whose action is set in May of 1957 and therefore situated on the coming wave of the civil rights movement. Kelley's novel is a spectacular meditation on the trope of migration, the psychology of apartheid, the tenuousness of minority leadership, and the illusions of nationhood. Its premise—the evacuation of all African Americans from a region situated in the American South—is the utopian fulfillment of the black Exodus, an inversion of the proposal periodically advanced by the Communist Party, the Nation of Islam, and others that a separate black republic be created within the borders of the United States. Kelley imagines instead a super-migration and erasure of black life from an imaginary state situated between Tennessee, Alabama, Mississippi, and the Gulf of Mexico produced when, all at once, the state's African Americans simply rise up and leave, stranding the white population in a mock enactment of the racial supremacy that has underlain their laws and social philosophy for nearly four centuries.

The migration that leaves the state without any black population is sparked by Tucker Caliban, a fifth-generation descendent of the story's original, unnamed African, a statuesque maroon whose legendary resistance to enslavement sets in motion the deep historical action of the book when he is hunted down and killed by his would-be owner, Dewitt Willson, at an unspecified date in the early nineteenth century. Suddenly one day in 1957, Tucker Caliban, who has not long before purchased from Willson's great-grandson the parcel of land on which his African ancestor was slain, abandons his apparent intention to farm the land. Tucker Caliban salts his fields, slaughters his animals, destroys his furniture, and burns his house to the ground before setting out with his wife and child on a journey apparently to the North. Within a matter of days, the entire African American population of the state, inspired by Tucker's strange act of prophecy and revolt, follows him in what one white observer calls a "strategic withdrawal," leaving the whites in a bizarre quandary: "It was like attempting to picture Nothing, something that no one had ever considered. None of them had a reference point on which to fix the concept of a Negro-less world."

Carrying to its ultimate conclusion the Hegelian thesis of the master's dependence upon his slave, the ironic bondage that Orlando Patterson has represented as a kind of inverted parasitism, Kelley creates a world in which the racialization of America—not just of the South—stands forth in striking clarity. Without blacks, what is left of white thought, white culture itself? The novel's rich play on the long African American tradition of anonymity and invisibility, from the legends of folklore to Bert Williams to James Weldon Johnson to Ralph Ellison, comes to rest in an illustration of James Baldwin's contention, in *The Fire Next Time*, that "the black man has functioned in the white man's world as a fixed star, as an immovable pillar: and as he moves out of his place, heaven and earth are shaken to their foundations."

Tucker Caliban's revolt symbolically recapitulates the Exodus paradigm that has dominated African American history, whether in the form of escapes from slavery, periodic mass migrations, nationalist schemes for colonization in Africa or Central America, or voluntary expatriation, as in the case of intellectuals such as Richard Wright, Chester Himes, Baldwin, and later Kelley himself. But it also inadvertently fulfills the dream of radical racists that blacks be driven from the land altogether. The result for the white world is an abrupt negativity. The departure of blacks from the State is voluntary and falls short even of preliminary Nazi schemes to make Germany *judenrein* through mass deportation (to Madagascar or elsewhere) rather than mass extermination. Enmeshed in a deeper meditation on diaspora, Kelley's allusion to modern Jewish experience in the novel is no less important for being largely subliminal. By hypothesizing a complete rupture with the world of slavery and segregation while leaving blank the future of this new black diaspora, Kelley's totalizing migration creates a white South that is, so to speak, *negrorein*. In doing so at the very moment that America's confrontation with the

Holocaust assumed a public dimension, Kelley threw the modern meaning of the Exodus into mesmerizing relief.

The compass of Kelley's vision is evident in the title of the opening chapter, "The State," which provides an almanac history of the anonymous territory from which the Exodus is enacted. In addition to the allusion to Thoreau's own private resistance to the "State"—evident first of all in his novel's title, drawn from a famous passage in *Walden*—Kelley's evocative phrase sums up the battle for African American equality. Not just the hypothetical southern state of the novel's primary action is encoded here but other tropes as well: the actual or virtual state of slavery from which African Americans had migrated in multiple reenactments of the journey to the Promised Land; the nation state from which black Americans, in varying degrees, had long been politically and culturally excluded; the jurisprudential conception of the state as an entity lying outside federal oversight, which had been at the heart of interpretations of the constitutional reach of the Fourteenth Amendment from *Plessy* v. *Ferguson* through *Brown* v. *Board of Education*; and the imagined territory of nationalist aspirations by which a subject people might hope to define itself—in the case of African America a diasporic geography coextensive with the history of slavery in the western empire summoned up so vividly by Kelley's naming, in Tucker Caliban, Shakespeare's *The Tempest* as his own master source.

Tucker Caliban has no announced philosophy, but *A Different Drummer* makes no secret of its appeal to Thoreau, in its title, its epigraph, and its dramatization of "a movement . . . started from within . . . at the grass roots." One of the most famous passages in Thoreau's "Resistance to Civil Government" (popularly known as "Civil Disobedience"), is, of course, a prescription for the univocal rebellion of a Tucker Caliban: "If *one* HONEST man, in this State of Massachusetts, *ceasing to hold slaves*, were actually to withdraw from this copartnership, and be locked up in the county jail therefor, it would be the abolition of slavery in America." The uncertain utility of Tucker's act illustrates the double-edged meaning of Thoreau's example.

On the one hand, Thoreau became a celebrated (and well-marketed) catalyst to 1960s activism, in the civil rights movement and otherwise. King's inspiration by Thoreau became legendary—witness his reflection on his organization of the Montgomery bus boycott 1955, in which he expressed his conviction that the boycott was true to Thoreau's argument in "Civil Disobedience": "We were simply saying to the white community, 'We can no longer lend our cooperation to an evil system.'" Or consider John Lewis's instructions to activists preparing for the historic 1960 Nashville sit-ins, where he concluded with the admonition: "Remember the teachings of Jesus, Gandhi, Thoreau, and Martin Luther King, Jr." Such modest but heroic resolve is captured well in Kelley's portrait of the common folk gathered at the bus depot to head into exile: "A few sang hymns and spirituals, but most stood quietly, inching forward, thoughtful, triumphant, knowing they couldn't be stopped." On the other hand, Thoreau's exhortations were abstract to the point of futility, a limitation brought home by one strain of Stanley Elkins's argument in his landmark book *Slavery*. Overshadowed by his infamous use of the Nazi concentration camp as an analogue to southern slaveholding, Elkins' chapter on the politics of antislavery was equally provocative. The Transcendentalists' focus on individual conscience and moral abstraction threatened to drain antislavery of its ethical meaning, said Elkins, leaving each man, like Thoreau, privately at war with a State whose very leniency protected his right to protest that the State had no authority over him whatsoever.

With the exception of Tucker's private war against the State and the Exodus it initiates, the novel depicts floundering and paralysis on both sides of the color line. The puerile philosophy of white segregationists, the stagnation of Left progressivism, and the entire range of activist black leadership associated with the NAACP, Marcus Garvey, Father Divine, the Nation of Islam, the Southern Christian Leadership Conference—all are implicitly held up to suspicion in *A Different Drummer*. The "men on the porch," a white choric group called to witness the migration but otherwise inactive until their manic outburst in a hateful lynching at the end of the novel, follow the sophistic dictates of Mister Harper, a failed military man whose despair has reduced him to a self-willed paralytic life in "a wheel chair as old and awkward as a throne." (Harper is distinctly reminiscent of the homegrown fascist Percy Grimm in Faulkner's *Light in August*, of whom the author said that he had "created a Nazi" before Hitler did. He also points forward to Dr. Strangelove, the mad German émigré scientist, bound to his wheelchair, in Stanley Kubrick's famous 1964 film.) David Willson, the socialist renegade of the patriarchal family, sacrifices the ideals formed during the Depression through his friendship at Harvard with the West Indian black nationalist Bennett Bradshaw to weakness and tradition, becoming a self-loathing rent collector for the family's sharecropping properties. And Bradshaw himself, following a flirtation with a group called the National Society for

Colored Affairs, from which he is purged because of his Communist leanings (much as Du Bois was driven away from the NAACP), becomes a well-heeled religious showman, founder in 1951 of the Resurrected Church of the Black Jesus Christ of America, Inc., which displays a familiar litany of anti-Semitic lore and styles its doctrine on a mix of "Mein Kampf, Das Kapital, and the Bible."

The subconsciously militarized atmosphere of the *A Different Drummer* illuminates the Exodus as a story about the power of a state over a subject people, particularly as it draws upon the escalating counterpoint between federal authority and the claim of states' rights in the battle over desegregation. In addition, the trope of "marching," borrowed from Thoreau and resonant throughout *A Different Drummer*, places the novel within a rich symbolic history. During and after World War II the equivocal militancy of "marching" was foregrounded in the long contemplated March on Washington (first envisioned in the early 1940s by A. Philip Randolph but not realized until King's historic event in 1963) and in renewed calls for blacks to abandon the Jim Crow South. The phenomenon, of course, had a long history, in the modern era dating to Robert Abbott's 1917 exhortation in the Chicago *Defender* that southern blacks must begin "The Flight Out of Egypt" (within two years some 65,000 had moved to Chicago). Until *Brown* v. *Board of Education* and the advent of the modern civil rights movement, the Promised Land remained the geographic North, a theme prevalent in black fiction and poetry, and exemplified in Adam Clayton Powell, Jr.'s book *Marching Blacks* (1945): "As soon as World War II is over millions of marching blacks of the southland must pack up and move. Freedom road is no longer an unmarked trail in the wilderness. It is a highway." Although the North is not yet Canaan, said Powell, the South is ruled by "Der Fuehrer, King Lynch," and those who have been "suckled with the milk of freedom" must turn their backs on the Egypt of the South and renew the "American Exodus."

Well beyond World War II the South appeared to many not simply as an alliance of states bound together by their resistance to federal authority, but, for that same reason, as a kind of "State" in its own right. Although black predictions of true genocide have usually been incredible, the power of the southern "State" to authorize and conceal racial violence in the era of Jim Crow is hardly in question. What Roy Wilkins, editor of *Crisis*, wrote in 1938 remained true through the era of *A Different Drummer*: "The South approaches more nearly than any other section of the United States the Nazi idea of government by a 'master race' without any interference from any democratic process." Kelley's insertion of Thoreau's pacifism—or, more accurately, his eccentric libertarianism—into this setting underscores the tensions growing unbearable as the non-violence of Martin Luther King, Jr. and the Southern Christian Leadership Conference advanced on a collision course with the varying strands of black militancy represented in SNCC (the Student Non-Violent Coordinating Committee), the Nation of Islam, and the Black Panthers.

It is a reminder, moreover, that the militancy of civil rights heroes did *not* take the form of abandoning a fascist state. The historic marches of the civil rights movement—King's March on Washington, the 1965 march from Selma to Montgomery, among others—both recapitulated and redirected previous calls to enact a black Exodus from the South. In this respect, they were marches in which *flight* to a new homeland is superimposed upon reclamation of *rights* to a homeland—namely, the Constitutionally guaranteed rights of the United States. They were a kind of Exodus in place, one in which the homeland was here and now, if only the marchers, as southern activist Lillian Smith said in reflecting on the Freedom Rides just beginning in 1961, had the courage to "climb into the unknown."

By tracking the narrated lives of the modern-day Willson family and Bennett Bradshaw back to the radical politics of the 1930s, *A Different Drummer* alludes not just to the galvanizing effects of totalitarian orthodoxy upon black civil rights in the United States but more specifically to the Communist Party's ill-fated "49th State Movement," which envisioned that southern counties with a majority black population be banded together and converted into a southern Black Belt republic. Neither George Schuyler's ridicule of what he called the "Separate State Hokum" nor the Cold War entirely put to rest this "cartographic fantasy" of a black republic, as Eric Hobsbawn has labeled it. In April of 1968 the National Black Government Conference, a radical black caucus convened in Detroit and later featured in *Esquire* magazine, rejected emigration to Africa and promulgated instead plans for the "Republic of New Africa," a sovereign land modeled on Tanzania's purported cooperative economy and comprised of the five southern states of Louisiana, Mississippi, Alabama, Georgia, and South Carolina, which were to be purchased county by county, like Palestine, through "Malcolm X land certificates" worth $100 each, to a total of some $400 billion. If necessary to secure the new state, armed guerillas and nuclear weapons acquired from China would be deployed.

The bizarre unreality of such a scheme obscures the abiding power of separatist fantasies in the African American imagination. Such a temptation motivated Sutton Griggs's vision of a secret black republic in Texas in his 1899 novel, *Imperium in Imperio*, a book likewise preoccupied with the inability of the federal government to enforce the Fourteenth Amendment; and it led Communist Party member James Allen to speculate in *The Negro Question in the United States* (1936) that the creation of a "Negro Republic" would give southern blacks, as in the Soviet Union, "the right to choose freely between complete independence as a separate state and federation with a state or group of states." Inverting such a promise, Kelley forecast something beyond contemplation, locking utopia and dystopia into a kind of tautology. By writing without reference to a future land of milk and honey—that is, by initiating an Exodus but identifying no sought-for homeland—Kelley exaggerated the pain of the continuing black diaspora. Severed economically, psychologically, and culturally from a homeland, *A Different Drummer* suggests, African Americans are left in a condition of perpetual wandering. Conceivably, the novel is silent on the subject of the Promised Land because Kelley found or anticipated it to be a bankrupt illusion, a mere redesigning of the space of segregation in urban terms that had already been well imagined, for example, in works such as Richard Wright's *Native Son* or Ann Petry's *The Street*, and that Kelley himself had already portrayed in several short stories collected in *Dancers on the Shore* (1964), where the Promised Land for some of his novel's characters turns out to be the Black Belt of Chicago. Or it may be that he saw Tucker's act to fall within the tradition of western messianism whose signal feature, as Michael Walzer has written, "is the apparent endlessness of the Exodus march."

Begun while Kelley was a student in John Hawkes' writing class at Harvard, *A Different Drummer* was almost certainly inspired by an episode in Ray Bradbury's *Martian Chronicles* (1950) entitled "Way in the Middle of the Air." Set in 2003, Bradbury's story begins in the conversation among white men on a hardware store porch in the South—a tableau, just like Kelley's, that could refer to any time within the previous one hundred years—about the shocking exodus of all the "niggers," who have secretly saved their money and built rockets to take them to Mars. Like the episode's title, which echoes a black spiritual, the names ascribed to the rockets by a taunting white man—*Elijah and the Chariot*, *The Big Wheel*, and *Over Jordan*, among them—underscore the biblical meaning of this delivery to the Promised Land of Mars. (The story also echoes Elijah

Muhammad's teaching that Mars was inhabited by a colored race and his enduring prophecy that the reign of a new black civilization would begin, after an apocalyptic destruction of white people, with the arrival of the celestial Mother Plane adumbrated biblically in Ezekiel's Wheel.) Paying one another's debts, maintaining an unfailing courtesy to the white folks, and abandoning their possessions in neat piles along the road, a vast "black tide" of the South's African Americans disappear "straight up into the blue heavens," leaving the white men to contemplate life without a cheap black labor force and the nightriding pleasure of the Ku Klux Klan: "The men on the porch sat down, looked at each other, looked at the yellow rope piled neat on the store shelves, glanced at the gun shells glinting shiny brass in their cartons, saw the silver pistols and long black metal shotguns hung high and quiet in the shadows. Somebody put a straw in his mouth. Somebody else drew a figure in the dust."

Comparable plots would later reappear in Douglas Turner Ward's 1965 stage farce *A Day of Absence* and then again in Derrick Bell's 1992 parable of black expulsion "Space Traders."[1] Bradbury's prescient story set a high creative standard, though, by fusing black migration and civil rights militancy with the aftermath of the Holocaust—the complete removal of a people as though they had disappeared into the blue heavens. At the same time, "Way in the Middle of the Air" posits, even if it does not portray, a homeland—a planetary state that will presumably afford African Americans the rights denied them on earth, much as post-Holocaust Jews were afforded a homeland only with the founding of modern Israel.

Kelley's strange abridgment of Tucker Caliban's revolt registers this ambiguity in the historical moment. As America's Jews, blacks had long since adopted Exodus as their foundational narrative, and they were increasingly prone—whether in sympathy or in a twisted contest—to claim that slavery forged their kinship with those who had suffered the Holocaust. Yet the absence of their own Israel, a national state to which African Americans could make *aliyah* under a Law of Return granting them immediate citizenship and cultural identity, pinpointed the transforming power, not of the Holocaust alone, but particularly of the creation of a Jewish state. African nations to which American blacks had emigrated in the modern era, such as Liberia and Ghana, remained tenuous outposts, bearing no resemblance in their economic and military relations with the United States to the state of Israel. "Unlike Zionists who after 2,000 years of wandering in the wilderness have found their home," wrote Lenora Berson a few years later, "the Black Nationalists have only just begun their odyssey."

For African Americans, however, the "State" that mattered most was the United States. *Brown's* draining of power from states long accustomed to ruling by legal and customary codes of racism changed profoundly the meaning of both states rights and the power of the nation-state for African Americans, even though, as Kelley's dwelling on the white reaction to the new Exodus prompted by Tucker Caliban suggests, the state abandoned by black Americans was first of all a state of mind. ("Come out from under the mind of a slave," said Louis Farrakhan at the Million Man March in 1995, invoking the perennial themes of Exodus and black historical amnesia.) For Kelley, the new Exodus would throw off both the black state of servitude to a racial ethos and the white delusion of black faithfulness, the fantasized agreement to segregation that has so marked the history of supremacist thought.

Although Exodus logically implies the exchange of one state for another, *A Different Drummer* has nothing to say about the imagined future of its black characters. Appearing at a time when the consequences of the civil rights movement could not yet be envisioned—when no more than six percent of southern schools had been desegregated, when the Civil Rights Act was still in the future, when a peculiar extremist named Malcolm X, catapulted into the national consciousness by the 1959 television documentary *The Hate that Hate Produced*, still appeared more often on network news than Martin Luther King, Jr.—Kelley's novel was a startling but mystifying exercise of the teleological imagination. For all the historical depth of the novel, Kelley wrote paradoxically in a prophetic mode but without prophecy. At the end of the 1950s, the future for racial equality remained a blank. For whites and blacks alike, perhaps, thinking of a world without segregation was indeed "like attempting to picture Nothing."

The conflict between integration and nationalism that reverberates throughout the novel might be interpreted in light of Kelley's autobiographical representations of black identity. Kelley was a native of New York City, the son of a one-time editor of Harlem's *Amsterdam News* but also a young man of relative privilege, educated at the mostly white Fieldston School and later at Harvard University. David Bradley calls attention to the searching irony in the fact that, while the nine black students who integrated Central High School in Little Rock were being cursed and spat upon in the fall of 1957—*A Different Drummer* is set in the spring of 1957—Kelley matriculated at Harvard into a very different September world. In the words of Kelley's revealing 1963 *Esquire* essay,

"The Ivy League Negro," the world of Harvard Yard was one where "the leaves on the trees were dark green; the grass too was green and I remember thinking that it looked like the view in an Easter egg."

A bittersweet reflection on the combined, but asymmetrical, racial and class alienation likely to be experienced by a black student at Harvard in the late 1950s, "The Ivy League Negro" also affords a different but no less demanding calculation of the metaphors of state and nationhood at the center of *A Different Drummer*. Several elements of Kelley's schooling at Harvard, as desultory as Thoreau's own, are echoed in the novel. The autobiographical fate of the black intellectual described in Kelley's essay involves nowhere near so cruel a revelation of racism as the lynching of the West Indian nationalist Bennett Bradshaw that concludes *A Different Drummer*—though the Bradshaw character is vaguely modeled on one of Kelley's friends at Harvard—but the "state" from which Kelley the student finds himself excluded and to which he finds his identity sacrificed is no less a reincarnation of the authority of the master. Whereas his privilege and isolation within a very small world of black university students estrange Kelley from what he calls "Negro consciousness" and the race pride it might imply, his color leaves him stranded between Africa and America, between "a race he feels he has grown away from and a [white] class which will not fully accept him."

The essay's poignancy is less striking, however, than its meditation on the paradigm of African American alienation. Unlike other minorities in America, Kelley writes, "after six or more generations, the African 'immigrant' remains one." In composing his variation on the common African American theme of double consciousness made most famous by W. E. B. Du Bois, Kelley explicitly echoed Langston Hughes, who wrote in *My America* (1944): "This is my land, America. Naturally, I love it—it is home," but who lamented the fact that his fourth-generation American family had fewer rights than European immigrants right off the boat. Just so, Kelley anticipated the psychology of alienation diagnosed in *Black Rage*, an influential work of the late 1960s—and still selling today—which argued that African Americans, unlike other immigrant groups, have no culture of their own. Whereas the Jew appeals to religion and tradition, the "black man stands alone," wrote William Grier and Price Cobbs, "forbidden to be an African and never allowed to be an American." In this respect, Kelley's argument that "the Negro was so completely cut loose from Africa that next to nothing is left of it in his culture," sounds like nothing so much as the notorious contention of U. B. Phillips, a southern paternalist of the early century, that African

Americans were "as completely broken from their tribal stems as if they had been brought from Mars." Even if one takes Kelley's statement as a rhetorical ploy, it remains a fair indication of his haunting construction of "Negro consciousness" in *A Different Drummer.*

By the time he embraced the separatist philosophy of Black Power, Kelley had set aside any remaining ambivalence about the source of his alienation. In rejecting the politics and aesthetics of integration—in denouncing older black writers, except Richard Wright, for working too much in a Western rather than an African literary tradition—he also condemned his former self as "one of the most integrated people that the society has produced . . . I was one of the most messed up mentally, one of the most brainwashed. All the private school and Harvard education I've had is something I've had to get over." In the early 1960s, however, Kelley wrote against a backdrop of personal educational privilege very much in tune with E. Franklin Frazier's landmark work *Black Bourgeoisie* (1957). Frazier described middle-class blacks who, in their desire to forget the Negro past, had become "exaggerated Americans" inhabiting a world of intense ambivalence about emulation of whites, a world of make-believe and deep-seated inferiority that strands them between two worlds, "in the process of becoming NOBODY."

In a 1962 preface to his bestselling book, Frazier noted that his Jewish friends found his portrayal of black alienation within a "white" world to describe their experience as well. Unlike Jews, however, African Americans in the late 1950s were far from the point at which appeals to an African cultural past could shore up, much less embolden, a sense of transnational identity. Indeed, one of the most famous—later one of the most notorious—reflections on black America by a prominent American Jew, Norman Podhoretz's essay "My Negro Problem—And Ours" (1963), asked why blacks should wish for pluralistic survival as a distinct group, when, unlike the Jews, they were not bound by "a memory of past glory and a dream of imminent redemption." Rather, said Podhoretz in expressing the growing anxiety about black militancy among Jews sympathetic to the civil rights movement, the Negro's "past is a stigma, his color is a stigma, and his vision of the future is the hope of erasing the stigma by making color irrelevant, by making it disappear as a fact of consciousness."

Podhoretz to the contrary, the necessity not just of integration but of assimilation would soon become anathema to many African Americans. More to the point, the erasure of color and its historic stigma was, in the era of "The Ivy-League Negro," a greater challenge than the post-

Holocaust dismantling of anti-Jewish quotas and legal covenants. A telling remark by Harvard president Lawrence Lowell in early 1920s remained relevant in Kelley's day: "Cambridge could make a Jew indistinguishable from an Anglo-Saxon; but not even Harvard could make a black man white." To be a Negro in such an America, concluded Kelley, is to spend "much time in painful contemplation on the meaning of difference," the meaning of the "negative" value assigned blackness by an unfathomable white world. To be a Negro is, in Kelley's allusion to the Liberty Paints episode in *Invisible Man*, "to be a man waking up in a hospital bed with amnesia," willing to accept any name "because it is better to have a name, even one which holds no meaning, than to have no name at all." No doubt *A Different Drummer* registers Kelley's own middle-class alienation from an "authentic" blackness, his immersion in the world of "exaggerated Americans" described by Frazier, but it also registers a new moment of consciousness among African Americans. Writing at a moment when some black nationalists argued for casting off the slave names of the past in favor of African names—or for canceling out the master's name altogether in a signature X—Kelley's portrayal of the consciousness of nationhood had to balance his rejection of the Muslims ("who have turned the American Nightmare of irrational prejudice on its head and made it a Faith") against his unnerving invocation of African American historical amnesia.

A Different Drummer records this struggle with cultural amnesia in its fragmentary recovery of an African past. The legend of the African maroon from whom Tucker Caliban is descended stands in counterpoint to the almanac's history of the state's most famous citizen, General Dewey Willson, son of Dewitt Willson and a Confederate hero—the archetypal southern patriarch. Yet the importance of the African as a heroic liberator, an alternative to white history, is hedged by his betrayal from within by a seeming compatriot ("I'm an American; I'm no savage," the slave traitor says), and his murder by a white man before he can prevent his infant son from being enslaved. Named First Caliban by Dewitt, a reader of Shakespeare, the black child raised by slavemasters in the New World breeds a race enslaved by law and custom until Tucker's singular revolution undoes Caliban's curse and reverses the design of slavery's empire.

Although Mister Harper, who renders the legend of the African, ascribes Tucker's revolt to the "blood" of the African acting in him, the novel understands blood not as biology but as a figure for the achievement of cultural consciousness. Tucker Caliban's act, though its practical outcome remains unimagined in the novel, is thus a true "revolution." To the extent possible, it turns full circle, through the amnesia of history, back to the moment at which the African family lost its own name and accepted the name of Caliban.

When he takes buys the land on which his African ancestor was slain, Tucker is also given the mystic white stone recovered from the site where the dying African had tried and failed to murder his infant son in order to prevent his enslavement—a stone held in trust by the Willsons, so it seems, as a symbol of mutual dependence and bondage, an enigma to be grappled with by generation after generation until such time as enslavement might end. But Tucker finds that property itself is not identity, that he has nonetheless "lost something." Or, as Bradshaw more accurately puts it: "I think he meant that he had been robbed of something but had never known it because he never even knew he owned what had been taken from him." As Bradshaw's convoluted proposition suggests, *A Different Drummer* places itself on the horizon of a future that is also a past.

Tucker Caliban's act of renunciation, like Thoreau's temporary migration to Walden Pond—and even more like Ike McCaslin's renunciation in Faulker's Mosaic saga, *Go Down, Moses*—places a premium on the relation between property and identity. Whereas Thoreau sought to describe a geography of the self in which complete sovereignty might be imagined (if never achieved), Tucker's renunciation maps, for African America, a comparable space of sovereignty in fittingly negative terms. By buying and then destroying and abandoning his property, Tucker declares that what has been taken from Africans can never be given back. Like "The Ivy-League Negro," the novel implicitly argues that consciousness of African identity among American blacks is predicated upon inventing a collective sense of African memory—an invention rendered at once intense and precarious by the fact that slavery forever differentiates African Americans from other immigrants. The dilemma of black Americans, notes Gerald Early, is that "they are bound by the prison of self-consciousness about the meaning of their once having been African, while realizing that they can never be African again."

Indeed, so far as the novel tells us, Tucker Caliban does not discard his name. His renunciation creates a blank domain of historical mourning, a space that may be provisionally filled by legend and memory but never be fully healed, no more than the life and possessions stripped away in centuries of enslavement and racism can be fully returned, or a rootedness in Africa entirely recovered. His purchase of the land brings an "end" to work for the white man, marking a rejection of the racist pastoral promulgated by the southern Agrarians and constituting a clear break with the sharecropping past; but it does not, as he discovers, permit him and his family to "free ourselves."

Among the possessions that Tucker destroys is an antique grandfather clock taken off the slave ship along with the first African (and likewise belonging to Dewitt Willson) and eventually passed into the Caliban family as a reward for service. When Tucker chops up the clock with an ax, he annihilates both the time of bondage and the false recompense of property. He also provides a fitting figure for the paradox of the novel's creation of a pathway from amnesia to memory, its struggle to narrate the temporal plot of African American life in a way commensurate with a history of estrangement that cannot be undone either by Tucker's revolt or by Kelley's storytelling. Time—Nation Time, as Black Power would say—is not recovered in Kelley's novel but rather suspended. Egypt is no more, but Canaan is nowhere in sight.

Tucker's act points to a world without segregation, but the underside of this dream, the "Negro-less world" left behind in the white "state," is perfectly captured in the mirroring action that ends the novel, the lynching of Bradshaw. The original African is killed by Dewitt Willson because he cannot be possessed, will not become part of the white man's property, like his clock, and live in his time. Bradshaw, in contrast, is killed by the men on the porch as an outside agitator mistakenly thought responsible for the migration. But most of all he is killed as what the men perceive to be "our last nigger, ever. There won't be no more after this, and no more singing and dancing and laughing." Whereas the African had seen something akin to a look of masculine respect in the gaze of Dewitt Willson before he shot him, Bradshaw sees, as though in a short circuit to the historical present, paternalism degenerated into racist fury—a stare that is "completely blank, that very blankness a sign of the renunciation of alternatives, of tenderness or brutality, of pleasure or pain, of understanding or ignorance, of belief or disbelief, of compassion or intolerance, of reason or unswerving fanaticism; it was a gaze which signals the flicking off of the switch which controls the mechanism making a man a human being."

Incorporating the totality of victimage—as though the eliminationist philosophy of the Holocaust were contained in a single murdered Jew—Bradshaw at once depletes the reservoir of sacrificial victims and inaugurates an age of wrenching paternalist nostalgia. In this respect, Kelley's scenario is reminiscent of George Schuyler's *Black No More* (1931), where the disappearance of the nation's blacks through a skin-bleaching vogue leaves a southern community with "nothing left to stimulate them but the old time religion and . . . clandestine sex orgies," until a last pair of bleached Negroes is discovered whose mutilation and burning provides a final act of communal gratification. If Tucker Caliban's revolutionary act of exile reveals the metaphysical trauma of whiteness deprived of blackness, Bradshaw, as the white community's "last nigger, ever," reveals the brutal underpinnings of whiteness.

One could argue that these southern killers are "ordinary men," that lynch mobs, as Christopher Browning and more recently Daniel Jonah Goldhagen have argued of the Nazi Holocaust, were composed of common people wrenched by circumstance into a capacity, even a lust, for diabolical acts. Whatever *A Different Drummer* tells us about the continuum between casual racism and genocide in the white southern psyche, however, Kelley's rendering of black consciousness is all the more terrible and sobering because even its annihilation is contained within white consciousness. The men force Bradshaw to dance and sing a grotesque minstrel tune before hauling him off in his own limousine (his driver, like the original African's black compatriots, deserts him) to an undescribed ritual death, narratively rendered only by its distant screams, on Tucker Caliban's abandoned property. The young white boy in whose narrative consciousness the peculiar night sounds of the lynching are registered, leading him to imagine a festive party prompted by Tucker's return, closes the novel on a harrowing note.

Year by year as Kelley was writing, the African freedom movements sparked by war against European colonialism galvanized the civil rights movement in the United States. By 1961 more than a dozen former African colonies, beginning with Ghana in 1957, had achieved independence, yet even these historic events provided but a shaky foundation upon which to build a pan-African ideology of liberation, let alone a strategy of "repatriation."

Tucker's migration leads nowhere—yet. And his past tells no usable story, for it is not he, but others, led by a white demagogue, who narrate it. Black consciousness remains in eclipse, time is momentarily frozen on the brink of a revolution that cannot be enacted, and the white men's sacrifice of Bradshaw suggests that, once one people is accustomed to the elimination of another, migration and murder draw closer together.

Migration cannot be fully conceptualized in *A Different Drummer*, not because there are no models available—indeed, black American history is a history of such models—but because, in 1962, Kelley could not see where this new march toward freedom would lead. As actor Ossie Davis would remark in 1969, in a tribute honoring the prominent Zionist Avraham Schenker on his emigration to Israel: Just as "you have found and pinpointed in time and space your Jerusalem," we, too, seek our Jerusalem. "Think of the pathos of men who stand on the corner and dream of free Southern States that they want to call their own. Think of the sorrow and sadness of men who stand on a ladder in Harlem and preach of the desirability of returning to Africa some day because they will never find in this country what it is that will make them complete men." William Melvin Kelley the writer might retreat to Harvard Yard, if not to Walden Pond, but for William Melvin Kelley the African American, there was no Exodus.

[1] In Ward's *A Day of Absence*, staged by a black cast in whiteface and costumed in red, white, and blue, the sudden exodus of the African American population leads to chaos in a southern community that "has always been glued together by the uninterrupted presence of its darkies." Economic paralysis is followed by near social disintegration when it is revealed that some prominent white citizens who have been passing are also missing—among them city council members, a college football star, and the chairlady of the Daughters of the Confederate Rebellion. The mayor's televised passionate appeal to the missing blacks to honor their "sacred" obligations to the Jim Crow South dissolves into a white riot; but the next morning all the blacks are back, as though they have never been gone and nothing has changed—except, presumably, the consciousness of the white townspeople. "Space Traders," published in Bell's *Faces at the Bottom of the Well*, is an allegory of exile set in the year 2000. An extraterrestrial power offers the United States gold to pay its government debts, chemicals to clean its toxic environment, and a safe nuclear energy source in exchange for removing all African Americans from the nation. Refusing to let the trade be the "final solution" for blacks in America, Jews organize in protest, promising to hide blacks away according to plans drawn up by the Anne Frank Committee; an unarticulated concern is that, in the absence of blacks, Jews will become the nation's principal scapegoats. Ultimately, a constitutional amendment allowing the trade passes with 70 percent of the vote. On Martin Luther King, Jr. Day, all African Americans are forced to leave: "Heads bowed, arms now linked by slender chains, black people left the New World as their forebears had arrived."

A Passion for Playwriting

Claudia Allen

In the early summer of 1999 I was slipping into Victory Gardens Theater through the dressing room when I suddenly paused and listened. I realized I could hear rehearsals wafting at me from both the main stage and the studio theater. A one act called *Change* was in the studio and Julie Harris's glorious voice could be heard rehearsing *Winter* on the main stage. I wrote both plays. That's as good as it gets for a playwright. I just stood there listening.

I've been a Chicago playwright for the past twenty years. I've been a "success" for the past twenty minutes. I've been declared the Best Playwright in Chicago by *Chicago* magazine. How did I reach such a pinnacle? And what took so long?

Seduction

At thirteen, I fell in love with theater watching a high school production of *My Fair Lady*. My sister fell in love with and eventually married Henry Higgins. One school auditorium, two grand passions.

I spent the next eight years immersing myself in theater—devouring plays, reading as well as watching them, even treading the boards as dowdy, middle-aged women in high school musicals. But then I stumbled onto my true calling. I was in my senior year at the University of Michigan, all set to take a year of Shakespeare, but I quickly realized the instructor was no one I wanted to inflict on myself for a year, so I went hunting for a better class. Just down the hall was Dr. Peter Bauland and his playwriting class. Within a few sessions I had once again fallen hard. And after Dr. Bauland told me I was the best student dramatist he'd ever taught, I was a goner. All the words, the stories, the characters, the voices just came flooding out. I knew if I didn't give playwriting my best shot I'd regret it the rest of my life. Besides, I couldn't stop myself.

Entrance

Convinced—well, hoping—that the theater world was waiting for me with baited breath, I moved to Chicago in 1979. After much deep thought and the pricing of Greyhound bus tickets I chose Chicago because it's close to Michigan and it's big. As it turns out I dumb-lucked my way into a burgeoning theater town, but in years to come I'll probably change this story and lie, eventually convincing even myself that this move was all part of a brilliant grand plan. But no, I left my beloved Ann Arbor because Chicago is a large city in the Midwest, I had friends here, and I wanted to stay a bus ride from Michigan to be close to my family and my muse (often one and the same). When I had my epiphany in playwriting class and realized I had to write plays I was stunned to realize most of them were going to be about small-town Michigan. I couldn't wait to leave my two stop-lighted hometown for college, but when I started writing plays small-town Michigan was what I wrote about. I could leave physically, but I was imprinted. Willa Cather lived in New York for decades, but Nebraska held her soul. Ditto Michigan for me. So I needed to be able to hop the bus up there every so often to listen to Grandma Allen's stories—"Ella Horrup's sexless marriage" was a personal favorite. I needed to stroll the cemeteries at Memorial Day with my parents pointing out stones and telling the stories buried there. One about a man who built his own casket in his backyard and tried to hire someone to shoot him gave me just the character I needed for my play Deed of Trust. My voice is a Michigan voice, a Midwestern voice. Moving to Chicago allowed me necessary proximity but it also gave me perspective.

And I had friends from college living in Chicago. (Network early, network often.) Bob helped me find an apartment. Diana introduced me to her aunt Sandy Eisen who was a director at the Playwrights' Center.

Please Read My Play

Scary words.

I've taught for years and I try to create a nurturing, nonthreatening workshop space, both at the University of Chicago and at Victory Gardens, because I remember how hard it is, how vulnerable you feel walking in a door and saying those words, "Would you, could you, please read my play?"

Luckily for me, the Playwrights' Center did. In 1979, Chicago was a happening theater town but not for local playwrights. The soon-to-be-famous Chicago actors preferred to strut their stuff via Sam Shepard. And in 1979 the women playwrights in town could and did fit in a small living room. But the Playwrights' Center on Kinzie Street gave me staged readings and a first production of my first full-length play, *The Freedom Rider*. I was on my way. I was hot. I was not produced for another six years.

In the Desert

Talent counts but endurance and perseverance count more. To be a good playwright you must possess and encourage a heightened sensitivity; you must let the world in. To survive all the rejection, all the blows that come with building a career in the arts, you have to throw a cloak over that raw sensitivity and somehow keep going.

A play isn't complete until it's produced; same goes for the playwright. I spent the next six years writing, obsessively writing plays but not getting produced. I would come close. One theater was going to produce *Raincheck* but then folded. The Burt Reynolds Dinner Theatre almost did *The Long Awaited*, but Eileen Brennan got a sitcom. The literary manager at the Goodman Theatre, the wonderfully named Peregrine Whittlesey, was friendly. She invited me to the Goodman Christmas party, but then she moved back to New York City, and I haven't been invited to a Goodman Christmas party since. Theodore Mann in New York wrote encouraging rejection letters.

Most theaters have several levels of rejection letters, from the blatantly Xeroxed to the cunningly Xeroxed (that appear personal but aren't) to the real thing: hand-scribbled rejection. I read the hand-scribbled "Waiting for the next one" so many times I started to write a play called "Waiting For the Next One." Of course, those dismissive Xeroxes were worse. Or the snotty Xeroxes informing me I should just send a synopsis next time. Like I said, talent's great, but what you really need is the hide of a rhino.

For much of the Eighties I was the best-known unknown playwright in Chicago, lucky to get a staged reading with quality actors sitting in folding chairs, scripts in hand, reading my play to a packed house of fifteen or twenty. But for a couple of hours, hearing my words aloud, I got a taste and remembered why I do this. More than once during this time I took a long look at myself and my calling and tried to quit—but couldn't. It's not about making a sensible, well-reasoned decision. It's about passion.

I had stories to tell. I wrote because I couldn't not write. I broke my thumb one summer in the Eighties, but I was "with play" clenched the pen clumsily between finger and brace and scribbled away, finishing that first draft in ten days, not because there was a deadline or because anyone anywhere had any expectations, but because I was fertile and that play had to come out. I'd write anywhere: standing in line for a movie, waiting for a doctor's appointment, crossing the bike path in Lincoln Park, at work . . .

I've come to understand that those "failure" years of the 1980s were vital to my creativity. If attention had been paid, if a bright, warm light had shone on my work too soon, I might have written plays to conform to what a Claudia Allen play was expected to be. With virtually no one paying attention I was free to write whatever the hell entertained me—and all sorts of things do entertain me. I've written a number of family plays set in rural Michigan, as well as madcap comedy (*Cahoots*), romps (*A Gay Christmas Carol*) and *Xena Live!*), and steamy lesbian sagas (*Movie Queens* and *Hannah Free*). Eventually I found that these plays written to entertain me also entertained an audience. But I had to write them for me first—better to write for myself than to someone else's scale.

Those six very productive, unproduced years gave me my core as a writer and a hide like iron. And when productions finally did come, I knew enough to appreciate them.

Mentors

The 1980s weren't all Reagan and sorrow because I met the two most important people in my theatrical career.

Sandy Shinner, the Associate Artistic Director of Victory Gardens Theater, befriended my work and me and now directs all of my main stage productions at Victory Gardens. In the mid-1980s she gave me readings and she gave me hope. In the years since, she has been the person I turn to with a new script or a life crisis, and she brings her ferocious focus to bear.

Then there's Julie Harris. I've always been a believer in sending plays any and everywhere, so—goofy as it sounds—I sent the great Ms. Harris my play *The Long Awaited* care of "Knots Landing." Well, stupid as that sounds, Julie got the play and she read it and got in touch. Having a Broadway legend like Julie Harris tell me I was a wonderful playwright sustained me for years. And it wasn't just one friendly postcard. It was fifteen years of correspondence, fifteen years that led to her appearing in *Winter*.

So despite appearing to languish among the unproduced during much of the 1980s, I was laying the groundwork for my later career. I created a body of work and established some of my most profound professional relationships. When Julie Harris came to Chicago to appear in *Winter*, two of the four actors in that show, Meg Thalken and Nancy Lollar, were women who'd done countless readings for me in the 1980s and Sandy Shinner directed. Never forget.

Broadway—Well, Not Quite

My first New York production was a badly acted off, off Broadway production of *Movie Queens* in 1986. But how amazing to be produced in New York. How amazing to be able to say I was being produced in New York. I had a show running in New York. . . . Back home in Chicago I'd always be aware of the time of night when my show was running in New York. I take things like that, take too much, for granted now.

Later that same year, *Movie Queens* was done in Chicago and *Deer Season* was presented live on Channel 5. Both productions featured some perfidious intrigue behind the scenes, underscoring for me how very much I needed to find a collaborator I could trust and enjoy (enter Sandy). *But* both shows were still fun. I love being produced. I love hearing the words.

Collaboration

I'd had readings at Victory Gardens Theater for years but finally saw my first short play done there in 1987 as part of a noble but short-lived festival of new work, The Great Chicago Playwrights Exposition ("Play Expo"). *They Even Got the Rienzi* was about an old Chicagoan, Mr. Ponazecki, who finds out they've ripped down his transient hotel home just as he's about to be released from a long stay in the hospital. It's a play about loss and it resonated. Eventually Studs Terkel, the great Chicago voice, performed it on his radio show.

In 1989, Victory Gardens chose to produce its first full-length play of mine, *The Long Awaited.* (Since Victory Gardens had done its first reading of The Long Awaited in 1982, we took to calling it "the long awaited 'Long Awaited.'") In the 1990s I became a member of the Victory Gardens Playwrights Ensemble and the theater produced more of my plays: *Still Waters*, *Ripe Conditions*, *Deed of Trust*, *Hannah Free*, and *Winter.* In 2000, Sandy Shinner will direct my seventh Victory Garden Main Stage production, *Cahoots* (starring Sharon Gless from "Cagney and Lacey").

I had finally found my home theater.

On the Road

Of course I also love getting produced out of town. In fact, I knew I was finally getting somewhere when I couldn't get to all of my out-of-town productions. But I go when I can. It invigorates me and revalidates what I do. I get to meet people from Ft. Worth to L.A. to Bloomington, Illinois, and they're never strangers because we have the play in common. And even the worst, most amateurish production can be useful to see.

The hardest but best way to see whether the message, the humor, the plays themselves work is if they can survive even the most abysmal deer-in-headlights acting. And of course when I get back to Chicago people are impressed that I was produced in L.A. or New York or Oregon—they don't need to know the production sucked. I enjoy seeing my plays produced in Wisconsin or Arkansas more than in L.A. or New York—less attitude, more pure love of theater. I have met some just wonderful, dedicated theater people doing their bit for the Sheboygan Theatre Company and the Port Austin Community Players, not to mention my favoritely named Snapdragon Ozark Feminist Theatre and Detroit's Pissed Off Women (POW). Just think, the Snapdragon women do one play a year in Fayetteville, Arkansas, and one year it was my *Hannah Free*.

Pitfalls

Just in case I'm sounding too upbeat, let me now wax on about some pitfalls of the playwriting game.

Rejection. If you can't take the sight of your mailbox jammed with rejected manila manuscript envelopes, don't be a playwright. If you can't take the sight of an artistic director recoiling in terror when they realize you want them to read your play, don't be a playwright. I remember going to a panel discussion in the Eighties on women and theater. I listened to Pauline X pontificate on the dire need for women playwrights, but when I approached her afterward, an actual specimen of the breed, she recoiled like a snake bitten. And even now that I'm hot, oh baby am I hot, I'll get things back with those huffy requests that I just send a synopsis and sample pages next time. And just last year, after a couple of seasons when I was produced out of town but not in Chicago, a local journalist approached me at a function, beaming, and asked me where I was living these days. You're never safe from that kick in the solar plexus. The question is, do you keep getting back up?

The One Play Syndrome. Don't stop at writing just one; people will notice. Literary managers appreciate a writer who can write more than one play, in more than one style, on more than one subject. And they get tired of reading your newest draft (those minute changes that mean so much to you) of The Opus that you have too much riding on. Remember when they write that they're looking forward to reading the next one it is good to have a next one.

Bitterness, Resentment. Don't waste your energy resenting all those writers who had it easier than you, because it's a waste of your energy and probably not true. Try to be gracious even if you know you're a far superior playwright than that dim wit who just got your grant.

Speaking of Dim Wits. The press. So-called critics. First remember that if it comes from out of town it's better even if it's not. Also remember that your final critic is the audience because they actually paid for their ticket. Some Chicago critics actually love the theater and try to encour age new work; others are a blight on humanity. But I'm not bitter.

Money. Anyone who takes up playwriting for the money is an idiot. Poetry pays worse but playwrights spend more on Xeroxing and stamps. I proofread corporate law for most of the 1980s to pay my rent and Xeroxing costs. Try to read the print on a bond sometime and you'll know just how much I wanted to be a playwright.

No Regrets

Growing up, I knew too many old guys (i.e., people my current age) who would sit around the VFW hall and bitch about life opportunities they'd had to miss because their wife (or—fill in the blank) wouldn't let them take that job in New Orleans (or—fill in the blank). When I realized I had a passion for playwriting I followed it because I didn't want to meet myself at 45 if I hadn't. This past summer I felt like I had.

My parents and I were in Mackinaw City, Michigan, killing time at a touristy little bookstore before going to a musical review at the theater across the way. Browsing I gradually realized the snazzy jazz voice I was hearing wasn't coming from the radio. Sitting behind the cash register was a melancholy woman in her fifties doing just wonderful song stylings to what was playing on the radio. "They're writing songs of love, but not for me." She said she'd been offered a job singing when she was eighteen, but her dad wouldn't let her take it because it was in an iffy neighborhood. Years later she came in second in a Karaoke-Barbra Streisand Look Alike Competition. She was sure that the contest was rigged because she lost to a woman with an "in" at the radio station but no voice or resemblance to Streisand.

So here was this talented woman who'd let a couple of no's stop her; here she was singing, "They're writing songs of love, but not for me" at a cash register, singing for her own pleasure, at least she was still singing, but she'd let the world—and herself—stop her from pursuing her dream. I'm glad I didn't.

Curtain

Angels in the Shadows: Identifying Millennial Drama

Susan Booth

On the campus of the University of California, San Diego, there is a large stone building. Architecturally unremarkable, it is encircled by a neon banner—near its top—that alternately flashes the seven deadly sins and the seven cardinal virtues. (An interesting test: ask the averagely literate person to list the former. Then ask them to do the same with the latter. They will succeed only on step one. Bet you.) This is the Pres Five Story Building of the Powell Labs, where sundry structures are subjected to earthquake-like shakings of different Richter levels. Think of it as the site of stress tests for buildings: "How far can we go before the center will not hold?"

Outside of the building, in a kind of ersatz sculpture garden, stands a collection of damaged columns. Some are merely chipped concrete things—looking not much more desultory than your average standing underpass. Others are marvels of destruction—a kind of nasty inverse of Michelangelo's lane of emerging figures at the Academe in Florence. This line of figures, too, is about possibility, but what emerges from these columns is not the miracle of David, but a visual insistence on the possibility of decay.

Possibility's the wrong word. Inevitability is better.

> *And so from hour to hour, we ripe and ripe; and then from hour to hour we rot and rot. And thereby hangs a tale.*
>
> —Shakespeare
> *As You Like It*

There is so much talk about beginnings and endings just now.

Seemingly clear lines of demarcation between where we have been and where we are soon to be going. (I rather like imagining chronological border guards who will greet me at midnight on December 31st, 1999 and demand my papers. "I'm sorry, Ms. Booth, but you've not been properly authorized to enter New Millennium,"—this border being, in my imaginings, a geographic destination one could locate on a map—"you'll have to turn back." And the vision I will see as I look over my shoulder like Lot's wife walking back to a future to be spent in the past, will be one of Technicolor pastoral beauty. The place will look suspiciously like a cross between Disney Quest and Dorothy's first glimpse of Oz's poppy fields and the shining city beyond. And I will sigh. "Ah, New Millennium. I had so hoped to visit.") But it is a different place I wonder about right now—this place we inhabit just now—this place between now and then, between here and there, between the provinces and Moscow. It is a place marked by the inevitability of decay, but touched by the promise of . . . something. But what? Not the unknown, surely, for here in this cusp of time we have frighteningly extensive knowledge right at our fingertips. Here we have the postmodernists telling us that we have all been there and done that. And here we have the dramatist—as ever before—holding the mirror up to nature. But here the dramatist would seem only to find a reflection of people holding up mirrors of their own.

> *Well, it's all over now. Not only are we no longer the still centre of God's universe, we're not even uniquely graced by his footprint in man's image. . . .*
>
> *Man is on the Moon, his feet on solid ground, and he has seen us whole, all in one go, little—local . . . and all our absolutes, the thou-shalts and the thou-shalt-nots that seemed to be the very condition of our existence, how did they look to two moonmen with a single neck to save between them? Like the local customs of another place.*
>
> —Tom Stoppard
> *Jumpers*

As surely as their mallmap counterparts, the plays of the twentieth century have shouldered the responsibility of telling us "You Are Here." In a time when walls are falling and the previously mysterious is becoming pedestrian in its commerce, we are enamored of anything that might place us against this staggering degree of knowledge—something that might give us locus. When the humanists rediscovered the individual in the prose and poetry of the nineteenth century, they did so against the emerging cogs of an inhuman revolution of industry. When Donne celebrated the soul, he did so as a member of a collectivizing society that had nearly lost the thread of community's genesis. The "You Are Here" address provisos of the plays of the twentieth century are different; they tell us in equal measure about the landscape as the figures in the foreground. In the very beginning of this century we were proffered the emotionally denuding statement of "you are yearning" in Chekhov's *Three Sisters*; a few decades later came the political challenge of "you are greater than this" offered by Odet's *Waiting for Lefty* and the fearful "You may not be here at all" caution inherent in Beckett's *Waiting for Godot*. And as the aforementioned magic millennial marker is approached, the message becomes increasingly personal and profoundly dark as dramatists shine demanding flashlights into the hoary corners of both the natural universe—Tom Stoppard's *Arcadia*, Michael Frayn's *Copenhagen*—and the larger universe of the soul. Eric Bogosian's *Suburbia*, Mark Ravenhill's *Shopping and Fucking*, Mike Leigh's *Ecstasy*, and Paula Vogel's *How I Learned to Drive* all seem to offer unsettlingly transitory road signs reading "You may well be here, but you won't be here for long and nobody cares overmuch, so get solid or get lost."

So many clues. Perhaps the wisest thing is first to identify the questions being asked—and the first to the surface seems to be "Where are our passions?"

The easiest answer to the "what consumes us now" question is bifurcation. We have become a people so entrenched in the validation of the individual—in the "I'm okay, you're okay, and really, I'm only interested in the fact that I'm okay" school of near narcissism—that our millennial drama is foremost the drama of the embattled individual. And that theory holds, up to a point, when we examine what the theater—as opposed to the playwright—is producing. Look at 1999 Broadway, where the current emotional zeitgeist has intersected with a body of antecedent classics in the most telling of fashions. A Willy Loman for the millennium struts and frets to attenuated nonexistence when attention is not paid in the celebrated revival of *Death of a Salesman*; Eugene O'Neill's Iceman once again cometh, to take us to the darkest of dark edges—the precipice of individuals stripped of dreams. (Perhaps the most bleak of emotional prognostications came last year in the surprise hit revival of Terrance Rattigan's overlooked masterwork *Deep Blue Sea*, in which our heroine learns the devastating lesson that one can, in fact, live without hope.) These are all plays of the gray zone, plays in which the personal is the political insomuch as the polis has become only so large as our immediate grasp and our immediate grasp would seem to have disintegrated to a space not much larger than what our skin can hold. But these are, as said, revivals of plays of the early reaches of the century. Something a little different seems to be happening with the works written in more immediate response to our present threshold. And the question seems to be shifting from "Where Am I?" to "Why Am I here—wherever that might be?"

> *God creates us free, free to be selfish, but He adds a mechanism that will penetrate our selfishness and wake us up to the presence of others in the world, and that mechanism is called suffering. To put it another way, pain is God's megaphone to rouse a deaf world. Why must it be pain? Why can't He wake us more gently, with violins or laughter? Because the dream from which we must be awakened is the dream that all is well. . . .*
>
> *We're like blocks of stone, out of which the sculptor carves the forms of men. The blows of His chisel, which hurt us so much, are what make us perfect. The suffering in the world is not the failure of God's love for us; it is that love in action. For believe me, this world that seems to us so substantial is no more than the shadowlands.*
>
> —William Nicholson
> *Shadowlands*

Am I suggesting the playwright as spokesperson for divinity? No. Well, not quite. But playwright as an instrument of divine forecast and guidance? It worked for the Greeks, didn't it? When the polis needed to know why the gods of Troy and Sparta allowed ten years of violent devastation, Euripides had a suggestion. When just such battles allowed the emergence of mortal heroes and society had a new need to know the cost of overweening pride, it fell to Sophocles to suggest a divinely ordained penalty. And regardless of a particular society's multifaceted definitions of divinity, there seem always to be a few playwriting Cassandras in the shadows, telling us stories we may or may not want to hear.

I read plays. It is what I do for a living. Somewhere between 800 and 1,000 manuscripts a year find their way to my office and must be listened to. I sift these texts through a template of questions that go something like this:

> Could this story only be told in this medium?
> Does the plot transcend the immediate lives of its characters?
> Have I read this story before, and if so, was it told in this way?
> Has the writer spilled the play with a sense of urgency?

But as the days go by, and the stacks of scripts to be read (large, always large) transforms into the stack of scripts to be paid attention to by the theater in some substantial way (smaller, sadly, smaller), I stop being the one asking the questions. The plays coalesce into one literary behemoth that turns inquisitor itself. "What do you see recurring in our worlds?" they ask. "What common bells do you hear ringing?"

And in the beginnings of finding my answers, I find myself with yet more questions.

Why do the plays of late twentieth century evidence a clear trend toward poetry (a language drama speaks in quite sporadic and utterly particular times)? Because in the works of Luis Alfaro, Kia Corthron, Jose Rivera and Mac Wellman—playwrights very much on the hit list of America's regional theaters and playwrights always populating the aforementioned smaller stack of scripts—the syntax is thick with poetry. Particular poetry—celestial imagery, abstractions of desire, and elliptical searches that round further and further in on themselves. Back to that oft used and even more oft misused idea of postmodernism, again. Traditional narrative structures like chronological sequence, extended scenes built on conversational dynamics, singularly developed plot structures—how can these forms of communication possibly hope to be universally understood by a generation that channel surfs? What does a conventional three act play structure employing Aristotelian unities of time, place, and story offer to a listener/viewer raised on cinematic fragmenting, MTV sound bites and advertising-speak that equates a Nike swoop with the larger idea of "just doing it"? Perhaps even words themselves have approached a sort of saturation point in our communication frenzied times. The simplest linguistic exchanges have become impossibly complex as "I love you" has evolved into "I love you, but I need to know if you've been tested." "I love you but everyone knows that the old institutions for the signifying of that love—marriage, say, or family—have broken down like so many earthquake shaken columns." And so the poets of the theater look for new combinations of words. New ways of signifying ancient human emotions that depend upon actions and metaphorical images rather than a hope for a shared perception of what is meant by a shared vocabulary. Because "family" doesn't mean what "family" used to mean. And "home" doesn't look like "home" used to look. And a whole lot of the archetypal signposts of spoken exchanges can no longer simply be said and heard, but must have the poetic equivalent of quotation marks put around them. And perhaps in that way we can understand that we are talking about some unarticulated resonance that "love" still has—

even if the word itself has become fragmented into near non-meaning by its placement against a profoundly cynical landscape.

And about "landscape" . . .

In that same small stack of plays that seem to have discovered a way of speaking a late twentieth century language, there emerges a different sort of poetry. Not the poetry of language, but the poetry of place. Of context. Because how can anyone talk about the plays of the end of this century and not wonder at the phenomena that is the "American Cycle" of August Wilson—a cycle that emerged in 1982 with *Ma Rainey's Black Bottom* and appears to be going strong with the scheduled fall of 1999 premiere of *King Hedley*? Here is the landscape of little and local—enormous human dramas played out in backyards, around greasy spoon tables. Here are cataclysmic crises erupting over seemingly pedestrian stakes—a new shoe stepped on, a promised ham withheld. And, ironically, for the same reasons that Wilson would seem to be placing the embattled human soul against the most familiar of landscapes—so that we may see a person whole—other dramatists are eschewing logical landscapes entirely. Because in the landscape deconstructions of the works of Robert Wilson and Peter Sellars—directors who have blurred the line between the idea of director and writer by recontextualizing stories we thought we knew—the individual is again explored anew. The potentially limiting mandates of postmodernism are subverted by this tool of deconstruction and new tales are being told in spite of all we know. Because of all we know. When Sellars turns *The Merchant of Venice* into The Merchant of Venice Beach, and shows videos of the Rodney King beating while Shylock is culturally excoriated, we can no longer smugly place Shakespeare's story into the "I know this story" camp. We cannot sit back as the casual observers of an oft-told tale. The audience's engagement is demanded as people coincide with place in unexpected fashion. God, it would seem, truly is in the details.

And about "God". . .

Why, in so many of these late twentieth century plays, has the sacred become secular? Why now, in a time of such knowledge-laden cynicism about believing in anything devoid of empirical proofs, does faith in the unseen come raging to the fore? Rachel Rosenthal writes of immediate deities; Erik Ehn writes of topical saints; Paula Vogel invests her chorus players with omniscience usually accorded only the divine; and in attention demanding fashion, Tony Kushner gives us titular assurance (or warning?) that the millennium is approaching and there are angels in America.

> *Chaos is our natural state. But we hold Nature at bay to give ourselves the illusion of order. In my own microcosm I've tried to keep Chaos at bay. Oh, how I've tried. Yet things persist in flying apart! I will take a shamanic journey. Answers aren't always surface. To go in depth, one must pierce the crust. The Lower World is a place where that can happen. There is always some risk involved in shifting realities. But animals and humans yearn for altered states, and this particular practice does not involve restricted substances. . . .*
>
> —Rachel Rosenthal
>
> *Pangean Dreams: A Shamanic Journey*

Today's playwrights are informed by the same precarious sense of the individual that fueled the earlier plays of Miller and O'Neill, but their desired panacea is not simply the self-satisfied divinity of the Lord of the Self. The plays of the end of this millennium seem to favor a willing placement of the individual soul on a larger continuum—and favor, too, the accepting of a lower rung on that cosmic ladder. The tragedy of Willy Loman is rooted in an implicit belief that the individual should triumph over circumstance, but that he, sad man, has failed in the endeavor. In marked contrast, the child of Naomi Wallace's *One Flea Spare*, the violently beleaguered women of Diana Son's *Stop Kiss*, the passionate sisters of Michael Henry Redwood's *The Old Settler* (all three plays the product of this decade and recipients of multiple productions) are all denizens of the margin. These are people who have taken the full pulse of their time and place and said with lyric beauty, "I am only here. And it is as far as the gods will let me go, so here I will build my house." But lest these examples suggest a genre of surrendered dreams, these characters are not articulating the acquiescence of despair; this is the acceptance of scale. This is the embracing of margins larger than our all knowing world can know, because they are the vertical landscapes of individual desire, rather than the horizontal landscapes of a described society. And lo and behold, we're back to the Greeks. Back to Moira and hamartia and all of those ideas that we'd relegated to the myopic realms of "another time, another place."

You see, we have seen ourselves whole. We have subjected ourselves to rigorous shakings and measured the inevitability of decay. And we have stood on the moon and seen ourselves for nothing more than the skin and bone and spirit amalgams that we are. And brewing in that last ingredient—in the face of all that we know—we still have a kind of hope. It is, sometimes, the near desperate hope of the traveler who believes there is water around this next curve—not because a billboard has told her so, but because there simply must be. Or crawling deeper still, it is perhaps the hope of that same traveler having rounded the curve, found no water, but continuing her journey. Walking still. Walking further, with her eyes wide open.

> PAUL: *(in a low whisper) An angel appeared, and I lifted my hat, because above all else I wanted to be polite to angels.*
> *(THE ANGEL has slowly pointed to his own head. Then the lights flash and fade. THE ANGEL slaps his head and then points to it with his finger.)*
> THE ANGEL: *Angels know not from politeness.*
> PAUL: *Now I know. Before I didn't.*
> THE ANGEL: *So your hat is not in evidence.*
> PAUL: *Correct.*
> THE ANGEL: *Did the angel stay?*
> PAUL: *Yes. It integrated itself inside me. It's here.*
> *(THE ANGEL comes beside him, and blows once into his ear.)*
> THE ANGEL: *It's inside you.*
> PAUL: *Yes.*
> THE ANGEL: *Is it speaking?*
> PAUL: *Yes.*
> *(THE ANGEL touches PAUL gently on the shoulder and PAUL is magically thrown to the side of the room.)*
> THE ANGEL: *I believe you should cast it out, Paul.*
> PAUL: *An angel is a higher being.*
> THE ANGEL: *But it isn't you, Paul. As a human being, your destiny, I would assume, is to realize yourself rather than to escape yourself.*
> PAUL: *To have an angel inside me is my ideal. Because where I am, or was, is a void.*
> THE ANGEL: *Grow into it.*
> PAUL: *I am trying. With an angel.*
>
> —Richard Foreman
> *The Mind King*

Social theorist Mikhail Bakhtin wrote about an oft-recurring phenomenon of social fervor that exists in the marginal spaces between defined times. There was, he felt, a particular human energy that emerges just before the revolution yields a new social order. It was a time he called the "Carnival." Here was a wondrous, fertile, and thoroughly dangerous notion that in the fault line between the known and the unknown (and the soon to be known) there is frantic activity of the generative kind. Of the seismic kind, that shakes the object upon which it works—not for destruction but for revelation. Because as the excess is shaken away in an act of clarifying decay—a core is revealed that shines with a previously unarticulated truth. There is a chaotic kind of play going on in that gray space between here and there, between "been there, done that" and "what, do you suppose, is just over that hill?" And if the horizontal distance between traveled and untraveled territories may appear to have been foreshortened by millennial omniscience, then the vertical depths of the traveler herself must be further plumbed by those wanting to tell a story right now. In this place. There is an energy of searching, of wanting the wheres, whys, and hows attended to, that fuels the playwright. That necessitates the play. Always has been, always will be. These writers are our earth-shakers, our anthropologists, but they are in the uniquely precarious position of being the exact thing at which they are looking. No safely removed "man on the moon" vantage point for them. No safe place in which to stand. And what the playwrights of the late twentieth century seem to be articulating in word, gesture, and image is that the unknown no longer lies "out there" somewhere. It is right here. It is us.

And there is so much left to be known.

Robert Lepage's Theater

Edited by Leigh Buchanan Bienen

It's truly a great pleasure for me to be here tonight, and I would like to thank Northwestern for inviting me and those responsible for the Hope Abelson Artists in Residence program. I have been very busy, and it has been crazy trying to slot this into my schedule. The reason why I accepted was not because of the money, but because it is an opportunity for me to stop and think, to think out loud with an audience, to interact with an audience. Don't worry this is not going to be a solo piece or a monologue. Eventually there will be a question and answer period and we can exchange views on the subject matter that we're going to be treating tonight. The thing that preoccupies me the most, not just during these days, but that has been preoccupying me for the last few years in my practice, is what's going to happen to this extraordinary artistic expression called theater. I am someone who is very much enamored with that form of expression. I believe in it very much still today. I think it is an extraordinary, vibrant, crazy form of art. The most difficult thing is not to convince audiences to come and see my shows, or to convince audiences that theater is an extraordinary form of art, a form of expression, but to convince theater people that theater is the most fantastic thing. If we want to move into the twenty-first century and help this form of expression evolve and grow, and become something even more extraordinary, we must now reflect amongst ourselves, as theater crafts people.

What is theater? Why is it still alive? It's not going to die, and why? These are questions that I necessarily can't ask of the people with whom I'm working, because we're way too busy putting on shows, too absorbed in all those crazy production schedules. So the only people whom I could actually ask these questions, and interact and have a dialogue with, are either journalists, but of course they have their own tainted way of approaching things, or the audience, which of course is the most important intellectual entity with whom it is interesting to dialogue about theater. The audience is as much a part of the theater phenomenon as the theater artist, and we'll go deeper into that later. The reason why I'm talking about trying to convince theater people, or theater crafts people, that theater is an extraordinary form of art is that I meet few people who still believe in theater as a form of art, as a form of expression.

People do theater for all sorts of reasons. People do theater in the meantime. People do theater because they can't afford to do film, or can't afford to do TV. A lot of playwrights whom I know write plays because there is money for writing plays in Quebec, and very little money for writing novels. They would like to write novels, but they don't. They write plays. So, I don't know what the situation is here, in the United States, but I can tell you that where I come from plays are being sold in book shops without ever being staged. It used to be that you'd buy a play because the play had not only been written by someone, but it had been staged. It had been through the meat grinder of the theater production context. It had been through the meat grinder of the actors. It had been through the hands of the stage architect, of a director, and all the others who worked on it. That's not the case now, at least in the French speaking world, and in the Latin countries. You can now buy a play that's never been staged. And it's better that way anyway because the authors don't want their plays to be staged. They don't want directors changing things all around. They don't want actors to be breaking the play into pieces and doing their own things with it. Of course, these authors don't want their play to be a living thing.

For me that is symptomatic of what I have come across. I don't want to sound pretentious, but I work all around the world. My personal work is being shown internationally on tours on a regular basis. I also have had the opportunity in the last fifteen or twenty years to stage productions in Tokyo, Germany, France, Sweden, and England. Of course I haven't done the whole world yet, but I have a pretty good impression of what's going on in the western world, or the western theater world, the western part of the theater world.

My impression is that theater is this kind of almost-dead fish that smells funny. When it's really, really, really good, it still smells. It is even a stranger object for a lot of people. People are kind of doing this in the meantime. I'm very interested in this. Let us ask ourselves what is going to become of theater in the twenty-first century. The twenty-first century is at our door. It is something that we can foresee, something we can evaluate. We are responsible for what's going to happen to theater in the twenty-first century. I can't talk about what's going to happen to theater in the twenty-first century without referring to what has happened to the theater in this century, and trying to compare that with what will happen to the theater in the twenty-first century. I'd like to start by explaining something that for me condenses my feeling about theater nowadays.

In the nineteenth century, French romantic painting brought painting as a form of expression to new heights. Until the invention of photography in the middle of the nineteenth century, the painter was the chronicler of his time. If you wanted to keep traces of the heroes, the historical figures, the political figures, the great battles, if you wanted to depict elements and details of a certain era, painting was the form or art which did that. Painting really conveyed what that epoch was about, whether it was the sixteenth century, or the Italian Renaissance, or the German and French romantic movement.

Then photography comes along and it seems to perform this function better. The technology of photography allows you to go click, and suddenly there you have it. You have the great battles. You have the political figures. You have the historical figures. It seems that photography is going to become the better chronicler of its time. It's easier, it's user-friendly, as compared to painting. You don't need to study that much to be a photographer. Of course, it's black and white, but there's something about it that's so close to reality, especially compared to the transposition of painting.

For about half of the nineteenth century, painters think that painting is dead, that the art of painting is finished, and that it has become a lesser art compared to photography and the possibilities of photography. Photography eventually moves into another realm with color and movement and becomes in certain ways a form of art, a form of expression that's very close to what painting was in the nineteenth century. So, for about half a century, a lot of painters thought their art was dead and could never surpass that extraordinary new technological advancement which was photography.

After that half a century suddenly painters understood that painting had been liberated by photography. A painter doesn't need to be the chronicler of his time anymore. He doesn't have to do these realistic renderings of political figures and battles. Painting moves into a form of expression that has never been expressed before. Painters start to express emotions and ideas that have never been expressed before. Painting becomes dadaist, cubist, surrealist, impressionistic, all these extraordinary things at the turn of this century. Suddenly we move into a complete, different realm, and painting is this avant-garde, crazy place to be.

I think the same phenomenon is happening to theater right now. We're stuck in the middle of a period where people think that theater is like painting in the nineteenth century. Theater is this "dead rat," that there's nothing to be done with this form of art. Whereas I really, really feel that theater is this avant-garde, crazy thing that still remains to be explored. Theater doesn't have to be the chronicler of its time anymore. It can move into dadaism or cubism. Now we have freedom as theater artists to express emotions and ideas, and things that have never been expressed before. This is a big idea to sell to theater artists nowadays, because people are preoccupied with scheduling seasons, selling tickets, and acting. I hope by the time we get into the twenty-first century that people, theater artists, will understand that we are part of a crazy form of art that has been liberated by film, that has been liberated by television, and not been killed by film, not been killed by television. You can even observe the same phenomenon in film, when film people today begin to understand that television does it better: if you want information, watch television; if you want to see things live, as they happen, watch television. Film is a form of art. Film can express things that television cannot express. Even television is changing with the Internet, with all the new technologies, and all the new forms of art that are developing thanks to these new technologies. Television itself is questioning itself. What is the TV for now? And we are witnessing amazing changes right now. We are accepting things on TV that we didn't accept before and that has its own pace. We'll let the TV people wonder about that.

There are very few people in the world right now who have chosen to do theater for theater, who have chosen to do theater not as a normal process towards film, as a normal process towards television. In order to convince people that theater is this extraordinary crazy form of expression that hasn't been discovered takes a lot of work. I think that twenty-first century theater has to take into account the idea of cross-breeding. Now, there are cross-breedings at all sorts of levels. The first form of cross-breeding was to embrace the cross-cultural, the world culture. Cultures from all over the place are clashing and colliding and merging, and of course in theater too. If you want to understand what theater is going to become, you have to observe new trends in theater and incorporate theatrical techniques coming from different societies and different cultures.

Now, it may sound like I'm trying to make divisions in theater, that there is the Italian theater, the British theater, the American theater. Of course all of these are different expressions of the theatrical art, but there are some profound divisions in the different types of theatrical expression that we must take into account. It never really occurs to us at first, but I am someone who has worked with Japanese actors, worked with Latin performers, and with theater people from the English speaking world—and being myself a strange animal because I come from a country where culturally we are living a kind of schizophrenia, we are both completely Americanized and at the same time completely European. So I feel that I'm in a very privileged position at least to observe that phenomenon. One of the first things I observed, maybe ten years ago when I started to work in England at the National Theatre, is that I was always talking about "the spectator." What will the spectator think, because I'm French, and the audience is a "spectator." We don't say "audience," we say "spectateur." Then in the Latin speaking countries, it is "spectatori." The term implies that people come to *see* a story. They come to *see* a spectacle, to see something that's going to happen in front of their eyes.

In the English speaking world you say the "audience." That word implies that people come to *listen* to a story. It seems as if this is playing on words, but about ten years ago this was a key thing for me to understand as to what the English theater was about. This helped me understand why it was difficult to direct English actors, why they were from the neck up, and why the Italians and French were so difficult to understand when they spoke, why they were always doing this hand clapping thing, because they are so much into visual theater. There are these profound divisions in theatrical art, and we have to take that into account, and we have to try to understand how these two things can merge. In the early twenty-first century we will have to accept that historically based, traditional types of theater—whether English speaking, French speaking, German or whatever—are going to be shaken, are going to be clashing with other forms of theater.

I found a form of satisfaction in this cross-breeding of visual theater and text-based theater when I had the chance to work in Japan. I've been doing quite a lot of work in Japan. For me it has been very interesting because there's a lot of hope in Japan right now in the theater world. Japanese culture embraces, has always embraced, these two aspects. I've been learning Japanese in the past five years, and it's a lot of work. You cannot begin to understand, or to grasp, or start using that language, without understanding the visual communication of Japanese, as well as the verbal, the sound based, the auditory part. I'm sure there are other cultures where the same phenomenon occurs, but my small experience only made me identify it in Japan. You can feel that Japanese theater now is welcoming to both these forms of expressions, trying to blend them in a special way, a certain crafty way. This is one of the reasons why Japanese theater is so interesting, but it's also baroque, because of that phenomenon. And it doesn't travel well. People say, "Well, we never see Japanese shows in international theater festivals because they're too expensive." That's not true. You don't see Japanese shows in international festivals because it's a tough nut to crack, it's a difficult thing. The Japanese have developed this extraordinary, baroque culture. They are embracing their own traditions, and they are also embracing the western world. They are embracing sound and image. The Japanese experience of theater is way ahead of us, not because they are doing better theater than we are, but because they have their two feet into the experiment that is awaiting us in the twenty-first century.

So, if you want to know what's awaiting us in the early twenty-first century, look at what's going on in contemporary theater in Japan. They are really dealing with both the visual and the auditory tradition on an everyday basis. They are interested in opening markets. They are interested in exporting their theatricality, and they are also very interested in exporting their traditions. So are we all, whether we come from the United States, Canada, or Europe or wherever. We all have a form of theater tradition that we want to bring with us. I feel very *Quebecquois* even if I do a show in Japan, or in Germany. I want to convey a certain way of doing things but at the same time I'm ready to embrace world culture. So that for me is a very important phenomenon.

We have to be aware that we are living in a big CNN world, where someone comes on TV and says, "This is what's happening in the world, ladies and gentlemen." Well, yes, that is what's happening in the world according to *your* view, but there are other views, and there are other ways of looking at events. I think theater can be an extraordinary forum in the twenty-firsty century for that kind of experience to happen. I always refer to the Elizabethan period, to Shakespeare's work. There you can really feel, if you see the plays from a French point of view, or German point of view, or Gaelic point of view, you really feel when you're trying to translate these extraordinary Shakespearean plays that here is a language that was being created as he was writing these plays. He was taking all of these influences from all over the world and kind of putting them together. Probably Shakespeare was going through what we're going through as theater artists today, trying to deal with this brave new world. We have to see these fantastic theater periods in history as if they were dealing with the same phenomenon that we are dealing with today.

Another form of cross-breeding that we have to take into account in order to understand what's going to happen to the theatrical form of expression in the next century, is that there are two ways of telling stories. There's the live version. I could be on stage, as an actor, telling you this story, and this happens in a spontaneous, interactive, three-dimensional way, and it's called theater. Or, it's called the stage, and I'm including dance in that, and opera. Then you have the other way of telling the story nowadays, where it's canned, it's on film, or it's on tape. It will not move. It will not interact with you. If I'm a character on the screen right now, I'm just light. I'm not for real. I'm not made of flesh NO MATTER WHAT, whether you laugh, if the room is empty, if it's full, if you applaud, if you boo, you will never interrupt what goes on the screen. So that form of telling a story, in French we call that the "électronique" whether it's video, whether it's cinema. And these two ways of telling stories, whether we want that or not, whether we accept it or not, or it converges slowly, as the Titanic and the iceberg (and there was a lot of discussion of that in the workshops today), and so you have these two forms and they're going to meet. Is it going to be a clash? Is it going to be a merger? I don't know, but that's what's waiting for us and coming soon.

The reason why this is happening is because the audience commands that. The audience wants the theater to be more filmic, not because the audience likes films and projected videos on the stage. It has nothing to do with that phenomenon. The audience wants film narrative structure on stage because the audience now has a new way of listening to stories, a new way of digesting stories, a new way of understanding stories, of following stories with a film made vocabulary that is much richer than what audiences had twenty and thirty years ago. Today audiences know what a jump cut is, and a flashback, and a flash forward, through rock videos and commercials, all these are things that people didn't necessarily see twenty or thirty years ago. Then most people saw film and TV. Look at how people try to sell a car today. Try to follow how the stories go. It's not point A going to plot point on page 28 going to plot point on page 30. No, it's not that at all. It's like this, you know the information, you grab it, and you do your own thing with it. Similarly, with rock videos and Tarantino movies. This is what the cinematic and television narrative vocabulary has done to the theater audience. I'm not saying that we have to give in to that, because film has a stronger influence, that out of fear we have to invite cinema on stage. But what I am saying is, take into account what the audience is used to dealing with. If theater doesn't take that into account, it will die. That is not compromising, it's just being aware of the time in which we are living.

This is why I am desperate to understand what people understand when I do a play. Sometimes the audience is at the end of the play before I am. Well, the audience should be, actually, it will always be saying, "Follow me, follow me." Then that's not what happens. For me that explains a lot of empty rooms where the audience doesn't feel that its intelligence is challenged, in putting the pieces of the puzzle together. People come, sit and see a play as if, of course, that's going to happen. The actor opens the door there, and then comes in, and says whatever. . . . And people are at the end of the play long before we are as actors and performers, For me that's a big problem. I think that the solutions to that dilemma give way to a very interesting form of theater.

Of course I don't pretend to have the answer. I'm trying things. Other companies are trying things. I'm trying to respect that. For me that's one of the forms of cross-breeding that's awaiting us. If we want theater to survive in the twenty-first century, we have to accept that a piece of theater is something that goes on as much in the room, as it does on stage. The audience is part of the writing process. The audience is part of the theatricality of the piece. The audience has to be reinvited back into theater, and to the theater craft.

Now it may seem that I am opening my arms and saying that you all are welcome to say what you think of my play. It's not that. It's finding a way to do theater so that people can give you feedback. It doesn't mean laugh or not laugh, applaud or not applaud, scream, or, another kind of response. It's finding ways to develop a piece over a certain period of time, so that critics, reviewers, theater writers, whatever their opinion, whatever they have to say is reinjected into the piece. Right now, we have imprisoned ourselves in a system where opening night happens, and after that, you're a dead duck! The guillotine of the opening night falls, and that's it. So if you didn't eat too much before the opening, and if the main character didn't have the flu, and if everyone wasn't too nervous, and the actors didn't have too much stage fright, and, all of these elements which don't have anything to do with the theater, then decide the fate of a theatrical piece. This is completely absurd!

In my own way I've been defying that. I've been trying to bypass the rule of the guillotine. I develop my work in a work in progress fashion.

Of course that's not new. A lot of people have been working in that way. We have a system called "the public rehearsal" where we show up unannounced, and people show up. There aren't reviewers in the room, and we rehearse in front of the audience. The audience interacts with that rehearsal. Afterward, we have a party and we drink beer. At the party people come up, and they say audience things, and you don't expect them to be artists. You don't expect them to be theater crafts people. They tell you what they feel and what they think. Of course, what they have to say about what you do is as important as your first intentions. That interaction has been largely removed from the theater in the twentieth century. Today the audience is a market. Period. You have to attract them with arguments such as, come and see us and you will not have to think. Come and see us, and you will forget about your life. Come and see us, and you will relax. Which of course is the last thing an audience member wants when he buys a ticket. Of course, if you ask a member of the audience he will say, "Well I like to come to the theater because I like to laugh, or I like to relax."

Of course, we've put that in their minds.

But the audience comes to the theater because it likes a work out. Look at people who work in office buildings from nine to five, and then ask why are the gyms full nowadays, how come everybody's training? It is not just because they want to look good. It's because they have this amazing energy, this amazing physical energy. People go to their work, and that doesn't use any of that energy. They go into jobs where, you know, they have a certain energy that they give. They know they have jobs where they feel creative. Sometimes they have jobs where they feel challenged physically, or energetically, or their brain feels challenged. But nonetheless they must train because they have this massive energy that hasn't been used. They want to feel alive. They want to feel challenged. They want to feel more energetic the day after when they train. I think people come to the theater for exactly the same reasons. People come to the theater because they want to be challenged. They want this part of their brain, or this part of their body, to be used. Unfortunately, it all won't be in spite of user-friendly computers and all of that. A lot of the knowledge being used by the computer takes care of a part of that energy and develops a certain kind of logical thinking. And of course there is expertise in this new way of living, but people want to feel intelligent. That's the reason why, for example, in French Canada they sell more tickets doing comedy. It is not just because people want to forget about their problems. Comedy, at least a certain kind of comedy, challenges the wit, the intelligence with all these puns and jokes. Of course, theatrical people put that down, they say "Oh, that's just trash." But it's not true. I think that an audience member would feel as challenged by a Greek tragedy if the people on stage would have confidence in his intelligence, if the people on stage would trust the audience to be, not cultured people, but intelligent people. Right now, the way theater is marketed, the way it's sold, is with this pretension that you have the "culture," ladies and gentlemen, to see this thing—which is not true—but you don't have the intelligence to understand it. So we'll masticate it for you. We'll serve it to you but you won't have to bite it, we'll do that for you. We'll serve it up to you once it's masticated and digested and all of that.

I think it's the other way around. If theater people take the attitude of saying, well, of course you don't have the references. We're doing a Chekov for God's sake. Half the people here wouldn't understand the context of Russia prerevolution and the Stanislavsky School. We don't ask that from an audience. I trust that people are intelligent enough to relate what they see to something else in their life, and make the connections, and feel that when they come to see a play, they're active and not passive participants. For me this is one of the great reconciliations that we have to keep aiming for if we want theater to be an extraordinary, alive, vibrant place to be in the next century. We have to reconcile with the audience. We have to take into account the audience and stop thinking that theater is something that happens here on stage and there's a fourth wall. The fourth wall is just a convention, but it's getting thicker and thicker and thicker, as theater companies are funded from external sources and become hostage to development and marketing strategies. So for me those are the great kind of cross-breedings or convergences that are awaiting us in the theater. We have to be brave enough to take this upon ourselves as theater people, whether we are writers, directors, designers, or performers. We have to take on that responsibility, and say, well, theater will survive if we believe in theater, and if we believe in the audience, and if we believe that theater is still one of the rare, democratic social events. Theater is a social, collective form of entertainment.

Just to touch on film a bit. Ten years ago I started to do a bit of film work. I've always been curious about what's the difference between telling a story in film and telling a story in theater. And it's radically different. That doesn't mean that film and theater should be done by two different kinds of artists, and that doesn't mean that film and theater should be done by two different kind of performers. But these are two different forms of communication. Only when we understand these are two very distinct ways of telling stories can we begin to think of merging them together, as we try to understand how we can make film more interactive, more two-dimensional, more alive. How can we make theater more filmic, in a good sense, not in a bad sense. For me one of the main differences is the relationship between the audience and what goes on, on the stage or on the screen. Theater is *always* a collective event. There's a group of people out there in time and space. As a collective they have a strength. They have a power. They can change what goes on on a stage. Of course, they can't change the set or the furniture around, but they can change things by their energy, by the collective energy of active participation in front of another collective group, which is the actors, the people who put on a play, the people that have written it, directed it, staged it. So it's a meeting of two collectivities and everything that happens, even in a one-man show, is a collective thing in that circumstance. So it's a very, very, very different way of conveying a story from film.

Film is a completely individualistic relationship. It's a one-on-one way of telling a story. I don't remember going to see a Woody Allen movie. I wouldn't be able to tell you if the house was full or empty. That doesn't change my way of understanding the film. I don't know if people laughed or not. The collective, the actual reality of the audience in time and space does not get reflected in a film. Of course, people will say, "I went to see 'Titanic' yesterday and it was full." Of course, it is always full. But so what, the fact that it's full it doesn't change your relationship with the film. You didn't forget the people that accompany you when you go see the film. The main reason why is because you cannot change what is going on in the film. You do not have an existence as a group, so you can't change that. Even as a director I feel that it's a very, very individualistic thing to do film, compared to doing a theater piece. In the theater I feel I'm part of a collective of artists who are trying to convey a story. In film, even if there are zillions of participants, it's always your film, what you as a director, or as a filmmaker, have to say about this or that. So that's radically different, and those things are very difficult to reconcile. These two ways of conveying stories are very, very, very different. They are made of two very different things. So I'm very, very interested to see how these things can cross.

Technology helps create a kind of interface. Theater people used to be completely forbidden from film sets, and, of course, theater people would keep out the film world. They would accuse the film of not understanding what the stage world is, and of course that's wrong. Now, as a theater artist, I feel much more welcome in the film world and vice versa. That understanding has happened a lot because of the common technological basis, the instruments we use on stage, and the instruments we use on the film set, are starting to be the same. We're starting to have that versatility. When you start using the same equipment, and the same rooms, to convey stories, that means you're starting to share. Maybe they're just instruments and equipment and money and budgets, but it is a first step. At least, it's a starting point. It used to be, for example, that a puppeteer and somebody who does computer animation were in two different worlds. The puppeteer belongs to the theater world, he belongs to the world of sculpture, where matter is used like clay. It's a completely different artistry than doing computer graphics used to be. Now computer graphics have been transformed into a very, very user-friendly medium. Now the sculptors and the puppeteers are welcome again into the world of animation. The technology people have invented this thing called meta-clay that can only be sculpted by people who know what sculpting is about. And the animation is now three-dimensional. I get calls from all over the world now to do film from companies who want to do three-dimensional communication. They know that the people whose only experience is from the film world have difficulties dealing with this idea of a three-dimensional reality, or with the concept of interactivity. For me this is very encouraging. I don't think the two worlds are actually moving apart. Quite the contrary, the technology is forcing these two worlds to come closer, to share experience, and to try to convey ideas together. It's very difficult to talk about because I don't have clear examples of that phenomena. I only have little snippets, little examples, but I bump into these examples more and more often. I really do think that the theater world will have to accept that the film world is going to be invading the stage, and vice versa. The film people will have to accept that there are theater rules that will be applicable once again to filmmaking.

To be a good observer, or a good user of this new phenomena, I've decided to create a new company called Ex Machina. Of course, the name indicates that we believe in the machine, that we believe that we can extract miracles out of technology, or extract miracles out of the machine. I used to be a part of a company called Théâtre Repère in the good old days when we used to do theater in a very subsidized way, doing our regular four shows a year, etc. Then I wasn't satisfied with what was going on in the company, because it wasn't taking into account, wasn't taking into consideration this new trend. This new reality is a crossbreeding of multimedia, film, television without forcing it, but taking into account that all of these are going to have a great influence on the theatrical form of expression. So I created this company called Ex Machina four years ago. We have a laboratory in Quebec City. It's an old fire station that can be transformed into a film studio, and twenty-four hours afterward can be a performing space again. This is a place where we do operas for Japanese and French companies. It's a place where we do CD-ROM, where we do web sites. It's a place where we have music and music performances. We have all of these people who usually work in different places, all under one roof now, trying to find a way to connect. They are connecting anyway because the tools that they have, to write their stories, or to write their musical scores, or to edit their films, are becoming the same tool. It's not that I'm a complete worshiper of technology, but I do try to understand. I do try to listen to the technological advancement. Then I try to read into that, and try to identify what the technology is trying to tell us. It's really trying to tell us that eventually we won't have any excuses not to understand each other's worlds, and each other's rules.

That's what we were doing this afternoon in the theater workshop. I did a workshop with a group of students, as always starting a new project from chaos. It really becomes fun when you have rules, when you're playing a game. It's interesting right now in our new building, to ask a filmmaker not to edit his film in a filmic way, but to think instead in a musical way, in a theatrical way, in more interactive CD-ROM way, in a website way. All of these ways of thinking actually bring in new rules, new games to play, and the art that comes out of that is sometimes, quite extraordinary, almost revolutionary. So for me, it was very important to create a center, a place where all these people from all over the world, from all sorts of disciplines can get together. To exchange ideas and try to see how they can use each other's mind structures and rules, to try and make their own form of expression a bit more permissive, a bit more modern, a bit more connected with today's realities.

I have just finished my third feature film. With my first film, "The Confessional," I did the standard recipe. You sit down. You're in your hotel room, and you're writing your film script. Then, you give over the script. Then they budget it and give the money. Then you go and shoot it, etc. The last two films I've done I've been more connected to the theatrical process of the film. That means, for example, that the film I just finished editing was first a theater piece. On the set the actors were still improvising and trying things around. Then, the actors collaborated on the editing process. We opened up all of the process. The film rooms in major studios usually have two seats, maximum. One for the editor, and one for the director. We created an editing room with many, many seats because all the people came in and tried things in the editing process. One of the things that helped create this new film is that we had to do the play. The play was way over budget. So we signed a film deal because there's more money in film. We took the film deal and did the play. In order to do the film we had all these amazing multimedia subsidies from Quebec. So we took the multimedia subsidies, and we did the film with the multimedia budget.

There's a lot of money in multimedia these days. But there is a kind of lack of content. There are all of these amazing grids. Microsoft may phone and ask, "Hey, do you want to come live in Seattle? We'll give you a desk and you'd just have to have ideas, ideas, ideas, ideas." People want content. So this money for multimedia projects is a rich gold mine right now. People in theater don't know that. People in film don't know that. Spike Lee has been doing films for the web because he understood that's where the money was. And not just the money, but the web doesn't have censorship. You don't have to go through all these boards, all these meetings, or have people approve what you do. They just give you the money, and say, "Fill in the grid." We've developed a system at Ex Machina. The web site helps do the film, and the film helps do the play, and the play helps do the web site. The web site forces us to do the film in a web site structure. We have to approach the film with a hypertext way of thinking, and that changes the way you do films. I'm working on *The Tempest* right now. I'm developing a 3D *Tempest*. We have all these multimedia and video people who are used to doing things for commercials. They do the virtual 3D things, and then they say, now you have to import that onto stage.

The stage is a three dimensional world. So we have *The Tempest* with real actors, and the set is this virtual, 3D world. The screen, the virtual world is always extremely clean and sharp. Then actors are out of focus, because, depending on where you're sitting in the room, you don't necessarily see their faces clearly. But you can see something on the screen even more sharply. So the virtual reality people have to adapt their rules of sharpness and their vocabulary to the theatrical vocabulary. These are little examples; they're not really significant. But they show there is a will for all of these ways of telling stories to get together and say, well how can I make my craft evolve. Can I make it clash with another form of art? So that's what Ex Machina is doing right now.

The Tempest is just one of these projects. We deal with recorded material, and things that are live. The recorded material is not completely recorded, because it's run by computers. That means that you can interfere with it at any time and change it. What you see projected is a film, but it's not a film. Nothing is locked as in a film. You can actually stop the visual images, the film, and actually make it go faster, or you can change it. Or you can change your mind as you do in theater. The main thing allowing for all of these changes is the flexibility of the new technology.

Doing period plays in modern costume and modern dress is not being connected to our times. That's just changing costumes and scoring points. If you take a Roman play and set it in 1920s, and then say the crash equals this, and this equals that, but nothing equals anything, that's not being contemporary, quite the contrary. The technology today helps us better understand the classics. What's on stage could actually be even more classical than you've ever seen, and in a more accurate way, with a different understanding. Always Shakespeare is an example. I was working in Stockholm doing Strindberg in Swedish. I could feel how very little they knew about Strindberg. Of course, it's *the* big museum of Strindberg. They've been doing it in their way forever, as though time had stopped. And the world has continued to evolve, and Strindberg is such an extraordinary writer. His works are amazing. These aspects never found an echo. They have continued to stage his works as the first director, or as Strindberg himself would have performed them.

You have to take into account that theater is something that changes all the time. When I see one of my films, it's like seeing the ghost of an old ideal. My god, what is this? Why am I here tonight? Something I shot four years ago. Something I wrote two years before that. I was completely someplace else. "I" in the theater, even if you wrote something fifteen years ago, it's still here, in the present. It's still being changed. It is always about who you are at that moment. You could take the same approach to a classical repertoire. Take what you want from the classical repertoire. If you want it to be alive, you have to accept that half of it drops away. It's really weird. This year in Berlin the hundred-year anniversary of Bertolt Brecht is being celebrated. He wrote reams of pages about how there should never be museums, everyone should rip off everybody else, and all of that. And they're doing this big Brecht centennial. They want Communism to be this big monolith, which has never changed. We know what Communism is, and we know what it became after Brecht. Everyone is pretending in Berlin now that the work still must echo today in this way and that form. But some plays hold up, and some plays don't. You have to be iconoclastic, to approach these works as an iconoclast, considering the new realities of today, and not just put on a costume that a person would wear today. That doesn't make a play modern, not at all.

The Frank Lloyd Wright project for example, was inspired two years ago when I spent a lot of time in Chicago. I know Chicago quite well, and I went to Oak Park for the first time two years ago. I had always been a great admirer of Frank Lloyd Wright's work, mainly because of the organic aspect of his work, because he always spoke of an organic architecture, whatever that meant in those days. I've always kept the pretension that my work was organic theater. You let things happen by themselves, taking into account the environment in which it was being done. So I thought it was appropriate at one point for the group that had been working with this "organic theater" method to do something about Frank Lloyd Wright. Our theater piece has nothing to do with "organic architecture." It's called, *The Geometry of Miracles*. It's about Frank Lloyd Wright, but it's not about all of his life and his philosophies. It's about a certain period of his life. Not the period when he was the greatest architect of the nineteenth century, but the period when he was the greatest architect of the twentieth century, the second part of his life. It is about how Frank Lloyd Wright tried to establish an American architecture with a Jeffersonian way of thinking. He was actually extremely Russian in his approach. It's a lot about spiritual quests, quests for immortality, about counting and geometry.

As a theater person, I don't believe that you write theater alone. "Writing theater," that's one idea, one generalized idea that we have about theater, that theater is something that a writer does on his own. It's a collective process, and theater only exists if there's an audience. My work starts being written the first day it's being performed. I never publish any of my plays. I've done many, many plays, but rarely published them. There's always a theater reviewer somewhere who wants to have the script for some reason, as if *that's* the true play. For me, if there's no audience, if there's no reconciliation with the audience, if there's no survival of the relationship between the stage artist and the audience, then there's no theater. As an artist, I cannot write by myself anymore, because all of the rehearsal process resembles exploration and improvisation. The night that we decide to open, it's because we feel that we have a kind of a semblance of structure, and the audience will actually inform us what the show is. So you have to have a lot of humility to do this. You have to accept that the work is bigger than you are, that what you have to say is probably much more interesting than you are. You have to accept that. The word is that at the end of a tour at some point, you will get an idea of what you were trying to say. We live in this European, colonized mentality, where the director enters and says, "I know where I'm going, you all shut up and follow me." That's my problem with the German system. The director comes in and everyone wants you, the director, to scream and say, "You are nothing, and this is where we're going!" I say, well, I'm sorry, this is not the way I work. You know that happens very, very late into the process, if at all. In America the bottom line is very important. If you can figure out a way for people to want to see this show, fine, but if you do it and nobody comes, the producer says good-bye. Well, that's a bit of a Catch 22. Of course you can't convince people that what you do is good if you don't have an audience. You have to find a way to attract an audience, so you have to be good first. Here's an example. We offered a show called "Dragon's Trilogy." We had a three-hour version and a six-hour version. We toured the world a couple of times with this show. We would ask the promoter, or the director of the festival, which version he wanted. On the first tour they would all want the three-hour version because they thought nobody would want to spend six hours in the theater. So we would do the three-hour version, and it is great theater. People loved it, and it's fine.

So then some festival people would invite us again the year after. They'd say, "Well, it was so good, some people asked us if you could do the six-hour version."

So I'd say, "Well, are you sure you want to do the six-hour version?" It implies technically the full day. There are three intermissions. It says six hours, but it's eight hours total. What time do people finish their jobs? You can only do two, maybe three performances a week, not five. Suddenly, you bump into all these practical considerations. So then people say, okay, we'll settle. We'll do two three hours, and we'll do two six hours. Okay, we got a deal. So, we do it, and the tickets for the six-hour version sell like crazy. The three-hour version we play in front of half houses. There's a reason for that. People go to the theater because they want to enter a world. They don't want to come to the theater and say, okay, it's an hour and a half. First half hour, where's the car parked? They're still in that frame of mind. Then, they miss something, and, okay, what was that about? And then after that second half hour, okay, the babysitter. Oh my god, the babysitter! And it's like the whole evening goes, and then okay, we had a great time. Where's the car? So, what we're trying to do is bad film. We're trying to pretend that theater can be like an evening at the cinema: You park your car, you come in, you get it all, and then you go home. And that's not how theater works. "The Seven Streams of the River Ota" is seven hours long, seven and a half hours long. People rushed to it like crazy because people want that to happen to them. And when we think for them, we're always saying, "Oh people will never want this, or people don't do that, or people are not into that." We don't know that. What I know is Shakespeare. His plays used to go on forever. Hamlet was five hours. There were intermissions, and dinner breaks, and people got drunk and said, "Well, who was Gertrude?" And that was expected, because it is a social occasion. That's what intervals are for, because the audience feels it is a part of a community. "The Seven Streams" was great and is still touring Australia right now. People come in. They know they have seven hours, or seven and a half hours, to be sitting there. So you don't sit down in the same way. You go, okay, this is going to be seven hours, so you spread your energy around in a different way. It becomes fantastic. The actors feel they can tell the story at a certain pace. They go into details you could never go into in an hour and a half, or two hours. Then there's a break.

In the break people say, *well* wait a minute, I didn't get that. Well, that character's related to this character. Oh yeah, okay. Then it becomes a social event, and after three intervals, they're intimate. They know each other. They're happy to be a part of this. Then they eat together. They're anxious, and they all rush back into the theater together because they want to see "Part 5" and they all want to be there together, and that's what theater is. "The Mahabarata" was nine hours of theater. People say, "It's Peter Brook, and Peter Brook has a name." That's not true. Peter Brook doesn't have name in Perth, Australia. People go because they hear they're going to spend a complete evening. They bring blankets. They're going to be in a quarry. They are going to see the story. It's complicated, and it's about India. People want that to happen to them! Mnouchkine and Peter Stein have all understood that you can decide. You can decide, to do a five-hour show or, a three-hour show. You can decide that if there's a time to tell the story, that's what it takes. If it means doing only two performances a week, it's two performances a week. The tickets will be a bit more expensive. It means all of these practical things, but there's an audience for that and I believe in that totally. The Frank Lloyd Wright pieces people are asking, "Well, are you sure that we can slide it in between 7 and 9:30 because after we want to have a talk?" I don't know how long it's going to be. It's going to be the time it takes to tell that story, period! Now people say "Oh yeah, well, you have a name, or you have an international reputation." It's not true. People who come to see my shows don't know who I am. They've never heard of me. The majority of the people come because somebody said, "I saw this show yesterday, and it inspired me, or it was interesting, or I had a great time." That's why people come and tickets sell. The theater system, the actual theater system that is completely copied from the film logic of marketing is completely wrong. It's killing the whole theatrical experience.

In Chicago at the International Festival a few years ago they did "The War of the Roses." Everybody was worrying, I'm *not* going to see seven hours of Shakespeare. I hope I *am* going to see seven hours of Shakespeare. At last I'm going to understand this. At last I'm going to become accustomed to a way of speaking, to a style, even if it's badly performed. It's an event. And that for me gives way to so many possibilities. Right now, we're doing all these two-hour shows without interval. I think there's a lot to be learned about what to do with the classical repertoire. We're keeping all the wrong things from the classical repertoire. We're not keeping the essential things from the classical repertoire, such as spending a day in the theater. People felt privileged. They said, "I'm going to see this . . ." Now people have film and TV, but people still feel privileged if they come to see a good piece of theater where there's space for their own way of understanding. Some people understand quickly, some slowly, but, if you have an hour and a half, you're only satisfying one half of the audience.

You can do what you want if you're the artist. When you're a painter, you paint in an oval or you paint in a square. What I think is interesting, is, why this frame? Why did film go from the 1:3 ratio that was closer to painting, to become this amazing Panavision thing. So, I really try to avoid putting up work that accommodates a standard room. There's no real standard anywhere. We're working in an intuitive way, instead of using the usual intellectual approach that says, Well, this is the theme: the theme is war. I mean, war, the Gulf War. Okay, so of course there are all of these intellectual and political opinions, and things like that. I try to avoid all of that. I hope that these things will come at the end. At the end you may have an opinion.

Somebody who works on one of my shows eventually develops an intellectual position and opinion. Usually we start with something that you can't discuss really, that you can't agree or disagree on. I use the example of a card game. You can't agree or disagree with a card in a card game. But everyone can have different impressions of what a card game does to you. For some people, it is fortune. For some it is cheating. For some people it is the royal families. Once people start arguing there's no way you can find a consensus because we are all different people. We all come from different backgrounds. Half of us are men, half women. Some people come from a rich background, some have a poor background. By the time you've sorted all of that out, you've watered down your subject so much that you can't even start doing art.

My method is based mainly on selecting things that we all feel are starting points, that we feel are rich, that are juicy. People will actually go in all sorts of directions. We explore. We include every aspect of the production into the exploration. We have the set designers, the lighting designers, the director/writers, whoever, the musicians, everyone is there from day one, even the technicians. They bring what they can bring to the explorations, and it takes all sorts of forms. We try to find what will eventually be the language of this new form, and try to serve that, instead of trying to make it fit into three weeks of rehearsal. We don't try to fit into a proscenium stage, or fit into somebody else's schedule or marketing plan. It's not a courageous thing. It's easy to do, you do it once and it works. Often people say, "My God, you've been defying the rules." But people do it, and they feel free to do it again because it works. I mean it really works. It isn't as if you do extraordinary things every minute. So, it's not that much of a risk.

I don't understand the American system of training. The facilities here at Northwestern University, for example, are amazing, and the participants in the workshop are extremely talented and versatile. I was a bit surprised. Where I come from when you're in training in the university, the opportunities are not very good. We have a conservatory system with specialized classes in a school where you *only* do theater. You can also train in the university, but in the university you're stuck with all these other academic classes and requirements. I feel generally that training is much too disconnected from the professional world. It's the same problem everywhere, whatever the country. For me there's one exception that I always praise. And everybody hates me for it. It's the slave system of Japan.

The Japanese have this extraordinary system of training artists, and I hope we'll understand and get it one day. I did quite a lot of work in Tokyo. This is their system. Well, it's not really a system. Here's an example. They had an actor playing the main character, the guy who was playing Prospero. He comes in and he imposes on the production that this young guy and this young girl must have a small part in the play, otherwise he won't do the play. The director then decides, okay, okay, the young girl will play a fairy. Or, he'll play a fairy. And eventually you begin to see that these young people are always around this actor. They're bringing him water. They're prompting him. They're recording him and all of these things. Then the rehearsal room starts to be full of all these slaves. They are all over the place. They come in, and they're there. Some guy that I never met a week before the opening is on stage, and he's prompting one of the actresses. Then he brings in his cassette and he says, "I'm also a singer, if you . . ." And the room is full of all these people. The worst thing is that you go into production week and the wings are full of all these guys you've never seen. They're waiting with a towel. And this other guy's there with something else. And you go, "What is this? This is completely ridiculous." Then you discover that it's a fantastic system. Because if somebody really admires an actor, he says, Mr. Mashita, I'm a great fan, a great admirer of your work. If one day I become an actor, I would like to act like you do, to learn from you, so can I follow you around? And the actor says, "Yes." And that is how the slave comes into being.

It's fantastic because you're in the rehearsal, in a room full of extraordinary artists. You would never be in these people's presence if you were in theater school. You see how production works. You prompt people. You make yourself helpful to the production generally and eventually you get in contact with the professional world. Sometimes you get to say a line or two, and it's fantastic. So, the first time I saw this in operation I was revolted because I thought, this is so feudal, from another century. Eventually I started to appreciate what was happening. I don't mean that I need a slave waiting behind me with a towel. You could feel it. There's a sense of a master class. We come from such a democratic society in North America we would never accept that kind of training. It's not politically acceptable. Sometimes I reflect on my own training. I was trained at the conservatory, and I had the works. But I never learned as much as the time when I asked a director whom I admired, "If I could just go in and observe, and be helpful. I'll make some tea." Of course, you learn humility at the same time. I don't want to generalize because I know it doesn't work like that everywhere in Japan, but the few companies I worked with in Japan had that kind of system, and I found it fantastic! And people really come out of there knowing something. Of course they buy you gifts, you know, so the actor doesn't have to buy you gifts. People really want to make it, and they're very devoted and they learn.

France, on the other hand, is such a literary culture. Where else except France would you invent a phone where you write to each other. They have mail twice or three times a day, and then they visit and write, and write and visit. And in France the whole theater system is controlled by this playwright's thing. My big problem with this is that too many plays are being published without ever being performed. It's a big divorce. There's a divorce between the playwright and the stage right now all over the world. Another problem with the literary, the writing aspect of theater, is that it is encouraged by the critic's world, that is itself literary. That's a "big problem." I share this opinion with Peter Brook who has said, the "big problem" right now in the twentieth century is that we are trying to do theater, which is a completely, physical thing, a visual thing, a sound thing, which is all these languages even before it's literature, and the only people who judge us, who say go and see it or not, the only people who leave traces of what you've done, are people who are writers. So of course they glorify writers. I have to admit there are some theater writers who have enough insight, and are intelligent enough, not to judge things strictly on a literary basis. But this literary logic that controls the whole system is part of the problem. It creates a big divorce.

This is one reason why directors want to write, because you can no longer stage what is being written. In the tragedies you no longer go into Duncan's room and come back with your hands covered in blood. Shakespeare was such a fantastic writer because he wrote for the stage and for nothing else. He wrote his best soliloquies because there was a set change, and the actor would just get up there and talk, we have, "To be or not to be." Or, Fortinbras was getting behind there, or a funeral is going to come in, so I have to pass the time. I'm exaggerating, but all I'm trying to say is that, when you stage Shakespeare, it's easy because it's been planned for the theatrical reality, the production reality. People walk out on a stage because they have a set or a costume change, and he took that into account. Maybe those are only the traces of Shakespeare. Today you read plays and they're not capable of being staged. They're not the reflection of a reality that is called "the stage," and includes the costumes, the audience, and whatever.

What you call a company here is, of course, a group of actors. Maybe you have a company of 20 actors or 60 actors. What we call a company is just an official name. There's not enough money where I come from to support a company system like you would have here. There's a nucleus of maybe 20 or 25 people that we keep using in different ways, keep collaborating with. Of course they're free to wander off and do something else and then come back. They're not linked by any kind of contract to the company. They maybe linked to a project. We like to keep it open because all sorts of weird accidents happen. We have this amazing dramatic soprano that I worked with in an opera once. She's fantastic. She says, "I like the way you work and I have stories to tell." And, she found her way into our work. Other people come in and they say well, I'm not necessarily an actor. Or I'm not necessarily a writer, but I'd like to contribute. People are interesting. What's important is that people are interesting, if they have things to say, if they're brave enough to explore new forms and ideas. So there's no official company.

We were talking about the Japanese, and Asian influence in general in my work. I guess it's just personal interest and personal taste. I was a kind of Japanese theater specialist when I was in the conservatory, although I'd never seen a real Kabuki play. It was only very late when I finally got to work in Japan and to see the real thing. I discovered it had nothing to do with what I had seen on film, or what my teachers had told me, it was a totally different experience. There are many reasons why I'm influenced and interested in Asian theater, Japanese theater most specifically. One reason is the great discipline based on the responsibility of the actor. That has changed my way of approaching and directing actors. It is difficult to explain. First, you have to see it. We all imagine that acting in Japan means the same thing as it does here. It doesn't. In Japan actors are extremely responsible. They are the storytellers. They take on that responsibility. I bumped into this thing also in the Western style theaters that exist in Japan.

You have that extraordinary moment in Kabuki where the curtains open, and the character comes in, and everything stops right there. People applaud and scream. In fact, they're not just acclaiming the great actor who just came in. They're evaluating his choice, because, he chose the costume. People know the repertoire. In Quebec, we know the repertoire of Moliere, and Shakespeare. So it's, Okay, how is he going to *do* Hamlet. How is *he* going to do Hamlet? The actors come in, and it is just that first visual impression, that first choice, and you freeze it there, saying, "This is what I'm responsible for." People applaud or boo or whatever. Or, they say, "Okay, this is what you want to try. Okay, we're with you!" The actor comes in, and he walks very slowly. He slowly gets into gear, and he's completely responsible for telling the story. He takes that on himself. Even if he's been directed or he's been helped or he's been designed, or he's been whatever, you really have this sense of responsibility. This is a great thing that happens in the Kabuki. It used to be this way in the West. Then they discarded it.

Then there's a moment where as you get deeper into the drama of the character, and the more difficult the piece is for the actor to perform, he will not continue performing it if he's not helped. If you are sitting in the theater for the first time, you're wondering, "What's going on," because somebody might scream something, perhaps a name. And you want to say, Shhh, the guy's concentrating and that doesn't exist anymore. What they are doing, they are screaming his actor's family name. It is a clan system. Your name is Yamashito, or Yamamoto, but you are part of the Kendo family of actors. People scream that name, meaning you are worthy of that name. Your choices are good choices. We're going to help you and push you farther into that. And the actor kind of takes that in and continues. So, theater becomes this dialogue, even in the worst, the most difficult passages. The actor says, "Help me." And the actor just takes it on, and gives it back. *That* has been a great influence on me and my work. I always say to actors, you're doing terrific work, but the audience is not invited into that. That is often how I feel when I go to the theater. I feel that things are going, seem to be going quite well on the stage, but I'm not invited in. You say, Oh, you know, great acting. But there's always this very thick fourth wall. I'm sorry, I don't want to intrude here, and you applaud and leave. And that's the twentieth century. It's psychological drama and it's all a bad interpretation of Stanislavsky. It's a century of actor's studio technique, where we're supposed to admire the effort and not the result. Emotion is something that goes on on the stage, but not in the audience, when that's *where* it should be.

Etchings and Monoprints

by
Mark Strand

Big Island, 1998
Etching
Published by Harlan Weaver

Sea with Islands, 1998
Etching
Published by Harlan Weaver

Eight Islands, 1998
Etching
Published by Harlan Weaver

Central Cloud I, 1999
29 3/4" x 22 1/4"
Monoprint
Published by Goya-Girl Press, Inc.
Baltimore, MD

Central Cloud II, 1999
29 3/4" x 22 1/4"
Monoprint
Published by Goya-Girl Press, Inc.

Central Cloud III, 1999
29 3/4" x 22 1/4"
Monoprint
Published by Goya-Girl Press, Inc.

Big Cloud, 1999
29" x 38 1/2"
Monoprint
Published by Goya-Girl Press, Inc.

Two Clouds, 1999
29" x 38 1/2"
Monoprint
Published by Goya-Girl Press, Inc.

A Cloud with a Story, 1999
38 1/2" x 29"
Monoprint
Published by Goya-Girl Press, Inc.

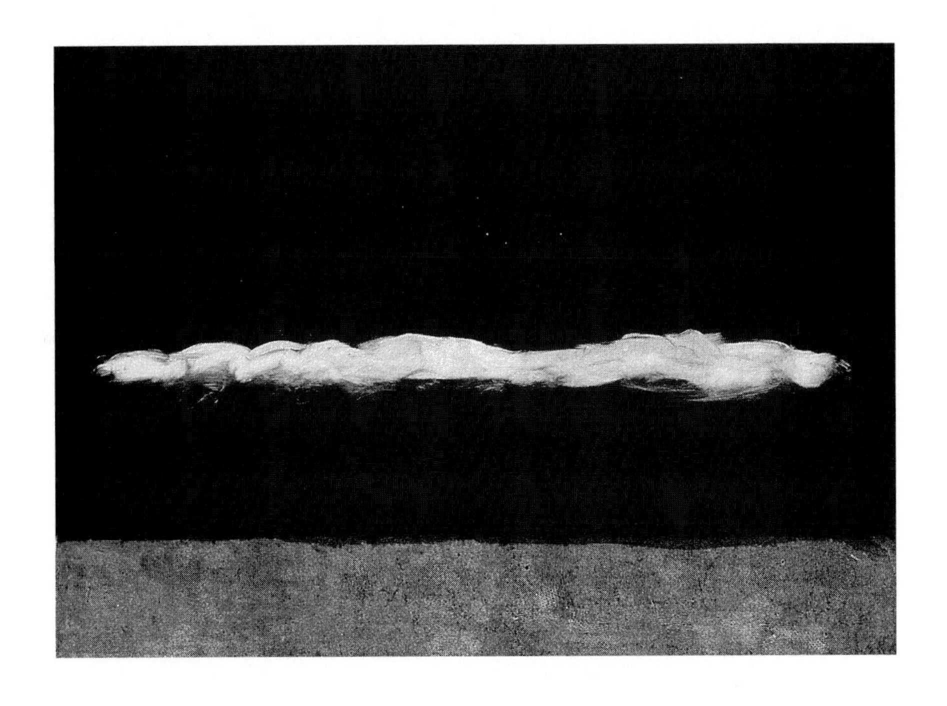

Italian Cloud, 1999
29" x 38 1/2"
Monoprint
Published by Goya-Girl Press, Inc.

Odd Clouds I and II, diptych, 1999
Each 29 3/4" x 22 1/4"
Monoprint
Published by Goya-Girl Press, Inc.

Very Stormy Sky, 1999
29 3/4" x 22 1/4"
Monoprint
Published by Goya-Girl Press, Inc.

Extremely Stormy Sky, 1999
29" x 38 1/2"
Monoprint
Published by Goya-Girl Press, Inc.

Some Bright Stars, Some Dim Ones, 1999
29 3/4" x 22 1/4"
Monoprint
Published by Goya-Girl Press, Inc.

One Bright Star, 1999
29" x 38 1/2"
Monoprint
Published by Goya-Girl Press, Inc.

Dream with Billie Holiday

Aliki Barnstone

In dreams East is West. The Pacific reaches
toward the land with passion.
I squat beside a tide
pool,
feeling the anemone close around my finger. Cliff-spray flies
with the gulls and I'm with a lover I haven't seen
in decades. That first night in his room,
hearing her
voice
in the dark as if her hands stroked his whole body
and the dark were night waves,
I was quiet but overcome by something like what holds
waves up a moment so high before the boom and sibilance.
"Who's this?" I asked. "Billie Holiday," he said.

Now it's much the same;
his body still wiry, his hair still black,
he bends bare-chested over his guitar.
I only see
the years intervene in the expression on his face.
The old longing warms me like a sip of seven star brandy,
like Lady Day and her rich swoony tunes.
At last I say, "We weren't so nice to each other."
"I've heard that complaint before," he answers, a bit resigned.
"I meant me," I say, "I wasn't so nice."
Then to punctuate
the half-lie I press my palms into the small of his back.
And I hear waves breaking in my hair, in the pillow,
and in our illicit kiss.

Back then we kissed and told,
so all our kisses were new.
When he slept with a dental hygienist who slept with the dentist, he
smiled ironically, playing his thin fingers
across my hip as if it were his guitar.
I saw a swan
floating in each of his teeth and wondered
why the god
transformed himself into a gaudy, stupid bird,
why
his eyes
were green as the new leaves outside the window sparkling
with temptation. Even as I wanted him all the more,
the swan
enraged a memory of his bragging. He read only the old poets
and thought all the new bad. So
I was bad.
One morning I
came to him. I kissed his neck
and he kissed mine and
found an illegible haiku there. "Tell," he said. "No."
"Tell," he pleaded. "No," I laughed.

Decades years later in a place we never were,
we are as wild as we were that morning. I hear
sea lions moan from the boulders and piers
and the room
is loud with ocean and the moon-face fills the window
with an open-mouthed sigh.
Then I see Billie Holiday standing in the door,
mock-shocked, laughing behind her hand, singing,
I've been seen with someone new,
But does that mean I'm untrue?
Then I'm back East.
It is the January thaw in Wisconsin. The sunlight tricked me.
I stood beneath sunny but frozen buds and remembered
something. I stopped myself where this dream began.

Three Poems

David Breskin

Escape Velocity

Thrust then blur, ripe speed, a gentle pricking
of atmosphere into the black yonder:

carrying a payload of past-due bills
from father, mother's invoice of regret,

the backyard family trash exploding up
out of a watery basement, where shelves sag

under the weight of time, you muscle past
aimless geese and grazing clouds, staking claim

to a future unpredicted by corner
commentators, those who'd have you flail

and fall. It could be ghetto. Could be bones
splintery since birth. Might be cross-eyed stairs

you couldn't climb, unsolved story problems,
the needle of hunger. Or just every

dull day flattening mind into a thin broth
of *No*. Find fuel. To trigger ignition

in such conditions requires X. You are
Y. Go ahead and throttle Z round Z's

fat neck: smell the aggression of incline.
While your visored helmet rattles and fogs—

eyes hammered into sockets—a snaky
tether feeds your vitals to the watching

few and the greater world awaiting. Life's
not cheap at this burn rate. Out here there's

no air save your own breath. You've gone so long
not talking, words feel like food in your mouth.

Literary Fiction

A perfect stranger, he arrived with a suitcase.
But one guest lounging under the doom palm,

near the pool, knew what was in that suitcase.
She was a sulky testatrix—her purple

lips a volva of desire—and being that,
she bided her time. She wasn't asking

for trouble . . . she demanded it. Not
the trouble eustasy would cause her ex

shacked up in his beachfront bachelor pad,
but trouble still. She took a banaustic

drag of her Lucky, and watched, as the tall
man with the suitcase vermiculated

past her to his balcony room facing
the pool. Room 233. To get that suitcase

from him, she'd have to create the kind
of casual and innocent gallimaufry

at dinner he might suspect. That was her
chance. That was her choice. When the band

started to shout, she'd slip something into his
olla podrida and into something more comfortable

herself. Soon, he'd be having a thrombus
fit for a Southern senator and she'd be picking

through the vomitus for that little suitcase key
that would change her life. She'd have to get

the good stuff quick, throw all the tired bumf
on the firedog, light a match and leave. Oh,

and burn her hot satin black dress, putting on
some old galligaskins to throw the dicks off

the trail. What she didn't know, what she *couldn't*
know, is that the man with the suitcase, now dressing

for dinner in the shadowy light of Room 233,
knew well of her fissiparous plans for his jack,

and vowed he'd never let this Jill get so close
she could hurt him in that way. Never. *Never.*

As the bleeding sun dripped below the horizon
and the poolside band struck up its first koan

of the night—a ballad for no dancers, just the
empty strophes of windblown water splashing—he

took his own measure in the steamy bath mirror:
had redintegration ever felt quite like this

before? Here he was, all his furious smurfing
finished, his long lost facture tight, and now,

at the fag end of the job and perhaps his days
as well, here *she* was . . . again. Yeah, he could

deconstruct the privileging inherent in his gender
role, but how would that unwind his bind? And how

would that trim her sails, with him still trapped
in the sweaty genre scene he knew he'd been *born*

for? He shaved, finished dressing. From his window,
he could see her, a long-legged kudu with flashing

eyes, standing so peccant, smoking by the deep
end of the pool. He slid his suitcase under the king

bed, told himself she'd be the tutee and he the tutor
on this night, walked downstairs and dove in smiling.

"Cheat Sheet" for "Literary Fiction"

doom palm: a palm native to the Nile Valley of northeast Africa and having oblong or ovoid fruits the size of an orange with a distinctive aroma and taste (also called doum, gingerbread palm)

testatrix: a woman who has made a legally valid will before death

volva: a cuplike structure around the base of the stalk of certain fungi

eustasy: a worldwide change in sea level

banausic: merely mechanical; routine

vermiculate: to adorn or decorate with wavy or winding lines; having a wormlike motion, especially the wavelike contractions of the intestine; twisting or wriggling; sinuous, torturous; infested with worms, worm-eaten

233: the number produced by combining and conflating the jersey numerals of Michael Jordon and Scottie Pippen, creating a certain synergy; that is, a condition (or site) in which desire, talent, triumph, fame, riches, glory, and luck are always present, albeit in varying degrees

gallimaufry: a jumble, a hodgepodge

olla podrida: a stew of highly seasoned meat; assorted mixture; a miscellany

thrombus: a fibrous clot formed in a blood vessel or a chamber of the heart

bumf: (or bumph) printed matter, especially of an official nature and deemed of little interest or importance; toilet paper (short for bum fodder)

firedog: andiron; also called dog or dog iron; any kind of metal supports holding logs in a fireplace

galligaskins: loosely fitted sixteenth and seventh century britches; loose trousers, leggings

fissiparous: reproducing by biological fission; tending to break up in parts or away from a main body; fractious

koan: a riddle in the form of a paradox, used in Zen Buddhism as an aid to meditation and a means of gaining intuitive knowledge

strophe: the first of a pair of stanzas of alternating form on which the structure of a given poem is based; a stanza containing irregular lines; the first division of the triad constituting a section of a Pindaric ode; the first movement of the chorus in classical Greek drama, while turning from one side of the orchestra to the other; the part of a choral ode sung while this movement is executed; (sometimes also called the turn)

redintegration: (psychology) the evocation of a particular state of mind resulting from the recurrence of one of the elements that made up the original experience

smurfing: the practice of substituting a great number of smaller denomination bills for fewer large bills, especially when laundering money from drug or other illicit transactions (slang, from the "Smurfs," very small cartoon characters of the 1980s)

facture: the manner and method of which something (as an artistic work) is made; the execution

fag end: the frayed end of a length of cloth or rope; an inferior or worn-out remnant; the last part

kudu: either of the two large African antelopes having a brownish coat with narrow white vertical stripes and, in the male, long, spirally curved horns

peccant: sinful, guilty; violating a rule or an accepted practice; erring

Welfare Reform

Mr. Full, I'm Mr. Empty. Rub my bones
together to spark a wispy fire. Swallow

your pride, keep yourself warm on the oil
of my intestine. Try a little garnish

of wages on the side. Not like North
Korea where they're so hungry women eat

their own afterbirth. Always worse
somewhere else. Here, just plaster

from project walls, Twinkies with food
stamps, rich kids eating ecstasy

by the lake. Oh, those happy happy kids.
Mr. Empty on the cellphone, without two Franklins

to rub together, coming to you live. I'm
moving in. I'll be on your wraparound

mortgaged porch. I'll be walking Billy
to school, keeping him out of traffic

and trouble. I'll be your sleeping bag, your
makeup kit. The Lakota used every piece

of the buffalo and I expect no less
from you. If you rub me hard enough

against the rough concrete of the voters,
my skin comes off like grated cheese.

Recover that chaise. Patch the frayed cord
of the tennis net. Resole that old soft shoe.

Metaphysical Trees

Christopher Buckley

I still had two friends, but they were trees.
—Larry Levis

I went out into the woods today, and it made me
feel, you know, sort of religious.
—William Matthews

I'd like to have a eucalyptus,
a pale and slender one bouncing its loose thoughts
off the blue—
                    and maybe an avocado
with boughs like an anaconda,

and one expansive sycamore reaching out
for everything.
                    Yes, and a jacaranda,
its violet shade each June edging
the eternal past . . .
                         and a pomegranate,
I want a pomegranate with Spanish flame-
red blossoms dazzling as all get-out
in dim December.
                       While I'm at it,
I'll have an acacia, and a few Russian olives—
their aqua-marine leaves recalling, of course,
the implacable sea.

And a podocarpus,
those leaves Leonardo invented
to dovetail with the aureate cloud of light
backing up the renaissance.
And all this
in a little valley arrived at through mustard weed
and fennel, white and lavender blooms of wild radish
recalling the loosely affiliated clouds,
the preliminary stars. . . .

We stepped down
from that quantum shine
clueless as to how
our bodies might be simply pronouns,
how we stood for—
part and particle—those astral antecedents.
Right off, looking up,
comparing ourselves
to the lustrous night, we complained
of our unadorned
surroundings;
we would have towers,
would crawl back up the stellar imbrications
despite a prohibited tree
and all the knowledge
we would assume,
despite the gardens
of Nebuchadnezzar and Assurbanipal where
the dim substance of the soul was
elucidated
against the incomparable chastity
of the sky.

And though Socrates tells us that we can learn
nothing from trees—
only from the moral man—
what about steadfastness, fortitude, perseverance,
loyalty, tenacity, not to mention
modesty, grace,
their spiritual arms,

and a dozen other abstractions
for which men die miserably?

Still, we are not that bad off
if we can get out
one afternoon and find a faithful conifer
or two to praise,
or can let the lacy shag of a pimiento
sort out the sun,
or especially if we can recall
the arboretum of childhood
and keep the camphor trees,
the pittosporum hedge in perspective
against the vanishing point
on the air . . . .

But something was kept from us,
held over our heads, it seems, ever since—
incantations,
the chalk and diagrams of constellations
blowing by

until Latin phrases for all we were sure about
in the firmament
were inscribed in stone over
the cathedral doors and
set down darkly in orthodox

moveable type,
and the world divided, and so many
taking refuge for ages in the woods . . . .

Nevertheless, coming over the dark plateau,
there is our old town
spinning alone in light,
blister of a moon
against midnight, white static
of starlight across the desert, the salt coming
to the surface,
the ice caps evaporating,

and it's November
in Palm Springs, where I go walking in the morning
to uncloud my heart,
to keep its tumbling,
root-like
chemistry clear,
to see four wild parrots fly
from palm to palm
as I pass the convention center,
the steamy perfume of stalks and delphiniums

rising from the moist beds
and I am 7 or 8 again
wearing a red bow tie and stiff blue
business suit
for Easter,
the glory
of the manifest world
arranged in sunlight.
Above me, the mimosa and lemon boughs,
and no text beyond that—
I mean we're protected
from the vast void of space
by nothing more than air,
and when the night calms
down to darkness
we listen
for the planets whirling by
and it's only the trees
giving us back our breath. . . .

I take those wild parrots, brilliant and green
as Eden,
as a sign from God,
admittedly
a God largely uninterested, unsure perhaps
of what more
we could possibly want—
magnolia, banyan, yew?

Maybe an indifferent sign,

indecipherable,
inadvertent,
but there are at least these four green clues
to some happiness beneath the sky . . . .

If I can't have trees, then perhaps someday just
a few yards of dirt
some fennel bushes and nasturtiums—

that portion of childhood still volunteering from the roadside,
beckoning in the winds of traffic.
For the time being
I'll take these parrots appropriating
the tops of the royal palms
as if everything were still ours
equally before the sun.

Take what you can,
you know what God will do—
he will let the complaints rise
like a little smoke
dissolving against the dawn,
he will turn away,
thinking perhaps
of another universe.

The oceans will warm
and drive the sail fish north,
the last log
will be rolled out of the Amazon—
it will all go
to hell
in a corporate hand basket
as we're tipping the brim of our hat
over our eyes,
nodding-out on the bench
in the blue
absolution of shade,
beneath the last trees
of our forgiveness.

Milk, Flux and Wand

Michael Chitwood

> Human language is like a cracked kettle on which we beat out tunes for bears to dance to, when all the time we are longing to move the stars to pity.
>
> —Gustave Flaubert

10 am
Congratulations.
Children are God's message to the world.
This one, pink-edged, cardboard gilt,
postage due.

4 am
Jean's milk not in yet,
the colostrum, with its load
of live antibodies, gives you
the knowledge of your mother's body.

12:30 pm
Babies are God's way of saying I Love You.
Who is this love-sick God,
who tongued our bodies,
the direct objects of His desire,
for His own syntax?

7 pm
A child is an act of Faith.
The breeze is unseen yet works
the poplar leaves, the tiny gold
feathers of the finch.

11 pm
I'm walking the floor
not over you but with you over
my shoulder, a reverse knapsack,
since I carry you on my chest
and you won't go to sleep.
Knapsack, now there's a word for you,
not where we store naps
but, usually, something to eat.
Our constant, constant mouths.

1:30 a
Surely God didn't *take* the second child,
this one's ghost sibling,
fourteen weeks and the ultrasound technician,
technician is the right word,
says flatly "No heartbeat."
Jean was still on the table,
the wand still inside her,
"No heartbeat."
Jean moaned ultrasound,
pure meaning, pure grief.
"God doesn't sweat the details,"
she said months later.

6 a
Faith is
the other side of the intransitive verb,
always metaphoric when rendered
into language.

8 a
Her wordlessness,
her blue stare.
These are God's eyes,
not innocent, searching.
What am I to her?
Now I remember
the night just passed,
the moonlight bright

enough to make shadows
among the pines.

12:30 p
Sometimes it seems
she just wants her mouth
comforted.

5:30 p
After she finishes nursing,
I offer the useless nipple,
tip of my index finger.

9 p
God's message to the world is inconsolable.
We've fed her, changed her,
are walking her and still. . . .
No, wait, now she's sleeping like. . . .

Midnight
The sound of her nursing:
pigeons, a mid-summer brook,
a screen door spring,
someone humming inside a tent.
God of lists, what else?

3 a
God of Abraham,
God of Isaac,
God of Jacob,
God of the first name basis,
unnamable,
let her sleep.

8:30
"Maybe she's wet."
"Maybe she's too hot."
"Maybe she's already hungry."
These are the False Premises
for prayer.

Noon
Breast calmed, milk stunned,
even the damp wipe won't wake her.
She lets go a spurt of piss.

4:30
Whiff from the compost pile,
maybe the shrimp husks
like the skins of flayed thumbs.
Act of faith?

8:30
I've just remembered Jean
beside Grandma's fresh grave,
two weeks from delivery,
the twin mounds.
Grandma's sixth child,
the tiny tombstone beside this large one,
died of what was known as flux—
diarrhea—extreme dehydration.
Wallace Cordell Hall.
Cordell, a painter Granddad admired,
we think. Flux, change, a transfer
of energy across a given surface.

10:30
Mustard stain in the wet diaper,
God's little miracle shits seven times a day.
The miracle? It *doesn't* smell.

12:30
The old boogie book,
literal, hefted weapon
of my childhood's revivalist,
says "Make a joyful noise."
Noise. The piercing cry
that makes milk drop
from Jean's nipples.
"You are stately as a palm tree,
and your breasts are like its clusters."
"Knock it off."

3:30
Shhhhhh, honey, what's a matter?
"To get the baby interested
you may want to hand express
some milk." Instruction
manual. Hand express.

5:30
Lydia on top of the Kenmore.
We try its knock and warmth,
advertised as "Soft Heat,"
to see if it speaks
a dialect of Jean's body.

8:30
Stunned with vistas,
early American painters
substituted landscapes
for religious themes.
After this feeding,
I notice deer have cropped the azaleas.

12:11
"If I drew a cartoon of her,"
Jean says, drained, sleepy,
"it would be all mouth."

9:30
Lydia has a blanket
on which
the bears are dancing.

4:30
The paper, in its protective sheath,
is already at driveway's end.
Even with the drizzle, I can read
Papal panel says souls can't be cloned.
The Pontifical Academy of Life
said the spiritual soul, "the
constitutive kernel" of every human

being created by God, cannot be
produced through cloning.
The Pontifical Academy of Life!
I apologize for our adjectives and nouns.

1:30
"Oh God, is it time?"
"No, no, it's raccoons at the compost,
discussing the watermelon rind."

12:00
God of flux,
God of Montgomery glands,
God of conjugation.
Lydia's cry, ultrasound,
makes milk let down.

3
Sometimes when she's crying
if you walk outside the sudden
light makes her stop,
and sneeze.

1
Dark again. Stars pontifical.
Bears dancing. A transfer of energy.
The inarticulate mouth
being understood.

Room in Winter

Billy Collins

As I lie in bed in the dark,
my hand blindly

studies my face
as if it were memorizing it,

runs down
the proclamation of the nose,

circles the gelatinous
bulges of the eyes,

and moves across the indented lips,
cold lump of chin,

before it becomes downhearted
and goes limp at my side.

And there my hand lies
in the moonlight

wondering how long
this body will last,

how many mornings and nights
will it have to itself

to walk into deep woods,
to stand on a shore,

the twin brothers of the arms folded,
legs forked apart,

the ears open
to the sounds of water and birds,

the two eyes exploring
the icy surface of a lake together.

Vespers

Stuart Dybek

Wearing a surplice of billowing curtains
an altar boy kneels ringing a bell
at the shoreline of an undertow.
A black umbrella opens with an angry blow

bruising the underside of clouds.
Rain stirs the backyards to broth.
A barrow of soup bones sets off
like a blood clot late for a stroke.

*

Above back-alley roofs, stalagmites of spires
vanish, dismantled
                                        from bottom up by fog;
            a labor of eons erased in an afternoon.

Through the cracked lampblacked spectacles
of a cellar window,
                                    poisonous pulpits,
            erected by drizzle, ascend.

*

  We ran beside the carriage,
a rusted shoppingcart whose sole passenger stood
  regal as a queen in rags
            on her way to the guillotine;

she blessed the spitting rabble
while to the rap of a snare
a somber procession of blackbirds
marched behind,
wings
clasped like wringing hands behind their backs,
pausing only to bow

to the undigested seeds
of grass
in steaming pats of manure.

*

What was the record wingspan for a crucified Christ?
Maybe in the old Polish church on Ashland:
they didn't have a Black Madonna there who wept
real tears like a doll,
or a sister with the stigmata,
but their Christ with his long sinewy arms
that ended in the punctuation of nailed palms
was second to none.
By the flicker of vigil candles
he seemed to be flying.
In the glow of the sanctuary lamp
his wounds were varying relfections of red
as if his bare, agonized body had been kissed
by different shades of lipstick.
Once, when I thought I was in love,
I was sure I recognized the imprint of her lips
on the wounds of his feet.

*

Under a daylight moon, the bag lady
children called Hag
foraged half-bent beneath the weight
of the hump she lugged everywhere.

Were she the Goddess of the Hunt,
forever young, lithe as bow, half-bare,
the gilded fall of her undone chignon
would have concealed her nakedness.

As it was, a gray flow of matted
hair—perhaps, her lifetime's work—
swept the pavement before her every step.

A dogpack ran, further clearing the way.
Her battered straw purse proudly swung
from the mouth of a dirty white chow.

*

In a room the sepia of sunset-beaten shades,
she was wearing only pearls;
anointed with sweat, her girlish body
straddled his as if they were riding.
The pearls whipped them to a furious pace
until she snatched her necklace out of air
and held it in her mouth, and he could hear
the sound of their bodies sliding together
mimicked by the sound her lips made
as one by one she sucked the pearls
against her tongue—not unlike the way
an old nun, he unaccountably remembered,
blissfully fingered each blessed bead—
before she finally bit down.

*

After they report their own absence
to the Department of Missing Persons,
and the crime of nostalgia
seems the only defense against amnesia,
then it's to this street the prodigals come
to live out those final days before
they are reduced to seeking forgiveness.

One last nuzzle against the shoulder of night
along which stars are sprinkled with the disorder
of freckles beneath a bra strap.
Soon enough the sailors come floating home
from around the block, face down
through the old neighborhoods that lie below
a sea of flooded basements.

What's all this suffering for, Father?
Nothing, my Son . . . the same as all this love.

*

I tried to pay
for a link of sausage
with a rosary

snarled in what I'd thought
was a pocket
of loose change.

Three Poems

Sandra M. Gilbert

Hurtigruten[1]

1. Alesund: North

(To the west you can see the open Atlantic Ocean and the islands with their ancient settlements.)

The doors fly open and in flow
the skeptical airs of the north:

damp air of the troll cave,
mushroom breath, bog wind,

ice breeze bruising early
certainties, asserting freezing

nots—
not south, with its silken

collisions, its tumbles of gold,
nor west, so simple

[1] *Hurtigruten* means *Coastal Express*. All epigraphs are taken from Erling Storrusten, *Hurtigruten: The World's Most Beautiful Sea Voyage* (Bergen: ERA-Trykk AS, 1996).

in waves of yearning,
nor east, whose doughty

dawns circle like gulls,
insisting that *is* and *possible* are one,

but north, and strict
in rigorous doubt,

and now the steep houses
huddled in smoke

hunch against questions
that hoot like great gray geese,

and now the lips of the cliff
open and beckon,

and now a tall white sky
stoops to the shadow

that follows the aged sailor set
adrift today in a single wistful

meadow, smiling his random
icefloe of a smile.

2. Ornes: Midnight Sun

(All along the coast, you'll find former trading posts which remain untouched by progress.)

and broad daylight has a special meaning:
like the French *plein ciel*, daylight
spreads its heavenly apricot *confiture*

far and wide across the righteous houses
that would sleep if they could
but must wake in the fat flash

of a sunset that settles in
like a beaming cousin
come for a too-long visit,

and the ice on the gables gets all helplessly
rosy as if seduced despite
its austere principles,

while travelers from darker places
look out in delight
at the edge of town

where the still ordinary
ordinary is
what really surprises—

a steamer unloading lunch for a giant,
a flag saluting, a little sheepishly,
as a boy in a shiny anorak

rides a bicycle around
and around the wharf
in widening circles.

3. Salt Fjord: Arctic

(The strait is only negotiable two hours after high and low tide.)

North of Auden's north and the north
of the sagas, even the meditative
north of Rilke—

north where the spectrum
vanishes, and memory, its vast
harvests of color,

north where minutes are only latitude,
and the tongue of the traveler
begins to trill despite itself,

The people who come of this ice
cannot be like us, surely
they speak in cries like seabirds,

surely they have toes as fierce
as the roots of pines that tighten
around sheer rock,

surely they creak in the wind
like old ships passing the skerries
as they journey, forgetting themselves,

among great boulders of absence.

4. Lyngstuva: One AM

(Beware of Lyngstuva, a mountain protruding 390 m from the sea between Ulls Fjord and Lyngen Fjord.)

The exhaustion of the inexhaustibly
beautiful!

—the effort it asks
with its ceaseless

look and *listen*, its imperious
call for scrutiny—as here,

this crag, with its difficult
partitions, how they shine,

as if from within, as if
a translucent new geometry

might form right here,
among sea and sky

and stone in the unwavering
pupil of a sun we

have to keep looking at
hour on hour just as

framed in the ice
of indefatigable difference

it has to keep looking
back at us.

5. Trollfjorden: Gerda

(To the south, the peak of Trolltindan soars 1,045–1084 m above sea level, and its sheer sides pose a permanent threat of rock falls. To the north is Blafjellet. . . . To the west is the lake of Trollfjordvatnet, filled with chunks of ice even during the summer.)

"Then as we went further north
it grew brighter and colder

in the enormous
gaze of the ice

and I who once was little Gerda
in my land as blonde as cream

cried out toward where
you aged in the embrace that was

no longer snow but fixed as a cliff
in its greed for you,

I cried, I cried out twice
for little Kay, who was my

mate in what might have been
a meadow, and all the aching

buzzing gold,
all the buttercups and thistles,

all the night moths and dawn eggs
in the meadow of old

Gerda, gripping her twisted stick,
cried out for old Kay,

whose naked mouth yawned wider
and wider now

in an O
that could swallow nothing."

6. Nordkappbanken: Open Sea

that will not freeze
though the snow fields creep to the shore
and the crawling glaciers

glint and lure
that will not freeze
in the Arctic dark

when the great
lights seethe and flash
and the humped winds

plunge against black
hooks of rock and stranger
backs that neither

flinch nor grunt
that will not freeze
in the clasp of polar

ice that hisses
across abandoned
nests and bones

that will not freeze
that pulses with fish
that pulse with life

that streams invisibly
on and on
again and on

Omens

A sky electric with geese.
My sudden pulse.

You're coming. Back.
The rumor of your return

bearing down like the great wheels
of a jet descending.

You to whom a glittering
splash of sparrow,

a shriek of jay,
are minor portents.

You who have never entirely gone away.
You who have never been completely here.

You're coming.
Your enormous baggage of lights and clouds

littering the mountains,
your shadowy ladders

unscrolling sentences
step after step.

Even the least shiver of my breathing
seized and used

in the shrill wind of your arrival.

Want

1. *Kilninian Kirkyard*

Up on the moor what's empty
speaks beyond the speech

(whatever *speech* might mean)
of sheep and birds, speaks

with voices outside the long
long-suffering bleats, the hectic

twittering, and tongues of air
that lick the gravestones clean.

Against the ontology of bracken,
ground bass of hissing thistles,

how absurd the murmurings
of sunstruck wind, its weary natural

history that coils like an adder here
and there above the bog!

And now the sheep set up
their old hilarious clamor

for food and sex and maybe
even eternal life.

2. *The Dead*

The enormity of them, their
endless arrogance:

the granddad who won't smile
except in dreams, the husband

eternally enraged, the pretty
aunt whose last grimace

is carved in stone,
the newborn bound in a curve of need. . . .

Pour your libations, humble ones
in the sun, pour blood or wine—

and the dead still smile their clever
semblances, false love

in frescoes, photos, friezes—
while their glassy eyes askance

say *no*, say *want*,
say tall in their caves, they want

every cell that never was theirs.

Pour or pray:

the long blank granite family
turns away, dines in the silence

that grips the sullen
spine of the night sky,

3. *I Am*

At the kind west edge
of Mull, green inner island
where a blue flat glimmering
palm of the Atlantic

opens as if in
supplication, as if
begging the land for what
only land can have—

an end to motion, a silencing
of all those dizzy
whispers back and forth
across the shingle.

Grapes on the beach.
And thoughts of the dead
while the summer trippers flail
their kites and sails.

I am.
In a hollow of sun among
the dunes. Behind me
a swath of bitten turf.

Am. Without
so many who
opened their sleeves
to the salt the sea

flung toward them once
in hollows of sun
below the high blue
shuddering air. Am.

In the western isles,
July, the sun still high
and the tide rising.
"D'you like the temp.?"

asked the walker I met just now
at damp sand's edge.
"The air's so cold
the water's warm," I said.

"But it's really cold," he said.
"Cold and it comes fast.
Ten meters in half an hour.
Very cold. Very fast."

Smoke Follows Beauty

Jeffrey Harrison

we used to say, standing around a campfire roasting marshmallows,
or, a little older, just sitting and telling stories, laughing,
or listening to a guitar, some of us singing, others just staring
into the flames—until one of us got up and moved away,
hands rubbing eyes, then dodged to one side, fanning the smoke away,
and it was then that someone would say, "Smoke follows beauty,"
and whoever it was standing there would smile through tears.

We said it without thinking, without knowing where the saying
came from, or what it seemed to be saying: that there was no use
trying to get away, the smoke would follow you
away from the fire and into the night, and into the next day,
and through all the days of your life, shadowing your years,
until one day you succumbed to its smudged touch,
the pungent smell it leaves on your skin, and to tears.

Three Poems

Paul Hoover

Family Romance

You like
showing photos

blind as
light, decades

ripped to
shreds and

littered in
an album.

The future
is present

in history's
window, where

the brief
green world

observes its
turning. An

apple is
yellow at

the edge
of red.

In the
pallor of

the storm,
someone is

rouged in
distance. Your

mother and
father just

after marriage
smile at

the light,
their eyes

dark as
a harvest.

Form is
deep in

portions your
whole life

long—no
winter shadow

thin as
sin, just

broken stones,
a tottering

ghost. Ragged
as pleasure,

rain stabs
water. A

lighthouse on
the prairie

does no
less. What

is life,
what world

born five
miles back?

The *this*,
the whole

boat. When
your heart

is beating
and the

porch is
soaked, you're

drowning in
arousal and

always in
the frame.

Commemorative Gestures

> Then he told me he knew who his brother's killer was,
> and that he sometimes saw the man around Kigali.
> —Philip Gourevitch, "Letter from Rwanda"

In the town of Nyarubuye, among the million
killed, a young man lies in front of a mission
where his body was left as a sign to others

several months ago. Beneath the outspread arms
of a statuary Christ, photographed at ground level,
his face has shrunken back to bone, so that,

wearing a white tennis sweater with perfect
Oxford stripes, he becomes an aesthetic object
in the planned collision of art and history.

Lipless and eyeless, he reminds children
passing to school or heaven that no place is safe,
all policy horror. Yet somehow this is beauty

in the Christmas *New Yorker* a few pages
from Helmut Newton's portrait of Loulou de la Falaise
wearing a couture ensemble as she hurries

to a meeting, her pinched face hidden.
In her neurotic stride, the aging woman
moves through death toward fashion

on the virtual ground of the lens.
Buried in our senses as in a public place,
we hurriedly turn the page to something

less cruel than sight. The guilty sleep
soundly tonight on a nest of broken machetes,
but we, in our condos and lofts, need only watch

the skies for signs of children flying.
The perfect sentence won't change the blood-soaked facts.
Loulou de la Falaise knows the camera is empty:

the photographer pours darkness into his eye.
So it's not just murder that matters.
As the world's grey grass gives birth once more,

I'm also alarmed by the photograph's intentions,
framing that skull in arms of mission plaster;
how empty the park appears as the empty woman passes.

Gilded Instruments

At the hour
of unleashing,

local and
baroque,

earthen angels
cry in stone.

The mouth
writes desire

on the body
in question;

a man is
beaten like

the prophet
of the town.

What verbs
are needed

by devastation's
measure, what

silence thick
as pleasure?

The precipice
is a harvest.

In the strictest
of senses, you

are never you
but a cloud

quotation in
a borrowed parlor.

The rigor of
matter, like a

black magic feather,
eats at decorum

and natural history,
remains American

as your old
man. At water's

sharp edge, the
fraught world

bends its vines
and senses,

feeling if it can
the nothing

gather. Down
comes the cold.

Comes of itself
a small persistent

longing. In each
pleasure, the

tensions minded
and what are

years for? You
found and secured

nothing your
own. A white

mouth open.
Indecent as

a sculpture
of fur and bone.

Low against
the sun, on

what was once
a lake, crayfish

appeared out
of small hollows.

The temper
of the light,

fine and ashy,
moves you now.

Two Poems

Mark Irwin

An Autumn Essay

Everything happens at once, a world sifting its yellow
leaves to sing a lessening sun. The tulle wrapped around
the goldenrod and pupa
like a veil only found in cloudish

ways. On TV Sister Wendy spoke about Botticelli
his name means little barrel. He stole gold
leaf from his father to paint Venus' hair. And while Sister Wendy
spoke, Lisa's caterpillars hung from each of several

stems. Their larval bodies were beginning to change
as the first snow dusted the mountains, a fire
in us that said "go there." Someone we knew
was dying. He drove a silver Corvette for hundreds

of miles to watch the stars. His long white hair
blew in the wind while a monarch caterpillar
hung from a thread. Its green body
would swell and mummify to some pellucid

capsule, clearer and beyond, till one morning
we noticed the tiny inlaid gold beads haloed
about the crown, and then—barely visible—
the apricot, yellow and black-striped

wings. Plato came to mind as I drove to see
my white-haired friend. We went fishing
at Monument Lake, and when the trout hit the elk
caddis, I knew it lessened the pain, just as the snow-capped

mountains and his mistress from Texas did.
She cooked fried green tomatoes with bacon with
trout. Another friend opened hundred dollar bottles
of wine. We smoked cigars and looked at the stars. No one

asked about the pain, but we remembered
the lake and fish. Everyone agreed it was the best
meal we'd ever had. We got drunk but no one
asked. We danced. We turned the ranch upside down

and Joe forgot for awhile. He talked of his family.
I remember he had a dog named Rocket, dead now,
but boys still call its name. We went for a walk
in the night and it was long and we all laughed

when Joe pulled out an expensive toy, a global
positioning device, which by flashlight gave his
longitude and latitude, his elevation and speed.
Never had we walked so slowly. Joe stopped to kiss

his girl, and we all stood mateless, alone beneath the icy
pulp of stars, then moved slowly away, watching
our shadows stumble and rise across the field,
saying yes to the joy that we were still unfound.

Even Now

Still I try to remember when you first caught
fire, the barely visible flames about shoulders and arms
accentuating everything you touched, and I first saw
through words. I watched you reach for a glass dissolving
in air while your sight tore holes in an April world drowning
with rain and flowers. We walked through a park where
you stuck your hand in a young retriever's mouth, feeling
the hot pink gums and new teeth, while a little girl
wearing a lady-bug cape swooped, singing over the grass
as bees droned "is, is" over the jonquils. We drove
to the country and walked through fields and meadows
and stood beneath an orchard's new gauze where you
talked of the past, picking chunks of time like invisible
fruit, and I could feel the rivers and trees engrave us.
We entered a half-built house, flooded with sky, and you
said, "There, there, and there bodies will blossom."
I remember how it began to rain but you did not get
wet. How the fragrant wood smelled like a ripening fruit.
The sun came out as the evening grew long, and where
you lay down in the field to sleep, there was only a red glow,
resembling coals in a fire, a warmth I can feel, even now.

Marina Tsvetayeva's Last Cigarette

George Kalamaras

1.

To one day return from the grocer's. To remove your raincoat and hang yourself. In the kitchen. To calmly smoke a cigarette first, tearing the wrapper from store-boughts, struggling with cellophane that sticks to this finger, then that. To have scrubbed the floor an hour before, thinking *I am really not a roach*, then to have chanted your mother's maiden name three times over a pan of kidney beans. To have washed the beans beforehand clean of gravel, like searching for copper or silver, sensing a catch in your throat and the dust of a truck grinding passed. To have sat on the stool, peeing first, smelling last night's asparagus as warm sulfur springs. To have sighed deeply even earlier that morning after checking the almanac for weather, oddly comforted that it would rain. And that it would be a good year for wheat.

2.

As a little girl, Marina Tsvetayeva loved flowers. Marigolds. Poppies. Mums. Every May 1 she'd check the doorstep for love. What May Day basket might bring secret plans of marriage? What marigold might mean a young handsome Cossack with yak fringe? What mum, a handsome prince from old St. Petersburg waving and calling to her from a droshky? What poppy's dark center might rake the pollen and cull the bees? Every May 2, the empty stoop. That clawing green kerchief holding all but a stray patch slipping across her forehead in place. Iron combs keeping the braid. Holding her tongue. Sunlight, like fog, blurring her eyes. Poppies at market on the way to school bending toward her in faint Moscow wind, a most brilliant red. A most moist spot of black fur. A bee sucking the center like a pulsing thorn.

3.

Never, never, never. Poetry for the State is just that—poetry for the State. Ice in the peanut vendor's beard. Black lice in the floes resembling pepper. Raincoat collars turned up against the curb. A narrowing flat like stepping inside after blinding sleet. *Always, always, always.* The roach at the sink is an armored kidney bean? The dill and boiled eggs still too warm to add for salad? How could things have gone so wrong? Mixed up, say, like endive in the lettuce? Endive in your toes at night? Oh God, what was it below in the sheets? What did the feet expect after all at midnight, with no moon. *Never, never, never.* The asparagus on the counter under the knife. Cossacks cringing somewhere at the thought of a gelding. City men crunching caviar on a saltine at the thought of a steer. To cross one's legs and mean it. What does the body shut out without even knowing? A cigarette ash as long as an unkempt fingernail. How long can one hold on?

4.

To be a good year. To be wheat. To be wheat in that good year. To be a book and know what you are supposed to know. To have been all that is within you. An almanac is weather forecasting and, strangely, weather itself. To have peed during the day that long satisfying middle-of-the-night pee when the urethra, finally relaxed, fully expands. To have washed the beans, thinking *I am truly not a roach.* And feel the armor dissolve and the gravel slip off into someone else's voice. To have had your husband of 29 years shot as a counterrevolutionary. To be exiled to Elabuga, your poems burned. To be 49 and 49 and 49. Like a mother's maidenhood forever preserved—but how? To have scrubbed the floor, hearing in each scrape the sound of your infant steps. To calmly lick the cellophane from your hands and then spit it out directly into the trash. In the kitchen, yes, in the kitchen. To strap your raincoat on the hook and hang your entire life up to dry with it. Smoke trailing off the almost-fallen ash in the tray, dust clouds roused by the gravel passing of a truck churning diesel.

Three Poems

John Kinsella

Night Heron Manifesto

for Robert Adamson and Coral Hull

Incarceration diatribe via lens of camera
as per art, or animal fat in the tyres,
irony travels only so far as the bird's bravura

spikes a namesake or thin fish, frogmouth criers
heralding and syncopating thick dressings of gnats
and lardish smoke rising blue in the yellow desires

of the barbecue crowd, night heron stats
collated to back up a sampling of DNA, essential
repository and data-bank should the species collapse;

eyeballing or verballing, sculptured pose, eventual
transfiguration into literature and television,
sanctioned presence, ordination—substantial

presence on the international stage—canonisation
before time, rumours pandemic. Architecturally
it's the Swan River, or Bateman's jetty, realisation

of a speculator's dream—almost a nineteenth-century
hobby farm where in high trees left-over rookeries
bloom, of this and that bird but always the incendiary

night heron, rufous and archetypal, compact mythologies,
with personal aesthetics, ethics, and namings,
cool as—well, stealth—saturating analogies

with points of style, signifiers in every solitary's defaming
of the madding crowd, deployed like products and lies
of faith against film's gelatinous coating, inflaming

backwaters to sunset pink, as if death factories
develop unassisted: below their flight-paths, guts
& garters splayed and pegged tanned and stretched bodies,

eye-catching dilation of harmonic, internal parts
and clocks taking stock or heat sensors:
sound: syrinx-driven the hunting hawk's cones sparking hearts

and other transplanted body parts as Dolly the Night Heron stores
identity and every other heritage from the phrenologist,
his skull collection and possible rehydration of laws

of art and flesh and the names of birds long since lost,
the lost tribes and forbidden worlds and Lost City
of the Incas in the fringe suburbs of Perth, as out of mist

the Nyoongah words of forgiveness make the pretty
lawns of Parliament House greener than green,
the government fighting land claims and identity,

glossing over the slaughter and conflation; deep fixation
in windows parafoveal suprasegmentals voiceless plosive
just squeeze the trigger Alexander Graham Bell's frisson

at stimulating his talking head in the aviaries of missive
and (my) empire, quails scurrying over the floor,
while overhead the 28s and budgies, the corrective

psychology of new prisons—public and private—Zipf's law—
inverse relationship between wordlength and frequency,
body's balance, oppression of protestors, madonna-whore

gender codex, codes writ translatable—easy!
two photos of a solitary with complex social interactions,
out and about in brilliant daylight, replete with decency.

Conflated Memories: a list

for John Forbes

On Hilton stationery
the streets of San Francisco
are a jetlagged schematic
of recall and heart-crunching
gradients, hesitation
before lunging momentum—
it's for you, this poem
I couldn't write in Cambridge—
here where Trans-ams
and Rancheros agitate at crossroads
like martinis shaken, not stirred,
where the corner of Mason and Geary
brings in the New Year
and riot police incite
revellers to infamy;
homeless and living with AIDS
a gentle tremor is felt
and Metallica plan a pas de deux
with the San Francisco
Symphony Orchestra.
In Borders every tree is a book,
in Macy's every shopping bag therapy;
newspaper vending machines convolute
on Market Street—safety in numbers,
multi-lingual, polymorphous,
earthquake-tolerant highrise culture,
rental cars, phone cards,
massages, all nomenclature
just off Union Square,
irony bobbing like toe-tags off The Rock,
valet parking as glitzy as you'd expect.
In the King Deli a Bud sign flickers
not with uncertainty but confidence,
knowing, and knowing

so rapidly, saying
"the military has left the Presidium—
a few buildings and a strategic
array of views reminds
us it was there"—and the bit
you'd have liked best,
keeping up the history
in case you might decide
to believe in God:
the God of Grace, the God of
the First Church of Christ, Scientist,
Pacific Heights, the God
of imported European Cars
and a burgeoning economy,
the God that brought down the Alamo
somewhere else, CNN reports
of further strikes in the Gulf,
loveless rooms floating
with seismic confidence.

Glare

for Xavier Pons

As if whipped up by the water itself,
or molecules of air coated with glass—
the sun fragmented and stuck inside,
frantic to get out, or the brightness
inside your head turned all the way up.
Full blown, making a place snow-bound
and twenty below conceptually the same
as a space burnt to dunes of white sand.
In painting this universal portrait
of landscape, such that the deflection
of light off a pond in the Tuileries,
or snowburn from a drift in Alberta,
or the intensity of solarium hills
on a forty-degree day near Sydney
all fit comfortably within the same frame,
without frontiers or contraries,
we must paint with the essence
of place, or what illuminates.
In the light of day it is the intensity
of sight, or resistance to—the glare
that counts as constant. And so great
is that given off by our standards—Greenwich,
the platinum Metre, that we
see nothing: just a blank—
so bright we dare not look.

Between Heaven and Earth

Anne Marie Macari

Not from philosophers or tarot cards or from a stringy-haired
woman caressing my palm. I who tore apart

cloud after cloud looking for a sign. Who practiced Bach
with stiff fingers trying to hear, and dug

in riverbeds and peatbogs, and walked and walked
and counted hundreds of thousands

of severed hands and gouged-out eyes. In the woods I found
an abandoned nest and peeled half the shell

off an egg, making a cradle. Inside a chick lay curled
in the position of hope, with a blotch of blood on its belly,

its head tucked, its speck of a beak pointing at its heart.
Give me a hint, just

a word to suck on, I'm so hungry and this
is taking so long. I refuse to renounce a damn thing.

I refuse to take it on the chin again or to adjust my methods:
I leave cataloguing to people who need

to keep busy, let them play with fragments
of parchment trying to match dust to dust. I stay off ladders.

I go after the TV with a shotgun
and bury it without prayers because when the time comes

it's the radio that will surprise us
with its access to other worlds and then the sense of smell

will finally return, as it was eons ago,
and the odor of milk, sweet and sticky, blue

and reflective in its puddles on the floor from a mother's sobbing because
she knows everything

is whole and broken at the same time which is why
they want to drug her at the moment

her vision is most clear and her pain the worst,
when she's bearing down, crossing the boundary,

they want her to behave, they hate screaming
and her body arching like that. Always, a world

between worlds. Something holding me down like his leg
hooked over my hip, two passengers on the torn sheet,

the hissing of pipes all night
to accompany us. The sky moves through the window

and the cold, more and more, wears me out, making me
take up my fear the way some women take up knitting—

though I believe in the near-death of snow
and all it buries, even if trees are laughing at me,

their bare fingers pointing up,
even if the dead are walking on us, talking behind our backs,

and the pond is frozen and animals inert in their burrows.
When it comes down, heavy and white,

I want to stand inside its sadness. The snow
won't speak of where it came from. Though I'm listening,

my ear pressed against wind,
trying to catch the very moment it passes into this world.

Four Poems

Cleopatra Mathis

White Primer

Even the clock is a liar:
the clouds' blank ceiling
claims whatever light falls from the sky.
I wake to the day, an arrow
aiming for the hour to call the nurse,
caretaker of the new white world
where my daughter lives, all her color
stripped in the name of health.
Doesn't the snow come to let the good earth live?
So too will they cover the girl with white,
all that raging blossom of the self.

Don't ask me to believe in this season.
White nametag, white gown, the red lesions
like roads going nowhere. Covered, you see,
by the weather of this place,
its mindful preparations, hypnotic lesson:
you will not, you will not, you will not

until she hears it like a heartbeat in the white tempest.
All passion spent, all will,
she is good enough for the allowed visit,
the allowed room. Led to her,
I can't read the map of her cold face.
Nothing reveals the child I know
but the hopeless tangle of her hair.

"as if mad is a direction, like west . . ."

Margaret Atwood

I'm caught in March, the humdrum
ice-snow-ice fusing to one gray.
I live on the road, headache

reeling to backache, hospital
to home, no-where hours, hinged
and strung to her string of hours

in an unmapped hell. Where's the lock,
thread to the ultimate
pattern-maker, puppet-master

of the wires that make her jump?
I navigate the rut, my numb feet
dance on the brake, on the gas—

leaping the back-road curves. I'm
programmed in a moving blur,
mother emblem, a stick-figure

doll to the daughter who jerks
and cries. Bent behind the fixed wheel,
I'm a blond smile in a black car,

unstitched. She's got the needle.

Old Trick

Spring wants me back,
and I should know better than to heed
that old goddess, the hag
disguising herself with the first green
she can muster. Hanging around, her true self
gray, icy, bent, gazing from the corners
while I glory in the fine scribble
skimming the trees. I let her
bear the weight of my heart,
not my first mistake: every year she promises

to bring back what I love, and for awhile
she does—a flower here, another there,
fast-talking me through the price
I'll pay later. It's one panorama
followed by the next, the returning
birds in a parade, finches
twittering at dawn. They too

make me think I can trust them:
look at those nests, their faith
at my feeder, but I can tell you this,
keep an eye on the children.
September will come, the ripe business
whirring, too many things
you can't see in all the greenery,
its constance already tinged: a slight cast,
a whine. Your own girl will vanish
under that yellowing wing.

After Persephone

Heaven got sweeter, its paperweight curve
star-crazy at its purple center.
She'd found a god, a weapon in the works.
Something I hadn't noticed in the field
fought out of the layers and took her.
I tore away the land's every color,
withered the smallest grasses. Every heartbeat
went blank, I dismantled the ticking.

They only say what I took, not what I gave:
roots and strong light, glory
in the single shoot, green currency
of the just-born. From the irredeemable,
the buried—this is how a self gets made.
Remember, that darkness contained the seed
sealed in the swollen red globe.
Hell had to pay.

Kissing

Michael McFee

The mouth's elegy to itself.
—*Adam Phillips*

"It's a pity I can't kiss myself," Freud says

we're saying when we seek out another mouth
as children and later as sublimated adults

in this "softened hint of the sexual act,"

and maybe he's right, but it really does seem
that there's nothing *less* selfish than kissing:

even the most routine hello or goodbye buss

is a surrender of self, a willing sacrifice
of voice and sight and a moment's control,

to say nothing of lovers resuscitating each other

so long their slick lips ache from sharing breath
and teasing it out to one slow crescendo

of lick and suck and smack and salty bite

after another, the kisser and kissee
disappearing into a single body

as Rodin showed us in unbroken stone,

the man's huge hand on the woman's thigh
and her left arm pulling his head down to hers

part of the same mass as the roughhewn rock

they rise from like Adam and Eve discovering
how sour and sweet a mortal kiss can be,

farewell and welcome, betrayal and betrothal,

the smothering of speech and yet a kind
of articulation, a wordless word, unutterable

except by two human beings who agree

to stop and join their mouths in such a manner
that they begin saying the *yes* that is a kiss.

Two Poems

Campbell McGrath

Florida

If they'd had a spark of wit or vision
it would be known today as Cloudiana,
in honor of the mighty Alps and Andes
assembled and cast westward as rain
and thunder each and every afternoon.

If they'd understood the grave
solemnity of the sublime
it would be named for the great blue heron:

for longevity, the alligator;
for tenacity, the mosquito;
for absurdity, the landcrab.

If they had any sense
of history
it would be called Landgrab,

it would be called Exploitatiania,

for the bulldozed banyans,
lost cathedrals of mahogany and cypress,
savannahs of sawgrass and sabal palm,
mangroves toiling to anchor their buttresses,
knitting and mending the watery verge.

Beautiful and useless, flowers
bloom and die
in every season here, their colors dissemble,
soft corpses underfoot.

If there was any justice in this world
it would be named
Mangrovia.

The Florida Anasazi

From above it's a dickie or a verdant tie skewed sideways, banana or schlong, skull of a prehistoric mammal with lower mandible removed and Okeechobee for its eye, a moth-eaten pennant hemmed with blue water, a peninsular thumb bruised a dozen shades of green, emerald fronded jungle and sandy palmetto veldt and the predominant olive dun of once-cleared land reverting to scrub. And from the plane one sees, throughout Florida, titanic etchings upon the ground, quadrants of scarred earth that in their obscure figurative squib resemble the sacred patterns of a primitive mythos, the song lines of aboriginal Australians, or the vast animal figures of the Nazca plateau, or the pictoglyphs of the ancient Anasazi, sun-bleached ochre against canyon wall, fertility symbols and animal visages, banded armadillo and antler flange, mischievous coyote, flute-bowed Kokopeli, so different from the local totems, backhoe, chainsaw, roadkill, stripmall, the alligator-headed figure known to us as The Developer who works his trickery upon the people of the tribe, pilfering communal goods, claiming to produce that which he despoils. This is his signature, these marks upon the earth, a palimpsest of greed and grand plans gone wrong, a promissory text of spectral subdivisions, roads and cul de sacs that never were, premonitory ghost cities rising like the ruins of the Anasazi in reverse, abandoned pueblos, cliff dwellings slipped into empty rungs on the ladder of need, a civilization as inconspicuous as lichen, vanished after centuries with little to mark its tenure but rock drawings and the shards of earthenware vessels, a midden heap of piñon nuts, a loom shaft carved from juniper wood. The Florida Anasazi aren't here yet, but you can tell they're coming. The mark of their ruin has preceded them, to help them feel at home, and so that we may know them when they arrive.

Worker's Prayer

Edward Nobles

The rat, gnawing at my wrist,
gives me a reason to stir. I am thankful.
For you too cockroach
nibbling the crumb upon my lip—
I am thankful. The lord protects its creatures.
Then I wake and scream for water, my mouth so dry.
This cell is cold and dusty. Nothing audible
emerges from inside. Nothing harboring here is certain
whether I live or die. I dress and proceed to work.

The night before I stood above
the iron, its hissing love notes,
and made presentable thirteen hour's
worth of wear. The night before
I made a sandwich and poured out cereal
for the morning's meal. This morning
I showered, shaved, and selected a disguise.
Next day, same as above.
Dear Lord, you make my meaning as I make my bed.

The ride over is a way across.
The time clock is a wonder, the way
it moves on, marks for you my every move.
I smile as I slide open
the metal door. Everyone greets me as they expect me
and I make my way to my machine.
Strapped in, I am home.
Dear Lord, forgive me if I was mistaken.
Dear Lord, forget me in my work.

The Birth of Venus

Alicia Ostriker

I

Huge shell the remnant of my great-grandmother dragon,
Split open to form the world,
They have made a boat of it
And set me here.

The effect is of scarcely tolerable pleasure.

II

If I am anything I am young, so young.
As I arrive on this shallow scalloped sea
Zephyr huffs flowers at me, frowning.
The effect is to deepen my reverie.

My face emerges from another world
Behind the picture plane, a world
Of light and clouds, volumes of clouds.
The artist has set it at an impossible angle

Upon my impossibly swanlike
Neck, my impossibly sloping shoulders.

If I am anything I am unreal.

III

Some further hints: the patchy blues of sky
Filled in behind me, the sensitive penciling of the hand
With which I touch myself, as against the crudely dashed
Bronze accents on foliage to my left, wings to my right,

Same gorgeous color as my hair, a wheat
That might nourish a province, and, where a shoulder's edge
Meets a pale background, traces of draughtsmanship
Reveal revision, which is a kindness, or an insolence

Or a looseness . . . beyond perfection.

IV

I am a factory of flowers. Lilies without, roses within,
I will be loved, the hunters will shoot me,
The gardeners pluck me, I must fade, I must die

To assume an immortal order,
You must write about me. Unforgettable,
That is what I am, and I must die

To be remembered, I must reappear
Fresh, moist as April garden plots, soft outdoor earth
Delved and planted around a hothouse, a navel.

V

The navel, smallest of circles, at the latitude of the horizon,
Echoed by nipples.

VI

Hair uncoiling in breeze,
Oval belly, little globular breasts,
And the great shell

Imply a categorical
Encyclopedia of curves,
A Pythagorean feast.

Scallops imply an open universe
Like the bit of open sea
At the back of the canvas.

VII

Knees together, slightly inturned . . .

A plump foot, but with a peasant's long capable toes . . .

A woman steps from the forest.
She looks Roman, a matron under orders
To wrap me in patterned cloth.
Presently, everything blows with the wind.

VIII

I dream I am a warrior, a revolutionary.
Can this account for my glazed-ceramic look,
A girl's chaste fantasy?

How vast it seems, an abyss of time
From her to myself.
I carry neither spear nor gun

Circle after circle, history after history.
Do you feel that I am wistful, ineffably melancholy,
That I appear to ask pardon for my beauty?

IX

Now that I am here I will proliferate.
I will be poorly copied
But I will not object

(I object to nothing, I have no complaint)
For the next six centuries girls will pose like this
To represent innocence, trailing one foot.

But I am neither love nor innocence,
I am only exquisite.
Nobody is ever loved enough,

Our mothers say. I am less than skin deep,
No deeper than canvas, an undercoat
And these thin areas of gilt, sapphire, white.

X

It is one thing to gaze, from the self's jail, at things.
Another to be a thing, an entity, a self.
Lastly, to fuse the two, be the self's self. The soul
At once all-seeing and utterly blank, meaningless

As a cloud or river.

Now look at my eyes. Be pitiless,
Use me as your mirror.

XI

Before my birth you were an animal,
Or supposed yourself one.
You lived among the pigs in mud and straw
Having forgotten almost everything

Pertaining to the gods.

Before my birth, confess it, you were savage.
Seeing me now you forsake your appetites,
Drawn by the gentle half-lit tenderness
Of my inward gaze,

Subtly indented nostrils, coral lips,
The weightless gravity of my porcelain face,
The contemplative pearl of my form, my air of trust—

XII

The limousine that dropped me on your street
Has driven away through an arch of palms.

The driver finds his eyes in the rearview mirror
Like opals, adjusts his cap, undoes his tie.

Now I have paced your narrow front walk,
Glanced at the pansies, the geraniums in your yard,

Mounting the three unpainted steps of your porch
I reach the screen door of your memory:

Cease to resist,
This bed here, this belongs to me

*****

And the shore onto which I am about to step

*****

Power

Ricardo Pau-Llosa

for Austin Hummell

The will—absent
from the tilting canopies of oak
and the slicing leaf of giant lily
that feels like cash,
and the jammed metronome of patio umbrellas—
asserts its human testament,
bent on direction. Call the hand
toward or the foot away, point the head
or eye and whim is enough. Mocks
the spirited wind that cannot know itself
amid ornate measures of pressure and knots.
The hand is simply made to rise, zip
a few dozen small leaves from the poinciana
and turn them on the palm like the coinage
of dark and light moons tumbled
beyond calendar and freedom. Weight,
the surgical sun and the thermostat shade,
the vehicular breeze all frame
what the will makes of nature.
On campus with my poetry students,
I traverse the grounds, walk attentively,
my body a butterfly gathering of radars.
By will I am open to the sudden hairline rivers
of the concrete ramp I've walked in the numberless.

By will its ghosted treadmarks dawn.
It is clear, by din of note and stare,
that fading too is rigored by an art
or punishment of laws. I see the blueing
chalk of graffiti names that love other blues
and make them kin by the arc of a glance
to watermarks on a cement gutter, their veils
of brown made lyrical by a dry spell
and their rust washed by wind into a thin gold.
But then, there is a human face to ruin language:
paint chipped on the rim of the pick-up,
the palm-polished centers of the brass doorhandles,
the cloudy milk of tread on the frequent pavement,
the flint path of bald sand on the lawn
all denote the archeology of use
because by merely living we wear ourselves
as kind if not as selves into codes and permanence.
Ours is the art of slow halting into nothingness
read as habit and probability. As singulars
we are the full stops, the drunken stare
of the disconnected fan, the blind sleep
of aluminum planes, noon tungsten, angling
a faintly reptilian pattern across a dashboard.
In the will's drama among the elements
there is yet another arrangement, complicitous.
Behold within the grammar of intention
the hunched gardener feeding the onyx belly
of his trashbag with nature's refusals,
or three lipstick-bloomed cigarette butts
punctuating a sentence of fallen leaves.
Behold the frozen fireworks of white cobwebs
on the flat iron capital of a lit column.
They've signed their fossil tattoo
where a diurnal island broke the mandate of night
and fed them. Human and natural do at last
conspire to blur each other, as in the grave,
language and the hope of law come riding
into all our crevices to rule and parcel out

where the fade of this meets the bend of that.
Dreamt or otherwise. Let such chambers be
a cradle like the oak leaf edge-curled,
thick green yet artifice in feel and weight.
Insect shell, bottle cap, husk and painted nail.
Where we glean we will, abandon pray.

Repair

Molly Peacock

You have broken yours, haven't you?
In the dim peeling of years
below the dim ceiling of years
squats a toybox
padded in yellow oilcloth
fresh without a build-up of grime.
Backward in time. . . .
You have broken yours, haven't you?

Broken the clock to find the tick,
dissolved the stamp to find the lick,
plucked the lips off a doll,
torn the leg from Sleepy the Fluffy Lamb,
bent the tail of the metal pony,
the sheer examination of what you love
its destruction:
Texas peeled off the puzzle map,
its statehood
scrolled up like snots.

Breaking
is constructive.
You see how things work
in the moments they are destroyed,
like the prongs of a ring
that once held a birthstone
now not only empty
but . . . withered somehow,
the tiny tines twisted

so the pearl dropped to the stone floor
beneath the pew
where a child dug at her birthstone
which rolled away
and in its absence
she saw its presence made the ring whole.

. . . Bicycle wheels
headless tulip stems

divorces . . .
So this is why!
Then why, why, why, why, why
did it have to break?
If only . . .
My only one . . .

You might recognize repair as
a square-snouted dog
with one eye.
At least it has one eye.
Poor Morgie the dog—
but he can still see
from that felt pad anchored by a button.
Damaged but understood.
Damage is a kind of understanding:
Look what you've done.
You have broken *yours*, haven't you?

Five Poems

Carl Phillips

The Lost Chorus

One saying

We faltered, we
loved, oh—

we sailed—

the wondering
only is which,

and which one of us first

One saying

Because I
could not

Because I could

Because

(Rain somewhere, and the snow—
fitful, here.)

One saying

There's the bell again,
sounding like nothing remotely

like silver

Another
One of us should answer it

Another
Who?

One by
one by

more

(who have always been everywhere
about us,

we had only to notice)

do they
come to us,

each restively harboring the same gift:

a fish

carved out of something cloud-
milkish,

neither soapstone and

not jade.

The all of them—

Sometimes holding the gift
out to us.

The gift throwing routinely up into sudden

relief

their invisible hands.

Yours, and the Room After

I admit to entering them
both—no
force behind me

except my own—
but have since come
to believe I meant each time

nothing by it,
unless a kindness: granted,
a hard one. Prizing

clarity, I am rarely
without it, yet I have been
often not quite

understood—
The light
afforded by grand

windows, the as-if-
indecisively
thrown sheets, styled

tokens of dishevelment:
these become the facts
only insofar as they

misrepresent me. Can't
there always be found,
somewhere,

a sconced mirror in three
panels, say, to confirm
what is known

already: how many-sided is
the body, how inadequate
every mirror . . . ?

The rest, however—all of it—
sure, call true: did I
intend the single orchid,

do I intend
still its five flowers
open, its four

shut ones? Yes:
Water inside a budvase the color
of water.

Chosen Figure

"That was the winter of three
instances of
birds colliding
with the one window.

Each time—

superstition, or
else wisdom—I
asked, aloud,

Who has died?

                    Each time, the glass
held, for answer."

*

Like any man wanting
in instruction, he
did not say at first
the correct words,

for he didn't know them.

Later though —
knowing them—that he did not
say the words
correctly:

            —That we found
unforgiveable.

*

Nothing, understand, to do with
you, who could be
any man now—now and wanting.

No questions. Not so much

Down-on-your-knees, as
Down-on-your-knees-*Sir*, had you

forgotten. A mirror likeness,
and what its glass holds, for answer.
A darkening spot upon

                                        your brow,
where the Lord has touched you.

Revision

Which is worse—not being
myself, for long hours, able to

account for my own absence; or
not having been, by anyone,

asked to—I can't say. As when
the leaves have but to angle

in direct proportion to the wind's
force, times its direction,

and the mind, whose
instinct is to resist any

namelessness, calls
all of it—leaves, leaves,

and the wind's force—
trust, at first, then *disregard*

until, suspecting the truer name is
neither of these, it must

stop naming. Or as in
the days, reportedly, of

the gods having dwelled
among us—always

people invariably not knowing
and then (some irreducible

odor, an abrupt
solidity to the light) only then

knowing, but too late,
their faces changed

forever after by the difficult
weight of mere witness,

of having none but their own
word for it. . . . If mistake, possibly,

yet mistake this
afternoon seems less

a river than a barely contained in
spite of everything

belief: there's another ending.
In this one, I recognize you—

and the recognizing has the effect of
slowing down that

part of me that would
walk past, or as if away toward

another ending—   You

speak first. And I'll answer.

Perennial

Something to do with thunder,
but the rest of it—*clap*, *cloud*—

the wind taking or,
as likely, had I stopped

listening? Either way, the name
each time wrong for the tree's

appearance, which was pink
blossoms entouraged by

a dullish shade of maroon-to-
brown leafage, all of it like

some wordless because at
last not requiring words

statement about context, or
propriety. We had

argued again—again and
terribly—just

that morning: what
was it? As easy

to ask and not answer as
If to do with thunder, then

how come sky
nowhere figuring?

Tiger-lilies,
ten pots of. Mint, you said,

for the smell of it; for its
taste, loveage—for

how they hold in small
beads the rainwater hours

after a rain, lupines, and
—and two scotch pine seedlings,

which of course, no sooner
home, than we were planting,

you determining the correct distance
apart with an absoluteness

that was neither fate nor
the truth itself except in

its effect, which was
to render—to seem to

render at first meaningless all
alternatives: foresight, or a wild

confidence, blue or yellow, how
could it matter, the rule was

everything, though it leave, it
must come back—

from Minding the Darkness: A Poem for the Year 2000

Peter Dale Scott

III.iii

April 14, 1995

Good Friday! I lie in bed
in a millennial mood
without a heart to choose

between those who in the name
of enlightenment and peace
have thrown off all restraints

from ritual and text
(Kant's rigorous distinction
between the phenomenal world

and the noumenal — *Lilla 38*
leaves *the hereafter*
emptied of what *contains*

the slightest breath of this world
and ourselves *transported*
toward a "cataract") — *Benjamin '95; Lilla 39*

and those who now revive
old memories of hate
of jihad and crusade

(attempting to build up
Messianic intensity
in the order of the profane) *Benjamin '78 312*

Tempted to reprove
both sides for having lost
dialogue with the voices

of sanity in the past
I am minded to go back
for the first time in two decades

and celebrate Easter
in the church across the street
(returning to that glimpse

I had of a new life
as Dante had inspiring
me to pray among the jonquils

of a Morvan monastery
just as the earth itself
by Dante's calculus

now returns to its first point
in the *ordo saeclorum*) *Dante Inf 1.38–40; Virgil Ecl. 4.5*
except that in this year

by some exotic computation
of progress and return
Easter and Pesach coincide

This year I will choose Pesach
and in truth as a Christian
just because both religions

bring us to atonement
I prefer this time to hear
the never silenced phrases

When Israel went out — *Psalm 114:1*
(the words of Dante's pilgrims
insieme ad una voce — *together in unison; Purg. 2.47*

Out from the house of bondage — *Exodus 13:14*
a message from the past
for those who had been slaves

that tells of liberation
within not just outside
the linear course of time

and projects it forward
You were aliens in Egypt
you shall not oppress an alien) — *Exodus 23:9*

in the Pesach service
perhaps from a sense of guilt
the keynote of this age

echo of bloodstained madness — *Benjamin '78 256*
having read when I first met Ronna
how in this Easter week

of the year 1264
(and its blood-libel rumor
of the young Hugh of Lincoln

crudeliter crucifixus — *Walsingham ad ann. 1255*
or *slayn with cursed Jewes* — *Chaucer 164*
as recalled for English Lit

by Chaucer's prioresse
with her *tendre herte*) — *Chaucer 18*
a number of London Jews

estimated at hundreds
were killed on the eve of Pesach
the customary date — *Roth 61–62; Sachar 199*

Ronna would have me convert
        but I have this need to stay
   with the sins of my fathers

(if I could convert
        could I still be
   a dual-spiritual

as I could a dual-national?)
        and in any case both of us
   will continue to chant

the Buddhist refuges
        now increasingly disfavored
   from Burma to Japan

Should I rebuke myself
        for always celebrating
   as a green card alien

or is this the necessary
        atonement for self and world
   where as Augustine said   *civis sursum, peregrini deorsum*

by grace we are aliens   *Aug. City of God 15.1*
        from the time of Jesus' death
   to *Strasbourg on the Sabbath*

when *eighteen hundred Jews*
        were dragged to the cemetery
   and burnt alive

and in this final age
        the Easter massacres
   unleashed by fearful tsars

with the same blood-libel rumor
        child's blood for matzoh-dough   *Sachar 320–22*
   which searchers for folklore

have found in America
I think of how World War Two
eclipsed my father's vision

Dundes 233–42

of enlightenment and law
and roused him to new gloom
Christ in the darkness dead

P.D.Scott '95 298–99

his hope for man too soon
sealed with the outer stone
and feel myself succumb

F.R. Scott 190

to that nostalgic rhythm
which sees all fates as one
death and liberation

the ritual demise
of Pharaoh in the flood
and of the Second Temple

with its animal sacrifice
of Baghdad in its prime
and then avenging Rome

passionate to defend
the Bible with the sword
and now of the holy cities

of Shi'ite Sikh and Kurd
the vision beyond reach
becomes the grave of each

from which our hopes are risen
Time is a hologram
in tension between return

F.R. Scott 190

and the power from despair
to emancipate *quotations*
from their *demeaning bondage*

Benjamin '78 xxxvi

discovering liberation
        not just in escape from time
    (of heart and by wisdom — *Digha Nikaya 230, 566*

like Orpheus in his descent
        empowered by his lyre) — *Virgil Aeneid 6.119–20*
    but in the *ordo saeclorum* — *Virgil Ecl. 4.5*

and not just in the end of time
        (that millennial Easter
    when God shall be all in all) — *I Cor 15:28; Milton Par. Lost 3.341*

but now in this jubilee year — *2000*
        which for us as for Dante — *1300*
    is a year of forgiveness — *Dante Purg. 2.98–99*

to proclaim liberty — *Leviticus 25:10*
        you shall not sow nor reap
    but shall return everyone

unto his possession — *Leviticus 25:11–13; cf. Virgil Ecl. 4.40–41*

Four Poems

Tom Sleigh

Newsreel

It was like being in the crosshairs of a magnifying glass
Or in the beams of the planets concentrating in a death ray
Passing right through me, boring a hole between

My shoes through the concrete floor all the way
To the far side of the earth. Yet it was only not knowing
Where I was and how to get where I was going,

I'd gotten lost in the parking lot on the way
To the cinder block bunker where my mother
Worked the snackbar, my father the projector.

The drive-in movie screen stretched horizon
To horizon, the whole of Texas sprawled around,
The cathedral-like De Sotos and great-finned Pontiacs

Flickering and sinister in torrents of light flooding
From the screen. Frozen in that light, I
Might have been the ancient disconsolate

Ageless stone-eyed child ornamenting a pillar
In a dead Roman city high up on a desert plateau.
I wasn't even as tall as the speakers mumbling

On and on the way now in my dream of extreme
Old age I hear voices mumbling interminably. . .
Where was it, my refuge, grotto of my swimming pool

Lapping in the infinite leisure of the newsreel?
At last my mother appeared from among the cars
And led me back to the snackbar but I was still

Out there, turned loose among the shadows'
Disembodied passions striving for mastery
Above the tensed windshields. There was

Marilyn Monroe movie star enjoying her fame
In the voluptuous, eternal, present tense
Of celebrity being worked over by hands

Of her masseur. Bougainvillea was overgrowing
Her beach bungalow retreat of peace and pleasure,
The screen nothing now but layer on layer

Of flesh the fingers kneaded in a delirious ballet
Pushing, pulling, palms slippery and quick,
Ambiguous instruments of comfort or of pain.

The rush of blood to her face began to cloud
Into white light as the film stock jerked across
A void half coma blackout, half nightmare aura:

The film jammed, raw light pulsing like a bandage
On a face wrapped round and round in surgical gauze.
Wherever I was, I wasn't there among the candy bars

And gum wrappers blazing under glass. The movie poster
Death ray stopped the earth revolving, time had stopped,
My mother's black slacks and my father's not yet grown goatee,

My own hands shaking nervously about were silently dissolving
In that ray bombarding from beyond the galaxy
Being invaded by the screeching, beseeching noises

Of alien beings searching for a planetary home.
Then up there on the screen, frenetic in the light
Was a hair trembling between two cloven lobes

Of shadow that were part of the projector's
Overheating brain, its brilliantly babbling, delusional,
Possessed by shadows, dispossesed brain.

For Robert Owen Sleigh, C. F. C., 100th Division

The men you killed with a grenade that day
Come back in dreams: Gold-epauletted conductor
Punching your ticket on a train, black-vested waiter

Bowing to recite "The house specials."
But it was your own story, not some "war story,"
You wanted me to understand . . . the way going

To the dump after the War made you feel
At home—among gulls scavenging, foxes
And raccoons rummaging all night . . .

Red light leaking from behind your windowshade:
Color of blood of all the murdered dead.
Midnight ashtray smoking, butts heaped and twisted

In a mounting pile . . . Their voices rising in
Your throat, the old warriors try to speak, Sitting Bull,
Achilles, Colonel Sussman who ordered you

To follow him across an open field, bullets
Kicking up divots at your feet. In your
Underwear and T-shirt lit by the refrigerator light,

You grope for the ice water, lay the sweating pitcher
Against your sweating face, the fluent,
Ever shifting nuances of your voice

Harrowing my ear: As a German soldier approached
Through mist, you bent to tie your boots,
So scared you knotted the laces together

And tripped when you leaped out of the foxhole,
Your M-1 sliding into the mud at the man's feet.
He handed you your rifle, turning the barrel

Toward his chest the way someone passing
A butter knife holds it out handle first.
"Danke schön," you said; "Bitte sehr," his reply,

Holding out his wrists to be bound: Deadpan,
You shrugged, " . . . and they gave me the Bronze Star."
Surrender to your memory freshens your absence

Wafting from your fading uniform.
You let me put it on when I was a boy,
The sleeves so long they seemed to dangle

In defeat, gravity so heavy in the pockets
The coat could have been the uniform
Of all the dead barracked in together . . .

Voice from an empty bottle echoing
Among the darkened rows of bunks, make the dead
Lie still! Colonel Sussman, Sitting Bull, Achilles . . .

Forever in Elysium I see them standing by you
Listening to how you ran across that field,
Swearing under your breath but obediently loyal

To that "fire-eating old fool." Survivor
Whose voice is balm, casualty of time
My voice can't plumb, oh huddler

In foxholes, happy eater of K-ration
Chocolate bars, scoffer and stumbler, come out
Of the pickle barrel in the bomb-blasted cellar:

The SS man, his Luger drawn, lies dead
On the splintered stairs and there's a hole
Blown through the wall just your shape and size.

This Day Only

i

Zone innavigable of being, unforeseeable zone,
whether you wear a friend's face or grin back at us
from the mirror or the blankness of a computer screen,

every instant I feel you trying to lure me down:
You crackle with feedback from Jimmy Hendrix's guitar,
empty snail shells reverberate with your cataracting roar.

Everywhere I look this brilliant hot July, between shafts of sun
you insinuate yourself deep into the day:
A man I know is about to die, today, maybe tomorrow;

his voice on the phone is interrupted by your static
as if he were marooned on a mountain top
or shouted up from the bottom of a crevasse . . .

The rich stink of carrion that wafts from the garden,
slugs indomitably traversing the wet grass,
the couple strolling, their aura frangible, incalculable,

hint at your vibrations both visible and invisible.
Isn't this all part of your ambiguous shining, a blossoming
and withering so particular it can't be argued over?

ii

Whether we are or aren't immortal, whether we know
who pulls the strings or it's this day only that the light falls
inexhaustibly, the whole prison feeling of too much

within too little dissolves into sun
scaling the telephone pole. On a morning this calm,
Medusa's midnight mask of stone is only a snarl

of kite string marooned in the maple's crown . . .
Everyone's sitting around having a good time,
the table is set with beer and wine, cheese and cake—

between the table slats, ten thousand fathoms down
we sense in your vacuity an intelligence
working us as if we were threads woven on a loom:

To name you is to name the cold that won't relent,
the vertigo, irremediable, that rises up to meet the wings
of a jetliner suspended above the ocean dark.

You bat us this way and that in the heaving atmosphere.
Whatever we do, wherever we are,
we're creeping along the edge of your abyss.

iii

Your comings and goings, your heavens and hells.
Your minions rush into the vacuum that attends you,
they hover like the balloons advertising

this Sunday's yard sale, THIS DAY ONLY . . .
July eleventh, the air so clear
I can see to the very bottom of the sky!

You lead me down into your cold that shivers up
through the fur coat wanly sprawled under the balloons,
your depths so precipitous in the swirl of the fur's grain

it's like diving into the gulf between each atom . . .
This morning the leaves are too flagrantly green—
green as the respirator mask Charlie breathes through

on his scaffold, his mask making him look
like a serpent god or simian angel, his white shirt
blending with the wall he's painting such

an insidious white it seems he's being
swallowed stroke by stroke, that whiteness subtle
and ungraspable flowering from the paint can.

Tracks

an installation by Jin Soo Kim

Evanescent engine in its ether-housing,
The soul pulls out from the Depot of Unknowing:

Moment outside time, moment of pure relation
Where coils of nerves lit up like bare bulbs

Glow all night in the abandoned station . . .
No conductor, no tickets, no golden spike

Glinting in the desert where track meets track,
No signal, warning beacon, no switch or switchman,

No boxcar, caboose, flange, no piston,
Nothing but the soul's own eccentric motion

Along rails converging to a vanishing point,
Rusted ties and spikes drilled and threaded

Through by snaking black cords slithering
And coiling to end in bursting lights.

Beyond that point the Museum of the Invisible
Holds spirits from Lödz, Vilna, Warsaw,

Riding the rails to where the rails sink out of sight . . .
Spirit of Matter, casual anti-angel

Whose smile or frown means that we live or die,
Your will racing at the speed of thought

And carving through chaos and inanition
And the finest shadings of space and earth,

Can't catch that tiny, brave, flickering engine
That keeps improvising its destination,

Smokeless in its path through nowhere and nothing,
Arriving at each moment beyond as far as it can go.

The Superflux

Bruce Smith

There was a wind the color of chrome that came down the gorge like a Buick. It blasted the petals to sepal and stigma. It ruined the rose. It was the end of a season in the West, three hours behind the season in the East, where I had learned the *Please, Please, Please* and the dance, The Camel Walk. James Brown and the tenth reincarnation of The Famous Flames came to the Rose Garden like a comet that's seen now as a smear of light above the city. I am sorry, now, I did not scream the screams or pass through the sequined wardrobe chest like a child in a story. I am sorry I did not fall terribly down with the Godfather of Soul, refusing the cloak. The comet was just some noise and not the call. The singer had been pressed with charges: wifebash, gunplay, joyride in Georgia, fisticuff, suffering the Sunday after the Saturday night. The song itself a felon.

There was wind in the reeds by the river. Wind through the reeds of the sax. Wind peeled the paint off everything: the trailer and the big yellow house where she lived with paintings of the annunciation. Wind made the dogs clairvoyant, and it angered the wolves. There was too much for us to breathe. Us: that complicity. She was the reason for the shouts and grunts. Night wind blowing the horn. The wren divined the chimney.

There can be too much of the rose hips and dogishness and the music—too much being. Enough is not ever enough. Not ever. The romance was story in the first degree. And the wind released the lupine seeds from their furred pods. It stuck our eyes shut and vexed our throats. I am sorry, now, for the shrieks and whinnies and whispers, for the bass line broken and using the voice as a drum. I am sorry for walking the walk. I am sorry, now, for not dancing the dance.

Three Poems

Charlie Smith

Santa Monica

Someone was writing this incredibly personal poem
and I was reading it over his shoulder
Santa Monica was in the poem
but you could hardly tell
and the devastating loss of integrity
his wife ranting
his cowardice—these were in the poem
and he was sweating as he wrote it
and looking around as if for spies
I am amazed he didn't see me
but sometimes they look right through you
he went on writing his act of contrition
and memory
expressing his extreme embarrassment and sorrow
at how he selfishly used loved ones
lost the money and the house
sat in the car out in the driveway the last morning
and couldn't think where to go
until someone, a cop maybe, suggested
he get something to eat, and then after that he drove
to Kansas. There was a weeping blue cypress in the poem
and at one point he was very accurate about how it feels
when on the street the beloved turns you away.
Sometimes, he wrote, *I stand unnoticed at a counter, waiting.*
At last the woman looks at me and asks what.
It was a struggle, for both of us, to get to the next part.

Green Life Where It Goes

I go off and visit the trees,
the gray-green one,
& the complicated cucumber tree
I thought was a magnolia.
Late fall's an explanation
someone's left off arguing about,
a declamation on a lonely corner
around suppertime, unprovable.

You can go on telling someone
their ragged and misinformed
way of looking at things
won't wash, but they never
listen. You have to
step out into the yard,
really get into the stars, the dew
and the peacock cries.
It will probably get better,
though there's no guarantee of this,
and besides, today's the day.

Where's my frothy ebullience
now when I really need it? What
helps if not dreaming about real estate,
about sunlight on blue formica tables,
and bare tanned legs? Someone,
somewhere, is entering his heyday.
He'll go on through it
to the sick coughing and regrets
of eventide, but why furnish
your head with that just yet?
There's no way to be careful enough.

From the middle distance a shout—
warning or hopeful cry?—
perhaps a friend wants to let us know

he's about to start up
again. I didn't know I could
grieve love's loss
so long, I had no idea.
Find someone else, a friend says,
but I can't, or won't;
I'd like to cry every tear first.
Or simply not let go.
Or pretend absence is presence,

that old routine. The day leans
against me and asks for a hit.
I'll follow green life where it goes.
I enjoy saying this and rub the heel
of my hand with my good thumb,
think about an aria I heard
where the tenor went on past
the grief into a credible exactitude
vis à vis solace and hope. A silence
fell then, not stunned exactly, but as if
those around him didn't know what to say.

Honesty

Maybe Anna won't arrive.
Maybe mordant self-concern will become love.
O you who know things
never change. I imagine
E. A. Poe kissing his child bride, thirteen year old girl
her mother standing in for his mother
sweet tempered raking roast potatoes from the fire,
and shiver with tension and morbidity.
He was appalled by loneliness
by scary apartness, shuddering with resentment
and an alarming sense of smothering.
He lived a while in a bee glade,
high on the island, in NYC.
Anna is
Anna Karenina. Maybe
she won't reach the station.
I used to think the fact my
crazy mother was still alive
meant there was hope. A fool's notion.
She became unreachable
long ago.
In the untidy southern village I come from
this is not unusual.
People are set.
Vietnam was so great, my friend says,
because folks who would never
get a chance to change their minds, did.
Like my friend's father fat ex-Air Force sergeant
who at last, weeping at the grave,
cried Please God end this, it's no good.
Not the *end this* important, but the *it's no good.*
A change of heart.
Not Vronsky saying okay
I didn't mean it, forget the war,
I love you let's get married raise a family,
but Anna.
It's no good. And Edgar Poe,

this weeping into my hat, tugging the sleeve
of a dead child woman: It's no good.

Once in my junkie days I kept a cattle herd.
It was winter in the mountains,
prohibitive, rage like a canvas shirt caked in ice,
I pushed hay bales out of a truck.
The cows, fretful women,
their bony hips, moaning, snotty,
when they snuffled up
I'd punch them in the face.
I wanted to punch
my wife
and the side of the mountain
and my life snarled like a deer in a fence.
I was filled with longing
for joyful permanent fixations, and insight,
for play and a secular individualism,
a spiritual life and some unnameable
opportunity like a right I vaguely
remembered and couldn't get purchase on.
It was no good.
It took me years and one mistake
after another to realize this
and even then I simply got washed out,
put aside
I didn't really learn a lesson.
I know it's not so much the mistakes
not the divisions, or cultural impediments,
the threats and isolation techniques
we run on each other
it's the heart. The nutty way we grip
and won't let go, and the way,
despite what they tell us, *we can take it.*
My father went to his grave unchanged.
So did Poe.
And beautiful Anna Karenina.
And Ovid. Consuela Concepcion, too, my piano teacher.
They say in the end
Mussolini was so terrified his mind seized and he couldn't speak.

He sat there swelled-up and bug-eyed. This is not it.
Or anyone drowning or
lurching from the fire shrieking he didn't want this to happen.
There is so much gibberish. And imprecision.
No wonder we lock in.
Like you, I get scared.
I used to go to my friend's house,
sink into the old sofa on his back porch
and read all day. His family
and the ducks and dogs would pass by,
let me be—discreet love—I'd feel safe.
It was just after I stumbled out of my second marriage,
grieving and
struck dumb, war paint still streaking my face.
My friend practiced a religion
remarkable in its narrow-mindedness. He inserted
his children into this olla-podrida
like a man stuffing leaves into a shoe.
It hurt to see it.
Broken saddle bronc of a beautiful face he had
and his wife a slim twist of blonde girl cunning
and fretful without shame
about anything—I spoke up eventually and got tossed.

I've spent years watching television.
I lie on the couch
eating chocolate and watching television,
arguing with some woman in my head.
Television says the world is not a mysterious place.
Don't worry, it says,
you don't have to change a thing.
And then I remember digging wild leeks,
buying eggs from a crippled old lady
who glanced into the next room sadly
as if a great novelist was dying in there,
and went on
talking, like Kissinger after the war.
And how scary things became when my wife
got up close. Change of heart.
Love leeching the lining away, exposing the pulp.

Stupidity and malice
and a fitful generosity,
shortsightedness and painful posturing,
and things continue just as they are,
nut cases, disputes,
overbearing stupid
claims, modernity hamming it up,
life someone says only a device for entering other realms
—all these in the hopper.
And the tough decisions.
Poe dreaming of a cold finger
picking the lock. Anna stuffing screams back down.
Let go, or stay with it?
The Dali Lama saying *Sure, sure, I'll take the sprouts,*
including the Chinese in everything.
My girlfriend stunned by the power of her own rage,
nothing she can do about it yet,
rebuking paradise, groping for the dog.

Au Claire de la Lune

R. T. Smith

for Geroid Ó Cathain

In the gray Fifties—the wake
of the Great War, the shortage—
the last child on the Blasket—
no playmate but conies
and a calf, no sport or rival
but the graceful gulls—
was told the tallow ration
was too meager for reading
or keeping at bay the dark.

At his studies by day he found
an old story in the Irish tongue,
how the island fishermen
filled a shell with mackerel oil
and ran a rush through it
to wick the spark.
Sprawled across his pallet
with books and a tablet,
he learned the work of French,
maths, Scheherazade
by the mollusk lamp's light.

His science page called
the shell an *atremis*.
A shy creature lived inside,
alert for the moon's *open sesame*.

It followed the tides and kept
his secret. Under the spell
of its midnight flicker
the boy grew fluent, his ear
keen, eyes astute as a lark's.

When at last the door opened
and the island was abandoned,
he sang the song he'd learned—
je n'ai plus de feu . . . pour
l'amor de Dieu—and crossed
the salt water to the world's
green feast—ink-smudged,
fish-smelling, Aladdin's lamp
shut snug in his valise.

Gods of the Second Chance

Kevin Stein

I like the humble maker who'll suffice
with yardstick and upholstered plywood slats,
a little lever to lean the back back,
and *voila*, Mr. Shoemaker's got something
even he can't name. His Name-the-Chair contest
offers up *The Slack-Back, The Sit'n Snooze,*
The Comfort Carrier, his winner blessing it
The La-Z-Boy, whence Bubba culture weds TV.
Add massage, built-in phone/modem/remote,
and who need leave its cushioned heaven?
Be thankful he wasn't Sir Thomas Crapper,
plumber-inventor whose throne we close
the door to mount in regal privacy,
his legacy the flush chain and clean gutters.

All this I've gleaned from one of those
sour millennial surveys of who invented what,
a book whose subject is less invention
than the author's envy of who did what
she didn't, and thus history's envy so often
involves knives, black sheep of problem solving.
The book blames Shoemaker for abetting
the beer belly, sloth, and Super Bowl spousal abuse,
though like any mortal a petulant god makes his goat,
he had limited options. Even a god can't undo
what another god does. What consolation
to be a goat, yes, but one graced to foretell
the future? Who, knowing what eventual evil

we'd wreak of it, would ever invent a thing?
What if Gutenberg could've imagined *Mein Kampf*?
What if Curie envisioned Teller's H-Bomb?
Even Univac, balky but infallible,
couldn't compute the microchip or Internet porn.

Oh please. Stop the sniffing and pawing,
all the muzzled, puddled pleading.
We're the dog at our own basement door.
Come up into what scant astigmatic light
February delivers. We, dear readers,
are not the first to thus screw up!
From fire, did Prometheus suspect napalm
and the cigarette? Amidst the millennial
lists we quaver over, let me praise my old Fender amp
and yellow Telecaster, to whose accompaniment
I wailed much best left unheard by dancers
and parents alike. Guitar whose feedback cloaked
my chimey rhyming of "moon" and "June"
with "Julie Calhoun." Amp whose blaring fare
did not spare my own ears, so now I nod
and smile at what my daughter pinches through
clinched teeth, hearing only a muffled sigh
of harmony coalesce paternal sense
I don't possess. Let's praise the eraser,
god of the second chance, without whom
Einstein's flawed formula might've cubed
our dark night's failure before he squared it.
Let's praise the delete key's beautiful impunity—
our knack for the right word held back,
the wrong keyed too freely. Let's praise
the blunt butter knife, ladder I offer
this beer-addled gnat to rise from my mug,
dry his wings in Einstein's light, then try again.

Vision and What It Was

Gerald Stern

I looked at the sun as Huxley did according
to the teachings of my cousin Eo whose name
in Pittsburgh was Israel when we were sitting on Boulevard
Raspail in order to change my vision and saw as
Huxley did the marvelous elements of the sun
including purple animals with heads like
crocodiles and tails like lions and wings that
appeared and disappeared the more I pressed my
lids or rubbed my eyes and I was wearing a
blue shirt when I leaned back and the tears
just poured down my cheeks and into the creases, Eo
at all times encouraging me and lecturing me
on vision and what it was, breaking it down
the way Huxley did and staring himself at
the sun and weeping like me, the color patches
just patches after awhile as we went back to
homunculi or sperm just swimming slowly
from west to east, in my case it always started
that way, against the stream, as it were, though I
would never stare directly, even with the thick
old glasses, though Eo was pushing me, and Huxley
would never be that mad. I did my palming
and blinking instead and taught my mind how to move,
and I remember a man who took his glass eye out
so for two blocks I put my glasses inside
one of my pockets and went without looking. I talked
to a white larva, I talked to Vasco da Gama,
I talked to Robespierre, for I could see in

one case how cruel one bastard was in velvet
pantaloons and in another how small the
severed head was, but it was after all
the sun that burned and I who walked down a filthy
stricken street in one of my stricken cities
with one hand over my eye and counted to ten
before I shifted hands and squeezed my lids
now that my glasses were off, the way I did when
I first had to stare at the harsh lights
with the door closed and saw in streaks and made the
beams that lie in objects elongate themselves
by narrowing my eyes or made them go double
just by relaxing a little and had my first
obsession then and longed to be by myself
so I could see double and I could squint and that was
the start, for me, whatever it was for Steve
Berg, blazing pages he says, or Willis
Barnstone staring all night at the Crisco sign
across the Hudson with the flashing clock
a part of the flashing firmament or Ted
Solotaroff working all winter in his father's glass shop
under a naked light bulb, to name just three.

Deep Fish

Brian Swann

White sky like curtains
in a headlong dive onto
fields & farms. I look out
from windows cut down to size
where a broken wheel is
grinding over glass alongside
a whiplash of streams,
where whirlpools twist
leaves & detritus in
on themselves, like ecstasies
unmoored or abandonments
without consequences & in the room
behind me I can still pick up
rustlings in the pianola,
the canary I freed picking
to pieces wax flowers in the
parlor & the pedal-organ
playing hymns by itself beside
the conservatory & its tomatoes
forced by bull-blood, thinking
me thinking them, & in my pockets
pebbles & stones, plans for gravity,
& airraid shelters eaten by evening
& a voice like my mother's
coming at me, deep fish swimming up
from night to drown
in white sky

Two Poems

Pimone Triplett

As of Two Ancestors, 1845

Story goes, cattle fattened, the wheels in rut,
goods borrowed or bought on credit, the bulk ready,
she slipped from staggered hides down the wagon
packed to hosannas, breaking an arm,
and so it was decided he should go on without her.
Home-bound then, the joint set in haste,
elbow throbbing always part of her to hostage,
she started the chiseling of instances, her ledger
of staying in place. Each thing mirroring
the mind alone, she'd keep track, try
to memorize the moments beyond
the garden weeding up all season, the plot
of dirt bricking below a lack of rain. Days,
wanting to see deeper into, say, the paper wasp
riding unseen waves in sage bush, or the lop-
sided columbine's snarl of petals dropped
in heat, she wrote the record he could
come home to. At night, checking her own
face reflected, warped wide in the mantle's
urns of ash—his mother, his father—
she waited to hear, trying to listen hard
within the fire's crack of falling
back on itself: stubborn, mouldering,
stirred by chimney's lesser wind.

Meanwhile, head bent to a breeze scanning
the broad plain, his mind moving, truing its brocade out in the elsewhere.

Back a stitch to her now,
then forth into the forward, a turning and turning, always about to complete.

Not sleeping, not wanting
the day's end, orchestral, echo of bats, their screech and round, a rough

hum of gnats
in swarm above him. Evenings, out to overtake the end, straddle what he couldn't

see, there, behind the two-tiered stack
of tree line half-hatched out of the mist it makes: the forest's

final catacomb, the secret
starting up from a story. Restless, he wrote her how, not far from the rock face

where he'd carved their name,
the mule, after braying for hours, gave out—a sound of steel grated live in the lungs,

followed by long quiet.
Hunting, he said, most days, wolf skins for county wages, out westering, still

looking for the right
spot, a new home—*it's possible*, he kept repeating, *for free*. In his mind a dream of dirt

piled in straight lines,
long doors unhinging his one desire, below the beds of sand, silt, worm, water,

lay a perfect dark: *land*, its sprawl
and secret, all the furrows a winged plow could portal into. . . .

Then upwards she saw the end: snow wrapped
as a cast binding beech limb, red oak, linden.
Having wintered long enough in his absence,
one night she emptied out the urns.
His mother, his father. Wrote down
how first she let their bodies'
chunks and rubbish fall
into an empty bucket, then fed
all his letters to the fire.
Later, she walked away from the house
craddling the ash and grit
of her missings in the small tin pail.
Knealing to the ground then, she put her hands
into the mix, smeared some onto her chest,
more onto her lips. Flung half
into the air, half into the waiting
dirt. After that, she lay down as never again—
the palm to cold cheek to still
colder stone—though the ground,
frozen, could not hold her,
not hold her yet.

Late Century, Long Drive with Stutter

So that each time I look out I'm following
the little storms of snow roadside, watching
the headlights have at it, slice of white
rivening the proximities. I try it slow,
wrist at the wheel. Everywhere a parsing
of particles (no two alike) seconds before
I drive the whole spinning thinness to disappear.
Meanwhile, voices on the radio
sputter up bits of the stories, the shootings
and bombs on target again,
more madmen, someone just said (at tether's end).
I can hear about the ones forced to stay
and the ones forced to flee. But when some mile
or mountain pass makes the girl's cries go
static for me, I lose that daughter
weeping through war and bad translation,
telling how they wanted us for *who we were.*
Can't say when the small shame sets in (always),
this not being able to listen anyway as the atrocities,
all too familiar, come on, the far off cruelties
going abstract, the girl hard to hold. Outside,
(a swirl) snow's up in arms, until I can't see
its filching of the visible.

Although I remember
(pulling over) how once I thought I heard inside it,
something huddled under the distances.
Heard it happen to—with—a stranger. I was
a child, at home. Came in the night, this rip,
the sudden almost whistle note waking us—
was it a teakettle—was it a siren—? Then everyone
running through the hallway to find it, father, mother,
me (parsing), each of us hearing in our turn
no, it's a scream (lock myself inside now).
Someone back then opening the front door
(snow, that flurry outside), and then her

falling into us. She a *she* all *red*, I thought, then
    no, all blood—blood running with a face behind it.
Her scramble and scrittering into the corner.
    Each of us trying to do something, trying to find
the right thing to do (windows steaming up now).
    Can remember mother at the phone,
father checking outside (the white on white,
    a swirl) and me on the floor with her face.

Her jacket flapping blood and glass,
    her arms around me, gripping, the storm
of her still screaming, rising up at me
    (starting to stick), then the room
bleaching white, all the lights coming on until
    I saw it from above suddenly, each of us
locked inside, spinning out, the different directions,
    each of us hurt, but her more so, sliced open
somewhere—where? the opening, her wound
    was where?—Each of us a privacy scraped wild,
and my wanting her off me by then (I admit),
    for her to shut up now anything but this
fear gone full throttle up from the voice and guts of her.
    Soon I heard further within maybe
(no two alike), something blank, sickening—no
    core at the core—no pulse and spin
under the skin, all her quiet
    deafening in the little hall—

        (And I let her go.)

            Later the police came, pieced
in the details, how she'd been kidnapped, car-jacked, forced
    (the long drive). How he'd laid her down in lawn
after lawn (a red on white). And now in the distance
    horizon's nothing, gone slipshod, smudge,
and I get the snow in dribbed bits
    off the interstate. A crackle and I get
the voices back on, updates on the updates, whirling
    (and the listening deep enough is?). She lived
in the end, thank god, on her way out kept

stuttering up from the stretcher: he was just a kid,
he was a child, she tried, he wouldn't
listen (and the is inside the is
is?) And if I open the door
this very second, climb down
on my knees into the gully, cup the cold flakes
in my two hands, couldn't it be for
the melting, the stillness, that finishes—
I catch a quick blinding
up from the ice bank outside,
then the squall shot surface, disturbed, circling.

At the Door

David Wagoner

All actors look for them—the defining moments
When what a character does is what he is.
The script may say, *He goes to the door*
And exits or *She goes out the door stage left*.

But you see your fingers touching the doorknob,
Closing around it, turning it
As if by themselves. The latch slides
Out of the strike-plate, the door swings on its hinges,
And you're about to take that step
Over the threshold into a different light.

For the audience, you may simply be
Disappearing from the scene, yet in those few seconds
You can reach for the knob as the last object on earth
You wanted to touch. Or you can take it
Warmly like the hand your father offered
Once in forgiveness and afterward
Kept to himself.

Or you can stand there briefly, as bewildered
As by the door of a walk-in time-lock safe,
Stand there and stare
At the whole concept of shutness, like a rat
Whose maze has been rebaffled overnight,
Stand still and quiver, unable to turn
Around or go left or right.

Or you can grasp it with a sly, soundless discretion,
Open it inch by inch, testing each fraction
Of torque on the spindles, on tiptoe
Slip yourself through the upright slot
And press the lock-stile silently
Back into its frame.

Or you can use your shoulder
Or the hard heel of your shoe
And a leg-thrust to break it open.

Or you can approach the door as if accustomed
To having all barriers open by themselves.
You can wrench aside
This unauthorized interruption of your progress
And then leave it ajar
For others to do with as they may see fit.

Or you can stand at ease
And give the impression you can see through
This door or any door and have no need
To take your physical self to the other side.

Or you can turn the knob as if at last
Nothing could please you more, your body language
Filled with expectations of joy at where you're going,
Holding yourself momentarily in the posture
Of an awestruck pilgrim at the gate—though you know
You'll only be stepping out against the scrim
Or a wobbly flat daubed with a landscape,
A scribble of leaves, a hint of flowers,
The bare suggestion of a garden.

Three Poems

Alan Williamson

MLA Notes (1988)

for Joanne Feit Diehl

We agreed we could always spot us at a distance—
tweed-buffered, bemused
not consciously angry, out of place at street corners
as an armed statue, and unlike,
say, scientists—who've never
been told they aren't, or should be, sexy—somehow fussily
self-fondled at the edges . . .
"What
kind of convention *is* this?," as the whore
said to my friend in the ladies' room . . .

Is it our uselessness, our failure
to be good at, say, machines; or a peculiar
second-handness toward life itself, gives our faces
that permanent aging childhood, that apologetic
arrogance around a void?

The very fluid
of life, passions, crises, imaginations,
how one thought hooks to the next—to which we add
nothing we stand behind, nothing that's purely ourselves—
coursing through us; and turned to no purpose, unless

making others love the same superfluous
quickening to the essence, is
a kind of turning . . .
                    Certain forms of magic
have always been handled by the epicene.

MLA Notes II (1998)

Of course, Pavese said it: "to hear people
of the same profession,
trade, religion, sex, talking about it
among themselves, arouses disgust." And still, I'm back.
On the BART crossing
under the Bay, there was a man haranguing
everyone and no one. Hatred seemed
the impetus, to judge by the twist among the mouth-hairs,
though one could argue for energy, a ceaseless
need to expel, discharge. . .

Everyone in this room would side with him
(I thought), not with the mother
who kept her small son's wide alertness carefully
turned somewhere else—his head so blond it showed
hers was once, *really*;
lourd et bourgeois to them, as the Frenchman said
by the subway exit . . . Arcana for ourselves, trash culture
for everyone else. Yet I'm here. Let's face it: power,
even small power, intoxicates, and gossip,
and being mirrored; hotels

with their turning corridors are the image
of the possible; young women
do shine, in their black suits and eagerness; this—
what to call it?—small whirlwind
of molecules trying harder
no more or less real than the one out there where *death*
isn't a trope but something lurking
in the cold of the air, the welder's fire, the edges
of metal things; at some not too distant day
quite unambiguous.

The Pattern More Complicated

The world becomes stranger, the pattern more complicated
Of dead and living.
Eliot, "East Coker"

I have my places, now, in every city.
The Wyndham Hotel. The Sutton Coffee Shop.
East Arlington. Cafe de la Mairie.
Circuits of habit, of self-comforting
for past desperation, of—*meaning*, even,
it takes half a lifetime's moving on
to lay down on the globe.

Arriving at the Wyndham, familiar soot-sting
of Midtown, some indeterminate change of season,
I set myself down and make my phone calls. I
am a man who sets himself down and makes his phone calls,
assuredly, though the bellboy has left the room.
Stiff lampshades watch me, and faded horsey pictures.
When I address the postcards to young women—
those I never had, those I lost in months or days—
I see their faces, not to see Someone
laughing, over my shoulder, at the List.

And most of them not born yet when—when—
I dream
often of the house in Haverford, now it's sold.
I drive past to look at it once more, but something—
sky-high windbreak woven against my gaze,
green, indestructible . . .
Before Dick and Marcia
moved out, new workmen, tearing up the kitchen,
discovered the wall of the old farmhouse, ending
at the pantry . . .
I keep thinking, we lost it, though I,
of course, had nothing to do with that divorce.
Like coffee stains on old fabric, heat-curdles on old wood,

it whispers, *our generation can't keep things*. They kept it,
Alfred and Isabel, whatever else they lost—
heart, lungs, esophagus; Alfred known at last
more for his dirty jokes and inappropriate
confidences, than anything else, except his parties . . .
But still a house in the old sense, *grands seigneurs*,
with a sweep of white newels down to the front door,
where we knocked, younglings, and were given sherry.

Jonny and I, and Dick, and Joel . . . I
could still walk that torn-up kitchen and find anything,
tumblers, tall stool to sit on, warmth-fields of several ghosts;
screen door, dog yapping to be let in or out.
Loss woven unnoticed into the whole pattern . . .

The last time I talked with Isabel, she could hardly
sit up at all, but we sat under the grape arbor
in the Eastern summer night—windless, stagnant, full—
and talked of how the dead go on, an ancestress' recipes,
family turns of voice . . . a thought ingrained in her
as the farmhouse walls embedded in the pantry's.
Trouble was, I'd known we'd have that conversation
as long ago, at least, as my early visits back.
It had nothing to do with just how much had gone wrong.
I loved her, but time had exhausted it,
too soon.

What do you do when you walk into
a new restaurant in San Francisco and meet C.,
whom you brought to that house in your mind, *unseen companion*,
since *even (especially) impossible love* makes
you *see things twice, see for the absent other*?
Thirty years. You don't recognize her,
her husband, the headmaster, recognizes you.
You're with a younger woman, it looks worse—
or better—than it is, but you can't explain.
She has multiple sclerosis. The beautiful proportion
of her eyes and nose is there, but contracted, somehow,

seen through the wrong end of the telescope.
Living in L.A. now. The headmaster's house
built for a short man, little squat pillars.
Finally started to write. Alone all day,
and the kids kept saying, "Mom, write that down!"
"What do you write about?" "Me. Don't you write about you?"
I'm sitting—the restaurant is so full—at her feet
on a small step, a posture
which seems oddly permanent—spring evening,
the two stone steps, the Haverford library. . .
And it's only when I get home I realize "Nancy,"
who died suddenly of an aneurism last year,
isn't the squat Nancy, the confidante,
but the wild one, with the dark glasses, the special car.

When I'm in the great house in Haverford, I'm lying
in bed, alone but thinking about the others . . .
One of my visits from Cambridge. It's early summer,
the room has no shades, I've never been anywhere
with so many birds, so all my thoughts are Eros,
that brimful Eros, straining through perfect images
like all the birdsong in the world, that starts to vanish
after twenty-five . . .
Or it's at night, I've left the party early—
I can't stand, even then, to have such a hangover twice—
but sleep holds off, and I'm holding, reinterpreting
them all in my mind, as the timbres of their voices
drift from downstairs . . . I think I go back to this easily
because time seems already past, so infinitely
arrangeable . . . C. and I? Starting writing so late,
diffidently . . . not to have had to smash a marriage
to feel the brimfulness release, suffuse . . .
Wherever
they went that night—friends, a hotel room—I so equally
wanted and didn't want her to stand apart where
rain stung a window . . . (Last scene of "The Dead.")

In my dreams the lost places grow enormous,
childhood apartments with tapestries for wallpaper
and chapel-alcoves, climbed to through ship's rigging;

or installations, worlds of airy fibre
that need to be thought in, and anchored, from outer space . . .
The vertigo Proust speaks of, the amazing
foreshortenings at the base. (Did Cal die
less than ten years after my father?)
But also his sense of a cathedral growing—
new shadows, amplitudes, as the arches close
and the *fleche* sharpens . . . (Did Jonny and I
address a multitude, ringing Buddhist bells?)

It's never quite mine, though—at best some enigmatic
ungiving other self's; or else I'm given
a little room to write in, off the kitchen.

The view out my window, at the Wyndham,
is like those archaeologies of my life,
strata whose lights and colorations are
unthinkable to each other. Men in yarmulkes
stand past dusk at long tables, tinkering small machines.
Mornings, one floor down, a secretary
bustles in with coffee and sits facing the airshaft,
by her potted plant. One day
the boss calls her out; she comes back and just sits there, glum.
I watch her not just because she's pretty, or reminds me
how my student once worked a job like that, in New York—
the delight of strange detail, and then the loneliness—
but something else, that for a moment makes
the "change" or "happiness" that was all we wanted, younger,
quite immaterial. Life, beyond my knowing.

Can't You Spare Me Over? (Smithsonian Folkways #40090)

David Wojahn

Coal dust webs the lungs & from them slurs the plea.
The banjo notes are nails stabbing pinewood: Dock Boggs
pleading, high and lonesome: **O Death,**

O O Death. Not the archipelagos of Hades.
But surely jet-black water carves the hollows
of Eurydice's bones. **O Death won't you spare me**

over 'til another day. The tape is spooling
on a porch in Lechter, Kentucky. & Death insists,
of course, that we follow standard protocol.

I bind your feet so you can't walk. I sew
your mouth so you can't talk. You can feel Him
wet His needle, hover at your lips, stitch & slither

against your jaw, the work as patient
as silicosis. & now a kind of twilight
mists the earth, on the hollows & the company stores,

coal cars rolling the narrow gauge & the barren
Churches of the Nazarene, where not even
bones shall be permitted at The End to rise

& dance & hair from the skulls forever
shall sprout. O Death, give us comfort at least
as the souls drift confounded up & down

the thermals of such mist. In these beds
the I.V. tubes prohibit movement. When I last saw Jake
he tried to pat the nurse's ass, but the chemo drip

was in his way. The request for lemon pie
was bluster & wildly his eyes looked about.
I was elsewhere for the fever which brought

the coma & you know the rest: bedside with my wife,
her mother at vigil in a metal chair & the sodden
April light of Birmingham. Entubated tremble,

machine whirr & the tics & twitches, lips & tongue at work
but silent. **I sew your mouth so you can't talk,**
I bind your legs. For weeks you search the riverbank

for a boat to give you passage. This shape you've taken—
how new & wavering it is, surging like the sawgrass
as it bows to wind & always it is noon, full summer

though nothing warms you & the sleek
dark berries which line these banks are not
for you to taste. They rain upon the ground

without your hands to reach for them or blue
the creases of your palm, or weave down your beard
to stain your shirt. A kite unmoored, you billow

& those who seek you, reading magazines & thrillers
by the nightstand in their vigil, are figures you can barely glimpse,
waving from the pineys & the milltown smokestacks glinting

from the camelbacked foothills behind you. & forward you inch
but cannot walk & lo you hover on the placid shimmer,
the luminary blues. Everywhere water,

& the jon-boat or trireme you've found
sways oarless in the sun. Peaceful now to drift this way,
the tide lapping slow. You are permitted to remain

as long as you shall require.

(Jake Watson, 1931–99)

Cavafy Museum, Alexandria ("Asend The Stare: On Top Floor Please Ring Bell")

As if Christo wrapped the courtyard stairs with dripping sheets

*

& traffic noise, from where your guide has circled lost. & off the tourist

*

map, as you suppose it always shall be. Pinstripe-narrow street

*

("bordello for the Flesh & church for Sin—& the hospital

*

where you go to die"), chair upturned on the cafe table, polis of little intrigues, Ptolemic

*

gossip, & the boys (so beautiful) on the cusp of ruin. & his pen, to balance

*

the Yes & the No—Adonis losing at 3-card monte, but chiseled immortal in mimeograph

*

& stapled in a pamphlet to the poet's name. & the moist sheets ripple, valanced

*

with handkerchiefs & socks, stained faintly, salted with the pathos

*

of human fluids. & the cotton t-shirts, roiling in a line, graven still with the shapes

*

of pectorals, tremor of nipple & the clothespinned sleeves. O pentimento-ed

*

tan-lines & the torsos resplendent, white in attic marble & white on the beaches

*

of el-Montazah where the rough & temporal Gods still throng.

*

Above dwells Eros, whose province is Longing. Part these curtains and ascend.

The Art of Poetry

for Roger Mitchell

In the beginning, desolation everywhere.
Hulking, glaciered, dishwater gray, the rocks
loom up from a spit of beach.
Here the men will winter & await the rescue ship,
relieved to stand at last
on solid ground. Eleven months
they've drifted on the floes, **Endurance**
squeezed to sticks of timber as the pack ice
tightened: "Elephant Island."
Shackleton may save them or he may
be dead. & everyone is sick to death
of penguin steaks. On "Mount Snowden"
they've set their flag, & in the hour
of August twilight that is day, they scan
the burged horizon for a sail
or swath of smoke, they gobble
imagined feasts. Today, a Yorkshire pudding,
conjured Homerically, gravy bubbling
on the dumplings & potatoes,
aubergines in curry & a starygazy pie,
apple tarts, the Devonshire cream aswirl.
Great buckets of claret & frothy Guinness
wash it down. The Woodbines
& cigars are lit, brandy in the club rooms
& the smoking cars. Blackboro's
right foot may well be saved,
but the toes of the left are surely gangrenous.
So on this first warm windless day
the main tent is cleared, hoosh pot
filled with ice to boil & crates in a line
make a kind of gurney. Penguin skins
sizzle white on the stove, & all the blubber lamps
glow. Macklin & McElroy strip
to undershirts & Blackboro breathes
huge draughts of chloroform. His toes

are black, the flesh almost mummified.
Now the incision, snaking & laborious
along the foot. McElroy peels back
the skin. He tests the forceps & the toes
spin down into a bucket,
clanging one by one. Blackboro,
waking groggy, wants a smoke. Will someone
please read to him awhile? & from
the salvaged three-book library
they choose **Britannica, N-O.** Numerology
gives way to Numismatics, McElroy
bending in the lampglow
to point out burnished coins
in rows, Xerxes & a Ptolemy
with laurel crown The Nutmeg
is tropical, hard & aromatic
is its seed. Blackboro drifting,
his hands unmittened & from Nutrition
come the Nymphs: Dryads who haunt
the forests & groves, Leimoniads the meadows
& in waters dwell the Naiads, Potameids
& Hydriads. But Nyx, Thrice-Great Nyx,
world-making Nyx, of whose breath
the earth & firmament were formed, whose realm
is All Things Of The Night, born of Chaos
& Mother of Aether, is a goddess
most fearsome, even by Zeus revered.

On Privilege

C. *Dale Young*

The rampant cane fields rife with disease,
the ocean carrying only shells to the altar,
a beach left to penitents, their easy sweat
cursing the sand that brought an increase
in tourism. Could this scene be altered?

Next to a pile of seaweed, the ubiquitous gull
ate from a plate of dead things, rejections.
Up in the cane fields, sitting beside an anthill,
a young and foolish version of myself had once hid,
scratching in the dirt his tired testament, his will.

To my firstborn, I would leave the sea; the sand,
to my future love. But my father's grim shovel
I would bury under a palm tree, under tendrils
of clematis, its showy blooms filled with poisons.
One should not be alone in the cane fields, its evil

captured in its wide paragraphs, its evil refined
like sugar. At a resort staggered down a cliffside
to yet another beach, I sat one morning studying
the flowers of the crown-of-thorns, its bloodletting
worthy of an entire chapter in a book

on phlebotomy. In the air, I smelled privilege.
I remembered the cane fields. The years rewind
so easily for one who is a visitor in his own home.
The sea silences these false lines and mocks me
with promises of splendor and bright fish, reminds me

I am a fisherman, casting an empty hook.

You, I, Them: A Confessional Poet's Dissolution

Jana Harris

My conjecture is that if you come from a family that has a strong "denial gene," and if you inherit only trace amounts of this genetic material, your chances are greater of developing the compulsion to become a writer of the genus poet, species confessional. This phenomenon holds particularly true if one parent is substance-addicted or mentally ill and the other parent is the guardian of the secret. In the beginning, you start out innocently enough harboring a growing obsession to document your side of the story, something to serve as a sort of testament as to what you perceive as the truth. You are still very young at this point, so you still imagine that there is a truth, or only one truth, at any rate. Besides that, you can't—due to the weak denial gene—contradict what your eyes see. Like all children, you are taught never to bear false witness. But early on you figure out that you don't get punished for lying to keep the secret. You only get swatted, sent to your room, or threatened with foster care if you tell your truth, which is labeled a tale. And when you persist, you are branded Dirty Little Liar. Thus, you learn the art of subterfuge.

Later in college when you take a freshman creative writing class, the assignments seem almost effortless, because you're already an adept storyteller. Besides, it's the late sixties and every bumper sticker yells at you to let it all hang out. This message cleaves to you like a religious text and becomes your mantra. Sophomore year you get a little lazy and don't make anything up. Voila, you discover that you get points for your confessions, your depictions of altered states of reality, your dramatic moments which more and more often take the form of lines of uneven length scrawled across the page, unhampered by the restraints of punctuation. Unfortunately for you these narrative efforts aren't entirely off the cuff sketches ripped from the pages of your diary. One problem is that you are told to include a lot of what feels like boring, insignificant detail. The other is that the story of your life and the people around you seems so mundane that it hardly feels interesting. Who would want to read something about a person whose life has been slightly southwest of normal? Then, during your junior year, it dawns on you that not everyone had a Joan Crawford or a Marie Antoinette or Joseph Stalin or Henry VIII as a parent. Okay, so you suspect one or two of your good friends did—which is probably why they're your good friends—but not everyone sees their parents in a clear critical light and still fewer feel compelled to write about them. Better to call up what strength you can from the recessive denial gene, bury the past (or invent a new one), and move on.

But the truth-telling itch prevails. Like-mindedness jumps out at you from the lives of others. You learn to recognize the citizens of Planet Abuse. If not consciously, then unconsciously. The Mainstream Mind tells you that you've a skewed vision, a perverse sense of what's important, that instead of forgetting the bad and remembering the good (as your parents promised would be the case), you have an affinity for the worst possible scenario if not the hideously bizarre. Society blames you for this wrong-thinking. But that's okay, you're used to being the scapegoat. Some call this state of mind Clinical Depression. You call it Reality and are bent on the world seeing your side of the story. Consulting the psychiatric world seems beside point. Under the microscope of your cynical eye, mental health practitioners appear more screwed up than you are and you suspect they sought out this branch of medicine to fix what was broken in their own heads. Besides, if you spent all your time bleeding across some shrink's couch, you wouldn't have any fluids left to ink your pen. By now typing out lines of uneven length describing the inclement weather of the heart seems more cathartic than talking to gray-beards excited about the prospect of buying pontoons for their Cessnas enabling them to tie their aircraft to the boat dock in front of their homes. Now, they tell you gleefully, they'll get out from under the high price of renting airport hanger space, which they really need to do in order to catch up on those killer alimony payments.

Back in class, you and your narrative poems and stories shoot for a degree in English. But the study of literature is plagued by cultural prejudice, and the Powers That Be are bent on labeling you Little Miss Sick-o as a pseudonym. The red ink sniffs: Are rural and working women really valid subjects for literature as seen from this point of view? You switch your major to mathematics, a discipline where a correct answer is possible and even when not achieved, the method by which you arrive at the last line—the reassuring QED—is what's important. However, unlike your comparative literature seminars where there's at least safety in numbers, there are only three women in the entire department. The lack of camaraderie aside, the study of mathematics tells you that it's always possible to find some order amid chaos and, further, that the truth is not only attainable, but remains true. What the Greeks proved four thousand years ago is still true today. Almost as importantly, Mathematics isn't culture-based. It's the faith you've been searching for. Besides, you only cover 45 pages of well defined symbols per semester as opposed to 400 pages of text which, according to your Twentieth-Century Literature professors, you never seem to be able to interpret correctly.

Confessions ooze from your pen like serum from a septic wound. In your senior year at Overcrowded U of State, you sneak into Honors English, which because you're a math major is verboten, discovering Sylvia Plath and Anne Sexton and Jack Kerouac. Fuel for your fire. But back in those dark days, academia had not yet allowed domestic complainers into the canon of modern poetry. Unthinkable that Jack, Sylvia, and Annie might rub elbows with the likes of Ezra and T.S. The words needlessly self-indulgent glow in red ink in the margins of your poems. You try writing nature poetry—projecting human courage and foibles onto plants and lower invertebrates and vice-versa—but your perverse vision is deemed unacceptable. In a huff, you switch from honors poetry writing to honors short story workshop and in amongst all the Fitzgeralds and Hemingways, you discover Flannery O'Connor and Carson McCullers. You write stories about the mill town where you attended high school and assign your pain to others, then consider taking on a man's name as a pseudonym. In the spring, the English Department invites William Stafford to read at the library. You, and the thirty other students who attend, learn that sane, average-seeming people also write lines of uneven length and that road kill is a valid subject for poetry. Just after the Senior Prom, Allen Ginsberg tours your campus. He is not invited by the English Department and he does not read at the library, but in the gym which is filled with patchouli incense and a thousand students with tie-dyed hair. From Allen you learn that non words can be used in poems along with those snippets of language that play over and over inside your head.

With eyes glazed the color of Ginsberg's saffron robes, you graduate into the real world and head for the Haight-Ashbury. By now it's the 70s. Women have been liberated. Fewer and fewer graybeards tell you that it's not okay to write about the female inhabitants of Northwest mill towns. Nobody bothers to change the names to protect the innocent. As one of your new found contemporary West Coast writer friends, Mary Mackey, puts it: the guilty don't deserve it and the innocent don't need it. Besides Mary, you bond with other members of your planet, Valerie Miner, Faye Kicknosway, Jack Marshall. You attend local poetry readings and discover Susan Griffin, Adrienne Rich, Pat Parker, Ishmael Reed, Simon Ortiz, Judy Grahn, June Jordan, Alta and her Shameless Hussy Press. You get a job through the University of California teaching algebra to people who are called "culturally deprived" and live in "transitioning" neighborhoods. Some of your students are interested in learning about set theory, binary number systems, and the associative and commutative laws of multiplication, though all have more pressing concerns, such as: Is my bike getting stole? Has you got a knife? Or, what do that cross between the number three and the number two mean? Their inner landscape feels oddly familiar. You keep your well-paying, part-time job and moonlight on Fridays teaching through the Poetry in the Schools Program in the same neighborhood. Now you can drop the pretense of numbers and symbols and get down to the brass tacks of your students' "Has You Got a Knife?" stories. At least you think you can until their regular teacher informs you that real poetry rhymes. Monday, when you return to teach the same students algebra, you notice that the teacher never lectures you about the Real Number System. While she is out of the classroom you run with the idea of surreal story problems and the logic of Salvador Dali: What Do You Get When You Cross a Gynecologist and a Xerox Machine?

The endless sunshine and long California days give you and your feminist poets' army time to march the streets of Berkeley in high top, waffle sole, hiking boots. Somewhere along the line you move from a bad parent-child relationship to abusive love relationships. After all, what's intimacy without mistreatment? At about the same time you drop the pretense of the second person plural and embrace the first person singular. I become proficient in writing about the underbelly of things, the sow-bug-and-maggot-egg undersoul of life. A reviewer calls the tone of my work menacing. This word exudes power, inducing a high even more intense than the peyote buttons Allen prescribed.

By now it's the late 70s and the 60s are almost over. I consider myself a feminist confessional poet par excellence. My literary compadres tell it like it is in print. We have our own bookstores, bars, radio programs, and

New York magazine. This truth-telling centers more around what has been done unto us and less of what we have done unto others. What we do unto others is a thread that will be taken up all too soon by the next generation. I enter into an "alternative marriage," because, He tells me, conventional marriage is demeaning to women. My partner in crime edits my work, thriving on its nastiness and the fact that He is the wellspring of my "Daddy" and "Viciousness in the kitchen!" poems. He even lends one of his buddies the money to start a press to publish my first book, which to this day is still "forthcoming." On a Poetry Circus Sideshow Tour, I meet some of the world's "five-star poetry pigs," Bukowski and Hughes among them, and discover they're not Satan. In fact, God strike me dead, some are absolutely charming. My mother had attended something called Charm School, where she'd learned how to walk like a goddess in high heels with an imaginary string tied from her pubic bone to heaven. She also learned the proper etiquette of eating pie (from point to crust) and soup (always spoon away from yourself), things that as a teenager had made me roll on the floor with laughter. My mother's charm school lectures were about the only comic relief I got during my adolescent, no-saying years where, due to circumstances, my family lived in a garage. Not just any garage, but a three-car garage with a Lincoln Continental in the center berth. We kept our clothes in waxed baby coffin-sized boxes, which my father brought home from the slaughterhouse where he worked, and ate TV dinners which I had to share with my younger siblings. When you need adequate nourishment and shelter, eating Banquet frozen pie in tiny bites and always, like Scarlet O'Hara, leaving a tad of crust on your plate to show off your tiny appetite seems beside the point. But after meeting Bukowski and Hughes I'm left with the sinking feeling that my mother and her charm school mentality may have been on to something. Maybe I should have paid more attention to her helpful hints (putting a pair of underpants over my head to protect my make up and clothes while dressing). When she threatened to stop speaking to me unless I started using a lipstick brush, maybe I shouldn't have given up my rummage sale Revlon altogether. For reasons I did not want to fathom, being so bowled over by Ted's and Charles's charm depressed the heck out of me.

Back on my own domestic front, which now fuels the blood spurt that is poetry: My significant other and I join the organic gardening and back-to-the-land craze. We leave Berkeley, come back to Berkeley, leave. In order to support ourselves and our art (he is a landscaper, specializing in people's parks and sculpture gardens), we work on fishing boats in

Alaska. I cook, he's a deck hand. The ill treatment and slaughter of salmon the size of children spawns many poems. There isn't much to do on board, except to listen to fish die and watch men bend their elbows too often. My new MFA degree in creative writing not only helps me think up names for the variations of green that proliferate Sitka and the Alexander Archipelago, but also names for drinks made by odd combinations of liquor. Better to spend as much time as possible on shore where—surprise—I discover there's almost the same number of females in Alaska as males. Many of these women are elderly and sequestered in The Old Pioneer Home where I spend the day on the front steps listening to their yarns.

My alternative marriage's bad end generates even more confessional poetry. Oddly it is here that I reach a turning point, the beginning of the end of my career as a confessional poet. This time my catharsis is not more (and more) "he said /she said" poems, but a novel about the women who helped build Southeast Alaska. Finally finally the stories of the trials and tribulations of others seem more interesting, more important, more healing than my own. But only in fiction. Across the English-speaking world and beyond, first person, eye-witness-account poetry dominates the 1980s. From all quarters confessions come as thick as mosquitoes in August. More and more horrific abuses leap out of the cupboard. The winds of confession howl a single two-syllable word: incest, and with it the nightmarish tales of dysfunction escalate.

By now I've published enough so that I can give up trying to teach Algebra and begin to teach creative writing in a university where the confessions of my students halt me in my tracks. I feel like a magnet for their unburdening. Some of their stories even our National Enquirer news-hungry society isn't ready for (at least I'm not ready for them). Like a serial killer who tortures his victims longer and in a more gruesome fashion with each successive attempt, the crimes confessed in my student's stories and poems become more and more hideous. And my confessions seem more and more insignificant—at least I can't make them appear significant events in literature or even in my own life. My writing starts to sound like an add-a-pearl necklace of complaints and excuses.

The end of the 80s brings me a much more stable life. I live on a farm in the Northwestern foothills of the Cascade Mountains where my new husband and I raise horses. I have to rise every morning at six in order to care for beasts ten times my size, which is better than any antidepressant that I know of. I become strong, healthy, lean, tan, disciplined, learn to live on little sleep. Learn also that I am always always at the mercy of the elements. I come to know that there is such a thing as God's will, because sometimes little foals born with the deck stacked against them survive only because they have a tremendous willingness to thrive. I learn to be vigilant, to read the tiny nuances that, bunched together, bud into change. On a farm, reading between the lines of the proverbial writing-on-the-wall becomes a necessity to survival. But I am what's not so aptly termed a gentleman farmer. Which means that I don't support myself by this endeavor and probably never could. I marvel at the lives of those who had to and did, which consists of most of the people who populated the planet before the twentieth century. Indeed, remnants of nineteenth-century life surround me. People still pan for gold in the Skykomish River that runs near my door. The hollow eyes of silver and copper mines stare out from Haystack Ridge, an area rapidly being clear-cut by the timber industry. Like the nature poet I had tried to be before finding my niche in the confessional, I wait for those Wordsworthian sounds of spring—migrating geese and night croaking frogs—only to be confronted by their chainsaw and bulldozer conquistadors. I hear the unmistakable crash and aftershock of trees falling, which is followed by days of inhaling nothing but a pall of blue smoke generated by burning stump piles.

At first thinking about the last century is a means of escape, then it becomes a valuable tool for coping with farm life. It's an economic given that those who monopolize the powers of transportation rule. Up until the advent of the internal combustion engine, beasts of burden and the wind propelled people and cargo from one place to another. A horse was an important beast of burden. Much of the art of horse husbandry was developed by non-literate people and never written down. What little was documented has been out of print for more than a century. I begin combing pioneer journals for information on blacksmithing, handling, and just out-and-out telepathic communication with equines. Because horses can't speak to tell me where it hurts, I have to learn to read their body language for signs. Modern veterinary science is just that, a science. What I want is information (even the tiniest tidbit) concerning the art of healing and caring for these beasts.

In January of 1990, as I devoured pioneer reminiscences of anyone who had either made the trek by ox or horse across the plains or had been connected with the cavalry, I get the idea of writing a novel about a late nineteenth-century woman miner. I want to set my tale in Washington or Idaho, not the overused venues of Alaska, which I have already written about, or California. As I go about my winter chores, I try to imagine her day-to-day life; washing clothes in glacier run-off, rubbing the soil out with sand, drying her skirts on rocks. During a January mountain snow storm, winds rage at more than eighty miles an hour, bringing down a hundred-foot tree which crashes across the power line and onto a hundred feet of my back pasture fence. No electricity for a week, which means no heat other than wood and no water from my well. No stove, no lights, no oven, no shower. A horse should drink 15 gallons of water a day. My husband and I break the four-inch thick ice on our pond with a hammer and chisel, hauling hundreds of gallons of water about a quarter of a mile by handcart. Most of it sloshes out of the buckets and turns to ice, which makes our next journey to the barn even more interesting. It takes all our energy to keep warm, clean, the horses and ourselves fed and watered. Roads close due to ice and downed power lines, so going to a friend's or a motel isn't possible. No telephone, therefore no moral support. It stops snowing. Temperatures plummet. Trees encased in ice explode when another storm blasts through. The sun sets at about four in the afternoon and rises just after eight the next morning. What we have is long Walkman nights and a short daytime crush to get everything done during the few hours of light. Frozen Red Baron pizza warming on the woodstove proves especially good the following morning with tea made from pine needles steeped in pond water. Then an unforeseen variable: it's the year-of-the-swine-flu and my husband is one of the first casualties.

I imagine my novel's main character, her life and the lives of her neighbors: Endless years spent surviving winter, compounded by new babies and growing children, perhaps a sick or injured husband, and endless isolation—a far cry from the leisure-driven lives of the late twentieth century. Restored to life, my phone rings. A girlfriend calls to complain that her car won't start, she misses her leg waxing appointment and can't get to the tanning booth. While waiting for the overdue tow truck, she's spent twenty extra minutes on her Nordic Trak. I can barely contain myself. I haven't had a shower in six days. In the dugout my main character has cut into the side of a hill near her mineral claim, it's been too cold for three months to do anything but soak her hands and feet in a bucket of melted snow heated by the fire she built.

The county maintenance crew sands and salts the road to my farm. My husband takes fluids and a little day-old pizza crust, but getting out of bed for more than five minutes isn't possible. I drive the two miles to town in a small Japanese car where I buy a dozen lemon bars before trying to fix the smashed fence. I also buy my first latte in days, Handiwipes (which are a poor substitute for a shower, but never mind), and more lantern batteries so that I can plan my lessons for the new semester which begins next week. Because I teach school, I begin reading the reminiscences of Virginia Grainger, a school marm and an early graduate of the University of Washington where I am an instructor of creative writing. In 1890, during her first year homesteading on the other, eastern, side of the Cascade Mountains, directly opposite my farm, she and her husband had no barn. When the snow crusted and temperatures dropped to 60 below, the only cattle to survive were those they brought into their log and stick hut. A March thaw left every coulee filled with the bloated carcasses of white-faced cattle. Typhoid broke out. Virginia's husband was so afflicted he looked more skeletal than anyone at Andersonville Prison and could not rise from his bed. The remaining cattle were too weak to graze on the sparse blades of spring grass and often fell down, unable to rise. Virginia, ill herself, had to crawl out to them with her baby on her back and raise each cow with a fence rail. A hundred years later, my husband is now able to rise and feed the woodstove. As I contemplate the fallen Alaska spruce in my back pasture, the image of Virginia moving hand over hand through the mud in long skirts and bloomers haunts me.

I've never raised a fallen bovine, but raising a cast horse (one that is down and can't get up) is difficult and dangerous. Foals and young horses often cast themselves in the corners of stalls or paddocks by rolling over to itch their backs and then getting trapped against the wall or under a fence rail. It usually takes two people, a rope, and sometimes a two-by-six to raise the beast. I've done it alone, and recall the danger of the hind legs kicking out at me just before the frightened, angry, disoriented horse scrabbles to its feet, lunging—teeth bared—in my direction, holding me accountable for its grief. I can barely accomplish this in good health and can't imagine raising a thousand pound animal while malnourished, so ill I had to crawl, and with a year-old infant strapped to my back. On this day, as the sun sets behind a lacy fringe of hemlock, my husband is well enough to walk to the car, turn on the ignition, and drive to the airport for a week-long meeting in a foreign city leaving me to cope with the storm's wreckage. The novel I intend to write about a woman miner seeps away and the idea of a book of poems concerning the imagined confessions of women like Virginia Grainger takes its place.

When winter quarter starts, I face a fresh sea of faces. Among them a new voice, the children of the children of the sixties who write about what they knew best: poems which sport such titles as: "A Year of Living on Peanut Butter." In this piece, a budding male poet writes in a conversational style concerning communal life with his artist mother and his eight half-brothers and sisters. Their life in a wrecked school bus came to a dramatic close after a visit from Child Protective Services and the author never saw the siblings left in his care again. In another poem, "Men of Color: Agent Orange and Gangrene Green," an angry young woman chronicles her life with a seriously disturbed Vietnam vet of a parent who used his Chronic Combat Fatigue Syndrome as an excuse to deal drugs from the family home.

Sometime while my back was turned, the confessional voice kicked up another notch and was now speeding toward a galaxy far beyond my own. Had my generation done unto the next an exponentially more frightening amount of abuse than our parents had done to us? Are my new students' wounds of a crueler variety, or should I take solace in the fact that they've been given a platform on which to build their narratives? The above student writing is interspersed with coming-of-age-during-the-Epoch-of-AIDS poems. Until approximately 1980, the wages of sin was birth or disease. Now the wages of sin is death. I think about my own work. A poem I have just written concerning a woman shopping at Nordstrom's on the Feast of the Epiphany, trapped in endless after Christmas lines amid a sea of other women trying to look younger and thinner. In the pale January light cast by my fresh-faced students, my work lacks even the power of a complaint and, after a long teaching day, a difficult commute, and late night barn chores, reads like the whinings of a middle-aged, fat-bottomed suburbanite who couldn't see farther than her crows feet. Artful? Possibly—after all, I've been crafting these poems for years. Important? I give it a "2" on the one-to-ten scale.

I delve deeper and deeper into the lives of my pioneer ladies, looking for common ground which begins to leap from the pages. When Virginia Grainger and her friends weren't besieged by weather-related difficulties, they pondered problems as varied and timely as childcare, race relations, alcohol and drug addiction, gangs, health care, drug trafficking, equal pay for equal work, even the problems of having children of different ethnic backgrounds in the same classroom.

Childcare was particularly straightforward; children were tied to chairs, bed posts, wagon wheels, looms; all of which was preferable to the alternative—if left at large they ran the risk of falling into the fire or the river. The question wasn't, To Tie or Not To Tie, but How To Tie. There was the exception of a Pierce County, Washington woman whose husband had been the sheriff. She had her spouse bring home a convict Indian shackled to a ball and chain to mind her children while she edited the local suffragist newsletter, *The Echo*. Why, I wonder, a convict Indian? I become hungry for these lost minutiae of the past and start constructing poems around gems such as this.

The reminiscences of one-room schoolteachers beckon to me. My counterparts in the nineteenth century preferred buildings with thatched roofs, because thatched roofs gave them clout. The professor, as they were called, pulled thrashing rods from the ceiling any time a discipline problem arose. Otherwise, he/she was advised to keep a bundle of hazelnut sticks in all four corners of the room. Why hazelnut? Another lost tidbit cries out to me to be saved and resurrected. Hazelnut, I find out, because after the first strike, the switch returns to its original position and the second, third, and forth blows have as much sting as the first.

Of particular interest to me are the elderly who were interviewed by the WPA Federal Writer's Project in the 1930s. What strikes me about these memoirs is the comparisons made between the deprivations of the 1930s and the privations of the interviewee's post Civil War recession childhoods. The respondents all seemed to be of one mind and that mind was that though they had suffered economic losses after the stock market crash in 1928, their lives during "these recent troubles" were plentiful as compared to their childhoods. As children they had had nothing. The difference between the late 1860s and the 1930s was that as children, it felt as if we all had nothing alike, that there was not the wide (and widening) discrepancy between the haves and have nots. That snippet of language, we all had nothing alike, jumped at me and stuck in my head together with other fragments of language. One of my favorite snippets from the WPA Federal Writers Project archives is: " If you don't worry the bottle of Blue Ruin [corn liquor], you'll never mistake pig weed for amaranth."

The isolation of farm life often makes me want to reach for the bottle of Blue Ruin myself. Gazing at the fallen mastodon spruce in my back pasture, I settle for another dozen lemon bars instead of hot tea spiked with Jim Beam. The big question is how many treats to eat before trudging out to try to fix the smashed fence and how many to save for afterwards. The dead souls whose voices have begun to haunt me had no local bakery; indeed, no mercantile for hundreds of miles, no credit or currency if they did, and no antibiotics to treat their TB or pneumonia, no tetanus or typhoid vaccine, and no running water, except for a creek which, like my pond, froze over several months of the year. When things failed, the answer was try again, try harder, because failure could spell death—what we in the later half of the twentieth century have euphemized down to the bland Saltine wafer of "collateral damage." And it is here in the area of problem-solving that my common ground gives way. The residents of yesteryear were better problem solvers than their descendents. Today our all too common solution seems to be: buy a new one, buy more.

I begin reading for problem solving, finding lots of inspiration but, as I suspected, little common ground. Also I begin visiting my hundred-year-old neighbor and get more inspiration. Her father had raised horses which he sold to miners outside of Boise. Three days before she was born, the family's house burned down. On a snowy February evening, my neighbor came into this world in a stallion's stall. Bud, the stallion, had been moved in with a mare. My neighbor said that her mother once told her that the thing she remembered most about the birth was the mare rubbing her tail against the wall next to her. This kernel of information was one of the only tidbits she had from her mother, who died of heart failure while scrubbing the floor when my neighbor was only six. Her father's new wife bloodied her with a stick for no reason when no one was looking. My neighbor imparts these stories to me while her daughters drop in to praise the afghan she's been crocheting. When they leave she lowers her voice and tells me about what happened when she went to live with her older sister. My neighbor had been sent to work in her brother-in-law's trading post, sorting apples and potatoes. In her words, the brother-in-law was always trying to get her to himself and feel where her breasts would be. He told my neighbor that if she said anything to her sister about these "touchings," it would kill her. The brother-in-law was held in high esteem in the community. And for this reason, my neighbor tells me, she never put much stake in public opinion. She tells me this story many times with never a word altered and never a relative within hearing. It feels as if she cannot take this story to her grave, but even at age one hundred has not found a confessor. My unspoken thoughts tell her: I will be your witness.

Shortly after my electricity and well and shower and heat are restored, I discover that the daughter of one of Virginia Grainger's neighbors is still living, age one hundred and one, and I decide to visit her. I couldn't call on Signe on a Monday, she told me when I telephoned to arrange an interview, because she works Mondays at a rest home, teaching ladies how to knit receiving blankets for newborns. She lives alone, making dolls in her spare time. When I arrive at her sparkling clean apartment, I admire the photo of her 100th birthday celebration on the table next to me. "That's my good dress," Signe says of the navy blue velvet, semi-formal gown she wears while seated at a table heaped with flowers and surrounded by relatives. Signe raised seven children alone. Her husband worked building boats at the Tacoma docks during and after World War I. When he deserted the family, she sold the milk cow and yearling calf for one hundred-and-fifty dollars in order to buy a house, because no one would rent to a single mother. No milk, but they had a roof over their heads and saved apple parings from the tree in the front yard to make vinegar. After Signe had put all her children through the University or vocational college, she went to nursing school. When she graduated, she bought herself a good dress—ten dollars, a terrible extravagance at the time. But she just had to have it, she told me, because it was the same midnight blue of the early hours of Armistice. On the eve of the end of the First World War, her only daughter had gone out with a friend and not come home. The neighbors had found the girls playing on the swings at the schoolhouse. "Do you think those children would be found alive today?" She asks me, then continues; "I'm still not over the fright. And when I saw that dress in the same color as the evening sky the night they found my daughter safe, I just had to have it." Signe points to herself in the framed photo of her hundredth birthday party and asks if I'd like to see her gown. I'm speechless. I think of my many closets of clothes. I think of my now seemingly ridiculously unimportant poem about shopping at Nordstrom's.

On the two-hour drive home from visiting Signe, my troubles pale into a realm beyond the trivial. Instead of writing a novel about a woman silver miner, or poems concerning the life of a gentleman farmer, I decide to become a miner for the forgotten minutiae of everyday life of the past, for Common Ground, for snippets of lost language. These set the pitch for the chorus of voices ringing between my ears. Virginia Grainger and her neighbors speak to me, their trials flowing out through my pen. I know about isolation and cold weather and endless hours of chores. Virginia and her contemporaries often wrote about these in their diaries—or later in reminiscences—with the lack of emotion of someone composing a grocery list. But my eye is keen and I pry out the tokens of abuse, the marks of addiction, and the theater-of-the-absurd logic of dysfunction. Under careful scrutiny the messages my foremothers scrawled between the lines of their diaries become more and more clear. What was it that washed these women's souls of the dust of everyday life? I imagine their confessions and then I start to write in the first person in a voice I choose to own, but a voice not my own.

The Man Who Rode Away: What D. H. Lawrence Means to Today's Readers

Gary Adelman

1

In fall 1997 I taught an undergraduate honors seminar on D.H. Lawrence in which we read *Sons and Lovers*, *The Rainbow*, *Women in Love*, *Studies in Classic American Literature*, Volume II of *The Complete Short Stories*, *Sea and Sardinia*, *Etruscan Places*, selected poems (especially *Pansies*, *Nettles*, and *More Pansies*), and *Lady Chatterley's Lover*. I was unprepared for the hostile reaction of the class. Nothing here, one would think, nor in the mandatory packet of critical essays (by Kinkead-Weekes, Graham Holdernes, Joyce Carol Oates, etc.), could explain the antagonism that began to gather with *Women in Love* and literally exploded with *Studies*. I assigned one-page responses every week and had students keep journals for their more private reactions to the experience of reading Lawrence, for I wanted them at the end to be able to write as honest an analysis as they could of their reading experiences. Only two students in the class of thirteen expressed a positive view of Lawrence in their final papers.

A few general remarks: The students were juniors and seniors, ten women and three men, all of them high achievers as indicated by their GPA's. A few had read a short story or two, "The Rockinghorse Winner," "The Horse-Dealer's Daughter"; only one had read a Lawrence novel. This is not surprising. None of my colleagues teach Lawrence other than the occasional short story. They will say that they have let go of the Leavisite version of Lawrence as a secular saint with some privileged understanding of life, and that if they think of Lawrence at all, it is as a crude, historical curiosity. Lawrence was shocking to my students, who came to him innocently, and found his "thought adventures" insulting. Just about all of them adored *The Rainbow* and confessed (reluctantly) to enjoying *Lady Chatterley's Lover*. I've already mentioned the souring that began with *Women in Love*. Many of the students were bothered by Lawrence's preoccupation with incest and anal sex, labeling it "twisted" and "perverse," and this uneasiness probably fed their growing exasperation with him. For the bulk of the course, all but one of the women hated him, which their final papers make very clear:

"Feeling trapped in his crazy, created little world. His works affect you like a virus, a poison challenging everything you ever believed. He's antidemocracy, anti-American, anti-capitalist, anticonventional marriage, antisocial, and antireligious."

"I hate him for his overt sexism, his cynical view of love and heterosexual relationships, his fascination with incestuous language and immature flirtation with homeroticism, the constant vexation and negativity present in all of his works."

"[*Studies in Classic American Literature*] was the writing of a definite and obvious fascist. I was shocked at his honest belief that there are intrinsic leaders who command our submission."

"He describes women [in his essay on *The Scarlet Letter*] 'as sending out waves of destructive malevolence which eat out the inner life of a man like a cancer.' I was overwhelmed with hatred at Lawrence's desire to not only insult and degrade, but attempt to completely annihilate the female essence from the world."

"Who wants a relentless forcing of personal ideology and a multitude of obsessions thrust on them? Descontruction, Marxist, and gender theory are all invested heavily in questioning textual authority. The current English major is trained to dig as deeply as possible into a text to find anything that suggests social implications, and Lawrence's views on women, class, race, and homosexuality are blatantly sexist, fascist, racist, and homophobic. So it is completely unrealistic to expect anything other than general hostility towards Lawrence."

"I loved *The Rainbow*. The Ursula of *Women in Love* is too easy. If she was as real as she was in *The Rainbow*, she never would have given in to Birkin. I look at her as a sell-out. What she gained was a man, but what she lost was her soul. She lost everything that made her who she had been. She merely became attached to Birkin who was attached to another man. I really hated Lawrence for this. I felt the betrayal because I felt such a connection to Ursula initially. I felt that Lawrence was implying that the strength and independence of her character was something fleeting. It was something that a woman could have only temporarily. . . . Time and again I felt that I could not handle another word in which he was destroying everything I hold important in life."

While I was teaching this hostile seminar, I initiated a correspondence about Lawrence with 110 novelists, of whom forty-four responded. Subsequently, I sent these forty-four respondents the above-quoted reactions of my students. I'd like to present now a sampling of *their* reactions to my students. Almost every author responded to the quotations: at least a polite "you certainly have your work cut out for you," or "I'm glad I'm not trying to teach Lawrence in this climate," or "is what we used to call 'reading' dead?" or "they [the politically correct students] and their professors need their heads examined."

Most of the novelists were put on the defensive by the students' criticisms. Doris Lessing, for example, remonstrated that one cannot separate Lawrence's misanthropic writing of the twenties from his illness.

Gail Godwin quipped, "Maybe it [*Studies in Classic American Literature*] should be put on the academic 'index' (i.e. forbidden) until students have passed a maturity test." In her mind,

> *Studies* is best appreciated by readers a) with a healthy sense of humor, b) with a strong sense of self so that they can revel in Lawrence's punches without being insulted or threatened by him, c) who understand that great literature is a *conversation* of voices and not any one writer's monologue.
>
> A Lawrence diatribe is a welcome balance to a Jamesian reflection or a Kafka rumination, and so on. . . . No student or reader, however infected by –isms, or –osms, or gender studies, can deny him his energy and passion.

Steven O'Connor was one of a handful of writers who felt a strong affinity with the students:

> What interested me most about your students' reactions to Lawrence was how different their critical vocabulary and concepts are than those I would have employed when I was their age and, like them, reading Lawrence for the first time. I suspect, however, that despite the different terminology, many of your students may be responding to the same things that bothered me. Some of what they call sexist, cynical, and immature may well be

what I thought of as false, dishonest, neurotic, overly romantic, pretentious, and so on. If this is true, then it might not be feminist criticism that has sunk Lawrence, but some larger failing that we are simply hearing about now in feminist terminology, and will soon hear about in the terms of the next fashion in criticism.

Three of the most strongly worded letters came from Ursula K. Le Guin, Helen Benedict, and A. S. Byatt. Ursula K. Le Guin wrote:

> Of course he was a sexist. He was a working class, white Englishman born in the nineteenth century. He was a sexist and a racist, is there any argument? A man who wrote (I may not have the exact words of the quote), "fucking a black woman would be like fucking mud"? . . . Your students seem to be giving it to him and reacting to him with honesty and forthrightness. The last student quotation in your letter is, to me, right on the mark. Between *The Rainbow* and *Women in Love* he began to sell-out, somehow. . . .When I was eighteen, as I wrote you, like that kid 'I loved *The Rainbow*,' and like her I felt terribly betrayed by *Women in Love*, but I thought—as I was supposed to—that it was my fault. I did not have her clarity of mind and heart, perhaps because I did not have the social support as an 18-year-old girl that she has, that would have let me say when I read it, "no, I'm not just stupid or insensitive, I've been betrayed: he's letting me (and my namesake, Ursula) down. He's selling women out." Maybe that's the difference between the time when I first read Lawrence and "the contemporary moment." In 1947 I didn't have—as she has, and as you and I have—all the feminist critical thought of the last three decades to support me. Other people have worked hard to give you, her, and me the freedom to think such thoughts in 1998. Certainly as a feminist my wish would be to see Lawrence's readers get past mere judgmentalism, mere "condemnation," to try to find what has become unacceptable, and what is still valid for contemporary readers in the work of an immensely flawed, frequently despicable, frequently silly, very interesting, very powerful writer.

Helen Benedict wrote,

> Stephen O'Connor, my husband, showed me your letter about D.

H. Lawrence and I felt compelled to respond. I am a writer also (my two published novels are *A World Like This* and *Bad Angel* and I have written four nonfiction books). I am English and have read all of Lawrence's works. Stephen and I differ in our opinions of him. I have always loved Lawrence's work.

In reading your students' comments about Lawrence I was struck by their lack of historical perspective. He was one of the very first working class writers in England to be published and taken seriously, no mean feat in that class-ridden society, and much of his work is about class struggle, particularly *Sons and Lovers* and *Women in Love*. Do you know his trilogy of plays about life in a mining family? Brilliant, and virtually forgotten, as far as I know. It is easy for students nowadays to accuse someone of Lawrence's generation of modern sins such as sexism, but without understanding the historical and ideological context in which he wrote, such criticism is practically meaningless. In fact, it can be argued that Lawrence's recognition of women's sexuality was advanced for his time— even liberating. I am writing this as a feminist and author of feminist non-fiction books, you understand, but, nevertheless, I think students' charges of sexism are woefully uneducated. I blame this less on Women's Studies than on the inadequate education in history most American students get . . . What was happening in England before and between the wars was nothing short of class revolution. World War I broke down many class prejudices because men of all walks of life were thrown together in horrible conditions. This resulted in a burst of art and literature at the time that rejected traditions of the upper class and looked at working class life as respectable and human for the first time . . . Many artists and writers of the time wanted to be shocking. They wanted to explore poverty, portray the working class as fully human, grovel in humanity's sordid worries. (Stephen Spender, George Orwell, Wyndham Lewis, Walter Greenward are the authors I'm thinking of. Vorticism was one of the revolutionary art movements of that period.) Lawrence was ahead of his time in all this—indeed, he spearheaded much of it . . . The idea that students are dismissing Lawrence because he doesn't fit contemporary ideas of a pleasant person is deeply shocking. Go that route and we'll have no one left to read but Danielle Steele.

A.S. Byatt sees both sides:

> I am . . . very interested in your project . . . on whether we can read what past writers wrote as they wrote it. I think we can, but need to relearn "saturation readings" and the postponement of judgment. Modern students (and many teachers) have spent so much time reading postmodern, feminist and deconstructionist theory that they simply don't have the range of reading in the original literary texts to get an ear for them. I was painfully amused by your student who wrote "Who wants a relentless forcing of [personal] ideology and a multitude of obsessions thrust on them?" and goes on to list with approval what I regard as relentless ideological preoccupations, political if not personal, and certainly thrust—deconstruction, Marxist, and gender theory. We are embedded in a very subtle and violent field of stock responses which make true judgment and patient and generous reading almost impossible. . . .
>
> I was complaining in the British Council's Cambridge Seminar one year that feminism had weakened novels by women in my time—before me there were Murdoch, Lessing, Spark, Bedford, etc. and now most of the good writers in Britain are peacocky men. Terry Hawkes said that the women's creativity had gone into feminist theory, and I thought sadly that he might be right. . . .
>
> All the same, there is something silly and sinister about Lawrence's preoccupations. . . .
>
> It's odd that I feel angry with your students for saying what I myself might well say in conversation—I think it's because I know they haven't seen the art, the imagination, the power, as well.

2

My original letter to the 110 novelists sought to determine how Lawrence is perceived today. Here is how I framed the problem:

> Why is D. H. Lawrence no longer important? For some time now I have felt in my bones that he has "disappeared" as a point of

reference for writers, especially novelists. As a matter of fact, he has undergone a sudden, remarkable decline at the university. Not so long ago we thought him one of the most astonishing writers of our century!

What I'd like to know is how you feel about Lawrence, whether he clarifies things for you, whether you think of him at all? Apropos, I came upon a remark Milan Kundera made about Lawrence in a piece on Kafka:

> I am thinking about D. H. Lawrence, that committed eulogist of eros, who, in *Lady Chatterley's Lover*, tried to rehabilitate sexuality by rendering it lyrical and romantic. But lyrical sexuality is far more ludicrous than the lyrical sentimentality of the last century.

Is it ludicrous to believe that "the sexual act is for leaping off into the unknown as from a cliff's edge"? Fifteen years ago Lawrence was greatly admired for a kind of "furious honesty of observation," and also for that mixture of tenderness and reverence, a sort of "cosmic piety." He wanted very much to believe that there was a life force in people that his words could liberate. Silly?

Some of the writers responded that Lawrence was never important to them. But most acknowledged his early influence, for which they were grateful, and a number continue to read him. Many respondents rose to defend him as a writer whose work will outlast the fluctuations of literary reputation. Most of the replies entirely disregarded the sexism that repels students and faculty on my campus. It is possible, of course, that some authors have not read the fiction written between 1918 and 1926. The few occasions Kate Millet is mentioned, it is in the context of "the unfortunate gender politics of literary study in the last twenty years [which] have made him an embarrassing model" (A. S. Byatt).

A number of the writers feared that literature in general was in jeopardy. "You might have asked why is Joyce no longer important, or Nabokov, or Hemingway. Who *is* important, that's what I'd like to know," says Leslie Epstein.

Without exception, *Sons and Lovers*, when mentioned, is acknowledged a masterpiece. Rick Powers and Stephen O'Connor remark on its importance in their becoming writers.

Lawrence is frequently seen as a casualty of the permissive climate of our age, a climate he inadvertently helped to create. "Sex now is not such a big deal as it was for Lawrence in the days when more things were forbidden and had the glamor of being forbidden," says A. S. Byatt.

> Sex is now interesting . . . as a political phenomenon and as a passing pleasure not quite as good as good drugs [notes Eric Craft], but not as an adventure, a discovery, or a manifestation of the life force. People have had enough of sex. It's everywhere, and if overexposure has not quite succeeded in making it dull, it has succeeded in making it commonplace, and the commonplace is not . . . interesting.

"When Lawrence wrote phallus and [we] see only dick," Dale Peck writes, "then Lawrence will remain in decline."

This precisely is J. M. Coetzee's point in a chapter on Lawrence from his recent book on censorship, *Giving Offense* (to which he refers me in his letter). The crux of his argument is that taboo is a necessary condition for reader interest in *Lady Chatterley's Lover*. Coetzee has no doubt that in denying its transgressiveness, that is, its scandalous power, and claiming for it an improving moral purpose, Lawrence (and those who testified on his behalf at the trial and swayed the judgment of the ruling) robbed the subject of its glamor and mystery. Coetzee notes that nowadays, in our age of license, the force of the novel that Lawrence has written, "a novel embroiled in complex ways with taboo," has gone slack, and having lost its glamor, *Lady Chatterley's Lover* appears silly.

Dale Peck's remark suggests that Lawrence's attitude toward sex (and the mood of the 60s and 70s when he was so popular) is loftier than that of the present time, and if he seems silly, the problem is to be looked for in those who think so, not in him. Writing of Lawrence's declining readership, J. R. Salamanca contrasts his truly religious devotion to art and his passionate honesty with the new Puritans of the affluent middle class and their search for phony absolution.

Salamanca and Dale Peck write jeremiads against our present culture in defense of Lawrence, as if his decline merely testifies to the degeneracy of our time. Doris Lessing, John Fowles, Tim O'Brien, and others embrace Lawrence no less unconditionally but without mounting a political defense. In their minds he is synonymous with great literature. This point of view represents one side, the extreme side of an argument which runs through the correspondence like a debate.

The other extreme position regards Lawrence as dated, out of tune, "simply too grandiose for the modern era" (as Martin Amis puts it). "They [the novels] seem old-fashioned," writes David Huddle. "Lawrence's stylistic 'heat' is absurd to our 'cool' ear. His passion—once so thrillingly rebellious—now comes off as sort of Boy Scoutish." Rick Powers notes, "Earnestness has become the kiss of death in the 1990's academy . . . . The novels that critics most trust are those that build into themselves their own deconstruction."

"You feel him wanting to be an authority, a teacher, a sage. And sages date far more quickly than non-sages," says Julian Barnes. "His decline could have something to do with hormones," says Ursula Le Guin. "At fifteen Lawrence could be a revelation. At forty-five, well! Kundera is a nasty man, but he has a point there."

In other words, the correspondence tends to be polarized. On one side, Lawrence is old-fashioned and silly. On the other, the contemporary moment itself is to blame for his decline, the decades of the 80s and 90s, being "so hard-edged," as Margaret Drabble puts it, "so deterministic—defeatist in some ways, so merciless in others, and above all so cynical."

Debated also are several closely interconnected questions. Will Lawrence live on or is he finished, a voice gone dead? "Maybe much of his work is done," speculates Margaret Drabble. "He liberated us. And like bad children, we forget how hard and bravely he worked for us." Lynne Sharon Schwartz, Ursula Le Guin, William Gibson, and others say more or less the same thing.

John Updike wonders, "You might be misreading a temporary blip in his reputation as a permanent decline." Richard Ford says, "My faith, though, is that if he's got anything to say to young readers (and it's toward them that our sights are set) then he'll survive. If not, then that's all. His moment will have passed."

Then there's the question as to whether he will survive because of his art as distinct from his ideology. "One should read him as a writer and not as a preacher," says Umberto Eco. Supposing this possible, the notion that Lawrence will survive because of his artistic power as divorced from his "evangelizing" depends on whether he is, after all, appreciated as a great artist.

"Wading through Lawrence's thick, thick prose can be a daunting proposition," says Dale Peck. "Often I just can't do it, and when I do revisit Lawrence, I tend to read the shorter work." And, "I never liked

D. H. Lawrence, could not see excellence in his writing. I find it turgid and dull," says Annie Proulx. "Of course that was thirty years ago. No idea how he would read today, and I am not tempted."

"But what I love about him," writes A. S. Byatt in defense of his art, "are the perfectly constructed, irreducible encounters between people, the placing of people in landscapes, the light, and not the pronouncements."

Says John Updike, "But as a writer, a magical writer in the way that a fierce wind blows through his work and picks up a scene, a face, an exchange, he cannot be erased from the English literature of this century."

"And then his extraordinary ability to put down words and create a landscape or building or human figure—as Monet might put down paint," says Helen Dunmore. "There's scarcely another writer to touch him there in this century."

The most eloquent defense of Lawrence by a novelist is John Fowles's afterword to the 1994 Ecco Press edition of *The Man Who Died.* He begins by saying that for him, Lawrence remains "a peak in the Everest range . . . much too lastingly significant to be forgotten," but that there had been a time when he too was caught up in "the universal disparagement." Lawrence was impossible to swallow, so cock-sure, "too easy to make fun of, to mock," and aspects of his writing, especially during his last decade, were "near impossible to defend or justify, indeed sometimes near the ridiculous."

Fowles now confesses he had been "stupidly wrong" to jeer at Lawrence and to have behaved so crudely to a fellow novelist. No one excels him, Fowles says, in his ability to feel and venerate the "existingness" in things.

> Our philosophies and religions, our pleasures and pastimes, both our cultural and commoner routines and habits . . . it is almost as if they are deliberately (devilishly!) designed to blur and abstract the fact that I exist—or better, that the 'I' exists. . . . It was his acute and often raging horror at the insanely blind folly of humankind, especially of its more fortunate and better educated, and their total failure to see the reality of their situation, that must be seen as the constant drive behind Lawrence for most of his adult life. (96–97)

Fowles continues, in Lawrence's fight against modern civilization, he placed passion and the quality of sensations before intellect, and was given to excesses, the worst being his brush with fascism; and though his extremism was a consequence of the risks he was willing to take "to save us," it was no less repellent for all that. Fowles is also repelled by Lawrence's "often rather painfully obtrusive masculinism-phallicism" and "rashes of anti-Semitism," and finds his descriptions of sex embarrassing.

Even so, Fowles concludes that virtues of Lawrence's writing "enormously" exceed his defects. For the world "is very sick, and has become several times worse since Lawrence himself died," and whatever it is that makes him seem a mirror for the reader, in part "his hyper-awareness, his 'existingness,' his soul energy," and also "the almost hectic seriousness with which [he] saw mankind's deep-rooted psychological and emotional problems," make him all the more terribly significant now (89–101).

My students hated Lawrence for personal and ideological reasons. My theory-minded colleagues refused to teach him because he was too crude: "Why should we dirty our hands with him?" It was left to Lawrence's fellow writers to take on the complexity of the connection between art, the artist, and history.

A. S. Byatt:

I think it is precisely his combination of prophecy and art which has caused the decline in his reputation. Also he has gone under the microscope of politically correct scrutiny and some of his prophetic stances do look uncomfortably similar to various fascist ones. . . . And then *Lady Chatterley* became much more central as a point of reference for readers of his work than it should be, because of the trial, although Leavis was surely right in saying it was a minor work and not even very good.

I think this is a pity because if you can disentangle the slightly ludicrous prophet from the very powerful artist he remains one of the very great novelists. (I know you can't really disentangle them, any more than you can with Blake.) I think of my own work as a novelist in a tough visionary line that goes through George Eliot, Balzac, *The Rainbow*, and *Women in Love*, and he means more to me than either Forster or Virginia Woolf. . . .

I wonder if you know the novels of David Storey? I think *Radcliffe* is one of the major novels of my time in this country, and I think it may be forgotten because it is a Lawrentian novel and has become involved in Lawrence's curious disappearance.

Ursula K. Le Guin:

You have a good question there, I think—at least, I had asked it of myself a few years back, when I looked at the Lawrence novels in my bookshelves and realized that though I had loved them passionately in my twenties, I was never going to reread them, nor my copy of his complete poems, and wondered why.

It may be that Lawrence was one of these writers who is genuinely important, necessary, for a certain period, and unimportant outside that period—like, off the top of my head, Bulwer-Lytton; or indeed Lytton Strachey? It's as if their work was done, the road is built, everybody walks on it. I would venture that James Joyce was a very new and useful road, that led us somewhere new but that is really not much use walking back over; whereas Virginia Woolf is a vast and still only partly explored landscape. Maybe Lawrence was a road?

But he *did* "liberate my lifeforce," when I was 18 years old and got high on *The Rainbow*—I have no wish either to make easy fun of Lawrence or to dismiss him. I'm grateful to him. Even when he was dead wrong it was exciting, I had to argue with him, engage my mind and soul with him. Wrestling with the angel—one of his pet images, no?

Erica Jong:

D. H. Lawrence remains important to me—as does Henry Miller even if the Academy scorns him. We live in the age of political correctness—which in every epoch is antithetical to art. The real artist is a born upstart, will never (willingly) wear a rosette in his buttonhole and pontificate at symposia of disgruntled old men (who today are sometimes also women).

Hey! You can teach Lawrence and refute Kundera (who is also trendy but for a fleeting moment). Remember—Shakespeare also went out of style in my beloved eighteenth century and they even rewrote Lear and gave it a happy ending! Forget about literary fashion. If words live, they live. If not, they turn to dust. Like their authors.

Doris Lessing:

Who has said D. H. Lawrence is no longer important? He seems to have fallen foul of some ideologues. But as we all know, ideology is the most changeable thing in the world. And there is another thing—the United States is not all there is—I think at least some Americans seem to think that outside the United States is some kind of cultural vacuum.

D. H. L. wrote at least two books which are among the greatest of our century—*Sons and Lovers* and *The Rainbow*. I have recently reread both—they are wonderful. Other novels have good bits—but there are people who swear, for example, by *Women In Love*.

He has also written some of the great short stories of our literature. Also good poems.

Some female hysterics have decided that they are not "politically correct"—but as far as I am concerned anyone who uses that phrase at all is not a serious person.

Stephen O'Connor:

I am afraid that I am evidence of Lawrence's declining literary fortunes. I loved *Sons and Lovers*, which I read when I was in high school, but not since. While I no longer remember the plot very clearly, I do remember being fascinated and a little shocked by his portrayal of working class British life. I was especially interested in the relationship between the sensitive protagonist and his brutal (as I remember him) father and his desperate but supportive mother. This was one of the books that inspired me to be a writer, both because of the son's desire to be an artist and because I felt that through this book I had been shown "real life" by an author with a keen vision, uncompromising honesty and a sense of beauty.

I am afraid, however, that I have never had that feeling about the other novels by Lawrence that I have read—*Women in Love*, *The Rainbow* and *Lady Chatterley's Lover*. There is too much mysticism in his portrayal of sexuality for me, and he tends to romanticize what seem to me to be some of the more neurotic elements of male–female relationships. It is hard for me to be more specific, because I haven't read these books since I was in college. The truth is that I never felt that Lawrence was showing me "real life" in these later books. I didn't find his vision keen or feel that he was particularly honest—especially by comparison to the other writers whom I discovered at about the same time and continue to love today: Tolstoy, Kafka, George Eliot, and Dostoyevsky. I was so turned off to Lawrence, in fact, that I never bothered to read his other novels and never went back to reread these. It is possible that I have been unfair to him. My opinion of him was formed in my early twenties, and Lord knows I've changed a lot since then. But even the quote in your letter bothers me. Portraying sex as a "leap into the unknown," especially a leap from the edge of a cliff, just seems impossibly grandiose to me. I take a much more earthy view of sex, I guess. I prefer to see it as much more like every other form of intercourse between human beings. It can be funny, phony, slap-dash, disgusting or lame, as well as thrilling, beautiful, scary and fun. Can it be magnificent? Maybe. Sublime? Can anything that happens between two human beings be sublime? I tend to doubt it. In any event, it seems to me that grand abstractions like "life force" and the "cosmic" are for angels—or gods and goddesses—not for men and women. So, yes, I do think it's all a bit silly.

Dale Peck:

I think he was always a rarefied taste, always a bit hard to teach (especially in a typical academic environment, where college students still giggle when a teacher uses the word *phallus*). Lawrence is one of very few British writers who didn't write his books for the classroom. He didn't want them taught: he wanted them *lived*.

But if Lawrence is in decline, I think it's due primarily to the incorporation of a perverted version of his idea(l)s into everyday thinking, indeed, into everyday life. Call it the sexual revolution or whatever, but it's pretty clear that people are now fucking with the, um, *frequency* with which Lawrence hoped they would fuck. What most people haven't managed to do, of course, is lose their Victorian hang-ups about sex, and I suspect that if Lawrence were here right now he'd be producing tempered if not actually temperate versions of his vision. I think Lawrence saw his work as a correction of the Sadean impulse to re-enact the power inequalities of political life in the bedroom, but the great sex propagandists who came after him, people like Durrell and what's his name, Henry Miller, not to mention those awful Beats, returned to Sade. It's the easier—I want to say *lazier*—route for philosopher as well as for practitioner, so it should hardly be surprising that it proved more popular than Lawrence's stern idealism. And I do think it was stern: Dionysian excess is fairly easy to achieve—just about any frat boy or sorority girl can do it—but a conscious, conscientious move beyond rationality is exceedingly difficult, practically oxymoronic, perhaps impossible, perhaps only an ideal. Nevertheless, Lawrence thought it was a worthy ideal, and what is fiction if not an area in which to explore the ideal and the impossible?

Tied to this issue is one of non-sexual politics. *Lady Chatterley's Lover* (speaking of which: it's so like Milan Kundera, a lazy half-wit if ever there was one, to point up a writer's failing by attacking his second- or third- or fourth-best book) is "ludicrous" not because of its lyrical sexuality, which is laughable only in the way that great passion seems laughable to those unable to feel it, but because of the simplistic incorporation of Lawrence's socialism into the book. The economics, as it were, corrupt the romance, and these flaws to the best of my memory aren't present in *Women in Love*, in *The Fox and* "England, My England," in the great short story, "The Prussian Officer." In fact, "The Prussian Officer" is a prime example of how people like Kundera miss Lawrence's whole point, which wasn't merely that one should love—and show love, and make love—with true abandon, but that one should transcend rationality in all things, that the individual's true master should be his or her natural, body-driven impulses (problematic terms, I know, that two decades of feminist, queer, and post-structuralist cultural critics have been struggling to make sense of). In other words, where Lawrence wrote *phallus* Kundera sees only *dick*, and as long as the Kunderan reading prevails then Lawrence will remain in decline, since, viewed in those terms, his novels seem like nothing more than a dated version of MTV, or chaste Harlequin romances. . . .

There is a passage in *Women in Love* that I've never forgotten in the decade or so since I first read the book:

"If you are walking westward," he said, "you forfeit the northern and eastward and southern direction. If you admit a unison, you forfeit all the possibilities of chaos."

For a long time, I've wanted to write a nonfiction book called *Forfeiting the West*. It would be about how the late twentieth-century liberal vision, with its simplistic notions of unity, equality, and sociality, has failed, because it refuses to recognize the chaos at the heart of the human psyche. But that's where we are: we've embraced "the west," embraced "unity," and until we let them go then we must forfeit every other direction, forfeit chaos, and forfeit Lawrence.

And finally,

William Gass:

In my opinion Lawrence has fallen out of favor because (1) most writers do during the generations immediately following their deaths. James did. Woolf would have if she hadn't caught the feminist wave, which saved her from some proletarian criticism; (2) because the present P/C climate rates work according to its correctness, which Lawrence lacks; (3) because Lawrence is sentimental, insufficiently ironic and relatively old-fashioned formally speaking; (4) because Lawrence's ambiguous sexuality in comparison with his perceived fascist inclinations worries women and gays equally. Lawrence preaches, but P/C likes preaching if it likes what is preached, whereas I don't like preaching regardless of what is hullaballoo'd. P/C ignores esthetic quality unless it finds it keeping company with disapproved ideas and attitudes, and, when it does, that conjunction makes matters only worse.

I detest Lawrence's anti-intellectualism, but as a formalist, his ideas are irrelevant to me (so long as they don't disrupt the art); they are only material—givens. Lawrence can't be left out of the rusty old canon. Some of his poetry is as good as it gets. The prose of his travel books is as sensuous, paced and observant as any in English, and there are pages and pages of the novels which cannot be surpassed for beauty and sureness of touch. Few rival him as an informal letter writer—maybe Byron. P/C will pass, and when it does Lawrence will be back. It isn't readers who decide, because something suits their mood, that it has quality. Quality determines quality, and it is up to us to discern it for ourselves. Lawrence may be a flawed artist (how many aren't?), but he is a great one—and like General MacArthur, he will return.

3

With Lawrence's presence felt more as an absence or negativity in academe, it appears ironic that Cambridge University Press has produced scholarly editions of twenty-five volumes of Lawrence's work and seven volumes of his letters since 1979, thirty-two volumes in twenty years, an almost unparalleled rate for editions providing meticulous textual accuracy and containing copious explanatory notes and references. Ten volumes of works and an index volume to the letters are still forthcoming, including (in the 1999 schedule) a two-volume set of Lawrence's plays, separate volumes for each of the first two versions of *Lady Chatterley's Lover*, and the 1916 (first completed) draft of *Women in Love*. Add to this the completion in January 1998 of the three-volume Cambridge biography of Lawrence, the definitive Lawrence, the labor of a team of three scholars each authoring one of the volumes. All this furious activity, as if Cambridge were staging a spectacular theatrical performance to a near-empty house!

Or will these publications help to rehabilitate Lawrence? "Writers, posthumous and otherwise, need their champions," Gail Godwin wrote me. "Maybe it's part of a teacher's mission to champion the writers who kept him alive, on the quest."

I admitted to my hostile seminar, meeting their antagonism (which was also directed at me because they felt that I was excusing him by not taking a definite stand), that much of the writing Lawrence produced between

1918 and 1926 is corrupted by an archaic and absurd sexual philosophy. But did I believe this? Were *The Fox*, "The Princess," "The Ladybird," and "The Woman Who Rode Away" aesthetic failures because they were philosophically unpalatable? I said, why isn't it possible for you to separate out the "good" from the "bad" Lawrence and continue to admire the former? Those were empty words. I was not interested in making distinctions: I wanted them to understand what happened to his thinking, how it evolved during the War. I wanted to kindle their admiration so I could say: And after all, has anyone been more central as a critic of society, as a psychologist of culture, yes, and as a prophet of the risks ahead? I would have liked to hear them pick up on his pure acetylene.

I was not out to convert the students to Lawrence's "final, achieved figuration of the truth of the world" (as Fredric Jameson puts it). I only wanted to give Lawrence a fair chance. In any event, they backed away from my explanations. I might as well have been piping in canned music. They were wary of being tricked into admiring any facet of "perhaps the most pathologically sexist author that the modern English canon . . . has managed to produce" (in the judgment of Terry Eagelton).

Twenty-five years ago Lawrence was read (to the shame of many a cultural critic today) as a prophet and seer, as an absolute. But the postmodern literary left has awakened, they will say, like an adolescent from his dreaminess to the necessities of the mean bread and cheese question: What has Lawrence to do with real political goals and ethical reform of the world? How can teaching Lawrence play a part in the averting of fascism? The charisma of style and personality coupled with a systematic world view—his unmistakable signature—are things of the past, archaic, flawed and irrelevant. The vigilant critic will be more discerning about the means of social control and political subjugation without him.

No wonder, then, that while dissertations on Woolf have tripled since 1980, and those on Joyce and Conrad have doubled, the numbers for Lawrence have remained about the same, half of the dissertations, significantly, being hostile to him. No wonder that *The D. H. Lawrence Review*, for thirty years the storehouse of criticism, reviews, and information, is on the brink of extinction.

In addition, my undergraduate students were hostile for another reason: they felt betrayed. They revered *The Rainbow*, identifying with the authoritarian voice of the implied narrator as if that voice were their own conscience, a transcendental presence, and then continued to hear it as a tone of exhortation, of imperious command, in subsequent works which they hated. They then read back into the early Lawrence they loved a forecast of the later, doing so with the embittered emotions of innocence betrayed. They did not want to hear explanations, which they regarded as excuses. They were mad as hell and wanted revenge. Any encounter with the private language of his personal mythology exasperated them.

Why take it as a personal affront? I argued. Can you only read what you agree with? How are you ever going to learn about anybody's mind but your own? Great writers paint in gradations, not just black and white. None of these arguments was evoked with sincerity. I did not believe like William Gass and Harold Bloom that people who are put off by ideology do not know how to read. I simply was not going to allow Lawrence to be reduced.

I could not rehabilitate him—would that I could. Out of my life-long love for Lawrence, I wrote to practicing novelists, seeking reassurance. Here now is a further sampling of what they said.

Leslie Epstein:

My own feeling for Lawrence, it's true, has undergone a change. I always loved the stories. Immensely. Perhaps I still do. I think I'll read a few of the great ones to see. I even admired his plays, which I saw produced marvelously in England. For years I taught *Sons and Lovers* in a course on Psychoanalysis and Literature and felt uplifted each time I read it (perhaps the decline, if there is one, parallels that of Freud's reputation—though I am still a believer, if not in the therapy, then in the man and his thought). *Women in Love* was an important book for me in college. But it's true, I haven't much read Lawrence in the last decade or two decades, except for that last novel and, to my own amazement, I felt myself growing detached as I did so. I found Gerald and Ursula and Birkin, et al, if I've got the names right, somehow interchangeable. They picked up each other's ideas by a kind of contagion. At the same time, paradoxically, they seemed to be part of a program that ought to make this osmotic shifting of stances impossible. I suppose one could argue for Lawrence's integrity but I found myself annoyed. Do you know what I liked best? The very beautiful description of ferns, flowers, rain, dew. But I found myself backing away from those great themes and tortured characters, as if I were listening somehow to program music.

Lynne Sharon Schwartz:

First of all, the feminist movement has done its fair share in making Lawrence seem a trifle, shall we say, quaint? Right or wrongly, I and others recall Lawrence as viewing women as some kind of earthly receptacle, necessary for men's achieving cosmic, mystical experiences through sex. I even remember that women, in Lawrence, were not supposed to feel or do very much sexually, so as not to violate their role as conduits. Even if I'm exaggerating, this is so absurd that one can't even feel irritated, but only laugh. . . .

I tend to agree with the quote from Kundera that you cited. Lyrical sexuality, at least the kind Lawrence went in for, strikes me as silly, yes, and even though I may have been guilty of writing some lyrical sex, I think I always undercut it or at least intermingled it with some nod to reality. Anyway, for young readers, whose experience of sex is so unlyrical, alas, this aspect of Lawrence cannot mean very much. His views, in the abstract, seem pompous, naïve, didactic (all very unfashionable) and, paradoxical as it may sound, lacking in self-awareness or self-scrutiny.

However, reading Lawrence is quite different. I remember *Sons and Lovers* as immensely powerful, one of the books that shaped my sense of what novels could do, and there was a time during and after college when I read several of his novels and was enormously impressed. A few years ago I went back and read *The Rainbow*, just to check whether it held up, and indeed it did but I feel no urge to go back to him. I read him, this recent time, historically, as I might read someone like Cervantes, not expecting to be influenced by the views therein, but simply to see how people thought at the time. In fact Cervantes is not such a bad comparison, though the exaggerated idealism there is more acceptable than Lawrence's, and is happily mixed with other strains. Lawrence is such a one-noter. And that too, is alien to our esthetic of fragmentation and collage. . . .

Lawrence is a "hot" writer (passionate, I mean); our tastes are "cool." After the political and social upheavals of the century, we live by irony, skepticism, disillusion, a distrust of earnestness that is expressed as scorn. I am not fond of the extreme "coolness" of some of our younger writers, but I do think Lawrence's heat has earned our distrust.

Tim O'Brien:

I wholly agree with your estimation of D. H. Lawrence's high place in world letters—a brilliant artist, hardly a "eulogist"—and I had no idea, in fact, that he had tumbled so quickly, so far. His books and poems, I must believe, will far outlast the nonsense that comes of (willful?) misreading.

Cynthia Ozick:

Your Kundera quote is wonderfully telling: "lyrical sexuality is far more ludicrous than the typical sentimentality of the last century." *Lady*

Chatterley is a silly book. *Sons and Lovers* remains a masterpiece. I can't imagine that it will ever "disappear."

You speak of "a point of reference for writers, especially novelists." Is there such a thing as a point of reference any more? That requires a cohesive culture, an idea that's gone into vapor, nowhere more than in English Departments, which are themselves, in part, responsible for the vaporization.

Lady Chatterley is an infantile dream, and *Anna Karenina* is permanent, despite the total dissolution, in our society, of Anna's social norms. Is this possibly because *Anna Karenina* attends to "conduct," and *Lady Chatterley* to "self-expression"? And that the novels that last take a communal view of the world, rather than a creaturely view? In Lawrence, what you call "cosmic piety" can also be described as the-self-as-god. There's a touch of fascism in that life-force business: Lawrence had it, and so did Shaw. And Conrad saw this, and loathed it.

But *Sons & Lovers* is crystalline. Do your students read it, and like it? (Or are they *really* reading Tom Clancy?)

Rick Powers:

I read *Sons and Lovers* at 21, and the image of the author that stays with me still from that book is not the "eulogist of eros" but a kind of prophet of unrelenting, ravishing earnestness. I found the last third of the novel viscerally rearranging, and it taught me that our intensity of inner states requires, for its depiction, a stylistic awe and compassion the very opposite of fake interiority, in fact, to my ear, a sensibility—however lyrical—almost discursive in its forthrightness.

Now for a variety of reasons including overprofessionalization, earnestness has become the kiss of death in the 1990s academy. In the age of the absolute apotheosis of irony, it may be this earnestness, as much as any "lyrical sexuality," that has touched off the wholesale Lawrence devaluation. . . .

Seriously, I'm not sure I quite get Kundera's distinction or his objection. (Surely he can't be denying that literature has hinged on idealized eroticism since the very beginning?) Everything I've written, but most specifically *Gold Bug* and *Galatea*, is predicated on the belief in a biological energy that is not only released by words but also responsible for the desire to articulate in the first place. Sexuality and the urge to idealize it form a pretty powerful two-stroke engine driving the whole human vehicle. The problem, again, is that in an era of license, anyone who was once seen as a prophet of transgression is likely to seem dated in a way that blinds potential readers to any other subtleties he contains.

Gail Godwin:

I wasn't aware that DHL had fallen out of favor in the universities. How do you know this? Have you tried to teach *Women in Love* to a class of 20 year olds? That would be the test.

I re-read *Women in Love* every few years. I'm also fond of Lawrence's essays—iconoclastic, extreme, totally his own! For instance, his screed on the Book of Revelation.

An author is dead when his/her work is seen as smaller than the contemporary consciousness. The contemporary (average) consciousness still has light years to go before it can catch up with his view of the psyche. The chapter "Shortlands" alone is proof of this. . . .

As for the Kundera, there are plenty of snide statements about Lawrence floating around—many of them based on *Lady Chatterley*. Its notoriety has overwhelmed the real value of his work.

(I used to divide people into two lots, back in my graduate school and early teaching days. The ones who dumped on Lawrence, I recognized as my visceral enemies, and it usually turned out to be the case!)

Margaret Drabble:

. . . I have been thinking much of Lawrence lately, partly because I am working on a novel which goes back to my mother's childhood in a small mining town in South Yorkshire. My parents read his works as young people and admired them. So did I. Yet I agree he has, perhaps temporarily, almost disappeared from sight. Why? Because the mood of the 80s and 90s has been so hard-edged, so determinist-defeatist in some ways, so merciless, in others, and above all so cynical—a world in which DHL does not fit. We came to distrust his faith in power and therefore also his faith in love? We have been drowned in pornography? Battered by sexual warfare? I don't really know. If I come to an answer I will work it into my work in progress.

I haven't read much Kundera but have to say that I tend to find some contemporary mid-European writers, even celebrated ones, sexist in a way that DHL never was. I can't see anything wrong with sexuality, but like DHL himself I see much wrong with certain forms of pornography, machismo, etc. But then one has to be so careful about how one expresses this. . . .

In Lincoln last week I thought of him. He wrote wonderfully of that cathedral.

Richard Ford:

. . . Lawrence's sensuality, and his literary attitudes toward sensuality, plus the escapade that was his life, all made him a sort of 60's hero—uprooting to New Mexico, Mrs. Dodge, Frieda, the apparently wild side of things, plus that great, great intensity he instilled in his books. Plus again, Lawrence was a man for manifestoes, that impulse in people which wants to say, "I don't just feel this, I also think it," as a way of giving greater application and even substance to what might seem "mere" sensuousness. He wanted to do what he wanted to do, and he also wanted it to seem like the most intelligent thing to do. That, I think, is an impulse in mankind that prospered in the sixties, but that doesn't prosper in academe today.

Also, I'm quite sure, that Lawrence has been a casualty of, well . . . political correctness. His apparently thorough-going male sexuality (as distinct from hetero) isn't very popular anymore. His ledger doesn't seem to balance in gender terms and I rather doubt if a generation of female scholars and their eager-to-please male counterparts would be as initially interested in him as it would be in, say, Kate Chopin. . . . Lawrence meant great literature to me when I was in my middle twenties. I still have a little photograph of him in one of my studies.

But I haven't read him in years. Maybe if I went back now I'd find he didn't mean great literature anymore. My attention span is noticeably shorter now, and it's possible I might now think that Lawrence should've said everything more economically. What he was writing about, reading him in my twenties, was new to me. Now it's not. . . .

J. R. Salamanca:

. . . These are pursey times, and not many of its celebrants are disposed to rejoice in poems like "How Beastly the Bourgeois Is," or stories like "The Rocking Horse Winner," or the scores of others he wrote about the obscenity of money. Lawrence and Hardy are two of the novelists who have been my most constant and profound inspirations and influences, largely for the reason that they share the same passionate honesty—a virtue to which the middle classes have always paid mouth honor of the most perfunctory kind. Wealthy Americans will pay millions of dollars for a Van Gogh painting they don't really like or understand, as a kind of absolution of the guilt they feel at their own undeserved affluence; I think there is a similar kind of guilt among the present generation for the exuberance and excesses of the Sixties and Seventies, and along with the rise of the religious right in this country, American Puritanism, which lives always in the body politic like a retro-virus, has re-emerged in a fresh malignancy, like shingles after years of quiescence of the chicken pox virus. AIDS and herpes have added to the zeal with which the middle classes have bought Puritanism, much in the way that the wealthy buy Van Goghs, and critics are not immune to the phenomenon. It's a phenomenon that afflicts artists, as well, and I think it's very deviously manifested in the work of Kundera, whom you interestingly quote. The darkness and disingenuousness of his concept of sexuality is probably best expressed in his disturbingly morbid story "The Hitchhiking Game," a story which has come to be included in virtually every anthology of short stories, whereas tales like *The Fox*, "The Prussian Officer," and *Sons and Lovers* sink ever further into obscurity. . . .

So many writers use their work as vehicles for their virtuosity—art serves them; but Lawrence always serves his art. He puts his vision and virtuosity at the service of his stories and poems, with a humility that is truly religious. I think he tries to express this *sine qua non* of genuine art in his little book Pornography and So On in a typically impatient rejoinder to his critics . . . rest assured, there is nothing "silly" about the man and his beliefs.

Helen Dunmore:

. . . I hope that you have enjoyed *Zennor in Darkness*. I think in the novel I wanted to show Lawrence before he was greatly changed by the disillusionments of the First World War, and by the sense that he could no longer feel at ease in an England which had been so thoroughly militarised, and had treated him like a spy, along with Frieda. It was also very important to me to show Frieda as the complex, quick-thinking, deeply emotional woman she seems to have been (even though she must have been maddening upon occasions!). I think she has suffered greatly from anti-German feeling, even among literary critics. The caricature of her as the great big plum pudding who swallowed the gold ring of Lawrence has proved surprisingly enduring.

I really don't know the answer to your question about Lawrence's steep decline in popularity in the universities. It's a British phenomenon, as well as an American one. I think he is too complex, too contradictory, too uneven, too ambitious for current student taste—too infuriating, sometimes, as well, in novels such as *The Plumed Serpent*. . . .

P.S. I first became interested in D. H. Lawrence when I was at school—at Nottingham High School for Girls—opposite to school L. attended—so we knew all Lawrence places and landscapes well.

4

In July 1998 Taos was the site of the biennial international Lawrence conference, attended by some 160 scholars and devotees. I had come to participate in panels on strategies for teaching Lawrence in a climate hostile to him and to read a paper about the written responses of current novelists to Lawrence's decline. When our group arrived by van at the Kiowa Ranch (given to Frieda by Mabel Dodge Luhan), we found the caretaker sitting on the porch of the Lawrence cabin in the shade of the very pine tree under which Lawrence used to write. He was speaking scornfully of Lawrence's abusive behavior to some six or seven of our group.

"O yes, it's quite true," I piped up, "I don't know that he indiscriminately beat animals, but he did lose it at times in fits of uncontrollable rage." A nasty incident came to mind, which I sucked in, controlling the temptation to ride the negative side of my ambivalence towards Lawrence, much of it in any case discharged by the obstreperous antipathy of the resident caretaker himself. The Lawrence that lived in his imagination was a swine who beat Frieda and who tied down animals and beat them, too.

He said he knew what he was talking about, personally knew from Frieda herself, and Mabel, and Dorothy Brett, an artist who resided at the ranch with the Lawrences in 1924. "*Everybody* knew," he said.

I knew that one of the most repellent incidents occurred at the nearby Delmonte Ranch in the early winter of 1923, and was reported in the memoir of a perfectly trustworthy witness, Knud Merrild, one of the two Danes staying with the Lawrences their first winter in New Mexico. The facts are these: Lawrence quite literally adored a little bulldog, a clownish, merry female that loved everyone indiscriminately. All humanity was like jam to Bibbles. This "disloyalty" irritated Lawrence. When the dog went into heat and ran off with a small Airedale, he became violent. Merrild describes him entering his and Göetzsche's cabin the following day without knocking, and making a beeline for the dog who had taken refuge there after its night out. Lawrence punched Bibbles from a chair to the floor, and then went on his hands and knees grasping for her where she had taken cover under a sofa. Both Merrild and Göetzsche stood transfixed by his fury. When the dog shot out the door that had been left ajar, Lawrence strode after her. Poor Bibbles made the mistake of leaving the trodden path and soon was hopping helplessly in the drifts of snow. Lawrence kicked her, and picked her up and hurled her from him as far as he could. Bibbles stopped trying to escape. After Lawrence's kicking and heaving her a second and third time, Merrild stepped in between him and the dog.

The caretaker, Al Bearce, knew the story, and implied that he knew many others which we, who had come distances, might not know. He asked us if we had examined Lawrence's jacket, which was hanging on a nail in the cabin along with his hat, the point being that Lawrence was "a little man." No doubt this explained why he beat women and domestic animals, but would never have dared to turn his rage on a man.

Yes, he was a slight, narrow-shouldered, weak-chinned, pudgy-nosed figure of a man, I thought, repelled for the moment by the "privilege" Lawrence allowed himself, to vent whatever he was feeling. Artistic privilege, was it? Emotional honesty even at such a cost?

Al Bearce sat smiling primly, his hands folded on his stomach. A small figure, he wore a peaked cap, a red-and-white checked gingham shirt, and pants with suspenders. I asked him if he had seen black and blue marks on Frieda's body. I meant the question facetiously, since Lawrence had been dead twenty-five years when Bearce came on the scene.

"I saw enough," he said.

A woman asked if she might take a picture of him. Al Bearce refused, and refused a number of others during the hour I sat on the porch of the Lawrence cabin beside him, engaging him intermittently while he discoursed with others.

He said that he hadn't driven down the main street of Taos more than six times in ten years. Hated the place. Ditto for Santa Fe. He hated everything changed from its earlier state, everything "improved" by so-called civilization. Our conference hotel had once been a nice place—evidently before it became a conference hotel.

By then he was reminding me of Mellors. "I'll bet you have a dog," I shot in. Of course I knew he had a dog; it was barking. "I'll bet you named it Flossie!"

He corrected my misguided guess. The dog's name was Nipper. It seems that for thirty-eight years, ever since the University of New Mexico officially committed itself to maintaining the ranch, Al Bierce had been living there alone with a dog. The president of the University at the time was a fishing buddy, he said. That's how he was installed in the job. But he usually got to do whatever he wanted. He claimed to be eighty-four, and claimed the same number of teeth he had had when he was twenty, and said he had no use for college kids, especially those sent to the ranch to help with the work.

I asked him what he thought of Lawrence's books.

Yes, he had read them. He thought them "overwritten," *Lady Chatterley* especially. He didn't think much of any of them.

"Cripes," I said, "I can't believe it! You're the perfect person for this job. Lawrence would have loved you. I mean it, really. There was a side of Lawrence, a very pronounced side, that was just like you."

Al Bearce was not impressed.

"The world was a horrible thing to him, too," I said. "And was he really such a monster? I think you know how generous he was to his wife after he became sexually impotent. I'm talking about Angelo Ravagli."

Al Bearce had known Angelo Ravagli and didn't like him. "He was a bigamist," he said. "He had a wife and children in Italy and married Frieda because he was afraid of being deported. Anyway, he got what he wanted." (I gathered he meant that Ravagli inherited half of the Lawrence estate and became a prosperous Florentine landowner, dying in the arms of his wife and family twenty years after Frieda's death.) "Frieda let everyone take advantage of her," he said.

"Wasn't it courageous of Lawrence," I asked, "to allow the thing to go on without making the least little face?"

He was unmoved. He considered Lawrence the devil. He also, two minutes later, told someone that he was personally responsible for the location of Frieda's grave, which was just to the left of Lawrence's stone.

"So close to the devil?" I inquired. "Why?"

This question had him speechless for a minute. "She liked the view," he said.

Somebody asked Al how many visitors came to the ranch on an average day. I suggested after listening to his various calculations, "Are you saying about ten thousand visitors a year?"

"That number certainly," he said.

"Ah, so you're proud of the fact that people come all this way drawn by Lawrence," I said. "Honestly, what do you think of us, scholars and students of Lawrence come from all over the country and from other countries as far away as Japan and Korea: are we crazy?"

"I don't mind people," he deadpanned.

At a gift shop adjacent to a Franciscan church, we found a framed painting celebrating the miracle of Our Lady of Guadalupe. The miracle led to the raising of a church and the bringing of Christianity to old Mexico. The painting shows Indians turning away from the sun and the moon to Our Lady and angels; but not, Lawrence believed, turned altogether away, entirely lost, as was sun and moon to the white race. He had come to North America to have the sun and moon again, that was it in a nutshell, the sun and moon as the pre-Christian Old World had known them, as the white child would certainly have known them had he not been colonized by his mother.

When Lawrence wrote "The Woman Who Rode Away" at the Kiowa

Ranch in 1924, he was being polemical, using all his literary genius to score points against white women, Western women, for performing spiritual incest with their boy children; training them to live statically from the intellect; cultivating them to be spiritually intense, adoring husbands; destroying in them, as in the miracle of Our Lady of Guadalupe, their cold, lordly insouciance of maleness. He probably wrote the story in a mood of sardonic glee. A white woman seeking release from nerves and exhaustion slips away from her marriage to ride up into the mountains. At an incredible altitude, she is taken captive by a small remnant of untamed Indians. At issue for them is the extinction of maleness that has befallen all the other nations of men who have lost the sun and the moon. The woman who rode away is made their emissary to the god of the sun, a propitiatory sacrifice, to ask that the sun return power to the people. She is drugged, ceremonially conducted to an altar, and has her heart cut out. Lawrence spares the reader the actual knifing.

In her memoir, Mabel called "The Woman Who Rode Away," "That story where Lorenzo thought he finished me up," recalling the day in June of 1924 when Lawrence handed her his new story to read. It was amusing to think when visiting Mabel's home—a big, cozy adobe house in the style of an Italian villa—that she never got from Lawrence what she would have liked, which is not to say that the spirit of the place failed to draw from him a powerful imaginative response. She wanted him to glorify the native American Indians; but those he saw when staying with Mabel she had made her servants, including her newest husband, Tony. Lawrence dashed off a skit, "Altitude," which wickedly parodies Mabel's colonial attitude toward the Indians.

With his back to the pine tree at the Kiowa ranch in 1924, he wrote *St. Mawr*, about a mother and a daughter who resignedly, despairingly in the case of the mother, give up ever finding a real man. The daughter doesn't know life like the mother so she still hopes. She buys a ranch in the mountains not far from Taos where they go to live. What is missing from her life and from her mother's, Lawrence evokes in the spirit of the place, so painfully beautiful, remote, and destructively potent. But poor Rachel Witt can feel nothing any more. No man has ever mattered to her. She has scarcely been singed. In desperation she proposes marriage to a druidical little man, a Welshman, the groom, because he is not namby-pamby—because every other male in the world whom she could possibly touch is namby-pamby—but he rejects her.

O, such a little masterpiece Mabel had given the world by being such a benefactress and inspiration! She was behind Rachel Witt, of course, and strapping Tony had been squeezed into a diminutive Welshman who did not/would not bring in drinks on a tray. (Or was Lewis the groom, with his gigantic beard, Lorenzo himself?) The idea of an untamed Tony with but a remnant of the ancient god-force Mabel claimed to worship, had given rise to something much more vicious than satire in "The Woman Who Rode Away."

We climbed to the rocky cave which inspired the final scene of the story. The cave was like an amphitheater wide open at the entrance. There was the waterfall, now dropping a clear stream of water across the entrance, and there the shelf where the woman who rode away had been laid out for sacrifice. Above the high shelf one could still make out a painted sun; for it was an ancient and ceremonial cave, though I do not think its history is known, only that (just as in Lawrence's story) the sun lights the altar at the precise moment of the winter solstice, shining through the ice of the frozen falls. Perhaps it is no wonder, I thought, that some young female members of the Lawrence Society are ashamed of their enthusiasm for him and often keep their research a secret from their colleagues.

The decline in Lawrence's reputation occurred with dumbfounding swiftness during the 1970s, though it took another fifteen years for Lawrentians to acknowledge it. Lawrence went out of fashion along with a whole school of literary criticism, the liberal humanists, the quasi-religious exegetes who believe that a work of art has the power to ennoble.

The new schools of criticism, gender studies and deconstruction in particular, disdain Lawrence for being crudely obvious. Ah, precisely, new schools of criticism! Lawrence has sunk, and the willingness to allow that there is more to him than the crude ideological content of occasional pieces, has disappeared. The future is out of our hands. Conferring with colleagues about strategies to keep Lawrence from dropping into oblivion is preposterous. It was not only the folly of the enterprise, but the sadness, the pity of it, that contributed to my testy mood at the conference.

If the most renowned of the living Old School of Lawrentians, Spilka and Daleski, did a can-can kicking in time while singing, "We are not has-beens," and someone recited a poem about the ghost of Leavis, saintly father of Lawrence criticism, tirelessly searching the underworld for a certain plant that has the potency to confer immortality on the Leavisite Lawrence, the performance would capture the essence of a memorable plenary session. It took courage for a star like Spilka to say to a crowded audience that graduate students are no longer interested in what he has to say about Lawrence or about literature in general; but bugger them all, he's proud to be out of fashion in the stellar company of D. H. L.

I guess I'm grieving over a lost love. Then he was all in all: a genius. He let everything hang out in the open; no pussy-footing about his feelings, but instantaneous detonation if he felt like detonating. We embraced his rage. We were not sufficiently trained before gender theory to recoil from stories like "The Woman Who Rode Away."

A Conversation with Charles Johnson

Interviewed by Rob Trucks

Novelist, short story writer, essayist, screenwriter, and cartoonist Charles Johnson received both his bachelor's degree in journalism and his master's in philosophy from Southern Illinois University before studying with the legendary John Gardner at SUNY-Stony Brook. Johnson has published two books of cartoons, a book-length essay entitled *Being and Race: Black Writing Since 1970*, and serves as coeditor for a collection of essays, *Black Men Speaking*. His published fiction includes *Faith and the Good Thing*, *Oxherding Tale*, *The Sorcerer's Apprentice*, and *Middle Passage*, a novel which garnered the National Book Award, making him the first African-American male to capture the prize since Ralph Ellison won for *Invisible Man* in 1953.

Johnson is currently the Pollack Professor in the Department of English at the University of Washington and is a recent recipient of a MacArthur Fellowship.

I interviewed Charles Johnson three days before his fiftieth birthday in his Manhattan hotel room, as he toured in support of his new novel, *Dreamer*.

Q: I got tired just reading over your list of accomplishments. It almost doesn't seem fair that you're still alive.

A: Well, you have to take one day at a time, man. I've been working since I was seventeen years old, as a publishing artist. I've worked steadily.

Q: I'm amazed that you find time to breathe. My point in bringing this up is, Do you ever feel pressure in your work, whether fiction or non-fiction, to please more than Charles Johnson and his immediate family?

A: No, actually I think I just write to satisfy myself. My friend, August Wilson, you know, he's got these rules for writers. There are four of them. One of them is, There are no rules for writing. That's one. The second one is, The first statement is a lie so pay attention. The third one is, You can't write for an audience. The writer's first job is to survive. And the fourth one is, You can do no wrong but anything can be made better. As simple as those are, I think they make a lot of sense. You have to write to satisfy yourself, first and foremost. Who else could you possibly write for? The Audience? What is that exactly? You see people who come into bookstores and they're from all walks of life, all backgrounds and all ethnic groups. All religions and race. So are you going to target one group as opposed to another? No, you're going to write for yourself.

When I write, I think about people who I've worked with in the past, or known. I'll say to myself, Now if John Gardner were alive, he'd like that line. If my wife reads this, she's going to like it. Or if my buddy over there looks at this little passage on martial arts, since he's a martial artist, he's going to like it. That's about as big as the audience gets for me, because you can't know all these invisible people out there who you've never met. So you have to work for yourself to satisfy yourself.

Q: I'm trying to figure a way to ask this next question without sounding like I'm fawning.

A: Well, it's not even about that. See? Here's why I'm a Buddhist, man. None of this is about ego. None of this is about career for me. It never has been. I have no interest in that. I've just loved to create, ever since I was a kid. First with drawings, and then later on I discovered I could write. And there's specific things that I do want to write, particularly philosophical fictions, for a number of different reasons. Because that's my training and background, in terms of formal education, and also because we didn't have a whole lot of that in African-American literature, except for Jean Toomer, Richard Wright and Ralph Ellison. So I figured there was a gap. There was a void. I could fill that void. And that's what it was about, enriching our literature through, I hope, books like *Dreamer* and the previous ones.

Now I also do other assignments and those were, primarily, to see if I could do them, in fact. Like public television and other kinds of things. To see if I could write a different kind of thing, just to challenge myself. You can also make some money that way, too.

Q: You hit on a couple of points there. The assignments like *Black Men Speaking* and *Being & Race*. Maybe when I say institution, I'm asking if you feel any kind of responsibility other than to yourself.

A: Responsibility? Keep going. What do you mean by responsibility?

Q: When you say that you've done assignments for the challenge, to see if you could do them, it seems like that might have been a concern early on, but not now. It seems like the motivation to create *Black Men Speaking* has to come from another place than just "to see if you could do it." Does the non-fiction provide as much enjoyment as fiction?

A: *Being & Race* is actually one of the most enjoyable things that I think I've done, primarily because that was going to be my dissertation at Stony Brook. I did all but the dissertation. I got hired by a writing program and they said, You know, you're publishing. You don't need to finish the Ph.D. because the M.F.A. is a terminal degree. And I said, Okay, fine. That gives me free time to write, literary fiction and other things, but I still wanted that dissertation on phenomenology in respect to Black American literature. And also, not as a dissertation, but something a bit more readable than a dissertation is. So that's why I went back and did *Being & Race*. The third reason was because I thought some of the reviews of earlier books were just abysmal. I thought that the book reviewers were, aesthetically, just totally at sea with an original work of art. So it's a manifesto of sorts.

Q: When you say "earlier books," you're referring to your earlier books?

A: *Faith and the Good Thing* in particular. *Oxherding Tale* threw a lot of people because they didn't know to do with this book. They didn't understand it. People seem to think ideologically, very often, about Black art, and they have presuppositions in their mind, and all kinds of sociological clichés. Ellison addresses this very eloquently, and other writers as well. But that's what *Being & Race* is largely about, the first half of it. It's an aesthetic in the first half and then in the second half I talk about writers, and assess various texts, in a capsule kind of way in some cases, for people who may not know who those writers are. Or those times. Or those books. So that book was something I enjoyed doing and I still like it, very much, among all the books that I've done.

Black Men Speaking was another matter. That was requested by my friend, John Gallman, at Indiana, and came from his desire to do that kind of book, and my desire to deal with the plight of young black men in the eighties. Again, my son has just entered that critical age group, sixteen to thirty-four, at the time, that's been labelled an endangered species. I wanted to work through all that mess, all those statistics that were so bad, and then get other writers to address those same questions, but in a fresh way. And not the usual kind of writers.

I owe the way that book looks to John McCluskey, who was able to put more time into it than I was, because I was busy with other things, like *Dreamer.* John was very interested in not getting academics, and not getting published writers, because those are the voices you usually hear in an anthology on Black men. He wanted grass roots people. He wanted people who were not writers and that meant that we, he and I, all had to work very carefully with the writers to bring the prose up to speed, because they didn't have a literary background.

I think some of the pieces are really quite fine. My colleague Joe Scott's first piece in there, on growing up in Detroit in the thirties, called "Making a Way Out of No Way" is really fine. Everybody loves that piece. And David Nicholson's piece is really good. Of course, David is a Washington *Post* reporter so it's going to be good. John got some good people to participate in this particular project, and to tell the truth. Basically a lot of people don't want to deal with those statistics. They want to deny them, or skip around them, but they're real. And until somebody just looks at it, and accepts it as being the case, nobody can move forward so, to me, that's a different kind of a book, but I feel very strongly about it. I feel a certain passion about it.

Q: You said, a few minutes ago, that one of the things being a Buddhist helped with was not having an ego.

A: Well, you work at it. It's an illusion anyway.

Q: Do you ever feel competitive with your fiction?

A: Competitive in what sense?

Q: I'm thinking of a particular section from the introduction to *Oxherding Tale* paperback: "The 1980s began as a decade when the work of Black male writers was systematically downplayed and ignored in commercial, New York publishing. For example, *Oxherding Tale* appeared the same year as Alice Walker's *The Color Purple*. I leave it to readers to decide which book pushes harder at the boundaries of invention, and inhabits most confidently the space where fiction and philosophy meet."

A: The reason I've never felt competitive with other writers is because I know exactly what I showed up to do, and it's basically philosophical fiction. That's my background. And, once again, everything I've done in the way of my own, self-generated projects, novels and short stories, have always been, I hope, in that area where fiction and philosophy meet. I don't even write a story unless it's philosophically engaging to me, or addresses some perennial question in Eastern or Western philosophy. I'm not going to write my own stories unless they do that.

But if there's anybody that I'm competitive with, then that's me, and that's it. To say that writers are competitive, what does that really mean? Are they doing the same thing? Is that what they mean? And so they're competing with each other? If that's the case, then you have two writers doing the same thing and you don't need one of them.

Q: But you seem to have a special pride for *Oxherding Tale*.

A: Definitely. If I had not done that book, I would not have gone on to do the other books. I know that. That's a very special book for me for a lot of reasons. That is the book I wanted to write when I became a writer. That is to say, I wrote six novels in two years prior to *Faith and the Good Thing*. They weren't the books I wanted to write because I hadn't figured out how to write out of a philosophical sensibility.

I met John Gardner while I was writing *Faith and the Good Thing* and I was beginning to understand what that could be. This place where fiction and philosophy merge. Because we divide things, I think. This is this and this is that and that thing's over there. And that's bullshit, because everything really is one whole, one unit. I hadn't figured out, exactly, how to carve at that until *Faith and the Good Thing*, but that still didn't satisfy me. John didn't really understand Eastern philosophy. He was actually kind of opposed to it. In fact, he was a lot opposed to it, at the time, though he changed later on, in his writing, and even wrote a piece called "Meditational Fiction" for a book he translated by a Japanese writer by the name of Kikuo Itaya, a book of short stories. John brought his work back here, had SIU Press publish him, did the introduction, mainly to say, He didn't understand these stories, which were very anchored in Buddhism, but he loved them. That's the kind of human being he was.

But at the time I was working with John, he didn't really understand and I didn't go that far, philosophically, in *Faith and the Good Thing*. For me, whenever I write a book, and this is probably a very difficult thing for some people to understand, I don't write a book just to be writing a book. I write a book as if it's the last thing in this world I'm ever going to do, the last statement I'm ever going to make. I take this final manuscript, when it's done, and I put it in the mail, and it's my Last Will and Testament in language. That's what this is. For me, it's got to be total when I do a book. I mean, total. Every emotion, thought. The best emotion. The best thought. The best technique. I'm going to have to learn something new from it and draw off of everything I ever knew. Pull up emotions I haven't felt before. I'm going to have to feel differently. I'm going to come out of this process different when I do a novel. It's a total thing. And one of the things dearest to me in my life, since my teens, ever since I got into martial arts, has been Eastern thought, Eastern philosophy. And I'm thinking about all kinds of things in respect to Eastern philosophy and its emphasis on personal liberation. And all the things that go into Buddhism, and then I'm thinking about the slave narrative, which had never been the form used for a novel. You know what I'm saying? And how you go about updating that and go philosophically deeper into it and focus on questions of freedom in a deeper way. Other kinds of slavery, such as psychological, sexual, metaphysical. All of that is something I just really had to deal with, in some book, somewhere, and that's *Oxherding Tale*.

I was looking at the "Ten Oxherding Pictures" from my late teens, when I was a cartoonist. I'd look at all kinds of art and that one is a seminal Buddhist text. That was important to me in grappling with this subject. So all of that went into *Oxherding Tale*, and why doing this book as opposed to something else.

My editor at the time, whose name I won't mention, I pitched the idea to him that maybe I could do a family drama, a black family drama, and he was like, Oh yeah, I can sell that idea. And then I told him, I never intended to do that. I just wanted to see what you would say. I'm doing this book. I said, It's this book or nothing. If you stick with something, fortunately somebody will understand it. That's why I have this long relationship now with John Gallman at Indiana University Press. I feel indebted to John for making that book a reality because I really would not have written anything else, in the way of a novel, unless I had gotten that book done. Everything I do refers to that in some way, if not to the novel then to the complex themes of Eastern philosophies, Taoism and Buddhism, that animate the book.

So that's sort of, basically, the story of that novel. I threw away two thousand four hundred pages as I wrote it. It had to be this book in our literature or I wasn't going to be happy.

Q: Compared to most writers, your novels have long gestation periods.

A: It depends on the novel. I used to write novels one every ten weeks when I first started writing fiction. *Faith and the Good Thing* took me nine months.

Q: Maybe I should follow that lead. What's the difference between the first six novels that you wrote and the seventh, *Faith and the Good Thing*, which was the first novel published?

A: The first six are easier. They're not philosophical novels. That's one thing. When I wrote *Oxherding Tale*, I sped read every book on slavery in the State University of New York at Stony Brook's library, just because I wanted to immerse myself in that, in all the slave narratives. I spent six years just reading stuff on the sea, reading literature on the sea for *Middle Passage*, everything from Appolonius to *Voyage of Argo* forward to Conrad. All of Melville I looked at again, nautical dictionaries. Everything about the sea, because I didn't know that stuff. That was '83 to '86, but, prior to that, going all the way back to 1971, I'd been collecting stuff on the slave trade, from the time I was a discussion group leader in Black Studies at Southern Illinois University, when Black Studies first started there. There was a big lecture class and we divided the students up and some of us undergraduates were discussion group leaders when I first saw the image of a slave ship projected on an overhead projector, a cross-section of a ship with those silhouetted figures. So one of the first six novels I did was on the slave trade. It's like number two, so it would be like 1971 or something like that, and I wasn't ready to write it. It was just too early. But I had the research. Anything related to the slave trade I collected or took notes on, from '71 all the way to '83, and I began *Middle Passage* in '83. So, again, a lot of history.

Dreamer, I hope, embodies a great deal of history and biography. Every take on the life of the spirit is in this book. The Christian tradition as well as Moslem, as well as Hinduism, Buddhism, Taoism and so forth. Because I like to learn, that's one thing, as I'm doing something. I mean, I come out with far more knowledge on a particular subject than I can get in that book. And that's just very enriching. I don't know if the next novel I do will have so much history as its foundation, as one of its conditions for coming into being. If that's the case, then give me maybe two years.

Usually I don't write autobiographically. I don't do that because it just doesn't interest me. I'm interested in other things. This novel, *Dreamer*, oddly enough, does have a couple autobiographical things in it. The sketch of my hometown in the fifties.

Q: Your great-uncle makes an appearance.

A: My great-uncle's in there. And that trip that the character makes with his mother, down South, that was actually a trip that my parents made. I usually don't pull out stuff like that because I'm interested in other subjects. I don't think the gestation period for a non-history-based novel would be too long.

But I'm very demanding about other things, too. As Sartre once said, Every sentence is a risk. I think everything needs to be compressed. I tell my students all the time, the French have a term, *remplissage*. It means literary padding. I don't want any of that in my book. I want this compression that happens when you have a lot of material presented poetically, distilled. It's like philosophy. You don't have a line in philosophy that doesn't advance the argument or, in this case, the aesthetic feeling. It's got to justify itself in some way. Every paragraph has to do that, and not just in one way, in two or three ways. So I tend to throw out a lot of stuff. Probably about three thousand pages for *Dreamer*. I know it was about three thousand pages for *Middle Passage*. Scenes, approaches that just didn't really fit. Characters that didn't develop. Who knows? Out of one page you might have one sentence or one paragraph that's really useful, for this fiction or for something else. I mean, I got to the point in this novel where I'm following this character, this King-like character, Chaym Smith, and he starts shooting up. I didn't know he was going to do that. Where did I learn about shooting up? Well, that's in a novel, one of the first six I did in those first two years. I remembered that. I did the research before. I pulled out the drawer of my filing cabinet and there it was, everything I needed just for that one description. So I never throw stuff away, because it might be one little thing on a page. One image, one idea that'll make a lot of sense.

You know, there's a phrase in *Dreamer*, "isomers of the divine presence," that King uses when he's thinking about spiritual immanence. That was actually the title of the last three books of the six novels I wrote between 1970 and '72. It was a trilogy that ran nine hundred and fifty-eight pages. That was the last three of the six I did in two years and it was called *Isomers of God* because I was thinking about isomerization and spiritual things all at the same time. But that trilogy is in my filing cabinet. All I got out of it is that one little phrase in that particular chapter of *Dreamer*.

Q: But the second of the six unpublished novels became *Middle Passage?*

A: Yes. The first one was actually called *The Last Liberation*. It was about a young black man, studying at a martial arts school like the one I was in when I was nineteen, and this whole other universe that opens up to him. You start with practice and you train the body, then you train the mind, train the spirit. And it was a first novel that just didn't work although I've returned to that subject, really, in short stories.

Q: Like "China"?

A: "China" and a couple of other things that've moved beyond the original premise. It didn't work but I do revisit some of the earlier subjects and themes with different characters. But I'm sure I'll never go back to the trilogy. It was about the childhood, adulthood and middle age of a black musician. That's what that was about. Again, I used to write ten pages a day so I could do a novel in ten weeks, and they would go through three drafts. I didn't know how to really revise until I met Gardner, though. I'd just go back over the whole book again, from the start to the end. But the second book in that series was accepted by a some little publisher here in New York and I asked Gardner, while I was working on *Faith and the Good Thing*, Should I publish this book? I'd found a publisher. And the book was very different from *Faith and the Good Thing*. And he said, You know, if you think you'll ever have to climb over it, then you shouldn't do it. So I asked for it back. The reason that they liked it was because it sounded like James Baldwin. It was very Baldwinesque. Those were just sort of my models in the back of my mind—Baldwin, Richard Wright, John A. Williams and so forth. And I took it back and I'm glad I did. It doesn't fit. It doesn't fit within the body of work that I want to develop. It was a good training novel, teaching me how to write. Do this and do that. But I didn't know enough about music to write something like that.

Q: It seems extraordinarily patient for a young author to turn down an offer to publish.

A: Everybody's got this hunger to publish, as a writer, but I don't. I don't have a hunger to publish. I have a hunger to create certain things along the lines that I've been telling you about, but not just to publish for the sake of publishing.

Now, I *was* like that when I was a cartoonist. I was panting, as a teenager, to publish. Anything anywhere. And that's really why I started so early. I used to come here to New York and stay with my relatives in Brooklyn, and take my portfolio of drawings all around to the cartoon editors and comic book companies, but I couldn't really do much assignment work because I didn't live here and, again, I was fifteen, sixteen years old. So I had a hunger to publish as a cartoonist. Anywhere and everywhere. I did a lot of that. I published a thousand drawings, two books and had a TV series by the time I was 22, so basically the thrill was gone in terms of seeing my name in print. It's fine but you have to ask yourself, *What* am I publishing? What is it that my name is attached to? Is it something that I can hand to my kids and say, Well, this is about the best your dad has been able to make out of his journey through existence? That's the kind of book that means something to me. That's the only kind of book that I would want to put my name on and release to other people. So it's not about the hunger to publish. That doesn't mean much.

With *Dreamer*, I made a promise to Lee Goerner, my late editor, who passed away before the book was finished. I made a promise to Lee. I said, Lee, I'm going to do the best book I can for you, so my feeling now is, Okay, I think I did that.

All my duties are discharged. All my promises are kept. I don't owe anybody anything, for the first time in my life. Nobody, nothing, nowhere. Not to former teachers, not to parents, not to colleagues, not to students. Nobody, nowhere. It's a clean slate, so fifty, for me, basically means all my debts are discharged and I can do what I want. I've always done what I wanted to do but I can do it a little bit differently now. Something may get moved to the side. It may be teaching. It just might be one of the balls I've been keeping up in the air for twenty something years.

Q: I noticed that writing wasn't one of those things that might get moved.

A: Oh no, never.

Q: Do you know what the next novel will be?

Q: No, I don't.

Q: I read a piece on you that was around the time of *Middle Passage*, and you were already talking about King.

A: I was. I was. This is how it happened. Lee said, What do you want to do next? I told him I'd been thinking about this short story I did on King and the issues that affect black people in America today, and looking back thirty years to recapture what the last few years of this man's life were like. So he called up the head of the company, whoever he was, and got an advance, and then we were rolling. But then I had to do the research. I didn't know the man. I just needed to immerse myself in King, while I was doing a bunch of other stuff right after the National Book Award. I was ready to start writing around '93. So the composition really took from '93 until September of 1997.

Q: Is there a stage during the research when you're tempted to try and put words down or do you tell yourself, No, this is the research stage?

A: Well, all of '92 I just was reading King. I was going off to do promotion for *Middle Passage*, lectures and stuff, and I would take the King books with me, so it was all going on continuously. I was accumulating. Going to the King birth house. I'd been to the Lorraine before, in the eighties, so I didn't need to go back, but I was just sort of gathering things. Documents, film stuff on the Civil Rights movement. Letting all of that stuff come together until I was ready to write, and the first thing I was ready to write was the Prologue. I just sat down and wrote it. Unlike with other books, I was basically working from the seat of my pants. I had a model for everything else. *Faith and the Good Thing* was a folk-tale, *Oxherding Tale* was a slave narrative, and *Middle Passage* was a classic sea story. I had no model for this book but the first thing that came to me was just that Prologue, just the feeling, and the feeling led me to where I needed to go.

I thought about this book, once, in terms of it being a classic gospel. You know, we have a whole tradition of literature written by monks writing to other monks about what you're doing with your life and how you should be a monk. I thought about that as a possible model but finally I decided on this structure, the alternating first and third persons. But maybe it still is a gospel. It has a structure that resembles one long prayer, you know, ending with Amen. And so that's the form it took, but I really didn't have a literal model for this particular novel. I kind of like to play with forms, literary forms, because you learn so much from doing that.

You bring in another aesthetic dimension from the nineteenth or eighteenth century and that's just a lot of fun. But I didn't really have that for this particular book.

Q: It's not nearly as cut and dried a process as two years of research followed by five years of writing, is it?

A: No. I just finished a piece for a magazine called *Commonquest* and there's stuff in there that's not in the novel because I was still thinking about King. I'm still thinking about the guy. I still read about him. I still try to improve my knowledge about who he was and what he represented. He really was a philosopher. In the past, you know, I might have a problem I'm writing about and I'd ask, What would Kant have to say about this or What would Hegel say?, but now it's pretty easy for me to say, What would King say about this? I have a sense now. Why did he say a particular thing? Well, I know why he said it. I think I understand a bit more about his intellectual foundation. That is now part of my literary repertoire. And I want to improve that understanding, to sharpen it. On this book tour, a guy gave me his Ph.D. dissertation and it's a philosophical analysis of "Letter From a Birmingham Jail." King is a philosopher and we should be talking about him in those terms. Not just as a Civil Rights leader.

Q: When you first started writing *Dreamer,* you had King and you had the *doppelganger,* but didn't the story change? I read that with at least one of your books you submitted an outline, but then the book changed.

A: They all do. But the only book where I've submitted an outline is *Oxherding Tale.* It changed, over the years, from its original incarnations, because you live with something for five years, it evolves as you evolve. You start with one interest and three years later you may have a different interest so the book has got to be capacious enough to contain your own changing perceptions and emotions and desires.

Q: I guess maybe I'm having a hard time understanding the patience that allows you to go through eight or nine drafts of a novel, and still feel something's missing, that something's not exactly right. With *Oxherding Tale* you went from a black protagonist to a mulatto protagonist and then from a more or less stereotypical slave owner to Flo Hatfield, however you would like to describe her. I'm interested in that moment of change.

How far, whether it's measured by length of time or number of pages or emotional investment, how far are you into *Oxherding Tale* when you realize the protagonist isn't black, he's mulatto?

A: Oh, there was a point where I was ready to leave it alone and just move on to something else. It was around Christmas. I didn't want another year to begin with me looking at this book. I literally sat down, this is between Christmas and New Year's, to give myself reasons for why this book was impossible. I said, First of all, to me, the narrator is boring. He's a typical black in the typical situation that a slave is in. As soon as I thought of that (because this is the way imagination usually works, I try to tell my students this a lot), I thought of a variation. Suppose he's mulatto? Ah. All of sudden he belongs to both the white and the black world. He's walking down this tightrope. He could fall either way, or be attacked from either side. Okay. That's interesting. But no, no, no. I still don't like the slavemaster. His name was Colonel Woofter, or something like that, and he was just predictable. He did everything you ever thought a slavemaster should do from Simon Legree forward. But what if, I thought, he's a woman? It's just a little thing but all of a sudden a door opens up. So I talked myself out of abandoning the novel. It was really the first of the year, January, and I said, Okay, I'm going to go back over this novel and I'm going to look at these new possibilities and chase them.

And, I tell you, much the same thing happened with *Dreamer*, because you're right, at the very beginning I had the double and I had King. The last layer of this novel went on early last year. Sometimes things just happen serendipitously. They're just pure chance. You know, I did that Bill Moyers show called "Genesis," where a bunch of writers came in to talk about Cain and Abel. A little before I did that there was a Black Writers Conference at Claremont McKenna College and Dr. Ricardo Quinones, who was the host, invited a bunch of people there. Shelby Steele was there and Walter Mosley, Ishmael Reed, and a few others, but as we were leaving he gave me a copy of his book, *The Changes of Cain*. It's the history of the character of Cain for 2000 years. And I said, I can't believe you gave me this. I've got a show to do and I don't know anything about the subject. This will help me.

I read a third of the book before the show and as we're sitting there, talking about Cain and Abel, I'm really getting interested in this story. I think I probably knew more than anybody else on that show because nobody else had time to do the research, or to prepare. So we're just kicking around ideas but I'm really getting interested and thinking, What the hell does it mean that the first two brothers are characterized by envy and murder? Cain brings murder into the world. Well, I still hadn't connected the dots. The show was over and I went back to work on this book and my agent saw the show and she had seen the drafts of *Dreamer* along the way, and she said, What about Cain and Abel? And I thought, Oh my God.

Q: So Cain and Abel wasn't there until a year ago?

A: Early last year. I said, Oh my God. And then I went back and finished Quinones' book. I looked at his sources. I went and read all these other stories about Cain and Abel, and it provided the *gestalt*, the glue between all the other elements. Chaym becomes Cain to King's Abel. It's all there. It's just all there. You know, sometimes writing is almost like the philosophical process. You're looking for that one last piece that will snap everything into focus so you've got a unified, organic whole. Otherwise, I was basically developing the double as a kind of uneducated guy, poor, from the South side of Chicago. I was having a really hard time with the double learning so much about King. Well, Chaym is way different. His problem is something else. It's a problem deep inside, one of faith. He's a mythic character. That gave me what I like to have in the novel, which is a kind of myth dimension. Because the other novels do have that as well.

Q: I want to know, before the answer comes, before the change of protagonist in *Oxherding Tale* or before you get the Cain and Abel connection in *Dreamer*, do you feel dissatisfied? Do you feel like something's missing? Are you physically writing or are you taking a break, waiting for some kind of intervention?

A: I think doing both. On the one hand, you're working with the idea you've got at the moment, to make it as good as you can, and the writing can actually be very elegant but it's still not what you want and you can feel that. Or, the other thing is, you just want to take a break for a while and work on some other assignment. One thing that's nice about having lots of assignments to work on is it's like being a poet. A poet works on a poem, hits the wall, puts it in the drawer, writes another poem, hits the wall, then puts that in the drawer and takes the first one out, working on it with fresh eyes.

Q: So the non-fiction does give you a break, a release?

A: It's like painters who work on several canvases. Ray Carver used to do the same thing with short stories. He'd put one away for a little while and work on a second one, and then six months later he'd pull the first one out, because now he's got an idea for where it should go. So moving from one idea to the other can be very refreshing. A non-fiction piece can do that, or an essay or a screenplay. It allows you to back off, for a moment, from the intensity.

Now, when I got back on this book, I worked on it night and day from July 1 to September 16th. That was it. I just told my family, Look, I'm going to go into one of these phases. I'll be here but I won't really be here, because I was just living it everyday, because I wanted it done for my fiftieth birthday. People say, Well, why is the book coming out now? On the thirtieth anniversary of King's death? Well, that wasn't the reason. I wanted it done by my fiftieth birthday so I could say, Okay, the slate is clear. This is no longer on my "to do" board. That was the reason so I worked on nothing else. I told people I couldn't work on anything else. I couldn't talk to them. Even friends. Actually, sometimes when I have a deadline on a screenplay it has to be that way, too. I'll just sort of go into that mode. Night and day. Work on the book until I'm exhausted. Sleep. Work on the book. It's just all day long like that. But when it's a long project, like a novel of this sort, I think you have to have time where you back away and then come back to it. Where you have something else to refresh yourself. And there's a lot of things you do that people can't understand exactly why you're doing it.

I remember Lee called me one time as I was studying Social Darwinism and he said, Why the hell are you studying Social Darwinism? You're still working on the King book, right? And I said, Believe me. It's got something to do with it. I read five books on acting because I was thinking, The double. He's got to be trained. So I got to learn some stuff about that. That may amount to half a paragraph in what remains in the book.

I was talking to my friend and former student David Guterson about this when he dropped by over Christmas so I could give him his present. He showed me what was in the trunk of his car. And it was some monogram, some academic paper from the forties, on nursing that he needed for the book he was finishing up. We both started talking about how this is where the real fun is. You learn so much more than you're going to put in a project because you don't know what you're going to need to know. Then finally it just gets winnowed out and scaled down. Yeah, there's stuff that gets left on the side that you find very enriching, but I personally believe that, even though a reader may be enriched by a book, nobody's enriched like the writer is, from having done it. All the things that you feel and have gone through and learn. That's the process. It's always intimidating with a novel, at least the way I like to do it, because I never know exactly what it's going to look like. I've often contradicted, at the end, everything I thought at the time I started it. It should be a process of discovery. If I don't learn, discover something that I didn't know before, I don't think the reader's going to have a sense of discovery. If there are no surprises for me, there won't be surprises for the reader. I'm convinced of that.

Q: Let me ask you to do a comparison/contrast of the process of writing *Oxherding Tale* and the process of writing *Dreamer*. I assume that you possessed a certain amount of faith, given your experience, while writing *Dreamer*, that the answer's going to come. Did you have the same confidence while you were writing *Oxherding Tale?*

A: Well, there's a faith in the material. There's a belief in what you're doing.

Q: What about faith in yourself?

A: Oh yeah, faith in yourself. Absolutely. The person I studied with, John Gardner, was the most incredible writing teacher anybody could have. The one thing that everybody I know who worked with John got from John was the sense that, if you're willing to sweat, then you can write greatly. You can write as greatly as the great literature of the past. And he could get you excited about the great literature of the past as well. If you were willing to work hard, and long enough, then you will achieve what you want to do. So it's not a matter of ever doubting yourself, because the wonderful thing about writing is you can rewrite. That's ninety percent of it. That's where the real joy is, as far as I'm concerned, going over something again and again. It's like sculpture. It gets more refined. It gets tighter. It's more precise. There's a greater fusion between sound and sense. The cadence of the line and the meaning of the line. That's where the real art comes in. Naturally you have to have faith in yourself, but that's not a hard stretch, because as long as you have faith in your capacity to work, it's going to come together.

Q: Gardner is known as one of the great creative writing teachers but there is that question about whether or not writing can be taught. If creative writing can't be taught, then what did Gardner give? What can a teacher do for his or her students?

A: He can't teach somebody imagination. I mean, a student's got to bring that himself. You can teach technique and Gardner was actually quite good about that. You know, in *The Art of Fiction*, all of those exercises in the back? My students have done those since I first started teaching. Maybe not all of them every quarter but at least two-thirds of them.

The other thing John taught was a passion, and he communicated that almost without even consciously teaching it. You just looked at how this man was working. You looked at his love of literature. He had a self-sacrificial capacity to give everything to the work. And once you got that sense, you could apply it to your own. And it should work this way. Once you're willing to go over something, like Hemingway, twenty times. Twenty times, we're told, he went over that last page in *The Sun Also Rises*. If you're willing to do that, then you can achieve the perfection that you're after. At least to your own satisfaction. It's just a matter of sweat. That's all it is. It doesn't even have to be a matter of brilliance.

Q: The amount of sweat that must go into an eight-year project. I know you've been working on a lot of other things but you've published a novel every eight years since '74.

A: Is that right?

Q: *Faith and the Good Thing* in '74, *Oxherding Tale* in '82, *Middle Passage* in '90 and *Dreamer* in '98. Of course, I have to stick with the novels. I have to throw out *Sorcerer's Apprentice* in order to make it work.

A: The stories in *Sorcerer* were written between '77 and probably '83.

Q: While we're here, have you done much short story writing lately?

A: I haven't really had a chance though I would like to put a collection together. I was talking to my agent about that. I've got twelve stories that I wrote in January that'll be in a textbook that evolved from a TV series called "Africans in America." The show will premiere in October of 1998 on PBS. The producer is Orlando Bagwell, a very distinguished man, I think, and the series, in four parts, four one and a half hour shows, will cover history from the Slave Trade all the way up to the Civil War. There'll be a lot of attention for this, believe me, in the fall. It should be late October. And they have a textbook tie-in that has been adapted from the series by Patricia Smith, who is a Boston *Globe* columnist, and they simply asked me to select moments in those four programs to write stories about. And they're all based on history, naturally.

For myself, to make it an interesting assignment, I wanted each one of those to be in a different form, literary form. I don't recommend anyone writing twelve stories in one month but I couldn't do them until I got all of this work out of the way for *Dreamer*. Then there are occasional stories, here and there, that I've published in various places. There's enough for a new collection.

Q: Backing up to the novel every eight years and the sweat that goes into it. The time that goes into it and the "totalness" that you mentioned before. What are you like on the day you finish?

A: Exhausted. Totally exhausted.

Q: It's more of a drained feeling than a celebratory one?

A: Well, there's a deep satisfaction, a feeling of, Okay, that is done, but it's like feeling empty. Somebody once told me that after Ralph Ellison finished *Invisible Man*, which he spent seven years on, he just took to his bed for a couple of weeks, like he'd just given a very difficult birth. And I always think about that at the end of a long piece because, for me, a novel has to be everything. If it isn't everything then I don't want to read it, let alone write it. There's a real feeling of exhaustion, but it's a good exhaustion, almost like a Zen emptiness, if you will. It's like in that one work is everything I could feel. And it's all externalized.

When I was a kid, the thing that used to fascinate me about drawing, more than anything else, was the way I felt, or thought, which nobody else could see was something. I could draw, and it was externalized on the page. And once it was externalized I was free of it in a certain kind of way. I could move on to something else. I feel much the same way about a novel. When I write a novel I literally have to go dead to the last novel. And when I say, Dead, I mean dead. It's like I never did it. I forget about it. I don't want to repeat the characters. I don't want to repeat the themes, but nevertheless that stuff still creeps in and you still find overlaps. That'll happen, but I have to say to myself, I've never written a novel before. I'm starting from scratch and I don't know what a novel is, and that's the way I approach it. Each novel I write has to be aesthetically different. Different in style and form and in its philosophical explanations.

For me, it really isn't a careerist or commercial kind of a thing. I wouldn't write fiction if that's why I had to do it. There's things I want to see in existence, and there are things in me that I want to see externalized, too, but other than that I wouldn't do it.

Q: I don't know of anyone who would accuse you of writing fiction for purely commercial reasons. I would think that the simple fact of only coming out with a novel every eight years is enough to dispel that argument. If you were in it for commercial reasons then you would've had a book out in '91 or '92 and probably your publisher would've been thrilled to be able to follow up so quickly on *Middle Passage* and the National Book Award.

A: The question is, What kind of book would it have been? I make money other ways. I teach, and have for twenty something years. I don't have to rely on art for money. I think you compromise art when you do that. It happens very, very often. I won't mention any particular names but I've seen it happen, and that's a sad thing. It's sad for the art and it's sad for the culture, in the long run. It isn't a contribution to literature.

Q: I was thinking before when you were talking about reusing characters. You know I just finished interviewing Russell Banks and he's a real threat to get those tie-ins in there, like the twins who miss the bus in *The Sweet Hereafter* end up living in that same bus in *Rule of The Bone*.

A: Is that right?

Q: And I noticed that Chaym Smith's lineage can be traced back to Baleka from *Middle Passage*.

A: It's better than that. You know the apartment where Smith lives? That he sets fire to?

Q: On Indiana Avenue?

A: Yeah, that's exactly where Bigger Thomas lived in *Native Son*. And Smith's landlady, Vera Thomas? That's Bigger's big sister. She's been living there all these years. She gives him the room. And the optic white? The paint that he uses? You know that, right?

Q: *Invisible Man*.

A: Right. Certainly those little things that pop up like that are fun but only for literate people.

Q: The Allmuseri tribe has appeared in all your fiction since *Oxherding Tale*. How did they come about?

A: Just by chance. I started a story called "The Education of Mingo," published in 1977, and I needed a tribe. I just needed a tribe for this boy from Africa. I read something like eighty books on magic for *Faith and The Good Thing*, when I was writing it, and in one of the books it said there was this little place in this African village called an Allmuseri. It was a hut, and magic went on in there. So I just copied that down in my notebook, you know, and I came back to it, and I said, Okay, this guy's got to be from a tribe. I think they're described as being a mystical tribe. And I needed another tribe in another story so I just said, Allmuseri.

Q: The title story in *Sorcerer's Apprentice*.

A: Yeah, the first story and the last one. Right. And then, with *Oxherding Tale*, I didn't want to designate a particular tribe, so I used the Allmuseri again. I developed Reb along these very spiritual lines, really Taoist. With him, the Allmuseri became more spiritual in its characteristics. So with *Middle Passage*, one of things I wanted to do was just to develop a tribe, top to bottom. Who's their god? What are their rituals? Where do they live? The whole thing. That was actually one of the fun things to do. It's interesting. People still think they're a real tribe. A guy I met in Memphis asked me if they were still living in Africa.

Q: You could have sold me on it.

A: I'm glad because I didn't make that stuff up. It's all culled from real, so-called Third World peoples—India, China, Africa, too—so none of it's made up, but there was just never a tribe like that. So that's how it evolved over time, and I like to play with them that way, in the story, if it fits. I thought about making King an Allmuseri but I thought that would be pushing it a little too far.

Q: Let's talk about the Book, the Book with a capital B in "Moving Pictures."

A: That's actually a story about Buddhist epistemology. No one ever gets that.

Q: That story is probably the least appreciated story of the collection.

A: I guess so. I guess so. I don't think people get it. They think it's just about a writer looking at the movie he's written but it's about Buddhist epistemology. Some Buddhist commentators and writers use that screen, the movie screen, to talk about consciousness, and the way thoughts and ideas and emotions are projected on it.

Q: Is it ever frustrating to be reviewed by people, who by definition, know less about what you're doing than you do? Do you read your reviews?

A: I do, just to see if you come across somebody who's really smart, and there are some smart people out there. I like to see the elegance of a really good reviewer. The reason I started reviewing is because I thought the state of it was really kind of bad in respect to Black American writers.

Q: Did you go into it hesitantly? Did you feel you might be crossing a line?

A: Not really, because there is a kind of literary review that isn't just a book review. The kind that John Gardner used to do. It's almost like a critique. It's the occasion for a critique, and you get an aesthetic. A theory sort of emerges from the review itself, and that's exciting, to me, as literary journalism. Not just a book review, because that's not interesting. But, for example, when I can do a piece on Albert Murray, who I've admired for years, and they give me his novel and his essay collection, then I get to deal with a contemporary writer who I greatly respect. You know what I'm saying? To try and let other people see what is a very nice work. To show them.

Q: Do you only write about novels or writers that you're fond of?

A: No, sometimes they'll send me somebody that's a turkey and at some point you've got to say it's a turkey. You have to look at it in terms of not imposing my own aesthetic on it, but to see what the logic of the book is from the inside, what its goals and ambitions are, and then see if it succeeds or fails on those terms. That's the better way to do it, and to quote liberally from the book so readers can see the real prose and the ideas and come to their own judgment, which might be different from the reviewer's. I think that's very important. You had another question, though, prior to that one.

Q: I want to ask about the Book, with the capital B. Probably it's most specific reference is in "Moving Pictures." As in, "You'd shelved the novel, the Big Book, for bucks monitored by the Writers Guild."

A: That's just some writer working on a book who decides to go do screenplays and not write fiction anymore.

Q: What about Evelyn Pomeroy, the writer in *Oxherding Tale?* She's struggling with her work. The guy in "Moving Pictures" has already lost his battle.

A: Yeah, he's not going to make it. Evelyn Pomeroy is working on a novel, fairly imitative, if I'm not mistaken, of Harriet Beecher Stowe.

Q: The Stowe part is interesting but I think, in a way, Evelyn Pomeroy can be taken a bit more universally than possibly you intended. "Every year past the publication date of her first book cemented her silence, confirmed the suspicions of critics—and Evelyn Pomeroy herself—that the magic had been a mistake that first time. A fluke." I think that applies to a lot of writers, though you also write, "none of this candies over the fact that Evelyn Pomeroy was crazy."

A: Eighty percent of first novelists never publish their second. That's a Gardner quote. Eighty percent of first novelists do not publish a second novel. Everybody thinks their first novel is the really important one to do, but it's really the second novel.

Q: Is it telling that Charles Johnson is writing about a woman's difficulties writing her second novel within his second novel?

A: Yeah, those are thoughts that you have. As a matter of fact, that's probably why I decided this second novel had to be something I truly believed in. It's not just a second novel. This says, This is who you are. You have an aesthetic. There's something you do that nobody else does. And that's very important, I think, for a writer to realize but still, the point of the matter is, the second novel is more important than the first in an artist's career. The first one could be a fluke. There are a lot of first novelists who do not publish second novels.

Q: Even though Evelyn is a comic character, even though she's crazy, I take her and her problem imitating Harriet Beecher Stowe seriously. I understand what she's going through. She has to have a love-hate relationship with Stowe. Something along the lines of, Look what you've done to my work.

A: Well, if you'd like, it's a Cain-Abel relationship. I hadn't thought about that in terms of Harriet because I haven't thought about *Oxherding Tale* in a long time, but there is that with Chaym and King. He can't do what King does, and I kind of tell you why that is in that novel. A lot of it has to do with faith and so forth, but this is different. This is art. But that's a Cain-Abel relationship, clearly, even though it's between two women.

Writers need good models. Everybody needs good models. They should have the best models. But more important than that is individual vision. More important than that is how you find individual vision within a tradition.

Q: Isn't that tough for a young writer to find?

A: I think it's enormously tough, because vision comes with experience. It sounds like a cliché. The point of the matter is that is what's hard to teach. You tell your students, You must find your own individual voice and vision. That's what you have to do. And finding that, sustaining that, breaking away from the models, which by virtue, actually, of finding your own voice, you might honor in terms of their influence on you. As a matter of fact, I'm thinking of King and there's a connection. I'm thinking of the sources for King, and where they were pulled from. Other ministers and stuff. Everything comes from the world in one way or another. It can be argued even that no one's work arises *ex nihilo*, from the egg, original, but it's how you bring all these things together and interpret them. And then you find the instrument for the expression of that vision. And that's why I think it's interesting to go from genre to genre in literary forms. Because each one can be a different vehicle for a vision, for modulating your vision in different ways. Read my book, *Being & Race*, the part on phenomenological aesthetics. You go from screenplays to essays to fiction, and each one, again, is a different vehicle that bodies forth the vision in an entirely different form. And that's discovery and the efflorescence of meaning. But you cannot think in commercial terms to do that, because commercial terms are always, What was successful yesterday? That's what we want today.

Q: Your admiration for Toomer, Wright, and Ellison has been duly noted. Did your admiration, when you were a younger writer, cost you anything?

A: Well, like I said, I wrote six books before *Faith and the Good Thing*. I had models in my mind. It wasn't so much Toomer then as the naturalistic writers, because my early novels were very naturalistic books. I felt there were dimensions of human experience I couldn't get to through naturalism. When I got to *Faith*, that's when I began to feel at least comfortable with the experiential possibilities of the characters in the novel, because, you know, it's magic, it's spiritual stuff, it's philosophy, it's folkore. All the kinds of things that I really delight in. The tale. I like the tale as a literary form because I heard them as a kid. There, for me, is when I began to get a handle on, at least for myself, of what my individual aesthetic/philosophical vision was, a blend of East and West, phenomenology and Buddhism. But that still had to be improved and refined over time. When I wrote that book, it wasn't refined.

My kids have had a big impact on the way I think about, and look at, the world. I think, probably, how I feel about my kids and so forth is what I invested King with, when he's talking about Dexter and little Marty. It's just the way a father feels. So, as you go along, what you see and what you feel deepens. It's a funny thing. We talk about individual vision but the truth belongs to everybody finally. It's not like this is your truth. It belongs to all of us.

Tolstoy's American Preachers:
Letters on Religion and Ethics, 1886–1908

Robert Whittaker

Early in 1890 Tolstoy described America as "the country most sympathetic to me," suggesting sustained interest and understanding on both sides.[1] Tolstoy's most direct knowledge of America came from personal letters, occasional visitors, books by Americans, and subscriptions to several periodicals. The constant flow of letters from America often concerned religious and moral topics. Ordinary citizens as well as religious thinkers gave Tolstoy warm support for his new Christianity, which had

---

This is the fourth in a series of articles presenting Tolstoy's correspondence with Americans, based on material from the joint US-Russian project "Tolstoy and His U.S. Correspondents" ("Tolstoy's American Mailbag: Selected Exchanges with His Occasional Correspondents," "Tolstoy's American Disciple: Letters to Ernest Howard Crosby, 1894–1906" and "Tolstoy's American Translator: Letters to Isabel Hapgood, 1888–1903" appeared in *TriQuarterly* 95, 98 and 102). Begun in 1986 under the auspices of the International Research and Exchanges Board, the Association of Learned Societies, and the Academy of Sciences of the USSR, since 1991 this project has been sponsored by the Gorky Institute of World Literature of the Russian Academy of Sciences in Moscow. The project has received major and essential institutional support from the Tolstoy State Museum in Moscow, especially the staff of its Manuscript Division. Activities of the project in the U.S. have greatly benefited from the support of the staff of the Slavonic and Baltic Division of the Research Libraries of the New York Public Library. The director of the project for the Russian side is Dr. L. D. Gromova, the chief editor is N. P. Velikanova; the activities of the American side are coordinated by the author of this publication, who expresses his gratitude to the staff of the Tolstoy State Museum and its Manuscript Division and to the Gorky Institute for assistance in this research.

dominated his thinking and writing for the previous decade. Ten years later he received a request for his views of America from the English author and critic, Edward Garnett (1868–1937), whose wife Constance had visited Tolstoy and was an important translator of his works. An American magazine had asked for an article on Tolstoy's novel Resurrection, which Garnett agreed to write if Tolstoy would provide some statement about the U.S. Assuming that Tolstoy held a negative attitude (not without reason, given the recent victory of militarism over pacifism in the Spanish-American War), Garnett suggested he address the topic of hypocrisy. Unexpectedly, Tolstoy responded with the same sympathy of a decade ago, now combined with gratitude, and qualified only by a note of disappointment. On the Fourth of July, 1900,[2] he wrote what has been called his "Address to Americans":

Letter 1: to Edward Garnett (July 4, 1900)[3]

Yasnaya Polyana
21–6
4–7 1900

Dear Sir,

Thank you for your letter of June 6th. When I read it, it seemed to me impossible that I could send any message to the American people.

But, thinking over it at night, it came to me that, if I had to address the American people, I should like to thank them for the great help I have received from their writers who flourished about the fifties. I would mention Garrison, Parker, Emerson, Ballou and Thoreau, not as the greatest, but as those who, I think, specially influenced me. Other names are—Channing, Whittier, Lowell, Walt Whitman—a bright constellation, such as is rarely to be found in the literatures of the world.

And I should like to ask the American people why they do not pay more attention to these voices (hardly to be replaced by those of Gould, Rockefeller, Carnegie, or Admiral Dewey) and continue the good work in which they made such hopeful progress.

My kind regards to your wife—and I take this opportunity of once more thanking her for her excellent translation of "The Kingdom of God is Within You."

Yours truly,
Leo Tolstoy.

Tolstoy came to write *The Kingdom of God Is Within You* (1893), the last major work in a series of religious and moral tracts, largely because of his correspondence with the sons of Garrison and with Adin Ballou, both preachers of non-resistance. Surprisingly, most of those who provided "great help"—and many of this "bright constellation"—were religious writers, several of whose names were already unfamiliar. Tolstoy's correspondence with these preachers as well as with a number of other American religious, philosophical, and political thinkers testifies to the breadth of their mutual sympathy.

Tolstoy explained to his English friend, translator, and biographer, Aylmer Maude, that great writers emerged from elevated moral feeling like that generated by the emancipation movement in America. This was why America produced such profound writers in the 1850s, but could not do so in the 1890s.[4] The writers and thinkers of America's Gilded Age and the Gay Nineties remained a disappointment to Tolstoy, not to mention the captains of industry, who represented no less an evil than the military. To the list of famous capitalists Tolstoy joined the name of George Dewey, recently made Admiral for his victory in Manila Bay.

Twenty-five letters written by Tolstoy to sixteen different Americans from 1888 to 1906 will be examined here. These exchanges provided Tolstoy with information and inspiration concerning Christ's teachings, notably on non-resistance and celibacy; with support from publishers and editors of spiritual and philosophical periodicals; and with the opportunity to influence social and political activities, especially in the area of the single tax and pacifism. This was a two way relationship: Tolstoy gave back in support to contemporary Americans what he had gathered from their own earlier, largely forgotten native thinkers. The "good work" which he urged in his Address to Americans was the spiritual, moral, social and political activity he believed characterized the country a half century earlier, and to which he himself would now contribute.

Tolstoy's Christian ideals resulted from his so-called "religious crisis" of the late 1870s, when he experienced depression and philosophical despair over the meaning of his life. He cured his depression and ended his despair by applying skills of self-examination, reasoning, observation, and textual criticism to religion, church writings, and the Bible. He saved himself by using just the skills he had wonderfully developed over the preceding three decades, beginning with short stories on war in the Caucasus and the Crimea, and culminating in *War and Peace* and *Anna Karenina*. The results of this "crisis" he chronicled during the next decade and published most prominently in eight works: *My Confession*, completed 1882 (appeared in America 1887); *An Examination of Dogmatic Theology*, 1880 (1891); *Union and Translation of the Four Gospels*, 1882 (1895); *What I Believe*,[5] 1884 (1895); *What Then Must We Do?* 1885 (1887); *On Life*, 1888 (1888); *Kreutzer Sonata*, 1889 (1890); and *The Kingdom of God Is Within You*, 1893 (1894). When translated and published in America, these works—especially the first, fourth and last three—proved influential, popular, even scandalous, and established Tolstoy's reputation as a spiritual and moral force that could not be ignored.

Each work described a stage in his recovery leading to the discovery of what Tolstoy called true Christianity, or Christ's Christianity. For guidance on how one should live Tolstoy studied the teachings of Jesus recorded in the Gospels. Through textual analysis and common sense reasoning, presented in *Union and Translation of the Four Gospels*, Tolstoy arrived at Christ's five commandments: "do not be angry; do not commit adultery; do not bind yourself by oaths; do not defend yourself by violence; do not go to war."[6] Of these five, the most important (and controversial) were total abstention from violence and from sexual relations, the latter being his ultimate understanding of Christ's teaching on adultery. His new Christianity declared that one can attain true, everlasting life by following Christ's teaching, "even were [one] alone in fulfilling it," and that this was possible now and was the only reasonable way to live.[7]

My Confession, *What I Believe*, and *On Life* brought Tolstoy numerous unsolicited expressions of support and testimonials of similar experiences. He responded to some of the letters, and exchanges developed on non-resistance, the nature of moral ideals, spiritualism, and celibacy. Letters on the latter topic helped him formulate his views in *The Kreutzer Sonata*, in which he defined adultery, illustrated its evil, and condemned marriage as an institution. This work of fiction focused attention on the problem, but failed to clarify Tolstoy's principles, and he later resorted to an afterword to explain himself. In *The Kingdom of God Is Within You* Tolstoy examined the principle of non-resistance, of not using violence to resist evil, and its misunderstanding by most Christians and the church. As a result he condemned all government and asserted that by not using violence against evil, men will find true freedom and the promised Divine Kingdom will come to pass.

In the midst of his "religious" writings Tolstoy came across one of the early American "voices"—Theodore Parker (1810–1860). In 1885 Tolstoy discovered this Unitarian theologian and social reformer, who resembled Emerson and other transcendentalists. He wrote to his wife in February of that year: "I am reading: today I found an American religious writer, Parker, and was very happy to find beautifully expressed my own thoughts of 20 years ago."[8] From his close friend Vladimir Chertkov he had received Parker's lengthy treatise "A Discourse on Matters Pertaining to Religion" and his sermon "A Discourse of the Transient and Permanent in Christianity,"[9] both written in 1841–1842. In the latter, for example, Parker declared that "in respect of doctrines as well as forms, we see all is transitory," and that in "the plain words of Jesus of Nazareth, Christianity is a simple thing, very simple. It is absolute, pure morality; absolute, pure religion; the love of man; the love of God acting without let or hindrance."[10] Tolstoy had himself rejected the church, its doctrine and all dogma in favor of Christ's teaching as the sole basis of belief, which he explained in his just completed *What I Believe*. He would focus these principles into a massive attack on all "transient" institutions of church and state in *The Kingdom of God Is Within You*, which he completed several years later.

I. Christian Non-Resistance

A more direct influence on Tolstoy's *Kingdom of God* came from another of "these voices"—the Unitarian pastor, Adin Ballou (1803–1890), with whom Tolstoy was able to correspond personally.[11] Among those who responded directly to *My Confession* and *What I Believe* by writing to Tolstoy was Ballou's son-in-law, Lewis G. Wilson (1858–1928).[12] Struck by great similarities between the two men's views, in June 1889 Wilson sent several of Ballou's works to Tolstoy.[13] In the exchange of letters between Tolstoy and Wilson and then Ballou himself, Tolstoy explained and defended a number of central points of his new Christianity.

In the name of Christian non-resistance, Ballou with thirty followers in 1841 had founded a community called Hopedale 30 miles west of Boston. During the next fifteen years this practical Christian movement grew into a commune of 300, occupying 500 acres in 50 houses. The roots of the movement lay in the Christian Perfectionism of William Lloyd Garrison, and as Tolstoy was to discover later, Ballou continued to publish Garrison's paper, *The Non-Resistant*, after 1844. Hopedale survived until 1856, when it was bought out by its wealthier members, and eventually it became an ordinary municipality. Soon after the failure of this experiment in moral perfectionism and non-resistance, Ballou and his teachings were forgotten. Twenty years later Tolstoy arrived at a similar doctrine of non-resistance and perfectionism, and his correspondence with Ballou on the essence of their shared moral principles greatly clarified the ideal and application of this doctrine.

Tolstoy responded to Wilson's gift with more than a simple acknowledgment. He insisted, contrary to Wilson's modest assessment of Ballou, that this was a significant thinker whose time would come. Then he objected to a number of Ballou's points in the works he had received:

Letter 2: to Lewis G.Wilson (July 5, 1889)[14]

July 5, 1889

Dear Sir.

I have seldom experienced so much gratification as I had in reading Mr. Ballou's treatise and tracts. I cannot agree with your opinion that Mr. Ballou "will not go down to posterity among the immortals." I think that because he has been one of the first true apostles of the "New Time"—he will be in the future acknowledged as one of the chief benefactors of humanity. If, in his long and seemingly unsuccessful career, Mr. Ballou has experienced moments of depression in thinking that his efforts have been vain, he has only partaken of the fate of his and our Master.

Tell him, please, that his efforts have not been vain, they give great strength to people, as I can judge from myself. In those tracts I found all the objections that are generally made against "non-resistance" victoriously answered, and also the true basis of the doctrine. I will endeavor to translate and propagate as much as I can, the works of Mr. Ballou, and I not only hope, but am convinced, that the time is come, "when the dead hear the voice of the Son of God; and they that hear shall live".

The only comments that I wish to make on Mr. Ballou's explanation of the doctrine, are, firstly, that I cannot agree with the concession that he makes for employing violence against drunkards and insane people. The Master made no concessions, and we can make none. We must try, as Mr. Ballou puts it, to make impossible the existence of such persons, but if they are—we must use all possible means, sacrifice ourselves, but not employ violence. A true Christian will always prefer to be killed by a madman rather than to deprive him of his liberty. Secondly, that Mr. Ballou does not decide more categorically the question of property, for a true Christian not only cannot claim any rights of property, but the term "property" cannot have any signification for him. All that he uses, a Christian only uses till somebody takes it from him. He cannot defend his property, so he cannot have any. Property has been Achilles' heel for the

Quakers, and also for the Hopedale Community. Thirdly, I think that for a true Christian, the term "government" (very properly defined by Mr. Ballou) cannot have any signification and reality. Government is for a Christian only regulated violence; governments, states, nations, property, churches,—all these for a true Christian are only words without meaning; he can understand the meaning other people attach to those words, but for him it has none, just as for a business man if he were to come in the middle of a cricket party, all the divisions of the ground, and regulations of the game, could have no importance or influence upon his activity. No compromise! Christian principles must be pursued to the bottom, to be able to support practical life. The saying of Christ that, "If any man will come after me, let him deny himself, and take up his cross daily and follow me," was true in His time, and is true in ours; a follower of Christ must be ready to be poor and suffer; if not he cannot be his disciple, and "non-resistance" implies it all. Moreover, the necessity of suffering for a Christian is a great good, because otherwise, we could never know, if what we are doing we are doing for God, or for ourselves.

The application of every doctrine is always a compromise, but the doctrine in theory cannot allow compromises; although we know we never can draw a mathematically straight line, we will never make another definition of a straight line than "the shortest distance between two points". I will take care to send you my book on "Life" and would be very glad to know that you and Mr. Ballou approve of it.

"I am come to send fire on the earth, and what will I, if it be already kindled?" I think that this time is coming, and that the world is on fire, and our business is only to keep ourselves burning; and if we can communicate with other burning points, that is the work which I intend to do for the rest of my life.

Many thanks for your letter, and for Mr. Ballou's portrait and books. Please tell him that I deeply respect and love him, and that his work did great good to my soul, and I pray and hope that I may do the same to others.

Your brother in Christ
Leo Tolstoy.

This letter not only defined his own position vis à vis Ballou, but also, more significantly, highlighted the absolute nature of Tolstoy's non-resistance ideal.

Tolstoy held that violence should never be used, even to restrain the insane, the drunk, the child, not even to protect another or to protect the attacker against himself. He allowed no concessions to practical exigencies: the "true Christian" prefers his own death to using any force, even in self-defense. Tolstoy's "perfectionism" exceeded the demands of other practitioners of non-resistance, who allowed for some exceptions. From this principle of absolute non-resistance Tolstoy deduced the inadmissibility of owning property: unwilling to defend his ownership, the Christian must abandon any such claims. Indeed, this same rejection of all violence prevented the Christian from participating in government—local, state, national—for these were only "regulated violence." Furthermore, since it supported institutionalized violence, Tolstoy included the church, which, especially in Russia, cooperated closely with the state. The true Christian "must be ready to be poor and suffer," for this is the inescapable consequence of avoiding all violence. The Tolstoyan twist to suffering—that it is a good test of the true follower—suggests some perversity in his perfectionism.

Tolstoy only conceded that the practical application of this ideal would be imperfect. The true Christian would necessarily fall short of his ideal, but the ideal must remain perfect. In hopes that they might better understand this point, Tolstoy had a copy of his recently published and translated work on practical ethics, *On Life*, sent to Wilson and Ballou.[15]

His closing sentiments about "fire" and "burning" places Tolstoy among the millennialists or premillennialists (the latter awaited heaven on earth as imminent). Tolstoy did not expect any Second Coming or new Messiah: the promised Messiah was Jesus, and he announced that the Kingdom of God had come. This was sufficient for Tolstoy, who saw this promised Kingdom in each true believer.

A response to Tolstoy's criticism did not come immediately. Wilson wrote in August to thank Tolstoy for the copy of *On Life*, which he was reading, and promised to respond to Tolstoy's criticism in the July letter and to share his impressions of the work just received. No such letter survives and it was apparently not written. Rather, on January 14, 1890, Ballou himself wrote to Tolstoy in answer to the latter's criticism. However, before doing so he mildly objected to Tolstoy's enthusiastic insistence on his future fame and glory. Ballou wrote:

I am an old man of little distinction or fame in this world, and must soon pass into the realm of the Invisible where the ambitions of this world are of small account. It gives me little concern to know that a mere handful of mankind concur with me in this

sublime doctrine, and that the vast multitude, even in the so-called Christian Church and State hold it in contempt; for I am none the less certain it is divinely true and excellent, and will finally prevail.

This quiet, realistic appraisal of the future of non-resistance captures an essential difference between the American and the Russian. Patient and pragmatic, Ballou defended his own understanding that Christ's teaching must be achievable, in contrast to Tolstoy's absolute and admittedly impossible ideal. In six numbered points, Ballou countered that "the employment of beneficent physical restraint" is consistent with Christ's teaching, that the context of this teaching limits non-resistance (which was never "absolute passivity to all manner of evil") and allows legislators, governments and "worldly-minded individuals" "the resistance of evil by uninjurious and beneficent forces." In the matter of human imperfection, Ballou objected strenuously: "In ethics, I think, no doctrine, theory or prescribed duty is sound that cannot be put in practice uncompromisingly." To allow for human weakness is "a dangerous concession to make to human tergiversation, that a moral precept—strictly right is expected to be compromised in application to actual practice." Tolstoy and Ballou viewed "moral precepts" differently: for Tolstoy the moral law was absolute, ideal, and actual in an abstract sense; for Ballou such laws are practical and must be practicable in order to be effective. At the root of this difference lay contrasting views of human nature. Ballou wrote of governments, property, and churches:

But these things are realities. We cannot ignore them as non-entities. They are outgrowths from nature, however crude and defective. Man is a social being by natural constitution, he is not and never can be a solitary, independent individual being. He must and will be inevitably more or less a socialist. Families, governments, states, nations, churches and communities always have existed and always will. Christ came to establish the highest order of governmental association, a purely fraternal social order—a church "against which the gates of hell should not prevail.". . . Non-governmentism, non-organizationism, sheer individualism is no part of true Christianity. It is impossible, unnatural, irrational—a chaos. We should aim, with our Master, to transform by the moral forces of divine fundamental principles, uncompromisingly lived out, all barbaric, semi-barbaric and unchristian social organizations into his ideal one—the true Church, wherein the greatest are least and all in unity of spirit

with him, as he with the universal Father. If in this holy aim we must dissent from the selfish and warlike multitude, let us follow him even unto death, till the final triumph arrive.[16]

By nature Tolstoy was not willing to recognize these practical realities: "sheer individualism" for him was not chaos, but the true, ultimate position of man. He believed that social forms—organizational, governmental—distracted man from his true situation in life. His anarchism was more thorough than what Ballou had ever professed.

Finally, in this letter of January 14, Ballou responded in kind with three questions about Tolstoy's *What I Believe*. The first concerned the nature of Christ and what Tolstoy meant by describing Him as "homogeneous with God." The second, "Is Reason really and absolutely God, alone to be worshipped?" And finally, he objected to Tolstoy's claim: "Jesus affirmed only this, that whoever lives in God will be united with God; and he admitted no other idea of the resurrection." Ballou vehemently objected: "I have diligently studied the Gospels for myself more than 75 years, and these assertions are . . . utterly contrary to the sense in which I have understood many passages in those Gospels." Tolstoy responded, but refrained from direct confrontation with Ballou on theological questions. He wrote this undated letter to Ballou in March, some six weeks after receiving the latter's first letter:

Letter 3: to Adin Ballou (March 1890)[17]

Dear Friend and Brother:—

I will not argue with your objections. It would not bring us to anything. Only one point which I did not put clearly enough in my last letter I must explain to avoid misunderstanding. It is about compromise. I said that compromise, inevitable in practice, cannot be admitted in theory. What I mean is this: Man never attains perfection, but only approaches it. As it is impossible to trace in reality a mathematically straight line, and as every such line is only an approach to the latter, so is every degree of perfection attainable by man only an approach to the perfection of the Father, which Christ showed us the way to emulate. Therefore, in reality, every deed of the best man and his whole life will be always only a practical compromise—a resultant between his feebleness and his striving to attain perfection. And such a compromise in practice is not a sin, but a necessary condition of every Christian life.

The great sin is the compromise in theory, is the plan to lower the ideal of Christ in view to make it attainable. And I consider the admission of force (be it even benevolent) over a madman (the great difficulty is to give a strict definition of a madman) to be such a theoretical compromise. In not admitting this compromise I run the risk only of my death, or the death of the other men who can be killed by the madman; but death will come sooner or later, and death in fulfilling the will of God is a blessing (as you put it yourself in your book); but in admitting this compromise I run the risk of acting quite contrary to the law of Christ—which is worse than death.

It is the same with property. As soon as I admit in principle my right to property, I necessarily will try to keep it from others, and to increase it, and therefore will deviate very far from the ideal of Christ.

Only when I profess daringly that a Christian cannot have any property, will I not in practice come near to the ideal of Christ in this instance? There is a striking example of such a deviation in theory about anger (Matt. V. 22) where the added word εἰχῆ ("without any cause") has justified and justifies still, every intolerance, punishment, and evil, which have been and are so often done by nominal Christians. The more we keep in mind the idea of a straight line, viz., the shortest distance between two points—the nearer we will come to trace in reality a straight line. The purer we will keep the ideal of Christ's perfection in its unattainableness, the nearer we will in reality come to it.

Allow me not to argue upon several dogmatical differences of opinion about the meaning of the words "son of God," about personal life after death and about resurrection. I have written a large work on the translation and explanation of the Gospels in which I exposed all I think on those subjects. Having, at the time—ten years ago—given all the strength of my soul for the conception of those questions, I cannot now change my views without verifying them anew. But the differences of opinion on these subjects seem to me of little consequence. I firmly believe that if I concentrated all my powers to the fulfillment of the Master's will which is so clearly expressed in his words and in my conscience, and nevertheless, should not guess quite rightly the aims and plans of the Master whom I serve, he would still not abandon me—and do the best for me.

I would be very grateful to you should you send me a line from yourself. Please give my love to Mr. Wilson. One of your tracts

is very well translated into Russian and propagated among believers, and richly appreciated by them.[18] With deep veneration and tender love, I remain,

Your brother and friend,
Leo Tolstoy.

Tolstoy tenaciously held to his metaphor of the straight line—an artistic rather than a philosophical tool. He would not cede the point that moral absolutes should be approximated in practicable rules, and this set him far apart from the pragmatic American.

Ballou responded in a conciliatory letter dated May 30, 1890, in which he tacitly objected to Tolstoy's view of "compromise in practice of an uncompromisable theory."[19] In the most basic of questions, however, the two saw eye to eye: "And I am confident of two conclusions. First, that Christianity will never enter its promised land till the nominal church re-embraces non-resistance as its cap-stone; and second, that this doctrine will finally be thus re-embraced." Whatever the nature of this principle, absolute or pragmatic, non-resistance remained the centerpiece of both men's philosophies.

Tolstoy wrote again to Ballou, on July 12, 1890, to reaffirm the principle of non-resistance and to ascertain in just what manner Ballou belonged to the movement of Garrison earlier in the century. Tolstoy's different understanding of the church as an institution perhaps reflected the contrasting natures of the Russian Orthodox Church and the Unitarian Church: the former virtually a state institution with rigid dogma, and the latter independent, protean in doctrine, and among the most liberal American Protestant sects.

Letter 4: to Ballou (July 12, 1890)[20]

Dear friend and brother, I seldom experienced such true and great pleasure as I experienced at the reading of your truly brotherly and Christian letter. I thank you very much for the books and tracts that you sent me. I received them safely and have read with great pleasure and profit some of them. The non-resistant catechism I have translated and will circulate it among our friends. It is remarkably well put in such a compact form the chief truths of our faith. What are your relations to the declaration of sentiments of the non-resistance society started by Garrison? Were you a member of it at the time? I quite agree with you that Christianity will never enter its

promised land till the divine truth of the non-resistance principle shall be recognized, but not the nominal church will recognize it. I am fully convinced that the churches are and have always been the worst enemies of Christ's work. They have always led humanity not in the way of Christ, but out of it. I think that all we can say and wish about church is to try to be a member of Christ's church, but we never can define the church itself, its limits, and affirm, that we are members of the sole, true church.

With true brotherly love and highest respect, I remain your friend and brother

Leo Tolstoy.

Ballou did not answer, for he had died shortly after receiving the letter, on August 5.

Tolstoy incorporated Ballou's pamphlet "Christian Non-Resistance: Questions Answered" under the title "A Catechism of Non-Resistance"[21] into the text of the first chapter of his *Kingdom of God*, as he did Garrison's "Declaration of Sentiments." Ballou's writings provided Tolstoy with the beginnings of this last and perhaps most radical of Tolstoy's religious writings. Just before this July letter Tolstoy completed an introduction to Ballou's work, and his work on non-resistance intensified after Ballou's death, as if in commemoration of the American's contribution. By the end of September he had incorporated comments on Garrison's writings and completed this statement on non-resistance in article form. Ultimately this article became the first chapter of *The Kingdom of God*, which he completed only in 1893. The link between the American preacher of non-resistance and Tolstoy had become so clear that his cousin, in a letter of 1889, described Ballou as "The Tolstoy of America."[22]

Under the influence of Ballou, Tolstoy revived his interest in the non-resistance writings of William Lloyd Garrison (1805–1879). Adin Ballou first joined the New England Non-Resistant Society in Boston in 1839, a year after its founding by Garrison, who wrote its "Declaration of Sentiments." Garrison preached Christian Perfectionism, a doctrine which combined anarchism and pacifism by refusing to cooperate with corrupt society or to serve or obey the government. The influence of Garrison on Tolstoy's religious thought, like that of Parker, was limited to published works, which his sons Francis and Wendell sent to Tolstoy. Prompted by reading Tolstoy's *What I Believe*,[23] early in 1886 Wendell sent him the recently published first two volumes of their own biography of their father.[24] In March or April Tolstoy replied with thanks for the biography and with questions. (The original of this letter has not been found; this text is from an incomplete draft in Russian.)

Letter 5: to Garrison (March–April 1886)[25]

Dear Sir:

I received your letter and books. I am very grateful to you for both the former and latter. To learn of the existence of such a pure Christian personality as your father was for me a great joy. I have not yet had time to read the entire book, but the Declaration of Non-resistance, in my opinion, is truly an epoch in the history of mankind. This Declaration, as it was constituted almost a half-century ago, fully expresses the sentiments which we now hold and which all people will hold, because they express God's eternal law for man as disclosed by Christ and which are bound to be realized when all is accomplished.

Allow me to address two questions to you and two requests. I would be very happy if I could pay you back with any kind of favor. My questions and requests are the following: 1) Is there not a short biography of your father encompassing his whole life? I would like as soon as possible to learn of his entire fate. 2) Does the society for non-resistance continue to exist. Where is its official publication, and who are its members? It seems strange to make this last question: the society of non-resistance is not an exclusive society, but it is properly a single church which began with Christ and can never cease. My question properly means: are there people who consciously profess the true faith and denounce quasi-Christians who accept government and the violence inseparable from it.—

Once again I thank you from my heart and hope that you will not refuse to oblige me even more by answering my two questions.—

Wendell and Francis responded immediately: the latter sent Tolstoy a biography of Garrison by Oliver Johnson and a memorial volume,[26] while the former wrote to answer Tolstoy's questions. In his letter of May 5, 1886, Wendell wrote:

The Non-Resistant was suspended, for want of pecuniary support, in the summer of 1842. The Non-Resistance Society held annual

meetings in Boston (but probably had little if any propagandist activity otherwise) down to the year 1848, after which it was probably dissolved. No similar society has ever risen to take its place, though a non-resistant "community" at Hopedale, Massachusetts, survived it for many years (its founder, the Rev. Odin Ballou, still lives at Hopedale).[27]

To this information Wendell added a clarification in his letter of January 9 the following year:

In regard to the Non-Resistant newspaper I am now able to add, that, after having been suspended in 1842, as I have already written you, its publication was resumed in 1844 by the Rev. Adin Ballou, at the Hopedale Community in Massachusetts. It again failed of support, however, and was finally discontinued with the eighth number.[28]

Perhaps because Tolstoy viewed Garrison as a precursor to Ballou, he considered him to be a Christian non-resistant first, and only consequently an abolitionist and antislavery activist. In his 1904 introduction to Chertkov's biography of Garrison, Tolstoy explained that the abolitionist placed non-resistance "at the foundation of his practical activity in the emancipation of the slaves" because he understood that "slavery . . . was only a particular instance of universal coercion." Furthermore, "Garrison did not so much insist on the right of Negroes to be free as he denied the right of any man whatsoever, or of any body of men, forcibly to coerce another man in any way."[29] (This view is not generally shared by recent studies of Garrison, which view non-resistance—together with woman's rights, anticlericalism, and perfectionism—as extraneous to his basic abolitionism.)

Tolstoy's interest in Garrison was stimulated again in 1890 as a result of his correspondence with Ballou on non-resistance. Nearly four years had passed since his first contact with the Garrisons when he undertook a translation of their father's "Declaration of Sentiments," the document he wrote for the Peace Convention of 1838 which had given rise to the Non-Resistant Society.[30] Tolstoy included the Declaration in the non-resistance article that was to become the first chapter in his *Kingdom of God*. At this time he wrote to Garrison's son Wendell and acknowledged their gift of the third and fourth volumes of their biography and sent them the requested portrait of Turgenev.[31] Tolstoy's letter of January 1890 has not been preserved, and correspondence with the Garrisons resumed only in 1892, when Francis, as secretary of a Boston organization to aid famine victims, began sending contributions to assist Tolstoy's efforts to aid the Russian peasants.[32] These letters no longer concerned the activities of William Lloyd Garrison, Tolstoy's concern with Christian non-resistance had been temporarily set aside, and his correspondence on the American founders of this movement had ended.

II. Christian Celibacy

In addition to Garrison and Ballou the first chapter of *The Kingdom of God* cites other sources: "Among the first responses called forth by my book [*What I Believe*] were some letters from American Quakers." This work stimulated a number of Americans to write Tolstoy with letters of support—over a dozen in the four years after the first two translations of *What I Believe* appeared late in 1886 and in 1887.[33] Among them were two Quakers who sent pamphlets, journals and books to Tolstoy to explain their view of non-resistance.[34] There also were letters and works sent by Shakers, whose ideas had an equally significant impact on Tolstoy's *The Kreutzer Sonata*. In this earlier, scandalous work on relations between the sexes Tolstoy tested ideas from his new Christianity which were no less extreme than his ideal of non-resistance, in particular the Christian ideal of a celibate life. The Shakers' view of celibacy provided significant support, if not influence on this point in Tolstoy's novella, which he worked on from 1887 to 1889.

Tolstoy had arrived at the ideal of celibacy independent of the Shakers, whose impact came late in his development of these ideas. The ideal originated in the second of Christ's commandments (as defined by Tolstoy): "Do not commit adultery." The Gospels present this principle in Matthew 19:8–12, where adultery includes divorce and remarriage. The key verse, in Tolstoy's interpretation from his own *Union and Translation of the Gospels* (1882), is the following: "The disciples say, It is better not to marry, in order that we may not have these sins. He replies, Yes, it is better: it is easy to say so, but not easy to fulfill it, that is, entirely to abstain from women."[35] In subsequent accounts of this second commandment celibacy is only implied, as for example in *The Gospel in Brief* (1883), where Tolstoy summarized his translation:

> **And I tell you that he who casts off his wife drives both her and him who unites with her into depravity. And by casting off his wife a man spreads dissoluteness abroad.**

And his pupils said to Jesus: It is too hard to be always bound to one wife. If that must be, it would be better not to marry at all.

He said to them: You may refrain from marriage but you must understand what that means. If a man wishes to live without a wife, let him be quite pure and not approach women: but let him who loves women unite with one wife and not cast her off or look at other women.[36]

In his earlier, close textual analysis, celibacy was "better, . . . but not easy to fulfill"; now it had become "if one wishes."

In *What I Believe* (1884) Tolstoy stated that "men and women . . . should unite with one another in couples and never under any circumstances infringe these alliances; so that the whole evil of strife caused by sexual relations is removed by the fact that there are not solitary men or women left deprived of married life."[37] A strong, pure marriage forms the concluding principle in his tract on poverty, *What Then Must We Do* (1885). Here Tolstoy advanced a strongly patriarchal view of a wife's duties—children, cooking, and (in place of church) upbringing. The work ends: "Women-mothers, in your hands, more than in any one else's, rests the salvation of the world."[38] It remains unclear exactly what prompted the change in Tolstoy's thinking from this traditional view to the emphasis on celibacy and women's rights, as expressed in *Kreutzer Sonata* (1887–89). Aylmer Maude, in his translation of *What I Believe*, provided a footnote to explain how Tolstoy could "fully approve of" married life in 1884 but then "in 1889 . . . express the opinion that man can best serve God and man by remaining celibate."

The explanation of his change of view lay in the fact that his wife disagreed with his wish to renounce his property, and he found that his union with her, and even their affection for one another made it hard for him to adhere to his principles. Marriage was therefore an obstacle to right life, and as such, it seemed to him, should be shunned by a Christian.[39]

There is little in Tolstoy's diary, letters, or other writing at this time to corroborate this assumption, but Maude knew Tolstoy very well, shared many of his ideals, and thus provides a reliable point of view. One can find some echo of Tolstoy's impatience with family life in his *Death of Ivan Ilyich*, written during this period, from 1884 to 1886. The wife thinks of her dead husband mostly in terms of property, and Ivan Ilyich himself discovers the falsehood of his former devotion to property and society, and of his family, only just before his death.

Another source—medical rather than moral—encouraged Tolstoy towards increasingly strict ideas of chastity: his correspondence with an American writer, editor and physician, Alice Stockham (1833–1912). In October and November 1888 Dr. Alice B. Stockham wrote Tolstoy on behalf of her magazine, *The Kindergarten*, to invite him to share his views on education and perhaps contribute a series of articles.[40] (Tolstoy's theories of education had appeared in a French translation, and an American journal published a commentary in 1888.[41]) With the second letter Stockham sent a copy of her own book, *Tokology: A Book for Every Woman*, with the explanation: "Your daughters may find some useful know-ledge in it."[42] This practical guide to childbearing and health had enjoyed great popular success—it "has had a large American role" wrote Stockham—and this immediately attracted Tolstoy's attention. He responded on December 12 with an enthusiastic letter about her book:

Letter 6: to Alice B. Stockham (December 12, 1888)[43]

Dear Madam.

I have received your book "Tokology" and thank you very much for sending it to me. I have examined it and found that it is, as far as I am competent, truly a book, not only for woman but for mankind. Without labour in this direction mankind cannot go forward; and it seems to me especially in the matter treated in your book in chapter XI, we are very much behindhand. It is strange, that last week I have written a long letter to one of my friends on the same subject. That sexual relation without the wish and possibility of having children is worse than prostitution and onanism, and in fact is both. I say it is worse, because a person who commits these crimes, not being married, is always conscious of doing wrong, but a husband and a wife, which commit the same sin, think that they are quite righteous.

Therefore your book (not speaking of its great merits) was very welcome to me.

I should very much like to have your book sold in M[oscow] and P[etersburg].

Entitled "Chastity in the Marriage Relation," chapter eleven advanced the absolute requirement of continence during nursing, strongly (if not unequivocally) defended sexual relations purely for procreation, and even supported the ideal of celibacy. Remarkably, Tolstoy had touched just this set of ideas in the "long letter" to Chertkov written November 18, 1888.[44] This letter, in a somewhat rambling manner, worked out in practical terms the nature of marital relations consistent with the Christian ideal as Tolstoy understood it. He had also expressed this ideal in an earlier letter to Chertkov of October 21, in which he returned to his understanding of Matthew 19:11–12. ". . . This means nothing else than, if a man asks what he must do regarding sexual feeling, what he must strive for? What, in our language, is the ideal for man? He answers: become a eunuch for the Kingdom of God. And he who achieves this will achieve the most sublime; but he who does not achieve this will also feel good because he is striving for it." Tolstoy concluded: "I think that for man's welfare, both men and women must strive for complete chastity (*devstvennost'*), i.e. consciously seek chastity, and then the outcome for man will be what should be.[45]

The particular significance of Stockham's work was that Tolstoy had found expert medical corroboration for his own moral and religious views (*pace* his often expressed skepticism for doctors). Immediately upon receiving *Tokology* he wrote to Chertkov again, on November 29, that the work "discusses in one chapter that very subject about which we corresponded and resolved the question, of course, in the same way we did. I'm happy to see that the question has been raised long ago and that scientific authorities solve it in the same sense."[46] These ideas as well as the principles enunciated by Stockham found full expression again in *Kreutzer Sonata*. It is salutary to keep in mind that, given all the intense scrutiny, including much significant research, of Tolstoy's attitude toward sexuality and sexual practices, the matter itself was for him primarily a religious question: how to lead a truly Christian life.

Tolstoy's enthusiasm for *Tokology* encouraged Stockham to take up his offer to have the work translated into Russian, for which she visited Moscow. She wrote him upon arriving in St. Petersburg on October 5, 1889: "More and more I see it is quite important that I should know something of Russian customs before *Tokology* comes out in Russian. Your habits and food are so different from ours that if the translation is exact there should be foot notes either by myself or someone familiar with both lands."[47] In Moscow she worked with a translator, S. M. Dolgov, in order to create a Russian edition. The translation was finished the next year, Tolstoy wrote an enthusiastic preface in February

1890, but difficulties with the censorship (principally because of the forward) held up the appearance of the work until 1892.[48] In his introduction Tolstoy recommended the book for its instructions to parents on how to bear and raise children in the best of circumstances. Of the science of childbirth noted that "after the science of how to live and how to die, this is the most important science."[49]

Stockham herself, who visited Yasnaya Polyana on October 14, 1889, made no less a positive impression on Tolstoy than her book. Their discussions concerned not medicine or sexual morals, but religion. Tolstoy wrote to a friend after her visit: "An American woman, Stockham, was here and left today. A smart and serious woman, formerly a Quaker, who wants to write a book about American religions. She supplemented in many ways my information on the American religious movement, and I very much feel like writing what I know and think about it."[50] The conversation excited him, he got up early the next day, and wrote in his diary:

> **1) Universalists, 2) Unitarians, 3) Quakers of the new construction after 1836—4) the majority of spiritualists, 5) Swedenborgians, 6) Shakers, 7) Zoroasters, 8) Spiritualists having their own churches, and finally 9) Broadchurch, which is represented by Herbert Newton, these are all one and the same thing. This all leads to practical Christianity, to universal brotherhood, and the sign of all this is non-resistance.**[51]

The entry continues with a discussion of Ballou's theories of non-resistance and of his differences with Ballou over the question of absolute moral standards and relative, practicable rules ("Practical Christianity" was a concept developed by Ballou and the title of a journal he published). The diary entry and link with Ballou illustrates, again, that the basic questions occupying Tolstoy in his contact and correspondence with Stockham were spiritual and moral. In the same entry Tolstoy noted that he asked Stockham "to help him gather information about America's religions." However, although she continued to write Tolstoy after her visit—13 letters from October 1889 to March 1906—the topic of religion did not come up again, and Tolstoy never responded.

In the spring of 1889, while still working on *Kreutzer Sonata* (by now Tolstoy was into a seventh version) and transforming views from *Tokology* into comments by his hero, Pozdnyshev, Tolstoy received the first in a series of letters from Shakers. He was working out practical questions of chastity, when on March 30, 1889, Asenath Stickney of the

Canterbury, N.H., Shaker community wrote, "Your radical views of Christ's teachings are many of them in strict accord with those which have been entertained by our Community for the past one hundred years." Her reaction to reading *My Confession* was that "the very texts the author quotes are continually repeated in our Church; are interpreted, and explained by our Christian advocates in the same way, almost in the same words."[52] She decided to send Tolstoy a series of Shaker publications, such as *Plain Talks upon Practical Religion*, *Sketches of Shakers and Shakerism*, a Shaker hymnal, and some issues of their periodical, *The Shaker Manifesto*.[53] Tolstoy expressed amazement in his diary for April 21, 1889: "Had dinner, read the Shakers. Wonderful. Complete sexual restraint. How strange that I received them now, when I am concerned with these questions."[54] The next day he wrote to Chertkov, "Do you know their doctrine? In particular, against marriage, but for an ideal of purity beyond marriage. This is a question which especially occupies me and namely as a question. I do not agree with the Shaker solution, but I cannot but admit that their solution is much more reasonable than ours—marriage—which is accepted by all."[55]

A week or so later Tolstoy read about the Shakers from the *History of American Socialisms* by John Humphry Noyes, founder of the Oneida community, who analyzed various religious communal experiments which had taken place during the first two-thirds of the century.[56] Tolstoy remarked in his diary with some satisfaction (on May 3, 1889): "Reading Noyes on communes. It's the same everywhere—freeing oneself from superstitions of religion, government, and family."[57] The account of the Shakers' in Noyes' history consisted largely of the eyewitness account of an anonymous visitor who spent four months in the community at Watervliet, near Albany. Tolstoy's reaction to this account, as distinct from the Shakers own writings, was more critical:

Reading of the Shakers: one is dismayed by the deathly monotony and the superstitions: dances and unseen visitors and gifts—eyeglasses, fruits, etc. I thought: withdrawal into a commune, the formation of a commune, maintaining its purity—this is all a sin—error. It is impossible to purify oneself individually or alone; if you're going to purify yourself, then do it together; to separate oneself in order not to get dirty is itself the greatest impurity, like feminine purity achieved through the labors of others. This is the same as cleaning or digging from the edge, where it is already clean. No, whoever wants to work, he will dig in right in the very middle where

the dirt is, or if he doesn't dig in, at least he will not leave the middle if he has ended up there.[58]

Tolstoy concluded that communes, whether monastic or socialistic, depended on force and coercion and were thus essentially at odds with the commandment of non-resistance.

Later that year, at about the time of Stockham's visit, Tolstoy received a letter and publications from a different Shaker community, at Mt. Lebanon, New York (also near Albany). The writer was Alonzo Hollister (1830–1911), who addressed him as "Apostle of God to your Nation" and assured him: "Your conduct and writings are stirring the religious thought of America to its very depths."[59] It was Tolstoy's advocacy of non-resistance that particularly attracted Hollister: "I write to strengthen your heart & hands, & to let you know there is a people who sympathize with your efforts to teach human brotherhood, and the principles of peace and non-resistance to evil—that is, not to resist evil with evil, but to overcome evil with good." (He had not read Tolstoy's works, but learned of him from published sermons on Tolstoy's ethics and from the accounts of a visit by an Episcopal clergyman, William W. Newton, which quoted copiously from *My Confession*.[60]) He also sent Shaker publications, several of which were new to Tolstoy.[61]

Hollister raised the subject of celibacy in connection with the principle of non-resistance. Although virtually all churches (he notes the exception of the Quakers) consider the commandment "resist not evil" to be impractical, the Shakers "have demonstrated its practicality for over 100 years, in a number of Societies, in different States of the American Union." This principle and the Golden Rule, if universally adopted, "would banish all war, crime, injustice, and oppression, & necessitous want from human society." However, behind these practical guidelines, lay a higher principle:

[They are] . . . merely an external remedy, which does not purify & remove the cause of evil from the heart. Hence for those who seek a higher & purer kingdom than that of the earthy, animal man who marries & propagates his species, Jesus taught the ethics of the kingdom of heaven—of the angel world—which descends from above & is not of this world—& which has a distinct social order, & a method for cleansing the heart from every desire & taint of sin, & from every shade & mar of selfishness & carnality.[62]

This interpretation of Christ's call to celibacy (Matthew 19:11–12) differed little from Tolstoy's, the language was very similar to his, and only the allusion to a world of spirits ("angel world") proved inconsistent with his views.

On October 31, 1889, Tolstoy responded to Hollister with thanks for the books and commented on aspects of Shaker belief. (The "new work about marriage" is, of course, *Kreutzer Sonata.)*

Letter 7: to Alonzo Hollister (October 31, 1889)[63]

Dear friend.

I got your letter, the books and tracts and thank you very sincerely for them. Last year I began a new work about marriage and thinking more and more on the topic I came nearly to the same conclusions as the Shakers. My idea to put it shortly is this: the ideal of a Christian must be complete chastity, marriage is the state of men and women who striving to attain that ideal could not reach it. And if the ideal is chastity the marriage will be moral. But in our society the ideal of men and women is marriage, and therefore our marriage is unmoral. You can think how welcome were to me your books and tracts. I agree with you in all your views of sexual relation[s] and got very much profit in perusing your speeches and sermons.

There are points on which I can not agree with you—that is, the revelation of Ann Lee, the belief that the whole Bible is inspired and that spirits can manifest themselves.

I am very sorry that it is quite impossible to me to believe in this, very sorry because in all other respects I greatly admire your life—non-resistance, vegetarianism, chastity, communism.

With brotherly love,
Yours Leo Tolstoy

Some months ago I received in Moscow, books, tracts, and photographs from a Shaker community; unfortunately I lost the letter with the address and could not answer and thank. If you happen to know who it was tell him that I am very sorry for it.

This letter confirms that Tolstoy had already come to the Christian ideal of absolute chastity. Tolstoy inserted in *Kreutzer Sonata* the example of the Shakers as a community which practiced celibacy. At the end of chapter 11, when Pozdnyshev introduces the ideal of complete chastity, the narrator interjects:

> **"I understand your thinking," I said, "the Shakers profess something like it."**
>
> **"Yes, yes, and they are right," he said. "Sexual passion, however it might be dressed up, is an evil, a terrible evil, against which one must struggle, and not encourage it, as we do. The words of the Gospel that he who looks upon a woman with lust has already committed adultery with her apply not only to other's wives, but namely—and chiefly—to one's own wife."**[64]

Incidentally, this exchange is missing from Maude's popular English translation of *Kreutzer Sonata*, which was based on the text in volume 13 of Tolstoy's collected works, edited by his wife and published in 1891 by special permission of the Czar.[65]

The eccentric nature of the narrator of *Kreutzer Sonata* and his peculiar manner of presenting Tolstoy's Christian ideals, most notably celibacy, caused some confusion about just what the work meant. At the urging of Chertkov and in response to numerous letters, Tolstoy decided to explain its significance in a special essay. This "Afterword to 'The Kreutzer Sonata'" stated plainly that Christ's teaching "points to absolute chastity as an ideal." Tolstoy restated the substance of Matthew 19:11–12, "that it is better for an unmarried man not to marry at all, to remain entirely chaste." However, if a Christian believer realizes that he falls short of this ideal (which is inevitable), he should strive to achieve it as best he can. Tolstoy made this same point in his exchange with Ballou: "It is not true that the ideal of infinite perfection cannot be a means of guidance in life." Here he used the analogy of a compass: to say that Christ's ideal is unattainable is the same as if a sailor who cannot keep to the compass bearing would decide either to throw out the compass or to fasten the compass needle so that it points where the ship is going. "It is not true that Christ's ideal is too lofty, too perfect and unattainable for us to use it as a means of guidance. We are unable to use it as a means of guidance simply because we lie to ourselves." The lie is "to replace Christ's ideal with external rules" rather to believe in this ideal.[66]

The Kreutzer Sonata seemed particularly difficult for readers perhaps because Tolstoy gave artistic embodiment to this contrast between the practical imperfection of human life and the perfect ideal. His hero, Pozdnyshev, is a powerful instance of human weakness: his story exemplifies physical sensuousness, violent jealousy, murderous rage. He has come to understand the Christian ideal (by a process of discovery that is not clear—to himself or the reader), and from this point of view he describes his former life as a horrible distortion of the truth. However, his own overpowering imperfections—including tics and mannerisms, using a narcotic (strong tea), and an emotional instability that is frightening at times—make his description of the ideal difficult to accept. It seems easier to understand and appreciate an ideal from one who is attractive and a model of moral and physical good. Tolstoy provided the opposite in Pozdnyshev.

Mention should be made here of an unusual exchange between Tolstoy and the publisher of a manual on sexual relations, Eliza Burnz (1823–1903). On October 7, 1890, she sent him a copy of *Diana, a Psycho-Fyziological Essay on Sexual Relations, for Married Men and Women*, a pamphlet written by Henry Parkhurst and published anonymously. Attached to the pamphlet was "A Private Letter to Parents, Fyzicians and Men-Principals of Schools" written by Burnz, who also advocated spelling reform (through her New School of Fonografy in New York City). In her letter to Tolstoy she noted: "Since the circulation, in America, of your work, "The Kreutzer Sonata," very many persons hav said, 'Diana carries out, and explains, and makes practicabl, Count Tolstoi's theories'."[67] At first Tolstoy believed this pamphlet represented still more support for his Christian ideal of chastity. He responded with a warm letter of thanks:

Letter 8: to Eliza Burnz (November 12, 1890)[68]

I received your letter and book safety and thank you very much for them. The book was very welcome and I think its propagation will do much good.

I immediately wrote a small article on its contents and made free to join to it your letter which I sent to a very popular journal the Week (Nedelya), from which it is reprinted in many periodicals. Although I do not quite agree with all your views, as you can see from my epilogue to the Cr<eutzer> Son<ata> I find your work very useful and thank you again for communicating it to me.

Tolstoy began his review, entitled "On Relations between the Sexes," by quoting Burnz's letter as an example of the many voices heard in support of the ideals expressed in "Kreutzer Sonata" and the "Afterword."[69] However, he qualified his approval of the pamphlet by noting that its thought reflected "not a Christian, but rather a pagan, Platonic outlook."[70] Indeed, the methods advocated by Parkhurst and Burnz turned out to be the opposite of Tolstoy's ideal of celibacy, as he realized later to his chagrin.[71]

Celibacy raised the specter of the end of the human race, should this ideal be universally realized. Tolstoy addressed this threat in the eleventh and twelfth chapters of *Kreutzer Sonata* with assurances that the ideal will not soon be realized. Furthermore, the total achievement of this ideal (given the fact that the sexual passion is the most powerful of all human emotions) could occur only after other true Christian ideals had been achieved (eliminating anger, violence, oaths, and war), at which point the purpose and perfection of human life will have been achieved. Until that time, however, there was much imperfect life left for humankind. Ballou had disagreed with his absolute Christian ideal and would accommodate human imperfection. The Shakers, however, expressed views much closer to Tolstoy's. Hollister used the following example to explain the gradual process of mankind's increasing understanding of the ideal and gradual increase in perfection:

> Do those who fear that the world will become depopulated by the gospel of virgin continence & purity—do they fear the Sea will become depopulated by fishing in it? Yet no fish which men take out of the sea, will propagate their species afterward. . . . A net allows the little fish to escape—enough, certainly to prevent extinction of the species.
>
> The kingdom is composed of volunteers, & only those who have reached a certain growth of understanding can become subjects of the spiritual kingdom.[72]

Tolstoy expressed his admiration for the image of the fish net in his next letter written to Hollister. He wrote on August 23, 1890, in response to Hollister's long letter of July 18, which had also expanded on the spiritualism that Tolstoy found unacceptable:

Letter 9: to Hollister (August 23, 1890)[73]

Dear Friend and Brother!

I thank you heartily for your letter; I expected it. I knew that my ideas about marriage would be approved by your community. Your books and tracts, especially "What would become of the world if all were Shakers" corroborated my views and helped me very much to a clear understanding of the question. I am very much astonished how a Christian can not approve of your and my view of marriage. In Corinthian 7 it is said in so many plain words. I admire very much your explanation of the comparison of the Kingdom of Heaven to a net, and the conclusion that the fishes taken in the net can/will not depopulate the sea, and that if they do it will be after the will of God, which in the form of our love for purity and chastity is written in our hearts like the love for purity and chastity.

I received one of your books, the Millenial church book, and I thank you very much for it,[74] but pardon me in brotherly love and spirit, I must tell you the truth: it was very painful for me to read in your letter the account of the influx of spirits from heaven and so on. It is painful for me because not only your faith (excepting Anna Lee and the manifestation of spirits) and your practice of life, as far as I know it is a true Christian faith, corroborated by your way of life—and it should have attracted to you all the people who crave for a true Christian life, but your peculiarities—manifestations of spirits—repel them.

God's truth has been known always in the old times, the same as now. The true progress, the establishing of the kingdom of God on earth consist not in producing new truths, but in sifting the truths that are known to us, by putting aside the lies and superstition with which they are intermingled.—You have put aside a great quantity of lies and superstitions of the external world, but I am afraid you have accepted new ones.—Put them aside. Analyze them. Don't keep to beliefs only because they have been beliefs a long time and are old. Put them away and your Shaker faith with your chaste and spiritual life, with your humility, charity, with your principle of moderation and manual work will conquer the world. Please pardon me if I have offended you. I have written this only because I think and feel it and because I love God, I try to love Him, and through Him to love you my brethren.

All that you say about the time fast approaching in which the Divine light will be spread over all the world and darkness dispelled is quite true. I feel it, and therefore write thus to you.

Yours in brotherly love,
Leo Tolstoy.

Hollister had explained at great length how Shakers communicated with the spirits not only of their own departed, but also of other departed individuals. He described a bizarre Russian connection with the spirit world: "In the time of the extraordinary influx of spirits from the heavens, & from Hades, to the bodies of the brethren & sisters in our meetings, from 1837 to 1848, Alexander of Russia was named as one of the spirits who bro't love from our Parents in heaven to their children in the body—& we felt greatly noticed & blessed, & of course encouraged thereby."[75] This sort of mystical, supernatural, and therefore non-rational experience and knowledge deeply disturbed Tolstoy, who felt it differed little from the official mysticism of the Russian Orthodox church. The Shaker way of life—their dedication to manual labor, their self-reliance and independence, and their principles of love and non-resistance—represented the same ideals he strove for in his own life and therefore this superstitious element seemed especially out of place. He responded positively to the phrase in Hollister's letter that suggested the coming millennium: "I believe the time is fast approaching, when the light of Divine truth will be so clear, & the darkness of ages of false customs & false reasonings, so dispelled & vanished, that all doubtful questionings will be settled, & all honest, persistent seeking for truth concerning man's destiny, & the best use of life here, will be rewarded with the finding." However, Tolstoy could not agree with the sort of authorities Hollister cited for his statement: "The words of spiritual Seers & the *signs of the times*, indicate a change approaching." For Tolstoy it was enough to rely on one's intuition.

Hollister, in his letter of November 16, 1890, shared his reactions to Tolstoy's *My Confession*, which he finally read. He noted that his own "spiritual illumination" came, beginning in 1851, through his belief in "spiritual manifestations" of the sort which he argued energetically in this and previous letters to Tolstoy. However, he continued, "had I not believed in spiritual manifestations, & been myself spiritually illuminated & instructed, I doubt if I could have been persuaded to live as Christ taught. Perhaps I could in some measure, if I had been instructed in the contrasts presented in Tolstoy's *My Religion*."[76] This is an extraordinary complement, indeed, to suggest that this work would have brought him to his present enlightenment, had it existed when he needed it. In the same letter Hollister commented on *Kreutzer Sonata* in such a way as to suggest that he approved of the work also and of its ideas, which is not surprising, since the work reflects much that is consistent with Shaker views. He wrote, "There are various opinions of the Kreutzer Sonata—more of them censorious than approbative—but that was to be expected, when the veil is withdrawn by iconoclastic hands, from the world's Idols." The "idols," presumably, are the social conventions of sexual initiation, courtship, marriage and family life: behind the "veil" is the animal, carnal existence of those who serve these conventions.

On December 9, 1890, Hollister wrote again to present his view of sprits in more detail. In this lengthy letter of many pages he demonstrated, largely by citations from the Bible, the reality of spirit intervention in human life. He summarized his views:

For us to deny, or ignore the agency of spirits in human affairs—or their power to manifest, would be as suicidal & weak witted, as it would be for a Professor of Science & Philosophy to deny the action of electricity & magnetism in the phenomena of nature, & to ignore all the discoveries & inventions made in the last 100 years to render those ordinary invisible, nonintelligent forces, serviceable to man, in the matter of driving machinery, giving us light, & conveying intelligence along a wire stretched thousands of miles.[77]

Tolstoy remained absolutely opposed to belief in anything incomprehensible by reason. Yet in his response he omitted any reference to spirits and spiritualism, perhaps out of respect and the recognition of this ideological impasse.

Hollister had also offered comments on Tolstoy's *What I Believe*, with whose basic ideas he was in general agreement. He complemented Tolstoy on his Greek translations and textual analysis, and he wrote at length on the nature of Christ. After summarizing his views, he concluded:

I think this harmonizes with the idea of the Christian life expressed by you in "My Religion," if I apprehend correctly your meaning. I think we agree with your idea of the *Son* of *man*—he is part of every man—or rather, every man & woman is part of him, who undergoes the process of dying to self & personal aims, & rising into that imperishable life which knows no partiality, but exists for all.

These comments on *My Religion* and the nature of Christ did not elicit a reaction from Tolstoy, who was disturbed by the extensive argumentation for spiritualism. He responded to Hollister's letter on February 15, 1891, with the following polite, brief note:

Letter 10: to Hollister (February 15, 1891)[78]

Dear Friend and Brother.

I received your long letter and have read it with interest, but I must confess that all your arguments taken from John's revelation do not convince me. I do not consider that book as a moral guide. I

think that God's revelation must be simple and able to be understood by the simplest soul. In general as I told you before, dear Friend, I agree completely with your practice of life, but not with your theory, especially about spirits. I hope that the open expression of my thoughts will not lessen your kind disposition to me.

With brotherly love
Yours truly
Leo Tolstoy.

With this letter Tolstoy ended his correspondence with Alonzo Hollister, who wrote him again for the last time on May 8, 1891. Hollister commented on recent newspaper articles about Tolstoy's religious writings: an account of an interview on the origins of *Kreutzer Sonata* with a *New York Herald* reporter whom he described as "'pigheaded' & pugnacious" and "stuck in sensual mud"[79]; and an article on Tolstoy's views of true and false Christianity, parts of which he agreed with. However, he emphatically disagreed with Tolstoy's idea, which he quoted from the article: that the Gospel "completely excludes outward worship, condemns it, & in the clearest & most positive manner repudiates proselytism of every kind."[80] Hollister expounded the opposite point at great length, citing numerous texts from the Bible in support of traditional preaching. Tolstoy was not inclined to argue the significance of texts whose validity he had already questioned, and so the correspondence found itself in a dead end.

Hollister had read Tolstoy's letter to another Shaker at Mt. Lebanon, Frederick Evans (see number 11 below), in which he raised the question of private property. This apparently prompted Hollister to suggest why the Shakers not only believed in property rights but also accepted government: "Where the rights of equitable distribution of property & possession are not recognized, there could be no order, no incentive to labor for more than bare subsistence—no crops could be raised, because of plunderers, like the Arab robber tribes, in some parts of Palestine. Hence so long as any considerable portion of men are beastly & unjust to each other, they must have some kind of government." In this case like Ballou, Hollister could not accept Tolstoy's absolute ideal of non-resistance, and thus their exchange came to an end.

Frederick W. Evans (1808–1893), an Elder of the Shaker community at Mt. Lebanon, wrote Tolstoy on December 6, 1890, to send him some of his own writings and to ask for comments.[81] He had been following Tolstoy's correspondence with Hollister, and he added a new viewpoint regarding spiritualism . "You are 'pained' at our ideas about 'Ann Lee, &

spirit intercourse' between parties in & out of mortal bodies," Evans wrote, and he noted that times have changed and so have Shaker views: "what they were, when the 'millennial Church' was written, leave to the people of those times," and he suggested these were childish things that belonged in a childhood long past.[82] He invited Tolstoy to come to visit, and ended on a millennial note: "A poor, illiterate, uneducated factory-woman [i.e. Ann Lee, the founder of Shakerism] has confounded the wisdom of all *men*-reformers, legislators, & scholars, who have come to nothing, as promoters of human happiness. Their systems have ended, in Christendom, as you now see it; & as Booth[83] & his companion who inspired him, saw it. The end has come! & Tolstoy & Shakerism remain, as the last hope of mankind."

Tolstoy answered Evans' letter, which lacked Hollister's argumentative edge, on February 8, 1891:

Letter 11: to Frederick W. Evans (February 8, 1891)[84]

Dear Friend and Brother,

Thank you for your kind letter, it gave me great joy to know that you approve of my ideas on Christianity. I was very much satisfied with your views upon the different expressions of religious sentiments, suiting the age of those to whom they are directed. I received the tracts you sent me and read them not only with interest but with profit, and cannot criticise them because I agree with everything that is said in them. There is only one question, that I should wish to ask you. You are, as I know, non-resistants. How do you manage to keep communial but nevertheless—property? Do you acknowledge the possibility for a Christian to defend property from usurpators? I ask this question because I think that the principle of non-resistance is the chief trait of true Christianity and the greatest difficulty in our time is to be true to it. How do you manage to do so in your community?

I received your tracts; but you say in your letter that you have sent me books, do you mean that you have sent me books and tracts, or do you call the tracts books?

I received more than a year the Oregon paper "Worlds Advance Thought". I have several times seen your articles in it. I am very thankful to the editor for sending this paper; in every No. of it I get spiritual nourishment and if it were not for some spiritistic tendency, which is foreign to me, I would absolutely agree with

all its religious views. Who is the editor and how long ago has it been founded? I like this paper very much. With sincere respect and love,

Yours truly,
Leo Tolstoy.

Evans did not send information about *World's Advance-Thought*[85] but its editor soon began a correspondence with Tolstoy.

The question of property rights and how to defend them deeply concerned Tolstoy, who had renounced his own rights in favor of his family and, for his works written since 1881, in favor of no copyright at all. Evans avoided a direct answer to Tolstoy's question of how the Shakers justified property rights. He suggested that abandoning such rights would only be possible when men reach perfection: "Jesus said 'Be ye perfect, even as your father in Heaven is perfect.' That is the *end of* our Christian travail. But is it the *beginning*?" And therefore, he implied, the existence of property rights is one "of the various transgressions and violations of the abstract principles of Christianity as you and I now see them."[86] They "manage to do so," i.e. to observe the principle of non-resistance, in this case by accepting their imperfections. Evans offered a similar comment on government, although Tolstoy did not ask how the Shakers accepted the powers and actions of the state. Without saying so, he suggested that compromise has served the Shaker community well:

We hold and defend our Communial property under the Civil Laws of the New Earth. But in no case, or under any circumstances, should we injure a fellow being. You see that our Civil government is the voice of the people—Vox populi, Vox Dei—And the people who are the Rulers, are more progressed than are the Rulers of Russia or of any Church-and-State Government on the face of the Earth, we—the Shakers—under the Am[erican] secular Gov't can carry out the abstract principles, taught by revelation of the Christ Spirit, more perfectly than has hitherto ever been done by mortal men and woman. Just as we do carry out sexual purity, notwithstanding the sexes are brought face to face, in every day life, living without bolts or bars, in the same Household of Faith. Come and: see what God hath wrought.[87]

Tolstoy did not answer this letter nor the subsequent short letters of greeting Evans sent in 1892 and 1893 (although in one letter he thanked Tolstoy for a postal card greeting).[88]

Evans died on March 6, 1893, shortly after his last letter to Tolstoy. A member of the Shaker community, Daniel Offord (1848–?), wrote to inform him of Evans' death and of his desire to write again and his invitation to visit Mt. Lebanon. Tolstoy was moved by Evans' last words for him: "But I have no doubt I'll meet him in the spirit-world. Give him my kind love and tell him how much I wish to write to him." Tolstoy responded in a letter dated March 27:

Letter 12: to Daniel Offord (March 27, 1893)[89]

Dear friend,

I can not tell you how sorry I am, not for the death of our dear and honored friend Ewans, but for you and for all those who loved him and were fortified by his spirit. I am one of them. I am very touched also by his kind remembrance of me. I loved him very much. Two days ago I wrote a [note] on my card to introduce to him one of my friends Professor Yanschul, who is going to America and promised me to visit your place. I hope you will be kind to him and to his wife.

Please, give my love to all your brothers and sisters, who have any idea of my existence.

Yours truly
Leo Tolstoy.

His correspondence with the Shakers had been intensive: from 1889 to 1891 Tolstoy had written five letters, and he had received thirteen, several of them very lengthy—a dozen or more sheets. Discussion of the same religious and moral ideals, however, continued with other correspondents, among which a prominent place was held by Lucy A. Mallory, editor and publisher of the Oregon monthly paper, *The World's Advance-Thought and The Universal Republic*. Tolstoy's impression that this publication and editor expressed views similar to the Shakers was justified by the fact that not only did Evans publish articles in it (see letter 11 above), but so did other Shakers, including Alonzo Hollister.[90]

III. The Spiritual and Philosophic Press

Of the American writers who influenced Tolstoy—Parker, Garrison,

Ballou, together with Emerson and Thoreau—the one writer he did not name in his Address to Americans was perhaps the most influential. Lucy A. Mallory was born in the 1843 and died, apparently, in 1919, having produced her magazine for 33 years, beginning in 1886.[91] Her childhood, which was dominated by the terror of a cruel stepmother and the tragic loss of a close Native American friend and inspiration, ended early when she married her schoolteacher at the age of fifteen and eloped to Portland. There he prospered and she undertook the publishing and editing of a monthly magazine of usually a dozen to 16 pages in each issue. This religious periodical advocated no established (or in its phrase, "orthodox") religion, but rather non-resistance and pacifism, women's rights, vegetarianism, and antivivisection. It supported spiritualism, but as a means to achieve religious understanding, not as an end. As Mallory explained in an article,

> **The phenomena of Spiritualism are for the purpose of arousing you to grow the faculties of your spirit. They cannot and do not give to your being the perfect satisfaction of your own soul's unfoldment. If you seek only the phenomena of Spiritualism with the idea that they will perfectly satisfy the soul, regardless of your state of life, you will find yourself mistaken.**[92]

One of the more remarkable programs of the journal was the world-wide soul communion: on the twenty-seventh of each month, at 12 noon Portland time, "the time fixed and inspirationally communicated through the world's advance-thought for Soul Communion of all who love their fellow men, regardless of race and creed—the object being to invoke, through cooperation of thought and unity in spiritual aspiration, the blessings of universal peace and higher spiritual light." For the synchronization of this communication, the equivalent times for major cities throughout the world were listed in a table (no time was given for Moscow). The goal of this monthly telepathic communion was realized suddenly when the Russian Czar, Nicholas II, called for a peace conference: "The Soul-Communion force has done its work so silently and swiftly that humanity is dazed, and must have a little time to realize how far it has advanced."[93] The advance-thought of Mallory's journal was the understanding of God as ideal, and the universal republic was the equivalent of the Kingdom of God—the universal republic of the mind.

Tolstoy began receiving *World's Advance-Thought and the Universal Republic* in 1888, when an Edouard DeJongh, who was associated with the periodical, wrote him to offer a subscription (he received the November and December issues of that year).[94] Tolstoy continued to receive the periodical, although somewhat irregularly, judging from the volumes that remain in the library at Yasnaya Polyana.[95] Apparently he wrote to Lucy Mallory in 1893 (this letter has not been found), and she responded in December:

> I shall be very glad to continue sending my paper to you. Your appreciation of it is great encouragement to me, for I know its value. You alone, of all the Teachers I know, either by reputation or personally, practice that which you advise; and the world is greatly blessed thereby.
>
> If you feel inclined I should like very much to have you send me some of your thoughts for publication, for they give light to whoever reads them.
>
> I am only a poor woman, not a man as you supposed, but I feel the misery and suffering of mankind, and know that there is no need of it, if one could only find the way. H.N. Maquire was with me the first year, but for nearly seven years now I have published the paper without assistance, in any part of it. I do all the typesetting, editing, mailing, making up forms, etc. myself, for this reason it is not possible to get it out regularly at a stated time.[96]

Tolstoy apparently did send some materials for publication, however none has been identified. In one instance, early in 1894 Tolstoy received a letter (in Russian) from William H. Galvani, a regular contributor to the journal on the topic of vegetarianism, who requested a contribution. Galvani wrote again on May 20, 1894, to acknowledge Tolstoy's letter of April 18 and his article, "On the Question of Freedom of Will," which he promised to translate and submit to several other journals as well.[98] Unfortunately, neither the letter nor any article by Tolstoy with that title has been found.[98]

In August 1904 Lucy Mallory herself wrote a short note of appreciation to Tolstoy:

> I want to express my appreciation of the noble work that you are doing for humanity. You are one of the Immortals who live forever in the hearts of the people.
>
> Your speaking and working so boldly for peace will be the means of liberating Russia, and help, finally, to establish the Universal republic.

The happiness and satisfaction that must be the result of your efforts is measureless and abiding.[99]

To this letter Tolstoy responded immediately:

Letter 13: to Lucy Mallory (September 3, 1904)[100]

Dear friend and sister, I am very glad to be put by your kind letter in personal intercourse with you. Though I can not agree with your belief in mediumship and occultism, I greatly value your moral teaching and always with great interest read your journal for which I heartily thank you. I find in it true and healthy spiritual food and very highly appreciate your activity.

Yours truly
Leo Tolstoy.

3.IX 1904.

Tolstoy had expressed his deep admiration for the activities and writing of Lucy Mallory to several American visitors (many of whom had not previously heard of the little magazine). Her impact can be seen in Tolstoy's *Circle of Reading*, an anthology of maxims, sketches and short pieces selected and arranged for the days of each month in the year. The collection covers the entire spectrum of literature, from ancient and medieval—Arabic and Persian writers, Greek and Latin writings including the Bible, Indian and Chinese sources, the Talmud—to modern (French, Italian, German, English and American and Russian) writers. There are over 250 selections from American sources, including Emerson (58 selections), Thoreau (34), Henry George (30) and Channing (29). However, the most often cited source is Lucy Mallory and her journal (67 selections in all). Tolstoy most frequently quoted her maxims and aphorisms which she published monthly during 1899–1902 in a regular column, "Key Thoughts."[101] While he was compiling this *Circle of Reading*, one of his memoirists recalled Tolstoy's remarks on Mallory: "A spiritualist, but how well she writes! One has to write compactly, but so that everything is expressed." A little later he elaborated: "How do the theosophists manage to perceive and express such profound truths: so that they remove individuality and say what is common, eternal. In every issue of *World's Advance Thought* I find remarkable sayings. It will be amazing when next to Kant and others in the *Circle of Reading* there will often be Lucy Mallory, an unknown individual from Oregon."[102]

In 1906 Tolstoy sent Mallory a copy of his *Circle of Reading.*[103] She replied with some surprise at the extent to which he quoted her writings. His praise, however, remained qualified by her spiritualism, which he could not accept, and yet which was an essential part of her philosophy. In her letter of thanks for the book, she wrote to explain how she herself discovered Tolstoy:

> **. . . all comes from the guidance of my Angel Teachers. My natural ability was very meager but they taught me how to develop myself and make the most out of what I had. I owe my first acquaintance with you to my spiritual vision. I want to tell you about it: It happened when I was in my fourteenth year. I was looking up at the stars one night when there appeared before my vision a vast army of men, and there was one that stood out more prominently then the others, with a light shining around him. As I looked I heard a voice say: "It is the future you behold. Tolstoi will be the cutting edge that will emancipate his country and that will be the leaven to raise the Universal Republic."**
>
> **You see with my experience I could not be other than a believer in the Communion of Spirits.**[104]

Tolstoy did not respond to this letter, nor to the several more she sent, save to thank her in a short note for sending her photograph.[105]

Tolstoy's religious and philosophical views brought him into close contact with another American magazine and its editor. Once again he republished material from an American magazine, but in this instance he mistakenly received credit for the authorship. This journal, *The Open Court*, edited by Paul Carus (1852–1919), published a number of Tolstoy's works and, of all American periodicals, it became the most supportive of his religious and moral ideals. It is not clear how he came to receive the journal or when, but an entry in his diary in June 1890 mentions the discussion of Bellamy's *Looking Backward.* Tolstoy, incidentally, shared Carus' negative evaluation of the immensely popular, optimistic utopian novel: he found the work naïve and Marxist.[106] His diary also notes two other generally approving reactions to articles in Carus' magazine in 1891.[107]

Although nowhere near as obscure as Mallory and her journal, Paul Carus, his literary and philosophical journal *The Open Court*, and the publishing house of that name deserve to be much better known than they are.[108] Author of almost 75 books and 1500 articles on philosophy, religion, history, literature, politics and poetry, Carus dedicated himself to bridging the gap between science and religion, even to establishing a religion of science. Among his significant contributions to American philosophic thought, perhaps most important were his efforts to make Oriental thought, and especially Buddhism, available to a wider audience of Americans. These efforts, most energetic from 1893 to 1915, brought him together with Tolstoy, who had begun to study Buddhism as part of his larger quest for religious and moral ideals.

The interests of Tolstoy and Carus coincided in the fall of 1893. Two matters prompted Tolstoy to write to Carus. First, Tolstoy had included articles from *The Open Court* in a list of projects for the popular publishing house Posrednik (The Intermediary), which he supported as a means of widely distributing inexpensive editions. Secondly, Tolstoy had become interested in the philosophy of Lao-Tze, and Carus was also engaged in translating the classical works of Chinese philosophy. Tolstoy probably included articles from *The Open Court* in the list of topics and materials prepared for Posrednik and given to P. I. Biryukov early in October. Later that month or early in November he wrote to the editor:

Letter 14: to Paul Carus (October–November 1893)[109]

Moscow, Hamovnik 15.

Honoured Sir,

I am very much indebted to you for sending me your highly interesting periodical. I have always wished to thank you & do it now, with all the more pleasure, that the editor's [i.e., publishing] firm—Posrednik —has the intention of reviewing and publishing under my supervision some of the articles which have appeared in your periodical.

I should be most grateful to you, dear Sir, if you were to continue forwarding me your paper.

Believe me, honoured Sir

Yours truly, Leo Tolstoy

On December 9, 1893, Carus responded with thanks for Tolstoy's "good intentions" and expressed his pleasure that his magazine's articles might be "reviewed or translated under the supervision of so distinguished an author." With this he sent a number of publications, apparently including his own lectures, philosophical sketches and stories.[110]

Exactly which articles were republished by Posrednik is not known, although the publishers doubtless used material from *Open Court.* Tolstoy personally was so pleased by one work, however, that he translated it himself, provided it with a short preface, and published it. This short tale written by Paul Carus—"Karma"—recounts a series of good deeds that reward not only the recipient but also the doer several times over, a series of misfortunes that turn into good fortune, and the benefits of selflessness.[111] Although Tolstoy in his preface described the work as a "Buddhist fable," the truths it illustrated were precisely those that he advocated in his Christian teachings. Specifically, these truths were: "that freedom from evil and acquiring good is achieved only by one's own effort," that there is no device or organization that can achieve "one's own or a common good" other than "one's own personal effort"; that "the good for an individual person is only truly good when it is good for all others"; and that "life exists only in the rejection of individuality." The latter, he noted, was one of the truths discovered by Christianity.[112] At just this time Tolstoy was deeply engaged in summarizing his own Christian views, working on a tract that was finally published in 1898 under the title "The Christian Teaching."[113] Also at this time he was studying Lao-Tse and his *Tao-Teh-King* and collecting various translations of the work in preparation for his own rendering into Russian. Tolstoy later received a copy of Carus' own translation of Lao-Tse and subjected it to detailed scrutiny; however, he never felt confident enough in his own translation to publish it.[114]

For some unknown reason Tolstoy never credited Carus as the author of this work. The title in *Severny vestnik*, where it first appeared in 1894, was given as "Karma. A Buddhist Fable. Translated with a Preface by Count Leo Tolstoy." Perhaps he never understood that Carus had created the work, and only considered him to be the translator. In any case, the story was widely republished, probably in several editions by Posrednik, and it proved popular enough to find its way into European publications as a story written by Tolstoy, not translated by him. Certainly this shift made it easier to publish the work abroad, since Tolstoy's renunciation of all author's rights to his own works written after 1881 removed any question of copyright violation. The fact that Carus' name was never mentioned made this "transfer" even easier. Eventually Carus learned of this situation and wrote to Tolstoy on July 12, 1897:

Dear Sir:—
I am preparing the German translation of "Karma: a Story of Early Buddhism," and should like you to write a few introductory words

which I might use as a kind of preface. You are perhaps aware of the fact that the story has been translated from the Russian version, which you made, into French, and from the French into German and English, in which form it circulated under your name. Now I am not at all jealous that writings of mine should be current under your name. On the contrary, I have heard of the adventures of my little story not without satisfaction, but it would be a gracious act on your part to reinstate the author of the story into the rights of which he has been dispossessed by a concatenation of strange circumstances.

In case you would do me the favor of writing a few introductory words to "Karma" which may be made either in Russian, German, French, or in English, I remain, with kind regards and profound respect,

Yours very truly,
P. Carus[115]

Tolstoy wrote back immediately with praise for the story and an apology for unintentionally receiving credit as its author.

Letter 15: to Carus (July 1897)[116]

Dear Sir:—

Your tale Karma so far struck me by its depth of thought and likewise by its simple and entertaining narrative, that, in order to put it within the reach of Russian readers, I translated it at once into Russian, and contributed it first to a magazine, afterwards publishing it in popular form.

I never thought that this tale, in its English, French, and German translations would pass for my work, because, when editing it, I took special care to state that it was a translation from the English. It was only through your letter that I learned it had been circulated under my name, and I deeply regret not only that such a falsehood was allowed to pass unchallenged, but also the fact that it really was a falsehood; for I should be very happy were I the author of this tale.

I am very sorry for not being able to comply with your wish, as I am much engaged with other works which I am eager to finish before my death. If you can avail yourself of this letter as a preface, you are quite welcome to it, and with this supposition I once more repeat: this tale is one of the best products of national wisdom and

ought to be bequeathed to all mankind, like the Odyssey, the History of Joseph and Sakai Muni.[117]

In conclusion, allow me to thank you for your journal. I always read it with pleasure.

With my apologies for not having written to you in person, on account of ill-health, believe me,

Yours sincerely,
Leo Tolstoy.

At just this time Tolstoy was deeply involved in completing his "What Is Art?" and felt trapped by the need to complete the tract, and thus he did not want to distract himself with another task.[118] Carus, however, was so anxious to receive an introduction from Tolstoy that he did not wait for a reply before sending proof sheets of "Karma" to Yasnaya Polyana and repeating his request. In this letter dated July 21 he also mentioned his own translation of Lao-Tze and the similarity he saw between the views of the Buddhist philosopher and Tolstoy:

I am at present engaged in publishing a translation of Lautsze's Tao-Teh-King, the book of reason and virtue, of the old philosopher who lived in China about 600 years before Christ. As Laotsze's doctrine in many respects bears a remarkable resemblance to your own religious views, I took the liberty of calling attention to it in the Preface, and of sending you the book as soon as it is out, or, if possible, send you advance sheets of the Preface.[119]

This letter commanded Tolstoy's immediate attention, especially since he had attempted his own translation of this work in 1893 (and only in 1909 published a collection of the philosopher's sayings). The connection between his own Christian principles and those of Buddhist philosophy seemed to confirm Tolstoy's observations in his preface to "Karma." In his response (written just days after receiving Carus's letter) he asked about the sources of the tale, suggesting that he was still not certain of the origins or authorship of the work:

Letter 16: to Carus (August 10, 1897)[120]

Yasnia Polyana
29/7/97

My dear Sir,

I am obliged for the proofs of Karma which together with your letter of 21 ulto. have come duly to hand. I have already replied to your former letter about Karma, but omitted to ask, whether your story is built on some eastern legend, or whether you invented it yourself.

Cf. Lao-tsze I commenced a Russian version (constructed from European translations) several years ago, but I was not quite satisfied with what I wrote and it is still unpublished.

Hoping that my former letter has reached you safely and will answer your purpose

Yours very truly.

On September 11, 1897, Carus wrote to Tolstoy, expressed his pleasure at using the first letter as an introduction to "Karma," and provided the following explanation of his authorship:

. . . the story Karma originated in my mind while I was compiling "the Gospel of Buddha," from the various sources of Buddhist literature. I was full of the subject, and the story dawned on me just like an inspiration. There are reminiscences of Buddhist thought in it, but it is very difficult for me to trace them to their proper sources. I have inserted in footnotes the references which are still remembered.[121]

He also sent Tolstoy a copy of his *The Gospel of Buddha* and a collection of stories, *Truth in Fiction*, of which he singled out one—"The Chief's Daughter"—as being similar in spirit to "Karma."[122]

Tolstoy responded with a brief note of thanks for the volumes received:

Letter 17: to Carus (October 24, 1897)[123]

Dear Sir,

I received your books and thank you for them. Some of them I know, the others I had not yet time to read. The Gospel of Buddha I like very much.

Yours truly,
Leo Tolstoy.

Tolstoy's copy of *The Gospel of Buddha* has extensive underlining and other markings showing careful study of the texts, several of which he used in his calendar collections of quotations in 1903 and later in 1905.

Information about Tolstoy's unfinished translation of Lao-Tsze reached one American translator of the Chinese philosopher's work, Isaac W. Heysinger (1842–?), who sent him a copy of his own *The Light of China, the Tao Teh King of Lao Tsze, 604–504 B.C.* in March 1903.[124] In an accompanying letter he wrote, "I think it is the first comprehensive endeavor to give this unexampled record to Western civilization, and to analyze its teachings. I know that you have studied this great record, in times past, and, I believe, once thought of translating it into the Russian language."[125] Tolstoy responded with a comment that reflected his own difficulties with the work:

Letter 18: to Isaak W. Heysinger (April 14, 1903)[126]

Isaak W. Heysinger.
Dear Sir,

I received your book and thank you for it. The translation seems to me to be very good, though I am not a competent judge of it. I have read many translations—French, German, Russian and English, and it seems to me that yours is one of the best. It produces the impression of profound wisdom which in its depth can not be quite clearly expressed.

Yours truly
Leo Tolstoy.

14 April 1903.

Heysinger was not a scholar or a professional translator, but rather a man of some historical and philosophical interests. He was a physician with homeopathic and spiritualist tendencies, an officer in the Northern Army during the Civil War, and the author of historical studies of Civil War campaigns. Little else is known of him.

Although Tolstoy's exchange of letters with Carus ended relatively early, with the 1897 letter (number 17), the relationship between him and *The Open Court* continued with much energy into the next century as the journal published works by and about him. Tolstoy first appeared in *The Open Court* in 1896 when his "Christianity and Patriotism," completed two years earlier, was offered to the journal by an otherwise unknown Russian immigrant, Paul Borger, who had translated this lengthy tract. Ironically, and perhaps significantly, given the pacifist nature of this work, Borger was serving at that time as an American soldier. Carus agreed to publish this important critical analysis and thorough condemnation of all forms of patriotism, but wished that the style and form of the translation be improved. This was done by a Thomas McCormack, who then wrote to Tolstoy (on May 28, 1896, at Carus' request) for permission to publish this work. Together with this request Carus sent a illustrated Japanese edition of "Karma" (this a year before the request for an introduction, see number 15 above). Tolstoy responded through his daughter, Tatyana:

Letter 19: to Carus (July 4, 1896)[127]

Dear Sir,

My father bade me write and tell you that he will be very happy for his sketch to appear in your journal, which he appreciates very much, and always reads with great interest and pleasure.

He received in due time the beautiful edition of Karma and thanks the sender of it most heartily.

Believe me, Sir,

Yours truly
Tatiana Tolstoy.

Borger's translation of "Christianity and Patriotism" began immediately in *The Open Court*, and then appeared in a separate edition along with excerpts from other essays of Tolstoy selected by Carus.[128] This edition gave Carus an opportunity to express his own reaction to Tolstoy's "Christianity and Patriotism." While Carus agreed with the attack on "the wrong kind of patriotism" (which he called chauvinism), he felt Tolstoy overlooked "a right kind of patriotism which consists in the love of one's own country and in the legitimate aspiration of preserving all that is good in the character and institutions of one's own nationality."[129] In fact, Tolstoy explicitly rejected this positive nationalism, calling it "patriotism as a lofty sentiment" and a "virtue . . . [that] demanded . . . devotion to the highest ideal , . . . that of the fatherland."[130] For Tolstoy, patriotism and patriotic sentiment were unavoidably linked to government, and because all government used coercion, patriotism could not be a positive force.

Carus continued to publish Tolstoy, albeit with occasional qualifications. Three years after his first translation, Paul Borger submitted another work by Tolstoy: "Money," which represented chapters from *What Then Must We Do?* and had been published separately in Russian.[131] Again, Tolstoy received a letter and page proofs of the translation with a request to check the heavily edited text. In addition, Carus wrote: "I might add that your views of money are very interesting, and, although written for conditions which are applicable in Russia, may possess a special bearing on the development of American thought."[132] After elaborating on the peculiar conditions governing U.S. monetary policy, e.g. the political question of silver vs. gold standard and the "Greenbackers," Carus informed Tolstoy: "While your article presents one side of the question, I wish that the other should be represented at the same time, and I have sent advance sheets of your essay to Lawrence Laughlan, Professor of Economics in the University of Chicago." Tolstoy did not answer the letter, and it is unlikely that the political nuances of monetary policies held much interest for him.[133] He did respond to one American who wrote to him on the subject of money and morality. Alfred B. Westrup, author of several books on monetary policy during the last decade of the nineteenth century, sent Tolstoy two of his works in October 1899 with a long letter on the nature of money. Here he presented his "new philosophy of money" based on the elimination of all interest for credit, which he claimed was the root of all immorality produced by money. He strongly condemned church and state together, calling them "the two thieves between which we are crucified" and believed that for purely moral reasons "mankind will abolish property in land except for occupancy and use."[134] Tolstoy's response addressed this moral aspect and expressed basic agreement:

Letter 20: to Alfred B.Westrup (December 27, 1899)[135]

Moscow.

Dear Sir,

I received your letter and your Essays on money and thank you very much for them.

I think your theory quite right. I wrote some 15 years ago about money and came nearly to the same conclusions.

I heartily wish success to your idea.

Yours truly,
Leo Tolstoy.

15/27 Dec. 1899.

It was this 1885 work by Tolstoy on money that Carus published shortly after this letter, in April 1900.

The next year Carus published (as "characteristic of his deepest religious convictions") Tolstoy's letter to A. Ramaseshan advising how to cure the evils of India, including how to cooperate with the British, and to preserve its "true religion."[136] In 1903 a somewhat edited version of Tolstoy's legend of Christ's descent into Hell, "The Overthrow of Hell and its Restoration," appeared, as did excerpts from his "Appeal to the Clergy."[137] And in 1904 Carus published excerpts from Tolstoy's article on the Russo-Japanese War, "Bethink Yourselves!" and his "Two Letters on Orthodoxy."[138] During this same period he also published articles defending Tolstoy, notably Maude's "The Misinterpretation of Tolstoy" and Crosby's "Tolstoy's Answer to the Riddle of Life."[139]

Carus gave his ultimate estimate of Tolstoy in a commemorative piece published in honor of his eightieth birthday in 1908. He concluded his "Tribute to Count Tolstoy" with the observation that

> **Tolstoy's ideas of religion, of the principles of morality, his preference for non-resistance to evil, his opinions on war, on the nature of the State, on the significance of money, etc. are subject to criticism, and among thinkers who are scientifically trained there will be few if any who would advocate any one of his bold propositions. But one need not agree with Tolstoy's propositions to admire the man, who is an extraordinarily typical actualization of the eternal problem of the soul which finds its highest expression in those nobler impulses that know nothing of self but are the expression of the social conscience, of the All-Spirit that has produced us, of God Himself, and whom we love and move and have our being.**[140]

This unusual mixture of profound admiration and circumspect qualification offered an assessment no less sympathetic than the view of Americans Tolstoy had offered in his "Address." Carus acknowledged here a soul that expressed God Himself and that advocated ideals too bold for "thinkers who are scientifically trained." In Tolstoy, it would seem, religious vision had overpowered science.

IV. Social and Political Activism

America in general was not listening to its voices of the 1850s, but there were still a few individuals who were "paying attention" to them and "continuing the good work" of Garrison, Ballou and others. Several of these individuals corresponded with Tolstoy, were inspired by his writings and ideals, and received encouragement from him directly. However disappointed Tolstoy may have been in America's current path, he joined with those who objected to the capitalists and militarists and opposed the influence of the Goulds, Rockefellers, Carnegies, and Deweys. In this way Tolstoy amplified the voices and non-resistance ideals of Garrison and Ballou in articles and letters preaching pacifism and attacking militarism and imperialism. He spoke out against capitalism largely through the voice and ideas of Henry George, who may have belonged to a later generation, but whose single tax Tolstoy believed could nonetheless continue the same "good work." Tolstoy's fervent disciple Ernest Crosby spoke for pacifism, against American imperialism, and for the single tax (see the second article in this series). Another social activist who benefited from Tolstoy's writings and supported George's radical theory of the single tax was Bolton Hall.

Bolton Hall (1854–1938), like Ernest Crosby (with whom he collaborated on a number of social issues), read *On Life* and came under Tolstoy's influence. Although Hall had the advantage of reading the work in a good English rendering (by Hapgood[141]; Crosby had read it in French), he nonetheless felt the translation did not adequately present Tolstoy's ideas. He decided to provide his own version of the work—but not a new translation, for he did not know Russian. Rather, in 1897 he attempted to recast, condense and even rework the book's ideas. Crosby sent Hall's work, titled *Even as You and I*,[142] to Tolstoy, who responded directly to the author.

Letter 21: to Bolton Hall (March 21, 1897)[143]

Dear sir:

I have received your book and have read it. I think it is very good and renders in a concise form quite truly the chief ideas of my book; I hope that this book in this new form will be useful in the sense in which I intended to be to a larger public than the original.

With my best thanks and wishes for the success of your book, I am, dear sir,

Yours truly
Leo Tolstoy.

21st March, 1897.

This reworking of Tolstoy's religious piece did in fact prove more popular than the original, perhaps because it was received more as a social than as a religious work. The correspondence between Hall and Tolstoy continued, developing principally the social aspect of Tolstoy's ideas. Hall wrote five letters to Tolstoy between 1901 and 1907 on non-resistance and on single tax activities. In February 1908 he sent Tolstoy a copy of the *Single Tax Review*[144] containing an encouraging article on the increasing popularity of Henry George's theories, and he sounded an optimistic note in his accompanying letter which ended, " I feel and these are great times to live in."[145] Although Tolstoy had not written to Hall, the latter was aware of his bewilderment at the lack of general acceptance George's ideas. Hall intended to provide Tolstoy with positive examples of social progress. Tolstoy responded with an account of his own attempts to support radical measures against capitalism in Russia:

Letter 22: to Hall (March 28, 1908)[146]

Dear Sir,

Thank you for your letter and the marked article in the Single Tax Review.

I am very glad to hear, that the question in your country seems advancing. The indifference in Russia to this capital question is an inexplicable puzzle for me. I have tried to propose the system to our members of the government and of the Duma, but they seem all so much occupied with all kinds of superficial matters, that they have no time and no sense for the capital question. But the question must be solved and very soon. So that I quite agree with you, that these are great times to live in.

Yours truly Leo Tolstoy.

28 March 1908.

Tolstoy had first addressed the agrarian problem and the failure of capitalism in Russia in 1906, when he offered a solution along the lines of Henry George's theories, and wrote an introduction on this topic to the Russian translation of George's *Social Problems.*[147] In July 1907 he wrote to the Prime Minister, P. A. Stolypin, with the suggestion that, were George's theories to be introduced to the Duma, this would be an opportunity to deprive the revolutionaries of a major source of support from the dissatisfied populace. Stolypin finally responded (after a second appeal) with a curt refusal and condescending reminder of the sanctity of private property.[148] Tolstoy's letter to Hall suggests that the problem had become acute, and that a solution would be found, one way or another.

The "good work" of Garrison and Ballou continued in the activities of pacifists, anti-imperialists, and anti-militarists. Tolstoy contributed his support to these voices so effectively that he gained the reputation of a political radical and attracted the attention and condemnation of conservative politicians, most notably Theodore Roosevelt.[149] Still, a number of liberal American politicians, local and national, numbered among the supporters of his Christian and pacifist ideals. Perhaps the best known American who preached Tolstoyan principles was William Jennings Bryan (1860–1925).

Already an influential political figure, lecturer and journalist, with two unsuccessful attempts at the U.S. Presidency behind him (1896 and 1900), the liberal Democrat and Populist Bryan undertook a world tour in 1903 to meet with world leaders in support of his anti-imperialist and anti-militarist ideals. The countries he visited included Russia, and the leaders—Tolstoy. He approached Tolstoy through a mutual acquaintance, James Creelman (1859–1915), a reporter for the *New York World* who had recently visited Tolstoy himself. Creelman wrote to Tolstoy in September 1903 to introduce Bryan, whom he described as "an uncompromising radical, a man of serious and incorruptible life—an elemental, total democrat."[150] Tolstoy responded immediately:

Letter 23: to James Creelman (September 19, 1903)[151]

Dear Sir,

I will be very glad to make the acquaintance of Mr. William Bryan if he comes to Russia. Excuse me, dear Sir, if I make a little reproach to you. It was very painful to me to know that you published my opinion of Mr. Harper and that I offended without wishing it a man who before your article could not have any ill feeling to me. In all other parts your interview is quite correct and very well written.

Yours truly
Leo Tolstoy

Sent. 6/19, 1903.

Tolstoy referred here to an interview, in which Creelman had quoted Tolstoy's unflattering opinion of William Harper, the President of the University of Chicago, who had visited him earlier, in 1900.[152] Harper had ascribed great significance to the millions of dollars contributed to the University by John D. Rockefeller, which had not impressed Tolstoy, who in turn found the President intellectually and morally unfit for his position, and had said so. No doubt Harper confirmed Tolstoy's belief, expressed at just that time, that contemporary Americans had failed to live up to their country's greatest thinkers.

In Bryan, however, he found a pleasant exception. His first acquaintance with Bryan's views came in a copy of a speech just delivered in London, which concluded with statements sympathetic to his own ideas: "The world is coming to understand that armies and navies, however numerous and strong, are impotent to stop thought. Thought inspired by love will yet rule the world. . . . There is a national product more valuable than gold or silver, more valuable than cotton or wheat or corn or iron—an ideal. . . . In the rivalry to present the best ideal to the world, love, not hatred, will control. . . ."[153] These ideas had been shaped in part by Bryan's study of Tolstoy's writings and the writings of his disciples such as Ernest Crosby.[154] Bryan arrived on December 5, early in the morning, expecting to spend a few hours with Tolstoy in Yasnaya Polyana before leaving for St. Petersburg for a scheduled audience with Czar Nicholas II. Tolstoy consented to meet him early, they walked and rode horseback, and Bryan was so taken by the meeting that he postponed his audience and stayed for the whole day and spent the night.[155]

Bryan wrote an article, "Tolstoy, the Apostle of Love," describing the meeting and later included it in his 1905 collection, *Under Other Flags*.[156] He made the pilgrimage not to learn of Tolstoy's ideas (which he knew already from numerous essays), but to learn through a personal meeting the secret of his great influence. Bryan concluded that,

> **notwithstanding his great intellect, his colossal strength lies in his heart more than in his mind. It is true that few have equaled him in power of analysis and in clearness of statement, while none have surpassed him in beauty and aptness of illustration. But no one can commune with him without feeling that the man is like an overflowing spring—asking nothing, but giving always.**[157]

This image of the spring, it appears, Bryan borrowed from Tolstoy himself, for he acknowledged as much in a letter of thanks after their meeting. He wrote on December 31, 1903:

> **I beg to assure you that my visit to you was most refreshing and helpful & I find in your essays many things similar to my argu-**

ments and the fact that you have used them confirms in the belief that the arguments are sound. I notice that you have made a most beautiful and effective use of the figure which represents life as a spring.[158]

In his account of their meeting, Bryan explained Tolstoy's religious principles based on love, his Christian ideals and striving for perfection, and his belief in non-violent resistance to evil. In contrast to Ballou, for example, Bryan could accept Tolstoy's absolute idealism: "While he recognizes that the best of efforts is but an approach to the ideal, he does not consent to the lowering of the ideal itself or the defense of anything that aims at less that the entire realization of the ideal."[159] In areas of government policy Bryan agreed with his rejection of militarism, protectionism and trusts, and he admired his support of Henry George's single tax. However, he did not accept Tolstoy's anarchism and opposition to all government, which he explained as follows: "His experience with the arbitrary methods of his own government has led him to say things that have been construed as a condemnation of all government. . . . it is not strange that the evils of government should impress him more than its possibilities for good."[160] Of all the European leaders he met, none impressed Bryan more than Tolstoy. The only two photographs in *Under Other Flags* both include Tolstoy, who was becoming an increasingly important influence on Bryan's thinking.

Tolstoy himself was positively impressed with Bryan. He was quoted as noting that "Bryan is a serious person. I find it strange that he can aspire to the post of President. In his views he is a very exceptional American."[161] Tolstoy believed that Bryan shared his belief in absolute non-violence, and he cited their conversation (and Bryan's acknowledgement) in his essay on William Lloyd Garrison, which he wrote as an introduction to V. Chertkov's biography.[162] Indeed, he thought so highly of Bryan that he offered support for his political activities, while also encouraging him to look beyond this career. Bryan received a warm response to his letter of December 31, 1903, in which he asked about Bondarev's book on work and idleness and an essay by Tolstoy "To the Czar and His Assistants":

Letter 24: to William Jennings Bryan (February 2, 1904)[163]

Dear Mr. Bryan,

The receipt of your letter gave me great pleasure as well as the reminiscence of your visit. If you wish to have Bondareff's book

and my letter to politicians please write to my friend Wladimir Tchertkoff, England, Hants, Christchurch, he will forward to you all, what you wish to have. I had in the Russian papers news about you. I wish with all my heart success in your endeavor to destroy the trusts and to help the working people to enjoy the whole fruits of their toil, but I think that this is not the most important thing of your life. The most important thing is to know the will of God, concerning one's life, i.e. to know what he wishes us to do and to fulfill it. I think that you are doing it and that is the thing in which I wish to you the greatest success.

Yours truly
Leo Tolstoy.

2 February
1904

Bryan later sent a copy of *Under Other Flags* to Tolstoy, who was not particularly pleased by one of the photographs—a collage of three portraits: Pope Pius X on the left, Czar Nicholas II on the right, and Tolstoy in the center. Tolstoy reportedly remarked, with a smile: "I protest against such company."[164]

Tolstoy followed Bryan's activities and asked about him, as, for example, in a conversation with a visiting American lecturer, Frank R. Roberson, who had traveled the Chautauqua circuit with this famous speaker. In May 1905 Tolstoy commented:

From June to August, every day, Bryan delivers speeches on the primacy of the American people. Firstly, they have freedom of speech, and secondly, they accept the Christian ideal. The Christian ideal includes freedom of speech. Bryan is smart and talented and has a religious bent, but this is forced labor, political work, newspaper work, disputes—and no doubt he hasn't moved forward for the last twenty years, and not only not moved forward, but moved backwards.[165]

Despite doubts about his political activities, Tolstoy's affection and respect for Bryan grew. The next year, when Bryan came up in a conversation with his daughter Marie, Tolstoy remarked: "Bryan is a nice fellow, smart, fearless, but like Europeans, he is badly educated. He has blinders." To Marie's comment, "His speeches are good," Tolstoy responded, "That's his profession."[166] As the 1908 elections approached, Tolstoy grew more interested and supported Bryan's candidacy against William Howard Taft. In May

1908 he was visited by Jerome Reymond, a professor of sociology, to whom he expressed his desire that the Americans elect Bryan as their President.[167] Later that year, in June, during a conversation with the American journalist Herman Bernstein, Tolstoy asked who would win the presidential election. To Bernstein's reply that Taft would win, Tolstoy commented that he had liked Bryan very much.[168] Shortly thereafter, in August, he received a letter from a Ryerson Jennings asking whom he supported for president.[169] He responded with a letter in support of Bryan:

Letter 25: to Ryerson Jennings (September 28, 1908)[170]

28 Sept. 08

Dear Mr. Ryerson Jennings,

In answer to your letter of 24 August I can sincerely say that I wish Mr. Bryan success in his candidature to the Presidency of the United States. From my own standpoint, repudiating as it does all coercive Government, I naturally cannot acquiesce with the position of President of the Republic; but since such functions still exist, it is obviously best that they should be occupied by individuals worthy of confidence.

Mr. Bryan I greatly respect and sympathise with, and know that the basis of his activity is kindred to mine in his sympathy with the interests of the working masses, his antimilitarism and his recognition of the fallacies produced by capitalism.

I do not know, but hope Mr. Bryan will stand for land reform according to the Single Tax system of Henry George, which I regard as being at the present time, of the most insistent necessity, and which every progressive reformer should place to the fore.

Yours faithfully
Leo Tolstoy.

Bryan made wide use of this letter in his campaign, and Tolstoy's support became well known and controversial.[171] When asked about the reasons for his advocacy, Tolstoy explained to a reporter of a Helsinki newspaper: "Bryan is a supporter of Henry George, an antimilitarist, and a sincere and smart man, and therefore I would like the American people to have him as their President."[172] This political activism, however unique in Tolstoy's relations with America, did not prove effective, or at least not effective enough to bring victory. Bryan thanked Tolstoy for his support in a letter written in May the following year, 1909:

> **I want to thank you for the letter which you wrote during the campaign. It was read at a number of meetings. I think the main cause of our defeat was the influence over the businessmen of the country and over the employees. However, there is nothing to do but fight and to hope that, however dark the night, the dawn is near.**[173]

The American people had chosen wealth over truth, in Tolstoy's opinion. He understood that Bryan still remained committed to change: "The capitalists won, but he nonetheless hopes that he will become President," he commented after getting news of the election results.[174]

Bryan continued his crusade, defending peace and preaching the message of brotherly love which he found so profoundly expressed in Tolstoy's writings.[175] He achieved his goals, in large part, only after Tolstoy's death in 1910. In 1913 Bryan became Secretary of State in Woodrow Wilson's cabinet, where he pursued the dreams of peace and a world without war which had marked his own Presidential campaigns. He succeeded in securing the agreement of thirty-one nations in individual treaties to employ arbitration instead of military action. But his activities as Secretary of State on behalf of pacifism and against militarism lasted only a little more than two years: he resigned in disagreement with President Wilson over the content of a protest note on the sinking of the *Lusitania*. As a private citizen whose popular support had fallen sharply after his resignation, Bryan lost his persuasive power for peace and brotherhood, and he turned his considerable oratorical talents towards support of Prohibition and religious orthodoxy. Ultimately he found himself, at the end of his life, defending creationism and literal Biblical revelation in the Scopes Trial of 1925.

Ironically, the leading lawyers at this trial—Bryan for the prosecution and Clarence Darrow for the defense—had both earlier preached Tolstoy's ideals of non-violence and pacifism. At the turn of the century Darrow had become "a devoted admirer of Tolstoy," and was "largely influenced by his remarkable books."[176] Inspired by Tolstoy's ideal of non-resistance, he wrote a study of non-resistance in relation to crime and punishment, which he published under the title *Resist Not Evil* in 1904. Reissuing the work 21 years later, after the Scopes trial, Darrow held fast to his earlier views, but qualified his belief in non-resistance. "Man can never reach a state of non-resistance. His structure is fixed and is moved by stimuli like all other animals, and under sufficient inducement the primal emotions will sweep away all the inhibitions and restraints that culture has woven around him."[177] This Darwinian belief in the primacy of natural forces over cultural conditioning was as inconsistent with Tolstoy's ideals, as was Bryan's fundamentalist belief in Biblical texts.

This coincidence illustrates the extent of Tolstoy's influence at its peak, and its decline after his death. The principal force silencing his voice and the voices of American pacifists, non-resistants and anti-capitalists was World War I. Patriotism and militarism easily drowned out these voices, to which America had already become largely indifferent. Late in 1906 Tolstoy himself anticipated this decline when he complained that "Americans have achieved the highest degree of material welfare and have fallen to the lowest degree of morality and religious awareness." He had just met an American, a novelist named Leroy Scott, who "did not know the best writers of his own country."[178] Not only had America failed to "pay attention" to a "bright constellation, such as is rarely to be found in the literatures of the world," but her own writers were no longer even aware of their heritage. For twenty years Tolstoy had done what he could to amplify "these voices." The record of his efforts survives in the letters he exchanged with America's preachers of non-resistance, anti-imperialism, anti-militarism and anti-capitalism; the measure of his success remains in their "good work" for which he felt such great sympathy.

Notes

[1] Letter to V. Chertkov, January 15, 1890, in Tolstoy, *Polnoe sobranie sochinenii* (Jubilee edition), v. 64, pp. 153–154. Hereafter abbreviated *PSS*. The American traveler Thomas Stevens remarked on this special sympathy when he visited Tolstoy in 1890 and ascribed it to the fact that America was the first of the English-speaking countries to translate, read and appreciate his works (*Through Russia on a Mustang* [New York: Cassell, 1891], p. 103); this same view was expressed by the English journalist, William Stead, in his *The Truth about Russia* (London: Cassell, 1888), see pp. 399, 405.

[2] Tolstoy gave two dates to the letter: June 21 and July 4, 1900. The first was the date according to the Julian calendar used in Russia; the second—according to the Gregorian calendar used in the West, which was 13 days ahead of the Julian calendar in the 1900s (12 days in the 1800s). All dates here are given according to the Gregorian calendar.

[3] Autograph File MS.L.S. #43M–192, Harvard University, Houghton Library; draft in the State Tolstoy Museum in Moscow (hereafter abbreviated GMT), copybook number 3, sheet 37 (hand of Arthur St. John).

The draft differs substantially from the final copy: the name of "Admiral Dewey" was inserted into the list of unworthy "voices" in the final copy. A version published at the time, in 1901, differed even more: instead of the list of names, the parenthetical phrase read: "hardly to be replaced by those of financial and industrial millionaires, or successful generals and admirals" (*North American Review*, April 1901, 172(533):503).

[4] He named the same writers and added Longfellow and Harriet Beecher Stowe. *Tolstoy and His Problems: Essays* (London: Grant Richards, 1901), p. 38.

[5] In English it was first given the title *My Religion*.

[6] From chapter 12 of *What I Believe* in Maude's translation, *A Confession, The Gospel in Brief and What I Believe* (London: Oxford University Press, 1971), p. 521.

[7] Ibid., p. 523.

[8] Letter of February 25, 1885, to Sof'ya Andreevna Tolstaya (*PSS* 83:486).

[9] Tolstoy named *Discourse on Matters* by Parker as having had a "great influence" on him. See his letter to M. M. Lederle of October 25, 1891, and note 32 (*PSS* 66: 68, 71), where he places this influence as having been after 1878.

[10] Robert E. Collins, *Theodore Parker: American Transcendentalist. A Critical Essay and a Collection of his Writings* (Metuchen: Scarecrow Press, 1973), pp. 94–95.

[11] Adin Ballou should not be confused with his better known relatives, both named Hosea Ballou – the one also a theologian and his nephew an educator, one of the founders of Tufts College and its first president.

[12] Wilson published much of their correspondence in an article "The Christian Doctrine of Non-resistance, by Count Leo Tolstoi and the Rev. Adin Ballou. Unpublished Correspondence Compiled by Rev. Lewis G. Wilson," *The Arena* (December 1890) 13:1–12.

[13] It is not clear what he did send at this time. In his commentary on the correspondence (see note 12 above) Wilson listed several works by Ballou (*Christian Non-resistance*, 1846; *Practical Christian Socialism*, 1854; *Primitive Christianity and its Corruptions*, 1872) and noted that he "had sent some of these works." Tolstoy did receive Ballou's *Christian Non-Resistance: in All Its Important Bearings.* (Hopedale, 1846), for it is clear from the context of their correspondence that Tolstoy had studied this work. The following works, most likely received from Wilson, are present in Tolstoy's library at Yasnaya Polyana: "The Bible: in Its Fundamental Principles Absolutely Divine. In Its Explicative Ideas and Language Properly Human" (Hopedale, 1849), "Human Progress in

Respect to Religion: Two Discourses, Delivered in the Chapel at Hopedale, Mass., May 26th and June 9th, 1867" (Hopedale: Modern age, 1867); "Lecture on the Inspiration of the Bible: Delivered in the Town Hall, Milford (Mass.) . . . January 16, 1859" (Milford, 1859); "The True Scriptural Doctrine of the Second Advent: An Effectual Antidote to Millerism, and All Other Hundred Errors" (Milford: Community press, 1843). It is likely that he had received several more works by Ballou and had given them to friends.

[14] Original unknown, draft in GMT, notebook 50, pages 208–209. Text published in *Arena* (see above, note 12) and *PSS* 64:270 with omissions.

[15] Tolstoy asked Isabel Hapgood to send Wilson a copy of her recently published translation, *Life* (New York: T.Y. Crowell and Co., 1888), which she did.

[16] Letter from Adin Ballou to Tolstoy of January 14, 1890, GMT T.c. 205 38. The entire letter can be found in *Arena* (note 12).

[17] Original unknown, no copy in GMT; text from *Arena* (see above, note 12), where its receipt is dated March 26, 1900. Also in *PSS* 65:34, where it is dated February 21–24 (Old Style).

[18] Nine months earlier, in June 1889, Tolstoy wrote to D. A. Khilkov of his intention to translate and distribute Ballou's works (*PSS* 64:278). He himself corrected one translation in January 1890 before sending it to a Moscow newspaper (*Gazeta* A. *Gattsuka)*, but the work was never published because of objections by the censorship, and the title remains unknown (*PSS* 51:174, N. N. Gusev, *Letopis' zhizni i tvorchestva L'va Nikolaevicha Tolstogo. 1828–1890* [Moscow: Goslitizdat, 1958, p. 745). Tolstoy had distributed several copies of this article, apparently, by April 1889 (*PSS* 65:64).

[19] Letter from Adin Ballou to Tolstoy of May 30, 1890, GMT T.c. 205 38, and in *Arena* (see above, note 12).

[20] Original unknown, text from copy in GMT; not included in *Arena* (see above, note 12), but printed in *PSS* 65:113.

[21] Ballou's pamphlet is undated; in the summer of 1890, Tolstoy asked N. N. Strakhov, who was visiting Yasnaya Polyana, to translate the pamphlet (*PSS* 87:32), and this translation was then corrected by Tolstoy and used in *The Kingdom of God.* At about this same time Tolstoy had asked Chertkov to translate Ballou's 1846 work, *Christian Non-Resistance* (*PSS* 65:105–106), which work was published only 18 years later as *The Doctrine of Christian Non-Resistance to Evil by Force* (*Uchenie o khristianskom neprotivlenii zlu nasiliem*, Moscow: Posrednik, 1908).

[22] Letter from Olive Ballou Day to Tolstoy of October 16, 1899, GMT T.

c. 205 39. His cousin's characterization would not have pleased Ballou, it would seem. In contrast to Tolstoy's enthusiasm, Ballou "was seriously disappointed . . . in both the man and his teachings": he found his theology "wild, crude, and mystically absurd," and his views of Christ's divine nature and of immortality to be "untrue, visionary, chaotic, and pitiably puerile." See William S. Heywood, ed. *Autobiography of Adin Ballou* (Lowell: Vox Populi, 1896; repr. Philadelphia: Porcupine Press, 1975), pp. 508–511.

[23] This is described in the Preface and Chapter 1 of *The Kingdom of God.* See *The Kingdom of God and Peace Essays by Leo Tolstoy,* trans. by Aylmer Maude (London: Oxford, 1960), pages 1, 5.

[24] Garrison, Wendell Phillips. *William Lloyd Garrison, 1805–1879; The Story of His Life Told by His Children.* Vols. 1–2. Boston: Houghton, Mifflin and Company, 1894.

[25] Original unknown. Text from draft in GMT. Published in *PSS* 63:333–334.

[26] Probably the following: Oliver Johnson, *William Lloyd Garrison and His Times; or, Sketches of the Anti-Slavery Movement in America, and of the Man Who Was Its Founder and Moral Leader* (Boston: B.B. Russell & Co., 1880) and Boston (Mass.) City Council, *A Memorial of William Lloyd Garrison from the City of Boston* (Boston, Printed by order of the City Council, 1886).

[27] Letter of W. P. Garrison to Tolstoy, May 5, 1886, GMT, T.c. 216 35.

[28] Letter of W. P. Garrison to Tolstoy, January 9, 1887, GMT, T.c. 216 35.

[29] "Introduction to a Short Biography of William Lloyd Garrison (A *Letter to the Editors: Vladimir Chertkov and Florence Holah)*" in Maude, *Kingdom of God,* op. cit., pp. 577–578. This introduction also appears in Chertkov, V. G. *A Short Biography of William Lloyd Garrison* (Westport, Conn., Negro Universities Press <1970>, a reproduction of London: Free Age Press, 1904), see also *PSS* 63:345.

[30] Tolstoy used the text provided in the Garrison sons' biography, vol. 2, pp. 230–234 (see above, note 24).

[31] See letters of Wendell P. Garrison to Tolstoy of October 8, 1889, and January 27, 1890, GMT, T.c. 216 36.

[32] Tolstoy wrote to Francis Garrison on February 18 and April 1, 1892, to acknowledge contributions to his program to assist famine victims.

[33] *My Religion,* trans. Huntington Smith (NY: T.Y. Crowell and Co., 1885); *What I Believe,* trans. Constantine Popoff (New York: W.S. Gottsberger; 1886).

[34] Letters to Tolstoy from Joseph Potts, 16 June, 1887, and from Helen

Harries of September 11, 1887, accompanied works by George Fox, S. Grellet and J. Woolman (GMT, T.c. 234 77 and T.c. 219 19). Tolstoy quoted from two other writers: the Quaker writer Jonathan Dymond, *An Inquiry into the Accordancy of War with the Principles of Christianity: and an Examination of the Philosophical Reasoning by Which It Is Defended; with Observations on Some of the Causes of War and on Some of Its Effects* (Philadelphia: Uriah Hunt and Son, [18—]); and a Mennonite (Reformed), Daniel Musser, *Non-resistance Asserted, or Kingdom of Christ and Kingdoms of This World Separated* (Lancaster, PA: Elias Barr, 1864).

[35] Leo Wiener, trans. and ed., *The Four Gospels Harmonized and Translated* (Boston: Dana Estes, 1904), chapter 9, vol. 2, p. 155.

[36] "The Gospel in Brief" in Aylmer Maude, trans. *A Confession, The Gospel in Brief and What I Believe* (London: Oxford University Press, 1940, 1971), p. 227.

[37] "What I Believe," in *A Confession*, op. cit., p. 378.

[38] *PSS* 25:411.

[39] "What I Believe," in *A Confession*, op. cit., p. 379.

[40] Letters of Alice B. Stockham to Tolstoy, October 29 and November 4, 1888, GMT, Ban 13530 and T.c. 242 7.

[41] *La liberté dans l'école*, 2nd ed. trans. B. Tseytline and Ernest Jaubert (Paris: A. Savine, 1888). See F. W. Farrar, "Count Tolstoi on Education," *Forum*. 1888.

[42] Published in Chicago by the Sanitary Publishing Co. in 1883. A resident of Evanston, Illinois (seat of the WCTU, an organization also devoted to alleviating women's suffering), Alice Stockham devoted herself to women's social issues, including suffrage. Born into a Quaker family in Ohio, she attended Olivet College, taught school, then in 1853 entered the Eclectic College of Cincinnati, the only medical college in the west at that time accepting women. If she had graduated, she would have been one of the first woman doctors in the U.S. She left the school to marry George P. Stockham, who graduated from the college in 1855. Alice Stockham did receive her medical license in Illinois in 1882 upon graduation from the Chicago Homeopathic Medical College, however she appears to have been practicing medicine prior to this. *Tokology* sold over 150,000 copies in ten years, which success led Alice Stockham to establish her own publishing house to publish her own works and the magazine edited by her sister, *The Kindergarten*. See M. Silberman, *Tolstoy and America: A Study in Reciprocal Influence* (Ph.D. dissertation, CUNY, 1979), pp. 287–308, for more complete information on Stockham.

[43] Original unknown, text from a copy in GMT, published in *PSS* 64:202.

[44] *PSS* 86:180–184.
[45] *PSS* 86:177.
[46] *PSS* 86:188.
[47] Letter from Stockham to Tolstoy of October 5, 1889, GMT, T.c. 242 7.
[48] The work was published under the title *Tolkologiia ili nauka o rozhdenii detei*. (*Tokology or The Science of Childbirth*) in Moscow, 1892.
[49] *Predislovie k knige d-ra meditsiny Alisy Stokgèm* ("Foreword to Dr. Stockham's Book") "*Tolkologiia, ili nauka o rozhdenii detei*", *PSS* 25:267.
[50] Letter to I. D. Rugin, October 15, 1889. *PSS* 64:314.
[51] Diary entry for October 15, 1889. *PSS* 50:153.
[52] Letter from A. Stickney to Tolstoy of March 30, 1889, GMT Tc 242 1.
[53] G. Albert Lomas, *Plain Talks Upon Practical Religion: Being Candid Answers to Earnest Inquirers, Including an Answer to the Inquiry "What Shall I Do To Be a Shaker?"* (Shakers [Watervliet], N.Y.: Office of the Shaker Manifesto, 1878.); Giles B. Avery, *Sketches of Shakers and Shakerism: Synopsis of Theology of United Society of Believers in Christ's Second Appearing* (Albany: Weed, Parsons & Company, Printers, 1883); *Shaker Music Inspirational Hymns and Melodies Illustrative of the Resurrection Life and Testimony of the Shakers* (Albany, N.Y.: Weed, Parsons, 1875); *The Shaker Manifesto* (Shakers, N.Y.: G.B. Avery, 1878–1882), *The Manifesto* (Shaker Village, N.H.: United Societies, 1883–1899).
[54] *PSS* 50:64.
[55] *PSS* 86:224.
[56] Philadelphia: Lippencott & Co., 1870. Tolstoy could have read here of Ballou and Hopedale, but he did not seem to recall Noyes' account when he corresponded with Ballou.
[57] *PSS* 50:71.
[58] Ibid.
[59] Letter from Alonzo Hollister to Tolstoy of September 23, 1889, GMT T.c. 221 26.
[60] Minot Judson Savage, *Christ's Christianity According to Count Tolstoi* (Boston: George H. Ellis, 1887); John White Chadwick, *The New Testament and the Higher Criticism: a Sermon* (Boston: George H. Ellis, 1897); William Wilberforce Newton, *A Run Through Russia: the Story of a Visit to Count Tolstoi* (Hartford: Student Publishing Co. 1894).
[61] In addition to *Shakers and Shakerism* and the Shaker periodical, Hollister sent: Daniel Fraser, *The Divine Afflatus: a Force in History* (Shirley, Mass.: The United Society, 1875; Boston: Rand, Avery, & Co.); Frederick William Evans, *Autobiography of a Shaker and Revelation of the Apocalypse; with an Appendix*, new and enlarged ed. (New York: American News Co., 1888).

[62] Letter from Hollister to Tolstoy of September 23, 1889, see note 59 above.
[63] Letter undated, postmarked October 19 (O.S.), 1889, Western Reserve Historical Society, Shaker Manuscripts Reel 21 IV:A–44; Tolstoy's draft of the letter, in GMT, differs substantially, and is much more extensive.
[64] *PSS* 27:31.
[65] Maude's translation, first published in 1925, is used most recently, for example, in Harper and Row's *Great Short Works of Leo Tolstoy*, ed. by John Bayley, 1967. The *PSS* edition (1933) incorporates the full and final ninth redaction, and is used by David McDuff in *The Kreutzer Sonata and Other Stories* (Harmondsworth, England: Penguin, 1985). On the Tsar's approval, see L. D. Opul'skaya, *Lev Nikolaevich Tolstoi: Materialy k biografii, 1886–1892* (Moscow: Nauka, 1979), p. 227.
[66] A. N. Wilson, ed., and Robert Chandler, trans., *The Lion and the Honeycomb. The Religious Writings of Tolstoy* (San Francisco: Harper & Row, 1987), pp. 72–76.
[67] Letter from Eliza B. Burnz to Tolstoy of October 7, 1890, GMT, T.c. 208 85/1.
[68] Location of the original is unknown. The text is a draft dictated by Tolstoy and written by his daughter Tatiana, located in GMT.
[69] The review, dated October 26, 1890, appeared in issue 43 of the journal *Nedelya* (dated November 10).
[70] *PSS* 27: 287.
[71] For a thorough account of this incident, including the relationship to Alice Stockham, see William Nickell, "The Twain Shall Be of One Mind: Tolstoy in 'Leag' with Eliza Burnz and Henry Parkhurst," *Tolstoy Studies Journal*, 6 (1993): 123–151.
[72] Letter from Alonzo Hollister to Tolstoy of September 23, 1889, GMT T.c. 221 26.
[73] Original in Western Reserve Historical Society, partial text in Flo Morse, *The Shakers and the World's People* (Hanover, NH: Univ. Press of New England, 1980), pp. 233–234. Text here from a photocopy in GMT (no. 11382) received from the Western Reserve Historical Society.
[74] Hollister had sent Tolstoy, with his letter of July 18, 1890: Calvin Green, *A Summary View of the Millennial Church, or United Society of Believers, (Commonly Called Shakers.): Comprising the Rise, Progress and Practical Order of the Society; Together with the General Principles of Their Faith and Testimony* (Albany: Packard & Van Benthuysen, 1823).
[75] Letter from Alonzo Hollister to Tolstoy of July 18, 1890, see GMT Tc 221 26.
[76] Letter from Alonzo Hollister to Tolstoy of November 16, 1890, see

GMT Tc 221 26.
[77] Letter from Alonzo Hollister to Tolstoy of December 18, 1890, see GMT Tc 221 26.
[78] Western Reserve Historical Society, Shaker Manuscripts, Reel 21 IVA–45; photocopy in Morse, op. cit., pp. 232–233.
[79] "Dr. Eaton on Tolstoi." *New York Herald*; November 1890. A clipping with this interview was enclosed in the letter from Alonzo Hollister to Tolstoy of May 18, 1891, see GMT Tc 221 26.
[80] *Philadelphia Sunday Press*, April 4, 1891. Cited by Hollister, without naming the author or title.
[81] Evans sent his own autobiography (see above note 61) and a copy of his letter to Judge Thayer, who freed the individual arrested for selling *Kreutzer Sonata*. See "'Kreutzer Sonata': Philadelphia Decision: Sales Not Illegal: Not Obscene." *New York Times*. 1890 Sep 25: 1 (col. 4).
[82] GMT does not have this letter, which was first published in the collection: *Shaker-Russian Correspondence between Count Leo Tolstoi and Elder F. W. Evans* (Mt. Lebanon, Columbia County, NY, 1891). The text was republished in Richard S. Haugh, ed. & intro., "The Correspondence between Count Leo Tolstoy and the American Shakers: Introduction and Texts," *Transactions/Zapiski of the Association of Russian-American Scholars in the U.S.A.*, 11(1978):236–237.
[83] Probably William Booth (1829–1912), founder of the Salvation Army. His companion was his wife Catherine, neé Mumford (1829–1890).
[84] Location of the original is unknown. Text first published in the collection: *Shaker-Russian Correspondence Between Count Leo Tolstoi and Elder F. W. Evans* (see above note 81), reproduced here from Richard S. Haugh, op. cit., 237–238. GMT has a draft of the letter by Tolstoy's daughter Tatiana (*PSS* 65:240).
[85] Published in Portland, Ore., from 1886 to March 1918, when it apparently ceased publication
[86] Letter from F. W. Evans to Tolstoy of March 6, 1891, original unknown (not in GMT), text from Richard S. Haugh, op. cit., pp. 238–240.
[87] Ibid.
[88] Letter from F. W. Evans to Tolstoy of February 1, 1893, acknowledged receipt of a post card. GMT Tc 213 76.
[89] Original unknown; text from copy in GMT. See also *PSS* 90:283–284.
[90] Hollister's letter to the editor, entitled "Appreciation from a Shaker" (vol. 5 no. 10, p. 155, May, 1903) expressed his views "against materialism and against slaughtering animals for food or for ornamentation...also vivisection, all of which practices are born of savagery and prolong its

right in the human heart." This periodical is quite rare and not all issues have been preserved; the articles by Evans have not been located.

[91] The few biographical details available can be found in *The Morning Oregonian*, in an article in the issue for April 8, 1919, "Mrs. L. A. Mallory Is Struck by Train."

[92] Lucy A. Mallory, "Spiritualism," *World's Advance-Thought and The Universal Republic*, 15, 9 (March–April, 1903): 136.

[93] Lucy A. Mallory, "Fruits of Soul Communion," *World's Advance-Thought and The Universal Republic*, 12, 1 (August-September 1898): 3.

[94] Undated letter of Edouard DeJongh to Tolstoy GMT Tc 223 9.

[95] According to the card catalog of journals in Tolstoy's library, created by the Museum at Yasnaya Polyana, various issues were received from 1888–1910, with rarely a full set per year, and some years are missing entirely, e.g. there is a gap from spring 1889 through 1893.

[96] Letter from Lucy Mallory to Tolstoy of December 4, 1893, GMT, Tc 228 29.

[97] Letters from William Galvani to Tolstoy of March 20 and May 21, 1894, GMT Tc 216 13; no such article appeared in other journals.

[98] The title, "Po voprosu o svobode voli," is not found among any of Tolstoy's written works or projects, nor is the title in a typical format for Tolstoy. It remains a mystery.

[99] Letter from Lucy Mallory to Tolstoy of August 8, 1904, GMT Tc 228 29.

[100] Original not located, text from GMT, copybook no. 6, p. 220. See also *PSS* 75: 158–159.

[101] See Nikolyukin, "Amerikanskie istochniki" (American sources), *L. N. Tolstoy: Krug chteniya*, vol. 2 (Moscow: Izdatel'stvo politicheskoi literatury, 1991), p. 345

[102] D. P. Makovitsky in his *U Tolstogo 1904–1910, Yasnopolyanskie zapiski*, 4 vols. (Literaturnoe nasledsovo, vol. 90, Moscow: Nauka, 1979), 1: 171, 297–298.

[103] Letter from Lucy Mallory to Tolstoy of June 22, 1906, GMT Tc 228 29, in which she acknowledged receiving the work in German translation, *Für Alle Tag.*

[104] Letter from Lucy Mallory to Tolstoy of September 27, 1906, GMT Tc 228 29.

[105] Mallory wrote on November 8, 1906, August 14, 1907, and January 27, 1910. Tolstoy's note is dated December 2, 1906.

[106] For Tolstoy's comments on Bellamy, see his diary for July 1, 1889, *PSS* 50:101–102. He had received a copy from Hapgood; his negative opinion was formed before he encountered the critical discussion of the novel in *Open Court*, see *PSS* 51:47–48.

[107] Tolstoy reacted with some self-criticism to an article comparing him to General William Booth, founder of the Salvation Army (Moncure D. Conway, "The Samaritan on 'Change'," *Open Court* 4 [January 29, 1891]: 2683–2685) and with approval to an article by F. Max Müller, "The Divine and the Human in Religion" (*Open* Court 4:2819–2821; *PSS* 52: 6–7, 38).
[108] For a thorough account of Carus' contributions, see Harold Henderson, *Catalyst for Controversy. Paul Carus of Open Court* (Carbondale, Ill.: Southern Illinois University Press, 1993).
[109] Original located in "The Open Court Collection" of Morris Library of Southern Illinois University. Tolstoy's letters to Carus have been located and published by Henry F. Fullenwider in "Leo Tolstoi and Paul Carus' *The Open Court*," *Russian Literature Triquarterly* 22 (1988): 221–237. The originals of Carus' letters are located in GMT; texts of his letters were available to Fullenwider only from letter press copies.
[110] Letter of Paul Carus to Tolstoy of December 9, 1893, GMT T.c. 209 66. The titles of the publications sent were not listed, however the following titles by Carus (published in 1893) are in the Yasnaya Polyana library. *The Philosophy of the Tool: A Lecture Delivered on ... July 18, 1893, before the Department of Manual and Art Education of the World's Congress Auxiliary* (Chicago : The Open Court, 1893; The Lakeside press-R.R.Donneley & sons); *Primer of Philosophy* (Chicago: The Open Court, 1893); *Die Religion der Wissenschaft : Eine Skizze aus dem philosophischen Leben Nordamerikas*, Extra edition (Philosophische Monatshefte, Band 29 : Heft 5, S. 257; and Chicago: The Open court, 1893; The Lakeside press—R.R.Donneley & sons Co.); *Science a Religious Revelation: An Address Delivered on September 19, 1893, before the World's Congress of Religions at Chicago, Ill.* (Chicago: The Open court, 1893); *Truth in Fiction : Twelve Tales with a Moral* (Chicago: The Open court, 1893).
[111] *The Open Court* 8 (September 13, 1894): 4217–4221.
[112] From Tolstoy's letter to L. Ya. Gurevich of November 29, 1894, which became the preface to the work when it was first published in *Severny vestnik* 1894, 12 (December): 350–358. Note that the letter differs slightly from the published introduction: 'organizations' is omitted from "devices and organizations" in the published version, probably because of the censorship which (correctly) understood this to mean the church and organized religion.
[113] *Khristianskoe uchenie*, begun in 1892, finished in 1896, and published by Chertkov in 1898 (see N. N. Gusev, *Letopis' zhizni i tvorchestva L'va Nikolaevicha Tolstogo. 1891–1910* [Moscow: GIKhL, 1960], p. 220). When asked by an American which of his works best reflected his own

religious views, Tolstoy cited this work: see his letter to Edward A. Braniff of October 14, 1900, (unpublished, GTM, Copybook 3, sheet 96) in response to Braniff's of September 5 (unpublished, GTM, Tc 207 101/1).

[114] See *PSS* 31:47.

[115] Letter of Paul Carus to Tolstoy, July 12, 1897, GMT T.c. 209 66.

[116] Fullenwider, op. cit., 229–230. The undated letter was probably written between July 20 and 29, 1897: the letter was written by Tolstoy's daughter Tatiana because of Tolstoy's debilitating stomach and gall bladder illness; a diary entry of July 29 notes that he took pleasure at Yasenki riding a bicycle. (See Gusev, op. cit., pp. 242, 245). Note that letters from the US reached Russia in a week to ten days, and Tolstoy's second letter to Carus on "Karma" was dated August 10.

[117] Shakyamuni, or Sage of the Shakyas (in Russian Sak'ya-Muni), the title of Siddhartha Gautama (623–544 BC), founder of the Buddhist religion, i.e. Buddha, or Gautama Buddha.

[118] See Tolstoy's letter to A. K. Chertkova of July 29, 1897, *PSS* 88: No. 455.

[119] Letter from Paul Carus to Tolstoy of July 21, 1897, GMT T.c. 209 66.

[120] Fullenwider, op. cit., p. 230. The letter was written for Tolstoy by his daughter Tatiana, who dated the letter according to the Julian (Russian) calendar.

[121] Letter from Paul Carus to Tolstoy of September 11, 1897, GMT T.c. 209 66, misdated in Fullenwider, op. cit., p. 230

[122] *The Gospel of Buddha: According to Old Records*, second edition (Chicago: Open Court, 1895); *Truth in Fiction : Twelve Tales with a Moral* (Chicago: The Open court, 1893). Both titles are in Tolstoy's library at Yasnaya Polyana.

[123] Fullenwider, op. cit., p. 231.

[124] Published in Philadelphia by Research Publications Co. in 1903.

[125] Letter from Isaac Heysinger to Tolstoy of March 14, 1903, GMT, T.c. 220 54.

[126] Original unknown, text from a copy in GMT, Copybook 5, sheet 159.

[127] Fullenwider, op. cit., p. 227

[128] *Open Court*, July 2, 1896–August 6, 1896. *Christianity and Patriotism with Pertinent Extracts from Other Essays*, Paul Carus, editor (Chicago: Open Court Publishing Company, 1905).

[129] *Christianity and Patriotism*, op. cit., p. 93.

[130] Opening of chapter 13 (pp. 510–511 in Maude, *The Kingdom of God*, op. cit.).

[131] Published in Geneva in 1887 by M. K. Elpidin under the title "*Kakova moya zhizn'?*"—"*Den'gi!*" and containing chapters 17–20 of the final version of *What Then Must We Do?*

[132] Letter from Paul Carus to Tolstoy of November 17, 1899, GMT T.c. 232 79.
[133] "Money," *Open Court*, 14 (April 14, 1900):193–200. J. L. Laughlin, "A Criticism of Tolstoi's Money," *Open Court* 14 (April 14, 1900):200–228.
[134] Letter from Alfred Westrup to Tolstoy of October 23, 1899, GMT Tc 246 10.
[135] Original unknown, text from GMT, Copybook number 3, sheet 59. See *PSS* 72: 274–275.
[136] "Tolstoi on India," *Open Court*, 15 (1901): 765–766. Tolstoy's letter is dated July 25, 1901, and was published in the August 1 issue of the journal *Arya* of Madras. See *PSS* 73: No. 120.
[137] "The Overthrow of Hell and its Restoration," *Open Court* 17 (June 1903): 321–324; "Leo Tolstoy's Appeal to the Clergy," *Open Court* 17 (August 1903): 449–457.
[138] *Open Court* 18 (August 1904):509. "Two Letters on Orthodoxy." *Open Court* 18(September 1904): (513–517).
[139] Ernest H. Crosby, "Tolstoy's Answer to the Riddle of Life: An American Admirer of Tolstoy," *Open Court* 17(December 1903):708–712. Aylmer Maude, "The Misinterpretation of Tolstoy," *Open Court* 16 (October 1902):590–601.
[140] *Open Court* 22 (November 1908): 702.
[141] *Life*, trans. Isabel F. Hapgood (New York: T.Y. Crowell and Co., 1888).
[142] *Even As You and I. Parables of True Life by Bolton Hall*, Boston, 1897. The work so pleased Tolstoy that he had it translated, and it appeared in two editions. The first appeared as Hall's own work ("Istinnaya zhizn'," Moscow, 1899), but the second appeared as Tolstoy's *On Life* ("O zhizni," Moscow, 1903), where Hall is named in the foreword.
[143] Original is unknown; Hall published the text in his *What Tolstoy Taught* (New York: B. W. Huebsch, 1911), p. 11. A copy at GMT differs in slight details and has an earlier date (see *PSS* 70:41–42). This book, *What Tolstoy Taught*, is a revised edition of *Even As You and I*, which had gone through several editions itself; Part 1 (of 2) is titled "On Life" and expands Tolstoy's work even more.
[144] *Single Tax Review*, 1908, vol. 7, no. 3. A copy is in Tolstoy's library at Yasnaya Polyana.
[145] Letter from Bolton Hall to Tolstoy of February 3, 1908, GMT Bl 2/1562.
[146] Letter dictated and signed by Tolstoy. Tolstoy Collection of Aylmer Maude, Rare Books and Manuscripts, Butler Library, Columbia University. A copy of the draft is in GMT, copybook 8, sheet 157 (see *PSS* 78:90).

[147] During September and early October 1906 Tolstoy worked on several articles for Posrednik: "A Solution of the Land Question (According to Henry George)" (*Reshenie zemel'nogo voprosa [po Genri Dzhordzhu]*); "The Significance of the Russian Revolution" (*Znachenie russkoi revolyutsii*) and the preface to S. D. Nikolaev's translation of Henry George's *Social Problems* (*Obshchestvennye zadachi*). See Gusev, op. cit., pp. 562–564.
[148] Gusev, op. cit., 592, 598. Tolstoy wrote on August 8, 1907 (*PSS* 77: No. 192); Stolypin responded October 6, 1907.
[149] Theodore R. Roosevelt, "Tolstoy: An Estimate," *Outlook* 92 (May 15, 1909):103–108.
[150] Letter from Creelman to Tolstoy of September 3, 1903, GMT T.c. 211 11.
[151] Original unknown, text from a copy in GMT Copybook number 5, sheet 257–58 (see *PSS* 17:185).
[152] *New York World*, July 23, 1903. Republished in *The North American*, 8 August, 1903, and in other newspapers and journals.
[153] "Thanksgiving Address, London, England," *Under Other Flags* (Lincoln, Neb.: The Woodruff-Collins Printing Company, 1905), p. 131. Bryan's speech delivered November 26, 1903, was sent to Tolstoy on December 14, 1903, by Samuel Smith, US Consul in Moscow. See Smith's letter to Tolstoy of this date, GMT Tc 240 45.
[154] See *Under Other Flags*, op. cit., p. 99. He wrote specifically of Tolstoy's essay, "Industry and Idleness," the first piece in the collection *Essays and Letters*, trans. Aylmer Maude (NY: Funk and Wagnalls, 1904). This was Tolstoy's introduction to the peasant writer T. M. Bondarev's work *The Agrarian's Victory or Industry and Idleness* (*Torzhestvo zemledel'tsa, ili Trudoljubie i tunejadstvo*), which work finally appeared in 1906. It had appeared in English, edited by Tolstoy, in 1890: T. M. Bondareff, *The Suppressed Book of the Peasant Bondareff. Labor: the Divine Command Made Known*, trans. M. Cruger (NY: Pollard Publishing Co., 1890).
[155] See the accounts in "Tolstoy, Apostle of Love," *Under Other Flags*, op. cit., 96–108; Makovitsky, op. cit., 1:110; also P. Sergeenko "Tolstoj i Braiyan" (Tolstoy and Bryan) in his *Tolstoi i ego sovremenniki* (Moscow: Sablin, 1911) pp. 243–251.
[156] "Tolstoy, the Apostle of Love," *The Commoner*, February 19, 1904, 4(5):3, 6. Tolstoy received a clipping from Bryan via Consul Smith in a letter of March 21, 1904 (GMT Tc 240 45).
[157] *Under Other Flags*, loc. cit., p. 99.
[158] Letter from W. J. Bryan to Tolstoy of December 31, 1903, GMT, Tc 298 61.

[159] *Under Other Flags*, loc. cit., p. 104.
[160] Ibid, p. 107.
[161] Makovitsky, op. cit., 1:110.
[162] "Introduction to a Short Biography of William Lloyd Garrison (A Letter to the Editors: Vladimir Chertkov and Florence Holah.)" in *The Kingdom of God and Peace Essays*, loc. cit., p. 579.
[163] Original unknown, text from a copy in GMT Copybook no. 6, sheet 39. See *PSS* 75:17.
[164] Makovitsky, op. cit., 1:110.
[165] Makovitsky, op. cit., 1:207.
[166] Ibid., 2:166.
[167] Ibid., 3:97.
[168] Ibid., 3:124.
[169] Letter from Ryerson Jennings to Tolstoy of August 24, 1908, GMT T.s. 222 64.
[170] The original is unknown; text published by A. Maude in his *The Life of Tolstoy. Later Years* (London: Constable, 1911), p. 638. See *PSS* 78:231.
[171] Much of the controversy was generated by Roosevelt's article (note 149), see: "Col. T. Roosevelt Accuses Count L. N. Tolstoy of Having Dangerous Moral Influence, for Campaign Support of Bryan Article in The Outlook", *New York Times*, May 14, 1909 1 (2); "Letter Scores Roosevelt for Accusing Tolstoy of Having a Dangerous Moral Influence," *New York Times*, May 23, 1909,6: 7 (3); "Mr. Roosevelt's Attack on Tolstoy," *Current Literature* 47 (July 1909),1:64–66; Thomas Van Ness, "Tolstoy—Another View," *Outlook*, 92 (June 5, 1909): 336–337; Ivan Narodny, "Tolstoy—Another View," *Outlook*, 92 (June 12,1909):380–382. In his letter to Tolstoy of May 27, 1909 (note 173), Bryan wrote: "You may have read Ex-President Roosevelt's criticism of you. He seems to have been angered by the fact that you favored my election. I enclose a brief editorial reply in my paper, The Commoner. You have found many defenders since the Ex-President's attack has been published." The article Bryan wrote is "Feeble Folk," *The Commoner*, 9(1909),19:1.
[172] Mokovitsky, op. cit., 3:225.
[173] Letter of W. J. Bryan to Tolstoy of May 27, 1909, GMT Br 2 1579.
[174] Makovitsky, op. cit., 3:429.
[175] For details of Bryan's activities and the influence of Tolstoy, see Merle Eugene Curti, *Bryan and World Peace*, The Garland Library of War and Peace (New York: Garland Publishing, Inc., 1971), pp. 135–148.

[176] Clarence Darrow, "Foreword to the 1925 Edition," *Resist Not Evil* (Montclair, N. J.: Patterson Smith, 1972), p. xxxv.
[177] Ibid.
[178] Makovitsky, op. cit., 2:298. Tolstoy had met this minor American novelist, Leroy Scott (1875–1929), author of a dozen novels principally set in New York City, early in November 1906.

Apple

Susan Stewart

If I could come back from the dead, I would come back
for an apple, and just for the first bite, the first
break, and the cold sweet grain
against the roof of the mouth, as plain
and clear as water.

Some apple names are almost forgotten
and the apples themselves are gone. The smokehouse,
winesap and York imperial, the striped
summer rambo and the winter banana, the little
Rome with its squat rotunda and the pound apple

that pulled the boughs to the ground.
The sheep's nose with its three-pointed snout,
the blue Pearmain, speckled and sugared.
Grime's golden, cortland, and stamen.
If an apple's called "delicious," it's not.

Water has no substance
and soil has no shell,
sun is all process
and rain cannot rise.
The apple's core carries

a birth and a poison.
Stem and skin, and flesh,
and seed, the apple's name,
no matter, is work
and the work of death.

If you wait for the apple, you wait
for one ripe moment. And should
you sleep, or should you dream, or
should you stare too hard in the daylight
or come into the dark to see

what can't be seen, you will drop
from the edge, going over into
coarse, or rot, or damping off.
You will wake to yourself, regretful,
in a grove of papery leaves.

You need a hillside, a small and steady wind,
a killing frost, and, later, honey-bees.
You need a shovel, and shears, and a ladder

and the balance to come back down again.
You will have fears of codling moths
and railroad worms, and aphids.

Scale and maggots and beetles
will come to do their undoing.
Forests will trap the air

and valleys will bend to gales—
cedars will bring on rust, so keep them
far in the distance. Paradise,

of course, was easy, but you and I live
in this world, and "the fruit of the tree
in the midst of the garden"

says nothing specific about apples;
the "apples of gold" in *Proverbs*
are probably oranges instead.

And so are the fruits
Milanion threw down:
an apple does not glitter.

If you're interested in immortality
it's best to plant a tree, and even
then you can't be sure that form

will last under weather.
The tree can break apart in a storm
or be torqued into pieces over many

years from the weight of its ruddy labor.
The state won't let you burn the wood
in the open air; the smoke is too dense

for breathing. But apple-wood
makes a lovely fire, with excellent
heat and aroma.

Fire will take in whatever it can
and heat will draw back
into earth. "Here is the fruit,
your reward and penalty
at once," said the god

to the waiting figures.
Unbearable, the world
that broke into time.
Unbearable, the just-born
certainty of distance.

You can roast late apples
in the ashes. You can run
them in slices on a stick.
You can turn the stem to
find the letter of your love

or chase them down with
your chin in a tub.
If you count the seeds to tell
the future, your heart will
sense more than your

tongue can say. A body
has a season, though
it may not know it
and damage will bloom
in beauty's seed.

If I could come back from the dead, I would—
I'd come back for an apple,
and just for one bite, one break,
and the cold sweet grain on the tongue.
There is so little difference between

an apple and a kiss, between desire
and the taste of desire.
Anyone who tells you otherwise is a liar, as bad
as a snake in the quiet grass.

You can watch out for the snake and the lie.
But the grass, the green green wave
of it, there below the shadows of the black
and twisted boughs, will not be
what you thought it would be.

Contributors

★★★ **Gary Adelman** is a professor of English at the University of Illinois. His book on Dostoevsky is forthcoming from Bicknell University Press. ★★★ **Claudia Allen** is playwright-in-residence at Victory Gardens Theater in Chicago. A collection of four of her plays, *She Always Liked the Girls Best* (1995), is available from Third Side Press. ★★★ **Aliki Barnstone**'s most recent book of poems, *Madly in Love* (Carnegie Mellon University Press, 1997), was nominated for a Pulitzer Prize. Her poems have appeared in *Agni*, *Antioch Review*, *Boulevard*, *Chicago Review*, and *Poetry*. ★★★ **John Barth** is the author of twelve books of fiction and two collections of essays. His latest novel, *Coming Soon!!!*, is forthcoming. ★★★ **Mitch Berman** is the author of the novel *The Time Capsule* (Putnam, 1987) and the multimedia CD, *The Search for Konkowsky*. ★★★ **Leigh Buchanan Bienen** is a writer, lawyer, and teacher of law at Northwestern School of Law. She is author of *Crimes of the Century: From Leopold and Loeb to O.J. Simpson* (Northeastern University Press, 1998) with Gilbert Geis. ★★★ **John Blades** is the former book editor and critic for the *Chicago Tribune*. His novel, *Small Game*, was published by Holt in 1992. ★★★ **Susan Booth** is Director of New Play Development for the Goodman Theatre. She teaches playwriting in the department of Radio, Television and Film at Northwestern University. ★★★ **David Breskin** is the author of a book of poems, *Fresh Kills* (Cleveland State University Press, 1997), a book of interviews, *Inner Views: Filmmakers in Conversation* (DaCapo, 1997), and a novel, *The Real Life Diary of a Boomtown Girl* (Viking, 1989). The poems appearing here are from a forthcoming collection, *Escape Velocity*. ★★★ **Christopher Buckley** has published nine books of poetry, most recently *Fall from Grace*, (Bk/Mk Press of the University of Missouri-Kansas City, 1998). ★★★ **Dan Chaon**'s first book, *Fitting Ends and Other Stories*, appeared in 1996 from TriQuarterly Books. A second book of stories is forthcoming. ★★★ **Michael Chitwood**'s most recent books are *The Weave Room* (University of Chicago, 1998), and *Hitting Below the Bible Belt* (Down Home Press, 1998). His poems have appeared in the *Threepenny Review*, *Ohio Review*, and *South Carolina Review*. ★★★ **Billy Collins**' latest collection of poems is *Picnic, Lightning* (University of Pittsburgh Press, 1998). He teaches at Lehman College (CUNY) and Sarah Lawrence College. ★★★ **Stephen Dixon**'s most recent books are *30* (Henry Holt, 1999), *Sleep* (Coffee House Press, 1999), *Tisch* (Red Hen Press, spring

2000), and *Story of a Story and Other Stories: A Novel* (Rain Taxi Press, spring 2000). He teaches in the Writing Seminars at Johns Hopkins University. ★★★ **Stuart Dybek**'s poems have appeared in the *Iowa Review, Harvard Review*, and *The New Republic*. ★★★ **Alexai Galaviz-Budziszewski** is a graduate of the Iowa Writers' Workshop. His work has appeared in *River Styx* and the *Alaska Quarterly Review*. ★★★ **Sandra M. Gilbert**'s latest collection of poems is *Ghost Volcano* (Norton, 1995). She is at work on a book-length study of the twentieth-century poetry of mourning, to be titled *The Fate of Elegy: History, Memory, and the Mythology of Modern Death*. ★★★ **Jana Harris**'s seventh and most recent book of poetry, *The Dust of Everyday Life* (Sasquatch Press, 1998), won the 1998 Andres Berger Award for Poetry. Her second novel, *The Pearl of Ruby City*, was published by St. Martin's in 1998. ★★★ **Jeffrey Harrison**'s most recent book of poems is *Signs of Arrival* (Copper Beech Press, 1996). He was awarded a Guggenheim Fellowship in 1999. ★★★ **Edward Hirsch**'s most recent books are *On Love: Poems* (Knopf, 1998) and *How to Read a Poem and Fall in Love with Poetry* (Harcourt Brace, 1999). He teaches in the Creative Writing Program at the University of Houston. ★★★ **Paul Hoover** is the author of six poetry collections, including *Viridian* (University of Georgia Press, 1997). He is editor of the anthology *Postmodern American Poetry* (W.W. Norton, 1994) and the literary magazine *New American Writing*. ★★★ **Mark Irwin**'s most recent collection of poems is *White City* (BOA, 1999). He teaches at the University of Denver and the University of Colorado. ★★★ **Ha Jin**'s most recent novel, *Waiting* (Pantheon, 1999), won the National Book Award. "After Cowboy Chicken Came to Town" will be included in his collection, *The Bridegroom*, forthcoming from Pantheon. ★★★ **Charles Johnson**'s novels include *Oxherding Tale* (Plime, 1995) and *Middle Passage* (Scribner), for which he won the National Book Award in 1990. He teaches at the University of Washington and is a recent recipient of a MacArthur Fellowship. ★★★ **George Kalamaras**'s book, *The Theory and Function of Mangoes* (Four Way Books, spring 2000), won the Four Way Books Intro Series in Poetry Award. He is Associate Professor of English at Indiana University-Purdue University Fort Wayne. ★★★ **John Kinsella**'s most recent books are *Poems 1980–1994* and *The Hunt*, both from Bloodaxe/Dufour. He is a Fellow of Churchill College, Cambridge and coeditor of *Stand*. ★★★ **Fred G. Leebron**'s novels include *Out West* (Doubleday, 1996) and *Six Figures* (Knopf, 2000). He teaches creative writing at Gettysburg College. ★★★ **Robert Lepage** is known throughout his native Canada and around the world for his prize-winning dramatic productions. His current one-man play, the *Far Side of the Moon*, is being produced in Quebec, and his next film, *Possible Worlds*, is due out next fall. ★★★ **David H. Lynn** is the editor of the *Kenyon Review*. His most recent book is *Fortune Telling* (Carnegie Mellon Press, 1998). ★★★ **Katherine Ma**'s work has appeared in the *Threepenny Review, The Crescent Review,* and *Other Voices*. She lives in San Fransisco. ★★★ **Anne Marie Macari** won the 2000 American Poetry Review/Honickman First Book Prize. Her book, *Ivory Cradle*, will be published in the fall of 2000. ★★★ **Cleopatra Mathis**'s books, all published by Sheep Meadow Press, are *Aerial View of Louisiana* (1979), *The Bottom Land* (1983), *The Center for Cold Weather* (1989), and *Guardian* (1995). She is a professor of English at Dartmouth College. ★★★ **George McFadden**, professor emeritus at Temple University, is the author of *Dryden, the Public Writer* (1978) and *Discovering the Comic* (1982), both from Princeton University Press. ★★★ **Michael McFee** has published five books of poems, including *Vanishing Acts* (Gnomon Press, 1989), *Colander* (Carnegie Mellon University Press, 1996), and *To See* (North Carolina Wesleyan Press, 1991), the latter a collaboration with photographer Elizabeth Matheson. He teaches at the University of North Carolina. ★★★ **Campbell McGrath** is a frequent contributor to *TriQuarterly*. He lives with his family in Florida. ★★★ **Edward Nobles** is the author of *The Bluestone Walk* (Persea Books, 2000) and *Through One Tear* (Persea Books, 1997), which was selected as a Notable Book by the National Book Critics Circle. His poetry has appeared in *Boulevard*, the *Gettysburg Review*, and the *Paris Review*. ★★★ **Josip Novakovich**'s latest collection of stories, *Salvation and Other Disasters* (Graywolf, 1998), won an American Book Award from the Before Columbus Foundation in 1999. He has received a Whiting Writer's Award and a Guggenheim Fellowship for Fiction. ★★★ **Joyce Carol Oates** is the author most recently of the novel *Broke Heart Blues* (Dutton, 1999) and the story collection *The Collection of Hearts* (Dutton, 1998). "Pin-up 1945" is an excerpt from her latest novel, *Blonde*, (Dutton, 2000) ★★★ **Alicia Ostriker**'s most recent book of poems, *The Little Space* (University of Pittsburgh Press, 1998), was a National Book Award finalist. Her most recent prose work is *Dancing at the Devil's Party: Essays on Poetry, Politics and the Erotic* (University of Michigan Press, Poets on Poetry series, 2000). ★★★ **Ricardo Pau-Llosa**'s third and fourth collections of poetry, *Cuba* (1993) and *Vereda Tropical* (1999), were published by Carnegie Mellon University Press. His most recent book of art criticism is *Rafael*

Soriano and the Poetics of Light (Miami: Ed. Habana Vieja, 1998). ★★★ **Molly Peacock**'s most recent book is *How to Read a Poem & Start a Poetry Circle* (Riverhead Press, 1999). She is the author of four books of poems, including *Original Love* (Norton, 1996), as well as a memoir, *Paradise Piece by Piece* (Riverhead Press, 1999). She has served as President of the Poetry Society of America. ★★★ **Carl Phillips** is the author of four books of poems, most recently *Pastoral* (Graywolf, 2000). He teaches at Washington University in St. Louis. ★★★ **Chaim Potok** has published seven novels, including *The Chosen* (Simon & Schuster, 1967) and *The Promise* (1969). He has won the Edward Lewis Wallant Award, the Atheaeum Prize, and the Jewish Book Award. ★★★ **Stephen Schottenfeld** is a graduate of the Iowa Writer's Workshop and was the 1998–99 Halls Fiction Fellow at the University of Wisconsin. His work has appeared in *Gulf Coast*, the *Coe Review*, and the *Crescent Review*. ★★★ **Peter Dale Scott**'s trilogy, *Seculum*, will be completed with the publication of *Minding the Darkness* (New Directions, 2000). Previous volumes were *Coming to Jakarta* (1989) and *Listening to the Candle* (1992). He has also published *Crossing Borders: Selected Shorter Poems* (1994), all from New Directions. ★★★ **Frances Sherwood**'s most recent novels are *Green* (1995) and *Vindication* (1993), both from Farrar, Strauss and Giroux. She has published stories in numerous magazines, including most recently, the *Atlantic*. ★★★ **Tom Sleigh**'s books of poetry include *After One* (Houghton Mifflin, 1983), and, from the University of Chicago Press, *Waking* (1990), *The Chain* (1996), and *The Dreamhouse* (1999). His translation of Herakles will be published this year by the University of Oxford Press. ★★★ **Bruce Smith** is the author of four books of poems, most recently *The Other Lover* (University of Chicago, 2000). He teaches at the University of Alabama. ★★★ **Charlie Smith**'s fifth book of poems, *Heroin*, will be out this fall from W.W. Norton. He has also published six books of fiction, including *Cheap Ticket to Heaven* (Henry Holt, 1996) and *Shine Hawk* (Univeristy of Georgia Press). ★★★ **R.T. Smith**'s books of poems are *Split the Lark: Selected Poems* (Salmon Poetry, 1999), *Trespasser* (Louisiana University Press, 1996), and *Messenger*, forthcoming from LSU. He is the editor of *Shenandoah*. ★★★ **Kevin Stein**'s new collection, *Chance Ransom*, will appear this fall from the University of Illinois Press. His book, *Private Poets, Worldly Acts* (Ohio University Press), essays on poetry and history, was reprinted in paperback last fall. ★★★ **Gerald Stern**'s most recent book is *Last Blue* (Norton, spring 2000). *This Time* won the National Book Award for poetry in 1998.

★★★ **Susan Stewart** is the author of three books of poems, most recently *The Forest* (University of Chicago Press, 1995). She recently completed, with Wesley Smith, a new translation of Euripides' *Andromache*, forthcoming next year with Oxford University Press, and her prose study, *Poetry and the Fate of the Senses*, is forthcoming from the University of Chicago Press, also in 2001. ★★★ **Mark Strand** won the 1999 Pulitzer Prize for poetry for his book *A Blizzard of One* (Knopf). A former Poet Laureate of the United States, he has recently returned to painting, drawing, and collage-making. ★★★ **Eric Sundquist** is Professor of English and African American Studies, as well as Dean of the Weinberg College of Arts and Sciences, at Northwestern University. His books include *To Wake the Nations: Race in the Making of American Literature* (Belknap Press, 1993) and *The Hammers of Creation* (University of Georgia Press, 1993). ★★★ **Brian Swann** has published in hundreds of magazines and journals. He is the editor of the *Smithsonian Series of Studies on Native American Literatures*. ★★★ **Pimone Triplett**'s book of poems, *Ruining the Picture*, was published by TriQuarterly Books in 1998. Her poems have appeared in such journals as the *Paris Review*, *Poetry*, and *Quarterly West*. ★★★ **Rob Trucks**' interviews with writers, including Rick Moody, Stephen Dixon, Robert Olen Butler, and Russell Banks have appeared, or will appear, in the *Black Warrior Review*, *New Orleans Review*, *Indiana Review*, and *Glimmer Train*. ★★★ **Justin Tussing** is a graduate of the Iowa Writers' Workshop. ★★★ **David Wagoner** edits *Poetry Northwest* for the University of Washington. His most recent book is *Traveling Light: Collected and New Poems* (University of Illinois Press, 1999). ★★★ **Robert Whittaker** is coeditor of Russian editions of the correspondence between Leo Tolstoy and Americans and of the letters of the nineteenth-century poet and critic Apollon Grigoriev (Nauka, 1999), and is the author of a biography of Grigoriev, entitled *Russia's Last Romantic* (Edwin Mellen Press, 1999). ★★★ **Alan Williamson**'s most recent book of poems is *Res Publica* (University of Chicago Press, 1998). He teaches at the University of California at Davis. ★★★ **David Wojahn**'s most recent collection of poetry is *The Falling Hour* (University of Pittsburgh Press, 1997). He directs the Program in Creative Writing at Indiana University. ★★★ **C. Dale Young** works as a physician and as poetry editor of *New England Review*. His first collection of poems, *The Day Underneath the Day*, will be published by TriQuarterly Books in the spring of 2001.